DRAGON DESCENDANTS

THE COLLECTION
BOOKS 1-4

USA TODAY BESTSELLING AUTHOR

J.L. WEIL

DRAGON DESCENDANTS

CONTENTS

Copyright   x
Written by J.L. Weil   xi

STEALING TRANQUILITY

Chapter 1   2
Chapter 2   9
Chapter 3   17
Chapter 4   27
Chapter 5   37
Chapter 6   45
Chapter 7   53
Chapter 8   63
Chapter 9   75
Chapter 10   87
Chapter 11   97
Chapter 12   107
Chapter 13   119
Chapter 14   131
Chapter 15   141
Chapter 16   151

ABSORBING POISON

Chapter 1   170
Chapter 2   177
Chapter 3   185
Chapter 4   195
Chapter 5   203
Chapter 6   213
Chapter 7   221
Chapter 8   231
Chapter 9   241
Chapter 10   251
Chapter 11   259

Chapter 12   269
Chapter 13   279
Chapter 14   289
Chapter 15   301
Chapter 16   309
Chapter 17   321

TAMING FIRE

Chapter 1   338
Chapter 2   349
Chapter 3   361
Chapter 4   373
Chapter 5   387
Chapter 6   399
Chapter 7   413
Chapter 8   425
Chapter 9   435
Chapter 10   447
Chapter 11   459
Chapter 12   469
Chapter 13   479
Chapter 14   493
Chapter 15   503

THAWING FROST

Chapter 1   522
Chapter 2   529
Chapter 3   537
Chapter 4   547
Chapter 5   555
Chapter 6   565
Chapter 7   575
Chapter 8   587
Chapter 9   597
Chapter 10   607
Chapter 11   617
Chapter 12   627
Chapter 13   637
Chapter 14   651

Chapter 15   659
Chapter 16   671
Chapter 17   683
Chapter 18   693
Chapter 19   705

A Note from the Author   715
Next from J.L Weil   716
About The Author   720

THE COLLECTION

COPYRIGHTS

COPYRIGHTS

Published by A Dark Magick Publishing, August 2022.
www.jlweil.com

WRITTEN BY J.L. WEIL

The Raven Series
White Raven, book 1
Black Crow, book 2
Soul Symmetry, book 3

The Divisa Series
Saving Angel, book 1
Hunting Angel, book 2
Chasing Angel, book 3
Loving Angel, book 4
Redeeming Angel, book 5
Losing Emma, A Divisa Novella

Breaking Emma, A Divisa Novella

<u>Luminescence Trilogy</u>
Luminescence, book 1
Amethyst Tears, book 2
Moondust, book 3
Darkmist,
A Luminescenece Novella, book 4

<u>Beauty Never Dies Chronicles</u>
Slumber, book 1
Entangled, book 2
Forsaken, book 3

<u>Nine Tails Series</u>
First Shift, book 1
Storm Shift, book 2
Flame Shift, book 3
Time Shift, book 4
Void Shift, book 5
Spirit Shift, book 6
Tide Shift, book 7
Wind Shift, book 8
Celestial Shift, book 9

<u>Dragon Descendants, A Reverse Harem Series</u>
Stealing Tranquility, book 1
Absorbing Poison, book 2
Taming Fire, book 3
Thawing Frost, book 4

<u>Supernatural Taskforce Academy</u>
*An Academy Series, Paranormal Romance Adventure From Authors
J.L Weil & Stephany Wallace.*
Scorpion Blood, Mission 1

Mystique Blaze, Mission 2
Immortal Shift, Mission 3

Divisa Huntress
Crown of Darkness, book 1
Inferno of Darkness, book 2
Eternity of Darkness, book 3

Elite of Elmwood Academy
Turmoil, book 1
Disorder, book 2
Revenge, book 3
Rival, book 4

Stand Alone Novels & Novellas
Starbound
Ancient Tides, Division 14: The Berkano Vampire Collection
Falling Deep, A Havenwood Falls High Novella
Ascending Darkness, A Havenwood Falls High Novella

ACKNOWLEDGMENTS

First and foremost, I want to thank Stephany Wallace for being more than an incredible PA and editor, but also being my cheerleader and friend. I wouldn't get through my edits without those comments that make me lol.

Another huge thank you to Allisyn, who constantly helps me grow in my skills as a writer. I really do take all your notes to heart, even if it seems as if I'd forgotten them.

I want to give a big shoutout to the YA Vets. You know who you are. This group is a resource I can't do without. Muawah!

And as always, a massive thank you to the readers and reviewers. You guys give me the encouragement to keep doing this and making me believe in my dreams.
I FLOVE all of you!

DEDICATION

This book is for readers.
I wouldn't be able to do any of this without you!
I FLOVE you!

JASE

STEALING TRANQUILITY

BOOK ONE

USA TODAY BESTSELLING AUTHOR

J. L WEIL

CHAPTER 1

My feet pounded the pavement as I ran down the street. A warm pizza box bounced in my hands while my Converse crunched pebbles, empty soda cans, and discarded fast food wrappers.

I probably shouldn't be running. It wasn't my forte. Any second, I was positive I would do a face-plant, and end up losing my first meal in days.

"Come back, you little thief!"

Thief? Okay, so technically I did steal a pizza, but in my defense, I was starving, and this was about survival.

The cook chasing me was bound to run out of steam soon. I hoped. The last thing I needed was to get caught.

Pushing myself, I bolted down Elm Avenue like my hair was on fire, dodging a couple walking their dog. I turned the corner, and a gust of wind slapped me in the face. Damn. If this took much longer, my pizza would be cold.

"I'm calling the cops!" he yelled.

Go for it. Good luck finding me. I would take my chances and called bs on his threat.

I knew the difference between right and wrong, and stealing was wrong, but sometimes, you needed to break the law to live, or starve to death. And I wasn't ready to die.

This wasn't the first time I'd stolen a meal, and honestly, I doubted it would be my last. When I came across the restaurant earlier, I had stopped and glanced longingly at the filled booths, seeing the happy faces as the patrons stuffed their bellies full of garlic breadsticks, and deep-dish pizza. At that moment, I would have killed for a hot slice of sausage with extra cheese, loaded with tomato sauce. My stomach rumbled (angry with me), telling me I needed to find food sooner than later.

That's when the plan had been born. Over the last few weeks, I'd become quite skilled at being invisible, and taking what I wanted. Wallets. Clothes. And pizza.

I had scampered down the pizzeria's alley, seeing the back door slightly ajar. From inside, I'd heard voices and the smells of baked dough, zesty tomato sauce, and Italian herbs. Peeking around the door, I had spotted an open box with a fresh-out-of-the-oven pizza sitting on the end of a metal counter. All I had thought was *Jackpot!*

My triumph had been short-lived, unfortunately.

Looking left and right, I had tiptoed inside, keeping below the counter. There had been a guy opening one of the many ovens and another spinning a ball of dough in the air. Both of them had seemed too occupied to notice me. Quickly, I snatched the box and backed out the way I had come in.

"Hey!" a voice had called behind me.

I hadn't bothered to look, and just started running, the pizza box tucked under my arm. It hadn't been a very thought-out decision, but rarely any of mine were. Stealing wasn't something I wanted on my record.

Hell. I didn't want a record at all.

At just a few months shy of eighteen, I would be shoved into a foster home or juvie, and I'd rather live on the streets. My legs burned, and my lungs ached from the chill, but I pressed on, glancing over my shoulder to judge how much distance I had gained. Not enough.

For a cook, the guy was persistent—not that I knew a lot of cooks, just what I'd seen on TV, but most of them didn't strike me as a *long-distance running* type of guys.

Just my luck that this chef would be the exception.

Taking the next right, I cut the corner sharply, and the bottom of my worn-out shoes skidded over loose rock. My hands flailed in the air as I lost my balance. Shit. This was it. The face-plant was imminent.

By an act of God, I managed to stay on my feet, keep the pizza in my hand, and regain my composure. *Smooth move, Olivia.* I took off down Oglesby Street.

"I better not see your face again!" the cook screamed, finally giving up. He stood panting at the corner.

Yes! Victory is mine.

A smile crossed my lips when I hooked a left around the corner, but I didn't ease up on my pace for another five minutes and refrained from jumping in the air. Being homeless stunk, and I wasn't just talking about my body odor. Being homeless in Chicago was plain insanity.

An icy breeze whipped through my hoodie, sending a thousand tiny pinpricks over my flesh. I huddled up against a brick wall, the smell of pizza stirring up hunger pangs that assaulted my belly.

I crouched in a corner behind a dumpster in an empty alley near the local college, digging into the pizza box with a sigh of pleasure. I savored the taste of sweet basil tomato sauce and mozzarella cheese, burning it to memory. This was a moment I didn't want to forget.

I swallowed, positive I'd died and gone to heaven.

When was the last time I had pizza?

Months?

I couldn't be certain. Hell, I didn't even know what time it was, what day, or if I would survive the night. What I did know was I was going to feast like a king and then find somewhere warm to stay before I froze to death. The boogers in my nose already had ice crystals forming on them.

On nights like this, it was hard to forget how my life had ended up so pitifully. It was never supposed to be like this, not for me, but fate had a way of throwing you curveballs.

Like the day I found out Mom had died. After she passed, her loser husband—not my father—had decided he no longer wanted a kid, especially an angry and lost one. Denny had his own life, his own plans, and those didn't include me. Not that I cared. He was an asshat. I didn't need him. That had been my mantra since the stepfather-of-the-year had kicked me out two months ago. I'd been on my own ever since.

My real father split when I was a baby. Mom sure knew how to pick them.

Good riddance.

I didn't need a daddy figure anyway.

My mother had been beautiful, silky honey hair that shone in the sunlight, curves that turned men's heads, and aqua eyes that glittered like the ocean. Everyone had said we looked like sisters, twins even, but our personalities couldn't have been more different. For all her flaws, I loved her immensely. We had been partners, best friends, and I missed her something fierce. She might have been flighty in love, but as a mother, she was everything a girl could ask for.

I was determined to not be so unlucky in love, which was why I planned to never fall into it. I was protecting my heart. Mine had bled enough.

After Mom's accident, my life as I knew it was over, but I never imagined it would be this bad. I blamed my stepfather for everything. He didn't even really qualify as one. The two of us never saw eye-to-eye. Mom had an older sister, but I knew very little about her and even less about my real father and his family. It was just me, myself, and I.

Those first few weeks after Mom passed were the worst. I'd never felt so alone in my life, and if it hadn't been for my best friend, Staci, I don't think I would have gotten through it. Staci and I were friends at first sight. Her personality matched her wild wardrobe, which looked like Katy Perry's stylist had sex with Marilyn Manson's makeup artist and Staci was the result. Her pink short hair, heavy eyeliner, black nail polish, pink boots, and tight jeans completed her everyday look, and yet she managed to appear adorable.

Staci had begged me to come stay with her, and as much as I wanted to, I knew her mom couldn't afford to care for me. She had her hands full, working two jobs to support Staci, and her younger brother, Aiden. I refused to burden my best friend. If I could get a job and contribute, that would be another story, which was what I would do first thing Monday morning—job hunt.

And for tonight, I would just try to survive.

As I downed my second slice, a mouse scampered out of its hiding spot, and stared up at me. I swallowed my initial squeak with a bite of pizza. "Hey, little guy, you hungry?"

Breaking off a hunk of crust, I dropped it onto the ground. Pipsqueak scurried over, and grabbed the offering in his two tiny hands, nibbling with an intensity that I understood far too well.

"Not bad, huh?"

Holy shit. I'd been reduced to talking to the local street rodents. At least he had better table manners than Denny. I'd take a dozen mice over him any day of the week.

I polished off half the pizza—my first real meal in two days—my belly felt fully satisfied for the time being. Licking the last bit of sauce from my fingers, I stood up, gathering the other half of the pizza as a blast of wind bit straight into me.

Ugh. This sucks. I cursed Denny to seven different kinds of hell as I shivered my ass off, but I didn't regret standing up to my stepdad. Screw him. He was a piece of trash.

Winter reared its ugly head, and the bone-chilling wind made me want to huddle forever in my hoodie, and never take it off. Leaning against the wall, my mind wandered to the days when I used to hang out with Staci. I missed her and her off-the-wall sense of humor. She worried about me… the only person who did.

Checking my phone I exhaled. No messages. It was hard not to feel unloved at the moment and utterly alone in the world. I didn't expect her to blow up my phone every five minutes, but the occasional *are you okay?* text would be nice.

The coolness of the bricks reached me when I rested my head back, and glanced up at the charming, and historical Brentley University. Remembering the application I had completed to attend this school, it was hard to realize my dreams had been swept away. I had left it sitting on my desk at the house Denny now occupied alone. It was probably crumbled and in the trash now, just like my future.

Throwing my backpack onto my shoulders, I moseyed to the end of the alley, gaining a clear picture of the campus courtyard. It was sad, but I used to sit on the benches, watching the throngs of students come and go from the dorms and classes, picturing myself among them.

Someday, I promised myself. Someday I would go to college, but first I needed to figure out how to finish high school, and I couldn't forget about that J-O-B.

A gaggle of giggles interrupted my drifting thoughts, and drew my attention to a group of college students whispering in a circle. I rolled my eyes, glad I'd never been one of those annoying girls, but still, curiosity got the best of me while my gaze followed theirs across campus.

Keeping myself partially hidden in the dark alley, I glanced at the parking lot, seeing a sporty black car. Leaning on the sleek vehicle was a tall, attractive man. His legs were crossed at the ankles, as he shot an award-winning grin at his fan club.

Leif Lexington. He had been a senior last year at my school and was smoldering hot with an ego the size of the Sears Tower. The pizza threatened to come back up. Guys like Leif made me sick. So what if he drove a stellar car, had perfect blond hair, and sexy scruff? I found it freaky. No one could be that perfect.

What a douche-sicle.

The clique of girls might as well drop their panties. Cringe.

Leif forked his fingers through his hair, giving it that messy, I-just-woke-up-like-this look that he probably spent hours perfecting. I swore I heard a chorus of sighs, even from my hiding spot.

The gag reflex started in the back of my throat. It was a train wreck I couldn't stop watching, like reality TV.

One of his groupies got the lady balls to approach him, her heeled boots clattering on the pavement as she strutted to the parking lot. A seductive smirk coated her cherry lips. Leif reached into the back pocket of his tattered black jeans—that probably cost more than the entire wardrobe hanging in my old closet—pulled out a lighter, and a small red box of Marlboros.

Gross.

How could they think that was hot?

With a flick of his thumb, the flame on the lighter caught, casting a soft glow over his flawless face, while he put a slim white cigarette into his mouth. He cupped the dancing fire with his hand, bending his face to catch the tip as he sucked in, sharpening his cheekbones.

If he could see me now, I doubted he would recognize me. I was repulsed to admit that at one time Leif had briefly dated Staci, which could account for 90 percent of my dislike for the guy. To this day, I still don't know what my best friend saw in him, but I guess she had wanted to give dating Mr. Popular a shot, just to say she had.

As if his nose was itching, Leif's sparkly silver eyes whisked to the alley, catching a glimpse of me staring at him. The corners of his mouth twitched. There was something aloof and pompous about the slight tilt of his lips. I jerked back, sinking farther into the darkness, and out of his eyesight.

Color heightened my cheeks. *Crap. Had he seen me?*

The last thing I wanted was rumors spread about me at school. Leif had a younger brother, and at my high school, gossip spread like cancer.

Worry ran through me. *I need to find something better than this.* Living on the streets couldn't be my life.

The girl with mile-long legs reached Leif, taking his attention, but not before I caught the sneer on his lips.

Ugh.

I pressed my back against the wall, arguing with myself. *Don't do it, Olivia. Just walk away.* But it was as if I was possessed. Turning against the brick building, I inched forward, taking another peek. Legs laughed at something Leif said, tossing her ebony hair over her shoulder, and then she placed a flirty hand on his chest.

I snorted.

What they were saying wasn't clear, but it didn't really matter; their body language said it all. Wariness held me back. Something in Leif's gaze made me shudder. He was a tad too controlled. Edging along the wall, I moved farther away from the couple, no longer interested in taking a trip down memory lane, and what he had done to my best friend.

My gaze dropped to my phone for the umpteenth time—nothing new. I noticed the date was the winter solstice. In high school, I'd been fascinated with astronomy. The beginning of winter was here… and the beginning of death for everything else. The plants, the trees, all of it would become stagnant, and here in Chicago, winter wasn't some little event; it lasted months.

A flutter drew my eyes to a shadowed corner near the dumpster. As I grew closer, I noticed it was just a discarded magazine, the pages flapping in the wind. My fingers grazed its pages when I bent down to pick it up. I could use some reading material—a form of entertainment to pass the long night ahead—but first, I needed to find a bathroom. That was one of the things you never thought about before becoming homeless—how difficult it was to do something as simple as pee.

Scooping up the gossip tabloid, a lock of blonde hair fell over my eyes, partially impairing my vision. I stood up and turned the corner, not thinking about where I was going, and smacked into a wall, spilling my pizza. I was always doing crap like that. Being graceful wasn't one of my redeeming qualities.

Son of a bitch. The last thing I need is a bloody nose.

Correction: It wasn't a wall. Just a guy with abs of steel, and I had barreled straight into him. Besides losing my next meal, the collision caused my bag to slip off my shoulder and on to a slice of cheese pizza. *Freaking wonderful.*

"Maybe watch where you're going…"

The rest of my snappy retort got stuck in my throat when my eyes slammed into his. I immediately shut my mouth, and stared into the prettiest eyes I'd ever seen. Bold and bright, they were an unusual violet color. My gaze roamed over the rest of his face, intrigue sucking me in. His cheeks jutted out at sharp angles that led to a defined jaw and full lips, which quirked at the corners.

What did he find so amusing?

I bristled.

I didn't care how jaw dropping he was. The look in his stunning eyes made me uncomfortable—their intensity overwhelming. Why was he staring at me? If he was expecting an apology, he would be sorely disappointed.

The guy towered over me, and my neck cramped from looking up at him. For some reason, he took a step toward me, forcing my back against the damp concrete wall.

The first strings of fear wrapped around my heart. Something in his eyes had my internal alarm going off. This guy was dangerous. He continued to scrutinize me, and my eyes shifted, taking in the rest of his appearance.

He had an obvious love for black. His dark pressed suit with a white cotton T-shirt underneath made him appear older than his smooth face. He couldn't have been more than a year or two older than me, which made me think he was a trust fund baby. An influential and dominating presence emanated from him, reeking of trouble.

His midnight brow lifted—the same shade as his windblown hair. "Are you okay?" His voice was cool and silky. It had a calming effect on my ears, almost hypnotic.

Did he just say something? I shook my head. "What?"

Shifting his stance, he allowed me a smidgen of space, his gaze still relentless. It felt as if he was dissecting me bit by bit with the ferocity of his eyes. I found them mesmerizing and difficult to look away.

"You know, you can stop staring now," I ground out. I needed to keep his gaze focused on my eyes, my lips, my boobs, any part of me that was distracting, so my hands were free to slip into his pockets. And voilà. Hopefully, I was bit richer tonight.

"And miss seeing your pretty face?"

Damn, did the sound of his voice have to be so rich and sensual? He grinned, revealing deep dimples on either cheek. His face now an inch from mine.

From this angle, I spotted a black leather wallet peeking out of his inside jacket pocket. To distract him further, I pushed his chest and, at the same time, I slipped his wallet into my coat pocket, and then folded my arms, needing some sort of defense from his body. Was he flirting with *me*?

"I'm not a hooker, if that's what you're looking for."

His lips thinned, no longer amused. "I'm not, but I am looking for someone."

"Uh, I'm definitely not her. So…" I hoped he would get out of my way and let me pass. I was wrong. What was with people? Did I have a tattoo on my forehead saying "Sucker"? My mouth started flapping before I could stop myself. "Um, do you think you could step back? I really need to pee." *Classy, Olivia. You run into a hot, rich guy and all you can think to say is "I have to pee"?*

Ugh. I wanted to crawl under the nearest bench. Heat crawled over my neck. I shouldn't have been surprised by his reaction, but I was as his lips curled.

"What are you doing out here alone?" he asked, ignoring my need for space. His eyes suddenly took on a new interest in me.

Major warning bells went off, and I scrambled to come up with something that would ward off any seedy ideas. "For your information, I'm not alone. I'm actually on my way to the dorms, which, last I checked, isn't a crime. I'm meeting my huge—I'm talking massive—boyfriend. Like he has muscles for days." Okay, I might have laid that on a little thick. He probably didn't believe me.

He leaned down, the scent of him assaulting my senses, like the sea after a thunderstorm, and I gulped. Why did he have to smell so freaking good? It derailed my train of thought. "Is that so?" he challenged me.

"If you make another move toward me, I'm punching you in the dick." Defense 101: Hit a guy where it hurts, and then run.

He chuckled, and my hands balled into fists. "This has been interesting." Those violet eyes bored into mine, and he lifted a hand as if to touch my cheek.

I should have made good on my threat, instead of just standing there like I'd never seen a guy before. My behavior was odd, but then again, so was this entire encounter.

I held my breath, waiting.

He dropped his hand, the muscles in his body suddenly tightening. Something other than me had his back prickling up, and I was curious what it was. Running a hand through his hair, those piercing eyes returned to mine. "Not possible," he muttered.

For a paralyzing moment, I thought I had been caught red-handed. Anxiously, I tucked my honey blonde hair behind my ears to keep it from hanging in my face and raised a brow. *What is he mumbling about?*

With an expression I couldn't pin, he turned and walked off. No apology. No "it was nice meeting you." Just a cold shoulder and a bizarre meeting.

I watched him strut across the perfectly manicured courtyard with purposeful strides. Wow. I was just going to pretend the last ten minutes had never happened, except my mind was plagued with questions.

What had he meant by "not possible"?

Who was he?

Where was he going?

What was his name?

I hated mysteries, and that guy oozed unanswered questions.

He never bothered to look back, and for some inexplicable reason, it irked me. One thing was clear, I needed to get off the streets and the hell out of Chicago. There was nothing holding me here, other than Staci, but she would be headed to college soon.

With a sigh of regret, I gave Brentley University one last glimpse, and went in search of a bathroom.

My mind mulled over everything I'd lost as I walked—Mom, my home, my friends, all sense of love and stability. No wonder I'd become so cynical. The measly amount of money in my bank account wouldn't last longer than a few days, and I was saving it to get out of here. California sounded heavenly right about now. Warm, sandy beaches. Bountiful opportunities. And miles away from Denny.

How could I say no?

Shifting my bag that housed everything I owned higher on my shoulder, I walked toward a building on the edge of campus. I jogged up the steps, pushing the door open to the commons of Cummings Hall. The ladies' room was to the left. I quickly took care of my bladder, and went to wash my hands, splashing warm water on my face. In the side pocket of my bag, I dug out my hairbrush and ran it through my snarled hair.

Feeling halfway normal, I stared at my reflection. Who would have ever thought the clumsy, sassy girl from Wrigleyville would end up here? Not me. Not in a million years. I would have laughed in their faces.

My aqua eyes were tired and puffy. No amount of cream would fix these bad boys, but a pillow top mattress and a solid ten hours of sleep would do wonders. The only thing saving me from looking like a zombie was my thick, dark eyelashes. I never had to wear mascara. The dusting of freckles sprinkled over the bridge of my nose had started to fade as winter approached.

I fitted a beanie over my hair to prevent the wind from knotting it, and my keep ears warm. Digging into my coat pocket, I pulled out the sucker's wallet and fumbled through the slots.

Son of a bitch.

There was nothing. No credit cards. No cash. Not even an ID. Who the hell carries around an empty wallet? A ghost, that's who, or someone with something to hide. And the mysterious stranger seemed to have plenty to hide. I still didn't know his name. Disappointed, I tossed the black leather billfold into the garbage, cursing my luck. I should have gone for the watch.

Sighing, I gathered my bag, and set out to find a cozy spot I could curl up in for the night. The train station was always an option, but I risked being kicked out by security, and I wasn't in the mood to deal with authority figures. My other option was an abandoned warehouse behind the convenience store that had come in handy, and I had often made it my own little sanctuary at night.

I hauled ass down the stone steps of Cummings Hall—not very

gracefully I might add—when a shiver wracked my body, as a jolt of icy wind whipped through me. Leif and his harem were nowhere in sight. Stealing a glance over my shoulder, I saw the sidewalks were vacant, but a sudden flight response rose up inside me. With each step, I couldn't shake the instinct, and instead of ignoring the feeling, I took a quick turn toward the courtyard—away from the campus buildings behind me. While trekking across the street, some jackass honked from his Mercedes, and I flipped him off, jumping onto the sidewalk. Chicago traffic was the absolute worst.

It was only a few blocks' walk, but as I passed Lou's Quick Mart, the prickly sensation of being followed increased tenfold. I turned my head around for another peek. Again, no one there. I bolted.

This was definitely one of my not very thought-out decisions, but I also didn't want to get killed tonight. Better safe than sorry. If I was wrong, no harm. Sure, I might feel silly afterward, and have a quick laugh, but I would be safe.

The sound of footsteps pounding behind me told me I'd made the right choice. I amplified my speed, flying over the grass. My Converse sunk into the damp dirt, and I lost my beanie in the process. Strands of my hair flung in my face as I ran. It didn't take long for my legs to burn and my lungs to ache from the exertion, but I pushed myself. Blood rushed to my cheeks as my heart quickened.

Terror clamped down on my chest and settled. Knowing this could end badly, like really bad for me, I refused to think of who was chasing me or what they wanted. Damn those horror books I'd been obsessed with in high school. My imagination was getting the best of me.

Money?

Rape?

Torture?

Slavery?

A million horrible scenarios raced through my head, clouding my ability to keep my wits sharp—a huge mistake.

"Who the hell is following me?" I asked myself as confusion set in beside the fear. The only thing I was certain of was I needed to get somewhere public at record speeds.

I cut the corner toward the multistory buildings, but realized my mistake, having turned right instead of left. I stared at a dead end alley.

Smart move, Olivia. Now what?

"Shit. Shit. Shit," I muttered out loud, trying to gather my thoughts through the slick feeling of terror. It gripped me, and for a second, I was afraid I would cower into a ball in the middle of the street.

I jerked around, hoping I had enough of a lead to backtrack before my stalker cornered me. No go.

A shadow stood in the mouth of the alley, blocking the exit. From the size of his form, it was a man… a very big man.

Trapped, I released a soft whimper. My breath came out in a cloud in front of my face. *What do I do?* Did I even have options at this point? What could I do besides cry for help, and hope someone came to my rescue?

I didn't like my odds. Not at this time of night or in this part of town. Everyone was in their dorms with the music turned up, and people were laughing, drinking. Who was going to hear the cries of a desperate girl?

I opened my mouth to scream, and that was when I heard a familiar voice. Someone I'd only met a short while ago, but was unlikely to forget.

"Just the girl I was hoping to run into," a deep and rich voice said from the darkness.

Son of a bitch.

I was going to cause him bodily harm for real this time.

The very last person I ever thought I'd see again, stood in front of me in all his pompous glory—the jackass with the dreamy eyes and sinful dimples, who had almost mowed me down in the last alley we'd shared. The one I had stolen the empty wallet from earlier. What were the freaking odds?

Pretty slim, I thought, unless he'd been following me.

But why would he do that? Why would he care about a wallet with nothing in it?

"You!" I accused him, a feeling of anger engulfing me, and giving me a dose of boldness. "You've been following me. Why?" I demanded, as my eyes bore into his First rule of being a thief: never admit to what you've done.

My mysterious stalker lifted a brow, his form dwarfing the entrance of the alley. Words couldn't do justice to how striking his face was—a truly unearthly beauty. His violet eyes were a stark contrast to his fair skin. "You intrigue me."

I wanted to berate him for scaring me half to death. I didn't need any more nightmares in my life. "The laws of nature intrigue me. Literature intrigues me. Stars intrigue me. But following people down dark alleys doesn't intrigue me. I think you might need some new hobbies. Stalking is creepy."

"It wasn't my intent to frighten you," he said, a smile playing on his lips.

He needed to stop doing that—flashing those dimples at me. I didn't like the way my belly flip-flopped. "Why don't I believe you?" I shifted my feet, dying to run again. The dreamy stranger made me wary.

"Because you're smart. What's your name?"

His voice sounded closer than it had before, but I hadn't even seen him move. I glared. "Sorry, I don't think names are necessary. I've got places to be." I started to walk around him, quickening my pace, but I should have known he wasn't going to let me go.

His hand shot out, gripping my arm, and twisting me so I was forced to face him once again. "I highly doubt it."

Heat pooled on my skin where his hand held me. "You think you know me? Please." I jerked away, dislodging his hand, but not because I was stronger, or had caught him off guard. He had released me.

"Your name," he insisted.

Geez. If it got him off my back, so be it. "Olivia Campbell," I answered in an even tone, resigned to my fate. If he had been following me for the wallet, why hadn't he mentioned it yet?

"Olivia," he repeated as if testing the sound of my name on his lips. "Now, that wasn't so hard."

Smartass.

"Happy now?" I snapped, prepared to go on my merry way.

He lifted a single brow. "We're just getting started, Cupcake."

"Don't call me that. I gave you my name, even though you haven't given me yours." Did I even want to know? He would probably give me a fake anyway. Damn. Why hadn't I thought of that? I shouldn't have given him my real name. That was so stupid of me. If I was going to survive, I had to be smarter than that.

His lips curved. "It seems we got off on the wrong foot. I'm Jase Dior."

I rubbed my arm not because it hurt, but just the opposite. Tingles radiated from where he'd touched me, confusing me. Jase, huh? He even had a sexy name. Not surprising though, it suited him. I shoved my hands into my back pockets, ignoring the strange sensation. "Why are you so interested in me?" I asked.

He blinked. "I haven't figured it out yet."

A snorting sound came from the back of my throat. "Can you at least tell me why have you been following me?"

"I have a weakness for pretty things."

"Like diamonds? Cars? The sunset?" I asked.

"No, blondes," he replied matter-of-factly.

I choked. An awkward silence descended, and I was still trying to come up with a better plan than my first to get myself out of this situation. I still didn't know what kind of situation I was in. Good? Or bad? "I'm not a natural blonde," I finally said, breaking the silence. It was a lie, but he didn't need to know that.

He crossed his arms, his muscles stretching the fabric of his suit jacket as they covered the taut chest hidden under his shirt. "I can be flexible."

Hell no.

"How old are you?" he asked.

Next, he was going to want to know my bra size, or my social security number. Either way, I wasn't dishing. "Does it matter?"

"No, not really," he admitted, angling his head to the side as he regarded me with those piercing eyes.

What the hell was he getting at? I definitely didn't trust him. Flipping the hood of my sweatshirt over my head, I covered my tousled hair. "You're really starting to weird me out. I'm not interested in any little sex rings you've got going on the side. So it was nice meeting you, Jase." *Hope I never see you again.*

Even as the thought left my mind, I knew it wasn't true. As much as I needed a ridiculous amount of therapy, I couldn't pretend there wasn't something about Jase that captivated me.

"Not so fast." A breeze blew down the alley, carrying his scent in the air. It reminded me of sea spray and moonlight, like a midnight beach party. "You don't belong on the streets."

I snorted. "Thanks for the unnecessary concern, but I do just fine on my own."

He moved forward, so that his warm breath danced along my cheek, and I flinched. "I'm not going to hurt you. It isn't my style to intimidate women," he admitted, shooting me a disarming smile.

He shouldn't be equipped with such a powerful weapon. For a moment, I forgot we stood in the street. That it was freezing outside. That I must look atrocious. The way he stared at me made me not feel alone for the first time in weeks.

"Okay, what is it you want from me? Am I a welfare project? Because I'm not interested in being your charity case."

He forked a hand through his dark hair. "Do you always jump to so many conclusions? I should just pick another girl, but I can't figure out why I'm drawn to you."

"It's the hair, isn't it?" I questioned, remembering his comment about blondes.

His lips might have twitched, but it was hard to tell in the night. "It definitely helps, Cupcake. I need you to come with me."

My brows pulled together. "And if I refuse?"

"It would be easier if you didn't."

My fear was now off the charts. I didn't care how perfect his face was. "Easier for who?"

His gaze locked on mine. "I won't hurt you. I give you my word."

"Sorry, but I don't trust you, and for your word to mean anything, I would have to trust you. So, you see, I think we find ourselves at an impasse." My eyes darted behind him. There was a very slim chance I could take him by surprise and run off. A knee to the groin usually worked, and would give me the window I needed to escape.

"Don't even try it. I will catch you," he warned me, his eyes darkening to a deep plum.

"If you don't let me go, I'll scream."

The stranger's jaw tightened. "Time is running out. We must go."

"I'm not going anywhere with you. No matter how cute your dimples are." I squeezed my eyes shut for a moment. Why did stuff like that always have to come out of my mouth? I needed to learn how to not blurt out the first thing that popped into my head.

He blew out a breath. "I figured you'd want to do this the hard way."

I was about to take my chances and give my lungs some more exercise, when he blew in my face. A cool mist that smelled of lavender and vanilla, and felt like the spray of a waterfall rained over me. I gasped—the worst possible reaction I could have had—inhaling a huge gulp of the mysterious mist. The effect was instant. A heavy calmness overcame me, making my eyes droop.

It took away my fear. It took away everything.

A shriek tore through the darkness, like a soul being tortured. My last thought was I might never get to tell Staci about the hottie I ran into in an alley. She would have loved every second of my discomfort.

I blinked several times, hoping to recognize my location. No such luck. This wasn't the first time I'd woken up in a strange place. However, it was the first time I'd woken up with my wrists tied together.

What the hell?

Thickly corded ropes bound my hands, and no matter how much I tugged, I couldn't loosen the knot. *Breathe, Olivia. You can figure a way out of this. Just Breathe.*

My body quivered, and a veil of panic came over me as my eyes followed my bindings to where the rope attached to a wall. I felt chilled, but unlike the cold I was used to in Chicago, this emanated from the inside.

Where am I?

How did I get here?

Jase! my mind hissed—the hot guy with the dimples who had cornered me in the alley. His face was the last memory I had before my mind went fuzzy. What had he done to me? I should have listened to the stupid voice in my head, the one that had told me to run when I'd had the chance. Now look what I'd gotten myself into—tied to a wall.

At least my clothes were still on.

But for how long? that little voice asked.

Shut up.

"Hello?" I called, my voice echoing through the silent room. "Is anyone there?"

The only sounds were my heavy breathing, and the pounding of my heart. My frantic eyes took in my surroundings: a plush bed in the corner, soft cream carpet on the floor, and flickering candles casting a soft glow.

At least I wasn't in a dungeon or a cellar. I had that going for me.

Opening my mouth, I was about to call out again—louder this time —when the clopping of footsteps approached outside the door. The knob turned, and I shifted straighter in the chair, prepared to fight if necessary.

But that implied I knew how to fight, and I didn't.

Four extraordinary guys strolled in, their eyes immediately finding me in the room. One I might have been able to handle, but four? How the hell could I take on four? They gathered around me in a semicircle. I had to crane my neck to look at them since they were all tall, built like football players, and extremely good looking. I had thought Jase had muddled my brain, but four of them? All coherent thoughts went out the window. Each was different in his coloring and look, but they all held a sense of power and importance.

Jase stood in the middle. At least I knew who to blame for my capture. To his left was a guy who looked as if he belonged in a punk rock band. His hair was spiked down the center and green-tipped. His emerald eyes twinkled when he noticed me staring at the metal ring in his bottom lip. He winked, letting me know he noticed I was checking him out.

On the other side of Jase stood a golden god—olive skin, whiskey-colored eyes tinged with crimson, caramel brown hair, and full beautiful lips. Beside him was the fourth. Whereas the others seemed approachable, the blond with icy blue eyes was the fiercest of the four, and also the biggest. His lips formed a thin line as he eyed me with disdain. He reminded me of an ice prince.

"Welcome to the Veil Isles, Olivia," Jase greeted, in that calm and sensual voice.

"She is quite beautiful," the one with the mohawk and hot lips added.

Golden God smirked. "Did you expect anything less from Jase? She fits his type to a T." His voice was like honey, thick and sweet.

"You better be right about her," the blond replied in a sharp tone.

"Trust me, this one is different, Issik," Jase assured him.

"So you said the last one hundred and ninety-nine times," Golden God muttered.

They had done this one hundred and ninety-nine times? Kidnapping girls? My eyes went wide with fear. What kind of crap did I get myself into?

"Don't look so alarmed. Who knows? Maybe Jase is right," Hot Lips said, rewarding me with a wicked grin. "You could be the one we've been searching for."

I didn't really care if I was the *one*. In all honesty, I hoped I wasn't so I could get as far away from these four as possible… and this place called the Veil Isles. "Can you untie me now?"

Jase lifted a dark brow. "Depends. Are you going to run? Because I'm not in the mood to chase you through the castle."

Castle, my mind echoed.

"He might not be, but I am." Hot Lips winked.

"Kieran," Jase scolded. "Do we have your word, Cupcake?"

The three guys on either side of Jase smirked, even the cold one, Issik, his lips twitching.

"Fine," I agreed, while cursing the four of them under my breath. "But call me cupcake one more time, and I'll be forced to introduce my knee to your junk."

A few snickers erupted as Jase bent down and fumbled with the knot, loosening it so he could slip it over my hands. "Better?" Now he suddenly cared about my well-being.

Rubbing my hands over my wrists, I tried to release some of the sting from the bonds. "Are you going to tell me what I'm doing here? What is the Veil? And why did you kidnap me?" I presumed it was because I had been living on the streets, and Jase knew no one would be looking for me.

He had assumed correctly, but I wouldn't admit it.

"You have questions, clearly," Jase added, sounding too calm and collected for someone who had just committed abduction.

Duh. I think I had made that point already. "Did you think I wouldn't?"

Issik scowled.

Kieran smirked.

Jase frowned.

And the golden god, whose name I still didn't know, coughed.

"I like her," Kieran said. "Can we keep her?"

Ice Prince's jaw tightened. He was every inch the image of a Viking. "It doesn't really matter if you do or don't like her. She is here for a reason. Don't forget that."

"And just what the hell is that reason?" I demanded.

"It's complicated," Jase answered. "I think we should get you settled in, let you clean up, and rest. Tomorrow will be soon enough to answer those questions I see swimming in your eyes. And before you argue, remember, there are four of us."

They all loomed over me, daring me to challenge them with their stern demeanors and firm abs. Damn the four of them to the deepest parts of hell. "It doesn't look like I have much of a choice in the matter."

Jase hovered over me, power exuding from his chest. "You have no reason to trust me, but I saved you. You no longer have to live on the streets or steal to eat. You don't have to worry about where you're going to sleep. Do us all a favor and don't do anything foolish."

I tipped my chin up, feeling my cheeks flood with color. He might not have meant to embarrass me on purpose, but he did so all the same. My pride refused to admit that what he offered sounded like an answer to my prayers. Too good to be true.

I was struck again by his handsomeness, but it didn't last more than a few seconds before my sanity returned. Me? Do something foolish? A glint in his expression gave me pause, and I couldn't determine why I wasn't demanding him to let me go, or why I wasn't threatening him. "What happens if I decide I don't want to stay? Am I allowed to leave, or are you going to stop me?"

The four of them suddenly couldn't look me in the eye, and I knew I had my answer. They weren't going to let me go. After a minute, Jase took a deep breath. "I give you my word no harm will come to you. You'll be under my protection."

"Protection from what? Am I in danger?"

Kieran crossed his arms and gave me a cheeky smile. "This one is a lot quicker and calmer than the others. We're keeping her."

"She's not nearly as frightened as she should be," Ice Prince added, his frown deepening.

Oh, there was a good dose of fear inside me. I was just better at faking it. I took a second to study Issik. He oozed bitterness—a warrior with a chip on his shoulder. His silky blond hair hung straight, just reaching his chin, which was covered with day-old stubble. It suited him.

"Don't let her doe-eyed face fool you, Zade. She's scared."

I wanted to wipe the smugness off Jase's pretty face after his words. Bastard. I was starting to really not like him, but at least I had gotten the last one's name—Zade, the one who looked like a golden god.

"Will the four of you stop talking about me as if I wasn't in the room?" I shouted.

That got their attention.

"This will be interesting for sure. Do you think she'll get along with the others?" Kieran asked.

Jase was no longer amused, the pupils of his violet eyes sobering. "We're keeping her separate until we know for sure if she can be the one."

Zade lifted a cinnamon brow. "Is that the only reason?"

I opened my mouth to complain yet again, but Issik beat me to it. "How old are you?" he asked, directing the question to me.

Under his piercing eyes, I fidgeted in the chair. "Why does it matter? If you have no qualms about kidnapping, I doubt my age is suddenly going to give you a conscience."

There were a few snickers.

Jase shook his head. "This room will be yours for the time being."

My gaze swung to the door. "Let me guess, there's a lock."

"You got it, Cupcake, not that it matters. There's no leaving the Veil Isles."

We'll see about that. If there was a will, there was a way. "I thought I told you not to call me that."

"Try not to—" Jase was interrupted by a loud shriek.

All four glorious heads swung to the balcony doors I had failed to notice in the room before.

What was that? It sounded like a bear being tortured. Their hard bodies stiffened as each of the guys' faces became dark scowls. A large shadow flew over the window, causing the room to go black for a moment as it moved past. It was a lot bigger than your average hawk or crow.

Sweet Jesus.

"Dammit," Jase growled, causing trepidation to dance inside my chest.

"What is it?" I asked, my eyes bouncing between the four of them. Each guy was glowering, so I could only conclude it wasn't good.

"A wraith," Issik hissed, swinging his frozen glare to Jase. "Did you forget to close the portal?"

"No, of course not," he replied. "I'm not an idiot."

Issik lips thinned as he strutted to the double doors that led outside. "How did it get through, then?"

Another scream echoed, both long and piercing. I didn't know what a wraith was, but I also didn't want to know. My mind was kind of still hung up on the word "portal." That couldn't mean what I thought it did, could it? No. It wasn't possible. Traveling from one place to another through a swirling black hole?

Jase sighed. "I've got it. Stay with her," he told Hot Lips and Golden God, walking toward the French doors. I caught a flash of something on his face before he spun away, and if I already weren't having the most otherworldly day, I would have brushed off the speck of worry I thought I glimpsed.

Angling my head so I could see around the bulky form of Issik, my eyes bulged. Jase tossed his cotton shirt over his head, revealing chiseled abs. *I won't lie, for a moment, my mind went blank and my mouth dry.* I stretched to the side for a better view, but the bellow of another roar outside snapped me back.

The wraith, as they called it, was clearly pissed off. I didn't know what Jase thought he could do about it. I knew what I wanted to do: curl up in the corner and cry. This day was taking its toll.

But my emotions were pushed aside as I stared at Jase, my mind rejecting everything it was seeing. Dark purple scales that were almost black appeared on his shoulders, multiplying until they covered his entire torso. His fingers went to the button on his pants and off those went too.

Um, this was way more than I'd bargained for. His violet eyes brightened as the transformation took over.

I bit my lip to keep from screaming, because some inner voice told me that was not the right response, and would only make this situation worse. Three other pairs of eyes all watched me with intensity, judging my reaction.

Claws exploded from his fingertips and toes. He was already a tall and muscular guy, but his body grew, filling out and lengthening. Scales covered his entire form. A massive tail unraveled from behind him and across the room from one wall to the other.

My eyes swept the length of him from head to tail. What Jase had changed into, nearly made me pee my pants. He was a mother-freaking dragon.

I held back a squeak as he angled his triangular head toward me, and if it weren't for those violet eyes, I wouldn't have believed it was possible. I felt positive this creature could do a serious amount of damage; his sheer height and powerful tail were formidable enough on their own. Then he took off, spreading his massive wings when he leaped off the balcony.

"I'm not letting him have all the fun," Kieran announced, whipping off his shirt.

Oh my god. Please tell me they aren't all going to get naked and shift into dragons. I didn't think my nerves could handle it.

Dragons! my mind screamed. I'd been abducted by a group of sexy dragons. Or at least two of them...

It wasn't possible, but I had just seen it with my own eyes.

Kieran walked across the room, and in a similar fashion, his body changed and stretched, but his scales were green with long spikes lining the end of his tail. Dipping his head, he followed Jase into the dark sky.

My heart hammered in my chest, and I expected, any second, it was going to jump out. This kind of stuff didn't happen to me. It only existed in movies and fantasy novels. Had they injected me with drugs today? What the hell had been in that pizza? Was I dreaming? That had to be it. This was a nightmare, and I would wake up at any moment alone in my little shack behind the food mart.

I squeezed my eyes closed, praying when I opened them that all this would disappear.

Crap.

Issik and Zade stared down at me with twin expressions of curiosity.

Dammit.

"She hasn't freaked out yet," Zade said to Issik, possibly impressed with my composure. If he only knew what was going on inside me.

Issik's lips pressed together firmly. "I wouldn't be so sure about that. She's probably in shock."

I shoved off the chair, not caring if they tried to stop me. I had to see what was happening with my own two eyes. Were there really two dragons flying around outside this castle? Was I really in a castle at all?

Neither objected when I stood, but they followed me outside to stand on the balcony. I gasped. The view was… breathtaking. I'd never seen anything like it in my life. I had to be at least six stories high, and directly below me was a body of water that surrounded the entire castle, almost as if we were in a stranded oasis. Beyond the flowing sea were dark trees of various heights, and further yet, I could just make out through the fog three other castles with multiple towers that jutted into the sky and disappeared into black clouds.

"What do you think of your first glimpse of the Veil Isles?" Zade asked, leaning so he could whisper in my ear.

A shudder rippled through my body, and I couldn't tell if it was because of his proximity or the shock, but I was rendered speechless. My hands gripped the edge of the balcony's railing as I searched the sky and found what I was looking for. Proof my eyes hadn't deceived me. The two dragons soaring in the night were easy to spot; their impressive wings spread wide as they glided in the air, circling a small figure. "Small" was only a relative term to the size of the dragons, because next to me, this dark creature would have dwarfed me.

The shadowy figure moved with a deathly grace that filled my veins with ice. Then again, Issik had moved closer. He could very well have been responsible for the sudden coldness running through my blood.

I didn't know which I should be scared of more: the dragons or the wraith. Or the two guys flanking me.

I thought the night would have made it hard to discern between the dragons, but I spotted Jase easily enough. His scales glistened in the moonlight, and it was difficult to believe only moments ago he'd been standing in front of me.

The breath in my lungs escaped as my eyes followed his movements. Jase and Kieran seemed to work together, taking turns swinging their claws at the wraith while they hovered in the air supported by their wings. I could hear the flapping as their wings beat, both powerful and elegant.

The wraith fought with precision and ruthlessness. With twice the speed of the dragons, it weaved between Kieran and Jase. Kieran opened his jaws, letting a stream of neon green fire expel from within him, straight at the wraith. The creature let out another bellowing shriek, but didn't run away. In fact, just the opposite. He apparently did not fear the dragons.

Me?

I was afraid of everything at the moment.

But even with the huge amounts of fear swimming inside me, I couldn't tear my gaze from the action. It was like the most engrossing movie of my life, but instead of watching from the comforts of a recliner with a bowl of popcorn, I was an active participant. Everything I thought I knew about dragons—which, to be frank, was all from fiction anyway—seemed to be wrong. What happened to dragons spitting red fire? Kieran's dragon breath was so much cooler.

If I thought I'd had questions before, it was nothing compared to the absurd number racing wildly in my head now.

Jase and Kieran kept a tight leash on the wraith, following it as the beast flew just under the balcony. A gust of wind blew my hair back as the trio rushed through the air. I leaned over the railing, stretching to see them, and the next thing I knew, I was tumbling, falling through the darkness toward the black sea below.

My scream rang out over the valley.

The dark waters were rushing quickly toward me, and I braced myself. *Oh God, I'm going to die.* That was really going to piss Jase off. He went to all the trouble of getting me here—for reasons I still didn't understand—and then I go and get myself killed. Classic Olivia.

But I didn't smack the murky sea as I'd expected. I landed on something firm and scaly when it swept underneath me, catching me before I cannonballed. As the air was forced from my lungs on impact, my hands fumbled to grasp something for fear of falling again. Clinging to the dragon's scales around his neck, I tried to catch my breath. Wind tore at my face, and I buried my head deeper against his neck.

I wasn't sure which dragon had rescued me, but if I had to guess, it was Issik, the ice prince, since the shimmering scales underneath me were a whitish-blue. Although the scales were not as rough as I would have thought. We were still diving downward at frightening speeds toward the water, but at the last second, he pulled up, letting his hind legs and tail skim over the surface.

"You're intentionally trying to scare the shit out of me, aren't you?" I yelled, when my heart started beating again.

"*Are you always this suicidal?*" Issik's voice sounded in my head, proving I had been right about which dragon had saved me.

"Depends if I'm having a good day or not. And let me tell you, today has sucked the big one," I muttered.

"*Think you can manage to hang on, while I get you somewhere you can't get hurt?*"

My legs tightened around him as if I was born to ride dragons. Just like riding a bike, I told myself. "As long as you don't do any loop the loops."

I swore I felt his body rumble in a laugh.

Holy crap. I was riding a dragon.

Now that I was safe, for the time being, I could see more of the land. I had been wrong about the castle being surrounded entirely by water. On the other side, black sand covered the ground, leading to a gigantic volcano. Billows of smoke rose from the top, dissolving into the black clouds. It was evident I wasn't in Chicago anymore. The land here was lush and vibrant, yet somber. Regardless of its beauty, it emitted danger.

The dragons flying around were proof enough of that.

Above us, Jase, Kieran, and the wraith came into sight. The shrouded creature screeched in rage. Jase thrashed his thick tail through the air, smacking the wraith and sending him spiraling straight at Issik and me.

"*Hang on tight,*" Issik advised me as he reared back.

My arms wrapped around his neck, gripping on for dear life.

Issik inhaled deeply, and my mind screamed in warning. What goes in must come out. He blew an icy mist directly into the creature's face, a second before it sunk razor-sharp choppers into the dragon's scaly flesh.

A whimpering noise came from the back of Issik's throat, but he held steadfast, never wavering regardless that he was hurt.

The wraith's ethereal body crystallized, turning into an ice sculpture. Kieran flew down, whacking the spiked end of his tail into the wraith, and shattering it like glass. The pieces rained down into the murky waters below.

That was the single scariest and coolest shit that had ever happened to me.

Threat averted, Issik flew us back to the balcony with Jase and Kieran close behind. *"You think you can manage to get down without hurting yourself?"* Issik asked with a bitter sharpness.

Out of the four guys, Issik was the hardest to read. He didn't really seem to like me all that much; yet, he was the one who had saved me. "As long as you stay still for a minute," I retorted, swinging both my legs to one side.

He tipped his head, and I slid down his neck. Zade was there to catch me. Once my feet were safely on the ground, I spun around to get my first full look at Issik in his dragon form. He was utterly stunning. At the end of his enormous white wings, where they sloped into waves, were talons. His icy blue eyes glowed brightly as they pinned mine. Everything about him reminded me of Chicago winters—cold, blistering, ruthless.

Jase and Kieran had already shifted back and stood outside the bedroom door fully dressed, watching me as I gawked at Issik. In a reverse transformation, the dragon shifted into a man, who became a naked Issik. He raised a brow as I continued to gape, my gaze wandering over him. Who could blame me? He was an incredible male specimen. It was like a shield came down over Issik—his brief flicker of amusement washed away by the hardness now reflected in his eyes as he slipped into his discarded clothes.

After all the excitement, the moment finally caught up to me. I huddled in the corner, my body wracked with violent shivers. I was a pretty open-minded individual, but this... this was way outside my scope of reality.

Four sets of eyes stared at me as if I might shatter into a million pieces at any moment. Questions spun like a windmill through my head. How in the world did they turn into dragons? Did it hurt? Could it be an illusion? Were they aliens from another planet? Or maybe a science experiment with dinosaur DNA?—Jurassic Park came to mind. And if there were dragon... er, shifters... then why not a wraith? But most importantly, why did it attack us?

If I could only get those thoughts to form into words... but my mouth was numb. Placing a hand on the nearest wall, I leaned my hip against it.

"So, how was she?" Kieran asked Issik, bumping his shoulder lightly against the ice prince's.

Issik frowned. "Wouldn't you like to know."

Not getting what he wanted from Issik, Kieran turned to me. "How was your first time, Olivia?" The way he asked that had my cheeks flaming. Something about how Hot Lips worded things and his playful tone gave off a sexy vibe.

I ignored him and finally found my tongue. "W-what just happened?" I stammered.

"It's pretty common, actually," Kieran answered, a lazy grin on his lips. It was evident he loved the thrill of the hunt, of flying, and of being a dragon.

"Which part? That thing that attacked us, or you turning into drag-ons?" I needed specifics.

"The wraith was a messenger," Jase supplied.

"A messenger?" I echoed on the verge of hysteria. "I'm guessing it wasn't a friendly message."

The four of them shared a look, and seemed to be deciding how much to tell me before Jase turned to face me with an expression of incredulity. "You're scared... but not because I turned into a dragon?"

Truth be told, I was terrified, but yes, I was way more scared of the other thing. The wraith had an aura about it akin to death. As weird as this was, at least they had turned back into humans. I couldn't say the same about the other creature. That had to count for something. "I would be lying if I said I wasn't scared. Nothing about what I've just witnessed seems real, and I keep waiting to wake up, but on the off chance this is not a dream, I'm also… curious, I guess. Do all four of you turn into dragons?"

"Pretty fucking awesome, right?" Kieran said, grinning like the shithead I felt positive he was. The others didn't bat an eye.

"And you each breathe a different kind of fire or… something?" I questioned, processing the assumptions tumbling in my head. I was trying to make sense of it all, but I probably sounded like an idiot in the process.

With slow movements, Jase walked toward me. "It's been a long night, Cupcake. Why don't you get some sleep? In the morning, we'll explain everything. I think you've had enough excitement. I don't want to push you too fast."

"This can't be real," I muttered to myself, laying a hand on my forehead.

"I know this might all seem impossible, but get some rest. You'll see things clearer after you've slept." Jase kept his voice smooth and level.

Will I though?

Would I wake up in the abandoned building behind the Quick Mart —alone once again? Could this all be a dream?

Something told me a good night's sleep wasn't going to make it all better.

Jase flashed me a set of dimples, capturing my eyes with his, so that the other three guys melted away. There was something mesmerizing and magnetic about Jase. "Rest, Cupcake," he whispered, and for the second time tonight, he blew a puff of purple mist into my face.

"Why do you keep doing that?" I mumbled, my eyes growing sleepy, and I knew I only had a few more moments before I wouldn't be able to stand on my own, but it turned out, that wasn't a problem.

Jase bent down, swooping an arm under my legs and lifting me up. I rested my heavy head on his shoulders, unable to support it myself. My face pressed up against his neck, and I inhaled the scent of him—

sand and sea. "Because your body needs to sleep, and you strike me as the kind of girl who is stubborn. I'm giving you what you need. Now, close your eyes," he demanded, walking me into the center of the room.

So much for insisting on getting answers. Jase had even taken that from me. Now I had no choice but to sleep.

Just who are they?

What do they want with me?

Damn. Damn. Damn.

I lost the battle with consciousness before he laid me down.

Snuggling deeper into the warmth surrounding me, I kept my eyes closed, telling myself to go back to sleep, to ignore the blissful sun glowing on my cheeks. I didn't want to stir, for that meant I would have to face the reality that my life had become a fantasy, and not in a good way. It was so much easier to keep dreaming and pretend I wouldn't wake to a nightmare.

Maybe if I wished hard enough, I would be back home in my own bed. Mom would be downstairs humming, and life would go back to normal.

It was such a nice dream.

A firm knock sounded on the door, and I threw the covers over my head, wishing he would go away. A frown pulled at my lips. I was miffed about having my sleep disturbed. The door creaked open, and I held my breath, staying as still as possible under the covers.

"You going to sleep all day?" a husky voice asked. "I thought you would be brimming with questions this morning." It was Kieran. The rocker embodying a dragon had the tiniest hint of an accent.

"Go away," I groaned, my voice muffled under the thick blanket.

Kieran laughed, and the sound made my belly cartwheel.

My scowl deepened. *Stop that,* I berated my body. *You should feel nothing but contempt for him… for all four of them.*

Light fingers tugged on the end of the covers, pulling them down so I stared up into Kieran's twinkling emerald eyes. His piercing glittered in the sun, and I wondered what it would be like to kiss someone with a lip ring. Would the metal be cool against my mouth? Would I be tempted to bite it?

I shook my head.

Why are you thinking about kissing him? He is holding you hostage, remember?

"I brought you something to eat," he offered.

My gaze was drawn to a small table where a tray sat, the smells wafting around the room. "Where's Jase?" I asked, giving up the pretense of sleep. I was wide awake now, and my stomach was growling.

Kieran lifted a brow. "Would you prefer him over me?"

He was impossible. I shrugged because I was sure his ego would take a hit. "It doesn't really matter. Am I still a prisoner?"

The mattress dipped to the side with his weight as he sat on the edge of the bed. "I like to think of it as a guest."

Linking my fingers together, I stared up at him. "You have a warped sense of hospitality."

"If you give it a chance, I think you'll enjoy living in the Veil Isles. Believe it or not, we aren't monsters."

"Right, because the wraith was so warm and welcoming."

His lips twitched. "They are pesky bastards. Eat. And then I'll take you to clean up."

A shower. My mind sighed. Warm food, a clean bed, a hot bath—were they trying to butter me up?

I plucked a piece of toast off the tray and had it to my mouth before I paused. "How do I know this isn't poisoned?"

Kieran grabbed the other half of the toast and bit into it. "Happy?" he asked, swallowing. "I don't normally poison pretty girls," he added with a wink.

I took a nibble from the corner, refraining from gorging myself by shoving the whole piece in my mouth. I studied him as I ate, thinking about what he'd said. "Is that your ability? Poison?"

A gleam of surprise leapt into his eyes. "You're perceptive. Maybe too much. Yes, I breathe poison; it's my curse."

I thought it odd he considered being a dragon-shifter a curse. "Issik breathes ice. Jase some kind of sleeping spell?" I guessed, listing off their abilities.

"Tranquility," he supplied.

"What about Zade?" I asked.

"Fire," he replied.

After polishing off the toast, I moved on to a cup of fruit—none of which I recognized. Still, my hunger at this point wasn't picky. "Where are the others?"

Kieran shrugged and seemed content just keeping me company. "Around. We each have our own kingdoms to oversee. This is Jase's, Wakeland Kingdom, and his castle, Wakeland Keep."

"So you all don't live here?"

Kieran shook his head. "But don't worry, blondie, you'll get to see plenty of me."

Again, his tone implied something wicked.

I scooted to the other side of the bed and stood up, stretching my legs. I had slept in my clothes last night, and was glad to see no one had tried to remove them. With my hunger now curbed, I thought about the mention of a shower.

"Come on. I'll show you to the bath house," Kieran offered, as I ran my fingers through my hair.

It was hopeless. Nothing but a bottle of deep conditioner and a brush would fix this mess.

Exiting the chamber, Kieran led us down a long passageway. The walls were made of dark gray limestone, and our footsteps echoed off the wood floors. The corridors were lit by torches hung in sconces. We turned a corner and descended a set of winding stairs. Inside, I couldn't figure out how to feel. Scared? Fascinated? Foolish? Should I be trying to escape?

There were no railings as we walked down the steps, and me being me, I stumbled, by not looking ahead, and spending too much time admiring the paintings lining the walls. My nails scrambled against the rock as I tried to catch myself from plummeting, but really, I had little to worry about.

Kieran's quick reflexes saved me, his hands landing on my waist. "You're going to be quite the challenge to keep safe, aren't you?" he whispered as he pulled me up against him to steady us both.

"Huh?" I uttered, my brain fuzzy. *What did he say?* It didn't really seem to matter. My eyes couldn't get past his lips.

His chest rumbled against mine. "Curious?" he asked, running the pad of his thumb along the side of my jaw, skimming just under my lower lip. His head dipped, and my lashes began to flutter closed. He was going to kiss me.

"Kieran!" snapped a cold voice.

Hot Lips kissed the tip of my nose instead, grinning down at my wide eyes. "Issik takes the fun out of everything."

My eyes glanced over Kieran's shoulder to see the tall blond stalking toward us with purposeful strides. I jumped out of the punk rocker's arms, standing on my own without his support, and immediately missing the strength of his body.

What the hell is wrong with me?

Kieran shot a lopsided grin at Issik as he started to walk again. "Relax, mate. Olivia and I were just getting to know each other better. Isn't that right, blondie?"

Issik wasn't buying it. "Get her cleaned up. Don't play with her."

I winced. *Asshole.*

I bit my tongue to keep from saying something that would anger him further. Issik didn't strike me as the type of guy who put up with nonsense. Kieran slipped a hand to the small of my back, urging me, with a slight pressure, to keep moving. I was all too happy to oblige. Issik gave me the chills.

The castle was bigger than I imagined. Left on my own, there was no way I would be able to find my way back to my room. We had to be close to the first floor when Kieran pushed through a set of doors, a wave of heat hitting me. Inside was a large room with ivory pillars that stretched to the vaulted ceilings. At the center of the space, steam pillowed over a square pool, much like a hot tub. It was open and big enough for six people.

The bath house was a public facility. Talk about medieval.

I spun on Kieran. "You guys don't believe in privacy?"

"You're not shy, are you?"

I shifted my feet, unwilling to admit any of my faults to someone who might use them against me. "I never said that."

His lips curved. "Once we're sure you've adjusted, you'll be free to wander at your will. Until then, one of us will be at your side at all times."

"Joy," I mumbled.

I moved behind one of the elaborate columns, slipping off my grimy shoes and socks. Kieran guarded the door, leaning against the wall, but from where I stood, he couldn't really see me. The shifter chuckled, knowing I hid from his eyes.

The heat in my cheeks heightened as I whipped off my hoodie and shirt, leaving me standing in my bra and jeans. My fingers fumbled with the buttons. I wanted to hurry up and get under the cover of the steaming, bubbly water. Slipping the rest of my clothes off, I stepped onto the first landing, the hot water floating over my toes. Closing my eyes and sighing, I took the next two steps in a rush. My foot slipped, and I belly flopped into the pool. Water rushed over my head.

That was one way to get clean.

I came up, sputtering and snorting, my drenched hair hanging over my face. Shoving the mass of blonde strands out of my eyes, I groaned. Kieran was crouched at the edge of the bath, shaking his head and smirking. "You gave me a fright. For a second, I thought you were drowning yourself."

My lips seemed to be in a permanent frown ever since I got here. "I'm fine," I assured him through my teeth.

"Jase really outdid himself this time," Kieran added, as he walked back to guard the doorway.

I exhaled. His hovering made me self-conscious.

Along the side of the marble tub sat a tray of soaps, oils, and lotions that would have made Bath & Body Works jealous. The bottles and bars didn't have labels, so I just plucked one up and began working it into my hair. As the soap foamed, the room was scented like coconut shells. The warmth and the exotic fragrance made me feel as if I was bathing in a Hawaiian waterfall.

I had just finished dunking my head underwater, rinsing the bubbles out of my hair, when a girl sauntered in. She had long golden brown locks, and lush red lips that made her creamy skin appear flawless. Without so much as batting an eye, she dropped the silk robe she wore, and like a swan, gracefully lowered herself into the bath.

I stayed as still as a statue, not pleased at having my privacy invaded, but at the same time, it was nice to see another face that wasn't male.

She eyed me warily. "So you're the new shade of blonde?" I detected traces of envy in her voice.

Her? Jealous of me? Was she insane? All she had to do was look in the mirror.

"I guess?" I replied, unsure how to answer. My hair was blonde, so…

She skimmed a slender hand over the top of the water. "I'm Harlow."

"Olivia."

"A bit of friendly advice, *Olivia.* I might not be the chosen one, but this is *my* house." The implication came through loud and clear. She didn't want me stepping on her territory. Nothing was welcoming about Harlow.

"Trust me, you have nothing to worry about."

Harlow shot hazel daggers at me. "That's what we all said."

I frowned. "How many are there?"

She chuckled, and not in an approachable way. "Here in Jase's kingdom? I've lost count."

As long as she was willing to answer, I was going to pepper her with questions. Pressing my back against the wall, I kept to my side of the bath. "Why are we here?"

"They haven't told you yet?" Hatred dripped off her lips while she dunked deeper into the water, resting her head back. I shook my head. "It isn't my place to tell you. Besides, from the looks of you, there is no way you can be the one they are looking for." Every word out of her mouth was meant to make me feel insignificant and naïve.

I'd had enough. It wasn't my choice to be here. "What the hell is wrong with me?" I shot back. Thinking Harlow and I weren't going to be friends, I let my irritation mask my disappointment. Hopefully, the other girls weren't all as *friendly* as the viper Harlow.

She sneered, standing up and letting beads of water run down her perfect frame—not a shy bone in her body. "It doesn't matter what I think. Just remember your place." Then she stooped down to pick up her discarded robe and walked off.

And what place was that?

"Later, Kieran," I heard her say in a husky voice before the door opened.

It was becoming clear that I had no allies, no one I could trust here in the Veil. I only had myself to rely on. At least that was not much different than my life in Chicago.

"Let's go," Kieran urged, interrupting my perfect dream of lying on the beach, and soaking up the sun as the water lapped at my feet. "The others are waiting for us." He held out a giant towel, stretching from one hand to the other.

My skin was as wrinkly as a raisin, but I couldn't have cared less. Since Harlow's disturbing visit, I'd been trying not to dwell on what little information I had discovered. I stared up at Kieran, crossing my arms over my chest. "Am I expected to go naked?"

His mouth tipped up into a one-sided smile. "I wouldn't object, but

I'm guessing you would. There is a closet of clothes just through those doors. Pick anything you would like."

"Close your eyes," I commanded.

The smirk on his lips deepened, but he did as I asked. Water splashed as I rose out of the bathing pool, quickly taking the towel and wrapping it around my body. I held it closed with one hand and squeezed the water from my hair with the other. Kieran opened his eyes, capturing me with his. I hadn't noticed that his hands had moved to my hips until his fingers pressed lightly, drawing my gaze downward.

"You can release me," I said softly.

The center of his bright eyes twinkled. "Promise you're not going to fall and break your neck?"

I rolled my eyes. "Do you want me to lie?"

He only shook his head.

Keeping the towel secured around me, I padded around a white column to the doors Kieran had indicated. They slid open to reveal a small room, filled with everything from dresses to undergarments. *Why do they have so many women's clothes?* I tried not to let it freak me out, but it was pointless. My breathing quickened as I scanned the apparel. *Where are the yoga pants and T-shirts?* My hand ran over the sheer fabric of what I thought was a dress, but it seemed to be missing some key parts. He didn't actually expect me to wear this, right?

I grabbed the first thing my hand touched, resolving myself to look like a harlot because, obviously, that was what they were into here. Trying to figure out how to get it on was a joke, and I absolutely refused to ask the dragon for help—eventually I managed.

The soft seafoam material draped over my body in a Greek goddess style, leaving my sides exposed.

"Everything okay in there?" Kieran called through the cracked doors.

I bit my lower lip, searching a rack of shoes for something that would fit. Grabbing a pair of slip-ons, I stuck them on my feet and turned to push open the door. "No. Everything is not okay. I'm stuck in a strange land. I've been kidnapped by four hot guys. And I have no clue why."

A smug grin split Kieran's lips, his silver hoop twinkling. "You think I'm hot?"

Shit. Did I say that out loud?

His eyes roamed over my body, adding more color to my already flushed cheeks.

"I'm sure some girls find you good-looking," I grumbled, crossing my arms over myself, but it did nothing to make me feel less exposed.

He gave a little jerk of his head to the side. "Come on. I think it's time you learn what you're really doing here."

Took them long enough.

Kieran led me to a room that looked like what I would describe as a den from the Dark Ages. No windows made the room dim; the only source of light came from the flickering hearth. Jase sat behind a wooden desk, leaning lazily in an oversized chair. Issik and Zade were sprawled with their legs out on two chocolate-colored couches. All eyes turned to me as I walked in, and my cheeks brightened under their scrutiny.

They continued to stare at me with something akin to curiosity. *What do they see when they look at me?* I jutted my chin out. *What does it matter what they think? Their opinion isn't important.*

And yet, I stood there, feeling awkward and self-conscious.

"Not half bad after a bath," Kieran offered, grinning as he took a seat beside Zade, which left me the only empty spot in the room—next to Ice Prince.

Issik watched me with cool eyes.

"Are my looks that important?" I snapped, not happy about being put on display for them to ogle. I quickly sat on the far side of the couch, leaving as much space between me and Issik as possible. He shifted, taking up most of the couch, so that our legs almost touched, and he had done it on purpose.

I glared.

"No, it's just unexpected," Jase finally spoke up.

Did he mean that in a good or bad way? "I could say the same about the four of you." I hadn't expected them to turn into dragons. Life was full of surprises.

Kieran laughed. "What Jase is *trying* to say, but bumbling it badly, is you're quite beautiful, Olivia."

The color in my cheeks deepened. "Oh."

"But then again, Jase is known as a collector of pretty things," Zade added.

"Like blondes? I'm not your trophy," I retorted, feeling a flicker of annoyance spark inside me.

Jase scowled at Kieran and Zade, his violet eyes darkening.

"Is someone going to explain why I'm here? Or are we just going to make faces at each other?" I asked dryly.

Jase sighed. "Fair enough. You know we're dragon shifters. Our kind has existed for hundreds of thousands of years. We once lived among humans, fought beside them, until our world—and others' like ours—were split from the human realm."

"What do you mean 'other worlds'?" I interrupted him.

"The Veil Isles isn't the only land to house beings with extraordinary abilities. There are many others hidden from the human world," Zade elaborated.

"Is that where the wraith came from?" I asked.

"Sort of," Kieran replied.

"The Great War drove us to hide our world with portals, or we risked seeing it fall to destruction," Jase continued, leaning forward so his elbows rested on the wooden desk. "Our fathers ruled the kingdoms within the Veil—Iculon, Crimson, Viperus, and Wakeland—and did so for many peaceful years until the uprising."

I had no clue what Great War or uprising they were talking about. I had learned none of this in school during my history lessons.

"A supernatural war came to our doorstep, spilling the blood of our people, of our families, and our friends. To end the massacre, our fathers enlisted a witch by the name of Tianna, to cast a curse on the portal into the Veil before they were killed, but the witch had an agenda of her own. Her betrayal cost the dragon shifters everything." A muscle along Jase's jaw thumped as he talked about the witch. He definitely harbored some nasty feelings toward her.

As I sat and listened, I tried not to think about Issik's cool leg against mine. His body temperature seemed to be set at freezing all the time.

Kieran clenched his hands into fists, tension lining his body. "Tianna sealed the portal as our fathers planned, but only to their direct lineage. Her treachery trapped us here, and while others could leave, they eventually never returned—either killed or enslaved by the wraiths that guard the portal. And there was nothing we could do about it."

"We've been stranded on this island for nearly a hundred years. Never allowed to age, have families, or escape, except for a single night, twice a year, during the summer and winter solstices. We've spent the last ten decades trying to unweave the spell Tianna cast. We're the last dragons in the world," Jase explained.

A witch?

A dying breed?

A curse?

My mind whirled. This was a heartbreaking and *tragic* story, but I still didn't understand what I had to do with it. "What happens if you don't return after the solstices?" I asked.

All four men stiffened.

"There was a fifth dragon heir: Tobias." Zade spoke up, after a few tense moments passed. His cinnamon eyes swirled. "He tested that very theory, regardless of the warnings Tianna had issued before she departed from the Veil. We knew it was suicide, but he was foolish, and believed he had enough strength to resist Tianna's hex. His might didn't save him. When he didn't return before sunrise the day after the winter solstice, his body burst into flames as the curse had forewarned, leaving behind only the bones of his dragon skeleton Tianna has taunted us with his death since."

I suppressed a shudder. Being burned alive was no joke. "What does any of this have to do with me?" I asked.

"The curse Tianna cast can only be broken by a girl who holds the key to our freedom," Kieran informed me.

"Are you talking about a tangible key or a metaphorical one?" I didn't have any magical key in my possession. Hell, I had barely anything in my possession. My cell phone was the most expensive thing I owned.

"We don't know," Jase admitted. "Tianna used a blood curse to trap us, and we believe the blood of the chosen will set us free from this prison. We've spent years searching for the one who can break it."

And they thought that person might be me—that was laughable.

I actually started to chuckle, until all four pairs of eyes pinned me with a look of, What in the actual fuck is wrong with her? "You can't possibly think that it's me," I rebutted.

"That's why you're here," Issik said, speaking for the first time. He left no room for questioning. His voice was firm with a bit of that arctic blast coming through.

They were serious.

"The sight of my own blood makes me faint. No, I can't do it." I shook my head.

Issik's piercing eyes were directly on mine. "We're not giving you much choice in the matter."

Well, damn. "And if I'm not the one to break it, I'm stuck here. Is that what you're telling me?"

"It doesn't have to be all bad," Jase said, drawing my eyes to him. His tone had softened.

"Shit," I muttered under my breath. "Can't you take me back with you at the next solstice?" I could agree to six months. That was reasonable. But forever? Uh. No.

"If only it was that easy. Our time is running out," Jase explained.

"What do you mean?" I asked.

Zade shifted forward, the leather groaning under his weight as he leaned his elbows on his knees. "We were only given a hundred years to break the curse—twenty years for each of us, including Tobias. Once the years run out, we are out of time."

A hundred years seemed like a long time. "How many years has it been?"

"Ninety-nine," Issik confessed.

I felt my blood go cold. What they were basically telling me was I was their last hope.

Damn.

They were screwed.

"B-but—" I stammered.

"Once the summer solstice arrives, the portal will never open for us again, and we will start to age."

Geez. No freaking pressure. My body was tense.

I thought living on the streets was tough, but this burden was possibly more than I could handle. "Why me? What made you think it could possibly be me? Other than I have blonde hair. Because if that is what you guys are basing your selections on, then no wonder you haven't broken the curse."

Kieran's lips twitched, but only his. Everyone else looked as if they wanted to wring my neck. "Jase has been our scout due to his ability. It's the easiest way to persuade possible candidates to the Veil."

Persuade my ass. "You mean by drugging them," I said straightforwardly. Harlow had implied the other girls had been brought here for the same reason and failed.

Jase cleared his throat, and I swung my gaze from Kieran to the purple-eyed shifter. "Something about you pulled me in. If you hadn't run into me, I wouldn't have given you a second glance..."

I scoffed. *Thanks for the backward compliment, asshole.*

"...but the moment I looked into your eyes, I felt it." His stormy gaze captured mine, and for a moment, a zing passed between us, and I knew what he was talking about. "You feel it too?" he asked, seeing the flicker in my expression.

"I don't know what I feel other than confused." I answered instead, shifting in my seat. "Everything that has happened in the last twenty-four hours seems more like a movie than reality." A really messed up movie.

Jase blew out an aggravated breath as if tired of rehearsing the same speech in this same room countless times. He probably had I realized. "I can assure you, we're very real. This place is very real. And the spell binding us is *very* real."

Tilting my head to the side, I was suddenly aware that these four gorgeous dragons had lived over a hundred years. "Just how old are you guys?"

Kieran cocked a crooked brow. "Before the curse? Nineteen."

My gaze appraised each one in turn, and I could see hope shimmering in their eyes, even Issik's. How could I let them down?

I was their last chance.

This was insane. It would crush them when they found out I was nothing more than a homeless girl.

But what else could I do except agree to help them as long as it didn't involve offering myself up as a sacrifice to the dragon gods? I had no idea where the Veil Isles were. No idea how to get home.

"What do I do?" I found myself asking.

The tense anticipation I didn't know existed in the room until now dissipated, the four guys visibly unwinding. "For now, just rest, relax, allow yourself to enjoy being somewhere safe," Jase said, leaning back in his chair.

If it were only that easy… Did Jase think he could just snap his royal dragon fingers and, like that, all my worries and fears would disappear? I could pretend to be on vacation? Have a little spa day? Read a book and swing in a hammock by the water? I must have snorted out loud, instead of in my head, because I drew curious glances from all four corners of the room.

"Sure. Whatever you say," I replied with a bite I couldn't mask, nor did I even really try to. "But after I'm done doing nothing but basking in the glory of being under the protection of dragons, then what?"

"You don't give up, do you?" Issik remarked, his tone like ice snapping.

"I like to know what crazy shit I'm getting myself into, especially if it involves my blood."

Jase blew out a breath. "Fine. Have it your way. On the next full moon, we'll take you to the place on the island that has traces of magic —the temple of our fathers. There we will perform the blood ceremony in hopes that it will remove the shackles that bind us."

Next full moon, huh? "How many days is that exactly?"

"Ten," Zade informed me.

Right. That made sense. The winter solstice had been last night, December twenty-first. It looked like I would be spending Christmas with a pack of dragons. I wondered if they celebrated holidays. I'd seen no evidence of decorations or anything festive in the keep, suggesting they didn't. Fine by me. I wasn't feeling much in the giving spirit. "What am I supposed to do until then? Twiddle my thumbs?"

"The castle is yours to roam as you wish, but only the castle. You won't step outside these walls." Jase's voice ended on a dark note of warning that I didn't understand.

"What is outside these walls?" I couldn't stop myself from asking. Anything forbidden immediately piqued my interest. I was the kind of girl who went looking for trouble unintentionally because I didn't like secrets.

Issik tipped his chin up, and the firelight sliced across his cheekbones. "That wraith last night was only a taste of the dangers you will find in the Veil." Caution punctuated his words.

But I was like a relentless child, always wanting to learn more. "How do I know you didn't say that to scare me into not running away?"

Issik's brow rose. "The wraith wasn't proof enough?"

Jase narrowed his eyes and folded his arms over his muscular chest. "Just stay put for ten days. None of us want to go chasing after you. We have enough to worry about."

It wasn't like they gave me much choice in the matter. I sunk into the fine leather couch, accepting that I wouldn't be leaving this place anytime soon. But after ten days, after they figured out I was not the one they sought, I *would* find my way home.

J ase escorted me back upstairs to my chambers, and this time, as we walked, I made a mental map so I could find my way back to the first floor. It would be wise for me to learn the layout of the castle and would undoubtedly come in handy one day.

We stopped just outside the doorway, and Jase's massive body seemed to relax. My skin tingled at his touch, when he invaded my personal bubble, brushing a stray strand of hair behind my ear. I tilted my neck to look him in the eyes, but the second ours connected, I realized my mistake.

"What is it about you that I'm drawn to? I can't figure it out." That made two of us. Something churned behind those stormy eyes, something that reached into my soul and wrapped around my heart, tugging me closer.

I didn't want to feel anything for my captors, and yet, my body didn't seem to share the same opinion. "It's probably the shampoo."

His chest rumbled against mine, reminding me how close he stood; my breasts tingled. His hand traced down my arm, making me tremble on contact.

Dear God. He is going to kiss me.

We stood with our eyes locked, and my breath stalled in my lungs. I didn't dare move for fear he would actually kiss me... or that he wouldn't.

"Go, before I do something neither of us would forget."

I blinked, dropping my eyes to the rich wood covering the hallway as the air whooshed out of my chest. *Did I want him to kiss me?*

I was afraid of the answer.

Before either of us did something stupid, I turned and slipped inside, shutting the door quickly behind me, just in case he decided to follow. Alone, I dropped against the wall, giving myself a few moments to collect my composure, and when I could properly think again, without a dragon shifter messing with my head, I contemplated what I should do: to run or not to run.

Sounded like Shakespeare.

My life did feel like a screenplay, tragic and dramatic, I had nowhere to go. And the unknown of what I would face outside the walls of the castle was enough to keep me in the confines of the four shifters… for the moment. I needed to get my bearings.

I nibbled on my lip, running the conversation through my head again. I had asked for the truth. Hadn't I? Staying was a risk, just as taking my chances out in the Veil were. Here, they could kill me. Serve me up on a silver platter as a sacrifice to the gods or Tianna herself—unlikely scenario, but then again, so were dragons. Or maybe it was all a ruse, and I was being punked. Or maybe I was reading the situation wrong. Or maybe this was the beginning of something monumental.

It didn't take long for a headache to form, my brain whirling. My mind churned over what would happen after the ten days were up. I told myself not to think about how they would react once they figured out I was no one special. For the time being, I was going to appreciate having a roof over my head, and food to eat.

Just think of it as a vacation, Olivia. One hell of a vacation.

Lying down, I closed my eyes only intending to rest for a few minutes, but I awoke hours later with the sun sinking over the western sky. I turned my head to the side, gazing out the glass doors. Orange rays brightened the heavens, casting the clouds in deep cobalt and bright turquoise.

A brief moment passed before the clarity of my situation seeped in. It didn't last but a few seconds, yet that was all it took for the pain of my life to come crashing down on me, which was then followed by everything else that had happened. I would never be back in my own room with Mom still alive.

Inhaling a deep breath, I rubbed at my eyes and sat up, swinging my feet over the bed. A tray of food sat on the little table beside me, letting me know I'd missed lunch. My stomach was used to skipping meals, but with the smell of something savory in the air, it rumbled. I lifted off the silver dome on the platter. A plate of bread and thin slices of meat laid waiting for me to enjoy. I tore off a hunk from the loaf and popped it into my mouth.

My gaze traveled around the room, really checking it out for the first time without fear or confusion distracting me. It was pretty, I guess—nothing grossly girly, but it had traces of a feminine touch. A fresh vase of flowers sat on the little wooden table beside the bed. Everything in the room looked handmade, from the sturdy oak bedframe, to the quilted white blankets wrinkled from my sleep.

I highly doubted Jase was responsible for the state of the room, which made me think the other girls here also helped keep up the castle. *Slaves. Maids. Victims.* The words rang in my head, and a surge of anger rose up inside me. I would be no one's bitch, certainly not to a pack of egotistical, unnerving, drool-worthy dragon shifters.

Why did my brain have to add 'drool-worthy'? Couldn't it have just stuck to their less than redeeming qualities?

Taking another piece of bread and a bit of salted meat, I stood up, needing to stretch my legs. Outside my door, a group of female giggles and whispers floated by. They passed on, and I was curious who they were. It might be a good idea to talk with some of the other girls… besides Harlow.

Testing the door, I was surprised to find it unlocked. Maybe they had been serious about me not being a prisoner, or they were the worst kidnappers in the universe. I stuck my head out, looking left and then right, sighing in relief when I didn't spot a mind-muddling dragon shifter keeping guard. Feeling pretty smug about sneaking out, I tiptoed into the hall, remembering the staircase was to the right. I edged around the corner, trailing my fingers along the cool, textured stones.

The voices carried down the stairwell, and I made sure to keep a safe distance. They were definitely female, but didn't sound the least bit distressed. How had they adapted so well to their situation? Being abducted and tossed aside when they were no longer needed wasn't something I could easily forget or forgive.

As I gnawed on my lip and had an internal conversation with myself about the stupidity of girls in general, I tripped over something that had no business being left on a staircase. I saw my life flash before my eyes. Who the hell left a shoe on the steps?

Holy shit. Oh shit. I'm going to break my neck.

Those were the thoughts repeating through my head as I started to fall forward.

A pair of arms swept around my waist, catching me before my nose hit the ground in a plummet that would have certainly shattered it. "And where do you think you're going?" asked a smooth voice that wrapped around me like a cloak of silk as he lifted me off my feet.

I didn't even bother to struggle. What was the point? The fire dragon, Zade, was superior in pretty much everything. "Nowhere. I was just doing some exploring."

Zade pressed his lips together, holding back a smirk that teased the side of my ear.

Asshole.

"It's probably not a good idea for you to go wandering off on your own." His breath was soft and warm on my neck.

My teeth ground together. "You mean you've been assigned to babysit me."

"Until the full moon, we agreed one of us should look out for you at all times."

"Wonderful," I mumbled under my breath, my feet still dangling as he carried me the rest of the way to the first floor. "So what? You just shadow me? Or do you also dictate where I go? And what happens when I have to pee?" I already knew what happened when I needed to bathe. They had no qualms about seeing me naked, and no respect for my privacy. Why should I have any for theirs? "Should I just follow you around like a puppy dog?"

His dark brows furrowed together. "You've made your point."

Then why didn't I feel victorious? I opened my mouth to say something smart that would have probably irritated Golden God, but my eyes shifted over his shoulder and I forgot what I'd been about to say.

I'd never seen anything so beautiful yet also wild and primitive. Through a pair of decorative doors was a circular courtyard showered with plants of vibrant colors and flowers as tall as me. Beyond the garden were the murky waters that seemed to surround the entire castle.

My feet were returned to the ground as I gawked, and I wandered outside, wanting to smell the exotic vegetation. "I've never seen flowers like this." The plants seemed to sing a gentle song that was ancient and hypnotic. It hummed around me, engulfing me in their fruity fragrance.

"Each region of the Veil has plants and trees that are unique to the land. The same goes for the wildlife."

I turned to see Zade watching me with a fascinated expression. What did he see when he looked at me? "Including the dragons," I said with a smile.

His lips curved at the corners. "You're not like the others."

"You mean out of the gazillion girls you've stolen over the years, not one had a snarky personality?"

"Is that what you call it?"

Was this dragon shifter teasing me? I walked to the edge of the water and sat down on a dock, letting my feet hang over.

"I would think twice about sticking a toe in that water," he warned me, looming over my shoulder.

"And why is that?" I asked, swinging my legs in the air—the tips of my toes so close to the surface because I enjoyed doing the exact opposite of what he said.

Zade watched me intently, almost as if he was afraid I would accidentally fall in. He had valid reasons to be concerned. "We're not the only mythical creatures in the Veil Isles. Others are able to travel between realms, even in water."

He suddenly had my interest. My mind immediately went to my favorite Disney movie as a kid. "Like mermaids?"

His lips quirked as if he'd read my mind. "Not the kind you think, but in essence, yes."

I stared at the water with more intensity, pulling my legs up to my chest, no longer feeling safe. "Am I in danger here?"

"Always," he said, sitting beside me on the wooden platform, and our shoulders brushed. Heat seeped inside my body like a roaring fire during winter, and the bits of anxiety I had felt slowly faded. He had done that. There was something about these dragons that made me feel safe regardless of how I came to be here.

Why?

"Jase said you would protect me," I told him, needing reassurance.

"We will," he answered with a fervor I found comforting.

"How many other portals are there?" I asked, satisfied with his response.

"Many."

Not the straight answer I'd hoped for. "And mythical creatures?"

"Griffons. Sirens. Gargoyles," he rattled off.

"Gargoyles?" I interrupted, my voice squeaking in disbelief.

A frown marred his face. "Nasty little buggers. They can be quite violent when not in their stone form, and stealthy as fuck."

My eyes settled on the bright orange ball setting over the dark waters, and wondered what I would do if I came face to face with a gargoyle. I bet Harlow would squeal like the little girl she was. "What about all the other women you've brought here? What happens to them?"

Zade shrugged, his gaze following mine to the horizon where the sun was about to touch the gloomy waters. "They are given a choice to stay and live in any of our kingdoms, or the few who wish to return can do so during the solstices. Issik, Kieran, and I take them back."

He made it sound as if most remained, and I couldn't help but be inquisitive. If the Veil was so dangerous, why not return home? "Where are your lands?" I asked.

His hand lifted, pointing to the west where the shape of a volcano could just be seen through the misty fog. "The Crimson Keep sits just at the base of the Titan Mountain—the only volcano in the Veil."

A puff of smoke drifted up into the sky in the distance. "Just a guess, but is it hot most of the time in your domain? Not just the volcano," I added.

His eyes lit up. "Very."

The sunlight hit something in the water, making it sparkle like glass through the mire. I couldn't take my eyes off the object that lay just a few feet from me. Like the garden, a lulling melody seemed to emanate from the waters, luring me closer. I placed my hands on the ground and leaned forward to get a better look. What was it? I wanted to touch it.

"Olivia."

I swore it called my name, and my hand reached out, itching to hold it in my hand.

"Find me, Olivia."

I didn't understand what was happening, only that I had to help.

Something splashed in the water near me, breaking the trance, and I more or less jumped into the dragon's lap. His strong arms came around me automatically, keeping me from falling into the water. "Olivia." Zade exhaled. "What happened? You wouldn't answer me."

"I-I don't know," I stammered. "I thought I saw something."

Frowning, Zade situated me more comfortably in his embrace. "The waters of Wakeland are not to be disregarded. They are dangerous as is most of the Veil."

Warning heard, and yet, I couldn't help but be intrigued. After one more glance, I turned to face Zade, finding him closer than I expected. I had forgotten I sat in his lap, and suddenly I felt his presence everywhere. His fingers on my waist made lazy circles over the material of my dress, leaving behind a trail of fire.

His already warm eyes flamed, and I couldn't look away. What was wrong with me? Ever since I stepped foot inside the Veil, I didn't recognize myself. But one thing I knew for certain, he was going to kiss me.

The simple brush of his lips sent a stream of heat spiraling through me, like a firework. It was a quick kiss, but it caused my entire body to come alive. When he pulled back, I leaned in toward him.

A hint of a playful expression crawled onto his face before he lifted me off, and brought us both to our feet, leaving me breathless. "Are you okay?" he asked softly, his cinnamon eyes bright as they searched my face.

I had just kissed a dragon. No, I wasn't okay.

The disturbing part was I wanted to do it again.

I never got the chance to reply, and my tied up tongue had only a part to do with it.

"What the hell is going on?" boomed a voice.

I leaped out of Zade's arms like I'd been burned with a frying pan… and maybe I had. My skin still radiated sparks.

Zade moved so he stood just slightly in front of me as if protecting me. Odd. Did I need protection from Jase? "Just making sure our little gem doesn't get herself in trouble." Zade cocked his head to the side. "Isn't that what we agreed on?"

The tranquility-breathing dragon stood inside the arched doorway, glaring at Zade with a mean scowl—his eyes so dark they almost appeared black. "Yes, but that doesn't include you seducing her."

"Since when do you meddle in my extracurricular activities?" Zade challenged him, with an edge to his voice.

It was my turn to frown. I was no one's extracurricular activity.

A growl rose up in Jase's throat. He stormed to where Zade and I where awkwardly standing. "She's off limits."

Golden God's lips formed into a tight line. "You forget, Jase, you're not king. There is no single ruler of the Veil anymore."

Things had escalated quickly, and I didn't want these two going into the dragon ring over me. "Hey!" I yelled, stepping between the two. Not the brightest of ideas, but at the moment, it was all I could think to do. I didn't want blood spilled over me.

A muscle began to thump in Jase's jaw. "Keep your lips off her."

Spreading my arms out wide between them, my hands flattened on their chests. "Okay. First off, I can kiss whomever I want."

Jase's glower deepened.

I rolled my eyes. This was ridiculous. Framing Jase's face with both of my hands, I rose up on my toes and planted one on him, just to prove a point. The joke was on me.

The moment our lips met, all annoyance vanished from within me. My eyes fluttered closed as I fell into the blissful storm that was all Jase. His lips were soft… and skilled, expertly moving over mine. His hands came up to cup either side of my cheeks, and he deepened what was supposed to be a peck. My mouth opened, letting him in, and a purr sounded at the back of my throat as his tongue swept inside.

I'd never been kissed like this before—so passionately and fervently. My fingers bunched his shirt, holding him in place just in case he got any ideas about pulling away. I wasn't done yet. Honestly, I never wanted to stop kissing Jase Dior.

Zade cleared his throat behind us. How had I forgotten about him? Jase pulled back, his breath as ragged as mine.

I glanced up into his eyes, seeing the violet in them glowing brightly. "There. Are you satisfied?" I rasped, swallowing a knot of yearning. *No more kissing dragons.*

"Not nearly." Jase's head dipped as if he was going to take possession of my lips again.

My hand pressed against his chest, keeping him just out of reach. "Oh, no. I think I've kissed enough dragons today." I could barely believe I had locked lips with two of them within minutes of each other.

What is wrong with me?

Even more surprising, my little stunt actually had defused the situation... sort of. Their eyes no longer glowed, they took a step back, and their puffed-out chests relaxed.

"What do you have to say about not kissing her now?" Zade shot at Jase, looking damned pleased with himself.

Jase's spine straightened, and I thought for sure shit was about to get tense again. "No one but me gets the pleasure of tasting her."

Sometimes it sucked to be right.

Anger quickly returned to Zade's eyes, specks of gold flashing within them. "Hell no. I kissed her first."

I closed my eyes for a second, swallowing a stream of curses. "No one is going to kiss me!" I shouted before taking a breath. "I think I've had enough excitement for the day, and since I'm stuck here, I'm going to my room."

On my way back to the conservatory, I found Kieran leaning against the outer wall of the castle, watching the show with sparkling eyes. Issik stood next to him, frowning, his eyes like winter's first frost. I brushed past them, not saying a word, not even when Kieran stepped in time beside me.

Argh. I'd had my fill of hot-tempered dragons.

Ten days seemed like a lifetime.

Flying out of the garden and toward the stairs in the main hall, I made it two whole minutes before I broke my vow of silence. I'd never been able to keep my mouth shut, and that usually got me in trouble. My annoyed gaze traveled to Kieran, who still trailed me. "Why are you smirking?"

He raised his brows as we ascended the winding stairs. "Zade and Jase never fight. That was the most entertainment we've had in... well, years."

I didn't know if I was headed in the right direction, and was sort of relying on Kieran to make sure I got to the right room. "Glad I could be of assistance," I grumbled.

Devilishness glittered in his gaze. "I'm looking forward to seeing what happens next."

I rolled my eyes. "Don't get your hopes up." And I meant that beyond just my entertainment value. There was going to be buckets of disappointment when they all realized I wasn't *the one*.

"You might surprise yourself."

"Oh, I've had plenty of WTF moments since I got here." I wrinkled my nose.

He chuckled, pausing at a door I assumed was mine. "It's true, you know—what Zade and Jase said; there is something unique about you. I can't figure it out, but we all feel it, and it is the first drop of hope we've had in a very long time."

My face fell, displaying all the dread that had suddenly dropped into my belly like a boulder. A spark in Kieran's emerald eyes cautioned me to be careful. "Good night," I said before another dragon tried to kiss me.

"Good night, Olivia," he replied, winking.

Holy crap. What kind of dragon drama had I gotten myself into?

Shutting the door in Kieran's face, I went to lie in bed, staring at the painting on the ceiling. The artwork centered on an angel with glittery wings of gold. The midnight sky behind her was dark blue with pops of maroon and a thousand sparkling stars.

One thought circled in my mind before I dozed off to sleep. After the ten days, I had to find a way back home. Staying here with the four of them wasn't an option.

They can't keep me here forever. Not like those other girls. I'm not one of those girls.

Nine days to go… and so the countdown began.

I pulled open the drawers in my room, rummaging around for something useful. I wasn't sure what I needed, except for anything that might help me get out of here when the time was right. I hadn't given up on the notion of returning home. Not yet.

Nothing but clothes, extra blankets, and female essentials—including lotions, lip balm, makeup, and a toothbrush—were to be found. It alarmed me how the entire room had been set up for a woman. How many other rooms were there like this? How many other girls had stayed in this room?

To be frank, I wasn't sure I wanted to know. Sometimes ignorance was bliss. This might have been one of those times.

Sighing, I padded across the room and pushed open the double doors, letting in the morning sun and the gentle breeze, as it carried in the scents of honeysuckle and sea salt. There was no denying that the Veil Isles was a mesmerizing place. Water lapped against the keep's walls below, and in the sky, a flock of birds cawed.

Securing my hair in a messy bun with a black hair tie that I kept around my wrist like a bracelet—for emergencies—my attention was pulled to the gloomy waters, and like yesterday, I couldn't shake the feeling that there was something down there, something watching me.

I would have expected myself to be creeped out, but I wasn't. I was fascinated.

Walking back into the room, I stuck my feet into a pair of slippers, and reached for the doorknob to the interior of the castle. I twisted, once again relieved to find it unlocked. Stepping out into the hallway, I examined my door, trying to pick out something unique to help me find it again. Two sconces on the wall across from my room highlighted a couple of paintings portraying fierce, proud dragons. I made a mental note and crept forward down the corridor.

"A map would be damn helpful," I muttered, and cursed under my breath as I turned down another corridor before finding the stairs. But that wasn't all I found.

A pair of girls turned the corner just as I reached the staircase. They both appeared to be a few years older than me—early twenties if I had to guess. One had the most gorgeous olive skin color with warm honey eyes. The other was fair skinned, curvy, and had legs that went on for days. Their gazes fell upon me.

"You must be Olivia," the one with dark hair said.

"The keep has been buzzing about you," Legs added, a gentle smile tugging at her lips.

"Wonderful," I replied dryly.

"I'm Kaytlyn," the one with the envy-inducing olive skin introduced herself. "And this is Davina," she added, gesturing to the blonde.

Standing awkwardly in the hall, I wondered what I should say to them. I came up blank. "Where's the kitchen?"

They both blinked at me before Kaytlyn widened her smile. "We're on our way there now. We'll show you."

I almost didn't trust them being so nice.

Kaytlyn and Davina started the decline to the main floor with me behind them. "I remember my first days at Wakeland Keep. It was so intimidating, and I could never find my room," Davina admitted.

"This place is a maze," I agreed. "How long have you been here?" I asked, the question popping out of my mouth. I was curious about everything, but I probably shouldn't have assumed everyone was okay with divulging personal information.

"Four years," Davina answered.

"This will be my sixth," Kaytlyn replied.

Luckily for me, Kaytlyn and Davina seemed to be chatterboxes.

"And you've never wanted to go home?" This was the question I'd been yearning to know the answer to. Why did these women all stay?

Kaytlyn shrugged, her hand running along the mahogany banister. "At first it was a lot to take in, but you'll find living in the Veil is not so bad. I had nothing at home. Why not start over someplace new?"

And dangerous, I mentally added.

"They let you pick where you want to live afterwards," Davina divulged. Right. After they brought me to the temple of their fathers.

Our thin shoes clattered on the stone steps as we continued to descend the never-ending staircase. "You mean with one of the dragons." I was testing their reaction to the still foreign word. They didn't so much as flinch.

Davina nodded, her blonde curls bouncing. "Most of the girls choose Jase's or Zade's kingdom."

"And why is that?"

They both giggled. "Have you seen them?"

Oh, yes, I have. Was that all these girls cared about? That they were extremely attractive? "So, they're smoking hot," I agreed. "But what makes Jase and Zade different?" I didn't see how they could choose. Presented with the option to pick one of the four, I didn't know which one I would rate higher than the others. Except for Issik. He had a tough exterior, but maybe under all that ice there was a heart.

"I don't know where you lived before, but we didn't have guys like the descendants in Wyoming," Davina explained. "Besides, it's not just the guys, but also where they live. You just got here, but you'll see for yourself. The other kingdoms tend to be harsher climates and landscapes."

"You have nine days until the full moon?" Kaytlyn prompted me. I nodded. "Soon you'll be in the cave." Her voice carried in an eerie tone.

"What cave?" I automatically asked.

Kaytlyn batted ridiculously long lashes, watching me with an expression that said she didn't want to be in my shoes. "It's deep in the Viperus Woods of Kieran's kingdom."

She made the trip to the cave sound ominous, and I had to wonder if it was. "This is insane," I muttered. Curses. Dragons. Wraiths. What else could I expect?

Davina and Kaytlyn both nodded in agreement. "Yeah, it takes a while for that feeling to wear off," Davina confessed.

I wasn't positive it ever would, and I didn't plan to stick around to find out.

The kitchen was bustling with people—mostly females. Different types of stones lined the walls and floors of the industrial-sized space, and the ceiling vaulted into a dome, giving the room a circular appearance. In the center was a long rectangular wooden island with storage underneath. Food was spread out on the countertop, filling the air with both sweet and savory scents, waiting to be delivered to the tables beyond in the great hall. My stomach growled as I glanced over the fare, fighting the urge to pluck something off the buffet. The variety of brunch foods was different, yet familiar—a combination of fruits, eggs, and sweet rolls.

The lively chatter and shuffling died when I stepped into the kitchen, and all eyes swung towards me. I didn't like the attention or the silence. Then the whispering started, and I hated that even more, knowing everyone in the room was talking about me.

My back straightened, and I stiffened my chin.

"They're all wondering if you're the one," a cold voice whispered in my ear, sending a chill down my spine.

Issik.

My head turned a tad, finding him close. Too close. "What happens if I'm not?"

I swore I saw the corner of his lips twitch, but it could have been a trick of the light. "We won't let anything happen to you."

"Even after?" I pressed him.

He turned me around, so I looked directly into his icy eyes. "Yes."

I didn't know if I believed him, but what choice did I have in the matter? If this went badly in nine days, I would figure something out, because the only person who was going to truly look after me, was me.

"Olivia, you'll be eating with me and my brothers," Issik announced to everyone.

Thanks for singling me out, asshole. The last thing I wanted was to be treated differently or special. "Like I have a choice," I mumbled, my tone flat. I really just wanted to eat in my room, away from the prying eyes and the glances of pity.

His sharp, blond brow lifted. "You'll thank me later." He bent down, his breath cool on my cheek. Cold fingers wrapped around my elbow, causing a chill to climb over my arm, and spread through my body. I wanted to shiver, but I forced myself to stay still. Besides the coldness, I found it strangely comforting.

The soft material of the pink dress I had worn today, swished over my bare legs as Issik and I walked into the great hall from the kitchen together. Staci would have gone gaga over the color. Would I ever get the chance to see my best friend again?

Jase shot me a disarming smile, complete with dimples, as we joined his table, and my breath caught, wiping away every single coherent thought from my brain. "Good morning. Did you sleep okay?"

Ugh. How did he do that? And with just a smile? *A very sexy smile*, my sort of functioning brain reminded me.

It was too early to deal with all four of them, and I was beginning to regret leaving my room. I took an empty seat across from Zade and Kieran. Catching the scent of freshly brewed grounds, my eyes grew big. "Is that coffee?"

Zade nodded and began pouring me a mug. "How do you like it?"

"The stronger, the better."

Kieran wrinkled his nose. "Can't stand the stuff myself."

I took the warm mug with both hands and brought it to my face, inhaling. "I can't function without it. It smells amazing. God, I miss that."

"I'll make sure the kitchen has plenty on hand for you," Jase said, passing me a platter of what looked like diced potatoes with sautéed veggies.

Setting the mug down, I kept my hands wrapped around it for the heat to counteract the cold remnants of Issik's touch. "That's not necessary. I don't want to be any trouble. I'm sure I can manage brewing a pot when the mood strikes."

"If you change your mind, you only have to ask."

This feeling of being waited on was unsettling. I'd always envisioned having a massive house with cooks and maids to tend to my every desire would be glorious, but that wasn't how I felt at all. I didn't feel like a princess, regardless of my royal treatment.

"I won't," I assured him.

Forks clattered as breakfast resumed, and after piling a plate full, I took my first bite. The food tasted as exotic as the Veil, and I found it to be better, fresher, and more flavorful than earthly equivalents, including the coffee.

"Can I ask you a question?" Kieran said, eyeing me from across the table. There was a glimmer of seriousness in his eyes.

"Sure, fire away." What did I have to hide?

"Why were you living on the streets? Do you have no family who cares for you?" He hadn't meant to drag up painful memories or judge me. I could see it in the softening of his eyes, but he was merely as curious about me as I was about them. And why shouldn't he be?

I swallowed. "I did have a family once. My mom... she was wonderful. She—" My voice hitched, getting stuck in my throat with the tears not far behind. "She got sick and passed away. I've been on my own since," I rushed out before I lost it.

"There's a reason you were brought here. You won't be alone ever again," Jase offered matter-of-factly.

Shit. They were going to make me embarrass myself. I wiped at my eyes, staring at my plate as I took a few minutes to gather my emotions.

Kieran captured my stinging eyes. "We've all lost those we care about."

It was true. The five of us all had parents pass away. We knew the pain of missing those close to us. Was that a coincidence?

A stirring wind came into the room, rustling the plants out in the courtyard and blowing the curtains covering the open doors.

"Tianna," Issik announced.

"It looks like we might be in for a storm," Zade added seconds before the screams began, and a flood of darkness took over. It descended upon the sky, wiping out any light. Instinctively, my body tensed as worry and unease set in. Something was very wrong.

"Blood bats," hissed Issik.

Uh. What?

Before I got the chance to ask what blood bats were, in swooped a swarm of flying creatures as black as midnight, with eyes that glowed like the fires of hell itself. My hands mechanically covered my head as I curled down to hide under the table. I felt fleshy wings brush my hair and squealed.

Nope.

I don't do bats, not of any variety.

My head hit the edge of the table in my scramble to get to safety. I was a disaster magnet. A hand flew to my head, to rub the now tender spot on my forehead, and I gasped at a quick pain that sliced over my arm. *Something bit me.* Forgetting about my head, I cradled my arm, feeling the warm, wet flow of blood.

The ground shook.

My gaze shifted outwards to find that one of the descendants had transformed. Zade. His dragon form was tall and fierce. His neck lengthened as he straightened to his full, glorious height. The scales covering his body were a deep red, almost brown.

Issik plucked me from my awkward spot, half under the table, and into his arms. "Hang on. Things are about to get toasty in here."

Bats circled the great hall with hunger in their beady red eyes. It was a damn good thing this room had vaulted ceilings. Actually, now that I thought about it, all the rooms in the castle had dragon-approved heights.

Zade crouched in the doorway to the courtyard—his tail inside and his long neck stretching outside. Opening his mouth, he expelled fire, lighting up the bloodthirsty bats trying to get in. Their shrieks echoed throughout the Veil, and I huddled deeper into Issik's chest.

The creatures fluttering inside the hall were rounded up by Kieran and Jase. They herded them outside where Zade could finish them off.

"Are you okay?" Issik finally asked after what felt like hours, his cool breath blowing over my hair.

"What was that?" I breathed in choppy pants.

Issik unfolded his arms from around me, a troubling expression in his eyes. "A warning from Tianna."

Fear trembled on my lips. "Well, that wasn't very welcoming."

The ten days were up.

I woke knowing today was going to be a pivotal moment in my life. It would determine what happened next. If by some ridiculous odds, like winning the lottery, I was the one to break the curse, would they let me go home? And if I didn't release them from the spell binding them to the island, the same questioned remained. I knew I'd probably never get off this island, and as if the land had sensed my somber mood, the sky was blanketed in dark clouds, hiding any sunshine.

Doomsday.

That was what today felt like.

The four dragon descendants waited for me in the hall, pacing back and forth outside my door. I was surprised they hadn't just busted in, demanding for me to be ready. I understood their eagerness, but I was nervous as hell.

Soaking in a hot bath for thirty minutes had done nothing to soothe the tension in my muscles. What I needed was a Valium. Stalling wasn't helping my situation, so I gave up and headed to the door, taking one last look at the room that had become my sanctuary for the last ten days.

The descendants might have needed me, but I also had grown to need them… more than I'd anticipated. It made me realize how much I didn't want to go back to my old life. I wasn't positive that I belonged in the Veil, but I knew for a fact that the streets were no place for me either. After today, they were probably going to discard me like all the others. I wouldn't be special, and a part of me was more worried about being cast aside and alone, than not being able to break the curse.

With a sigh, I opened the door. The dragons' eyes swung toward me with a hopefulness that broke my heart.

Within minutes, I found myself outside the front gate of Jase's keep, boxed in on all sides by brooding dragon shifters. *Well, this is going to be a fun adventure.*

A gust of wind whipped across my face, and I gasped. Stretched out in front of us was an endless forest of towering pines, maples, and weeping willows that seemed to canopy the entire land.

Jase grabbed my hand and pulled me along while the others followed us down a dirt path that snaked into the woods. Pebbles scattered when our footsteps fell. We entered the vast woods, surrounded by tall trees and thorny thicket patches. Rocks lined the dirt pathway, which led us deeper and deeper into the forest, and I found myself drawing closer to Jase. I couldn't seem to help it. There was a malevolent ambiance among the trees that made me want to crawl under my bed. Jase's arms would have to do.

As if Jase sensed my uneasiness, he pulled me fully against him, twining his fingers around mine. All things considered, it really wasn't a bad place to be.

"Why do you get to hold her hand?" Kieran pouted.

"Seriously? Does it matter?" I argued. Each step farther in, felt like one step closer to my doom.

"Maybe," the green-eyed shifter replied.

Jase's smug smile grew, only irritating Kieran more. "I'm just ensuring she doesn't trip or fall. No blood spilled until we get to the cave."

How freaking considerate.

"We should take turns," Zade suggested.

Oh my god. Not him too. I rolled my eyes. "We're *so* not fighting about my hand right now." I snatched my fingers out from underneath Jase's, and a surge of anxiety rushed inside me. I stumbled. Holy crap. What was happening? My feet were suddenly paralyzed and refused to move.

"Olivia," Kieran called.

"She's scared," Issik groused. "Jase, take her hand again."

Once Jase's fingers touched mine, it was like a switch had been flipped inside me, taking away all my fear and reservations. I tilted my head up, glancing sideways at him. "You're using your ability on me, aren't you?"

His brows drew together. "Not intentionally." The others had stopped, and stared at us. "Let's go. We need to get there and back before nightfall," Jase grumbled.

I didn't bother to ask why the rush, because I knew I wouldn't like the answer. Nor did I ask why we weren't flying. The density of the woods would have made it difficult for a dragon, but the sky above seemed like a fast route.

"Here." I offered Kieran my other hand. "I've only got two."

Kieran happily took ahold of my fingers, interlacing ours together, and now I walked sandwiched between two dragon shifters. Joy. No escaping now—not that I actually thought I had a chance of doing so.

The five of us continued to hike through the jungle, and I couldn't help but notice how at ease Kieran seemed to be. I tried once to wiggle my fingers free from the two dragons, but neither of them budged, and I really didn't want them to start fighting again over who got to hold my hand. Things had finally settled down… for the moment.

After what felt like forever, I was about to demand one of them give me a piggyback ride when we came to a tree. Not just any tree. The biggest I'd ever seen in my life. I was talking Jack-and-the-Beanstalk huge.

My breath hitched as I paused to gawk.

"It's beautiful, isn't it?" Jase's voice was husky, sending a stream of comfort through me.

Damn tranquility dragon.

I just nodded, not bothering to scold him for screwing with my emotions, and leaned my weight against him, my legs weak from the trek. I'd never seen anything like the plant in front of me. The very old tree with a trunk the size of a house—probably bigger—had large exposed roots at its base that were interwoven with each other into a maze. They arched upward, forming an entrance over a round dark hole that dissolved into a musty cave.

"It's magnificent. Is it safe to go inside?" I asked. I wanted to explore, and it was too dark from outside to see the interior of the cave. Whereas the woods felt spooky and ominous, something about the cave called to me.

"Yes. It's safe. This cave has been here longer than the dragons," Zade explained in a voice like molten lava.

Peeling my eyes from the tree, I looked left and right to see that the descendants seemed as enchanted as I was. "What are we waiting for?" It wasn't that I was looking forward to what came next, but more so that I wanted to get it over with.

Kieran's lips twitched before he tightened his fingers, laced with mine, and drew me inside the cave, toward a pinprick of light flickering deep within.

The moment we stepped in its depths, I wanted back out, but I found myself rooted to the ground.

"What's wrong?" Kieran asked me, his green, luminous gaze falling on me when he felt my resistance.

Tugging my hands free, I wrapped them around myself. "Take your pick."

"There's nothing to be afraid of," Zade reassured beside me.

I snorted. Was he kidding? I could think of a dozen reasons off the top of my head, including the anger in their eyes when they figured out I wouldn't be able to release them from this curse. Taking a deep breath, I nodded.

We kept on a straight path, following the light, until it finally opened up to a clearing. I could see that the light was actually a torch embedded in a stone pillar—one of many that outlined the space. I stood on the outskirts, mouth hanging open. Five statues of men with beards, wrinkled faces, and hoods that draped to the floor were assembled near the center. Roots wove over our heads in an intricate network, and twinkling gold lights shimmered softly on the ceiling, like a million tiny stars. At the center was a rectangular altar with ancient marks carved into the stone, and on the ground surrounding it.

"What is this place?" My voice echoed through the open space, bouncing off the rock walls.

"It's the temple of our ancestors," Jase offered, his chest rising in pride, "and the one place on the island that generates mystic energy."

"Do you guys come here often?" I asked, curious who had lit the torches. My eyes were drawn to them.

Kieran stepped into the middle, the flickering lanterns illuminating only half his face. "No, only twice a year." He must have noticed my focus on the lights because he continued. "The flames are imbued with the curse. They will burn until it's broken."

"So, what now?" They'd gotten me here. That had to be the hardest part, or so I hoped.

Jase turned to face me. "We bite you."

I blinked. "I'm sorry, what?"

The four dragon descendants stood in a circle around me, and silence greeted my question.

Shaking my head, I backed up. "Uh. No. I didn't sign up for being bitten. Let alone multiple times."

Fingers lightly touched my waist. It was Zade. "Your blood is the key."

"Yeah, I got that part, but can't you just—I don't know—take a vile and drink it or some crap?"

Kieran's lips twitched. Issik folded his arms. Zade examined his nails. And Jase sighed. "We must be in our dragon form. It will only be a drop," Jase assured me.

"I must be freaking insane to even contemplate letting four grown-ass dragons bite me," I grumbled to myself, and then I looked each of them in the eye. "Where?"

Four sets of brows rose.

"Where are you going to bite me?"

The room filled with deep chuckles. "Anywhere you like," Kieran responded.

I blinked, ignoring the flush that stole over my body. "Fine. But make it quick." I held out my wrist. It seemed the safest part on me.

Their broad shoulders relaxed. "Up on the altar. Lie down," Jase instructed me.

All those visions I'd had ten days ago about being sacrificed to some dragon god came rushing back. I nibbled on my lower lip, uncertainty spiraling within me as I stood staring at the stone slab.

Jase cleared his throat behind me and touched the small of my back, immediately filling me with calmness. I spun, looking him directly in the eyes. "There's no need to fear us. We won't hurt you. I give you my word."

I nodded, keeping my gaze steadily on Jase as he helped me up onto the cold block. While he was coaxing me out of a mild anxiety attack, the other three had stripped, and suddenly the last thing on my mind was dying. There were four naked men surrounding me. My eyes didn't know where to look… or not look.

Each man was so different in his own way—from the tone of his skin to his unique personality. I didn't dare torture myself, so I closed my eyes and waited. The sounds were enough to keep my active imagination going. Bones, muscle, and skin stretched, grew, and adapted. The cavern was saturated with heavy breathing.

I felt the first sting of a bite on my arm as the first dragon sunk his incisors into my flesh, and with it a jolt of power surged in my body, causing me to suck in a sharp gulp of air. I tried to gather up every particle of bravery inside me. I had worked up about a tablespoon when all five of my senses were suddenly supercharged.

The musky air became more pungent, and I shivered as another pair of sharp fangs pierced my flesh lightly. Then another. And another. A groan escaped from my lips, and I bit down, tasting my own blood. It was then that my lashes fluttered open. Four dragons encompassed me, each of them with their radiant eyes locked on me.

A light flashed behind my eyes, momentarily blinding me, and my head fell back. This couldn't be normal.

What is happening?

Am I actually breaking the curse?

No fucking way.

When the light faded, I stared at a witch with flaming red hair and alabaster skin. She posed on the edge of a cliff—her hands raised to the sky, bolts of angry lightning crackling around her, five dragons circled above her head. I couldn't believe what I was seeing. Or how.

No one had to tell me that the figure I beheld was Tianna, the witch who had cursed the descendants. I was being given a glimpse of the past.

Her raven black dress unfurled behind her as the wind howled and raged. Even from a distance, I could see the pure, unadulterated hate in her eyes. She held a scepter in her outstretched arms, casting the curse and striking each of the dragons with magical light.

"No!" I screamed, but it was useless. The vision was of the past, and there was nothing I could do to change it.

Why I was being shown this moment? Did this mean I had something to do with breaking the curse? Or did all the girls before me see the same apparition?

As quickly as the vision had appeared, it faded, leaving me shaken while the effects wore off, and my vision cleared. I gritted my teeth. Jase, Kieran, Zade, and Issik were all huddled over me, no longer dragons. Worry creased their brows. "Was that it? Is the spell broken?" I croaked, my throat dry.

The four shared an equal look of dread and disappointment. "No," Jase finally spoke.

My stomach sank like the cave had collapsed. "Then what the hell was that? All the flashing lights and…stuff?"

"I don't know," Jase admitted, looking at the others for answers.

No one had any, but it was clear from their somber expressions, they had experienced the vision as I had.

Just freaking dandy.

"You mean to tell me that I'm not the one?" I said, sitting up.

"It doesn't appear so, blondie," Kieran said flatly.

If they hadn't looked like I just kicked their puppy, I would have said, *"I told you so,"* but I wisely kept my mouth shut, remembering I had been their final chance at salvation. All of this was for nothing: my being kidnapped, trapped on a strange island, and doomed to spend my life as the girl who failed. I'd been their last hope; now they had none. They would die. And as I gazed into four pairs of very different eyes, a heaviness landed on my chest. I didn't want them to die. I'd only been with the descendants for a short time, but somehow they had weaseled their way into my life. I cared about them.

"I'm sorry. I-I don't know what to say," I mumbled, my emotions a tangled mess inside of me.

"It isn't your fault," Jase offered, trying to soothe my guilt, but it wasn't working, and when he reached for me, I pulled away because I didn't want him to take the dread I felt. If they were all suffering, why shouldn't I? He grunted, clearly displeased I wouldn't let him touch me.

"Dammit," Zade growled, and a moment later, his fist punched the side of the cave.

His display of self-pity—no matter how justified—only made me feel crappier. It also caused an avalanche within the cave. Pebbles and dirt rained down from the ceiling, flowing faster with each passing second. I lifted my hands over my head, but it offered little protection.

"We need to get out of here," Issik said, glowering at Zade.

Kieran slipped a hand around my waist, lifting me off the stone altar, and instead of setting me on my feet, he tucked me into his arms, shielding me from the destruction thundering down on us.

Even knowing I hadn't broken the curse, they still protected me. A lump of gratitude joined the fear inside me. Kieran hustled us into the dark corridor, and as we left the temple of dragons, I swore I heard a female voice laughing.

I twisted in Kieran's arms, glancing over his shoulders, but there was no one there—no witch with devious eyes. *Great. Now I'm hearing shit.*

"What is it?" Kieran murmured in my ear as he picked up his pace.

Behind us a cloud of thick dust kicked up, and I hid my face in the space between his neck and shoulder. "I thought I heard someone," I admitted as the earth slowly settled as we moved closer to the exit.

"A female?" he asked.

I nodded, staring at his face. My eyes were drawn to his lips and the silver hoop. "How did you know?"

"Tianna taunts us often, but never the girls we've brought here."

I didn't want to think about the others who'd been here before me, not when he held me in his arms. He had a way of making me feel as if I was the only girl in the world. "She was laughing," I murmured.

His eyes slid to mine, and the usual mischievous gleam was missing from them. "I heard her too. We all did, but after a hundred years, you learn to ignore her. Reacting only gives Tianna what she wants, so we've learned."

We had reached the exit of the cave, but Kieran kept ahold of me, trailing just behind the other three guys. "You can put me down now," I urged, even as my fingers twirled the hair at the base of his neck. The truth was I was comfortable in his embrace.

His emerald eyes twinkled. "And if I'd rather not?"

"Kieran," Zade scolded him, spinning around and glaring at the other shifter with dark, narrowed eyes.

Kieran stopped and slowly dropped me to my feet, letting my body glide down his.

Damn.

The last thing I should be thinking about was his ripped stomach or how I missed the feel of him against me. As it turned out, I didn't get the chance to dwell for long on the way my body responded.

Zade flashed in front of Kieran's face, and I was shuffled to the side. "Will you stop pawing at her every chance you get?"

Kieran's answer was a cocky grin filled with trouble, just like him, which Zade retaliated by shoving Kieran in the shoulder. This was going to get ugly, fast, if someone didn't do something. My eyes sought out the other two dragons for help.

Jase and Issik had been walking shoulder to shoulder. They stopped to turn and see what the ruckus was now. Neither seemed surprised it involved me. "Should have known," Jase mumbled, crossing his arms, but did nothing to stop the hotheaded Zade or the troublemaker Kieran.

That left me. "Mother-freaking dragons," I muttered, stomping to put myself between them. Not exactly a safe place for a seventeen-year-old, who was only five feet five inches tall.

Kieran no longer grinned. The change in his eyes was like a viper, lethal and swift, as was his fist when it connected with Zade's face.

"Jesus," I breathed out for two reasons. One, if I had been any faster—thank God I wasn't—I might have been on the receiving end of that blow. And two, I couldn't believe punches were being thrown over me!

That had never happened before. Ever.

With my arms out in the warrior pose, I pressed my palms to their chests. This was becoming a much too familiar situation—me between two guys. I should be grateful it wasn't all four.

Fire leaped quickly into Zade's eyes. "Get out of the way, Olivia. I don't want you to get hurt."

"That wouldn't be a problem if the two of you stopped acting like imbeciles," I argued, blowing a strand of hair out of my face.

Zade's response was to pick me up by my shoulders and move me off to the side, out of his way, but I wasn't having it and started squirming to break free. That was how I fell on my butt.

Fortunately, I landed on a patch of softly packed soil, instead of the twig beside me. I shuddered to think about... a stick up my ass.

Wouldn't that have been my luck? Four concerned dragons hovered over me, all offering a hand. It was ridiculous—so much so that I started to laugh.

"Are you okay?" Jase asked, those violet eyes studying me with concern.

Breathless, I grabbed the side of my stomach and smiled.

The sky above us turned black, and I squinted, alarm suddenly chasing away the warmth in my cheeks. "Is that a—?"

"Wraith," Issik hissed, his cold eyes having followed the line of my gaze. He slipped his hand around my waist, pulling me to my feet. "We must get her to safety."

"Lead the way, Ice Prince." I winced. I hadn't meant to say that out loud.

He gave me a funny look, but my nickname for the shifter was the least of his concerns. The wraith screamed a sound that made my ears want to bleed, and its obsidian shadow fell over our heads, skirting the treetops. "Run!" Issik ordered me.

Shirts were flying off for the second time today as two of the guys immediately shifted and took to the sky. This was my chance to escape. I didn't know why the thought popped into my head at that moment, but once it was there, I couldn't get rid of the idea. I had made a promise to myself, if I didn't break the curse, I would find a way off this island. However, I hadn't factored in the feelings that had bloomed for the four descendants over the last few days. There might never come another opportunity like this when I was left alone, and if I had any real chance of going back to my world, I had to take it while I could.

But I'd underestimated the Veil and its penchant for danger. I had been warned, and I should have listened.

R unning was something I could do. I might not be a track superstar, but these legs could sprint as long as there weren't fallen branches, tangled ivy, rocks, or basically anything I could trip on.

It just so happened that the woods were full of all the above.

Fricking awesome.

Did I mention it was also growing dark?

I was so screwed, but it didn't stop me from hauling ass. Sticking to the dirt path as much as possible, I headed deeper into the woods, uncertain where I was going. It wasn't long before my feet began to blister from rubbing against the slip-on. Branches and sharp leaves cut into my arms and legs, but I didn't stop, afraid of who would find me or who wouldn't.

Clenching my jaw, I bared the pain, and pushed forward. My heart beat rapidly from exhaustion and adrenaline, but through the treetops, I could hear the battle between the dragons and the wraith.

Out of nowhere, Kieran pinned me against a tree, shielding me with his body from the wraith that dove from the sky and through the tree-tops. Holy crap. Where had he come from? It was evident that Kieran didn't know his own strength. Pain seared through me, and I felt like a china doll that could shatter at any moment.

Everything about the dragon overwhelmed my senses, from the feeling of his muscular body pressed against mine, to the light scent of his woodsy aroma surrounding me. I could have easily forgotten the danger above.

His eyes swept over my face, and I stared back. "Are you okay?" he said.

I nodded, not trusting myself to speak.

"Stay here," he commanded me and then ripped his clothes off, shifting into a glorious dragon, taking off to help Jase and Zade in the sky.

Like hell I will.

My brain cells were just settling down after being shaken, when I pushed off the tree.

Finally, an opening came into view. Pale moonlight splashed onto the grass as I stumbled into the clearing, nearly falling and eating dirt. *That would have been a hell of a look, Olivia.*

I glanced around. Now what?

Did I keep running? Did I hide? And then what? I didn't know how to get off this island. I had been utterly foolish to think I could survive on my own. How long would I last out here? A few days? A week?

Five more minutes?

A twig snapped behind me, and I swung around, casting my eyes to the edge of the woods where I had come from. I found myself face to face with a wraith.

Holy shit! What's the plan now, smartass? Scream for help?

The shadowy creature shrieked, blowing my hair off my face. Its breath smelled of rotting flesh. *Someone needs a Tic Tac.*

Up close, the wraith was scarier than I'd imagined. Under its hooded cloak of rags, the creature had no face. Where I expected to see his eyes was nothing but darkness. Completely freaked out, I sprang into action.

Turning, I ran, but I barely got a few yards before cold, bony hands latched onto me. Grabbing ahold of my wrist, the wraith wrestled me to the ground.

I hissed in pain as my head hit the ground. *Son of a bi—*

My breath evaporated as coldness stole into my lungs, snaking its way into my chest and throughout my body. I shivered. And I couldn't stop.

What was it doing to me? The world around me seemed to turn gray, losing all color, and my only thought was of death itself.

Paralyzed by fear or something else, I wasn't sure how long I lay there on the grass with the wraith on top of me. When all hope seemed lost and I could feel the life vacating my body, the wraith was suddenly ripped off me.

Still, I couldn't move.

I no longer felt connected to my body, unable to wiggle a toe or finger. Everything that made me human and alive was fading away, piece by piece. Growls and shrieks resonated in the clearing, and I knew my dragons were fighting the wraith. A white film had moved over my eyes, washing out the clarity of the world, just as someone sank to his knees beside me, and whispered my name. I thought I might have gasped, but I couldn't be positive it was me.

Sensing motion, I struggled to clear my vision and blinked rapidly. I was pulled into a man's arms—one of my dragons—but I didn't know which one, not until I felt the heat. He exuded heat like a bonfire. Zade. The fire dragon cradled me against his chest, and slowly the feeling came back into my fingers, my toes, and my lungs. My hands buried themselves into the hair at the nape of his neck, and I pressed my cheek against him, the coldness inside me melting into the warmth of him.

But it wasn't enough. I opened my mouth to tell him I needed more, but I didn't know what to ask for.

"Shh. Don't speak," he whispered in a terse baritone.

I could just barely make out the features of his face, but I took comfort in it, thinking I might not die after all.

Zade gently pressed his thumb to my chin, prying open my jaw and placing his lips to mine. This wasn't exactly the perfect time to make out, but once his soft mouth touched mine, it was all I wanted. Heat filled my body, and I finally understood what he was doing. His dragon's breath burned inside me, chasing away the lingering effects of the wraith.

His lips remained pressed against mine until they tingled. Everything tingled really. Zade pulled away. "Are you okay?" he asked.

"I-I think so, but don't let me go just yet." I still felt a little wobbly, but that could have been from his kisses.

"I wasn't planning on it." He brushed the hair off my face, keeping me tucked into his arms. "I'm used to girls freaking out, but you're not going to faint, are you?"

I wasn't planning on it either.

Much to Zade's disappointment, I didn't faint. Three naked dragon shifters stood around me. Thank God Zade had clothes on, because that would have been the height of my embarrassment. I didn't know what to say. "Are you guys always naked this much?" I mumbled, the words popping out of my mouth.

"Does it bother you?" Kieran countered as if the idea of spending more time in the nude with me appealed to him.

"How do you feel?" Jase asked, ignoring Kieran.

"She's… annoyed," Zade answered, while staring at me with a thoughtful expression.

How could he possibly know that? I wasn't miffed at them, but me. I had almost just died, and all I could think about was the four glorious shifters surrounding me—proof I needed my head checked. "And how would you know what I'm feeling?" I directed my question at Zade.

"I don't know. I sensed it." He rubbed at the center of his chest like what I was feeling was right there inside his heart.

"Is that something you guys do?" *And failed to tell me about*, I added silently.

"No," answered four unanimous, deep voices.

I was willing to brush it off. It didn't seem like that big of a deal since it was pretty common to read people's emotions. And then this happened.

"Okay, you've had her enough. Give her up." Kieran reached for me.

I still sat in Zade's lap, and although it had slipped my mind, it didn't get past Kieran's attention.

"Don't get possessive. She's ours to share," Jase answered, pulling on a pair of jeans but leaving the top button undone as he bent to pick up his shirt off the ground.

Since when did I become *theirs*? I wasn't having it. "You guys don't own me. I'm not anyone's. Especially not until you put some clothes on."

"The four of us are responsible for you now," Issik spoke up for the first time since the wraith attack. I was glad to see he had put on clothes… mostly. He was still shirtless.

I rolled my eyes. "And what does that mean? You're going to pass me around like a joint to share?"

"She's angry now," Zade said, studying me oddly.

Do I have something on my face? Why is he looking at me like that? "I have a right to be upset. I've traipsed through the woods, been pulled into a cave at the bottom of a tree trunk, been bitten four times by dragons, and attacked by a wraith. I'm waiting for my freaking badge of honor."

"Yep. She's pissed," Zade added. "I can feel her irritation rolling like waves. It's making the fire inside me roar."

The other three dragons all turned sharp eyes on Golden God. "What do you mean?" Jase demanded.

Zade forked a hand through his hair. "I don't know. It's like her anger is a part of me, simmering in my blood until it starts to build inside her."

"Here, let me try." Kieran pulled me to my feet and into his arms. Before I realized what he was doing, his lips were moving over mine. I touched his cheek and closed my eyes. I might not be a virgin, but holy crap, the venomous dragon knew how to work those hot lips. I sighed, leaning into him. My knees felt weak.

Kieran broke off the kiss, staring down at me with moonlight in his eyes. "I felt it too," he said, wide-eyed, rubbing the same spot on his chest that Zade had.

What is going on?

"Well, of course *you* felt something," Jase growled. "You just kissed her brainless."

Kieran sucked on his lower lip like he wanted to savor the taste of me. "It wasn't just chemistry, which there was plenty of. I could feel her passion inside me."

Zade had straightened to his full height and glared at the green-eyed dragon shifter. "What the hell. Why does he get desire?"

Seriously. Were they now arguing over my emotions? What next?

I stepped out of Kieran's arms before he decided to plant another one on me to test his theory some more.

"She might not have broken the curse, but something definitely happened in the cave." The silky smoothness of Kieran's voice had disappeared altogether, replaced by deep concern.

"I agree. When the wraith showed up, her fear was so strong inside me, all I could think about was finding her," Jase admitted.

My hands dropped to my hips, and the bitch came out. "Wait. A. Freaking. Minute. Are you telling me the four of you can now feel my emotions?" Oh, hell no.

"It's possible something happened when we took a drop of your blood," Issik concluded.

Please tell me this is a joke. I shook my head. "This can't be real. So I didn't break the curse, but I managed to emotionally entangle myself with four dragons. Jesus. How does this crap happen to me?"

"She's sad," Ice Prince said, looking at me strangely.

"Okay. Enough! Stop." I backed away from the four of them, not wanting any of the dragons to touch me. "I don't want to think about this anymore. I'm exhausted. Can we just go home?"

Home.

The word echoed in my head. Home was Chicago, not Jase's castle, yet it was the room in Wakeland Keep I had been referring to. This wasn't my home, I reminded myself, I couldn't forget it. This was only supposed to be temporary, but from the sound of things, the descendants weren't going to let me leave.

"She's right," Issik said. "We need to get her to safety before anything else shows up."

I didn't like his intimation of other things. Hadn't the wraiths been enough? What creatures should I be worried about, besides the four dragon shifters eyeballing me? I was getting sick of them constantly sharing glances that had double meanings. What were they keeping from me?

"Can you guys put the rest of your clothes on? Button up the pants. Throw on a shirt. It's very distracting." My eyes couldn't stop straying to certain parts of their bodies. I hadn't seen enough naked men in my life to judge what qualified as va-va-voom, but the dragon descendants had all the working parts.

"We're making her uncomfortable," Jase said.

Argh. This emotion-sensing thing royally sucked ass. I'd never be able to hide anything from them again. *I don't think they're sexy. Not one single bit,* I told myself. "They're not sexy," I accidentally let slip out. My hands flew to my mouth, and I groaned. Tell me I had not just mumbled something about being sexy out loud. I glanced up at four very smug dragons and groaned again.

Damn them.

They were going to be the end of me.

Zade crossed his arms and gave me a look. "What are you muttering about?"

My hand pushed through my messy hair, but it was a failed attempt. The numerous knots made it impossible to manage. "Nothing. It's not important."

Issik strode back into sight, his jaw locked.

"Do the four of you ever get along?" I asked.

"Yes," four deep voices answered together.

"Well, at the moment, I'm finding that hard to believe."

"Come on, Cupcake," Jase said as he started to move, taking me along with him. I didn't even bother to fight him. Maybe I was becoming used to being manhandled by the four of them.

I waited until we left the clearing and ventured back into the woods before peppering them with more questions. "What did it want?" I inquired about the wraith.

"You," Jase said in a very low voice.

Kieran slipped in next to Jase. "The wraiths are the dead of the Veil —our kings, our queens, our mothers, brothers, sisters, and fathers. Tianna's spell prevents them from moving on. They are as tied to the island as we are."

What was her deal? Why had she gone to such great lengths to curse the descendants and the island? There had to be more to the story. The dragons all walked with long, purposeful strides that I more or less had to run to keep up with. "What did it do to me?"

Jase's jaw grew tight, his cheek ticking. "Wraiths feed on humans, stealing their souls. They know why we brought you here and will do anything to stop the curse from being lifted at Tianna's command."

"But I didn't break the curse, so why would it try to kill me?" I asked, kicking a rock in my effort to stay with their pace.

Jase didn't answer at first, and I couldn't help but wonder if they were going to constantly keep me in the dark. How frustrating. I was here because of them and their stupid problems. The least they could do was tell me the truth.

"Because all hope isn't lost," Jase finally answered.

"I don't understand."

"The attack on your life, however distressing it may have been, means there is still a way to sever the tie that binds us to the island. You're the key; we just haven't figured out how you unlock the curse yet."

"So I gave you my blood for nothing?"

"Not nothing. You can't forget the link to your emotions," Kieran so kindly pointed out.

Again. That wasn't something I was happy about. "Is there anything else I should know about this spell?"

"There is one other thing," Jase confessed.

"Don't hold out on me now," I retorted.

Zade glanced down at me, a flash of anger in his eyes. "It also forbids us from siring children. If we don't find a way to break it, the dragons die with us."

So it wasn't just about their future, but also the fate of their race. "What do we do now?" I asked.

Jase shook his head. "There must be something we're missing, something we haven't thought of. And your blood..."

"What about my blood?" It drove me crazy when people didn't finish their thoughts. I didn't like suspense.

"None of us have ever tasted blood like yours. You are different, but it was more than the sweetness of it, it was as if you became a part of me," Zade finished. His body was still lined with anger, but the resentment wasn't directed at me.

"And the wraith's attack on you only proves it," Issik added.

So it wasn't just Jase who felt this way. None of them had given up.

"Tianna has the wraiths guarding the boundaries of the Veil. If they are hunting us, then we are doing something right." I could see flickers of fire and the promise of revenge in Zade's expression. He wanted Tianna to pay for what she had done to them.

My hand extended, and I found myself reaching out to touch the closest dragon. It was Issik. He stared down at my fingers. "Let me guess, this is going to be very dangerous, isn't it?"

The four of them shared one of their famous looks. "Yes."

"But we swear on our lives, we will protect you." Kieran rushed to jump in, and smooth over the mounting anxiety that had built in my chest.

I believed them. They had as much to lose as I did. Probably even more so. "Anyone have an idea of how to break this curse? This bitch is going down."

They rewarded me with four grins of pure sin. My dragons.

No. Not *my* dragons.

I was just helping them, and once we unwove the spell Tianna put on the dragon descendants, I would get on with my life.

Whatever that meant.

And my delusions of the future ran amuck in my head.

The journey back to the keep wasn't as treacherous as the trek to the cave had been. We picked our way through the woods, winding down the same path we had traveled earlier in the day. I started to lose steam quickly, lagging behind and tripping over my achy and exhausted feet.

After the third time of stumbling over a branch, Jase slipped an arm around my waist. "Hold on to my neck," he murmured, waiting for me to lift my arms.

"I can walk," I insisted, concentrating on putting one foot in front of the other.

"Are you always this stubborn? And clumsy?" he added.

My head whipped to the side and I glared. "I am neither stubborn nor clumsy."

He smirked, and I knew I was in trouble, not the life-threatening kind, but the why-does-he-have-to-use-those-dimples-on-me kind. "Good. Then you better hang on." Jase didn't give me a chance to argue. Dipping his shoulder, he put an arm under my legs and lifted me up.

I crossed my arms at first, refusing to give in, but it was awkward, leaving me no choice. My hands slipped around his neck.

Minutes later, my head became too heavy and I could no longer resist the urge to rest it on the space between his shoulder and neck. I sighed softly, comforted by the calming scent of him. Like the sound of the sea, he lulled me to sleep. I was pretty sure he'd used his tranquility on me, but I was too tired to care, especially when he suddenly brushed his lips over the side of my cheek. My fingers tightened at the nape of his neck as a surge of tingles danced inside me.

It was nothing. Just a simple kiss, and yet it felt anything but simple. If I wasn't careful, these four dragons would find a way into my heart. I didn't know how I could feel so equally attached to them, but there was no denying something definitely was brewing between us. Just what was I going to do about it?

My eyelids fell closed, and they didn't open again until my arms were wrenched off Jase's neck. He laid me down in my bed as I glanced up at him from half-lidded eyes. I rested a hand on his arm, not wanting him to leave just yet. "Are we home?" I asked groggily.

He sat on the edge of the bed, the mattress shifting to one side under his weight. "Yes, and it would be in your best interest if you stayed inside. No more escape attempts."

My fatigue vanished. I opened my mouth to say something in my defense and then quickly snapped it closed. How had he known? For all intents and purposes, I could have been just running aimlessly in the woods.

"The wraith has your scent. He'll be back with others too, and you're going to need our protection, Cupcake."

Shit.

Well, that just sealed the deal, didn't it? Jase gave me no choice. If I tried to run again, the wraiths would probably find me first. "Fabulous," I muttered sarcastically.

His finger brushed along my jawline, lingering just over my bottom lip. "Try and get some sleep. One of us will be near."

Was that supposed to provide me comfort? It didn't. Just the opposite. My entire body erupted in a heat similar to when Zade had blown his breath into my lungs. "How near are we talking? Like in my room?" The coloring of my cheeks morphed in the darkened room, and his eyes were drawn to them.

He grinned. "If you like."

Did I want him in my room?

I was afraid of the answer. "Is there a bed big enough for five?" I joked, but the gleam in his eyes made me sorry I had.

He raised a single brow. "Are you into that kind of thing?"

"No," I exhaled on a nervous laugh. "Definitely not."

"You sure?" he asked, trailing a hand lightly down my arm.

At the moment, I was only into him, but I shook my head, giving him the truth. "No. I can't explain it, but I'm all mixed up inside." And then there was the fact that the four of them could sense my emotions. I still hadn't digested that clusterfuck.

"Maybe I could help you clear things up."

The mischief in his eyes told me his idea of "clearing things up" would only complicate matters more and entangle my feelings deeper in the web woven by the descendants. *Don't look at him. Keep your eyes glued to the bed.*

"Look at me," Jase murmured.

His velvet voice pulled at me, and I lost the battle. Staring into his smoldering deep purple eyes, I held my breath and waited. He leaned down, a lock of dark hair cascading over the side of his temple.

My heart started pumping, and my fingers dug into the bed. He was going to kiss me. Dipping forward, my eyes drifted shut, and that was when I felt his mouth brush the tip of my nose. He sat back, a smile teasing his lips, and in the moonlight, I saw a flash of dimples.

Argh. He really knew how to torment a girl. My grip relaxed against the sheets as I exhaled and struggled with the desire to pull him to my lips. What did that say about me? I should be running far and fast from Jase Dior.

But I couldn't.

And from the smug grin on his face, he knew it. The jerk probably had kissed every girl here.

The thought was like being thrown in a bath of ice-cold water. My eyes hardened, and I pushed at his chest so he no longer leaned over me. "I'm not your current plaything, and that goes for all of you."

Irritation reflected clearly across his face. "Why would you think that?"

"You have a house full of girls just like me." They had been special at one time.

His expression turned to stone, masking any emotion. "The thing is, Olivia, none of them are like you."

"How do I know you're not just telling me what I want to hear?"

"For one, it's the truth. And two, we've never had a connection to anyone before." His hypnotic voice placated me.

How could I forget for even a second our emotional fivesome? "I just don't want to be screwed with," I confessed.

What I really wanted to do was demand to know how many of the girls he had kissed, how many he had slept with. Jealousy was an ugly feeling, but the vision of my dragons with other girls sent me into a tizzy. Ten percent of my frustration could be attributed to exhaustion, but the other ninety percent was all possessiveness.

"I don't know what is going on in that pretty head of yours, but I'm not just being a flirt. The way I feel about you is serious," he murmured.

How do you feel about me? I asked inside my head but couldn't bring myself to say the question out loud.

Jase tucked the corners of the blanket around me so I was cocooned in the bed. "Now, get some sleep." Standing up, he walked out the door, leaving me alone with my thoughts.

Which was a scary place to be. Almost as scary as the wraiths.

Feelings were weird.

Back in the real world, I'd never really had a boyfriend. I had dated a little, then Mom got sick and my love life no longer mattered. But when I looked at Jase, Zade, Issik, and Kieran, there was something unique about each of them that I found endearing. The four dragons struck different chords inside me.

What made me feel so possessive of them? Was it because they were dragon shifters and I'd never met anyone like them? Did they exude some kind of pheromone attracting me to them? That would make sense, but this need to be near them, to touch them, and do things to them that would have made my grandma blush, didn't make sense.

They had kidnapped me, and here I was thinking about their lips.

All four sets of them.

I had to think about this for a moment. What was I saying? Four?

That was quite a lot of dragons to handle, yet I couldn't choose one over the other. But I was totally getting ahead of myself. They might not even think of me as anything more than a means to an end—their freedom. So what if they had kissed me? Well, Issik technically hadn't —the only one of the four who had shown any restraint. Or maybe it was just lack of interest, but at times, he seemed to care about my well-being. That had to count for something, right?

My mind continued to make excuses on his behalf, until a new thought struck me.

What would happen if I somehow, by a million-to-one shot, managed to free them from the curse? Would they discard me like the other girls then? Would that be a bad thing?

Yes. The thought of living in the same house as one of them, and being cast aside as just another girl, filled me with dread. From the moment I'd arrived in the Veil, they had made me feel special, and I liked sitting on the pedestal they'd created. What did that say about me?

As I lay in the dark, my memory recalled each of their faces and how distinct they were.

Jase, with his dimples and calm disposition, was the levelheaded one the others turned to, even if they didn't realize it. A natural leader.

Kieran, the fun-loving and light-spirited dragon, had a wicked side to him that I was dying to unleash. The lip piercing, the tattoos, and those luminous green eyes spelled danger.

Zade, everything about the golden gold was hot, from his body to his soul. But he had a quick temper to match the fire in his eyes.

Issik, my ice prince—guarded and quiet. But under that frozen exterior was a heart waiting to be thawed. I surprised myself by wanting it to be me who would get him to open up.

Dear God.

I was falling for them. For all of them. How did that even happen?

Four guys. One girl. They would never go for that, would they?

Shaking my head I rejected the idea. No. They were proud and selfish—especially regarding me—but they were "sharing" me as they so eloquently had put it.

Just maybe…

I was insane. This wasn't happening. *Stop fantasizing about these dragons and start devising a plan to get the hell off this island. You still want to go home, don't you?*

That was the thing. Everyone had warned me I might like it here, but yet, I hadn't believed I would ever consider staying in the Veil Isles. The truth was, I didn't want to go back to the streets of Chicago. To the cold, harsh winters. To being alone. To fighting for my survival each day.

My life in Chicago hadn't been easy.

What did I have to lose here in the Veil?

The answer… nothing.

This could be my chance to start over, and do something meaningful with my life. It wasn't the life I'd imagined, but that didn't mean it had to be any less significant.

The image of four dragons, wrapped around me like a warm security blanket, engulfed me as I drifted off to sleep.

'd been cooped up inside for two days, and I was seconds away from throwing myself off the balcony, just to see which dragon would save me. My boredom had reached that crazy level where I was dying for excitement of any kind.

There was no TV. My cell phone didn't work in the Veil. And the four dragons that were keeping me captive in this room hadn't bothered to show their faces.

I hated being ignored. They were up to something, but I didn't know what. Why else would they disappear?

Maybe they are bored with you.

Maybe they don't need you after all.

Maybe my insecure self should just shut the hell up!

I finally got fed up with the silence, and went looking for *them*. I found Davina, Harlow, and Kaytlyn instead.

The three girls cornered me outside of Jase's office, which I had been about to barge into unannounced, and demand to know that he tell me what was going on.

"Everyone is talking about you," Harlow said as my hand reached for the doorknob.

I spun and pasted the biggest fake smile on my lips. "That's nice," I replied snappily. "Have you seen them?"

"*Them?*" Harlow drew out the word with a smile that was anything but nice.

Gag me. Girls like her used to make me sick in high school. "Yeah, you know, the four assholes who kidnapped us."

Kaytlyn snickered. Davina's hand flew to her mouth, and Harlow sneered. At least I had gotten a reaction out of them. This was the most interaction I'd had with people in days. "Are they ignoring you already?" Harlow tsked her tongue. "I guess the rumors aren't true then." She looked loftier than a cat who had just eaten the mouse.

I crossed my arms and planted my feet firmly on the ground in case things turned south. The fire in her eyes told me she wanted to go a round or two with me in the ring. And based on how I currently felt, I would welcome the release of anger. I angled my head to the side. "The one about the descendants being linked to me? It's true. You never know what will happen when you give someone your blood." My bitchiness had reached new heights and it was all *their* fault. Damn dragons.

Harlow stuck up her nose. "That's not what I heard."

"Then I guess you don't have a reliable source."

"But the curse hasn't been lifted," Davina pointed out, but not in a cruel way like Harlow would have. She sounded genuinely curious.

I shook my head. "No, but something else happened."

"We wondered what all the secrecy and commotion was about," Kaytlyn added, and was rewarded with a jab in the gut by Harlow.

So I wasn't the only one who'd noticed things were weird. "What commotion? Where are they?"

Harlow shrugged. "Gone."

"What do you mean 'gone'?" That didn't make sense. Jase had said they would protect me, that one of them would always be near, and yet here I stood... alone. My face fell, and I regretted the moment of vulnerability I'd revealed to Harlow.

Her expression was filled with smugness. "They all left two days ago. The night you came back."

I wanted to call bullshit, but from the looks in the other girls' expressions, she wasn't lying. Why would they leave? Where did they go? How could they abandon me without even saying goodbye?

"It was bound to happen. They tend to lose interest pretty quickly once they get what they want," Harlow gladly gloated.

She was lucky there were witnesses; otherwise, I would have popped her in the face. I wondered how pretty she would look with a broken nose. "I wouldn't be so sure about that." I was being cocky. I only hoped it didn't come back to bite me in the ass.

Flipping her hair in a dramatic fashion, she appeared indifferent. "Suit yourself. I was just offering a bit of friendly advice."

Ha. She didn't know the meaning of friendly. We both knew she didn't give two shits about me. "Don't you have someone else to intimidate?"

The smile that crossed her lips was one of victory. She'd gotten what she wanted—to get under my skin.

Drawing in a breath, I turned around, twisted the knob on the door to Jase's office, and stepped inside. The room was so quiet; the only sound was the water lapping outside. I inhaled deeply, taking in the scent that was all Jase—wild summer nights and ocean spray.

Curling into the deep leather couch, the smooth fabric cooled my cheek as I lay down and tucked my hand under a knitted pillow. I felt crushed, and I couldn't even rationalize why. From the moment they had flown into my life, my mind had been scrambled. It was all so much, and for the first time since I arrived in the Veil, I broke down. Tears I couldn't stop fell, streaking down my cheeks as I stared at the empty office. I lost track of time, but hours must have passed, and soon my eyelids grew heavy. It became a struggle to keep them open, and eventually, I closed my eyes.

For the first few seconds upon awakening, it felt like a fantasy —not sure of my surroundings—and then it all hit me. Dragons were real. I had some kind of emotional link to four of them, and for some reason beyond my comprehension they thought I could save them.

What a joke.

But it wasn't. This was my life.

I hadn't opened my eyes yet, still lingering in the dregs of sleep. Something tickled my nose, and I brushed it aside, not ready to face another empty room, but the feeling was persistent. I swatted the air near my face, and hit the tip of my nose. Snickers from around the room had me cracking one eye open and then the other.

I was no longer alone in the room, and the descendants were in deep shit.

"Where the hell were you?" I yelled at the four of them, bolting straight up on the couch as I shoved long strands of honey hair out of my face.

"She's mad," Zade said, smiling. He leaned against the wall, feet crossed at the ankle.

Four sets of eyes observed me, each sparkling different colors in the dark room. The hearth had been lit, and the wood crackled, casting a warm glow. "Damn straight I'm mad. You guys just LEFT ME."

"We have kingdoms that needed our attention." Issik exhaled as if irritated, but his eyes seemed to soften when they looked me over. He was the closest, sitting on my couch, while Kieran stretched out on the other sofa.

Fine. I understood they had responsibilities, but Jase? This was his home. "Where were you?" I asked him directly.

He folded his hands together on top of his desk. "Searching for answers."

"And just where the hell does a dragon go looking for clues about breaking a curse?" I was being a smartass, but I couldn't seem to stop myself. I was so relieved to see them, to know they were safe, but that relief had quickly turned to anger.

Issik's stunning features pinched together. "She's still pissed. Jase, do something to calm her down."

My hands shot up in the air. "Oh no. Don't you dare think about using your tranquility mojo on me."

"What are you doing in here? Did something happen while we were gone?" Jase asked, but I could tell by the darkening of his eyes, he wanted to ease my aggravation.

Yes. You left me here. That's what happened. And I think I missed you. But that wasn't what I said. "You told me one of you would be near, and then you all just disappeared. How am I supposed to trust anything you say?"

"We didn't want to disturb you—not after the day you'd had at the temple, and the attack from the wraith. We thought it best that you stay here and rest. Jase was supposed to—" Kieran realized what he was about to admit and quickly stopped himself.

I swung my glare of outrage to Jase. He was supposed to have tranquilized me. "You didn't," I accused him.

His brows drew together. "Does it matter? It clearly didn't work."

That wasn't the point. I frowned and sunk back into the couch. I tried to calm myself down before I did something drastic, but I couldn't erase what Harlow had said to me. "Do you guys get off screwing with me?" I mumbled to myself—an increasingly annoying habit.

"You make it far too easy, Cupcake." Jase flashed his wicked dimples to defuse my anger. "There is no need to be upset."

Says the guy who has an innate calmness. "Am I supposed to just sit here and pretend you can't tell what I'm feeling?" I asked. "You guys can't mess with my emotions like that."

Zade grimaced. "It was only our intention to keep you safe."

No longer able to hold onto my anger, I fumbled with the yellow dress covering my legs. "Did you find anything out about the curse?"

"She's worried now," Issik announced. No one answered my question.

I rolled my eyes. "You guys don't need to announce my every emotion. I know how I'm feeling."

Kieran didn't miss a beat. "But *we* want to know."

It was bad enough one of them would always feel what I was feeling. Now they had to share that information as well. We were going to nip that in the bud right away. "Some things are personal—emotions being one of them."

"Have you not learned to trust us yet? Have we not kept you safe?" Kieran questioned me. I wasn't sure what that had to do with my feelings, but I assumed they thought I didn't believe in them enough to protect more than just my body.

Did I though?

Zade shifted his stance against the wall. "Besides, we like knowing what you're feeling. It's the first real thing that has happened on this island in a hundred years."

"Glad I can be of service," I grumbled. So much for trying to get them to see my side of things. Ugh. Damn headstrong dragons.

Jase sat on the table in front of the couch and crossed his arms. "My staff told me that you barely left your room."

"You're spying on me?" I had been stewing and contemplating my options of escape, but they didn't need to know that.

A smile spread over Jase's lips, and it made me leery. "Let us make it up to you."

My eyes narrowed as I stared at him. "And just how do you plan to do that?"

"Since the Veil is now your home…"

I moaned a little too loudly, interrupting him. Four sets of eyes stared at me, and I shifted under their scrutiny, waiting for Jase to finish. *Way to make a spectacle, Olivia. This is your home now. Better get used to it.*

Zade took pity on me. "We thought you might like a tour, a chance to see the other regions."

My aggravation was forgotten as I sat a little straighter. "I would love that," I said, jumping at the opportunity to get out of the castle for a few hours.

"Good. You're not scared of heights, are you?" Kieran caught my gaze and winked.

What was he suggesting? "Depends if anything is trying to kill me."

Kieran swung his feet to the ground from his lounging position, a mischievous grin on his lips, and offered me a hand. "Let's go for a ride."

"I'll do it," the other three volunteered at once, causing Kieran to scowl.

Here we go again. This might not be a good idea, but I was too tired to care. I just wanted to get out of the keep, and I'd been dying to see the rest of the Veil Isles, even with the ever-present dangers.

The dragons bickered among themselves while I sat by watching the madness. If a fight broke out in this little room, we'd be in trouble. There was only one way to solve this problem—drawing straws. I glanced around the room, looking for something to use, as I was pretty sure the Veil didn't have plastic straws. On an end table sat a bowl of colored stones, I pulled out four, and placed them in a hat I found on the coatrack.

"Quiet!" I yelled and waited for the room to calm down. I turned to Jase. "Close your eyes and choose a stone. The one who picks this stone wins." I held up a flat turquoise rock before sticking it in the hat with the others. He arched his brows. "Unless you don't want to…"

His eyes snapped shut before I finished, and he snatched one of the stones out of the hat, immediately looking at which one he had chosen, a pearly smooth gem. The disappointment in his violet eyes tugged at my heart.

Zade pushed off the wall and waited for me to hold up the hat before he too shut his eyes and chose a stone. The rock crumbled to bits of dust when he beheld it, his anger destroying the small pebble. I gave him a half smile and touched his arm. It bothered me when they were upset, especially on my behalf.

Kieran toyed with the hoop on his lip, giving me a lopsided grin. "I'm liking my odds." It was a fifty-fifty chance. Not wasting any time, the poison dragon selected one. He grinned like a total shithead, the silver in his lip glinting off the firelight. The turquoise stone proudly held between his fingers. "Come on, blondie. I'm going to take you on the ride of your lifetime."

Zade scowled.

Issik stood to his full height, eyeballing Kieran with his usual disdain.

Kieran's warm hand enveloped mine as he pulled me out of Jase's office, through the main hall, and into the garden. Once we were outside, he began to strip.

"A little warning would be nice before you go commando on me," I muttered under my breath as I turned around, giving him my back.

"You've already seen us naked," he pointed out.

I had. Multiple times actually, and I was positive I would continue to see them in all their naked glory. Lack of modesty probably came with being a shifter, but for me, it was going to take a lot of time to get used to it.

Kieran stood behind me and leaned over my shoulder, his breath in my ear. "You can turn around now."

"Are you naked?"

"If I said no, would you believe me?"

"No."

He chuckled, tickling the back of my neck.

I pursed my lips, keeping my back straight. "Are you going to shift, or just tease me all night?"

"Impatient, are you?" His voice washed over me with a different inflection, indicating he had started the process that turned him into a poison-breathing beast with scales.

Yes, I was impatient. I was dying for some fresh air and the chance to ride a dragon again. Who would say no? And this time, there would be no wraith to ruin the experience, or so I hoped. I waited a few more minutes before I turned around, and caught the tail end of Kieran's shift.

He was a magnificent dragon. They all were. Kieran's form wasn't as bulky as the others', but he was still large and powerful. Dark green scales papered over his body, growing lighter in color at the tips. He dropped his head in a bow, his emerald eyes glittering with humor.

Eagerly, I climbed onto Kieran's back, and ascended it without any struggle. He leaped off the terrace, and entered a dive toward the water. My stomach lurched as my breath caught. It was a thousand times better than any roller coaster at Great America. At the last second, before smacking into the murky sea, he used his wings to pull us up, letting his feet skim over the surface and creating a trail of waves in our wake.

Wrapping my arms around his neck, I squeezed my legs together. *Holy shit storm. I'm riding on the back of a dragon.* Never in a million years would I have thought this would be my life. We climbed higher, leaving the castle in the distance. A balmy breeze blew over my face, whipping my hair. His scales felt sleek and smooth under my hands.

"Better hang on." His voice instructed in my head.

I hadn't thought much about it the first time I'd been with Issik when he saved me—how he had the ability to communicate while in dragon form. I'd been far too overwhelmed and scared to wonder how it worked, but now I was curious.

"How are you able to talk to me?" My body was more relaxed, and I seemed to move with him as he glided and flapped his wings, alternating between the two.

Kieran's angular head tilted slightly to the side. *"I can project my thoughts into your mind."*

"Wow. That's amazing." And so was the Veil. Kieran took us over the lush forest that backed up to Jase's kingdom, and a flock of birds fluttered from the treetops, swirling around us. Deep in the center of the woods was the temple of their fathers, and where I'd been attacked. I shuddered at the memory, not keen to relive those moments.

"Look to the east. You will see Viperus Keep."

"That's your home?" I asked.

"It is. You will love it." Evident pride sounded in my head through his voice. He cherished his home.

The setting sun was at our backs, casting rays of pinks and oranges over the lower half of the sky. In the distance, just over a cluster of evergreens, rose a triangular tower—Viperus Keep. As we flew closer, the outline of a mossy castle came into view. Vines clung to the sides of the washed-out bricks, dangling below arched windows and off balconies.

"It's beautiful," I whispered in awe. Vegetation of all shapes and sizes surrounded the entire estate, from tall to short and fat to sparse.

"I will take you there soon, but for now, it isn't safe."

"Because of the wraiths?" I asked.

"They are only part of the danger."

Beyond the forest of Viperus, to the northwest, was unmistakably Issik's region. At first, it was just the change in climate that tipped me off. Whereas Jase's and Kieran's realms both had pleasant temperatures that reminded me of spring and fall, Issik's was a blast of icy cold air. The closer we flew to Iculon, the more arctic the air became, making it almost difficult to breathe.

My teeth chattered as I huddled deeper against Kieran's long body, using his heat to stay warm and insulated. "Is it always this cold here?" I asked, shivering. It brought back those not so pleasant memories of living on the streets of Chicago.

"Always. Do you feel how the air is thinner and harder to inhale? That's what it is like for Issik in our regions. His body needs the cold, just as Zade's thrives in the heat."

"Is it common for all dragons to have abilities like the four of you?" I inquired.

He chuckled. *"There is nothing common about us."*

I rolled my eyes. "I know that, but what about prior to the curse?"

"Before Tianna meddled with our lives, the Veil Isles brimmed with dragon shifters all with a kaleidoscope of dragon's breaths."

Kieran lifted us over a mountain, and deep in the valley below stood a majestic castle that looked as if it was made entirely out of glass. Frosty windows glowed a soft aqua, casting prisms of light onto the blanket of snow that covered every inch of the land. "It's like something from a fairytale," I murmured to myself.

"Don't let Issik hear you say that. He thinks Iculon is harsh and unruly."

A fond smirk tugged at the corner of my lips. He would think that. "What is the fifth region of the Veil like?" I remembered them mentioning a fifth dragon who had died while testing the strength of Tianna's curse.

"It is nothing but a barren wasteland, completely uninhabitable. Nature has taken over."

"What was his ability?" I asked, curious about the dragon shifter I'd never have the chance to meet.

"Influence." A sadness I hadn't meant to cause crept into Kieran's voice. I immediately sought to erase it. Rubbing my face against him, I pressed my lips to his neck. "I'm sorry," I said.

Underneath me, his body gave a deep exhale. *"He would have loved you."*

"Were the five of you always friends?" I wanted to take away the sudden pain I'd caused this usually lighthearted man.

Kieran's laugh was vibrant in my head. *"No. We grew up hating each other, seeing one another as rivals."*

It both was and wasn't hard to picture their relationship. At times, they were fiercely loyal, and at others, they fought like brothers. "What about now?"

"I would give my life to protect them." He projected the thought with intensity.

I believed him.

Without warning, he began to speed through the sky, our surroundings a blur of pale blue and white. All I could do was hold on, and not get swept away by the rushing scene passing us by.

My eyes were unable to focus, so I didn't see what had him jetting off at first, but I sensed them. I wasn't sure how, but I knew the other three had joined us in the sky, other than by the quickening of my heart. I strained to peer through the flying strands of my hair and saw Jase and Zade on one side of us. Issik came up on the other.

"They just couldn't stay away." If dragons could scowl, Kieran was.

Yet, I didn't share Kieran's annoyance. In fact, I felt complete and bubbled with happiness.

My dragons.

There was no point in denying I wanted them to be mine anymore. They had quickly become a part of my life, and I wasn't going to let myself waffle on the issue again. "Can you blame them? Would you have stayed behind?" I asked.

He was silent for a moment, his formidable wings beating in the air. *"No. We all despise the curse that imprisons us, but we're proud of our homes and want to show them off."*

Only one region remained, Zade's, and I could tell he was excited.

Time went quickly as I enjoyed the thrill of flying. We left behind the cold and traded it in for an intense heat that had beads of sweat rolling between my breasts.

The Veil was so much bigger than my mind had drummed up. It

was amazing how the land shifted from one climate to the next so seamlessly. White powdery snow gave way to charcoal ash. The earth became cracked and filled with a glowing stream of lava that ran from an active volcano, and a hazy cloud of gray smoke billowed from the opening at the top, trailing off into the air.

Of all the areas, this was the one that was the most foreign to me and frightening. Fire was not my thing, but regardless of my fear, there was no denying its magnificence, like the dragon who lived here.

At the base of the volcano, surrounded by molten magma, was Zade's home. Made of obsidian, the castle pierced the sky with its sharp angles. There was nothing soft about the Crimson Kingdom.

My legs tightened around Kieran as he took a sharp right, tilting his body sideways. "You drop me and I'll come back from the dead to haunt you."

"Promise?" he teased.

I resisted the urge to kick him. He probably wouldn't have felt it anyway.

As we turned around, the sun was nearly gone and moonlight spread overhead, stars sparkling on the black water of Wakeland as we flew over. Jase's keep was in sight, and my heart sighed. From the sky, it looked lavish. Square towers rose up all in various heights with bluish-gray shingled peaks. A mystical mist hovered over the sea that bordered the castle on all sides, and an intricate bridge arched from the keep to the woods, connecting the home to land.

I'd become so enthralled by the glittering castle in twilight that I hadn't seen that we had company in the sky. It was Kieran who alerted me.

"Griffins," he hissed.

My head craned behind me, watching the dark figures descend upon my dragons. There were three of them—not as large as the descendants, but bigger than any bird on Earth. I was having a minor seizure. "What do they want?"

"You."

For the love of witches, could I get a break? "Let me guess. More friends of Tianna?"

Kieran dodged left, dipping his nose straight for Wakeland. *"You got it. Stay down, and no matter what happens, don't let go."*

Bracing myself, I latched my arms like a deranged monkey around Kieran's neck. Jase, Issik, and Zade flanked us on either side, and behind, forming a barrier around me. I couldn't believe these creatures really existed. Then again, I was riding a dragon. It shouldn't have seemed that farfetched, and I needed to learn to accept the outlandish.

One of the griffins managed to get directly above Kieran, and the ugly bastard raked the side of Kieran's back leg, causing him to stumble in the air.

"Kieran," I cried, but he quickly regained his composure. He was bleeding—not badly, but the sight had worry pitting in my stomach. "You're hurt."

"Don't stress. It is just a scratch, he reassured me."

Stress was my middle name.

My eyes scanned the skies, seeking out each of the dragons, and I exhaled when I counted three. They were safe, but we weren't out of danger yet. The griffins had rallied around Jase, circling him, and before the others had a chance to help, I watched as a nightmare unfolded.

In a uniform attack, the three birdy bastards expanded their spiny wings, and in a sonic scream that pierced my ears, they unleashed a fury of a thousand needles that shot from their feathers like a porcupine. The barbs embedded into the flesh of Jase's wings.

My heart stopped.

Without the use of his wings, Jase plummeted out of the sky, falling on his back toward the black water beneath us.

"Jase!" I bellowed, my voice echoing over the valley.

A tidal wave hit the shore as Jase's dragon form slammed into the water. I didn't think. I just acted, diving off Kieran's back straight into the dark ocean below.

My name was shouted in three different voices that grew distant as I plunged toward the sea. There were a million reasons why I shouldn't have jumped, including killing myself, but one reason overruled all the risks.

I had to save Jase.

It was ridiculous if I had taken a moment to really think about it. Me? Save a dragon? Laughable.

Splash! Cool, moon-bathed water rushed over my head. Frantically, I searched the murky sea for a large dragon flipping in circles. How hard could it be to find him? He was huge.

But Jase had shifted out of his scales and into his human skin. My heart quickened when I spotted him sinking farther into the depths of the ocean. I didn't hesitate, and started kicking as I dove deeper. The shoes on my feet flipped off, and I was thankful the dress I wore was lightweight, giving me the ability to move through the water.

Jase's body was limp. His head tilted forward. I didn't want to consider what his lifeless form might mean. The only thought racing through my head was how fast I could get to him. Time seemed to slow, making each second feel like minutes, and I began to fear I wouldn't be able to save us both.

Finally, my fingers skimmed over his elbow, and I nearly cried. As I slipped my arms under his, I saw a flash of something shiny embedded in the seafloor. I gave it nothing more than a cursory glance, but for a brief second, I felt a magnetic tug, making my fingers twitch.

Swimming toward the surface, I prayed I'd be able to hold my breath long enough to get us there. In water, Jase's muscular form was a fraction of the weight it would have been on land, but still, it wasn't an easy feat—not for someone who was only a hundred and thirty pounds soaking wet.

My lungs screamed for air, and no matter how hard I kicked, it seemed as if I wasn't moving. Panic set in.

I was going to drown.

We both were going to drown.

Some hero I was. What had I been thinking jumping in after him? That was insane, and I'd never done anything like that in my life. I don't know what had come over me, but seeing Jase get hurt, fall, and be in real danger caused an impulse in me—a batshit crazy one.

Just when I thought I couldn't move my legs one more time, a pair of strong arms enveloped my waist. I twisted my head to the side, making out Issik's face through the cloudy water. His frosty eyes glowed an eerie blue. Another set of arms relieved me of Jase's weight. Kieran. I relaxed into Issik.

Halle-freaking-lujah. We're not going to die.

I broke through the surface and took a welcomed gulp of air. Water rained over my face as I shoved my hair out of the way. Issik's firm grip was still secured around my waist as he swam to the edge with Kieran and Jase alongside us.

Zade was waiting on the shore and pulled me out of the sea. "What the hell were you thinking?" he growled.

"Is he okay?" I questioned, panic raising the pitch of my voice.

Zade lifted a brow. "Jase?"

Duh. Who else would I be talking about? Unless someone else had gotten hurt, but no, they were all accounted for. I had made sure.

Zade's arms tightened around me, and he tugged me against his bare chest. I was shaking. "Relax, Olivia. He's all right."

My head shook. I couldn't. The adrenaline was leaving my body, and I wiggled out of his embrace, needing to see Jase for myself. Zade let me go, and I darted to where Jase was lying in the black sand and dropped down beside him. *Is he breathing? Why isn't he moving?* My hands roamed over his torso, feeling for a heartbeat, and my relief nearly jumped out of my chest when I felt a steady pulse under my palm.

Three shadows came to stand around me. "He's breathing," I whispered.

"It would take more than a band of griffins to kill a dragon," Zade retorted, as if it was preposterous to think Jase could have been injured or worse.

Glad to see that they were taking this seriously, but then again, maybe I was blowing it out of proportion and Jase hadn't been in real danger of dying. They did have a lifetime of experience. I knew nothing about dragons except for what I'd learned the last few weeks.

As I was scowling up at the three descendants towering over me, a hand laced its fingers with mine. My eyes flew to Jase's. He was awake and smirking at me. "Jase," I sighed, dropping my head to his shoulder.

"Your fear awoke me," he murmured.

I wasn't sure how that made me feel, but next to Jase being conscious, it took a backseat. "Don't you ever get hurt again," I ordered, poking a finger into his hard chest. "You scared the shit out of me."

"She's angry," Zade commented, sounding confused by my sudden change in emotions.

Nope. I wasn't even going to argue about him pointing out the obvious. "I'm sorry. It's just not every day I see one of my friends get attacked in the air." And I didn't want it to become a habit.

Jase sat up, water glistening off his abs in the moonlight. "You'll get used to it."

That was the thing. I didn't want to. My heart couldn't handle it. Look what happened during a minor incident. How would I react if something major did happen to one of them? I didn't want to think about it.

"What you did… jumping in after me… that was crazy."

My heart swelled. "Thanks. I think my craziness has been established, but I couldn't let you drown."

His electric violet eyes blazed into mine. "I don't ever want you to do something like that again. Do you understand?"

Water dripped all over the ground when I stood to my feet. "Last time I ever save your ass," I muttered, miffed I wasn't getting a thank you or *Geez, Olivia, that was so brave of you.*

"Promise me you won't do anything that reckless again."

I stared at him, giving him my stern eye. "Fine. I promise. But next time, it will be your life on the line."

Jase shook his head as if I was the most confounding female he'd ever met, and the other three snickered at me. I didn't even want to know what they found so funny because I was almost positive it was at my expense.

Zade's amber eyes flicked my way, running over my body. The fabric of my dress was plastered to my skin like a rubber glove, hugging my every curve. I might as well have been standing in front of them naked. His gaze finally settled on my face. "Let me dry you off."

I shivered, but it wasn't from the cold. I didn't tell him that. As Issik and Kieran gave Jase a hand up, Zade blew a gentle, toasty breath over my skin, evaporating the beads of water. It felt like being under a giant hairdryer.

Combing my fingers through my hair, I turned to see Kieran and Issik assisting Jase inside. He wasn't making it easy. The proud dragon kept trying to shake them off, but whether or not he wanted to admit it, the pin-sized wounds his body had sustained had taken their toll. He needed rest.

Maybe someone should douse him with some of his own tranquility.

The thought brought a ghost of a smile to my lips.

If there was one thing I'd learned today it was no matter how mesmerizing the Veil appeared from the outside, it was only a cloak to hide the darkness lurking within.

Harlow, Davina, and Kaytlyn were in the kitchen when I sauntered down in the middle of the night looking for a snack. I couldn't sleep, not after the excitement. All eyes swung to me as I interrupted their little girl powwow. The hushed whispers and muted giggles died.

And who could blame them?

I would have run from the room. I was a hot mess—bloodshot eyes, flushed cheeks, and wild hair. There was probably seaweed still tangled in it. I'd been too tired earlier to do anything but go to my room, but now there was nothing I wanted more than a long bath, a hot bowl of soup, and a marathon of Supernatural… in that order. But I would have to settle for the bath and soup. Sadly, Dean and Sam Winchester weren't in my foreseeable future—one of the things I definitely missed about Earth—TV. The Veil struggles were real. As was this mutual loathing between Harlow and me.

"What happened? Did you get into a fight with a barracuda?" the devil herself sneered.

"Something like that," I muttered, really not in the mood for Harlow's shit.

"I hope you plan on cleaning up your own mess," she snapped, leaning her back against the cabinets, her palms on the counter.

The other girls couldn't meet my eye and glanced away, staring at a bowl of fruit as if it was the most interesting thing in the world. I didn't blame them though. Staying off Harlow's radar was the smart thing to do.

I wasn't a smart girl.

It should be noted that I hadn't even opened the cooler where perishable food was stored. I hadn't made a mess yet. With bare feet, I padded across the kitchen and plucked a roll from a basket. "I thought that was why you were here," I replied sweetly, half anticipating an apple to be chucked at my head. It was a good thing there were no knives nearby because Harlow's face had turned bright red with rage.

Someone better step between us. A kitchen brawl was about to go down. The door to the kitchen flew open and in walked Issik. His eyes bounced between Harlow and me. "Is there a problem?" He directed the question at me.

Didn't anyone sleep around here? It had to have been well past midnight. Only a million problems came to mind in response to his inquiry. "No," I said. "Harlow was just offering to clean up after I eat."

Issik's lips almost cracked a smile. "Is that so?" he asked, knowing just as I did that Harlow would never offer such a selfless, kind gesture, but the glint in his eyes told me he approved of my wit.

I smiled. "We're all just one big happy family."

Harlow crossed her arms, glaring at me, but she didn't dare act out in front of Issik, and I stored away that little piece of information for later.

Issik grabbed a chunk off the bread in my hand and popped it into his mouth, hiding the grin that I knew wanted to part his lips. "Glad to see you're making friends."

Davina and Kaytlyn choked.

Dragging my smug butt out of the kitchen, I moved through the halls, leaving a trail of breadcrumbs behind me. I couldn't have cared less about attracting ants.

I wandered my way down the hall into the bathroom with a bounce in my step. Shoving the last bit of carbs into my mouth, I slipped off my clothes and sank into the bubbling square pool in the floor to wash away the faint lingering scent of salt and musk. Steam curled over the aqua waters, and a light glowed at the bottom.

Tucking myself into one of the rounded corners, I laid my head back and let the heat seep into my pores. Blonde tendrils of hair snaked over my shoulders, sticking to my skin. I don't know how long I stayed like that—at least an hour—but the water never turned cold. It was bliss.

amn these long corridors and endless stairs. I just wanted to materialize in my room. Was that so much to ask for?

There was no one around to ask for directions—the castle asleep, as I should be—and if I ever found my room, I would fall directly into bed. I had more or less gotten the layout of the castle down in my head, but my brain had checked out, exhaustion finally creeping in. I was about to curl up on the floor and pass out.

The drafty halls were making me regret the decision to slip on a thin robe instead of something warmer. Gathering energy from some-where deep inside me, I tackled the stairs. While grasping the railing as if it was my lifeline, I swung around the corner and barreled straight into Jase.

Talk about a sense of déjà vu.

His arms dashed out, landing on either side of my waist. For someone who'd been shot by a dozen darts and fallen from the sky, he was extremely steady. I leaned into him, drawing on his strength. "Why aren't you sleeping?" I asked, genuinely concerned as I looked up into his handsome face.

Lowering his arms, he watched me from beneath thick lashes. "I should be asking you that."

I sucked on my lower lip and glanced away. "Couldn't sleep. Too much excitement."

Those deep violet eyes were on mine; his brows pinched together. "What you did was reckless, but I think you understand how dangerous it was."

About as hazardous as being alone in a room with Jase, and the last thing I wanted in the middle of the night was a lecture, but it turned out we weren't alone.

"What are you two doing sneaking around the halls at this hour?" Kieran asked, stealthily coming up behind me.

The sound of his voice made me jump. "For dragons, you guys are pretty fucking quiet," I mumbled, my hand flying to my chest as my heart thumped wildly.

They rewarded me with twin smirks of wickedness, and neither of them wore a shirt. Why did they have to torture me like this?

"I was hungry," Kieran replied as if lurking around the castle in the middle of the night was an every evening occurrence. His eyes took in my apparel or lack thereof.

My nipples puckered at his slow perusal, especially when his gaze lingered at the exact spot I was hoping he wouldn't notice. I crossed my arms over my chest, trying to hide my breasts from making any more of a spectacle, but one glance at the two shifters and I could see a sudden desire churning within their eyes.

Holy smokes.

Jase's eyes bored into mine, and my cheeks flamed. "I'm starved. You, Kieran?" he tossed the question to him. Jase took a step closer, and the lopsided grin on his lips told me he knew what was going on inside me. It was a look that said food wasn't on his mind.

Hot Lips came up behind me with green fire in his eyes. "I've never been hungrier in my life."

What had gotten into them? Or better yet, into me? Why was I just standing there instead of telling them to back off? I wanted to blame it on my near-death experience and the surge of adrenaline, but it was mostly just them. *All* of them.

I glanced down the hall to make sure no one else was wandering around the castle. Jase's finger came under my chin, bringing my eyes back to his. Behind me, Kieran's hands landed on the side of my hips. I couldn't move and could barely breathe, wondering in anticipation what would happen next. Any confusion or uncertainty I had was quickly outweighed by my curiosity.

Kieran leaned forward, his even breath tickling my neck a moment before his lips brushed the sensitive spot. My head automatically tilted to the side, giving him more access. Jase pressed his finger to my lower lip, forcing them to part, and the heat in his eyes had my lower body clenching, tingles cascading inside me.

Those tingles exploded when he took possession of my mouth.

What is happening? Am I really making out with two guys? At the same time? My mind reeled from the smorgasbord of emotions rocking within me. Every hair on my neck stood up, and I worried one of them would stop… or wouldn't stop.

"Is this okay?" Jase murmured, taking the lead.

"I-I think so." I reached out and wrapped a single arm around Jase's neck; the other one laced through Kieran's fingers at my hip. The gesture wasn't lost on anyone. I wanted them both to stay just where they were.

"Olivia," Kieran whispered in my ear, causing me to tremble as his tongue flicked out.

I was sandwiched between them, my body somehow molded perfectly against both of theirs. Jase's skin smelled like the sea and Kieran's like the woods. I closed my eyes when their hands roamed over my body, slowly kneading my skin while pleasure seeped into my muscles.

Kieran's hot lips scraped over my shoulder, brushing aside the material. "You've been driving us crazy since you got here."

It felt like I was in cloud nine. What were they doing to me?

Covering my mouth with his, Jase deepened the kiss, sliding his tongue between my teeth as I moaned. Kieran's needy hands wandered down my body, sliding into the robe as his fingers splayed across my belly.

Oh my god.

My knees nearly buckled and might have if the two of them weren't pressed against me on either side. I couldn't stop my body from responding, arching so my breast rubbed Jase's chest and my butt nuzzled into Kieran.

It was too much. My body yearned for release, but here in the middle of the corridor where anyone could walk out was not how I pictured our first time. Would either of them care that I wasn't a virgin?Should I say something and risk ruining the moment?

Kieran's fingers skimmed under the slopes of my breasts.

Nope.

Now was definitely not the time to bring it up.

Jase's lips moved from my mouth to drop kisses along my jawline. My eyes fluttered open, and over his shoulder, I caught sight of the three girls from the kitchen peeking at us through a cracked door. They all had stunned expressions on their faces, mouths agape, except for Harlow. She looked as if she wanted to tear my face off. The corners of my lips curved. I shouldn't be gloating. It wasn't my normal nature, but something about Harlow had turned me into a vindictive bitch.

It was clear she was jealous, that she wanted to be in the exact position I was—between two of the dragon descendants—but I wasn't willing to share, and I would fight her for them all.

Listen to yourself! my mind screamed. *They're not yours.* Not technically. Nothing had been discussed. So they kissed me. They desired me. But who was to say it would last? Who was to say they would be okay sharing me? It was hypocritical to expect exclusivity on their end when I wanted all four.

"Wait," I breathed, putting a hand on Jase's chest. He nipped at my earlobe before lifting his head to look at me questioningly. The girls closed the door they had been peering through, returning our privacy to us.

"What's wrong?" Kieran whispered, his lips brushing over my shoulder, making levelheaded thoughts impossible.

Other than I'd never done anything like this before in my life? "I don't want to just be another notch under your belts."

"That's not what this is," Jase assured me, and I wanted to believe him.

"You have an entire harem of girls living in your home," I reminded him.

"That may be, but most of them only work here. They have families of their own," he reasoned, dipping his head to silence me with a kiss.

"And the ones you've slept with?" I stopped him with the question.

Kieran snickered behind me.

I twisted to the side so I could glare at him too. "Same goes for you," I said, giving him a stern warning. "I might not have stepped foot inside Viperus Keep, but I hear the rumors about all of you. Issik might be the only descendant who doesn't have a reputation for being a slut."

"Did she just call us sluts?" Kieran asked with a smile.

"I'm being serious."

Jase forked his fingers into his messy hair, taking a step back from me. I immediately missed him. "I can see that," he replied.

"Maybe this wasn't a good idea," I muttered, dropping my hands and readjusting the robe to cover myself up. I clenched the material together at my neck.

Jase's lips pursed as the glimmer in his eyes faded. "This isn't why we brought you here. Seducing you was not part of the plan, and whether or not you believe me, you're not just another girl."

"There is something between us... between all of us," Kieran stated. "I think we're all curious about you."

I swallowed, feeling my body waver back toward them, but I stood rooted. "Maybe we can take things a little slower."

They both nodded. "We'd never do anything you weren't comfortable with," Kieran assured me.

"I appreciate that." What scared me was I was too comfortable with what we'd been doing. I didn't want to stop and might not have without the interruption from the three girls. "Good night, I guess."

The three of us awkwardly lingered for a few moments, uncertain what would happen next. I could see they both wanted to reach for me and pull me back into their arms. I wanted it too, more than I should admit. Biting down on my lip, I forced my legs to move and kept going until I was inside my room. Even behind the closed door and with them out of sight, it didn't diminish the strong desire in me. If they had followed me, I would have dragged them both inside and locked the door.

My brain no longer screamed at me to sleep, and after what had just happened with Kieran and Jase, I couldn't have anyway. The last thing I wanted to do was sit in my room replaying each touch and kiss we'd shared. It would drive me straight back into their arms.

In the days that followed, I saw very little of the descendants, and even though I told myself not to let my feelings get hurt, they were. Sure they were busy dragons, doing whatever dragons did, but without any friends in the keep, I was lonely… and bored.

I could only sit in my room and count the stars in the mural or wander aimlessly about the castle so many times. It would drive even the sanest person insane. I also wasn't the sanest person to begin with, so the going insane thing happened quicker for me. To pass the hours, my mind took it upon itself to come up with excuses for their absence.

Were they deliberately ignoring me?

Why would they do that?

Was everything they had said to me about being special a lie?

Was I being tossed aside like all the other girls?

To hell with that! If they thought they could kiss and ditch me, they had another thing coming. Dragons or not, their scaly asses were grass.

Were they secretly planning something they didn't want me to know about?

I stopped wearing out the wood floor in my room from pacing and strode to the door with purpose. Before I crossed the threshold, I glanced down at my attire to make sure I wasn't half naked. There would be no more wandering the halls in flimsy robes.

The door swung open viciously as I stormed out to hunt down the dragons, but as I rounded the corner, I found someone else. Harlow. The wicked grin on her cherry lips was all trouble.

For the love of peanut butter, I couldn't take any more drama. "Harlow, I'm not in the mood to mince words with you." I tried to pass her by, seeing as there wasn't a dragon in sight and that's whom I sought.

"You slut!" she hurled at me.

So much for being the bigger person, and walking away. I paused and took a breath before I turned around and faced her. "I'm sorry. I didn't know you had the authority to judge me."

Her hand flew back as if she was going to slap me, but I stared her down, daring her to touch me. "They'll get tired of you. They always do," she spat, her hand suspended in the air.

My gaze shifted to the left, staring at her open palm. "And let me guess, you'll be there to comfort whichever dragon will have you. I've got news for you, *sista*. I'm not giving them up. We have a connection you'd never understand."

Her face turned red. Not a pretty look. "You're nothing but trash. I heard they found you on the streets."

The fact that she knew that hurt. It meant one of them had talked about me to her, and I didn't like being discussed behind my back, especially with someone like the bitch-monster herself. But I refused to let her get to me. I lifted my chin. "In order for you to insult me, I'd have to value your opinion, which I don't."

"You little—"

I'd had enough name-calling for one day. I snapped my hand closed in front of her face. "Zip it. Now, get out of my way before I do something you'll regret." I jerked away and took a deep, cleansing breath that did nothing to stop the tremors of rage.

I should have known better than to turn my back on a girl like Harlow. In high school, Tracie Wilson had it out for me because she thought I had flirted with her boyfriend. So not true, but the point was Tracie had believed it. I had brushed her off and ended up flat on my face in the hallway with a split lip. She had shoved me when I turned my back on her. You think I would have learned my lesson.

Barely taking two steps, I felt a hand fist into my long hair and yank. Pain radiated from my scalp. I tried to steady myself and failed, pulled back like a ragdoll. I was going to kick her ass as soon as I got my claws on her.

Blindly swiping through the air, I attacked, just waiting for my hands to make impact, and once they did, I dug in, using my nails on her flesh. "What is your deal with me? What did I ever do to you?" I hissed, twisting her arm, and she released the fistful of my hair.

Her eyes were narrowed and filled with hate. "Before you came here, I was the one they came to."

Propelled by pride and fury, I took one long stride toward her. "Why you conceited, self-absorbed little—" Clumsy because of the ferocity of my temper, I missed my target, which had been her pretty face, and managed to spin in a circle. Not my finest moment, but then again, I'd never been much of a fighter.

I did, however, end up pinning her to the floor. So what if I accidentally fell into her, knocking us both down? It still counted. She went wild underneath me, scratching like a feral cat over my arms and face. There was definitely blood under her fingernails—my blood.

With a feral growl, I grabbed her wrists and stuck my knee into her gut, but I swear, she must have been a wrestler in a prior life. Girl had moves I couldn't even fathom. Swinging her leg into some kind of pretzel knot around my shoulders, she put me into a chokehold.

Oh my god. We're going to kill each other.

My face was turning purple when a pair of strong arms enclosed around my waist, pulling me off the she-devil, but Harlow wasn't finished with me. She came flying to her feet as I fought against my restraints. A cold chill sent tremors through me.

"Touch her and you'll deal with me," a hard voice said behind me. It was Issik.

Of all the descendants to see me in such a state, it would have to be the frosty one. He was the only one who hadn't warmed up to me, and still, I felt something between us when we were alone.

"Relax, little warrior. She won't hurt you," he whispered in my ear.

I reached for calmness and concentrated on the coolness radiating from him. The fight went out of me, and I sunk against Issik's firm body.

Harlow straightened. Her eyes shot daggers at Issik in an epic stare down. I had no doubt who would win. Issik had a severity about him that trumped Harlow's bitchiness. "Jase will hear about this," she threatened us.

"Yes, he will… from me," Issik assured her, not the least bit intimidated by her warning.

She flinched. "If you care so much for her, why don't you do us all a favor and take her to Iculon?" she challenged him, still trying to figure out a way to get rid of me.

"For someone who is so bright, a lot of dumb things come out of your mouth. That's not how this works, and you know it, Harlow." He said her name with a sharp bite.

"But she isn't the one," she argued, relentless as always. It made her sound like a petulant child.

Issik's hands loosened around my waist so that they held me out of comfort versus restraint, trusting me not to punch her in the boobs. "You know nothing of the curse. It still remains to be seen if Olivia is who we've been searching for. And it would be wise for you to remember your place in Jase's kingdom. The liberties he has allowed you will quickly end if you lay a hand on her again."

She huffed. "How dare you speak to me like that!"

"I think it's time you retired to your room. You've done enough damage for one day." I didn't miss the tension in his voice.

The second Harlow stomped her ass out of the hall I spun to face Issik. "Are you really going to tell Jase what happened here?" My voice quivered, fighting the tears that suddenly threatened to spill over my cheeks.

"Hey, don't do that." He brushed the pad of his thumb under both of my eyes, wiping away the water that had gathered there.

"Sorry. I hate crying."

"After the last few days you've had, no one would blame you," he said, keeping his voice low and leveled.

I sniffed, forcing the lump back down my throat. "I don't think I can do this." Everything felt so gloom and doom. I wasn't strong enough. I wasn't the one. They were all going to die because I couldn't break some idiotic curse cast by a jealous witch.

"Yes, you can. If you can jump off a dragon's back, in mid-flight, straight into Wakeland Sea, you can stick this out a little longer."

"I wish it were that simple." How I felt at the moment was anything but badass. I felt like a failure, and all I wanted to do was pack up my shit and go home. Screw the Veil. I didn't need this crap.

Issik kept me in his arms, allowing me to indulge myself in the cry fest of the century. If Harlow could see me now, she would have eaten up weakness. I let the bully win.

Through a haze of tears, I stared up at Issik. "Sorry about your shirt," I said, having left behind a big wet spot, but at least he'd been wearing one.

His eyes frosted over as he stared at a spot on my cheek. "She hurt you." The sound of his voice was strained, and he gently touched the raw scratch.

I shrugged, wary of the darkness I saw churning in his eyes like a blistering winter storm. "It's nothing. I'm fine."

"You don't think Jase should know that Harlow is causing problems?" he asked, his brows drawn together in confusion, but curiosity was there too.

"I don't want to add more stress to the situation. You guys have enough to deal with. This is something Harlow and I need to work out ourselves."

I couldn't make out the expression on his face, but that was typical when it came to Issik. "What did you do to get on her bad side?"

"Breathe," I replied dryly.

His lips cracked at the corners into what looked like a grin.

"Did you just smirk?" I teased him.

"No, definitely not." His lips returned to a thin line, but I could see he struggled to hold it in place.

Tucking my hair behind my ears, I shifted my weight to one side. "Just admit it. You find me amusing."

"I will admit no such thing, but if it takes the sadness from your eyes, then it might have been the smallest of smiles."

I beamed. "I knew it. You actually like me."

"So, are you going to tell me what happened between the two of you, or am I going to have to torture it out of you?" He wouldn't dare, and we both knew it—nothing but empty threats from Ice Prince, except in Harlow's case. Then he had been dead serious.

"She's had it out for me since I arrived." I avoided telling him about what happened to gain Harlow's wrath—the kiss with Jase and Kieran. What a kiss it had been. My mind was still reeling, and my emotions were a mess. I didn't want to go there. "I went to, um..." My brain searched for a plausible excuse. "...get something to eat and she cornered me. Started calling me names." That was as much of the truth as he would get.

His jaw twitched once, and I could see he was fighting back the urge to press me. "I told Jase he shouldn't mess around with Harlow. In case you haven't figured it out, she was sleeping with him, but he ended things before you got here, and hasn't touched her in weeks. She's jealous of you. Just a warning: be careful around her. I don't trust her. Never have."

Processing what I already knew about Jase's relationship with Harlow, I nodded, and ignored the pang in my chest.

This was the longest conversation Issik and I had ever had. What he said made sense, regardless of the fact that I didn't want to feel sympathy for her. I could understand Harlow's anger at Jase for suddenly ignoring her. It would put me in a not so pleasant mood, but I'd like to think I wouldn't act as she had. I would go straight to the source and ask what his deal was.

"Did you ever get to eat?" Issik asked.

"No." I answered, shaking my head. "The wrestling kind of killed my appetite."

"A good fight always makes me hungry."

"Does that include girl-on-girl fights?" I was razzing him, and it came naturally.

His eyes twinkled, and this time, there was no mistaking the smirk that spread across his lips. "Nah, that's a different kind of hunger, little warrior." He draped an arm over my shoulder. "Come on, I can't have you starving to death."

My lips twitched as I rested my head on his chest, letting him lead the way. I didn't expect him to take me to his room, only one of the million surprises I'd had recently, and I'd completely forgotten the reason I'd been in the hall in the first place.

Dinner wasn't anything fancy, but there was wine and candles. We sat on the floor with the terrace doors open, revealing a sky filled with glittering silver stars, which provided all the light we needed. The room was cool, but in a refreshing way, and we gorged ourselves on crackers and cheese. I drank the wine, but only one glass, and we talked for hours. There was so much more to the quiet shifter than I'd imagined.

I'd never been much of a drinker and sipped the smooth, cranberry liquid slowly. That was all it took to cause my eyes to become heavy. Feeling peaceful, my lips loosened, and I gave in to the questions that had been on my mind. "Do you have anyone waiting for you at home?" I asked Issik.

"Are you asking me if I have a girlfriend? No." He shook his head, his light blond hair falling around his jawline. "Iculon is a cruel and unforgiving land. Not many can withstand the constant brutal weather."

My heart grew sad for him. No wonder he was rigid and reserved. He had no one to care for him.

The coolness of his fingers brushed along my cheeks, seeping into my skin. "Don't feel sad for me, little warrior. I prefer to live alone."

Did he really though? How did he know if he had never shared his life with another person? "I think I would like to live in an ice castle," I murmured, my eyes blinking very slowly as my voice drifted off.

Soft lips pressed against my temple. "I would keep you warm," I thought he whispered, but the wine got the better of me, and right before I dropped off into a deep slumber, I recalled the reason I had left my room—damn dragons.

The sound of deep voices dancing around me woke me up— four of them to be exact. What were the descendants doing in my room?

And then I remembered I wasn't in my room, but Issik's. I must have fallen asleep. Oops. My cheek pressed against a pillow, and a thick blanket draped over my body. The smell of Issik's crisp scent lingered on the bed, and I found it comforting, unlike the dragon himself. Keeping still and my eyes closed, I tuned into the whispered conversation that was growing in volume.

"Did you sleep with her?" a low voice asked that I was seventy-five percent sure was Kieran's.

"No," Issik said with an edge. "But would it have mattered if I had?"

"Yes!" came three hisses.

A moment of silence followed, and I held my breath. "What is going on? It's been decades since we've fought. And never over a girl," Jase said.

I couldn't believe they were talking about me. Scratch that. Yes, I could. Arguing over me seemed to be a pastime they partook in frequently.

"We've never all desired the same girl before," Zade commented.

"There is that," Jase added. It sounded as if he was pacing the room.

"It must mean something because it's clear we all feel something for her," Kieran voiced.

"So what are we going to do about it?" the fiery golden god wanted to know.

"For starters, we need to put all our energy into figuring out what we're missing. Time is ticking by, and seducing Olivia is not going to give us our freedom, or save us from extinction," Jase lectured them, doing what he did best—leading.

A bunch of groans and shuffling feet responded, but eventually, there were grunts of agreement.

Don't I deserve a say in the matter?

"What's the plan? Do we have any leads? Something to tell us what direction to be searching in?" Issik asked.

A frustrated sigh resounded around the room. Jase. "We've been over every inch of this island, scoured every book in the kingdoms, tracked down every person with an ounce of magic, who are now all dead. What's left?"

"We have five months left to figure it out," Issik reminded him, not that any of them could forget about the sand quickly slipping through the hourglass.

"And five months to keep Olivia alive," Jase added. A cloud of foreboding lingered in the air.

"How hard can that be?" Kieran asked, in an attempt to lighten the bleakness that had settled in the room.

"Tianna's curse is complex, as we've learned. The closer we get, the more danger she will be in," Dimples explained.

"We can handle it," Zade reassured, sounding determined and confident.

"But can she?" Jase interceded.

"I think she can." Issik spoke up. "She's tougher than she looks."

Hell yes, I was, and I loved him for sticking up for me. We had shared a sincere moment last night, and it was nice to feel as if someone believed in me, even a little bit.

"With us by her side, we can take on whatever Tianna throws at us," Zade vowed with fervor.

"But that doesn't mean we can't be more careful. Mistakes cost lives," Jase reminded them, lowering his tone.

"I don't like this," Issik said, and I felt his eyes move over my pretending-to-sleep form.

"None of us do, but this is the only way. Enough is enough. We must end this curse no matter what," Zade retorted.

"I agree," Kieran's voice was determined. "But I'm not willing to risk Olivia's life for my own. We've lived more than a hundred years. She's only had seventeen."

"Even if it means it is the end of dragons?" Jase asked.

"The world already thinks we're fiction..." Issik let his thought dangle.

"Then we all agree?" Jase asked, waiting for someone to speak up.

I was dying to open my eyes just to take a quick peek to see what was going on. Were they nodding in agreement, shaking hands, or something else entirely? How would I know if they would forsake their lives for mine if I couldn't see them? And did I want them to?

I wasn't sure.

I had plunged into a lake from several feet up in the air to save one of them.

"How long have you been listening, Cupcake?" Jase asked.

Gulp.

Wrinkles spread over my nose, as I pried one eye open. "Not long." Sighing, I gave up the pretense of sleep. "Just something about the curse, less kissing, and blah, blah, blah."

Jase's lips twitched. "So everything."

I shrugged. "Maybe. What happened before Issik said he didn't sleep with me?"

A scowl settled on Issik's eyes, while the other three tried to maintain their unaffected postures. I don't know why they pretended with me. I could see right through each of them. They weren't as tough as they appeared.

Jase leaned against the far wall, faking an expression of consideration. "I think we were talking about how much trouble you are."

Grabbing a pillow from the bed, I chucked it across the room, not caring which dragon I hit, as long as I hit one of them. "You brought me here. Don't forget that part."

"She has a point," Zade agreed.

Of course I did. The pillow thumped to the floor, not hitting a single one of them. Wow. Pitiful.

A hint of a smile danced on Issik's lips as he sat at the end of the bed. "I guess there is no need to catch you up, little warrior."

Slowly, I sat up, keeping the blanket in my lap. "Next time, try not talking about me when I'm in the room, sleeping or awake."

Jase gave a quick nod. "Noted."

My eyes narrowed, making the rounds to each one. "Is there going to be a next time?"

"That we talk about you? Definitely." Kieran grinned.

Humor shone Zade's eyes as he stared at me from his spot in the corner. He was sitting in the only chair, his long legs stretching out in front of him. "You're stuck with us. We're not leaving your side."

That shouldn't have made me crazy happy, but it did.

"I think we need to hug it out," Kieran offered. A mischievous gleam that was ever present in his eyes glimmered.

My arms spread wide, letting a grin cross my own lips. "Group hug," I announced, singing it in a high-pitched tone.

The four shifters only wasted a single heartbeat before bombarding me on the bed, even Issik, the coldest dragon of them all, and I suddenly found myself engulfed in the world's sexiest hug as they all tried to wrap their arms around me. The bed groaned under the additional weight, and I thought for sure it would collapse.

In that moment, surrounded by the descendants, I didn't care what anyone else thought. They were mine.

"What happened to your face?" Zade demanded, seeing the red mark courteous of Harlow.

My eyes moved to meet Issik's and I swallowed. I had a feeling lots of roaring would be echoing in the castle.

When they had said they weren't leaving my side, I shouldn't have taken it literally, because in the next few days, they vanished—all four of them. Again.

The descendants were proving to be the worst protectors in history. Every time one of them took off, they had a million reasons why I couldn't tag along. It was pathetic. I understood they were worried I would get hurt, but being trapped inside the castle day in and day out wasn't good for my mental health, which was just as important. I couldn't possibly help them break the curse if I had mush for brains.

I hated being left alone. I hated being apart from them. I hated feeling sorry for myself, which was exactly what I was doing.

Pity party for one, please.

My foot connected with the innocent rock and I watched it skip over the dirt path of the courtyard. It was a good thing cell phones didn't work in the Veil, or I'd be blowing up theirs.

I avoided every part of the keep Harlow could possibly be in, and that really limited me to my room. Since our little hair pulling, nail scratching spat, we'd both been steering clear of each other like a plate of brussels sprouts. Neither of us had apologized, and I was definitely not going to make the first move. She had it coming. I wasn't sorry for my actions.

The grounds were fairly quiet today, everyone taking care of their daily responsibilities. I waved at Eve, the gardener, who was tirelessly trying to maintain the overgrown hedges surrounding the castle. The flowers and plants in the Veil seemed to grow at an alarming rate. Everything was bigger here, kind of like Texas. Raven, a sweet, shy elderly lady, gathered a bouquet of flowers for inside the dining hall, as usual. She didn't live in the castle, but in a small home on the edge of the woods bordering Wakeland. She had been one of the chosen girls many, many years ago and stayed, making a life here in the Veil Isles.

Continuing to stroll along the path that circled the keep, I enjoyed the sun on my face. A lazy cat wound its way in between my legs as I walked, keeping me company. Petra, I thought her name was—one of a few strays that hung around the kitchen waiting for Milly, the cook, to toss them scraps, which she did each day.

There was a routine to life in the Veil that I found comforting, yet mundane, and the existence I'd had before the kidnapping began to feel like it had happened to a different person. They were separate; one didn't bleed into the other, and I wanted to keep it that way. The girl from before, she didn't exist here.

Dropping down off the dock onto a small section of sand, I kicked off my shoes and sunk my feet into the tiny grains warmed by the sun's rays. A tender breeze blew in from off the sea, flirting with the hem of my dress.

My eyes were drawn to the sky, hoping to catch sight of the dark outline of a dragon. I don't know how long I stood in there, staring into the vast turquoise sky. Too long. Eventually, I sat down at the water's edge and hugged my knees up to my chest.

"Olivia Campbell..." someone whispered my name.

My gaze went to the aqua waters. I don't know what I expected to see, but there was nothing, only the gentle waves, a few fish, and lots of seaweed.

Am I hearing things?

To be safe, I scanned the area to make sure I was truly alone and Harlow wasn't screwing with me. There was no one around, and yet I couldn't shake the feeling that I was being watched as an inkling of unease snaked down my spine.

It was strange. Today the sea lacked its usual fogginess. The color of the endless sky reflected in the waves, allowing me to see into its depths. At home, Mom and I used to go to the beach every weekend during the summer, and sitting here now on the edge of the water, feet dangling just under the surface, I thought of her, of how much I missed her.

What would she think of my life now?

Would she approve of the descendants? Of dragon shifters?

The idea brought a tiny smile to my lips.

I highly doubted that when Mom thought of my future, she would have envisioned me entangled with four guys. And I know for a fact she wouldn't have believed in dragons.

Speaking of missing someone, it was awfully silent with the four of them gone. I hated it. I knew they had responsibilities and a curse to break, but I would have gladly helped, and it would have been much preferred to doing nothing.

My reflection stared back at me over the placid waters. My long, honey-colored hair fell over my shoulders, and as I leaned closer, the ends dipped into the sea. At first glance, I didn't recognize myself. My aqua eyes lacked the fear I'd gotten used to seeing in them when I was alone. My lips seemed naturally pinker and my cheeks peachier. I attributed it to the lighting, the glow of the sun giving my skin a dewy quality.

Have I changed that much since I've been here?

It wasn't solely my physical appearance, but also how I felt inside. I was different... older and wiser; that sounded so cliché, yet it didn't make it any less true.

"Olivia." The soft voice of a woman sounded again.

What the fuckity-fuck?

Okay, this time I wasn't imagining voices. Someone was trying to get my attention, and after the second eerie call, I was all ears. Problem was, I had no idea where it came from.

And then I saw something in the water.

It wasn't *something* I saw in the water, but *someone*, a woman rising from the bottom of the sea. I blinked and blinked again, convinced the sun and the reflection of the water was playing tricks on me.

Zade's warning about the sea and the creatures that lived in its depths echoed in my head. Sirens. Loch Ness monster. Things I probably couldn't imagine. Surely, what I was seeing was a mermaid, but her body was more fluid than solid.

She stayed under the surface, staring at me with white eyes that glowed like an oracle's. I found them freaky and struggled to look at them. Her vibrant red hair floated around her heart-shaped face in a tangle of waves.

"Olivia," she whispered my name again, but her mouth never moved. Her eyes fixated on mine. Her words transported into my mind. *"Let me help you."*

I couldn't believe I was talking to a woman of the water. "How?" I asked, unwilling to blindly accept some strange woman's aid. She could be dead for all I knew, or a siren trying to trick me.

"I have what you seek."

I shifted up onto my legs, my knees tucked beneath me. "What is it you think I'm looking for?"

She laughed, a melodic and airy sound like spring showers. *"What everyone on this island wants, to break the curse."*

"What do I need?" My heart quickened in my chest.

"I must show you," she insisted.

Did I look stupid? Were the letters s-u-c-k-e-r written across my forehead? "Let me guess. I need to swim in there," I said dryly, pointing to the sea.

Her head nodded up and down, causing her hair to float out behind her. *"It's the only way."*

Said every crazy person ever. My eyes roamed over the water, contemplating if I was insane enough to jump in. I already knew the answer because I had leaped in to save Jase, but now there was no one around to save me. "Why should I trust you?"

"Do you have any other options?"

Point taken. But that didn't mean I liked it. "Who are you?"

"My identity isn't important. What matters is you have something none of the others had."

"What do I have?" I asked.

Her eyes grew frantic. *"You must hurry. The sun is setting, and without the light, we will lose our opportunity."*

She was evading my questions, but I wasn't sure it really mattered who, or what she was. If there was even the slimmest of chances I could break the spell, or find something to help us, didn't I have to take it? Would Jase, Kieran, Zade, or Issik do the same?

They would without hesitation.

I had to do it.

"I'm so going to regret this," I muttered as I glanced down and grimaced. The mysterious woman had faded back into the dark parts of the sea, leaving the decision up to me whether I followed or not. I nibbled on my lip. The sun shone at my face, hitting the water, and that was when I saw it—the spark of something shiny.

What is that?

There was definitely something down there other than the mermaid, and it wanted me to find it. I don't know how I knew that; I just did.

I felt torn between taking a swim—I'd been warned to stay out of the water—or returning to the keep, and forgetting about the shiny object and the woman. There were so many reasons to not go after it. What if I drowned? I was a decent swimmer, but still, I didn't know how deep the water was. What if I was attacked? There were things in the lake I never wanted to come face to face with.

Shit.

Quickly scanning the grounds to make sure no one was around, I grabbed the hem of the slim dress I wore and lifted it over my head, leaving me in just my undergarments. I dipped my toes in and shimmied toward a set of rocks, dividing my attention between my own stability and glaring into the water.

It was dark, but not so dark that I couldn't distinguish between the grayish water and the gritty sand on the bottom.

You're fine. You can do this. Just swim down. Grab the pretty item. And get out. Easy peasy. You lived on the streets. How much scarier can a body of water be than that?

With all that nonsense chattering in my head, I held my breath and plucked up my courage, plunging into the sea. Water rushed over my head, gliding smoothly along my skin. I opened my eyes, giving myself a second to adjust, and kicking my feet, I dove onward toward the glittering object. My movements were jerky and graceless.

When something brushed the side of my leg, I tried to keep my cool but I couldn't repress the shudder. *Don't think about it. Just focus on reaching the bottom. Get in and get out.*

Pursing my lips, I stretched out my hand, ignoring the burning in my lungs, and the ache in my legs. I was so close. Just another few inches. The water around me rolled, and I realized with a jolt of panic that I wasn't alone in there anymore.

Please, don't let me get eaten.

I didn't let myself think about the dark shadow approaching me, and kept my focus on the object. A hum vibrated in my ears, and just as my fingertips touched the smooth surface of the translucent stone, another set of fingers brushed over mine.

My eyes glanced up.

Jase? What was he doing in the water?

All rational thoughts went out the window.

A thousand pinpricks sank into my body as a burst of colored lights haloed through the water like a disco ball. It came from the stone. Jase's hand clasped over mine, securing the rock between our joined fingers.

I gasped, inhaling a stream of water, and Jase reacted, wrapping his arms around my waist and launching us to the surface three times as fast as I could. Breaking through the water, I coughed, sputtering seawater from my nose and mouth.

A fresh wave slammed up against me, but before I could go under again, Jase lifted me out of the ocean and onto the dock. Coughing up the last bit of water, I collapsed on my back, eternally grateful to be back on land.

"What the hell were you thinking?" Jase yelled, barely giving me a second to catch my breath. "I told you to stay out of the sea."

He was beginning to sound like a broken record, which wasn't wholly his fault. I pushed myself upright, meeting his unhappy gaze. "That I could do something other than sitting around on my ass."

He drew in a ragged breath. "And swimming was the first thing that came to mind?"

"No."

"What were you doing then? You could have drowned."

Thank you, captain obvious. It was then I remembered the stone in my hand. My eyes traveled to my palm, staring at the glittering glass stone. It was smooth, serene, and lightweight. "I went to get this," I said, holding up the crystal that was purple in color, just like his eyes.

"A rock? Now I know you are nuts."

"I don't think it's just any stone," I said, unable to take my eyes off it. A pulsing rhythm thudded where it touched my skin as if it had a heartbeat. This was what the mysterious water woman had wanted me to find. She had led me to it.

"Let me see it." Jase's hand reached for the crystal, and that was when shit got psychedelic.

I swore the world stopped as a prism of light shimmered violet, dancing behind my eyes. The vibrant blend of blue and purple burst, threading around Jase and me, encircling us in a bubble of moonbeams. Our hands were connected with the stone between them.

My eyes immediately sought out his, and I gasped. I recognized his dragon, seeing the fierce creature that lived within him staring back at me. A surge of energy pierced my heart, and I braced myself for the searing hot pain I was sure would follow. But there was only pure stillness. It bloomed in the center of my chest, spreading to every point in my body—every muscle, every bone, every hair follicle. It wasn't just a feeling of tranquility; it was as if I *was* tranquility.

The swirling colors intensified to the point I worried about going blind. It built and built until... *boom.* They burst like a grenade blowing up a rainbow. Jase's eyes widened in horror as my name exploded in a roar from his lips, but it narrowly registered in my brain until his arms wrapped around me, shielding me from the flash. My face was plastered to his bare chest, and I thought, *I am going to die.* At least it would be in Jase's arms.

Not a horrible way to go.

For a few minutes, I remained still. I stayed planted against Jase, waiting out the wave of mystical energy. My legs trembled, but I didn't worry. Jase was there to keep me from falling. I was almost afraid to open my eyes, preferring the darkness to the dazzling colors.

"Olivia," he whispered, his gentle fingers coming to rest on my cheeks.

I blinked a few times, testing the brightness. Being blinded once was enough for me. "What just happened?" I asked, tilting my head upward.

The muscles in his shoulders tensed. "That rock isn't just a pretty piece of glass. I don't know why I didn't recognize it."

The stone—that was twice now that we'd touched it together, and made fireworks fly. Wiggling to put a little bit of space between us, I lifted my hand and spread open my fingers. I eyed the round purple crystal. "What is it?"

"The Star of Tranquility."

He reached to touch it again, and I snapped my fingers closed. His hand was suspended in midair as his eyes sought mine. A light of understanding dawned in them. Strange things happened when we both touched it, so for now, I'd hold on to it.

"It was lost during the Great War. Each descendant had a stone crafted by the gods, representing their power. They were embedded in the crowns of our forefathers, passed down through the generations, but they haven't been seen since the Great War when our ancestors were struck down. We all assumed they had been destroyed." His fingers dove into his damp hair, his mind traveling back in time.

"Does it have any magical properties?" I asked. Considering what just happened and, even now, the stone humming with energy it seemed likely.

Jase arched a brow. "It's been so long since I heard the stories, but it was rumored the gods enchanted the stones with fire, ice, tranquility, poison, and influence, giving the very first dragons their powers."

I couldn't imagine having such an amazing history, and to think I held the source of his power in my hand, this tiny little stone. "I'm assuming it hasn't lost any juice," I said, locking eyes with him.

"Do you feel any different?" he asked me, his stunning features darkening.

"I don't know. Should I-I?" I chattered, a shiver rolling through me, but as the words left my lips, I truly took a moment to take stock of how I felt from the inside out. I sucked in a deep breath, noticing a flutter stir in my chest. *What is that?* It didn't seem like a big deal and could have easily been from nearly drowning.

Retrieving his discarded shirt from the dock, he tugged it over my head, and I wiggled my arms into the sleeves. The material was warm and smelled like Jase. "It's hard to say, but I'm sure we will find out soon enough. The stones don't appear to have lost their abilities."

"I'll say," I muttered.

"We're going to talk about how stupid it was for you to jump into the water like that, but first, let me look at you." He took a step back as his eyes gave me a critical once-over from head to toe. The firmness crossing his brows softened, and I took that to mean I hadn't grown a second head or a third arm.

The sudden frown that grew on his lips spiked a bout of doubt, but he no longer looked at me. Jase rotated his wrists from left to right, staring at them with an expression of wonderment and disbelief. "It can't be!"

"What can't be? Because I definitely felt some weird magical mojo a minute ago."

"You did it!"

"What did I do?" I asked, squinting my eyes as I tried to see what I was missing.

"My bands… they're gone."

A funny look contorted my face. "What bands?" I prodded. Getting information from him was worse than going to Target on Black Friday.

A strangled laugh erupted out of him. "The ones that keep me locked to the island."

"Oh," I said. How had I not noticed them? Maybe they hadn't been physical bands, but some kind of magical ones. "Does that mean the curse is broken?"

"I-I'm not sure," he stammered. The man never stuttered. "We need to find the others," he announced, grabbing my hand without the stone.

I had to jog to keep up with him. We passed around the back of the castle and through the courtyard, barging in through the double doors. Kieran, Zade, and Issik were in the hall, sitting at the oversized rectangular table. Strands of wet hair clung to the back of my neck, dripping water down my spine.

The three dragon shifters stopped what they were doing and flipped their gazes to Jase and me. "What's wrong? Why are you both soaking wet?" Issik asked.

"You were supposed to find her, not drown her," Zade said, his tone dry and slightly annoyed.

Jase sat me down in one of the empty chairs. "I found her all right. At the bottom of the sea."

Three sets of eyes regarded me with disapproval. "Did she fall in?" Kieran asked, probably assuming I had.

Jase folded his arms and shook his head, enjoying the retelling a little too much. "No, I saw her jump."

He did, huh? "I went to get this," I butted in, throwing out my hand on the table so they could all see the Star of Tranquility.

Silence greeted me but was shortly followed by…

"Is that…?"

"It can't be."

"Holy shit."

Three different responses, but they all shared the same incredulity.

"It's the Star of Tranquility," Jase said, his violet eyes illuminating with the same glow as the crystal as if they recognized each other.

Kieran leaned closer to inspect the stone. "How? I thought—"

"We all did," Jase interjected. "But she didn't just locate the lost stone. Something happened when we both touched it. Look." He shoved out his wrists for the other dragons to inspect what obviously my human eyes couldn't see.

Their eyes volleyed from Jase to his hands and back again. Zade's brows scrunched together as he grabbed Jase's arms, turning them back and forth, much like Jase had earlier. "They're gone."

"The stone removed them. I felt it but wasn't sure at first." Darkness crept over Jase's face. "You still have yours," he said to the three dragons who were like brothers to him.

"Which means the curse isn't broken," Issik's powerful voice concluded, putting a dark veil over our short-lived elation.

Disappointment crashed inside me, and I rubbed the heel of my hand over my heart.

"That's exactly how we all feel, little warrior," Issik said, sensing my desolation for them. It hovered over all of us like a thick, black, ugly storm cloud.

"I don't understand. Why didn't it lift the curse?" Desperation laced my voice.

No one said anything, the silence thickened around us.

"Because we don't have all the stones." Issik announced, finally putting together the pieces. "There were originally five crafted. If the Star of Tranquility survived, it's possible so did the others."

"We need to find them," Kieran surmised.

Issik nodded in agreement.

"And I'm guessing you guys have no idea where to look." It had been purely accidental, stumbling upon the rock… or had it? The water woman. She had led me to the stone, but who was she? How could I summon and enlist her help again? I wasn't sure why I hadn't told them about her.

Zade heaved a heavy sigh. "They could be anywhere. The isles are quite large."

Having recently seen it with my own eyes, I could attest to the sheer size of the Veil. "It will be like finding a pot of gold at the end of the rainbow." I added to the gloom. Nearly impossible.

"For fuck's sake," Zade swore under his breath.

"But we have to try," I said, pleading with each one of them as I looked them in the eyes one by one.

Jase had both palms flattened on the table. "And we have less than five months to do it," he reminded.

Talk about a time crunch.

Silence followed.

None of us expected the sound of a female voice laughing in a husky, flirty tone, brimming with mockery. It came from all directions, surrounding us. My first thought was Harlow, but the pitch of the tone was wrong, raspier.

All four of the descendants bristled and shot to their feet, rushing into the courtyard. The expressions on their faces were murderous. I followed behind them, refusing to be left alone. They stood in a fierce line, strong and unified. I felt sorry for the idiot dumb enough to challenge them all.

I lifted up on the tips of my toes, trying to see over their broad shoulders. It wasn't easy, but I managed to find a hole in between Issik and Zade and weaseled my way in. A woman with flaming hair was poised in the gardens, a billow of white smoke at her feet, making it hard to tell if she actually touched the ground.

From my obscured view, her piercing gaze found mine. "You didn't think it would be that easy, did you?"

For an instant, a terrifying instant, there was only the sound of the sea and the wind and my own heart pounding. *Is she talking to me?*

A wisp of unease curled over me. I shivered and huddled back into Issik, instinctually knowing who the voice belonged to. He wrapped me in his arms, but the cold that settled into my chest wasn't from Ice Prince.

"Tianna," all four dragons hissed together, identical dark scowls marring their handsome faces.

Tianna?

The bitch finally came to show her face.

If I could get a firm grip on reality, I'd choke it. I felt as if the world had been spinning since I jumped into the sea, maybe even before then, and I couldn't catch my balance.

Panic embraced me.

What does she want? Can she hurt me? Hurt the descendants? Can they hurt her?

Question after question tumbled like rapid-fire bullets in my head. There was something eerily familiar about the witch.

The witch's lips curled into a grin. "So you finally found one of the keys. Took you long enough. I was beginning to think you'd given up."

"Never," Issik growled, his hands dropping from my back and fisting at his sides.

Every muscle in Jase's body was coiled and ready to strike. "Time isn't up yet."

Tianna pinned her gaze on him with a look of pure hatred. "No, you can still fail. And fail you will." Her hand lashed out and caught fire, lighting up her face in a green glow.

A knot of fear balled in the pit of my stomach. My hand clutched

Issik's arm, needing someone to keep me safe. I should have grabbed Jase. A dose of his calming nature would be divine right now.

My movement had Tianna turning toward me, a place I didn't want her to look. What I wanted was to be invisible. "Such a plain human."

I should have been insulted but that would imply I cared what Tianna thought about me, and I didn't. She was the source of all my recent problems, the reason I had been kidnapped and brought to the Veil. Or maybe I should have thanked her. Without the curse, I never would have learned about dragons or met the descendants, and now I couldn't imagine my life without them.

"I'd rather be plain than a vindictive bitch." Oops. The words just came tumbling out of my mouth. I should have thought about it before I opened my trap because she had powers.

But I had dragons.

Four of them.

I won.

Tianna lost her shit. With a flick of her wrist, she cast a flame of energy in my direction. Kieran threw himself in front of me, opening his mouth and blowing out a blast of emerald smoke. Poison expelled from him, fizzling out the sphere of fire.

"Pathetic," she laughed. "I've waited and grown weary of watching you through the curtain of magic as you fail time and time again, doomed to make the same mistakes."

Under my hand, Issik's arm flexed. The ice dragon was dying to freeze her lofty ass. "I'm assuming there's a point to this spontaneous visit?" Issik asked.

"I've come for the star," she stated as if we were all dim-witted peons. Lightning struck, the sky suddenly as black as Tianna's heart.

Jase's cool gaze switched from Tianna to me. "Is that what this has been about?"

"Whatever you do, Olivia, don't give her the stone," Kieran whispered into my ear.

This was something about they all seemed to be in agreement. My fingers tightened over the smooth rock.

With unblinking eyes, she let a long moment pass. "Did you

honestly think I cared about any of you? You have always been a means to an end. Sure, I had a little fun, but the games are over. Now, give me the stone, and I'll let your little pet live."

Only, by coming here and exposing her desire for the descendants' stars, she had revealed a weakness. Did her greedy heart want power so much she would destroy an entire race to gain it?

In Tianna's case, the answer was a big fat yes.

Holy shit. At Tianna's threat on my life, all eight of the descendants' eyes shone brightly with large, colored pupils.

"No. Not going to happen," Jase snarled, his voice reaching a low note I'd never heard before in a guy. It was more animal than human.

Tianna waved her magic-happy hand in the air, disregarding them like children. "Don't be foolish. It's the only way you can get the freedom you so desperately want."

"You've already cursed us. What more do we have to lose?" Kieran snapped.

"Her," Tianna hissed.

A wall of dragons formed around me. "Touch a hair on her head and you won't get what you want." Issik's words dripped below freezing temps.

Rage like I'd never seen before erupted from Jase, deep and vicious. "Trust me, we'll find a way to make sure we kill you."

"Are you willing to take the chance that I won't kill her?" Tianna tilted her head to the side, giving them a moment to ponder, not that any of the dragons needed time to think on it. "In case you need a reminder of how serious I can be..." She called a creature down from the sky to perch on her arm, skimming her fingertips over the ruffled feathers of its face. The griffin was about the size of a crow. She whispered in its ear, "It's time they heard you scream, dearie."

"Get her out of here!" Kieran yelled.

A ring of orange fire materialized, boxing us in. She threw her head back and laughed. "Not so fast. Olivia and I need to have a little girl time. You boys don't mind, do you?"

"Hell yes, we mind," Zade roared, his amber eyes flaming.

"You're not getting anywhere near her." Issik shifted into his alternate self beside me, not bothering to remove his clothes. His dragon loomed over us—glorious, fierce, and very pissed off. A stream of snow spouted from him, extinguishing the flames.

Kieran transformed next, following Ice Prince's lead. Jase and Zade framed me in between their bodies.

From above us, more griffins attacked, diving down at my dragons, their claws jabbing into the fleshy part of Kieran and Issik's wings, but they didn't show an ounce of pain. Using his tail, Kieran smacked one of Tianna's pets, sending the odd, bird-like creature sailing through the air and into the sea.

Jase looked at me, worry present in his eyes. It was then I finally saw it.

Fear.

He was afraid for me. Tianna had already cursed them, but she could use me to hurt my dragons. I wasn't going to let that happen.

"Olivia. Go. Now!" Jase bellowed, ducking as Tianna tossed another of her famous fireballs she was so fond of using.

All I could think was *I need to run*, and I begged my legs to work, but they were rooted to the ground. God, I was going to be sick.

I opened my mouth to scream, but no sound came out. Instead, a hazy, purplish mist I'd seen before expelled from deep inside me, rising up my throat and puffing into the air.

Tranquility.

How the hell had I done that?

The fighting stopped, and the Veil became eerily quiet for a few prolonged heartbeats. Everyone stared at me, except for the griffins. The feathery creatures were lying on the ground, sleeping.

I had done that.

"You!" Tianna hissed.

Uh-oh. She had on her ugly face, and I was in deep shit.

The air suddenly shifted, turning the dark sky foggy. Out over the sea, the winds picked up speed, morphing into a wicked twister, headed straight for me. Damn the witch.

"Olivia!"

"Olivia!"

"Olivia!"

"Olivia!"

Four voices bellowed, but they couldn't save me.

I was swept up in the tornado of magic Tianna had created, which twisted me off my feet and away from my dragons. I lost all sense of the world as I spun and spun in the center of the cyclone, Tianna's laugh echoing in my head like nails on a chalkboard. When my feet touched the ground, I was disorientated, my eyes unable to focus.

"Oh, come the frick on," I mumbled, my hands stretching out in the air to ground myself before I tipped over. I could tell I had been transported somewhere, but my brain was still too muddled from the trip.

"You're quite a funny human," Tianna's voice said in front of me.

I focused on the blur of red through all the muted colors of green, knowing it was the witch. *Where am I?* It could be nowhere good. Tianna stood in the middle of a forest as tall and powerful as any goddess, and maybe that was how she saw herself. With her arms thrown high, eyes glowing white, her fingers spit out tiny sparks of silver electricity.

"You're going to have to kill me," I said with a voice far steadier than I felt inside. My knees were trembling, and my stomach was still rolling.

She smiled coldly. "That is still an option, but I'm hoping more of your blood won't be spilled."

My stomach clenched in raw terror. "You need me to get the other stones, don't you?"

Her hands settled on her hips, sparks of energy still crackling from them. "What if I do?"

"Why me?" I asked.

"That's simple. Because they all desire you. You accepted them, not loving one more than the other, but the four of them equally."

It was true. I did care about them all. Love might be a far stretch, but really? This was the grand reason I was the key? Talk about a letdown. I'd been hoping for something dramatic. Special powers. An ancient lineage. Fireworks.

This couldn't be happening. How was I going to get out of here alive without handing over the very thing that would give the witch more power?

Tianna summoned a ragged-edged dagger. "Hand me the stone, and I'll go away... for the time being. I won't hurt you."

Like hell, she wouldn't.

I couldn't take my eyes off the dagger. It wasn't simply steel. Magic pulsed through the blade, etched into symbols I didn't understand. My pulse roared in my ears, and before I had a chance to doubt myself, I turned and ran. I didn't expect to get far. There was no moonlight to guide me, and I plunged heedlessly into the dark forest. I fled through the trees, my legs vibrating as I dashed down a slope. I was so blind with fear that I didn't see Issik's dragon until I rammed into him.

Relief poured through me. I was safe, right? The others would be here in moments.

Then it all happened so fast.

Issik let out a roar that echoed over the Isles—pure rage. He opened his mouth, expelling an icy mist of blue at Tianna, but the witch always had a plan. It was then I remembered the dagger in her hand. She cocked back her arm and let the blade go.

The sudden wheezing I heard left me confused. My frantic gaze searched for Issik. There in his chest was Tianna's dagger. A dragon's scales should have been impenetrable, but the magic imbued in the blade gave it the power to impale even the strongest of defenses. At the sight of blood, a strangled gasp parted my lips. She had hit one of my dragons.

NO!

Being so distraught over Issik's injury, it didn't register that I had been hit as well, but not with a magical sword. Issik's frost had struck me in the heart after he'd been stabbed.

I sucked in a sharp breath. Never had I been so cold in my entire life. It knocked the wind out of me, and all I thought was death couldn't be this painful.

"I will see you soon," Tianna's voice whispered in my ear, and then I was falling, as if from a great height.

"Olivia!" Issik shifted and somehow managed to catch me before I hit the ground.

Black spots danced behind my eyes, and then there was nothing.

Fire burned in my chest as I came to. The heat inside me exploded, pulsing in a giant wave that ran through my blood. It rippled like a solar flare straight from the sun.

With effort, I peeled my eyes open, and the first face I saw was Zade's hovering above me.

Holy shit. I'm not dead.

"This better be the last time I have to breathe fire into you, little gem."

"Is she gone?" I croaked, my throat feeling like I'd swallowed barbwire.

Zade nodded. "She vanished just as the rest of us showed up."

My relief was overwhelming, but I also knew it would be short-lived. Her promise echoed in my ears. She would be back. Her desire for the stones would keep her hunting and threatening me. Then I remembered I wasn't the only one who'd gotten hurt.

"Issik, he was stabbed. Is he okay?" I tried to sit up, but Zade pressed back my shoulders, keeping me on the ground.

"Not so fast," he scolded me. "You need a moment to let your body return to its normal temperature."

Didn't he understand? I didn't care about how hot or cold I was. If Issik was hurt, bleeding, we had to—

Issik sunk down to his knees beside me, his head resting near my face, but not too close, as if he was afraid to touch me. "You're alive," he whispered.

I blinked. What a silly thought. "Me? I'm not the one who got stabbed."

There was so much regret in his eyes, and it hurt my heart to see it there because of me. "I could have killed you."

"But you didn't. And it wasn't your fault," I stressed. "She threw a knife at you."

His blond brows furrowed together. "I never should have been so careless. Not with you, little warrior."

Kieran and Jase shuffled their feet behind us then, and I sat up slowly. "What's wrong? Why are the two of you so antsy?"

"Do you have it?" Jase asked, crouching down beside Issik.

The fingers curled around my palm slowly opened to show them the Star of Tranquility. It glittered under the starlight, vibrant and clear. It was safe. And so was I. Well, mostly. There was still the crazy thing that had happened when I screamed, but I was ninety-nine percent sure the cool stone in my hand was responsible for that.

A heartbeat later I found myself plastered against Issik's chest. "I'm so sorry. I thought we lost you." A look passed from him to me, and I squeezed him tightly, needing comfort as much as he did.

Pulling back, my eyes connected with his bright icy eyes. "Turns out I'm not that easy to kill, especially when I have four dragons around to save me."

Kieran lifted me off Issik and spun me around in his arms. "We'll always be here to protect you," he vowed.

I was counting on it, for I knew we hadn't seen the last of Tianna. We needed time to regroup, as did she, and next time we'd be ready for her.

To Be Continued...

KIERAN

Absorbing Poison

Book Two

USA TODAY BESTSELLING AUTHOR

J.L. WEIL

CHAPTER 1

Five. It was just a number. How could something so innocuous hold so much importance? It wasn't like we were talking about a gazillion. Many things could be associated with the number five.

It was the age I started kindergarten and demanded my mom braid my hair. It was the number of hotdogs Blake Cash ate in fifth grade on a dare, barfing all over the cafeteria. What had possessed me to sit at his table? It is the number of appendages most starfish have. It is how many senses humans are born with. But most importantly, it was how many months I had left to break the dragon descendants' curse.

Jase, Kieran, Zade, and Issik—the four dragon shifters had swept me off the streets, bringing me to the Veil Isles, a place as dangerous as the breath of the descendants. Before I came along, there had been five descendants. Tianna, the witch who cursed the dragons, imprisoned the last of them on the isles for a hundred years, except for two days a year when they could cross the veil. She took Tobias's life—well, her curse did, to be more precise. He tested the boundaries of her spell, and paid the price with his life.

And now there were four.

My dragons.

Since we learned what Tianna wanted and how to break the curse, plans were put into motion. The question we needed to answer was: Whose kingdom did we venture to next, to find the stone that held each dragon's unique power? That discussion, of course, broke out into a brawl. Living with dragons had its downfalls. Shit got broken. A lot.

I had to intervene. What other choice did I have?

Throwing myself into the middle of a circle of dragons, I extended my arms into a *T*. "Wait, before you break another vase or start breathing fire. How about we solve this without violence?"

"Where is the fun in that?" Kieran asked in a sexy Irish accent, grinning like the fool he was.

Heaven forbid I suggest doing something practical. I glanced into Kieran's moss-green eyes. The color seemed brighter than usual, but I noticed that happened when he got fired up, which didn't happen often. The poison dragon was as lighthearted as they came. He was free-spirited, a joker, kind, and probably sang in the shower when no one was watching.

"Fine. Kill each other. Then I won't have to break this stupid curse."

"Stupid, huh?" Jase countered. He was opposite of Kieran in the circle, and I had to spin around to see him. He shot me one of his famous raised dark brows. The dragon of Tranquility was smooth.

We were in Jase's study at Wakeland Keep. Zade had his arms folded over his broad chest, feet spread apart, and a scowl marring his full lips. Issik stood across from Zade like an immovable force. His blond hair was pulled back into some sort of man bun, keeping the silky locks off his gorgeous, but hard, face. It would take an act of God to cause Issik to flinch, or maybe flashing my boobs. That might work. He was frosty, not dead.

"Yes. When the four of you are acting like baboons, it's stupid." I scolded them, like a pack of two-year-olds.

None of them were fazed, least of all Zade. "Let me guess, you want us to pick stones again?" he asked.

"It worked well before," I defended with a shrug.

Four groans echoed through the room.

I rolled my eyes. "Fine, I have another suggestion. I'll close my eyes and Jase can spin me in a circle. When I open my eyes, whoever is directly in front of me gets to be the next victim."

I got no arguments. Amazeballs.

With that settled, I waited for Jase to put his hands on my shoulders. Zade, Kieran, and Issik shifted to even out the circle around me. It was like being burrito-wrapped in pure male sexiness. At Jase's touch, calmness radiated through me. After I closed my eyes, he spun me in multiple circles, and I lost my grip on gravity, my head spinning. His hands remained firmly on my shoulders to steady me. Otherwise, I would have stumbled like a drunken sailor.

When my eyes opened, I stared into irises as green as the rolling hills of Ireland.

Kieran—the dragon with the breath of poison.

"Hey, Blondie." Kieran's eyes traced over my face.

The warmth of Jase's body was still behind me, and the steady stream of serenity stemming from his hands still flowed over my shoulders. It seemed like second nature for him to use his gifts, especially when it came to me. "So, it's settled," Jase declared. "We go to Viperus next, to search for the Star of Poison."

That didn't sound ominous in the slightest. My enthusiasm was written all over my face.

Coming closer, Kieran lightly bumped his shoulder against mine, having to bend down to do so. "Don't worry. It's not as bad as it sounds."

"So there aren't creatures that could potentially eat, poison, or devour me?" I countered, being my usual smartass self.

Kieran's green hair was spiked down the center of his head, and the stud over his eye glittered under the waning sun streaming through the window. "No, there are, but you have four secret weapons: us."

That I did, and I would need all four of them to survive.

Releasing my shoulders, Jase walked to the desk. "We leave at first light. I know it doesn't need to be said, but we must be more alert than ever. Tianna is waiting for us to make a move. She'll do whatever it takes to get her hands on the stones."

The Star of Tranquility was carefully hidden away somewhere in Wakeland Keep. Not even I knew where it was, which was supposed to be for my own protection. At the mention of the witch, I shuddered. I was not looking forward to my next meeting with the redheaded whack job.

"Can't wait."

Did I say that out loud?

I did.

Wrapping the towel around my body, I secured it over my chest, tucking the terry cloth fabric in at the corners. I probably should have remembered to bring a change of clothes with me when I went to the bathing room, but such was my life. Forgetful should have been my first, middle, and last name. A closet full of pretty dresses sat in the corner of the room, but none of them were me. Give me sweats and a T-shirt, and I'd feel like a queen. I glared at the wardrobe door. Screw it. I was going to strut down the halls in nothing but a towel and pray for the best.

Still damp from the bath, I padded out into the hall. Coast was clear. Not a single descendant or staff member in sight. I exhaled and continued to the staircase. The halls of Wakeland Keep were drafty, scattering little goosebumps over my arms. It was very hopeful to think I would make it all the way to my room without being seen. The descendants were preparing to make the journey to Viperus—Kieran's kingdom. Hot Lips was my next dragon-curse-breaking victim. I might have been able to accidentally stumble upon the Star of Tranquility, but it was outlandish of them to think I could do it a second time. Or a third. Or a fourth!

They were all freaking nuts.

I was nearly as clueless as the first day I arrived in the Veil Isles. The only difference was I knew dragons were real, witches sucked, and I was probably never going home again. Finding the Star had been sheer dumb luck. I didn't have some kind of magical compass that pointed me in the right direction. I wanted more than anything to free the descendants from Tianna's curse. To give them back the life that had been stolen from them. To allow them to live, instead of constantly searching for ways to release themselves from the chains that kept them locked to the isles…

But how the hell was *I* going to find the next Star?

The four of them looked at me with hope and expectancy. I liked it better without the pressure. Now, I couldn't fail them.

I'd become so lost in my own head that I hadn't been paying attention to where I was going. Stopping dead in my tracks, I glanced around the long, dimly lit corridor, trying to determine where I'd wandered off to now. This didn't look like my hallway. In fact, I wasn't sure I'd ever been to this part of Jase's castle.

Fabulous. My last few hours in Wakeland Keep and I got lost. I swore to God, I didn't purposely do this shit.

Nibbling on my lower lip, I turned left and then right, deciding which way I should venture. Did it matter? I should sit down and stay put until one of the dragons found me. I'd have better luck of that happening, than finding my own way back.

A sigh escaped my mouth as I tightened my hold on the white towel, offering me little warmth. Did I really want to wait for one of them? If I did, I would have to listen to how I still couldn't find my way around, and that I needed a babysitter at all times. Blah. Blah. Blah.

I could actually hear their voices in my head.

Olivia, what are you doing?

Wow, that was way too real. It had sounded like Kieran was directly behind me.

Determining my best bet was to go back the way I came, I spun around, and ran into a wall of muscle. Kieran's husky laugh washed over me. The next thing I knew, my arms were flailing in the air, tangling with the descendant's as he scrambled to catch me. Not the smartest move. His reaction was a tad too slow, on account of him laughing at me. Legs got mixed in there as well, and then we were falling.

We went down in a heap. Somehow, Kieran managed to protect me from breaking my neck. I don't know how he contorted his body with such speed and accuracy, but he cushioned the brunt of my impact with his body. He was still chuckling, when I blew the damp tendrils of hair out of my eyes to stare down at his face.

He smelled delicious, like a woodsy waterfall, earthy and sweet. I basked in his scent, letting it encompass me wholly. I wanted to press my lips into the curve of his neck. Maybe I could ask him to carry me to my room. I wouldn't get lost, and I would get the added benefit of staying in his arms longer. Before offering the suggestion, I noticed he was distracted. His eyes weren't focused on me, but elsewhere.

The towel secured around me had slipped free, baring my breasts to the world, or in this case, Kieran's face. If he so much as moved a fraction to the left or right, he could have done wicked things that would have my body engulfed in flames, and not the kind Zade breathed.

I was stunned, but for a moment. A squeal flew from my mouth as I attempted to fix the towel and cover myself, but I made matters worse. My knee bumped into something, and I was afraid of what it might be.

His arms came around me, halting my squirming. I narrowed my eyes at him. He wore his shit-eating grin. "Stop moving, Blondie. You're making this more enticing for me."

I gasped as my fears were confirmed. "That isn't a cell phone in your front pocket?"

A chuckle rumbled his chest, vibrating my still bare boobs. "Definitely not, and if you don't want to find out more about it, I suggest you figure out a way to remove yourself from atop of me, without exposing more of yourself. Not that I mind the view." His green eyes blazed, brightening the longer I stared at him.

For the love of dragon's breath. Why do things like this keep happening to me?

My entire body sank into his, and I stayed motionless while I contemplated my options to remove myself and still keep my dignity, if that was even possible. Why couldn't he be flabby and have a potbelly like some guys get from drinking too much beer? Nope. Kieran had to be ripped and firm in all the right places.

The worst part: I was still mostly naked. "You can stop grinning," I grumbled at him. He was finding the entire situation far too amusing for my liking.

"You have beautiful breasts. They're perfect. You shouldn't hide them."

"I bet you would love that."

The grin on his lips spread. "I don't know a guy who wouldn't."

I couldn't believe we were spread out in the hall, discussing my boobs. Had there ever been a more awkward conversation in the history of dragon-kind?

Before I could say another thing, a dark shadow appeared over me. "What are the two of you doing on the floor? And why is Olivia naked? Or do I want to know?" Jase scowled, hovering over us, his voice deep and formidable.

Rushing to my feet, I jumped off Kieran to stand. My fingers scrambled to keep the towel from falling to the ground, but at this point, modesty had been thrown out the window. Why did I even bother?

I brought the white fabric up around the popular topic of the hour. I'd be happy to never talk about my boobs again. Ever.

"Nothing is going on. I fell," I quickly explain, my cheeks stained pink.

"On top of Kieran… naked?" Jase asked.

Kieran laughed and pushed himself to his feet, doing nothing to aid the situation. It seemed like he wanted Jase to think something was going on between us. This whole thing with the descendants was difficult to navigate. I didn't understand my feelings or how to deal with the four of them.

"Yes," I ground out, a damp strand of hair falling over my shoulder.

Kieran shoved his hands in his pockets, rocking back on his heels. "She's telling the truth. I found her wandering the halls, and the next thing I knew, she was on top of me with her chest in my face."

A shiver ran down my spine, but not from the cold this time. "Can we stop talking about my boobs for five seconds?"

"No," they both responded.

I'd had enough. "The discussion of my boobs is officially off-limits. Got it? This doesn't need to become one of those funny stories you tease me about later."

Kieran and Jase grinned at me. This was definitely one of those stories they were never going to let me forget. I groaned. Things had gone from sensual to awkward, to dire in mere seconds.

"I should get ready to leave."

"Do you need help getting dressed?" Kieran winked.

"If I didn't need this towel, I would whack you with it." I clutched the soft material as I collected my composure and stormed down the corridor. I still wasn't sure if I was heading in the right direction, but it didn't matter as long as no one was staring at my chest.

It took me ten more minutes to find my room, but the important thing was I had, and was safely tucked away behind closed doors—no dragons to make me feel like my emotions were tied to the end of a yo-yo. I didn't bother to put clothes on, but face-planted onto the bed as I let out a muffled shriek of mild annoyance and extreme embarrassment.

There. I'd had my momentary freak-out of the day. I had more pressing matters to attend to now. I'd been warned that the journey into Viperus's woods would be dangerous, not only because Tianna would use every opportunity to acquire what she desired, but the kingdom itself was perilous. Like the waters of Wakeland, the woods of Viperus were home to some unsavory creatures. The mention of snakes gave me the willies.

I shuddered thinking about it.

Letting out a pent up breath, I rolled off the bed to gather what little possessions I wanted to take with me. I slipped into the clothes I had arrived in—jeans, a T-shirt, and boots. If I would be traipsing around in the woods, I put my foot down on wearing a dress fit for a goddess. And to be honest, wearing my clothes gave me a sense of security, making me feel like myself, not like someone who was chosen to break a curse. Even though the material was washed, I could still smell me on it. Nostalgia and sadness whipped through me. Not a day went by that I didn't think about my mom, but in moments like these, when I was feeling alone and scared, it hit me harder.

Stiffening my chin, I refocused my mind on the menial tasks of tidying the room, and stuffing the few things I had into my bag. In a few hours, we'd be leaving for Viperus and the pressure was on.

No big deal.

I got this.

But I didn't believe a single word of it. Inside, I was trembling.

I took one last sweeping glance around my room. What had once been a prison was now a sanctuary. Leaving Wakeland was harder than I'd anticipated. I'd assumed I wouldn't form any real attachment to the kingdom I'd lived in for the last month, but I was wrong. After living on my own, not answering to anyone and homeless, I realized how much I'd been craving a family. And whether I had been looking for them or not, a family—no matter how unorthodox— was exactly what the descendants had given me.

It isn't the place that makes you feel safe. It's Jase, Kieran, Zade, and Issik, I reminded myself. If we were together, I'd be okay.

Taking a deep breath, I snatched my bag off the bed and swung it over my shoulder. I walked across the room and stepped over the threshold, heading to what was probably going to be my doom. Not the kind of positive attitude I should have, but some days it was hard to keep your chin up, when the task in front of you seemed so far from reach and daunting.

Downstairs, the four dragons waited in the great hall. Zade paced across the floor, muttering to himself, probably grumbling about how long it was taking me. Issik leaned against the wall, looking bored. Kieran stared out the window, and Jase was in the corner, lounging in a leather chair. I could tell tensions were high, and they were anxious to get going. No one wanted to find the next stone more than the four of them. Their lives depended on it.

"Who's ready for a little adventure?" I asked with a fake smile, as I sauntered into the center of the room.

Jase's violet eyes swept over me, brimming with exasperation. "This isn't a vacation or a camping trip."

"Good thing. I've never done either," I replied, looping my backpack over both my shoulders.

Four sets of eyes stared at me.

Shifting the straps on my back higher, I shrugged. "I'm not a fan of nature or flying, at least I wasn't before."

Kieran's pierced lips curled. "Imagine that. Olivia afraid of flying. You seem to have overcome that fear fairly quickly."

Yeah well, I kind of didn't have a choice, living with four dragons. "Watch it, or I'll hit you with my tranquility breath."

Kieran shook his head, but the smile on his lips didn't dull. "We need to teach you how to control your gift, without putting all the isles to sleep."

"And how are you going to do that?" It had been a few days since I found the Star of Tranquility and absorbed its power, giving me the same ability as Jase—to put people in a deep slumber. But I had no idea how it worked, or how to control this sleeping spell bestowed upon me.

As Kieran and I talked about my newfound ability to breathe tranquility, Jase, Issik, and Zade surrounded me, herding me out into the hall while Kieran kept me engaged in the conversation. It wasn't until the breeze rolling off the sea washed over my face, that I noticed we were outside the castle.

My feet stopped moving, staring at the vast trees towering in front of us. "We're really doing this?"

"We are, Little Warrior." Issik's cool voice tickled my right ear, and then we were moving again, straight toward the dense forest.

I cast a glance over my shoulder, toward the castle for memory's sake. Harlow stood in the doorway, eyeing me with disdain, and if I wasn't mistaken, her eyes glistened with tears. It could have been a trick played by the sun, but I didn't think so. She had a thing for Jase. Because of her treatment of me last month, it was hard for me to feel sympathetic. I definitely wasn't going to miss her sunny disposition. One good thing about going to Viperus was, I didn't have to worry about Harlow trying to stab me in my sleep.

The woods of Viperus bordered the southern part of Wakeland. Not long after we entered the towering trees, the air no longer smelled of sea and moisture, but of pine and earth. I'd made this trek once before when the descendants had taken me to the temple of their fathers. The journey was still burned in my memory.

"Why aren't we flying again?" I asked, tripping over a stupid twig for the twentieth time. The woods held us in a tight embrace, making me feel claustrophobic. I wanted space and air.

Zade strode up beside me, dwarfing me with his six-foot-plus frame, a scowl twisting his lips. "Tianna will expect us to be moving. She might not know which kingdom we've chosen, but you can bet your cute little butt she will have scouts watching."

"Can we leave Olivia's butt out of it?" Kieran called over his shoulder, amusement sparkling in his voice. He was leading the group, striding a few paces in front of us, and eager to get home. Who could blame him?

I ignored the comment about my butt. Too much talk about my body parts had already occurred, and I wasn't going to add fuel to the fire, but the tug at the corner of Jase's lips had me on edge. If I didn't steer the conversation back on topic, it would derail to my ass or, worse yet, my boobs. Hell no. I'd had enough embarrassment today. "But doesn't she want me to find the stones?"

"Yes and no," Jase added, clearing up absolutely nothing.

It was probably a waste of time trying to get inside the head of an evil sorceress, but what else did I have to do while schlepping through the woods? A couple of thoughts popped into my head, but none of them were suitable for hiking in the forest, and ironically, they all involved me nearly naked.

What is going on with me? I've suddenly become sex crazed.

Since the other night with the towel mishap, it seemed like all I could think about was getting naked. I couldn't stop reliving that moment... with a different ending. One where I didn't run away. One where Jase stayed. And the three of us...

Dear God, how much longer was this trip?

My cheeks deepened in color, and I prayed no one would notice. "That doesn't make any sense," I said to Jase, trying to reel in my thoughts.

"We're dealing with a witch. It's not supposed to make sense," Zade pointed out then.

And dealing with four dragons is?

"Are you feeling okay? You're looking a little flushed." Issik, the guy of few words, watched me with his piercing blue eyes. His blond hair was swept into a ponytail, making him look like a Viking warrior.

Damn these dragons and their ability to feel my emotions. It wasn't fair. Here I was tasked with freeing them from their cursed prison, and they got rewarded by having a direct gateway to my feelings. Since they had tasted my blood, a bond had formed between them and me. It was one-sided and unfair as hell. Each shifter could sense a different one of my emotions. Jase got fear, Zade anger, Issik sadness, and Kieran passion. But there seemed to be a bit of wiggle room.

"I'm fine," I grumbled, dragging my feet through a pile of fallen leaves.

"Here, drink this." Jase held out a container of water.

I took a swig and handed it back to Jase. Water was precious but also heavy, and I'd chosen not to bring any with me. It was hard enough carrying my own possessions and staying upright. "So what's it like in Viperus?" I directed my question to Kieran, suddenly feeling the need to be a Chatty Cathy.

"Buggy." It was Zade who responded.

"Green." Issik added, then.

Jase couldn't be left out, of course. "Untamed."

They all had their opinions of Kieran's kingdom, and I found it interesting that none of them sounded thrilled with the destination. Whereas my hesitation had little to do with the kingdom itself, the other three seemed leery of it, but then again, Kieran *was* a poison dragon.

"Don't listen to them. Viperus is lush and vibrant—full of life." Kieran defended his home with so much pride, that his chest swelled with it as he walked. "The plants that thrive in this part of the isles provide us with air to breathe, and rich soil for the cultivation of food."

"Do you have any crazy jealous girlfriends waiting to carve out my eyeballs?" I inquired. It was a justified question after my stay at Wakeland Keep.

"We give all the crazy girls to Jase." Kieran winked at me.

"Wonderful," Jase muttered, but his eyes twinkled with good humor.

I chuckled, some of the tension leaving my body, but the small reprieve of stress didn't last long.

Squawk. Squawk.

Dark shadows above the trees swooped down, their wings skimming the tops of the branches and shaking the leaves. All four descendants stopped and formed an immediate circle around me, causing the air in my lungs to stall.

Is it Tianna?

Has she found us?

The boys surrounding me tensed; ready to shift at any second if the need presented itself. An uneasy silence fell between us. My heart hammered in my chest as I waited to see what the creatures would do next. Time dragged by, and I was positive whatever was flying above our heads would swoop down and whisk me off my feet at any moment.

"It was a pair of day bats," Jase announced, his wide shoulders relaxing.

The others were quick to follow, stepping out of their defensive positions. "We might have gotten lucky this time, but you can bet Tianna is out there. We need to keep moving." Issik's raspy, cold voice had me forgetting my smaller problems.

No matter how much my feet and thighs protested, I pushed on without complaining. Walking had been something I'd done daily when I was homeless, but tromping through the woods of Viperus was strenuous. It could have been due to the numerous times I tripped. Each time I stumbled over a twig, a rock, or my own two feet, I swore one of the dragons would throw me over their shoulders any minute. We would have covered more ground faster if they had.

For the next few hours, things were quiet, and it gave me the chance to think. A scary place. Things should have felt easier now that we knew what we were looking for, but not in the fucking jungle. Viperus was vast and wild, and staring at the never-ending forest made it seem hopeless. How the hell was I supposed to find a tiny stone in here? Where was I supposed to begin? We hadn't even reached the castle yet and I wanted to give up so badly.

But then the descendants turned to fence me in from all sides, watching me with curious expressions.

Jase leaned in close. "Do I dare ask what you're thinking about?"

"I was thinking how impossible it's going to be for me to locate a single crystal in all this." My hands swept out over the woodlands. What was the point of trying to deny or hide what I felt? They could sense something was upsetting me anyway.

"We don't expect you to do this alone, Cupcake," Jase reassured me. "Don't despair. Let's take this one day at a time. Deal?"

"And as dragons, we can cover a lot of ground," Zade reminded me from behind me.

That was true, and it did make me feel slightly better, until I noticed Jase touching me. His hand had slipped behind my neck. "Jase," I rumbled.

Jase removed his hand, but not before giving me a little extra boost of relaxation. "You looked like you needed a pick-me-up."

Who could fault him for that? My mind had been traveling to a dark place. "We really are in the middle of nowhere," I remarked, admiring and feeling intimidated by the endless sprawl of woods surrounding us.

"Don't worry," Kieran assured me. "It's not as scary as they make it sound."

Kieran may not have believed his kingdom was eerie, but it would take more than his reassurance to shake the uneasiness that had settled over me. Deep down, we were all unsure about the next stage of the curse, and how it would affect our lives. The thought made me uncertain of the path we'd set ourselves on, or maybe it was that I couldn't shake the hunch we were being watched. By Tianna no doubt. The witch had spies everywhere, and she was biding her time, waiting for the right moment to strike.

I swiveled to look behind me while walking backward. I didn't know what possessed me to do such a thing, but Tianna had me on edge. On my next step, the ground was suddenly gone.

"Olivia!" Issik bellowed. He had been standing on my left, and his hands flew out to make a grab for me, but it was too late.

I was falling, and the scream that ripped from my throat echoed the entire way down.

Oomph.

I hit the ground, landing awkwardly on top of my foot, which was followed by a shooting pain, powerful enough to have me crying out loud. For a few terrifying seconds, I didn't move a muscle.

"Olivia!" boomed four voices from above my head.

A surge of anxiety tumbled through me. *I think I'm alive. I think I survived. Ninety percent sure I'm not dead.*

These were the thoughts that ran through my head as I took stock of what happened, and how I ended up underground. I'd twisted the hell out of my ankle; the rest of my injuries were scrapes and bruises—nothing that wouldn't heal—but damn if it didn't hurt like fatal wounds.

Cradling my ankle with one hand, I lifted my other hand to my temple and winced. My hand jerked away, blood staining my fingers. *Fucking fabulous.*

"I'm alive," I yelled up, hoping they would hear me. I deliberately left out the details of my injuries, knowing they would do something irrational to save me. But what I really wanted to say was, *Come get me before I bleed to death.* That wasn't an actual concern, except for in my head.

"Stay where you are. We're coming down to get you," Jase ordered me in his stern voice.

I had assumed they would, but it gave me comfort to hear them say it. Trying to breathe through the panic, I pushed slowly to my feet and grimaced, clenching my teeth as I put weight on my right foot.

"Shit," I hissed, my hand reaching out to steady myself on the rocky wall. My ankle was definitely injured.

My eyes swept the dark space, surveying my unexpected surroundings. I wanted to ensure I wasn't in any immediate danger. And with that thought, my mind drummed up a slew of horrendous situations, the hole caving in, being mauled to death by an ogre, twisting my other ankle trying to escape.

As I stepped out of the little grassy area I had landed on, I emerged into a cavern like nothing I could have ever imagined. Rock walls arched to high above my head from all sides, but they weren't ordinary stones. Flecks of green crystals shone like a million stars, twinkling underground. My mouth dropped open as my eyes scanned the open cave.

Holy dragon's breath! What is this place?

I felt like I'd struck gold.

Sounds of flowing water ricocheted off the stone, luring me farther into the cavern. Around the corner, a stream of water ran through a dark tunnel. The water emitted a green glow and lit up the pathway. I hobbled up to its edge and sat down, relieved to give my throbbing ankle a break. This was as good a spot as any to wait for the descendants. From behind me, I could hear pebbles and dirt moving about. It would be a matter of minutes before the descendants rescued me.

As I stared into the mesmerizing waters, a familiar hum trembled over the surface. Deep within the water was the sound of a woman singing in a hypnotic voice. The volume of her song was like a quiet whisper, and I strained to catch the words. Blinking, I determined I wasn't going crazy when a woman's face materialized in the pattern of the waves.

Long blonde hair haloed around her oval-shaped face as she came into focus. She looked like a mermaid floating under the water's surface, her skin glittering, but she had feet. They stuck out from under her flowing white dress.

"Olivia," she sang my name, a soft smile on her lips. She had an unusual lilt to her voice, like an ancient tongue no longer spoken. "You must save him," she begged me. Urgency was reflected in her green eyes.

"How?" I replied, my fingers gripping the rocky edge of the riverbank. I didn't know which descendant she was speaking about, but it didn't matter as long as I got a step closer to finding the Star of Poison, and if this woman had any information to help me, she better start spilling her spooky guts.

Her smile turned sad. "The stone you seek is buried deep in the unseen, but in plain sight for anyone to see."

How was I supposed to make any sense out of that babble? "I don't understand. Can't you just tell me where to look?"

Her face was bathed in a green glow from the water. "But I have. It's you, and only you, who have the power to do what must be done. The Stars have chosen you."

What did that say about the Stars? I didn't know how much stock I could put in them, if they picked me. I was no hero. "Who are you?" I whispered, extending my hand into the water. I wanted to know if she was real, a mirage, or a ghost. In the isles, you could never be sure.

The woman sank farther down, away from my touch and into the depths of the dark waters. I could no longer see her, but her voice rose up to me. "We'll guide you when we can. Take comfort in that."

Who were these women I kept seeing in the water? This one was different than the one in Wakeland, yet there was a similarity about the two of them. I believed they wanted to help me, regardless of their uncanny methods.

"Olivia?" a deep voice called, breaking through the bewitching encounter.

"Issik?" I croaked. He crouched down in front of me, staring at me with ice blue eyes of worry. I threw myself into his arms, never more ready to get out of this cave. His coolness encompassed me as his strong arms came around me. "What took you so long?" I murmured against his neck.

"Did you hit your head?" His fingers gently framed either side of my face, and he examined the cut above my brow. The frown marring his lips darkened.

Instinctively, I leaned one cheek into his touch. "I'm okay, but I twisted my ankle."

Slipping his hands under my legs, he lifted me, securing me against his chest. My arms automatically looped around the base of his neck. "Let's get you out of here before you do any more damage to yourself."

A chill entered his voice, making me wonder what I had done other than fall into a cave. Was he annoyed at the delay in our journey? Was he worried about me? Or was he just being Issik—cold and aloof? Even so, I knew Issik cared for me… Well, I thought he did most of the time. Of the descendants, Issik remained the hardest for me to understand.

The side of my face rested against his, wanting to thaw the chill that radiated from the ice prince. "I'm sorry," I apologized. For what, I didn't know, but it seemed like the appropriate response.

He tilted his head slightly, aligning our lips. My pulse quickened, and all I could think was, *Issik is going to kiss me.* Our breaths mingled, and our lips hovered there for a few heart-stopping seconds. The cave disappeared; the pain in my ankle vanished; and my mind filled with nothing but thoughts of Issik's lips on mine. The yearning to know how he tasted consumed me.

I should have known better. The ice prince had a resolve of steel. He was the only descendant who hadn't kissed me, and I couldn't help but wonder if he didn't desire me the same way I did him. I gave up pretending I didn't want to spend every waking moment locking lips with one of them. Who wouldn't? They were far too attractive for their own good.

The luster in his ice blue eyes faded as he turned his face forward again and continued walking. "You have nothing to be sorry for. It's Kieran who should be apologizing." His tone was gruff.

I tried to hide my disappointment, but it leaked into my voice anyway. "Why is that?"

"This is his domain. If he spent less time flirting with you, he would have sensed the change in the landscape. He should have been able to warn you."

Issik blamed Kieran. Of their own accord, my fingers twirled the loose strands of hair at the nape of his neck. I was compelled to touch him, and Issik didn't seem to mind.

"It was an accident."

He scowled. "You seem to have more accidents than normal humans."

I shrugged, a smile tugging at my lips. "Probably, but if I hadn't fallen, then you wouldn't be carrying me, and I kind of like being in your arms."

Issik's eyes flew to mine, and my heart pounded all over the place. When he looked at me like that, being stuck in a cave didn't seem so bad. "You're something else."

"So I've been told." Since kissing was off the menu, I inquired about something he said. "What do you mean Kieran would have been able to sense the hole?"

With ease, he moved us through the cavern toward the grassy patch. "We have a connection to our kingdoms through our dragon blood. The land is as much a part of us as the scales covering our bodies, or the breath we expel."

Fascinating. The more I learned about the descendants, the more I was convinced they couldn't be real—that I would wake up one day back on the streets, and everything that happened to me would be nothing but a dream.

"What kind of stone is this?" I asked, dazzled by the flecks of emerald we walked past.

"Did you touch it?" Issik asked with a sudden sharpness to his tone that took me aback.

I shook my head. "No."

His brows furrowed. "As pretty as the crystals look, they are poisonous."

I should have known. Kieran had warned me that Viperus was filled with plants, animals, and elements that could be lethal to humans.

We came to the spot where I'd fallen. "You ready to get out of here?"

Squinting against the beams of sunlight, I glanced upward. My other dragons waited for me above, and the sight made my chest swell. What would I do without them? "I thought you'd never ask."

The descendants made a makeshift ladder out of themselves, positioned every six to seven feet along the rocky wall. In their dragon form, they never would have fit through the hole. Issik lifted me up, handing me off to Jase. "Careful, she's injured her ankle," the Ice Prince told Dimples.

"What are we going to do with you, Cupcake?" he muttered, holding me in his grasp. He gave me a long squeeze before passing me to Zade.

Heat encased me. "We'll get your ankle fixed up, Little Gem."

Last was Kieran. Safeguarded in his arms, he easily lifted us out, but he didn't immediately let me go. Instead, he tugged me into his lap while he hugged me to death. "You scared the crap out of me, Blondie." His voice was like a whispered caress over my body.

I shivered, but not from the near brush with death. The descendants had a way of talking to me that made me feel seduced each time one of them opened their mouth. It could have been the stupidest of phrases and I would swoon. *It's raining today. What's for dinner? Olivia, are you listening to me?* I was a puddle of goo in their presence.

A light breeze ruffled my hair. "I scared the crap out of myself."

The others had made it out, hovering over Kieran and me. "We told you it was dangerous," Jase scolded me.

My neck craned to look up at the other three. "I thought you meant bears, snakes, and tigers, oh my, not that I would fall to the center of the earth."

Kieran's and Zade's chests rumbled. Jase's eyes twinkled with humor, but Issik's lips kept their straight line. "You didn't fall through the world," Jase assured me. "It is a chasm."

"Oh, in that case," I snapped back. Wiggling off Kieran, I pushed to my feet and instantly regretted it. Pain spiked through my ankle—a jolting reminder of why I needed to stay off my feet.

"We'll take turns carrying you," Jase announced, swooping in to cradle me against his chest, without me having to say anything. I had four of the most attentive boyfriends in the world.

"Why do you get to go first?" Zade complained, his possessiveness roaring to life.

They were arguing over me, a pattern I should be getting used to, competition ran fiercely among them. They had once been rival princes, though their current circumstance had thrown them together, forging a deep friendship.

As soon as Jase grabbed me, I knew I didn't want to be hauled around the woods like a swaddled infant. "Put me down. I can walk."

Jase already strode through the woods, expecting the others to follow. "Not going to happen, Cupcake."

I pouted at him, but he was staring at me with a dark and gloomy expression in return. "Why are you looking at me like that?"

"You're bleeding," he replied, the violet in his eyes becoming intense.

I touched my temple, remembering the cut. "It's just a scratch. I'm fine." The throbbing would eventually go away... I hoped. To distract myself from the pain, I pressed my hand over his heart, wanting to comfort him.

At the mention of my blood, Zade was suddenly at our side, cinnamon eyes searching my face. "We don't like it when you're hurt," he stated.

That made two of us… or actually, five. The dragons all wore identical frowns.

Issik, eager to get moving, pushed through the thick undergrowth of Viperus. The rest of the descendants shook their heads but followed.

I was passed from Jase to Zade to Kieran over the next few hours. One moment we were picking our way through overgrown thorns and brush, and then suddenly the path opened up again. Kieran set me down, allowing me to get my first real glimpse of the castle. My footsteps faltered, and I gasped. Up close, the castle was both impressive and frightening. The once white stone had become mottled with dark green, weathered from the infiltration of vines and moss. Torches lit up the walls, the soft glow of it a welcoming sight.

My eyes scanned left and right, trying to take everything in at once. "Holy crap," I muttered.

"It's something else, isn't?" Kieran replied, his voice coming from right behind me.

Words failed me. It wasn't only the sheer size of Viperus Keep that left me stranded in Stunned City. It was also the enormous stone statue of a viper that wound its way around the castle from the base to the tip-top of the highest tower.

Before I had a chance to mentally prepare myself for living inside a keep with a snake as the mascot, Kieran grabbed me by the waist, drawing me into the open field toward his home. "You're going to love it here, Blondie."

I highly doubted it, still, I didn't have the heart to tell him how uncertain I felt, but Jase knew. The tranquility dragon came up on the other side of me, taking my free hand in his. An instantaneous stream of calm flowed through my blood. Jase gave me a small smile of encouragement, using his gift to make me relax.

"Welcome to Viperus, Blondie," Kieran announced. Moonlight shone on the side of his face.

Zade's amber eyes flickered down to me. "If anything tries to bite me in my sleep, I'm setting it on fire," he mumbled.

Of course I could count on Zade to plant such a welcoming thought in my head.

"Don't be such a baby," Issik retorted, a small smile cracking his blank mask, before he strutted into the grassy clearing.

With Jase and Kieran's help, I hobbled through the front door of the castle. My pride was happy to be walking. As for first impressions, I didn't want to be seen as someone who couldn't stand on her own two feet. I wanted the staff at Viperus to respect me. The last thing I needed was another Harlow making things difficult. I didn't want any drama or trouble. Enough of that reigned in my life with the curse.

An elderly robust woman waited excitedly for Kieran's return. She reminded me of my grandma when she'd been alive. Her soft gray hair was fixed in a messy bun. Her brown eyes glowed at the sight of Kieran as she held her arms open wide.

A childish grin split his face. "Alice." Kieran picked her up, spinning her in a circle.

"Put me down, you imp." She playfully whacked him with a dish towel. From the smear of flour above her brow, she had just come from the kitchen. Kieran set her back down on her feet. "We've been preparing your favorite dinner, knowing how hungry the five of you would be after the day of travel." She in turn, gave each of the other dragons a long hug, before her sparkling brown eyes landed on me. "You must be Olivia."

I nodded, holding out my hand. "It's nice to meet you."

"She has manners, will you look at that. Not like the others you bring around here." I found myself engulfed in a warm hug. She smelled of cookies, sweet and homey.

I pinned Kieran with a look. *Others*, I mouthed.

Kieran cleared his throat. "Not to worry. They weren't who we were searching for."

Alice kept an arm around my shoulder and gave it a squeeze. "Ah, yes. But she is, I hear. And she's as lovely as a peach."

I adored Alice already.

The inside of Viperus Keep was laid out similarly to Jase's castle, which I found a blessing, but that was where the similarities ended. All of the doorway arches came to a point with the windows mirroring their tapered design, reminding me of a cathedral. Large chandeliers hung from the vaulted ceilings in the great room, casting soft flickers of light over the earth-toned tiled floors, and vines crept from the outside in, encasing the columns in green foliage and trimming the ceilings like garland.

"I can't believe you live here," I told Kieran, spinning around the room in awe.

"It's pretty spectacular. As a kid, I spent hours exploring the woods," he confessed, looking at the other dragons like they were wimps for being wary.

It was hard to think of them as little boys, given how long they'd lived, but I imagined the four of them were quite the troublemakers for their parents. And now they had lived on the isles for almost a hundred years, their lives frozen by a curse.

"I hope you brought your appetite, dear," Alice offered, looping an arm around my shoulders. She guided me farther into the castle, while the descendants followed close behind.

"I'm starved," I admitted.

Alice clucked her tongue. "Didn't they feed you in Wakeland?"

Jase made a snorting sound in the back of his throat.

How much did Alice know about me? She seemed to be well informed. Just how did Kieran have the time to come here and fill Alice in on all the details of my life? It was obvious Alice was someone he trusted.

We followed her into the kitchen where we were met by the fragrant smells of a feast. A girl with curly mahogany hair labored at the stove, peeling apples. A variety of pans steamed with meats, greens and potatoes rested atop the stove.

"Take a seat, and be quick about it before the food gets cold," Alice instructed us. "I won't let any of you go to bed hungry."

"You never do, Alice," Zade answered, taking a seat at the wooden table in the center of the room.

Chairs scraped as the rest of us sat. It seemed no matter where I was, the four of them surrounded me, but in a good way. I'd come to depend on it... on them. Two of the girls working in the kitchen appeared around us, each holding a plate of food. In a matter of minutes, the table was filled with meats, potatoes, fruits, breads, and other vegetables. It all looked delicious, and I wasn't sure where to start. I piled my plate, knowing my eyes were bigger than my belly.

As we ate, the four dragons caught Alice up on our last encounter with Tianna. No matter my efforts to dispel her from my mind, she wormed her way into my thoughts. Issik mistook my tiredness for fear… or so I told myself.

He leaned in close. "Don't worry about Tianna. We'll make sure she doesn't get to you."

And how did they propose to do that? She was a witch with magical means at her fingertips. I trusted the descendants without question, but there were some places not even they could shield me from Tianna—my dreams being one of those undefendable spots. Since the night she came for the Star of Tranquility, I hadn't been able to sleep. It wasn't a matter of if, but when, she'd pop back into our lives.

I pushed the potatoes around on my plate. "I know," I retorted, forcing myself to give Issik a small smile.

"How long do you think before she comes back for the stone?" Kieran asked the others. "We know she isn't about to give up that easily."

"No, that isn't Tianna's style. We'll worry about that when the time comes. For now, let's keep our focus on finding the Star of Poison," Jase instructed, his violet eyes catching mine briefly.

I swallowed. For the remainder of the meal, I stayed silent, listening to the four dragons strategize. It was obvious they had done this often, sitting around the dinner table discussing how they were going to kill Tianna. For me, plotting someone's death was a discomforting topic, even if the bitch deserved it.

Alice and the other two girls cleared the table, refusing to let me lift a finger, but having people wait on me made me uncomfortable. I didn't like not being able to pull my weight.

Issik stood at the same time I did, putting a hand at the small of my back when my legs wobbled. My ankle still throbbed, and my feet were blistered. "You look tired, Little Warrior," he stated, lines of worry creasing his forehead.

"You have no idea," I replied, leaning against his shoulder for support.

His hand slipped to my waist, partly lifting me up so my feet barely touched the ground, taking the pressure off my ankle. "To bed you go."

As glorious as a bed sounded, I longed for a bath to rid myself of the dirt, blood, and grime. "Any chance I could bathe before you tuck me in?" I asked wryly, as we left the kitchen with the others directly behind us.

"We could all use a shower," Kieran agreed with a wicked smile.

"That wasn't quite what I had in mind," I mumbled, shooting down the roguish dragon's insinuation.

"God, a shower would do wonders," Zade added, a look of longing sliding into his handsome features.

"You're telling me," Issik grunted, wrinkling his nose. "I can smell you from here. It's not pretty."

Zade cocked a dark brow, mischief in his gaze. "Is that so?"

I shook my head at the two shifters. "Fine, we'll all shower, just don't give each other bloody lips before we get there."

Four dragon mouths dropped open. "Is she serious?" Jase muttered, a look of surprise springing into his expression.

Kieran grinned. "Don't question it."

I rolled my eyes. Issik and I trailed behind the rest of them as we meandered through the castle. Kieran's home was like living in a greenhouse. The sound of gushing water tickled my ears as we reached a set of oversized double doors. Carved into the wood were a pair of ornate snakes twining into the shape of a *V*. Kieran pushed open the doors, revealing a beautiful, gently flowing waterfall. It rained over a cliff, dropping into a basin of fresh water, enclosed by swooping vines and bordered with white and blue wildflowers. The air smelled of clean moisture and sweet honeysuckle. Steam billowed from the basin.

My mouth dropped open in pure wonderment. "This is the shower?"

"Not too shabby," Zade whispered in my ear, his hot breath trailing down my neck.

Issik helped me approach the bank, and I held out my fingers, letting the stream of water run over my hand. The temperature was perfect.

"I want to live here. Right in this room."

Kieran chuckled. "It's yours to use whenever you like."

"I'm going to be the cleanest person in Viperus," I replied, grinning. Unlike the first time Kieran brought me to the bathhouse in Wakeland, I didn't hesitate to shed my clothes. It wasn't as if they hadn't seen me naked before, and I was absolutely dying to lose the sweat and grime. Flipping off my shoes and socks, I touched my bare feet to the rocky ground, which was smoother than it appeared. My shirt and pants were quick to follow, and I left them where they fell, leaving me in my undergarments.

Kieran folded his arms, not bothering to turn around while I made my way to the water, but neither did the others. Wading in, I closed my eyes and sighed in delight. I was bathing in utopia. Moving into the waterfall, the water cascaded over my face. This might have been worth the day of hell in the jungle.

When I opened my eyes, the four of them stood on the edge of the basin, watching me with mixed expressions. "What are you waiting for?" I called out to them, smoothing my wet hair off my face.

Suddenly, they were scrambling to disrobe and get into the water, like it was a race for the last slice of pizza in the world. I giggled, but the sound was overpowered by the splashes of the descendants jumping into the basin. Like a tidal wave, a surge of water came rushing right for me, and my laughter was washed away as I was pulled under. I came through the surface to find Kieran beside me.

"You look like a mermaid." His husky voice sent goosebumps over my arms. He came through the waterfall, dipping his head under the spray of water. His thick lashes stuck together, emphasizing the hue of his green eyes.

"I can guarantee you I don't swim like one."

A round of chuckles rumbled from the descendants.

Was I seriously bathing with four guys? What had possessed me to agree to such a thing? I was in over my head. "You guys think that's funny, huh?" I cupped my hands and tossed water into each of their faces.

For a stunned moment, they stared at me, and then I was sailing through the air. Kieran, who was the closest, had picked me up and tossed me to Zade.

Oh dear God. What have I done?

Zade, in turn, flung me to Issik, who launched me to Jase. Before he could pass me back to Kieran, I wound my arms around his neck. "No more," I warned, pushing his firm chest playfully. "You're making me dizzy."

Jase grinned at me, his eyes sparkling like the rascal that he was, but the glimmer swiftly shifted to something else as we both remembered our near nakedness. I should have loosened my fingers and floated away from him, back into neutral territory, but I didn't. None of us had discussed the other part of the bond. They could feel my emotions, but also we had an attraction between us. I didn't know how to handle it.

Was it okay that I wanted to kiss Jase, or would the others get jealous?

Was it okay that I wanted to kiss them all?

Did I even have a choice in the matter?

I acted on instinct, hoping it wouldn't steer me wrong. My arms tightened around Jase's neck, bringing his face closer to mine. The water lapped in a rhythmic motion against us, and I could feel his breath against my lips. "Don't you dare think about blowing any tranquility in my direction."

His smile returned, heartbreaking in its beauty. "I wouldn't dream of it. Now, are you going to kiss me?"

My head angled to the left, aligning our mouths. "I haven't made up my mind yet." I could sense the eyes of the others on us, and my blood raced.

I had no intention of playing favorites, but Jase was right here, tempting me with his dimples. His arms came to the sides of my hips, as the warm water licked over my breasts. The bra I had on offered very little coverage. Those violet eyes enthralled me, and everything else ceased to exist when Jase gazed at me. I didn't give myself the chance to think.

This was what I wanted.

This was what I'd dreamed about.

On the next wave, I pressed my lips to his and was met with resistance, as if he hadn't believed I would actually kiss him. But in the next breath, his will crumbled. His fingers dove into my hair, keeping my mouth to his, and my mind became filled with nothing but the taste and scent of Jase. I wrapped my legs around his waist, pressing our bodies together. The back of his knuckles stroked my cheek like velvet, and I deepened the kiss, needing more of him. My fingers played with the wet curls at the nape of his neck. I couldn't stop touching him. Stop kissing him. I was swimming in lust.

Parting my lips, I purred at the feeling of his tongue grazing against mine. I breathed his breath. How far was I willing to go? In the heat of the moment, I would have killed him if he stopped kissing me. So when his lips went lax against mine, I growled, wondering what I had done wrong. My lashes fluttered open, and I expected to see Jase's vibrant eyes gleaming at me. But they were still closed, and the arms that had been around me fell flaccidly to his sides. Trepidation reared its ugly head inside me.

"Jase?"

He didn't move, and his body was slowly sinking. Memories of Jase being attacked and falling into the lake rose up inside me, bringing panic with it.

"This isn't funny. Cut the crap."

Nothing. No twitching smirk. No dimples. No smart comebacks. In my arms, his body was lifeless and heavy, even with the help of the water.

What had I done to him? I racked my brain. We had only kissed. How could that render him unconscious? It was a question that would have to wait for an answer.

"Jase!" I yelled, shaking his shoulders.

As I shrieked, the other descendants surrounded me. They took one look at me then at Jase.

"What happened?" Issik demanded in a tone frosty enough to freeze over the basin.

"I-I don't know," I stammered, letting Zade take Jase out of my arms. The warm water suddenly felt frigid. "We were just… and then he went limp. What did I do?"

Snickers erupted from the three of them, and it took me a heartbeat to figure out what they found so entertaining. This was a life or death situation. I made one little comment about Jase being limp, and they got all childish on me.

"Grow up. That's not what I meant. How can you guys joke at a time like this?" I snapped.

Zade's brows rose as he pulled Jase's body to the edge of the basin. "I think you're forgetting one very important detail."

Kicking off in the water, I swam alongside Issik and Kieran. "What?" I urged him, feeling confused and scared for Jase.

"You were kissing," Kieran answered.

My gaze swung to the poison dragon, waiting for him to elaborate. "I fail to see how that is important." I knew the others were watching. That had been part of the appeal, but looking back, what had I been thinking? I didn't know what I was doing with these four guys. That was becoming quite clear.

"Maybe she kissed him to death," Issik offered, jumping out of the water to help Zade lift Jase out of it.

"Funny." Then I reconsidered it. "Wait. That's not possible, is it?"

Issik stood at the edge with his hands extended to pull me up. "Let's hope not."

I placed my hands in his, and Issik raised me out of the water like I weighed nothing. "Is he going to be okay?"

"Jase? Definitely. It is going to take a lot more than a kiss to get rid of this stubborn bastard." Issik handed me a towel before wrapping one around his lower half. I'd completely forgotten about our lack of clothing.

Securing the towel under my arms, I ran my eyes ran over Jase. He looked like he was sleeping peacefully, his chest rising and falling in an even pattern. *At least he is breathing.* I plucked a towel from a bamboo shelf and draped it over Jase's lower half.

Zade inspected Jase, beads of water dripping off his golden chest, before being caught by the cloth around his hips. "There doesn't seem to be anything wrong with him physically." His gaze slid to me.

"Why are you staring at me like I murdered your best friend?" He was being a little melodramatic. Zade's glare wasn't quite an accusation, but something made him suspicious of me.

"Damn," Zade cursed, forking a hand through his dark, wet hair. "We should have seen this coming."

My fingers clasped together. "Are you going to tell me what is going on?"

Zade grimaced. "We need to teach you how to harness your tranquility ability, or we all might be dozing."

I stared at Zade, taking in what he had said. *Tranquility.* It had been days since I found the stone and in return absorbed its power, but I hadn't thought much about it since. Apparently, I should have been more concerned with my newfound ability to breathe tranquility, because if I understood what Zade was saying, I had put Jase into a deep slumber.

Taking a step away from Jase, I shook my head. "I did this?"

"I'm afraid so, Little Gem," Zade replied in sympathy.

My bad ankle gave out on me, but Issik kept me on my feet. His hands grabbed either side of my arms, pulling me against his chest. My belly sunk. I was horrified. I couldn't believe I had done that without even knowing. Until I figured out how to control this power inside me, I wouldn't be kissing anyone. I was dangerous.

Kieran patted me on the back. "This is a first. You put the tranquility dragon to sleep. Priceless."

"What can I say? I can do the impossible."

"Don't despair," Issik whispered in my ear, feeling the gush of sadness inside me. "We could all use some sleep. It's been a long day."

I nodded. Words were unable to pass through the lump in my throat.

"You'll learn to control it. We all have," Kieran assured me, but it didn't do much to ease my distress.

Issik started to steer me out of the room. "Wait." I dug in the heel of my good foot, and Issik looked down at me with cool blue eyes. "We're not going to leave him here, are we?"

Issik glanced over his shoulder to where Jase still lay on the stone ground. Zade hovered over him. "Zade will make sure he is comfortable."

"Why don't I believe you?"

"It's not every day we get the opportunity to pull one over on Jase. We should be thanking you," Kieran added over my shoulder.

A practical joke? How could they conceive of such a thing right now? Sometimes they made me want to bang my head against the nearest wall.

Too tired to argue, I let Kieran and Issik lead me out of the shower room, and up the winding staircase. The curves reminded me of the snake curled around the outside of the castle, and I wouldn't be surprised if the layout mirrored the twining stone serpent's location. Kieran and I might need to have a talk about his choice of décor. Snakes were downright disgusting, but the inside of the keep redeemed itself. It was plush and a gardener's wet dream. Every corner had plants or flowers in it. Issik ducked under a vine hanging from an archway.

The most disturbing thought entered my mind as I watched him. What kind of critters lived in the vines and the plants? They were all over the castle. "Hot Lips, what is with the snake theme?"

Kieran didn't blink at his nickname. They'd gotten used to the names I'd given them. "Are you afraid of reptiles?"

Dumb question. "Snakes, spiders, bugs, all the usual creepy-crawly shit."

Issik smirked… well, a smirk for Issik meant his lips barely moved. "Just put them to sleep."

Kieran chuckled, and my hand automatically smacked him in the chest. The poisonous dragon frowned at me.

"Nervous tic." I smiled sweetly.

No one bought that excuse, but we had come to a door, and Kieran pushed it open, sweeping his arms in a welcoming gesture. "Your chambers await. Bug free, of course."

I walked into the room, looking around. "You swear? I don't want to wake up staring at an eight-legged freak." The bed in the center of the room was supported by bamboo stalks and covered in a soft sage duvet. Its cozy exterior beckoned me.

Kieran strutted into the room, drawing the curtains closed at the window. The room was submerged in darkness. "If you have any unexpected visitors, just yell. We won't be far away." He grabbed a clean shirt from one of the drawers, and slipped it over my head.

Pushing my arms through the sleeves, the towel fell to the floor. I padded across the floor and climbed onto the bed. "Where will you be…" My words got cut off as Issik dropped his towel to throw on a pair of nylon shorts, giving me a view of his butt. I swallowed. "…staying?"

"I'll be in the room next to yours, and Zade will be in the other," Issik answered me, completely oblivious of my jaw still on the ground.

"Maybe one of us should stay with her. If Tianna…" I locked eyes with Kieran.

He didn't need to finish the thought. We all knew what would happen if the witch showed up. T-R-O-U-B-L-E. That's what. Like the kind that would get me killed, thus getting the descendants killed. None of us wanted to die.

"We could take shifts. Rotate each night," Kieran proposed.

Did I get a say in this? How did I feel about having one of them sleep in the same room with me?

Hot.

Bothered.

And worried—what if I accidentally breathed on one of them in my sleep? The descendants would be no help to me if I constantly put them in a deep slumber. "I'm not sure that is a good idea."

Kieran arched his pierced brow, pushing his damp hair away from his face. He looked different without the spikes, but still handsome. "Two against one. You're overruled."

My head hit the pillow. "You guys are lucky I'm too tired to argue."

Issik came up to the edge of the bed, tucking the covers in around me. "We can discuss it in the morning." He turned to Kieran. "I'll stay tonight."

Snuggling deeper into the bed, I waited for Kieran to protest. It would be like them to start fighting over who got to spend the night, but he surprised me.

Leaning over the bed, Kieran pressed a gentle kiss to my forehead.

"Sleep tight, Blondie. Don't let the bed bugs bite." His lips curled against my skin.

My fingers gripped onto the blanket tighter. "I should breathe on you," I uttered without heat behind the words. I listened to Kieran's feet clatter over the floor as he left, probably smiling to himself the entire way, the damn devil.

I searched the darkness for Issik and spotted him in the corner, settling into a chair. Shadows danced across his face, giving him an aura of danger. "Are you planning on sleeping in the chair?"

"I've slept in far worse places. There's no need to worry about me."

But I did worry about him, and after the day we'd had, he deserved something better than being scrunched into a rickety chair in the corner. I fidgeted on the bed for another minute before I gave in and glared at him.

"This is ridiculous. I can't sleep knowing you're over there. The bed is big enough for us both." And I wanted him close, but not close enough I could unintentionally knock him out for good. I patted the bed beside me. "What are you waiting for?"

His long legs stretched out in front of him so that his toes almost touched the bedframe. "I'm deciding if it's a good idea for me to be close to you."

"Because of my tranquility?"

He shook his head. "Something like that wouldn't keep me from you."

The way he said those words—so possessive—had my pulse racing.

"I'm not sure I trust myself to sleep next to you."

"You did it before," I reminded him.

"And I didn't get much sleep," he stated dryly.

"Fine," I grumbled. "Be a stubborn, uncomfortable mule." I closed my eyes, telling myself to forget about Issik. I lasted less than five minutes. My eyes popped open to find Issik's gaze on me. In the dark, his light blue irises popped. "If I'm going to get any sleep tonight, you can't sit there staring at me."

"And if you keep talking, neither of us is going to sleep," he countered. Silence greeted us both as we engaged in an epic stare-down. Issik finally gave in, and inside, I squealed like a little girl at the candy shop.

He rose from the chair to walk around to the other side of the bed. The mattress dipped under his weight, making it so I rolled toward the center of the bed. Our arms were side by side when he lay down, and we both stared up at the ceiling. I angled my head to the side, checking to see if his eyes were closed.

He peeked at me from under half-lidded lashes. "Happy now?"

I grinned, snuggling deep into the blanket and closing my eyes. "Very."

He let out a long exhale.

As I was about to drop off into deep sleep, Issik's husky voice pulled me back from the edge of a dream. It had been a really good dream too. "So I guess you like Jase."

My shoulders moved in an unseen shrug. "I guess, but I like you too." My eyes lifted to his, gauging his reaction.

Like most things with Issik, it was hard to see what he was thinking. "We've never shared a girl before."

I understood how he felt. Unsure. Curious. And maybe even a little scared. "Me neither," I replied.

His lips twitched.

"That's not what I meant." I bumped my shoulder into his. "I've never had feelings for more than one person at a time before. Let alone four, but I can't choose between you. I won't." It was important I made that clear now.

"Haven't you already?"

Did I detect a hint of disappointment? Where was this coming from? I took a stab in the dark. "Why? Because you haven't kissed me? Not that it matters now. You couldn't kiss me even if you wanted to."

"Tranquility wouldn't keep me from kissing you," he answered calmly, ensnaring me with his cool gaze.

There went my heart, bumping in my chest. "You guys are going to drive me crazy."

A smile cracked his serious demeanor. "Now you know how we feel." Issik leaned over and kissed the tip of my nose. His wintery breath washed over my face, tickling my lips. "Goodnight, Little Warrior."

Now I understood what he meant about not getting any sleep. The scent of him teased my senses until late into the night, following me into my dreams.

When I woke, my world was washed in green, and my mind was muddled. A hundred different shades collided around me. Through the sheer curtains, beams of sunlight streamed across the floor. As I blinked, it all hit me at once.

Oh yes, Kieran.

I'd been whisked off to Viperus.

Just as I'd become somewhat familiar with Wakeland Keep, they threw me into another castle with as many corridors, stairs, and rooms. I was back at square one. And to make things more complicated than they already were, I had this ability I didn't know how to deal with or control.

Sighing, I felt something pinning my belly to the bed. Glancing down, I saw a muscular arm draped over me, and my heart swelled. Coolness radiated from the ice dragon, who in sleep looked less menacing and softer. I reached out, brushing a lock of blond hair off the side of his sharp cheek.

If I knew the descendants, today would be another long day. We had a stone to find, so I took these few precious moments of peace, to study the dragon who guarded his heart fiercely. He wasn't one to open up, but Issik made me want to be the one who melted the ice he surrounded himself with so fiercely.

I couldn't think of a better face to wake up to, and a smile spread over my lips. Our legs had intertwined during the night, and Issik must have some crazy leg hair because it tickled my thigh. Tilting my head down to look, I saw a bug the size of a Snickers bar scampering across my leg. I kicked as hard as I could, screaming. Long. Loud. And piercing. It sounded as if I was being held at gunpoint.

I was going to kill Kieran and his jungle.

If the bug didn't eat me first.

Issik jumped up, dragon scales peppering his torso. No sooner had he sat up than I was scrambling into his lap. The safest place to be during an invasion of critters was on higher ground.

"What's wrong? Where is she?" His frosty eyes glowed while his arms secured me against his chest.

I pointed my finger at the end of the bed, my bravery no bigger than a teaspoon at the moment. "There. I-it was a bug." I waited for him to kick into exterminator mode, but he just sat there, staring at my face.

"A bug?" he echoed. "Are you telling me that you woke me from a dead sleep, screaming at the top of your lungs, for a bug?"

"Shit. We don't have bugs like that in Illinois."

The door to my room burst open, and a shirtless Zade dominated the doorway. "What happened? Are you hurt? Did Tianna—" His voice cut off when he saw me situated in Issik's lap.

I groaned, dropping my forehead onto Issik's shoulder, who ran a hand through his hair.

"It was a bug," he told Zade.

The Golden God leaned a shoulder against the door, eyeing me with amusement. "I warned you there are bugs."

"You could have told me that they are as big as my hand!"

"This was more fun."

And there went my good mood. "I need coffee," I grumbled, removing myself from atop Issik.

That was twice I'd landed in ice prince's lap in less than twenty-four hours. It was twice I'd slept with him in the same bed, and yet, he was the only one who hadn't kissed me. Why did that bother me?

A fresh pot of steaming coffee waited downstairs in the kitchen for me. Alice was my favorite person in the world. Along with the caffeine kick were pancakes… and Jase, already on what appeared to be his second stack. His jet black hair was messy from sleep, and he turned those violet eyes on me as we walked into the room.

"How did you sleep last night?" Zade asked, razzing Jase.

Jase swallowed a mouthful of food, his eyes narrowing on Zade and Issik. "What the hell happened?"

Zade looked at me with a stupid grin on his face, while and Issik's lips twitched. Kieran chose that moment to walk into the room. "Did I miss it?"

"Olivia?" Jase called to me. "Do you want to tell me what these idiots are talking about?"

"Hmm," I replied, plucking a piece of fruit from the bowl on the counter, and shoving it in my mouth. If I was stuffing my face, then I didn't have to admit what I had done. "Not really," I confessed.

Setting his fork down, he folded his hands on the table. "I'm waiting."

My eyes darted around the table, looking at the others for help. They were useless. Taking my cup of coffee, I sat down at the table next to him. Giving him my "remember I'm just a girl" and "this isn't my fault" look, I told him what happened. "I might have accidentally put you to sleep when we kissed."

Jase didn't move a muscle. "You're joking."

"I wish I was," I muttered, taking a sip of coffee.

His eyes darkened, flickering around the table at Kieran, Zade, and Issik, who were all doubled over with silent laughter. I wished I had longer legs so I could kick each one of them in the shin from here.

"I'll deal with the three of you later." Leaning back in his chair, Jase focused back on me. "We're going to need to move up those lessons I had planned, it seems, but not today. Do you think you could avoid knocking any of us out for one day?"

"As long as none of you try to kiss me," I snapped back at him.

A sardonic twist spread over his lips. "Fair enough."

The table erupted in groans of complaint from everyone but Jase and me.

Jase picked his fork up to resume tackling his food, but first, he gave the others a lecture. "I'm trusting you guys can keep your lips off her for a few days. We can't afford to have anyone sleeping on the job, not when we're so close. Olivia needs all the protection we can give her. There is no room for mistakes."

We passed the food around and piled it on our plates. To an outsider, it would have appeared that everyone had ignored Jase, but that wasn't the case. They had heard him. They just chose not to comment. For one, it would piss off Jase to get no responses. And secondly, food was in front of them. Jase should have known better than to have tried to reason with them when food was involved.

I sank into my chair, nursing my coffee and assessing how I was feeling about the no kissing rule. It made perfect sense, but then why was I so put out about it?

My day didn't get much better.

As expected, after breakfast, Jase went into commander mode, barking orders, and then the five of us were back in the woods. It all happened so fast. One minute I was grabbing my second cup of coffee, and the next, I was ushered outside, barely awake and functioning. I didn't even know what the game plan was.

Throwing my blonde hair into a messy bun, I glanced up at the sun beating down on us. "Where are we going?" I whined.

Kieran startled me, suddenly appearing at my side. I'd been concentrating on the ground, looking for hidden holes. "These woods are filled with tombs and burial grounds of our people. It might be a good place to search for the stone."

Graves? Not the first hiding place that came to my mind. And honestly, I wasn't looking forward to disturbing the resting place of the dead. Talk about bad mojo. A witch had already cursed them. Pissing off a bunch of ghosts did not sound like a great idea. But what did I know?

"Are you guys trying to get me to fall through the world again?" My eyes continued staring hard at the ground in front of me. The last thing I needed was to twist my other ankle.

Speaking of which, my injured one was feeling much better. The pressure of my weight didn't seem to bother it. My explanation: one of my dragons had done something to speed up the healing process.

Kieran lifted a branch out of my way, waiting for me to pass under it. "How many times do I have to apologize?"

Mischief lit up my eyes. "How about a kiss instead?"

Zade and Jase laughed. I even got a chuckle out of Issik. Glad they found me so humorous, but it was Kieran's slow smile that dazzled me. Surrounded in miles and miles of dense woods, Kieran had never looked more in his element; he'd never looked more attractive to me.

"Don't tempt me."

They were the ones tempting me. "When do the dragons get to

come out?" I asked, thinking this would go a lot faster on a dragon's back.

Kieran shook his head, a smile tugging at his lips. "You're going to be very distracting."

"I could be annoying or boring instead," I offered.

His fingers brushed the loose strands of hair sticking to the back of my neck. "No, I think I prefer distracting."

A shiver danced down my spine, taking on a whole new meaning when a shrill vibrated through the woods. The sound was followed by two dark shadows flying over the towering pines. Their wings weren't quite as large as a dragon's, but they were still impressive in size.

"You might get your wish," Jase rumbled, his eyes glowing.

I knew what that look meant. He was about to shift.

In seconds, silvery purple scales papered Jase's entire body as his muscles and bones expanded. The end result was a pissed off dragon. His form was too large for the forest, and trees bent and crunched under his weight. Throwing back his angular head, he let out a roar from deep within his chest into the sky.

In answer, the squawking noise sounded again, and my elation at seeing Jase's dragon was overshadowed by the things circling overhead.

"Griffins," Zade hissed.

Oh, hell to the no.

I was definitely not a fan of the large flying birds with the legs of a lion and a serpent's tail.

"Stay with her," Issik instructed Zade and Kieran, who sandwiched me between their firm shoulders.

And then the viking ripped off his shirt, shifting into a fierce dragon with white and blue scales that looked like an ice storm— jagged and wicked. Kicking off his hind legs, Issik took to the sky, unfazed by the tree branches whipping him.

My arms wrapped around myself. "Does this mean Tianna has found us already?" I asked in a small voice.

Kieran's gaze zeroed in on the griffins. "I'm afraid so, Blondie."

"That was fast," I muttered to myself.

Craning my neck upward, I searched the sky. On the ground, under the thick foliage, it was hard to see what was happening. Then, of course, there were two giant men towering over me. I understood it was for my own safety, but it made keeping track of my other two dragons difficult. How was I to know if they were hurt?

"They'll be fine," Zade assured, reading the concern that had soured my expression.

I glared sideways at him. "I thought your emotion was anger."

A ghost of a smile appeared on his lips. "It is, but I don't need to feel your emotions to know you're worried. It is all there in your face."

Kieran breathed hard, vengeance shining in his eyes, which were a startling shade of emerald. "Tianna might send her goons to keep track of us, but they're no match for Issik and Jase."

I could sense his desire to shift and the resolve it took to stay in his human form. "I don't understand her. She wants the stones, wants their power, and yet, she is making it damn near impossible for me to find them."

Zade shook his head. "It is a waste of time to try and get inside the head of a witch."

Our discussion was interrupted, when something rammed into a tree off to our left. I whipped toward the direction of the splintering wood. Jase had slammed one of the griffins into a tree, and had its wing pinned with his claw. Feathers drifted down from the branches, while the beast shrieked, pecking at Jase with his large beak.

I was about to take action when Issik and the other griffin hit the ground like an earthquake. Grass and rocks trembled under my feet. Kieran caught my elbow to steady me as I lost my balance from the impact. My palms flattened on his chest.

Rendered immobile, I stood curled against Kieran and watched Issik fight the griffin. His jaws snapped like thunder cracking in the sky. More feathers coated the ground in a mangled mess. The griffin scored Issik's underbelly with its claws, and the dragon reared its head, letting out a roar of anger and pain.

I jerked into motion, running toward Issik, but Kieran and Zade were there to stop me before I made it two feet. Kieran wrapped his arms around my waist, pulling my back against his chest. "It's safer if you stay with us," he murmured in my ear.

Frantically, I flung my gaze back to Issik. *Is he okay? Had the griffin hurt him more?* My heart thrashed in my chest. I couldn't lose him. Any of them. Not now.

It turned out I had worked myself into a tizzy for nothing. As my eyes landed on Issik and the griffin, Issik opened his large jaw and wrapped his teeth around the griffin's neck. Jerking his head in one quick movement, he ripped the head from the creature's body. The ice dragon tossed his long neck, releasing the feathery head. It rolled on the ground before coming to a stop. A splattered trail of blood painted the earth.

I tried not to gag at the gruesome sight.

Burying my face in Kieran's chest, I turned away. His arms came around me, keeping me close. "Don't weep for her spies," he murmured, brushing his lips through my hair.

If Kieran had been Jase, he would sense it wasn't sadness or pity I felt, but fear. Peeking through my curtain of tangled and loose strands of hair, I saw Issik watched me with intense eyes. My actions might have seemed as if what he had done revolted me, which in a way it had, but it wasn't Issik I was disgusted with. He had done what needed to be done to keep us safe. I didn't fault him for that. If anyone was to blame, it was Tianna.

I projected my thoughts toward him, remembering he could hear me. *"Are you okay?"*

The ice dragon's angular head gave a curt nod. *"I didn't mean to frighten you."*

I took a step forward, but Kieran didn't let me go far. One more griffin remained. I huffed. *"I was taken by surprise. I'm not afraid of you,"* I assured him.

The beating of wings flapping in the air reached my ears. Jase hovered over us, a griffin clenched in his claws. Releasing it from his clutches, the beast fell to the ground. Zade stood over the creature and pounced, grabbing it around the neck. "She's ours," he growled at the griffin. "Take that back to your witch."

Damn straight I was.

Then he pitched the creature aside like it was worthless. The beast whimpered as it rolled on the ground, eventually coming up on its feet. It gave one long caw and pushed off the ground with its hind legs, taking to the sky. The descendants let him go to deliver a warning to Tianna.

Another crisis averted, but there was no time to rest. Tianna knew where we were, which would make finding the Star that much harder.

Jase and Issik shifted out of their dragon forms, giving me a nice view of their firm tushes, and I tried to remind my hormones that now were not the time to get excited. We had just escaped one of Tianna's famous attacks. I needed to focus.

The descendants had come prepared for the unexpected dragon shifts. Kieran tossed Issik and Jase clothes from the backpack he'd brought along. Issik was about to slip on a T-shirt when he turned around and faced me. Winter swirled in his harsh steel eyes. A red cut slashed across his chest from his right shoulder to his left hip. It was raw and beaded with blood.

A sharp inhale burned my lungs. "You're hurt," I whispered, moving toward him as I remembered the griffin clawing him. My hand extended, but I didn't touch him for fear of causing him more pain. "And don't tell me it's just a scratch."

Issik kept his gaze on mine, even when his fingers wrapped around my wrist, bringing my hand to his heart. "Well, it is. Griffin claws are sharp, but they won't kill me."

"I'd hug you, but I don't want to get blood on my shirt."

He smirked. "Good thing I don't care about your shirt." In the next breath, I was engulfed in his cool arms. And he was right: I didn't give a damn about my shirt.

He was alive. That was all that really mattered.

And finding the Star of Poison, of course.

One might think after an attack by a pair of griffins, we'd call it a day, and head back to Viperus Keep. Nope. Not Jase.

We pushed on, heading to one of the burial grounds.

Yippee.

I waded through the brush, pushing aside branches and swatting at bugs. "Remind me again whose genius idea it was to go traipsing around the woods midday?" This seemed to be the question on everyone's mind. An added bonus was it annoyed Jase.

"Jase," Issik, Zade, and Kieran groaned in unison.

"Do you want to break this curse or not?" Jase countered in his defense. "The Star of Poison is out here… somewhere."

"It might be easier to find a unicorn or the pot of gold at the end of a rainbow." My tone was naturally sarcastic—all part of my charm. The descendants loved me for it.

Kieran took a pause to wipe the sweat off his brow with the back of his hand. Zade and Issik continued walking a few paces up ahead of us.

"Why is it so hot today? It's not like we're in volcano country," I complained.

Despite the thin material of my clothes, everything stuck to my skin, including dirt, bugs, leaves, and anything else I managed to come into contact with then. "I'd trade my right arm for a pool right now."

"There will be no loss of appendages," Jase added sternly.

"Geez, Dimples, I didn't mean it literally."

"The sun is brutal today. Unusually so," Kieran admitted, glancing up through the green canopy of leaves. It offered little protection from the blazing sun. "Viperus is never this hot."

"Something is messing with the isles' climate," Jase concluded.

There were two things I could think of that might be responsible, Tianna or the stones. They were the only items on the isles that had the power to do something like this.

A scowl creased Kieran's brow. It was rare to the see the carefree dragon frowning. "It has to be the curse."

Jase nodded. "My thoughts exactly. We need to find the next stone sooner rather than later. I have a feeling things are going to get more complicated, if you know what I mean." He peered at Kieran over my head, sharing a look.

I raised my hand, wondering if it was a good idea to be doing that while walking, but it was too late. The deed was done. "No, I don't know what you mean. Can one of you explain?"

"Put your hand down," Jase ordered. "You're going to trip over something and break a bone."

Kieran flashed me a grin. "Don't worry, I'll catch you."

"There is no way in hell I'm going to trip," I proudly defended, tipping my chin up. "You guys act like I can't walk and chew gum at the same time." The truth was I probably couldn't, but that was beside the point. "I can walk with both my freaking arms in the air if I want to, thank you very much." I proceeded to show them how awesome my coordination was. "I'm far too poised to—" Then I tripped… over a tombstone nonetheless.

Really? What are the chances?

I miraculously stayed on my feet, but it was instinct for the descendants to save me. Kieran's hand stabilized my elbow, and I couldn't remember if it had been there before or after I tripped.

"You were saying?" Kieran asked, grinning like the devil himself.

I blew the hair out of my face and glowered at him. "Well, who the hell put a gravestone right in the middle of the path?"

The others gathered around. "Let's spread out, cover more ground."

Kieran shadowed my movements, and I assumed he was assigned Olivia babysitting detail, not that I minded. The only things we were going to find here were spirits wanting to possess my body, or talk to me from the other side. I'd had enough of ghosts. No need to encourage more.

"Do you sense anything?" Kieran asked, leaning close to me and whispering in my ear.

I stopped in my tracks and glanced over at him. "I'm not a stone detector. There isn't an internal beacon in me that sends an alert if there is a magical dragon crystal nearby."

Kieran straightened up, rubbing a hand over the back of his neck while pondering me. I tended to confuse the dragon descendants. It was obvious they'd never dealt with a girl from the city. Or I could be extra unique. "It doesn't hurt to try. Who knows what you're capable of? Did you ever think you'd be able to render people unconscious by breathing on them?"

"Uh, no."

"There you go." Kieran put his hands on my shoulders and steered me to the center of the misty graveyard. Carved stones were embedded in the green grass all around me. "Now close your eyes."

"This is never going to work," I stated, crossing my arms over my chest. My flimsy shirt was nearly see-through from sweat, but I couldn't have cared less. They had seen me naked before.

"We won't know unless you try. Now stop being stubborn and concentrate," he insisted.

"On what? I don't know what I'm supposed to be focusing on."

Kieran heaved a heavy groan. "Olivia, close your eyes. Envision a stone just like the one you found but emerald in color."

"That's not how this works," I told him. At least I was pretty sure it wasn't.

"Olivia," he warned me.

This was stupid, but the only way I would get him off my back was to do what he suggested, no matter how silly it seemed. Shifting my weight to one side, I let my eyes drift shut. Leaves rustled in the air with a gentle breeze that did nothing to relieve the heat. As I continued to listen, waiting for something fucking spectacular to happen, my mind wandered.

I wonder what Alice is making for dinner. Suddenly, I was famished.

Is that a wolf howling?

Are there wolves in the Veil? It's probably something way worse.

Then I got a whiff of Kieran and that was it. My concentration was shot to hell. I found myself leaning in toward the smell, drawn to him like a magnet. I had a beacon all right—a beacon for the descendants.

Kieran must have felt it as well. His body brushed up against mine, and I sunk into him. "What do you feel?"

My cheeks flamed. "You don't want to know."

The warmth of his chuckle breezed through my hair. "What am I going to do with you?"

I could think of a few things.

"Are you focusing?"

On the sound of your deep, husky voice, I thought, but he probably didn't want to hear that. Or did he? My eyes fluttered open after feeling absolutely nothing but the tingling awareness of Kieran's proximity. I turned to face him. He watched me with keen interest in his bright eyes. Nibbling on my lower lip, I savored his intense stare and soft mouth. The air was charged between us and had me wanting nothing more than to press my lips to his.

But I couldn't.

Kieran must have forgotten about my little ability to put people to sleep because he leaned forward, his passion pulling him to me like a baited fish. I opened my mouth to stop him, but Kieran swooped in, taking possession of my lips.

My hands steadied me on his chest while I struggled to control myself, but the need to melt into the sweet sensations he offered overwhelmed all my rational thoughts. The cool metal of his lip ring slid smoothly over my tender lips. I sighed.

And that was all it took to remind me what my breath could do.

I shoved at his pecs. "Kieran. You can't kiss me."

He blinked, staring down at me with heavy, half-lidded eyes. "Why? Because we might get caught making out on the job? Don't worry about Jase. I can handle him."

I snorted, shaking my head. "I'm not worried about Jase. I don't want to have to catch your massive body when I accidentally knock you out."

"It wouldn't be the first time I've been exposed to tranquility. I can't tell you the number of times Jase has hit me with his sleeping vapors."

"That explains a lot," I retorted, but my feisty tone went right over his Mohawk head.

Kieran took a step back from me. "Did you get anything before you decided to kiss me?"

A short puff escaped my lips. "First off, you kissed me. And secondly, I told you it wouldn't work."

"Or maybe you didn't try."

"Don't you think I want to find the stone?" Each word I filled with sharpness.

"I don't know what you want."

My arms flew up in the air. "You are impossible." I stalked away from Kieran to search out a descendant with half a brain. Zade found me first.

He strode beside me, bringing a wave of heat with him, not that I needed more. "Did you find anything?" he asked with hope shimmering in his cinnamon eyes.

My hands landed on my hips, and I narrowed my eyes as I scanned the sacred ground. "Only a bunch of graves and an imbecile."

Zade lifted a brow, giving me a funny expression.

"Don't ask. Can we go home now?" I'd had enough stone searching for the day.

His lips quirked. "You're definitely talking about Kieran."

"I'll never understand the four of you."

"That probably makes us even."

He might have had a point.

I nearly jumped for joy, when Jase and Issik found us a few minutes later to call it a day. If I never had to hike through the woods again, I would die a happy camper. I knew the likelihood of that actually happening was low, but a girl could dream. Days like today made the task of finding the stones seem impossible. We needed something to point us in the right direction.

I needed to fall down another hole, and have a chat with a spirit. They seemed to be partial to appearing in water. Why was that?

The walk back was quiet. Zade ended up carrying me most of the way. My little legs had given up on me. With my head resting on his strong shoulder, we reached the castle as the last slivers of dusk disappeared behind the trees.

It was hard to not let disappointment color my mood, even after a hot meal from Alice, the goddess of the kitchen. Unlike last night, I didn't suggest a group shower. I'd learned my lesson. The descendants were more than I could deal with all at once.

As I headed up the stairs to my room, my head continued to fill with negativity and defeat, but one smile from a dragon shifter at the top of the landing had the ability to turn my frown upside down.

Jase's fingers slipped under my chin, tilting my face upward to meet his gaze. "Why do you look like you lost your best friend?"

My shoulders fell, relaxing in his presence. "Sorry. Having a bad day."

He weaved his fingers with mine, leading me down the hall. "Compared to some of your other days, today wasn't half bad."

Maybe, but that didn't mean it still didn't suck some serious ass.

When we got to my room, the other three dragons were hanging out in front of my door. Breezing past them, I ditched my shoes and let down my hair, shaking it out. "So who's staying tonight?" I asked, spinning around to face the four descendants.

Everyone volunteered at once, including Issik, who had already had a turn. I should have known better than to open this can of worms. It would have been less complicated if I had picked one to stay, but I couldn't do that either. We needed a system, or I could count on fights breaking out each night before bed, which was the last thing I needed —more chaos.

They all talked over each other, and their voices were growing louder. It was only a matter of time before the chest bumping and fist flying started.

Standing in the middle of the room with my arms crossed, I tapped my foot, trying to decide which one I would punch in the dick first. How else would I get them to stop being complete animals? They were lucky I liked them... sometimes. I wanted to knock their heads together, but I was too damn tired to get physical with them.

"Hey!" I bellowed, my voice carrying out the door and down the corridor. "Enough!"

Four muscular men froze with their firsts in midair.

"If you guys need to beat the shit out of each other to figure out who is staying, take it downstairs. I'm going to bed."

I didn't wait for a response. I gave them my back, and went to the bamboo dresser in the corner of the room. Flipping my shirt over my head, I dug through the top drawer, pulling out an oversized T-shirt, and tugged it on. I wiggled out of my pants, leaving them where they fell. The silence I was appreciating erupted into dragon chaos once again.

Gah!

Rolling my eyes, I shuffled barefoot across the textured wood floors as I ignored the quartet. I climbed into bed, let my exhausted bones sink into the padding, and closed my eyes, coaxing my mind to sleep with the deep voices of Issik, Jase, Kieran, and Zade storming around me. It was hard, considering the stress of the last few days, and the loud arguing, but whether it was exhaustion or something else, my dreams pulled me under.

The streets of Chicago blurred as I came to the Veil, flying on a dragon, and of course, the witch was there. Tianna's face rose through the haze of images, becoming clearer as I fell deeper into my subconscious. She'd found a way to get to me where the descendants couldn't protect me.

Fucking bitch.

She stood inside an elaborate iron gate, her deep red hair blowing in the wind. "You can't run forever."

I put on my best impression of being as bored as rocks. "Who says I'm running?"

Her blood red lips curled. "Isn't that what you do? Run away?"

My toes dug into the dirt. "Don't pretend like you know anything about me."

Her hips swayed, in a sexiness I could never emulate while she sauntered toward me. "I know how much you care for the dragon descendants. I know how far you're willing to go to save them."

"I know a few things too. I know you're a bitch. I know you can't get the power you desire unless I find the stones. How's that working out for you?" I asked with a smug grin.

Her creamy hand flew in the air to strike me, but it stopped just shy of my left cheek. The sudden display of rage caught me off guard. I flinched. It looked as if someone had a bit of a temper simmering under the surface. Her eyes harbored flames of hate. "Watch what you say to me. My patience can be... prickly at times. I can make things very difficult for you, Olivia."

I shuddered at the way my name rolled of her lips. Hadn't she already been doing that? This time, I kept my trap shut, not brave enough to push the witch and her wrath. "What do you want from me? What is the point of you invading my sleep?"

Her red nails skimmed across her equally bold lip color. "I like that you're a get-to-the-point kind of girl. It makes our relationship less complicated. I want the stones. I thought that was clear. Time is running out, so I'm here to give you a gentle nudge."

I snorted. "A nudge? What do you think I've been doing? Knitting a blanket?"

"Just remember I'll be around to whisper in your ear, and give you a snippet of motivation from time to time."

That sounded ominous. I didn't like it. Not. One. Single. Bit.

I was about to tell her what she could do with her threat when a sudden pecking noise broke through my slumber, severing the dream. It sounded like someone was throwing rocks at my window. My first thought, it was one of the descendants trying to be cute, but would they go outside when I slept right next door? It didn't make sense, especially when one of them was sleeping beside me. I blinked, turning my head to see which one it was. Kieran had curled up next to me.

Slipping out of bed, I padded over to the window and peeked down into the courtyard below. A woman in a pale dress stood at the base of the castle—directly below my room. Her skin had an iridescent glow about it almost as if she was transparent. I was positive if I had been in reach and touched her, my hand would have passed right through her form. She looked like a ghost.

I recognized her. She was the same woman I had seen in the water after my fall. I was sure of it. Spinning around, I raced toward the door. If I hurried, maybe I could catch her. It was evident she wanted to talk to me, or why else had she awoken me? I desperately wanted to speak with her. She was my link to finding the Star of Poison.

As I bounded across the floor, my foot slipped on a discarded T-shirt. Kieran's. I cursed him to hell and back while falling backward. With a loud thump, I landed on my ass, a shriek escaping my lips.

Kieran woke up with a start, his green eyes wide and aglow in the dark. They zeroed in on me sprawled over the floor. "What are you doing down there?"

I scrambled to my feet. "I need to do something. Hang on." I threw open the door.

"Olivia!" he bellowed, but I was already running down the hall.

Please let her still be there.

"Olivia!" Kieran yelled again, but this time he was chasing after me and gaining. If he caught me, I might never get my chance to talk to the ghost woman.

Whipping around the corner, I wound down the stairs, doing my best to be quick and not tumble all the way to the bottom. Kieran grabbed me around the waist before I could reach the first floor. "Let me go," I screeched, my feet struggling to touch the ground.

"What the hell is your deal?" he growled through his teeth, his python arms pinning me to him.

My body wriggled like a fish out of water, trying to break free. "I told you. There's something I need to do."

He took us down the last few steps to flat ground. "If you tell me what it is that has you jumping out of bed in the middle of the night, then we can discuss if it is a good idea."

I rolled my head back, letting it rest on Kieran's chest. "Gah! You're so frustrating."

"Thanks, Blondie."

We were wasting precious time. If I was going to have any chance of talking to her, I needed Kieran to trust me. "I saw someone outside," I confessed.

I couldn't see his face, but I knew he wore a look of consternation. "And you thought you would go check it out alone."

Silence.

He set me down on my feet and spun me around to face him, but wisely kept his hands on my shoulders in case I decided to bolt again. "Do I need to remind you there is a witch out there who would do everything in her power to kill you?"

"She needs me alive to find the stones," I pointed out stubbornly.

"Fine. But there are a million other things she could do to you."

We could argue all night, but then I would miss my opportunity. "I don't have time for this. Release me. Or come with me if you're afraid it's a trap."

Kieran studied me before exhaling, and I could see he was reluctant to let me free. "I better not regret this."

The moment his grasp loosened, I was running, but Kieran was quick, slipping his fingers into mine. I tugged him along with me, urging him to pick up the pace. My heart was in my throat when we burst outside, the evening wind blowing over my face. I froze as I glanced to the spot where I'd seen the woman.

There was no one. No ghost. No woman in a white dress. Disappointment dropped in my belly like a heavy stone, and my brain was in denial, but my instincts told me the woman had been here; I wasn't losing my marbles.

"Tianna is probably playing games with you." Kieran's deep voice came from beside me, his fingers squeezing mine in comfort.

I couldn't deny he might be right, but I didn't think so. The witch had been screwing with my mind and invading my dreams, and this felt different. "Maybe."

Swallowing hard, I moved farther into the courtyard, needing to make certain she had disappeared. The trees surrounding the castle danced with the wind, and I shivered.

I'm not going crazy. I'm not going to let her win.

Waking up, I felt like something Tianna had dug up from a witches' burial ground, something half alive. No rest for the wicked. It would take a month of sleep before I was human again; I didn't have a month, and I wasn't sure I'd ever be human again.

Any more nights like the one I'd had would damage my mental health.

Peeling my eyes open, I expected a stream of bright sunshine to greet me, or at the very least, Kieran's sexy grin. I got neither.

Alone in bed, I flipped over, peering out the window. The sky was gray and moody, mirroring my own feelings. Rain plummeted against the castle in a torrential downpour. If it was raining outside that meant...

I jumped out of bed, thanking the storm gods. No traipsing around in the woods! It felt like it was my birthday. All I needed was for Alice to bake me a cake. Ooo. Maybe I could get her to make me one. Chocolate for sure.

Stepping into the hall after throwing on some clothes, I scratched my head, looking left and then right. *Crap. Which way is the kitchen again?* I really needed to start asking for a map when I came to these castles. It would make getting around much easier.

Finding the stairs was simple enough, and I wound my way down to the first floor. I found Jase at the base on his way up. His hair was damp from a recent shower and combed away from his face. Blue cypress and seawater scented the air around him, making me want to breathe deeply.

"Hey, I was coming to check on you."

My fingers ran through my hair, while I tried to remember if I had brushed it before leaving my room. "No need. I saved you the trip."

His soft lips spread into a smile. "I heard about your late night adventure."

I guess it had been too much to hope that Kieran would have kept it to himself. The moss green tiles suddenly captured my attention. "It was a misunderstanding."

"Try again."

I lifted my gaze to his. His stubborn face told me he wasn't going to let this go. It crossed my mind to lie. Tianna would love that, and it could end up driving a wedge between Jase and me, which I definitely didn't want. "I see people."

"What does that mean?"

Unsure of how to explain it, I shrugged. "I haven't been able to figure out if I'm seeing things, or if they're ghosts, or if Tianna has cursed me, but I've seen two different women. The one in the lake at Wakeland was how I found the Star of Tranquility."

He shifted his weight to the other foot. "Why didn't you say anything?"

"I didn't want to sound like a crazy person." Of course, after everything I'd learned and seen, it didn't seem that crazy. Not in the Veil.

He shook his head at me. "A little too late for that."

"Are you going to insult me all day? Because if so, I have better things to do." I moved to brush past him, but Jase caught my hand, and tugged me to face him again.

"Not so quick, Cupcake. You and I have plans."

I groaned. "I'm not going to like this, am I?"

"Depends on your attitude, but it can be fun, if you let it." The impish gleam sparkling in his eyes made me wary.

"Does this mean I'm not getting a free day to just hang out?" Once the idea was rooted, I desperately wanted to spend hours doing absolutely nothing, recharging, and being lazy. Jase didn't share my sentiments.

"Funny. This is the perfect opportunity to practice controlling your tranquility skills."

"Exciting," I replied in a flat voice.

"That's the spirit," he added, clapping me on the back with overexaggerated enthusiasm.

Jase led me to the south end of Viperus Keep, to a room with whitewashed bricks, and a circular tiled floor. It was unlike any of the other rooms in the castle. Ivy hung down the walls as the storm pelted the glass ceiling overhead.

"Where are the others?" There should be someone else around in case things went south and I put Jase to sleep again.

He released my hand but stayed planted in front of the doorway, blocking my only exit. "They're searching the castle for anything that might help us find the Star of Poison."

I cleared my throat. "Shouldn't we be helping with that?"

Jase's low chuckle washed away my evasive response. "This is just as important. If we stand any chance of finding the stones, you need to learn how to deal with the power you received from the first stone."

Interlocking my hands behind my back, I wandered aimlessly around the room. "I've been meaning to ask, what happens when I find the next Star? Will I suddenly start poisoning everything?"

He forked a hand through his tousled hair. "I honestly don't know. We'll deal with it *if* it happens."

I swallowed; realizing I could do nothing about it now, so no point in stressing. My eyes shifted skyward, looking through the glass. Heavy rains continued to drench the transparent ceiling.

"Is this Tianna's doing?" I wasn't sure what made me ask, but something about the storm and her warning last night left me suspicious.

Jase's gaze followed mine to the glass dome above. "It smells like her witchcraft."

"I don't get it. Does she, or doesn't she want the Stars?"

"Don't ask me to understand the inner workings of a witch. I'm already fending off a dull pounding in my temples from this endless rain."

Fair enough. I squared my shoulders and planted my feet. "Okay, let's get this over with."

"Your excitement is contagious." He flashed me a twin set of those adorable little dimples.

His damn dimples were weapons that made my knees weak, but it was too late to create a defense against Jase's secret weapon. I didn't even bother to try, and let my heart cartwheel.

With my internal gymnastics unbeknownst to Jase, he got down to business. "I'm not going to pretend to know exactly how this will work, but I am betting your ability is like mine. The mechanics, whether I'm a dragon or a man, are the same."

"You huff, and you puff, and you knock them all down." I tried not to giggle.

"Something like that, but what you need to learn is how to turn it off and on. Inside you is the source of your power. It's like breathing two different types of air. One is the air you need to breathe, and the other is your weapon. Once you identify the difference between them in your lungs, you'll be able to choose which one to expel."

Unexpected anxiety dropped through me. "That sounds complicated."

The heat of his body swarmed over my skin as he moved to stand in front of me. He put his hands on my shoulders, applying light pressure to encourage me to sit on the floor. I complied. Jase sat across from me and took my hand in his. "Close your eyes," he instructed me.

"Why?" I countered.

He let out a low breath in exasperation at my obstinacy. "I want you to try something, and closing your eyes will help you get in touch with what is going on inside you."

I didn't like imagining magical things happening inside me that I couldn't see. Trusting Jase, I let my eyes drift shut. It wasn't like he would smash a pie in my face. "Now what?"

"First, you stop talking and questioning everything I say. Just listen. I'm guessing you've never meditated before."

Deliberately not speaking, I shook my head in response.

My eyes might be closed, but I could sense those lips of his curving. "Not a problem. I want you to concentrate on your breath as it goes in and out of your lungs, filling your chest and then leaving."

For a few minutes, I did just that, listening to the sound and feel of my breath. It was surprisingly relaxing.

The texture of his voice was smooth and put me at ease. "Do you notice anything unusual in your lungs?"

That didn't really make sense to me, but I nodded anyway, desperate to learn.

Jase's warm chuckle tickled my face. "You have no idea what I'm talking about."

I opened one eye and peeked at him, finding his closeness unnerving. A tingling thrill spiraled into my stomach. "Nope, but I really want to understand."

"You don't lack heart, that's for sure. Let's try again. Close your eyes, but this time when you're breathing, I want you to be conscious of how the air feels moving through your lungs. Tranquility has a different quality. Oxygen is clean and refreshing; it's natural. Tranquility is slightly cooler and smoother."

Trying again, I focused on the rise and fall of my chest. It took more effort this time to get back into the "me" zone. Jase's fingers, interwoven with mine, were distracting me to no end. If he wanted my full concentration, then he shouldn't have been softly stroking the pad of his thumb over my skin. But somehow I made it back to the land of Zen.

Time ticked by, and I was near the point of giving up when something funny happened in my chest. It was subtle, a light flutter of calmness. If I pointed all my attention to it, I could isolate it from the oxygen moving within me. The normal air didn't stop flowing, but with my focus solely on the tranquility inside me, I was filled with a peace I'd never felt before. It was all-encompassing, radiating from my chest to the tips of my toes to the crown of my head. The longer I concentrated on that cool breath in my lungs, the more it built until I had to let it go or explode.

My eyes slowly opened, and I blew out a gentle puff of air away from Jase's face. I don't know which of us was more excited. A wide smile spread over Jase's face as a cloud of lavender mist glided from my lips. I watched with a grin of my own as the sleeping vapors swirled and floated before evaporating. My eyes returned to his sparkling ones, and I resisted the urge to throw myself into his lap.

"That was amazing." I would be lying if I said I didn't want to do it again.

Jase gave my knee a light squeeze. "See? All it takes is a bit of concentration."

Easy to say when it was second nature to you. "I can't believe I did it."

"Now to put it to the test, kiss me," he stated.

Jase didn't waste any time in his training methods. I'd managed to avoid not thinking about kissing any dragons for an hour, and here he was asking me to do just that. I blinked. "No."

He pursed his lips. "It isn't enough to identify the source of your power. You need to control it, and that comes with practice."

I tucked my hair behind my ears, nervous for so many reasons. Jase wanted me to kiss him. "And if I knock you out again?"

He tilted his head down to look me directly in the eyes. "Have a little faith, Cupcake. Isolate your tranquility and breathe."

How noble of him to willingly sacrifice himself. "Do you know who you're talking to? I can't believe you trust me. I don't even trust myself." Why was he taunting me? My mind was singularly focused on Jase's lips, and how addicting they were.

Dammit!

And he wasn't helping the situation. The pad of his thumb brushed against my lower lip, bringing my eyes to his. "You can do this."

I wet my lips. "Are you sure this isn't a ploy to get me to kiss you?"

He leaned in, bringing our lips closer. "What if it is? Still doesn't change the fact that you need to learn how to switch it on and off."

I rolled my eyes. "Fine, but if you pass out, it's on you."

His finger hooked the top of my shirt. "Shut up and kiss me, Olivia."

He'd asked for it. Taking a deep breath, I tried to calm the sudden nerves that had snuck up on me. *It is just a kiss. No big deal, so stopping being so dramatic.* The little pep talk didn't help.

I leaned in, keeping my gaze zeroed in on his lips as I brought mine closer. My eyes fluttered closed, and then a surge of panic hit. I yanked back, my eyes flying open. "Wait! I'm not ready."

Jase's irises glowed. "You can't possibly be scared. Not the girl who jumped from a dragon's back to save me."

He had a point. When push came to shove, I could be brave.

Resting my wrists on his shoulders, I scooted closer. My mouth landed on his, and I completely forgot this was supposed to be a lesson. His lips were supple and gentle at first, but within seconds, he was claiming me, demanding more. I didn't need to be persuaded. The only thing that mattered was Jase's mouth, and how he made me feel like a flower in a patch of thorns. I lost myself in him, and any thought of tranquility ceased to exist. His tongue traced along my lips. I parted them for him.

The moment his tongue slipped against mine, a low moan escaped the back of my throat. My fingers dove into the silky strands of his hair. Somehow I ended up in his lap with my legs wrapped around him —neither of us eager to move away.

Warmth emanated from him, but it was more than his body heat. Our breaths mingled in a way that seemed as if they were connected, our abilities reaching out to each other. I didn't know how else to explain what was happening inside me.

"Fuck," Jase muttered, reluctantly, pulling away.

His fingers stayed framed against my face for a few pounding heartbeats. He pressed his forehead to mine. He had more restraint than I did, for I was ready to dive back in for seconds. He must have noticed the longing in my expression.

"I don't want you to lose your control," he explained, slipping a single arm around my waist. He lifted me to my feet.

"How was it?" I asked with an arrogant smile. I was feeling pretty smug about the kiss. He was still awake, which meant the kissing ban was over as long as I could control my tranquility.

"It was… good."

My hands fell to my sides. I was looking for "mind-numbing" or "boxer-dropping." "Good" did not stroke my ego. "Gee, thanks. You know how to make a girl feel special."

A serious frown spread over his face, marring his handsome features. "I'm doing my best to keep my hands off you, and not strip you out of that dress. Is that *good* enough for you?"

I gulped, secretly pleased.

Holy crap. I had power. Like actual inhuman ability. I was a goddamn superhero.

9

The wind flew over my face as I squeezed my knees together, holding onto Kieran's back for dear life. Riding a dragon was the most exhilarating experience in the world. It wasn't possible, but I wished everyone could try it at least once in their life. I took advantage whenever a descendant was willing to take me. Today, though, had been a case of Kieran demanding I come rather than me begging.

A few days had passed since my lesson with Jase. Zade had stayed with me last night, and apparently Kieran couldn't wait because he had come bursting in to wake us up. Still half asleep, I had sat up in bed and rubbed my eyes, only to have a pile of random clothes tossed at me.

"Get dressed, Blondie. We're going for a ride."

Zade had rolled over and groaned, giving Kieran the middle finger.

I couldn't get dressed fast enough.

Rolling out of the extra toasty bed, I threw on the clothes, and rushed to follow Kieran downstairs and out the front door. He was already in his dragon form by the time I caught up to him, waiting for me to climb onto his back. His triangle head angled over his shoulder, to keep an eye on me as I positioned myself, and held on tightly.

Dark, ominous clouds painted the sky around us in shades of gray and green. Below us, various shapes of green leaves blanketed the tops of the trees. Kieran kept us above the woods to make our route more direct, but we flew close enough to them to take shelter if needed. So far, the coast had been clear.

No wraiths. No griffins. No witches. I enjoyed the peace for once.

"It feels wonderful to be outside."

His eyes trained on the cliffs in the distance. *"The storm isn't gone yet. It will rain again. And soon."*

The reminder of our gloomy weather turned my thoughts to Tianna. I didn't delude myself into thinking this was a joy ride. Everything the descendants did was for a purpose. "Where are we going?"

"There is a place that might be able to help." His voice sounded in my head. When the descendants were in dragon form, they could communicate through projecting thoughts. It was pretty kick-ass.

My fingers glided over Kieran's emerald scales as I lowered myself closer to his thick neck. "Why aren't the others with us?"

"They needed to check on their kingdoms. Make sure Tianna hasn't done anything insane in their absence."

Made complete sense to me, but I still missed them. It was always so quiet when we weren't all together. "So what provoked this impromptu trip?"

"Ever since you told us about the apparitions you've been seeing, it got me thinking. I don't believe they're a coincidence. The others

agree, and there is one place in the Veil that might give us answers about what they mean."

Kieran thinking… this should be interesting. At least they didn't think I was crazy.

"It is a place deep in Viperus. Hopefully, something sparks."

He was being awful cryptic, which made me uneasy, but flying on a dragon had a way of making it less worrisome. We flew for maybe another ten or fifteen minutes—my concept of time had been skewed since living in the Veil. They didn't bind their lives to the clock.

Kieran landed on his hind legs first before his front claws touched the ground. Jostled from the movement, I tightened my legs, and the bag strapped to my back slipped off one shoulder. I steadied myself, before trying to slip down the side of him. Kieran crouched flat, and I made my move, swinging both legs to the side so I could jump off him.

Safely on two feet, I wiggled the bag off my shoulders and waited for Kieran to shift. I couldn't help but watch. It was marvelous to witness the beast morphing into a man. How their bodies were capable of such drastic transformations boggled my mind. I didn't know if I would ever be able to wrap my head around it.

Or their lack of modesty. Being naked never seemed to faze them, unless I was naked. That was an entirely different ball game.

I handed over the bag, and Kieran pulled out the clothes he'd brought along. As he got dressed, I busied myself by taking in our surroundings. Kieran had dropped us outside a cave made entirely of trees. Thick, lush leaves formed the entrance. Compelled by a mysterious force, I walked through the arch of tree branches and into the mouth of the cave. At the center of the chamber was a pool with sparkling turquoise water. Humid air rose in a mist from the water's surface like a sauna.

"What is this place?" I asked, as my eyes absorbed the snippet of paradise.

And then a snake slithered across the grassy floor, right past my toes.

All hell broke loose.

I screamed, as I was prone to do at the sight of slimy critters with forked tongues. The shriek issuing from my throat was long and could have woken the dead.

Kieran was quick to react. Shirtless, he bolted in front of me, sealing my mouth shut with his hand. "Shh. It won't hurt you."

I begged to differ. Just its presence in the same room as me hurt.

With owl-sized eyes, I whacked Kieran on the chest. "Why didn't you tell me we were entering a snake's den," I hissed from behind his hand, which still covered my mouth.

"It's not a snake's den. It's the Mirrored Shallows." He removed his hand from my mouth, smiling the entire time.

My gaze shifted left and then right. "Is it gone?"

"Yes, the big, meanie reptile has left."

No longer feeling threatened or afraid of having a snake inject its venom into my calf, I strolled along the uneven ground. "What's so special about this place?" I couldn't deny its splendor, but I didn't see how it would help our current situation, and yet, if the descendants had brought me here, there must be a good reason.

"The Mirrored Shallows is said to be the thinnest point of the Veil. It is here where the living can see the dead, and…" He let his voice trail off.

"And what?" I prompted. He couldn't leave me dangling with something like that.

"And where the dead can summon the living," his deep voice finished.

I swallowed. Things were starting to come together. "You want to see if I can talk to the woman who keeps appearing to me since I stepped foot in Viperus," I concluded.

He nodded. "That is the plan. You game?"

My eyes jumped to the pool, studying it intently before darting back to Kieran. "Why not? It isn't the weirdest thing I've done since coming to the Veil." I walked up to the edge of the water with cautious steps and glanced down. "What do I do?"

Kieran's shadow fell over me, the spikes from his hair reflecting in the water. "You get in."

Nothing in the Veil was ever as simple as it seemed. There was always a catch, and I guessed the little hiccup would reveal itself in due time. "Have you ever gone in?"

He nodded. "Many times… especially after the war. I thought if I could see my father, he might be able to help us defeat Tianna, and break her curse."

I didn't have to ask the outcome of those visits, especially, when a touch of sadness moved into his eyes. "No chance you brought me a change of clothes in that bag, is there?" I quickly changed the topic.

"I figured you'd air dry on the way back."

Good thing I wore one of those flimsy dresses that were so popular in the isles. Kicking off my slip-on shoes, I hiked up the hem of my dress and dipped my toes in to test the water. The temperature was pleasant. Not as balmy as the bathhouse at Wakeland castle, or the waterfall shower at Viperus Keep, but it wasn't a deal breaker. Pushing forward, I went deeper into the pool, and a chill rushed over my legs. The eeriness increased until my skin was coated with it. I paused at the center, turning around to face Kieran. Water lapped around me while I treaded, but it quickly stilled. Almost too quickly.

"Now what?" I inquired, kicking my feet lightly to keep me afloat.

Kieran sat at the edge of the water—close enough to reach me if something happened—but he made sure to not let the water touch him. "You take a deep breath and go under, Blondie."

Letting my hands skim the surface, I stared down into the water. Even though it wasn't deep, I couldn't see the bottom of the pond. The color beneath me grew darker until it was nearly black. Inhaling a breath of air, I braced myself and dunked my head under the surface.

The first thing I noticed was the cold as the water touched my face, but then came the voices. It sounded like I was at a concert, everyone talking and screaming at once over the music. I wanted to plug my ears and push to the surface, but I forced myself to stay under the water, relaxing my limbs. My heart galloped in my chest.

One at a time, I yelled in my head.

No one was more surprised than me when the voices ceased for a blissful few seconds. *Finally, souls that listen to me.*

A soft female voice laughed in the water, the sound surrounding me from all sides. My head turned left and right, looking for the source of the feminine voice. A bright ball of light moved toward me, and I realized the voice came from the light. Her blurry form slowly began to take shape in the murky waters below me. Beautiful waves of blonde hair swirled around her face. Wisps of her white dress tangled with her feet. She was the woman I'd seen before.

"*Olivia.*" She spoke my name. "*You should not have come here. The witch is searching for you.*"

I didn't bother to ask how she knew who I was. "*I had no choice. We must find the Star of Poison.*"

Alarm captured her eyes. "*It is not safe here. She isn't the only one who would do you harm.*"

"*The other souls?*" I guessed, thinking about the mass of voices in the water when I had gone under.

Her round head nodded. "*They are restless, eager to be released from this world.*"

"*What do they think I'm trying to do?*" I shot back in aggravation.

Her pinkish-blue lips curled. "*The dead aren't reasonable.*"

Kind of like the descendants.

Her slim hand extended, caressing the side of my cheek. "*They don't care how the barrier is broken, only that it is. You will face many obstacles in your quest to release the dragons from their curse.*"

My body floated with little effort on my part, neither rising nor sinking, just suspended in the dark waters. "*Is there no way you can help me? I can't fail.*"

Despair radiated from her, and it stabbed me in the heart. "*No, you can't. We're all depending on you.*"

No pressure. "*I don't know what to do or where to look.*"

Soft aqua light haloed her body. "*The Stars are drawn to the hearts of the dragon descendants. They will return to a place of importance and meaning to those who rule the land.*"

Her idea of help wasn't very concrete. "*Who are you?*" I asked, still uncertain if she was someone trustworthy.

"*My name is—*"

I was yanked from the water by a pair of strong arms.

"Son of a bitch," I swore, shoving strands of dripping hair out of my face. I stared into Kieran's glowing emerald eyes. His arms were secured around me, keeping me pinned to his chest. "Couldn't you have waited a few more seconds before fishing me out of the water?"

"I thought you were dead," he growled, frowning at me. It took me aback. Kieran never scowled or scolded me. "You were underwater for far too long. And when I called your name, you didn't respond."

Really? It had felt like seconds to me. "I was fine… I think. I was doing what you wanted, trying to get information."

We were both soaking wet, our clothes plastered against our skin. Beads of water rolled down his chest. "You saw something?"

I bit my lip and nodded. "The same woman as before when I fell into the hole."

"What did she say? Did she tell you where to find the Star of Poison?"

Squeezing the water out of my hair, I looked at him sideways. "I was working on it, but you pulled me out before I could get more details. She said that the Stars are drawn to each of you, and would return to a place of meaning."

Kieran scrunched his face. "Is that all she said?"

"Do you want me to go back under?"

We both glanced over at the mystical pool of souls. "Definitely not. It's not safe."

"That's what she said." A shiver rolled through me.

Kieran's hands moved up and down my arms, bringing warmth to my skin. "It's time for us to go, Blondie."

I nodded, eager to get out of this little tree cave. The Mirrored Shallows wasn't a place I'd hang out at, or linger. As we crossed through the branched archway, a bolt of angry lightning cracked in the sky, coming awfully close to the tops of the trees that canopied us. Kieran's arms went around me, tightening. "The storm is back."

My body tensed. "I guess flying is out of the question."

Kieran gave the sky a dark glare. "It is for the moment. We'll wait out the storm until Tianna gets bored of torturing us."

Like that was ever going to happen. "It is going to be a long day," I said, stepping out of Kieran's embrace, and walking around the entrance to the tree cave that would be our shelter from the storm. A chill entered the air. If it kept up, I would freeze to death. My teeth started to chatter. Too bad Zade wasn't nearby; I could use a dose of his flames.

Kieran came to my rescue with a T-shirt in his hand. "We need to get you dried off. Here, put this on, and I'll see if I can start a fire."

As he gathered branches from the ground, I slipped out of my wet clothes and put on the soft shirt. It smelled of Kieran—exotic and wild. Dipping my head, I brought up the collar of the shirt to my nose, and inhaled, nuzzling the material against my face. How could any human smell so incredibly good? But the thing was, I felt exactly the same about the others. They each had their own unique scent that tempted me.

Within minutes, Kieran had a little fire going inside of the tree cave. Probably not the safest place, considering all the wood, but the alternative was no shelter. I stood beside the flickering flames with my hands out, letting its heat seep into my body.

"How are we going to let the others know we're okay?" I asked, concerned they might try to track us down in this magically induced shit-storm. It wasn't like the Veil had cell phone service.

"They'll know we sought cover. It's what any of us would do." Kieran seemed confident about the matter. I decided if he wasn't going to worry, then neither would I. "You should rest."

Spending the night in a cave filled with the souls of the dead creeped me the fuck out, I didn't know if I could do it. Sleep would not come easily. "Not happening. How do I know one of those souls swimming around in that pool won't try to possess my body in my sleep?"

"I doubt that would happen."

"Really? So far, everything I've seen of the Veil suggests otherwise."

Kieran gave the dark pool a distressed stare. "You might be right."

I rolled my eyes. That was likely the first time I'd ever heard one of them admit I was right about something. I wanted to treasure the moment, but the gleam that had suddenly sprung into Kieran's eyes had my blood racing.

"We'll have to do something else to occupy our time."

My head tilted to the side. "And what do you have in mind?"

He flashed me a grin, and hope fluttered in my belly. "I'm thinking you need more than a fire to warm you up."

"Ha," I breathed.

He still stood directly across from me on the other side of the fire, but he could feel the tension in the air between us, and the twitch of his lips told me he was going to do something devious. Wickedly devious I hoped.

"Is that a challenge?"

I shifted under his roguish gaze, wondering what he would do or say next, because I was a tangle of excited nerves. My eyes flicked to the fire, searching for something clever to say in response. I had nothing.

"Olivia," Kieran murmured my name, his voice suddenly so much closer.

I spun toward the sound, not expecting him to be at my side. How the hell had he moved so fast? My hands steadied themselves on his shoulders before I fell into the fire. Just what I needed: to go up in flames.

Blinking, I registered the warm skin under my fingers. *He is shirtless*, my brain reminded me. Why yes, he was. My eyes became distracted by his bronze chest. I'd seen all of the descendants naked, but it never grew tiresome. With hesitant fingers, I traced the tattoo lines on Kieran's chest. The black ink covered his entire right pectoral, trailing down to his flat belly and over his hip. The design spidered over his body, like the roots of a tree.

Air hissed through his teeth when my fingers skirted the band of his jeans. His hand shot out, capturing my wrist. My eyes snapped up, and the emotion stirring in his face caused my heart to pound. With a quick jerk, my breasts laid against his chest and my hips snuggled into his. Dear God. The feel of him pressed to the soft parts of me sent my pulse racing.

Wow. He was really hard.

And I wasn't just talking about his abs.

What am I doing?!

Flirting with danger.

His fingers framed my face, and I was hypnotized by the luminosity of his eyes. "I'm going to kiss you now." His husky voice melted my insides.

How could I say no to a kiss? "I might knock you out with my breath."

Bending his head, his lips curled. "I'll take my chances."

His soft lips closed over mine, and I felt like he'd drugged me. The storm raging outside, and the souls swimming in the bottom of the eerie pool were whisked from my mind. Every wonderful sensation brought on by the taste of his lips magnified in other parts of my body. His mouth slanted across mine, his tongue slipping past my inexperience. The velvety softness of his lips, combined with the rasp of his tongue, drew a purr from my core.

A blush stole over my body.

Kieran diverted his lips off to the side near my cheek. "I don't just want to kiss you, Olivia," he murmured in my ear, before taking my lobe in between his teeth. I pressed my lips together to keep from moaning. "Do you understand what I'm asking?"

Wait. What was he saying? If only he would stop doing that thing with his tongue. It was making it beyond difficult to concentrate, but when his words finally registered, a tornado of need swept through me. *Oh, my god. He wanted to sleep with me? Don't freak out. Do I want to sleep with Kieran?*

Yes! Yes! Hell yes!

But I needed to make one thing very clear. Waves of tension mounted inside me, as Kieran continued to rain succulent kisses down my throat, and over my neck. My fingers pressed at his chest, and I could feel myself slowly going under again.

No, not yet. You have something to tell him.

I applied pressure. "Wait." His mouth was reluctant to leave the alcove of my neck, but he peered down at me with heavily lidded eyes. "You need to know something before this goes any further."

"I want to make you mine," he growled, his eyes glowing brightly. "And I can feel how much you desire me."

Damn emotional bond.

His head dipped to take possession of my lips. He wasn't going to make this easy. My body was already leaning back toward him, but I pulled myself together.

"Kieran, if you kiss me again, I won't get this out, and it's important."

He had to know that I had feelings for the others. He would have sensed it, so what I was about to say shouldn't be a surprise.

I hoped.

Taking a shaky breath, I prepared to say what was on my mind. "I need you to know that whatever happens between us, it doesn't change my feelings for the others."

His lips skimmed my jaw. "I know."

It took me a moment to respond. "And you're okay with that?"

He gave a one-shoulder shrug. "For the first time in a hundred years, we have hope, and it is because of you. I don't know how this will work with the four of us, but I do know I need you in my life." Kieran stroked the pad of his thumb over my bottom lip, and I shuddered.

Good enough for me. I'd figure the *other* stuff out later.

Before I even finished nodding, he was kissing me. Leaning into his lips, my mind sighed. *Finally.* But my body was not appeased. It wanted so much more. And Kieran was happy to oblige. His hands slipped to my hips, gathering the hem of my T-shirt and pushing it up past my waist. Those fingers skimmed over my skin, leaving behind electric tingles.

I was going to come undone before we even got to the good stuff.

As his mouth claimed mine, I reveled in wonderment, I was about to have sex with a dragon in a tree cave.

Who would believe me?

None of that mattered.

I no longer gave two shits about what other people thought of me. Maybe my new attitude was also why I was so willing to accept my situation—me and four dragon shifters. It was complicated, sure, but being with Kieran like this made it seem worth it.

He secured an arm around my lower back and lifted me up. My legs automatically wrapped like a pretzel around his waist. It felt like I was flying. No, not flying. Kieran was laying us down, his body cushioning mine from the rock and dirt floor. I continued my exploration of his glorious body, running my fingers over the thick muscles of his arms. His golden skin was magnificent.

Kieran was a sweet intoxication and I couldn't get enough. My fingers fumbled with the button on his pants, brushing over a faint dusting of dark hair that led straight into his jeans. I wanted to be rid of all barriers. Kieran must have felt the same way. Within seconds, my shirt was up and over my head, discarded to some corner of the hollow. His pants followed, and just like that, we were skin to skin.

"I've never seen anyone as beautiful as you," he whispered.

Coming from any other guy, I would have blown off his admiration, but Kieran had never sounded more sincere or serious in his life, so much so that even I believed I was beautiful. I didn't know what to say. Thank you seemed too commonplace, so I laced my fingers in his hair and brought my lips down to his. The kiss seemed to last forever, a kiss filled with dreams, magic, desire.

Things escalated quickly.

I couldn't keep track of his hands as they roamed over my body, from my shoulders to my belly, to my thighs, and all the places in between. His lips spread fire everywhere they touched me, and passion burned between us. When his hot mouth closed over my breast, my spine arched forward as I reeled with pleasure.

What is he doing to me?

My hips moved, rubbing over the hardness of him with brisk, stimulating gyrations. I didn't know what I was doing, but I couldn't control myself. The amazing feelings were building and building. The primal need for release was overwhelming my sanity. And still, it frightened me. I'd never felt this kind of powerful emotion coursing through me.

But something I did recognize rose up inside me. Tranquility.

Breaking off the kiss, I turned my head to the side, to keep my breath away from Kieran's face. If he passed out on me right before the end, I would be pissed. He didn't seem to notice the sudden shift in my demeanor, but it didn't matter because he aligned our bodies. And slowly I was filled with heat, deeply, and completely filled. Kieran was enchanting, his hands, his lips, his body—the whole package. There was no going back.

His teeth scraped over my collarbone, and I arched against him, our bodies moving together in perfect harmony. I never wanted this night to end. My nails scored his back, and tendrils of wild desire rushed to the surface. Together we reached the edge, and tumbled over it blissfully. The orgasm rocked my entire body.

Glowing from the inside out, I purred in contentment, twisting into his arms. He pressed a soft kiss to my glistening neck and then to my cheek. A storm brewed outside, and I was curled cozily against Kieran, happier than I'd been in a long time.

Holy shit. I'd just slept with a dragon.

None of the girls at my old high school could say that. And Jimmy

Whitt had nothing on Kieran. Jimmy had been my first, and last experience with sex. I'd never wanted to repeat that painful deed again, until I met the descendants. It amazed me how vastly different the experience had been with someone who knew what he was doing. Now I wanted to experience all of them. Jase. Zade. And Issik.

Would it be different each time?

That thought generated another, not so pleasant, one. What would I tell the others? Should I say anything? I rested my chin on Kieran's chest, watching his face highlighted by the amber flames.

"Don't tell the others. Not yet. The last thing I need is you guys fighting over me... more than usual," I added.

He grinned. "That's not likely to happen. We're dragons. Fighting is what we do."

"Don't I know it," I muttered. "But jealousy won't help us find the stones."

His fingers brushed a lock of golden hair off my face. "If that is what you wish."

"It is." We lay quietly together, still absorbed in the afterglow of what we'd done. "Can I ask you a question?"

"Always, Blondie."

"How do you keep control of your poison in a... situation like this?"

Kieran raised an arm behind his head as a cushion. "You mean while making love?"

My fingers played with the fine hairs that ran down his lower stomach. "I guess."

"Were you afraid I would poison you?"

I shook my head. "I was afraid I would tranq you."

He considered my worried face. "It takes time. I've had over a hundred years to learn to harness my dragon gift. There will be times you'll forget or lose control, but at least tranquility won't kill anyone." I picked up on traces of remorse in his voice.

Had people died while Kieran had learned to master his poison?

I didn't ask, for the memories seemed painful, and I didn't want to tarnish what we had shared by drudging up the past.

The room had gone silent other than the crackling of the dwindling fire in front of us. "It sounds like the storm might be letting up," Kieran added. "We should get back to the castle before Tianna decides to flood Viperus in her bad mood."

If this was Tianna sulking, I didn't want to see what happened when we found another Star, because I was determined to show this witch up. Untangling ourselves, we gathered our clothes, and I got dressed by the glowing firelight while Kieran stuffed his in the bag. I wasn't sure if things were different between Kieran and me, or if it was my imagination. Should I say something? Thank you?

Definitely not.

Neither of us spoke, but it wasn't awkward like I remembered those moments following my first time with eight-seconds Jimmy being. I peeked up at Kieran, seeing him move toward the arched entrance. It was dark, but I could make out the form of his naked shadow as he stepped outside the Mirrored Shallows. He was preparing to shift, and it was a sight I didn't want to miss.

Rushing to catch up with Kieran, I grabbed the bag off the floor and secured it onto my back. The cool midnight air jolted my senses, and I huddled deeper into Kieran's T-shirt, letting the scent of him envelop me as I climbed onto my waiting chariot.

His wings beat, whipping the wind as we climbed through the air. Unfortunately, our flight home was not destined to be unadventurous.

We'd barely left the Mirrored Shallows, when a trio of griffins flew in from behind the gloomy clouds, flanking Kieran on both sides with one hovering directly over my head. I fucking hated these lion-birds. They were really making my life a living hell, and they had to ruin what had turned out to be a pretty mind-blowing night.

"Kieran!" I called.

"Hang on. Things are going to get a little rough."

Wonderful.

Kieran dodged left and then right, doing his best to evade the griffins as they attempted to claw or snap at him. It was too long before I figured out their plan, tricky little assholes. The two alongside kept

Kieran distracted while the one above me was waiting for his moment. It came before I had a chance to warn Kieran.

The griffin dove for me, his claws extended.

"Olivia, duck!" Kieran ordered me in a deep growl.

Quickly, I did as he instructed, flattening myself against his back, as the griffin above my head swooped down. His nails drug along my back, shredding Kieran's shirt and slicing my skin. I cried out but held on tight, breathing through the pain. Shit. That would leave a nasty mark, but their plan had failed… this time.

"That was close. Are you hurt?" Kieran asked, weaving through the air.

"I'm fine," I lied through my teeth, curling my fingers against him to keep the agony from my voice.

"I've got to get you out of here. We're going for the trees where we can hopefully lose them. I want you to run as soon as we touch the ground. Do you understand? They want to take you prisoner. I can't let that happen."

"I got it." My heart was jackhammering in my chest.

"Whatever happens, don't let go of me."

I didn't think I could hold on any tighter, but Kieran tested my strength. Diving toward the earth, he flipped around, exposing his underbelly to the griffins as we fell backward. He opened his mouth, releasing a mist of green poison.

Take that, you feathery abominations.

The trio of griffins squawked, scrambling to avoid the mist, but they had been following us too closely. Kieran's poison worked its way into their lungs, sealing their fate. I bet that would piss off a certain witch. The griffins' eyes bulged as if they were suffocating. Their feathered wings flapped haphazardly in the air before they completely stopped moving at all. Then they fell—nothing but dead weight.

We exhaled simultaneously. Using the force of his wings, Kieran spun us around, regaining control of our flight. *"Are you—?"*

Out of nowhere, a crack of thunder boomed like a god roaring from the heavens. It was followed by a spear of lightning so bright that I was blinded for a few seconds. In that short time, I didn't realize the bolt of light had struck my dragon.

Tumbling, spinning, spiraling downward in a breathless rush toward the ground, we fell from the sky. My fingers clutched Kieran as I hung on for dear life. The world became a dizzy blur of dark colors and fear.

Holy shit. We're going to die.

"I won't let you die."

I swore I heard Kieran's voice in my head, but his wings remained unmoving, and at any moment, we were going to smack into the ground.

Oh, my god. What am I going to do?

If there was a plan worth hatching, my brain was in too much shock to think of it. I did the only thing I could. Scream.

I don't know how he managed it, but right before we hit the forest below, Kieran spun. I was jostled off his back, free-falling. But not for long. His claws scooped me out of the air, brought me to his chest, nestling me against him. Panic tore through my gut.

Branches and leaves lashed his large form from all sides, snapping under his speed and weight. Our death was imminent. And all I could think was, at least I'd been loved fully and completely.

We hit the ground with an impact that shook the world. It rumbled like an earthquake, and the force of Kieran's fall seemed to crack the ground. The oxygen in my lungs vanished, leaving me gasping for breath.

And then nothing.

For a moment, I feared I'd died and all this fuzzy green shit I saw was Hell, but then my vision cleared. With the help of the moon, I collected pieces of my location, slowly remembering all the events that had led to this point.

I should be dead.

But by a miracle, I wasn't. In fact, I was very much alive and well. Sprawled over Kieran's underbelly, I pushed myself upright. Kieran had landed directly on his back in an attempt to keep me cradled, and safe from the brunt of the fall.

Stupid dragon!

He put himself in jeopardy to save me. I would never forgive him if he didn't wake up. If he...

I couldn't bring myself to finish the thought.

Scrambling up his long torso toward his neck, I used the scales on his body as handholds to prevent me from tumbling off him. He wasn't moving, and from what I could tell, he wasn't breathing either.

Don't do this to me. Don't leave me out here alone. You can't leave me. I forbid it!

I reached his neck, frantically searching for a pulse. Relief and wonder poured through me as I felt his heart beating strong against my ear.

Kieran was alive, but that didn't mean he was out of danger.

I needed to get help because—let's be real—how the hell was I going to save him? This wasn't the type of wound I could slap a Band-Aid on, kiss it better, and call it a day. He was unconscious, and bleeding in more places than I could keep pressure on at once. Not to mention dragging a dragon through the woods was an impossible task, almost like finding a stone. No way. I had to find help.

Flipping around on my ass, I slid down Kieran's side, landing on a pair of wobbly legs. I laid a hand on his dragon cheek, feeling the textured scales on my palm. "Don't move. Don't stop breathing. Don't die. I'm going to get you help and save you," I vowed.

Now was the time to be a hero. I wished I had wings. It would have made getting to Viperus Keep that much quicker, for time was Kieran's enemy. Without wasting another second, I took off, racing through the woods. The castle wasn't far—less than a mile or two. I never would have found my way if it weren't for the moonlight catching the eyes of the snake that wound up Viperus Keep. They glinted like a pair of twin lighthouses leading me home.

My legs were weak as I ran through the thicket of trees, keeping the top of the castle in view. I stumbled over rocks, twigs, and my own two feet more times than I could count, but I never stopped. The sounds of the woods echoed around me—crickets, animals howling, and the husky sound of a woman laughing.

Wait.

That wasn't normal.

I faltered.

Tianna.

Was she out there? Waiting for me? Or was she enjoying the torment she'd created with her spells and demented mind?

Truthfully, right now I didn't give a witch's tit.

Fueled by the desire to not let Tianna win, I continued running, and didn't stop until I burst through the front door of Viperus Keep. It was then I remembered what Kieran had said about the other descendants going to check on their lands.

"Hello!" I yelled, my voice carrying up to the high ceilings.

Please let them be back here. I didn't know what I would do if not a single descendant was here.

"Olivia, you're home," Alice said, stepping into the room. She wore a white apron around her waist.

"Are the others here?" I asked, breathless and anxious. "It's Kieran. He's hurt. Bad."

Alice's hand flew over her mouth, concern brightening her eyes. "Oh my. Yes. They are pacing the great room worrying about you."

Before I had a chance to head in the direction of the great room, Jase, Zade, and Issik stormed into the hall and pounced on me.

"Where the hell have you been?" Jase hissed. His dark hair was ruffled like he'd been raking his fingers through it, as he was known to do when stressed.

"Do you know how worried we've been?" Zade added, fire burning in his whiskey-colored eyes.

Issik gave me a frosty once-over, taking in my scuffed and battered state. "I'm going to kill Kieran."

My head shook back and forth, beseeching them with my eyes. "You might not get the chance. Hurry. You must help him."

Jase's brows drew together. "What are you talking about? What happened?"

Lurching forward, I grabbed his hand, tugging it with all my might. "I don't have time to explain. He's hurt. Tianna. We must go now before it's too late!"

Somehow through my broken, panicked phrases, they put together the pieces. Without another word, Issik burst into his dragon and took off through the front door to the sky. Zade followed with scales of crimson and gold papering his flesh.

I was no longer pulling Jase. He was dragging me through the doors of Viperus Keep. "You're going to tell me everything that happened as we fly."

I nodded. Fear choked my throat.

Jase tossed back his head, letting the dragon take over. He stood before me, his muscular form filling the courtyard, and his angular head standing tall and proud. Bright violet eyes stared down at me.

With a nudge of his head, he pushed me up onto his back. *"Where's Kieran?"*

"In the woods not far from here. There." I pointed off to the north where I'd emerged from moments ago. "He fell from the sky. The griffins attacked, and as soon as Kieran had taken care of them, Tianna struck him down."

"We'll find him," Jase vowed. He had never broken a promise to me. *"If he was seriously injured, his body would have changed back by now to heal."*

"That's a thing?" I asked, my voice shaking. I hadn't realized I was trembling.

"Yes, Cupcake. I'm told we're not easy to kill, not even by a witch, much to her displeasure."

"I was so scared."

"You're safe now. We never should have let you go." A tingle of power radiated over my skin. Tranquility, the ability I shared with this particular dragon. It connected us.

Jase landed in the clearing created by Kieran's fall. Issik and Zade were right beside us. Jase had been right. Kieran was in his human form, naked, and curled up on the ground. I bounded off Jase, rushing to Kieran's side, needing to make sure he was still breathing—that we weren't too late. Jase might be confident Kieran would recover—that his body would heal itself—but I needed to see it with my own eyes. Some magic needed to be seen.

I dropped down to my knees, running my fingers over his chest. He was shivering. "Blondie," he croaked, his voice rough and raspy.

My eyes flashed to his. Their usual bright sparkle was dull. I wrapped my hand around his. "I'm here. I brought the others as I promised."

His fingers gave a light squeeze against mine, but it was weak. "You shouldn't have put yourself in danger. I-I'll be fine."

Just like a dragon to think nothing could hurt him.

"You were struck by lightning and fell out of the sky," I not so eloquently reminded him. "I don't care who you are. You could have died."

His lips curled. "But I didn't."

Jase shifted while Zade and Issik both stayed in their dragon forms. "We need to get him back to the castle. He'll recover quicker in his home."

I wiped at my cheeks, surprised to find them wet. I was crying, finally letting the events of the day catch up to me. All I wanted to do was turn around and launch myself into Jase's arms, bury my face into his chest, and sob like a baby, but I couldn't. Not yet.

Kieran still needed me.

Stiffening my chin, I nodded. Together, Jase and I were able to get Kieran to his feet. His large frame leaned heavily on Jase for support. Issik flattened to the ground, allowing us to hoist Kieran onto his back.

Jase touched my shoulder, bringing my attention to him. He searched my face, and I could see he wanted to offer me comfort as much as I wanted him. Giving in, he wrapped me in his arms. "Zade will take you back to the castle. I'll make sure this fool doesn't fall off."

The crimson dragon was waiting for me. Jase released me and lifted me up onto Zade before hopping onto Issik's back behind Kieran, who was draped over the side. In a crisis, the descendants seemed to be able to coordinate together seamlessly without having to say a thing. It was odd and impressive, but at the moment, I didn't care how they did it, only that Kieran was safe.

I hugged my arms around Zade, resting my cheek on his neck. Fatigue crashed over me. My body ached, too worn to hold itself up. Zade was there for me—my strength, my wings, my protector. He kicked off, taking us swiftly back to the castle. The warmth of his body seeped into mine, and I reveled in the heat. I was so cold.

"We're almost home," he promised.

My cheek pressed against his scales. They were smoother than they appeared. "He's going to be okay, isn't he?" I knew what Jase had said, and I'd heard Kieran pretend like this was no big deal, but I couldn't shake the feeling that what had happened was monumental.

"Of course," Zade assured me, but his voice didn't hold the amount of confidence I sought.

"Do you actually believe that, or are you saying that so I don't worry?"

I was met with silence.

That's what I thought. My heart was battering against my chest, and what was a five-minute flight seemed like hours. I felt as if Zade was lagging behind on purpose, to give Issik and Jase time to tend to Kieran. But they kept insisting he would be fine. It was hard to believe. I wanted to trust that Kieran would be his healthy, smirking, flirty self in no time, but my nagging intuition told me something else was at play here, and the descendants didn't want me to find out what it was.

That was laughable.

If I could find the Star of Tranquility, a stone that had been missing for decades, surely I could uncover whatever secret they were hiding.

By the time I got back to the castle, and wrestled my way past the dragon muscle wall, Kieran was in his bed recovering. I crossed the room slowly, unable to take my eyes off his face. Most of the surface cuts and scratches had already healed. The only remnant of his trauma was the dried blood in his hair. Tears welled in my eyes, and my lower lip trembled. The adrenaline had begun to wear off, leaving me stunned at how close we'd come to dying.

"Those wouldn't be tears I see in your eyes, would they?" Kieran rasped.

Swallowing, I dabbed at my cheeks. "I think I deserve a sob fest."

The sparkle in his expression sobered, darkening his emerald eyes. "I put you in danger. I won't ever forgive myself."

Tears blurred my vision; I couldn't hold them at bay anymore. "That's bullshit. If you think I would have survived that without you— survived any of this—then you're crazy."

As I hoped, a small smirk emerged on his face. "That might be true, but I can attest that I'm somewhat crazy."

With care, I sat on the edge of the bed and gave a short laugh. "The four of you really are. Are you going to be okay?"

He shifted on the bed to sit up, but frustration overcame his expression at the difficulty of the everyday movement. Switching tactics, he stayed lying down, and reached for my hand instead. "Nothing a few hours of rest won't cure."

"How did I know you were going to say that?" He was nuts. I planned to sleep for a week, if only I could. Tianna made it impossible. I had a stone to find and couldn't afford to take off any time. Kieran might not die today or tomorrow, but unless I found that stone soon—very soon—he could still die. They all could.

And I would never be able to live with myself… live without them.

These four dragons had become not only the most important people in my life, but also the only people in my life. I needed them as much as they needed me, probably more so, and I refused to let Tianna take them from me.

Leaning over Kieran, I brushed my lips across his. "Get some sleep."

I needed to get to work ASAP.

As I got up to leave, Kieran grabbed my wrist, and I stared back at him. "I know that look. Don't do anything stupid," he warned me.

Best not to make a promise I couldn't keep. "The last thing you need to do is worry about me. There are three other dragons to do that."

His fingers gently fell away from my wrist, and I stepped out into the hallway. As soon as I was out of Kieran's sight, I let my tidal wave of emotions release. Boiling rage. Gut-wrenching sadness. Gripping fear. The powerful emotions swirled inside me, threatening to consume my soul. My lip trembled. My nails dug into my palms. And my heart quivered.

Just when I thought I would burst into a million fragmented pieces, I was engulfed by three sets of arms. Warmth, calmness, and coolness all surrounded me in a dragon-sized hug. They sensed my emotions, overwhelming them as much as they did me. My head came to rest on one of their chests—Issik's, judging by the frigid aura.

What would I do without them?

I never wanted to find out.

Lifting my chin, I met each one of their gazes. "We need to do something."

"We will. This isn't the end. A minor setback," Jase assured me, but he wasn't hearing me. I was talking about right now.

"Tianna thinks she's hurt us. She's wrong," I vowed with conviction.

Curiosity entered Zade's eyes. "Did you learn something new in the Mirrored Shallows?"

I relaxed my fighting stance. "Uh, not exactly."

"Then there really isn't anything for us to do at the moment. I suggest you get some sleep. You look like you're going to crumble to the floor."

My shoulders straightened to prove Jase, the know-it-all, wrong. There was still some energy left in this body. If they weren't willing to do anything right now, then I would. Couldn't they see we didn't have time to waste?

Brushing past Issik, I stalked down the hall, heading away from my room and toward the stairs. The descendants might not let me leave the castle, but there were many, many rooms in Viperus Keep left to be explored. The woman in white had said the stones returned to a place of importance and meaning, to the heart of Viperus. Maybe that meant somewhere in this maze of a castle.

"Where are you going?" Issik asked, falling in step behind me. Zade was right beside him.

I kept walking, not that I actually thought I would get far.

The descendants were, if anything, predictable. Zade's blazing arms came around me, and swooped me off my feet. "The only place you are going is to bed, Little Gem."

"Let me go," I ordered, torn between crying and screaming.

Thick, contoured muscle kept me secured against Zade's chest, and I gave up fighting fairly quickly. I was too tired. Too weak. And outnumbered. Not to mention, in pain. I groaned as the slashes on my back made themselves known. Crap. I'd forgotten about my own injuries.

"You're hurt," Zade murmured, carefully putting me back on my feet. He lifted my shirt.

From the corner of my eye, I saw Issik's hands bunch into fists, and his expression freeze over. "I'm going to kill her," he snarled in a voice so low I almost didn't hear him.

"Get in line," Zade growled. "She will pay for this."

Wiggling Kieran's tattered shirt back down over the cuts, I kept my face neutral to block them from seeing the pain. "It's a few scratches. They'll heal."

"And we can help. You'll feel better after you've slept," the fire-breathing dragon reasoned. "Jase?" Zade called.

I let out a string of colorful f-bombs, knowing exactly what was coming. Zade had his hands on my shoulders and spun me around. Jase was waiting for me.

Son of a bitch.

Not again.

My head shook back and forth. "Don't you dare open your mouth," I hissed.

His violet eyes bore into mine. "Cupcake, calm down before you hurt yourself more."

"If you do this, I won't ever forgive you," I seethed, narrowing my eyes at the tranquility dragon who was about to force me to sleep.

Bringing his face near mine, his fingers tucked a strand of hair behind my ear. "Sorry, Cupcake." Regret shimmered in his gaze, and I actually believed he was sorry for what he was about to do. Pain radiated from him, as if hurting me hurt him.

Poof. A cloud of purple smoke expelled from his kissable lips, except in this moment, I would have rather bit him than kissed him.

12

I woke up sweating my tits off, like my skin was melting off my body. Only one explanation came to mind, and no, it wasn't my hormones.

Zade.

God, he was hot. In more ways than just his body temperature.

Rolling my head to the side, I inspected my bed partner. Some girls might disapprove of waking up next to a different guy each day of the week. Not me. I enjoyed the variety, and I didn't really care what that said about me. Judgmental bitches could kiss my ass.

"How long have I been asleep?" I asked, stretching. I hated to admit that I *was* feeling better. The pain in my back was gone.

"Not long enough," Zade grumbled, yawning. "Do you know that you grind your teeth in your sleep?"

"It's better than drooling," I defended myself, rolling over onto my side. I doubted I'd ever get a normal night's sleep again. The descendants didn't seem to believe in a schedule.

His expression was thoughtful as his half-lidded eyes roamed over my face. "You're not mad," he stated, feeling my emotions.

Throwing off the covers, I contemplated whether or not I should also take off my shirt. Someone had removed Kieran's and slipped a clean one on me. Beads of sweat rolled between my breasts. "I'm too hot to be mad, but I still plan on killing Jase, by the way."

Zade's lips split into a grin. "I'm looking forward to it."

"I should give him a dose of his own medicine," I mumbled. My brain started to imagine all the ways I could get Jase back for knocking me out last night.

Zade moved closer, lifting up on his elbow so he was propped over me. "I'm supposed to bring you downstairs now that you're awake, but first…" His finger traced over my jaw, leaving trails of fire behind, and yet my face turned into his touch, craving more.

I was insane.

Dear God, is that all they ever thought about—kissing me? I wouldn't normally complain, but what I needed was a blast of Issik to counter the heat from Zade. "If you kiss me right now, I'm afraid I might spontaneously combust. It's so hot in here. Where's Issik?"

Hurt splashed into his eyes, but he blinked, quickly masking it. It hadn't been my intention to cause him pain or reject him.

"Shit. Sorry," Zade cursed, sitting up. He ran a hand over his face before climbing out of bed, and crossing the room to open a window. "I wasn't thinking," he admitted. His was back was to me as he leaned against the windowsill. "When I'm with you, it is so easy to forget you're human."

I got out of bed and padded across the room, berating myself for being so careless with his feelings. Laying a hand on his shoulder, I endured the wave of heat. Zade was worth being burned. "I didn't mean it to sound as if I preferred Issik over you. That's not the case. The truth is I have feelings for all of you. I don't want to hurt any of you."

Zade turned around and looked down at me. "This thing between the five of us is new. It will take some getting used to. And I'll try to remember to turn down the heat." He winked.

My shoulders relaxed, and I beamed up at him.

"We should probably find the others," he added, breaking the silent conversation we'd been having with our looks and smiles.

I was eager to see how Kieran was faring. Had his injuries completely healed?

Zade waited for me to toss on some clothes, before ushering me downstairs into the conservatory, a room made entirely out of glass. Kieran and Jase were sitting around a rectangular wooden table. Issik was standing, leaning against one of the glass walls. The sky was still gloomy and gray, casting somberness over the room. The conversation died when Zade and I walked in, making me suspicious. They were definitely hiding something from me, and it was time someone told me what the hell was going on here.

I brushed up against Issik, letting his natural coolness seep into my skin. He shot me a funny look.

My brow lifted. Was it so hard to believe I would pick him to stand next to? My critical gaze evaluated Kieran. Although he lounged in the chair with his usual carefree attitude, something felt wrong. His eyes lacked some of their luster, and his skin appeared paler.

Issik's hand landed on the small of my back, and the earth tilted underneath me as a gust of cold danced down my spine.

"Is someone going to say something, or are we just going to stare at each other?" I asked when no one began conversing.

Jase looked like a king at the head of the table. It wasn't even his house and yet it was clear which of the descendants was in charge. "Have you forgiven me?"

I frowned, my attention pulled away from Kieran, and coming to rest on the tranquility dragon. "Oh, I'll get you back, Jase Dior. When you least expect it."

"That's what I was worried about," he mumbled.

Issik's lips twitched as he loomed over me. "The witch isn't going to make this easy."

Jase tapped his fingers on top of the table, contemplating some scary-ass plan, I was sure. "When does she ever?"

"God, I can't wait to kill her," Zade added, the red in his eyes overtaking the soft brown.

Issik's scowl deepened, and darkness seemed to gather around him. "Get in line."

Jase stood up, pacing the length of the room. "We've wasted enough time. Going to the Mirrored Shallows cost us." That was an understatement.

"What are we going to do?" I asked.

An unrecognizable emotion swept through his violet eyes, and it worried me. "Comb every inch of Viperus if we have to. We split up and section off the kingdom. Every day we get out there—rain or shine."

My arms crossed over my chest. "Great. Now that we have that out of the way, what are you guys keeping from me?"

Four sets of guarded eyes met mine. "What are you talking about, Cupcake?"

"I know there is something you're not telling me. I can feel it."

No one jumped at the opportunity to fill me in on their secret. Suddenly, they had a keen interest in the grain of the wood table, or the texture of the stone floors.

I engaged my bitch mode. "Don't ignore me! I don't need to be coddled."

"We don't want to worry you," Jase eventually answered, his palms flattened on the table as he leaned on its corner.

"About what?"

Their discomfort was evident. Issik sighed beside me, iciness infiltrating the air. "She is going to find out sooner or later. What is the point in prolonging it?"

Jase's gaze went around the room, looking at each descendant. One by one, they nodded. A decision had been made. Finally, those eyes reached mine. "Our powers are getting weaker," he revealed.

My mouth dropped open. To me, they were nearly invincible. It was hard to imagine the four of them being anything but fearless, powerful dragons. "You didn't think that was something important I should know?"

The muscles in Jase's jaw tightened. "It isn't easy to admit, and we weren't entirely certain."

"Not until last night," Kieran added.

Meaning when he was struck down from the sky. From what I understood about the descendants, they weren't immortal, but nearly impossible to kill in their dragon form. They had healing abilities, and their scales were almost impenetrable, protecting their bodies from damage of all kinds—including a fall that would have killed a human. Something had been wrong with Kieran. This only reassured me that my hunch had been right, and that I had a valid reason to be so worried about him.

"As the deadline nears, we can feel the abilities inside us losing potency," Zade admitted in vexation.

Fan-flipping-tastic. Like we didn't have enough to stress about. It had seemed like an incredibly difficult task before, but doable. Now without them at full power to ward off Tianna's attacks, it felt hopeless.

"And you're afraid that if we don't find the stones soon, you'll be unable to defend yourselves against Tianna?"

Issik hooked a finger under my chin, lifting my face up to his. "It isn't just that. We wouldn't be able to protect you."

I swallowed. "You guys have to stop worrying about me. I'm not useless anymore. I have powers of my own."

It was all true, but none of us actually believed I could take care of myself. I wasn't a superhero. I wasn't ridiculously smart. I wasn't immortal.

I was average.

Jase straightened up, his expression shifting. "You might be on to something."

I didn't like the sudden lightbulb I saw go off in his mind. "I should have kept my mouth shut," I grumbled.

"Definitely," Issik agreed.

Jase ignored us, moving forward with his brilliant thought. "We're going to train you."

My brows scrunched together. "Train me for what? And when do I have time for that?"

"We'll make time. You learning to defend yourself might be what helps us stay alive."

Issik scratched the day-old stubble under his chin. "That isn't a horrible idea."

My eyes darted from one descendant to the next, unable to believe any of them thought this was an answer to our problems. "Are you guys insane? Have you been paying attention at all since I got here?"

"She has a point," Kieran spoke up, having spent most of the time quietly listening. "What if she hurts herself… or worse?"

The "worse" being I accidentally kill myself, which wasn't out of the realm of possibility. "Finally, someone who understands me."

"Olivia is often a danger to herself." Kieran shot me a faint smile.

Jase wasn't about to let the idea go. "I think it could make a difference. We can add it to your tranquility training."

My body sunk against Issik, recognizing I was outnumbered, as always. On the flipside, I could use my new combat skills to kick their asses. That was a perk I couldn't say no to. "Fine. It's your grave, Dimples."

Jase chuckled. If I didn't know better, I would have thought he was looking forward to it.

Regardless of my argument that Kieran needed to stay behind and rest, the five of us were hoofing it through the woods to another creepy grave site on the west side of Viperus. The never-ending search for the Star of Poison continued. As a kid, I used to love hide-and-seek, but now, the game grew tiresome.

Kieran and I hadn't said much to each other since the night in Mirrored Shallows, but a charge of electricity hummed between us. I swore he was playing with his lip on purpose to taunt me with his sexiness. I remembered all too well what it was like to have the cool metal touching me in the most intimate places.

My cheeks flushed. Christ, I was suddenly wearing too many clothes. "Stop looking at me like that," I hissed between my teeth, keeping my voice low so the others wouldn't hear me.

"I don't know what you're talking about," he replied as if he was an innocent lamb. His fingers brushed mine, and I jerked my hand away, afraid the others would pick up on something, but the light touch had done its damage, heightening the color in my face.

I scowled at the poison dragon, giving him a pointed glare. Didn't know what I was talking about my left butt cheek. I was on to him, and he had another thing coming if he thought he could seduce me in the woods with the others present. "I am not some prize you can claim."

"Is that why you didn't want me to tag along? Because you're afraid they would see how you feel about me, how I can make your body come alive?" he murmured near my ear, causing my belly to flip.

Maybe Kieran needed to realize he wasn't the only dragon who could make my blood sing. He might not be so cocky then, and once the thought took root, a reckless idea took shape.

We had caught Zade's attention with our odd behavior. "What is up with the two of you?" he asked, as we stumbled upon a clearing in the dense forest. "What's with the whispering and keeping secrets? You're both acting so weird."

Jase and Issik, who had been trailing behind, paused with the rest of us. "We are not," Kieran and I said at the same time, making us look that much more suspicious. We were going to have to tell the others what had happened in the cave eventually.

I preferred to do it later. Much later. When we weren't at the cusp of a spooky-ass grave. The area we stood in was filled with carved headstones, scattered across the grounds like the gravedigger had been drunk.

But Jase wouldn't let it go.

He eyed Kieran and me with intense scrutiny, which made me squirm with unease. "No, something definitely happened between the two of you."

"Knowing Kieran, he probably seduced her," Issik added in an offhand comment, but that was all it took to light a spark.

Jase's gaze was pure violet fire as he zeroed in on Kieran. "Tell me you didn't."

Kieran did the worst thing possible. He grinned.

Suddenly, Kieran was on the ground with Zade on top of him. I stood on the sidelines, nibbling my lip, and pondering if I should do or say something. Instead, I let them beat the shit out of each other. If the others weren't going to do anything, then screw it, neither was I.

Neanderthal dragons.

Would they ever learn fists didn't solve everything?

Zade's lip bled down his chin, and Kieran's knuckles were cut open when they finally broke apart and shoved to their feet.

"I didn't plan it, okay? It just happened. What was I supposed to do? Ignore her emotions? I can't help it you got anger instead of love. It probably has something to do with your temper."

I had to agree, but Zade didn't. The hotheaded dragon moved like lightning, grabbing Kieran by the shirt, and I thought for sure we were in for round two.

"Cool off," Jase ordered, intervening before any more fists were thrown. About damn time. "We're here for the stone. We can discuss Olivia's sex life later."

My mouth dropped open. "Hell no. No one is discussing my sex life—now or later." It was like I was invisible.

"Are you saying she picked you?" Zade challenged Kieran, flames licking in his crimson eyes. This wasn't a competition, and Kieran wasn't the winner, however much that twisted smirk on his lips said otherwise.

I cleared my throat. "I'm not picking anyone," I insisted, ready to change the topic to safer ground—like the stone. I might as well have been talking to a brick wall. No one listened to me.

It was time to take action.

Walking up to Issik—the only one who hadn't said anything—I placed my hands on his shoulders and lifted up to my toes. Before he guessed what I had planned, I sealed my lips to his in a glacial kiss like the first frost. I molded into him, sinking into his body.

From the moment my lips touched his, all I could think about was why it had taken me so long to kiss him. My fingers burrowed into his silky blond hair that came to his jawline. His taste was cool, minty, and addicting. My mouth tingled as his tongue parted my lips to dip inside. His cool caress against my tongue was refreshing, and I craved more.

My spine arched, seeking the comfort of his touch, and I wasn't disappointed. Issik's hands slid to my hips, pulling me against the length of him. A tender breath escaped my lips, as I succumbed to the heady persuasion of his mouth. What was meant to be a quick kiss had gained the power to snowball. It scared me—the ability the descendants had to make me tremble with desire at their feet.

And tremble I did.

A shiver rippled through me.

Issik slowly broke off the kiss to look at me with bright eyes that lit up in the dark. An emotion flickered through the need churning in his stormy, light blue gaze. Could it be hurt? "Why did you do that?" he asked in a strained voice.

I eyed him intently, wondering how I had hurt him. My fingers lightly traced the hard planes on his face, and I watched the way his irises darkened under my touch. "Because I wanted to."

"Good." His tone held a warning, but his arms were pulling me closer. "We're not finished yet."

We weren't?

Closing the distance between us, he fastened his lips over mine a second time. Pure white heat shot through me, tightening the lower part of my body.

"Enough," rumbled Jase. He slipped his hands around my arms, separating me from Issik. "We don't have time for this."

I blinked, giving myself a few moments to catch my breath, and when the ground was solid under my feet, I directed my gaze at Kieran. "Did you feel that?"

A deep frown marred his face. "You made your point."

With a slightly unsteady hand, I smoothed my tousled hair. "Like I told you before, I can't choose. The four of you are going to have to find a way to deal with that."

"You guys need to get your hormones in check, and stop thinking with your dicks. We have more pressing matters at hand." Jase rubbed his temples in exasperation.

"Hear! Hear!"

Jase shot me a raised brow, and I realized my snarky agreement hadn't been inside my head. "You're not helping either. Keep your lips to yourself. No more kissing anyone until we find the stone."

"Who died and made you king?"

Jase's jaw worked. "My father."

Ugh. I hated it when he was so literal, but it didn't stop the guilt. A parent's death was nothing to joke about. No one knew that better than me, and it didn't matter if it had been a month, a year, or a hundred years; the pain stayed with you.

Releasing me, he barked out orders. "Same drill as before. Split up. Find the stone. Stop the curse."

Without waiting to hear who would be assigned as my protector, I took off into the misty graveyard. There were times being surrounded by the descendants was overwhelming. They each had such powerful personalities and an enticing presence. My body didn't know what it wanted when the four of them were near.

I could feel Issik behind me. Hovering. One dragon I could handle, even the coldest of the bunch. My lips were still tingling from our kiss, and I touched my bottom lip, losing focus once again on why I was in a graveyard.

The wind picked up, blowing through the leaves and branches before tossing back my hair. Inside the whistling of the cool air, I heard a voice. It was trying to tell me something.

My entire body froze as I stretched to listen.

It's a trap.

S pinning around, I found Issik right beside me. "Did you hear that?" I whispered.

"I don't hear anything," he replied in a normal volume, scanning the area around us.

Lifting a finger into the air, I shushed him and waited, listening to see if I would hear it again. The wind did not disappoint. *Leave. You must go. Before it is too late.*

My eyes swept over the graveyard. "Someone is sending us a warning."

Issik's muscles tensed, and his mouth thinned into a straight line. "You're sure?"

I wrapped my arms around myself and nodded. "Pretty sure." The wind had died down, taking the whisperings with it, and leaving me a mess.

A spear of lightning lanced across the sky, making his face look sinister as he shifted into protector mode. "The sooner we find this stone, the closer I'll be to killing this witch."

Thunder cracked close to our location, and I couldn't help but think Tianna was responding to Issik's threat. I panicked, remembering the last time lightning had struck. My hands fisted into the material of Issik's shirt. "We need to get out of here. Now, Issik," I pleaded.

His arms came around me. "Hey, it's going to be okay."

My head shook. "You don't know that. This feels wrong."

With a tenderness he rarely showed, Issik ran his fingers over my hair. "Your fear is so strong, but you can't let it rule you. I need you to be brave. Can you do that?"

Inspired by the vibrant determination on his face, I nodded. Courage was the resistance of fear. I had read that once on a fortune cookie, and the words couldn't have been truer at this moment. I needed courage. It was the only way I could stand against the witch.

Hesitating, he laced his fingers through mine, keeping me close. "Good." Together we continued our exploration of the tombs.

"How did you win babysitting duty?" I asked, trying to take my mind off the fact that we were undoubtedly all walking into some kind of witch web.

"Because Jase thinks I'm the least likely to seduce you in a cemetery," he replied with the slightest traces of sarcasm.

I snorted under my breath, but a little louder than I had meant. Did that mean Jase didn't trust himself alone with me either? "He should be more worried about me making a move on you."

A smile tugged at Issik's lips. "My sentiments exactly."

In the dark, it wasn't easy to search for an object as small as the Star of Poison. I hadn't understood at first why the descendants thought the burial grounds would be a likely place to find the stone.

Not until I noticed the detail in a few of the headstones, particularly the ones that were nearly as tall as me. Besides ornate designs and beautiful symbols I couldn't interpret, many had jewels and other valuables encrusted into the stone or placed inside cavities.

"Does each kingdom have their own burial sites?" I was thinking if I had to spend the next few months rummaging among the dead, I might need to perform a few cleansing rituals.

"Not like these. We all have our own way of dealing with those who have passed on. Kieran's tradition buries the deceased, Zade's burns them, and Jase's releases them to the sea."

"And you?" I prompted.

Issik unwound his fingers from mine and jammed his hands into his pockets. "We freeze the bodies under sheets of ice."

I shuddered.

"Are you cold?" he asked, concern crinkling the corners of his eyes.

"No, not really. It's this place. It gives me the heebie-jeebies."

"There's nothing to be afraid of."

He received one of my bullshit glares. *Be brave*, I reminded myself.

Issik's massive shoulders gave a shrug. "Okay, so I lied, but I want you to feel safe with me."

"I do," I reassured him because he looked as if he needed it. My hand reached out to touch his arm.

"No touching!" Jase's voice carried from the other side of the clearing. The mist was too dense for me to see him clearly, but I could tell he was glowering.

I rolled my eyes. "We should make out just to piss him off more."

Issik's brows inched up. "It might mean a death sentence for me, but I'm game if you are."

Grinning, I walked around a triangular piece of stone in the ground, moving away from the temptation of Issik. What was I going to do with them?

That was a problem for another day, because a headstone a few feet in front of me captured my attention. I squinted, needing to make sure I wasn't seeing things I wanted to be there. Moving closer through the evening mist, I saw a sparkle of green under the moon's glow, causing my heart to batter in my chest.

In a kneejerk reaction, my hand shot out, grabbing Issik on the forearm. "Tell me you see that." It was comparable in size and shape to the Star of Tranquility, but as we drew nearer, a nervous feeling pitted in my gut.

"If you're talking about the hunk of emerald, then yes."

"Do you think…?"

His head angled to the side. "Only one way to find out."

With my heart in my throat and gobs of nerves shaking my steps, we walked to the tomb. I reached out, letting my fingers wrap around the smooth crystal. I waited for the jolt of magic, but in my heart, I knew this wasn't the Star of Poison. Nothing happened, and disappointment crushed my soul.

Lifting my gaze to meet Issik's, my shoulders slumped. "This isn't the star."

"No. That is not a star," he confirmed.

Following the setback, a fresh bout of frustration hit me. I chucked the crystal across the yard into the thick fog blanketing the clearing. "This blows," I huffed, letting my irritation leak out of me.

Something resembling alarm came into Issik's eyes, and my stomach muscles clenched. "Olivia, we need to go."

"What did I—"

Issik reached for me, slipped a hand onto the small of my back, and applied pressure, urging me back the way we'd come, but a movement caught my attention in my peripheral vision. My heels dug in, and my head whipped to the side. It wouldn't have mattered if I had kept walking or not, because all hell broke loose.

Literally.

Bodies rose from the graves. Wait. That wasn't quite right. They weren't physical bodies, but wisps of the humans they'd once been. Ghosts.

Holy rising dead!

My mouth hung on the ground at the sight, and Issik tugged on my hand. "What is happening?"

"Tianna is waking up the dead," Issik stated matter-of-factly, like it was as normal as rain falling.

"She can do that?" I screeched, drawing the ghosts' attention.

Issik's hand clamped over my mouth, and he pulled me to him. "Yes, she can," his frosty voice whispered in my ear. "And if you don't want those ghosts to try and possess you, keep quiet."

Good advice. I should take it, and I would take it.

And yet my innate concern for the others overruled my own safety. "What about Zade, Kieran, and Jase? We have to warn them."

Issik stiffened like a steel rod had been jammed into his spine. "They can take care of themselves. What we need to do is get you out of here."

I debated with myself while Issik steered us through the graveyard —run with Issik to safety, or turn and warn the other descendants? Maybe it was the shock from seeing a scene straight out of a horror film, but something inside me snapped. My brows drew together, and I yanked my hand free from Issik's. Before he had a chance to capture me again, I spun around, my hair fanning out in the air, and took off, running straight toward the gang of hovering ghosts.

"Son of a bitch," I heard Issik swear, followed by the pounding of his feet.

This might be a stupid idea, but I had to try. What was the point of having powers if I couldn't use them for good, like saving my dragons? No more chickening out for me.

I would fight.

Knowing I only had a second until Issik caught me, I opened my mouth and released a stream of tranquility from deep within my chest. The haze of purple swirled and twirled around the gang of ghosts.

Hell yes. Take that, you dead bastards.

I was a badass… for five whole seconds.

The mist began to dissipate, and instead of the spirits dropping off into a deep sleep, they shook off the dazing effect, and homed their blank gazes in on me.

"Shit. Shit. Shit. Why didn't that work?" I mumbled, backing up into a wall that turned out to be Issik.

His fingers were at my waist, keeping me from toppling over. "Because they're already asleep—an eternal sleep."

"That would have been nice to know beforehand." Our window of escape was gone, and I was to blame. Tianna's cackle echoed throughout the graveyard.

Issik shoved me behind him, taking a stand against the ghosts. Tingles danced in the air between us, indicating a shift was in the making. I backed up to give him room, and a hand touched my shoulder. I got a bad feeling along with a chill that was very different than Issik's.

Don't turn around. Don't do it, my mind chanted, but my body was already in motion.

A silent scream lodged in my esophagus.

The ghost in front of me wore a top hat, but that wasn't the strange part. He gave me a wobbly grin before he floated into me.

"Olivia!" Issik bellowed, but it was too late.

I'd been possessed by a mother-freaking ghost.

The coldness in my chest intensified, and I became a prisoner in my own body. My thoughts and feelings were mine, but someone else controlled my arms and legs. Unable to stop what was happening, my mouth opened, and the spirit delivered a message.

Deliver the stones, or I'll kill her.

Damn. Could my voice have sounded any freakier? I would have nightmares for years. Being possessed was certainly not something I would recommend. Not even once. Nothing else the Veil could do to me would shake me as badly as this had.

When the soul left my body, it felt like someone had a giant suction cup on my heart and then released the pressure, freeing me from its tormented possession. Trying to catch my breath, I sunk to my knees. Dirt and gravel dug into my flesh, but I didn't feel the pain.

In fact, I felt nothing.

I was empty.

No emotion. No thoughts. Just a black hole.

"Olivia!" Issik shook my shoulders. His eyes were filled with terror, and I could tell that it hadn't been the first time he'd shouted my name.

I blinked, feeling as if I'd awakened from a brush with death, and was amazed to be alive.

His fingers roamed over my face. "Is it you?"

Needle pinpricks radiated over my skin, starting with my toes and traveling to my head. It was the feeling you get after sitting on your foot for too long. My body was waking back up.

"It's me," I assured him.

He yanked me into his arms, pulling me into a tight embrace. "Little Warrior," he said it like an answer to prayer.

An odd noise, between a curse and a sob, left my lips. My forehead pressed to his chest. "I might be sick. God, I really hate throwing up."

Cool fingers took hold of my chin and tipped my face upward. "You're so pale, and your nose is bleeding."

My hand flew to my nose and wiped under it. Sticky red blood covered my fingers. The sight made me woozy. "I need a minute. Don't let me go." I shivered, my body not yet recovered fully from the possession of the spirit.

"You're cold." His fingers moved to rub up and down my arms in an effort to chase away the cold, which for him was a futile motion. "We need to find Zade." Issik bent down, scooping me up in his arms.

I could definitely use some of Zade's heat. "It's not you." I needed to explain the chattering of my teeth, so he wouldn't take it personally. "The ghost... he was so cold inside me." The air from my lungs came out in a white puff.

"A side effect from being possessed. It will pass, but quicker with Zade's help." His long legs ate up the ground.

My head rested on Issik's firm shoulder. The ghosts were wandering aimlessly; they no longer seemed interested in me since having delivered their message. Still, I doubted it was good for the Veil to have a bunch of dead running amok. They needed to be dealt with soon.

"What happened?" demanded a voice I recognized as Jase's. He was always demanding.

Issik handed me off to Zade, and I gladly entered his furnace. "She was possessed. Warm her up while I take care of the restless dead."

Nothing more needed to be said. The fire dragon spun me around to face him, his fingers coming to frame my blue cheeks. As his lips descended to mine, I caught a flash of Issik shifting. My eyes fluttered shut at the first touch of Zade's kiss. Warmth blazed back into me. From one extreme to the other, my body temperature flipped, now burning like the core of the sun. I felt as if I was glowing from the inside out.

"Better?" he asked after pulling back.

"Much," I agreed.

"I swear I don't know what we did around here for fun before you."

The snarky comment died on my lips, as I noticed a dragon missing. Where the heck was Kieran? I turned my attention back to the graveyard, searching for Issik. Jase and Zade stood shoulder to shoulder next to me, boxing me in with their tall bodies, which was obviously a protective maneuver in case another ghost decided to invade my body.

What was Issik doing? Sacrificing himself as a diversion? There were too many. How was he going to fight them all? I couldn't let him do it. I needed him as much as I did the others.

My blood pressure rose. "Are you guys going to just stand here?"

"Kieran is with him… somewhere," Jase answered.

The thick fog made it really difficult to see for any distance. "Great, you sent the wounded dragon to help."

Jase tilted his chin down to look at me. "You're more important than Issik or Kieran."

Frustration tore through me, only to be entangled by the strands of worry piling up in my stomach.

Issik circled overhead, dipping low over the clearing. Slivers of ice expelled from his chest, and the frost encased the ghostly forms, freezing them on the spot. Zade reacted. Wrapping me in his arms, he protected me from the cold, his body exuding an insane amount of heat, but it did the trick.

Teamwork at its finest.

The ground shook when Issik landed. A dozen ghost popsicles were scattered over the cemetery. *Swoosh.* His tail swung in an arc, taking out half of the ice statues and shattering them to little bits. The sky rained shards of their ghostly souls. He repeated the movement until every last one was gone.

I exhaled, breathing easily. "Can we go home now?" I asked, sinking against Zade. "I've had enough *fun* for today."

"There's always tomorrow," he replied with a smile.

"That's what I'm afraid of."

Tempers grew shorter every day. A week passed. The days drained away, and the dreams became a nightly occurrence since the possession. I didn't know what that witch had done to me, but I didn't like it. She could take her voodoo ways and shove them where the sun don't shine. And she could take the dreams back too. I was done with the restless nights, the torment, and the stress of it all.

Maybe that was part of her plan—to drive me mad.

Well, it was working.

This particular night, I had another one of my strange dreams, but it was different than the others; it broke through to reality.

A woman with wavy hair the color of wheat, that cascaded down her back stood in my room. Her eyes were milky and pale, hiding their true color. I didn't know why that particular detail stood out to me, but it seemed important somehow—like it would reveal her identity.

Crazy, I know.

But what dreams weren't? They never made any sense. It was as if my subconscious constantly wanted to fuck with me, but in this case, it was a witch.

The woman glided across the floor like someone from a horror movie, her tattered dress dragging on the ground. I scooted back in the bed, tempted to throw the covers over my eyes, and start humming to myself.

"You're not crazy," she whispered to me, except her mouth never opened. Her words projected into the air.

I tugged the blanket up to my chin, noticing for the first time I was alone. No dragon snored beside me. "I'm not sure how much weight that holds coming from a ghost in a dream."

This island was schizophrenic.

Some ghosts wanted to help me. Others wanted to possess me. What did she want? Was she a ghost? Was she someone important? Or a follower of Tianna? She could, of course, be a product of my colorful imagination.

"I'm not a ghost per se. More of a guide."

My heart beat so fast in my chest I thought I was going to be sick. "You're the woman from the cave?"

She nodded as her fingers played with a gold locket around her neck. "The stone is closer than you think."

She had my undivided attention. I tossed the covers aside and sat straight up. "Can you tell me where it is? I'm desperate."

"It is not far from the eye."

"Whose? Mine?" I frantically searched the room, looking for something to clue me in on where the star might be. Was it here in my bedroom? It couldn't be that simple.

She snuck up on me while I scrutinized every inch of my space, and finding her suddenly so close to my face startled me. I let out a little squeak of surprise, instantly concerned she might try to possess me. I stayed perfectly still, but ready to fight.

Her fingers reached for the back of her neck, unclasping the necklace she wore. "I want you to have this. Let it be the light to guide you through the darkness."

Did she mean figuratively or literally?

Holding the chain, she moved toward me, and I stayed motionless as she wrapped the necklace around my neck, fastening the clasp. The charm dangled between my breasts. I touched the gold locket and found it to be warm.

"I don't know what to say. Thank you?" My eyes lifted to meet hers.

The room had suddenly been sucked of all light. No moonlight filtered through the curtains. No candle burned on the small desk in the corner. Nothing but darkness and the sound of my heavy breathing filled the room. The woman jerked away from the bed and fluttered back and forth through the room. Her white dress was the only way I could track her movements.

Crawling to the end of the bed, I followed her sporadic pacing with my eyes. "What's wrong?"

"She's coming." Her voice had gone soft and scary.

"Who?"

Her eyes flew to the door, and she came to a harsh halt. "The witch. You must wake up. Now!"

Easier said than done. I couldn't just snap my fingers and boom I was awake. What was I supposed to do? Scrambling to lay back down, I closed my eyes. Wake up. Wake up. Wake up, I chanted. Regardless of the panic rising within me, I remained stuck in the dream, awaiting whatever horror Tianna had planned for me.

Hiss. Hiss. Hiss.

God. No. Please don't let that be what I think it is.

Everyone has fears. The one thing that makes them lose their shit— heights, spiders, blood. Mine was snakes.

I fucking hated snakes.

More than lima beans. More than winter. More than being homeless.

I got that a viper was Viperus's mascot, but that didn't mean I was thrilled to live in a castle with a snake carved into it. Yet, when it came to the dragon that lived in it, I would do anything to save him and the others, including dealing with a deranged witch... and her pets.

The vicious, venomous viper slithered across my floor like he owned the room. I didn't know when the woman in white had vanished, but she was no longer here, leaving me all alone with a brood of snakes. One after another, they slunk under the door, through the windows, and any other hole they could squeeze into with ease.

It might have been a trick of my mind or one of Tianna's hexes, but hidden in the hissing that echoed in the room was a voice. I was damn sure snakes didn't talk or, at the very least, they weren't supposed to.

Tick tock goes the clock. Ding-dong the key is dead.

Are you kidding me? Nursery rhymes? I had to still be dreaming. And they got the last line wrong. It was "the witch is dead."

In a puff of smoke, the nightmare faded.

I bolted upright in bed, cold sweat glistening over my body. The air in my lungs came out in quick short pants while I caught my breath. I told myself I was okay. Nothing could hurt me. But that feeling of security lasted a split second.

A shadow on the floor drew my gaze, and like my dream, darkness slithered over the wood planks. The dream might have faded, but the snakes had remained. They climbed up the side of the bed, forked tongues tasting the air.

A scream ripped from my throat.

Jase jumped out of bed like the castle was on fire. The bed sheet tangled around his legs, giving him a Greek toga vibe. In another situation, I would have appreciated the look on him—golden skin, tight abs, and eyes that glowed in the dark. Yeah, Jase Dior was definitely a rare breed of male.

"Get back on the bed," I yelped, thinking the snakes would bite him.

His body was rigid as he waited for an attack that never came. "What's wrong?" His sharp eyes ran over the room, trying to pinpoint the threat.

"Don't you see them? The s-snakes?" My voice tripped over the word. I refused to peek over the edge of the bed.

He raked a hand through his hair. "I don't see anything, Cupcake. It must have been a nightmare."

Oh, I didn't doubt I had been locked in a room of horror, but when that hellish room became reality, that was when you had a problem. Jase wasn't going to be able to convince me that what I had seen hadn't been real. The witch was toying with me.

Did that mean I was close to finding the key?

Or was she, in her sick way, trying to motivate me?

I curled up on the bed, hugging my knees. "I'm so tired. She won't let me sleep," I murmured, rocking back and forth.

Jase hiked the sheet up, freeing his legs, and climbed back into bed. "You mean Tianna?"

"Unless Harlow suddenly developed the ability to torture me in my dreams."

"Funny." His lips twitched as he gathered my distraught body into his arms. "The others have noticed the restlessness you've been suffering at night. Do you want me to help?"

For once, I was tempted by tranquility, but I shook my head. I didn't want to sleep. "Could you hold me instead?" Somehow my brain concluded I would be safer in his arms, as if he could chase her away.

"I thought you'd never ask." He settled back down, propping his head on the pillow and opening an arm.

Without hesitation, I nestled against him, resting my face in the space between his neck and shoulder. The tension and fear lingering from the nightmare began to clear. "Don't get any ideas and try that tranquility crap on me," I muttered.

His fingers ran through my hair. "Are you sure? A good night's sleep devoid of dreams might be what you need."

Under my hand, his heart beat steadily, and it comforted me, feeling his source of life, but a dark cloud nagged at the back of my head. *For how long?* it pestered. I didn't want to think about that. Not now. "This is better than sleep."

"Everything will be okay," Jase reassured, pressing a kiss to my forehead. "I promise."

How could he make such a statement? It might never be okay again. Without the stone, they would die. And then what? The last place I wanted to be was stranded on an exclusive island with a lunatic witch. None of us knew what would happen if the descendants died, but speculating about it wasn't going to change anything.

Sleep was out of the picture for the night, but wrapped up in Jase, I didn't mind. Lifting my head slightly, I saw the moonlight spill across the side of his face, illuminating his rugged sexiness, and I swore I heard the heavens sing.

"**W**hat are you wearing?"

The question every girl longed to hear. And Jase thought he had game. Hilarious. "Padding," I replied, patting the pillows strapped around my chest. "In case I fall."

Jase shook his head, clearly trying to figure out my madness. That made two of us. "I don't plan on beating the crap out of you."

"One can never be too prepared when I'm involved."

His eyes sparkled, and my belly squirmed in response. "Touché."

"Okay, I'm ready. Let's do this shit." Shit being self-defense or something like that. I'd been in a few fights, but I was talking about hair pulling and boob punching, nothing that required me to defend myself against wraiths and griffins. That was a new level I had yet to unlock.

Thick lashes framed his gorgeous violet eyes, and a slow grin pulled at the corners of his wicked mouth. The back of his knuckles feathered over my cheek, sending a thousand electrifying tingles over me. "You're almost too cute."

I blinked. Holy crap. A deep yearning that had been there since I laid eyes on him clawed at me. Jase had a way of leaving a stunning first impression. My head angled to the side as I regarded him. "Cute," I repeated, unable to stop my lips from curling. "You think this is cute?" I asked, my hand gesturing down my marshmallow torso.

He gave a slight shrug. "On you, it somehow works."

My hips rolled in the worst attempt at a stripper move. "I'm bringing sexy back." The words came out with a straight face, but it didn't last long before I busted out laughing. Sexy I was not.

"If you keep flirting with me, we're going to end up on the floor." His eyes roamed over my body.

This made me laugh more. Clutching my padded belly like Santa Claus, I tried to gain control of my laughter. "Are we really doing this?" I asked, glancing around the room. It had been cleared out with all the furniture pushed to one wall.

He stretched his arms out to the side and then over his head, his T-shirt lifting above his gym shorts to reveal his drool-worthy abs. "It's time for you to learn how to defend yourself. You didn't get padded up for nothing."

"Why do I need to learn? I have you for that." It had been a joke, but seeing the determination in Jase's face made me glad I'd gone the extra mile.

"Olivia," Jase scolded me in his no-nonsense voice. "It seems that no matter how much we try to protect you, Tianna finds ways to get to you. Last night is a prime example. You need to be strong mentally and physically."

Ugh. The snake dream. "Did you have to bring that up again?" I was doing everything within my power to pretend it had never happened.

"We can't let the witch get inside your head. Who knows what kind of damage she could do."

A shiver trickled down my spine at the idea of Tianna continually infiltrating my mind. My mind was a frightening enough place, without some vindictive witch getting her hands on it. It got me thinking though…

"What about the other girls? Do they know how to fight?" Maybe I wasn't the only one whom Tianna tortured with her mind games.

"Some of them, but most of them never had a reason to."

"I love being special."

Jase's lips twitched.

For the first half hour, Jase went over some basic footing and defensive techniques, which was honestly a waste of time and effort. I spent most of the time on the floor. It was embarrassing, but my balance was off-kilter with the extra padding. And Jase didn't help matters. The dragon could barely keep a straight face around me. This was the worst idea on the planet, but I wasn't a quitter. Jase moved on to lunging and attacking, luckily without any weapons, just getting used to the motions and learning the most effective moves for someone of my stature. I lacked the brute strength and towering height the descendants each possessed. He tossed in some tranquility lessons, testing my skill under pressure. That was the only test I passed.

But I did excel at falling on my ass and cursing.

"This has got to go," Jase said, pulling out my stuffing and tossing it behind him, all the while doing his best to retain his stern expression. The corners of his lips gave him away. They were dying to curl as he hovered over me. I was on the ground. Again. "I don't think I can watch you fall one more time. It's painful."

Lying flat on my back, I winced and sat up. "There is no way this is more painful for you than me."

He extended both his hands to help me to my feet. "Maybe we should try something else."

"You think?" I shot back, placing my hands in his, and with ease, he lifted me to my feet. It felt marvelous to be rid of the extra protection, like taking off my bra after a long day.

"Okay, smartass. Maybe this will grab your attention." Releasing my hands, he sauntered to the right corner of the room and bent down, picking up something wrapped in a cloth. He unraveled the material and straightened. As he started to turn around, I closed the space between us to see what he had been hiding.

My eyes popped out of my head at the first sight of the gold dagger, and I came to a jerky halt, nearly toppling over my own feet. "What the hell are you going to do with that?"

Jase flipped the blade in the air. "Teach you to use it."

I busted out laughing. "You want to give me a knife? Are you insane? What if I trip and fall on it?"

"She has a point." Issik's voice drifted in from the doorway, where he rested against the frame.

My hands went up in the air. "Thank you. Finally, a voice of reason."

"Issik, you're not helping. Don't you have something to do, like find a star?" Jase suggested between gritted teeth.

Issik gave a one-shoulder shrug. "Kieran and Zade went out."

I whipped my head toward Issik. "Without me?"

His eyes flicked to my face, but it was Jase who answered. "Afraid so, Cupcake."

I spun around, uncertain what I was feeling. Left out? I should have been glad they went out into the woods without me. All I'd done was complain about how tired I was, and yet, I was disappointed that I'd been left behind.

"Could you pick a different nickname? That one constantly makes me hungry," I snapped, feeling moody.

Jase lowered his lashes in a naughty look. "Me too."

Argh. They were devils. All four of them. The way their minds worked gave me whiplash.

Issik stepped into the room, breezing past me to stand in front of Jase. "This is why I'm staying. All anyone thinks about is seducing her."

"And you don't?" Jase challenged him.

"I didn't say that," Issik replied with a clenched jaw.

"Three *is* more fun than two." Did I say that out loud?

Crap.

What was wrong with my mouth? Why didn't it know when to shut up and keep things to myself? It was as if it had a mind of its own, spewing out whatever it pleased.

"Is that so?" Jase asked, tilting his head to the side. The two dragons stood shoulder-to-shoulder, eyeing me with twin quizzical expressions.

My fingers fumbled with the charm around my neck. "It's the lack of sleep. It's making me delusional. I don't know what I'm saying anymore."

"Uh-huh."

Jase's eyes bounced between the weapon and me before narrowing. "Where did you get that necklace? It looks familiar."

"Um, the lady in my dream gave it to me." Truthfully, I'd completely forgotten about it until now.

Jase and Issik both choked. "What are we going to do with her?" Jase grumbled as he and Issik both moved to get a closer look at the charm.

Issik's cool fingers brushed along my skin, causing my breath to catch. "I've seen this before as well, but I can't recall on whose neck."

"Why did she give it to you?" Jase asked.

"She said something about it guiding me through darkness." My memory wasn't so good, not with the two of them clouding my senses.

Issik let the charm dangle back over my neck. "Do you think it is safe? What if it's one of Tianna's tricks?" he posed to Jase.

Why hadn't I thought of that? I glanced down at the circle pendant. In the center was an intricate filigree design. Could it be this was a cursed talisman? I didn't want to imagine what kind of heinous things it would do to me if it were, in fact, hexed.

Jase sighed, looking troubled. "More questions we don't have time to answer. I can't explain it, but I don't think there's any sorcery at play here."

Good enough for me, and Issik too it seemed. And Jase was right, we didn't have time for another mystery. The clock was ticking, which meant I needed to pull on my ninja pants and get this shit done. When Tianna came, which was only a matter of time, I wouldn't cower at her feet. I stretched my arm toward Jase. "Hand over the blade."

Issik stepped to the side, eyeing the gold dagger. "You take that blade, and there's no going back." He turned his icy glare to Jase and poked a finger into his chest. "You better hope no blood is shed, or I am holding you responsible."

Flipping the blade so the handle was held out for me to grab, Jase offered me the sharp weapon. "This won't kill a witch, but it will do some serious damage to griffins, imps, goblins, and other nasties who are under the witch's rule."

My fingers wrapped around the smooth hilt. "Good to know." I then rewound the conversation in my head. "Did you say goblins?"

"We have all kinds of nasties in the Veil to be wary of," Issik stated.

"Delightful," I said dryly.

By the end of the day, my skills had improved very little. I managed to avoid hurting anyone, including myself, but I couldn't say I had any actual ability wielding a dagger. Flinging the blade toward the wall, I watched as it clamored to the ground, not even making a dent. My shoulders slumped, and I let my arm hang heavily at my side. The weapon might seem light at first, but after an hour of swinging, jabbing, and stabbing, my arm was about to fall off.

"Let's face it. I suck."

Jase came up behind me and massaged my aching shoulders. "You'll get better with practice."

I rolled my neck and moaned. If he stopped, I might threaten him with the blade. "There's no time, Dimples. This is hopeless. I'm in so much trouble, aren't I?"

"Depends on what kind of trouble you're referring to. I've had to spend the entire day trying not to think about kissing you." His seductive voice murmured near my ear.

Issik ran a thumb over his bottom lip. "I know what you mean. It's torture keeping her safe, when all I want to do is sweep her off to the nearest bed."

I was unable to look away, caught in the storm swirling in Issik's eyes. "Now is not the time for sexual innuendos."

Issik grinned—actually grinned, the Ice Prince and my breath caught. "There is always time for sex."

What was happening? They got a little sweaty and their minds went off the deep end?

I found myself sandwiched between Issik and Jase, and my blood pressure skyrocketed. This was supposed to be a training session, but I had a feeling the only thing I *would* learn was how to handle two guys at once.

"Is this a test?" My voice took on a husky quality I didn't know I possessed.

Jase lifted the blond hair off the back of my neck, gathering it to the side and over my shoulder. "The question is whether you will pass."

Now this was a test I could get behind. My hands lifted and looped around Issik's neck. "Is that so?"

Neither of them kissed me on the lips. They each bent their heads and went for opposite sides of my neck. Tranquility and ice swirled, encompassing me in an addictive cocktail I couldn't stop sampling.

Holy dragon babies.

What had I gotten myself into?

Issik's tongue traced along the pulsing vein on my throat, and I welcomed the sensations he created. I had been in a similar position before, just with a different mixture of dragons. What would it be like to try other combinations? My mind tumbled through the possibilities. Fire and ice. Poison and tranquility. Tranquility, Ice, and Fire. My math skills were on par with my combat skills, so I stopped trying to figure out the number of dragon mishmashes I could get myself into, and focused on what Jase and Issik's hands were doing to my body.

Issik had a rigid control I wanted to destroy; I wanted him to let loose, completely. I pressed every inch of my body into the full hardness of his, fisting my fingers into his hair. Pushing up onto my toes, I covered his lips with mine. Ice so cold it nearly stole my breath poured into my mouth, but I never faltered in our kiss. In fact, I took it further, letting him capture my low moan with his mouth.

"Fuck," he muttered, his fingers squeezing my bottom.

Victory.

It was sweet and oh so satisfying.

Issik spun me around, passing me to Jase, who was quick to pick up where Issik had left off. Jase claimed my lips with a hungry passion that nearly drove me straight over the edge. I wanted the release more than I wanted anything in my life. It didn't matter who delivered the fireworks, only that it was soon.

But the descendants like to take their time, and drag out the divine torture for as long as possible.

Dear god.

I might die in their arms.

It was at their mercy, and yet they only seemed to care about how they were making me feel. Neither was greedy nor combative, but they worked together to bring me right to the brink of desire. The release was right there. I bit down on my lip, my back arching forward when something fluttered over my arm. It happened again, soft and silky, pulling me away from the edge I so desperately sought. I was breathless, annoyed, and aroused to the point of no longer being held responsible for what I did next. My eyes slowly peeled open, and I gasped.

Obsidian butterflies swirled around the room in a stunning dance. Their velvety wings beat gracefully through the air, circling around the three of us. Our little intruders had seized the attention of Jase and Issik as well, but from the way their bodies had hardened against me, they weren't as infatuated as I was by them.

My head fell back as I followed their elegant forms. "They're beautiful."

Issik's fingers dug into my hips. "They're deadly," he informed me.

Exhaling, I turned my gaze to Jase in front of me. "Of course they are," I mumbled.

Issik picked me up like I weighed twenty pounds, and positioned me behind both of their massive bodies. "Don't touch them. Keep them away from your face."

I stared at his back, when all I really wanted to do was watch the mesmerizing butterflies frolic in the room. It was hard to imagine a creature I had spent summers chasing was harmful in another world.

The fierceness on Jase's expression just about stopped my heart. "The nightflies whisper commands into the ear of their prey, and the victim is powerless to do anything but obey."

"Mind control?" I shrieked. "But they're so small."

Issik nodded, never taking his laser focus off the little creatures. "They are born of a dark magic that doesn't exist in the Veil."

"She never gives up with her shenanigans, does she?" I retorted.

Issik scowled. "For almost a hundred years, she has tormented us with her tricks."

I swallowed hard, moistening my lips. "How are you not all insane?"

"Who says we aren't?" Jase countered with mischief in his eyes. He couldn't possibly be enjoying this.

But I supposed we all were a bit nutty at times. What we had been doing was incomparably the zaniest thing I'd ever done.

Jase twisted his head to the side so he could see me with one eye. "This is a great opportunity for you. Put them to sleep."

"No," Issik replied, rejecting the idea. "We're not putting her at risk. If something went wrong—"

My hand landed on his shoulder. "You don't think I can do it?" The urge to prove myself rose up strongly inside me. Issik had a right to be concerned. If I screwed up, I could potentially put myself in serious danger, and still, I wanted to do it.

I was tired of being useless.

A spark of willpower and confidence infused my blood. I blamed it on the descendants' kisses. They could make even the weakest of humans feel formidable.

Issik looked over his shoulder, careful to keep his gaze directly on me. "This has nothing to do with my belief in you."

"Good, then it's settled." Before I could change my mind, I stepped out from Issik's shadow.

"Son of a bitch," he swore.

But I already had my mouth open, blowing a stream of purple mist into the air above my head. Issik and Jase made the smart decision to stay behind me and not try to stop me. The fluttering, mind-control devils went berserk at first, flying in the air like they were tripping on acid. Then as the effects of tranquility took hold, the assholes dropped to the ground one by one.

I spun around and grinned, dusting off my hands. "Easy peasy." That badass feeling returned, and this time, it stayed with me. I wasn't helpless, and I needed to remember I had power of my own.

"Great. Do you know what you've done?" Issik accused Jase. "She is going to be putting herself in twice as much danger now that she thinks she can zap everything to sleep. What happens when they wake up?"

Oh, snap. I hadn't thought about that. "Can't we have Zade burn them?" I asked. Surely, they couldn't wake up if they were ashes.

Issik swung his frosty gaze to me. "We could if he was here. Who knows when they will be back. We can't take that chance. There's no choice but to get rid of them before the nightflies shake off the effects of tranquility."

Jase nodded in agreement, scratching a hand over his chin. "They might be small, but they are also resilient, even to my power. We might have an hour, most likely less."

I liked it better when I was feeling ultracool. "Okay, so what's the plan? You have one, right?"

Jase grinned. "I always have a plan."

"Gather the nightflies," Jase barked. "But don't let the powder from their wings touch you. We'll take them into the kitchen and cook them."

My nose scrunched up. "That's morbid and gross."

Jase lifted a single brow. "You got a better idea?"

"Not really. It's just we eat there."

"Speaking of food, I'm starving. The kitchen works for me." Issik didn't seem to share my disgust.

Rolling up my sleeves, I stared at Issik like he'd grown a second set of balls. "Oh, my god. How can you think about eating right now?"

Issik shrugged. "High metabolism."

"You think Alice is going to let us roast these in her kitchen?"

Jase slipped off his shirt and ripped it in half. "Once she knows what they are, she'll insist."

Ooookay. "What's with the hulk move? You're not expecting me to walk around the castle shirtless too, are you?"

He handed me half of his torn shirt. "The only people who get to see you naked is us. Tie this over your hand."

I did as he instructed, securing the fabric over my fingers in a makeshift glove to act as a barrier against the nightflies. Jase wrapped the other cloth over his hand, and together the two of us gathered the dark and deadly butterflies scattered around the floor. Issik had removed his shirt as well, holding it out like a hammock for us to put the nightflies in, and transport them to the kitchen.

It took a few minutes, and then we were on our way down the hall. The castle was quiet with Kieran and Zade gone. Viperus Keep didn't have the staff or the number of girls that Wakeland castle had, or maybe they did a better job at being discreet.

The kitchen was empty when the three of us arrived. Issik set the bundle of nightflies on the stove, and snatched a roll from a basket, tearing off a hunk with his teeth.

My hip leaned against the counter, as I shook my head. "I don't know how you can eat."

Taking another bite, he worked his way through the kitchen, opening a cabinet. "The body needs fuel, and so do you. Sit down. I'll make you something."

"I'm not hungry," I replied without looking at him. I was too busy watching Jase light the fire on the stove, and drop the nightflies into the flames.

"Olivia. Sit." Issik raised his voice, putting a chill into it.

I snapped to attention, weaving around the counter to the table. "When did you become so pushy?" I grumbled.

He pulled some cans off of the shelves. "The moment your health is at risk."

"Sometimes I think you guys care too much," I stated, sinking into a chair and letting my shoulders relax. It had been a stressful day. My body was sore and achy. I needed a hot shower, but I indulged Issik, knowing his heart was in the right place. Plus, I was interested to see what the Ice Prince could whip up for me.

Jase finished incinerating the nightflies, and I tried to ignore the smell of charred wings that lingered in the air. The foul deed was done. Tianna's little plan had been foiled. The sounds of Issik cooking in the kitchen relaxed me. Closing my eyes, I rested my head on the back of my chair, and kicked my feet up on the chair across from me. The one beside me scraped over the floor, and Jase's scent tickled my nose.

The warmth of the stove sent me into a stupor, and I might have dozed off for a little bit, because when I came to, the kitchen no longer smelled like putrid, burning insects, but of savory rich flavors. Butter. Herbs. Garlic. A mountain of pasta sat in the center of the table, next to a platter of chicken in a white sauce.

Zade, Issik, Jase, and Kieran were all sitting around the table. My gaze scanned over both Zade and Kieran. I sighed in relief, happy to have them back. They appeared to be fine, but starved. No run-ins with the witch. They each had a plate of food in front of them.

"You're back," I greeted still groggy, stretching out my stiff arms.

Kieran offered me a lopsided grin. "And you're just in time for dinner."

I missed hearing his slight Irish accent. They might have been gone for the day, but to me, it had been too long. I felt incomplete without being surrounded by the four of them, and sitting here at the table, my soul soared; I was whole.

"I'm famished."

Issik made a gruff sound in the back of his throat, and I grinned at him. Who knew the Ice Prince was a chef?

I listened to the others relay what had happened during the day as I stuffed myself. Jase told Zade and Kieran about the nightflies, which earned me a pair of dark scowls. Zade informed us how their trip had turned up nothing on the Star of Poison. Sitting at the dinner table, discussing our day, made it feel like we were a family. I wanted a hundred—no a thousand—more nights like this. I wanted to be their family, and I needed them to be mine.

Was it conventional? No. But it didn't matter. Not to me. How they made me feel was what mattered most.

"I can't believe Olivia took out a nest of nightflies. How the hell do I miss all the good shit around here and this is my house?" Kieran complained.

"I'm proud of you," Jase confessed, ruffling my hair.

My heart swelled.

J ase's soft snore filled my ears. I didn't understand how these descendants were able to fall asleep so quickly. Turning on my side to face the slightly ajar window, I watched the moon's rays filter through the curtains, casting a pale light upon my face. A cool breeze caressed my skin.

I finally slept and dreamed. Regardless of how I fought against the invasion into my mind, Tianna always found a way.

In the dreams, the Star of Poison burned like a furnace in my hand, and green toxins spilled from the stone. I wasn't alone. A black mass withered the ground, scorching it with darkness.

The dream shifted. I was cradling Kieran's lifeless body in my arms. The trees surrounding us wept with sadness, for the heart of their kingdom was dead. No matter how hard I cried, begged, or wished, nothing would bring the dragon shifter back.

My grief consumed me.

It had been days since we'd seen the sun. My face turned upward, soaking up the warm rays as they bathed my face. What I wouldn't give for a bathing suit, a bottle of Hawaiian Tropic suntan lotion, and a fruity drink with a pink umbrella. A perfect day lying out on the beach, the golden sun tanning my skin, and not a care in the world.

No curse. No deadlines. No impending deaths. That's what I wanted.

Lost in my fantasy, I twirled the charm hanging around my neck, strolling the grounds outside the castle. The pendant glinted under the sun, casting a ray of light out in front of me like a flashlight.

What the hell?

Looking down, I lifted the gold charm in my hand and watched in wonder as the light moved with my movements. Holy crap. This had to mean something, didn't it?

Like a kid with a new toy, I twisted and turned the circular charm in my fingers, watching as the beam bounced off everything it touched. It ran up the castle, tracing the winding stone snake, but as it got to the top, an unexpected flash of emerald joined the ray of light.

What is that?

My hand tilted the charm left and right, trying to reproduce that glint of green.

There! Inside the snake's eye cavity glimmered what I would have bet my left ovary was a gemstone—the gemstone.

I gulped. Why? Why did it have to be the creepy snake's eye? It had been right over our heads this whole time. How had we not seen it before? Other than the fact it was six stories high, and a vital part of a stone snake statue that twined around the main tower.

But I knew deep in my bones that nestled into Viperus's mascot's eyeball was the Star of Poison. I had found it, but getting it was altogether a different obstacle. Obtaining the Star of Tranquility had only involved holding my breath, and diving into the lake, but this was trickier. Still, it wasn't going to stop me.

Shielding my eyes from the sun with my hand, I stared up at the intimidating statue. Vines weaved around the castle like rungs on a ladder. I glared at the long journey ahead of me. The moment I grabbed the first strand of ivy, I knew this was going to end badly.

Me? Scale a castle?

Why would I even consider doing such a thing? The old Olivia wouldn't have contemplated it for two seconds. The old Olivia would have checked the new Olivia into a mental hospital. The old Olivia wouldn't have fallen for four dragons who had begun to mean everything to her. She also never would have talked about herself in the third person.

Before I could change my mind, I started ascending the castle. I was about six feet off the ground when a voice sounded behind me. "What the hell are you doing?"

My head whipped over my shoulder to stare down at Kieran, who had his arms crossed over his chest. "Climbing the snake," I hollered down, doing my best to keep my grip secure. The last thing I needed was to tumble to my death.

"I can see that. But why?"

My arms were already tired—a bad sign. "I found the Star of Poison," I announced. A triumphant grin split my face. In my excitement, my right fingers loosened, and I slipped a few inches down the side of the castle, losing some of my progress.

"Get down here before you hurt yourself," he growled at me.

"Did you hear what I said?"

"Olivia, now!" he boomed.

"Geez. Keep your boxers on. You really know how to take the *f* out of fun."

"Are you telling me you're having fun?" he challenged me.

Good point. "I hate you," I replied as I carefully made my way back to flat ground.

Kieran plucked me off the vine when I was within reach, placing me safely on my feet, but his hands stayed at my waist, anchoring me to him. "No one knows more than I how much you don't hate me."

My worry of falling vanished. "Rub it in, why don't you?"

Kieran turned me around. "Why didn't you ask one of us to take you to the top, instead of trying to scale a castle?"

Duh. I had four dragons who could flippin' fly. "I got so excited that I didn't think about it."

"Clearly," he chuckled.

"Soooo…" I drew out the word. "What are you waiting for? Let's get the stone before you-know-who decides to show up, and rain on my freaking parade."

"Have I told you how strange you are today?" he asked, sounding both amused, and exasperated all at once.

I rolled my eyes. "Says the guy who is about to shift into an emerald dragon, and spits poison."

Kieran winked. "Valid point. I think that's why we like you so much."

"Oh, I thought it was because I'm a blonde."

"There's that too." Kieran grabbed the hem of his shirt and lifted it over his head. "Do you mind holding these?" he asked as he wiggled out of his jeans.

My eyes were glued to his abs, and it took me a moment to process what he had asked. Then I noticed the pile of clothes in his hands. "Let's be real. You did that on purpose so I would drool over your naked body."

Wickedness sparkled in his expression, as he dropped his clothes, and lifted his thumb to brush the side of my lip. "Here, let me get that for you."

I smacked at his hand. "Stop flirting with me and do your thing already. We're wasting time." I couldn't believe he was teasing me.

Where was his elation at finding the stone? This was what we'd spent the last few weeks searching for frantically. I wanted an *Olivia, you're a genius* or some other type of accolade. My gaze narrowed as I glared at Kieran and realized something. He wasn't taking me seriously. Bastard.

"You don't believe me."

"I never said that," he quickly replied, seeing my brows draw together.

I let out a loud huff. "For the love of dragon eggs, shift so I can prove to you that I'm not kidding." And so I was no longer subjected to the view of his gorgeous body. Ten more seconds and I might have forgotten what I was supposed to be doing.

He gave a little bow as if he was at my service, and his silver lip ring shone under the brilliant sunbeams. "As you wish."

With a roll of his neck, his limbs stretched. His skin became green as scales formed over his body. The transformation from man to dragon was a seamless process, but I always felt this tingle of magic tremble in the air, and I couldn't help but be in awe each time. How a man could possibly become such a breathtaking and ferocious creature was beyond my comprehension.

I waited until Kieran shook out the shift and settled into his dragon form. He eventually brought his head and long body to the ground, allowing me to climb aboard his back. His wings spread wide as he rose up to his full height and kicked off the grassy ground, causing my hair to blow back off my face. The flapping of his wings whooshed in the air as we went upward.

We circled around the castle once before approaching the head of the stone snake. My anxiety kicked up a notch inside my chest. Kieran had gotten me up the six stories, but I still had to manage to get myself onto the head of the snake.

"Do you think you can climb onto the roof without killing your-self?" Kieran asked. There was no mistaking the worry in his voice.

"Definitely," I replied with as much enthusiasm as I would have had eating a plate of alfalfa sprouts.

"Fuck me. This is a horrible plan. You're going to fall. I should have gotten one of the others to spot you."

"Thanks for the boost of confidence," I grumbled as I swung one leg around to meet the other. Kieran in dragon form was too large to land on the roof. "Maybe I could use your tail as a slide." The comment was supposed to be to myself as I thought out loud, and tried to gauge my success rate of various options.

"No!" Kieran stated flatly. *"You might go too fast."*

My right fingers stretched out for the roof. "Can you get me any closer?"

He was all business, reminding me of Jase. *"What do you think I'm doing?"*

Okay, new plan. I flipped my leg back over, and scooted up to his neck. I threw my arms around him. "Fly to the head of the snake. I'm going to reach out and grab it."

"I should have strapped you on," he snarled, but he used his expansive wings to turn us so we faced the castle head-on.

While he positioned himself, I drew my feet up, and with care and wobbly knees, I began to stand up, keeping my arms secured around his neck. Once he was close enough for me to reach out, I leaned my whole body up against his long, thick neck, releasing one hand as the other clutched Kieran like he was my lifeline. And in a way, he was.

Anticipation trickled down to my toes. This was it. The moment we'd been waiting weeks for, ever since I'd found the first star. Being so close to our goal felt surreal—almost like one of Tianna's nightmares. My fingers grazed the stone, and I nearly jumped for joy. Wrong move. A gust of wind blew, smacking of magic, and it jostled Kieran, which then in turn made me lose my balance. I scrambled to get both my arms around Kieran or plummet like a ragdoll to my death.

"Olivia!" his voice yelled in my head.

I winced. "Geez. Not so loud."

"You're okay," he breathed in relief, shooting out a puff of poison.

"Yeah, but watch the toxic stuff. I don't want you to kill me before I get the star."

"Sorry, I lost it for a second when I thought you were going to fall."

"Me too. Quick, get me back over there before the bitch decides to grace us with her crazy presence."

"I think you might be the crazy one."

It was entirely possible, but I was willing to do anything to save the descendants, even tackle my fear of heights, and snakes at the same time.

Resituating myself, we went through the drill again—this time without hesitation. My fingers went into the hollow cavity of the snake's eye, and wrapped around the cool green stone. The very second I had a grip on it I yanked my hand back. It should have been a moment of celebration, but like most things in the Veil, nothing was as simple as it seemed.

A trail of green smoke exuded from the Star of Poison, climbing over my fingers, down my arm, and into my face. It cooled my skin— not like Issik did, but it dropped my body temperature nonetheless. Taking me by surprise, I inhaled, sucking up the smoke into my lungs.

Crap.

That was bad. Wasn't it?

It was called the Star of Poison, so the green mist had to have been poison. Right?

I guess I was about to find out.

Lucky me.

The urge to throw the glowing emerald crystal clutched in my hand was strong, but I held on, knowing that without it the dragons would never survive. My arms looped around Kieran's neck for stability as the poison in my nostrils worked its way through my body and settled around my organs. A jolt of energy slammed into me as soon as I had both hands around Kieran's neck. He must have felt it too.

"What the—" Kieran's head turned to the side, and I watched in shock as a milky film covered his bright green eyes. His wings went slack in the air and his body limp.

Oh, hell no.

This wasn't happening. Not again.

Like an airplane falling from the sky, gravity pulled the weight of his body toward the ground. "Kieran!" I screamed.

Only feet away from slamming into the ground, he activated his wings, pulling us back up into the sky. *"What the hell just happened?"*

"You tell me. You're the one who became paralyzed mid-flight."

"I lost control... of everything. My dragon. My ability. Myself. It all vanished until you called my name."

"It was the stone," I answered with confidence.

After circling once in the sky, Kieran flew us steadily toward the front of the castle. My legs clung to his body, and I gripped the stone tightly in one hand. I didn't allow myself to think about what was happening inside me. All that mattered was I had the stone.

I could sense Kieran's rush of joy as he realized we had finally found the stone, and it made me smile. Kieran landed in the courtyard on a soft patch of vibrant grass. The tingles of his shift from dragon to man danced in the air the moment my feet touched the ground.

I could barely contain myself, waiting for him to shake off the last remnants of his dragon. Not even his nakedness distracted me. "Do you feel any different? Have your shackles to the isles been removed?" I held my breath, waiting for Kieran to answer.

He had one leg in his pair of jeans and was wiggling the other in. The wait for him to pull them over his hips was torment. I was dying to know if it had worked as it did for Jase. Leaving his pants unzipped and unbuttoned, Kieran flipped his wrists over, front to back, staring at them. For whatever reason, the magic Tianna had chained them with was invisible to my eyes—all human eyes actually.

I started to tap my right foot as I waited for him to respond. "Hello? Did you forget about me?"

Kieran finally lifted his head, a smile playing on his lips. Suddenly, I was in his arms and my feet were dangling off the ground. "You did it. I can't believe it, Blondie." Then he was kissing me breathless. "God, I love you."

With my arms twined around his neck, I stared at him with stars in my eyes. Had that been a flippant comment? Like "Oh, my god, you saved my life, and I love you for it"? Or was he actually professing his love for me? I shocked myself by really wanting Kieran to sincerely love me—not like a friend or a girl who saved his life.

I wanted the dragon to be *in* love with me.

Holy shit.

I wanted them all to be *in* love with me because it became crystal clear… I was in love with all four of them.

My breathing became labored.

Someone save me from myself. How could I possibly be in love with four very different guys? It wasn't just their dragon forms that set them apart; each one was unique in the same way their abilities were unique. I'd become just like the other women on the isles. I no longer wanted to be saved or rescued from the Veil. I wanted to attach myself more and more to the dragons who ruled these lands.

I stared into Kieran's expectant, happy face. "We should find the others," I replied, wanting to hit my head on the side of the castle. Why hadn't I told him how I felt? Why hadn't I said, "I love you too"?

Because everyone you've ever loved has left you.

Being the key to the dragons' survival didn't mean I wasn't

damaged inside. Clearly, I was. The battle was far from over, and I might still lose those I held dear to my heart. Tianna could still win and take the descendants from me.

Then what?

I'd be left alone with a broken heart.

Again.

That was something I could not live through another time. Never again.

I had to protect myself, guard my heart, at least until the curse was fully broken. Then I could bare my soul, and I'd be free to tell them how I felt. I hoped when the time came, they wouldn't force me to choose between them. I couldn't. I wouldn't. But I would respect their decision. They meant that much to me. I would take them however I could get them. Not being a part of their life wasn't an option, regardless of how much their rejection might sting.

Kieran had yet to put me down on my feet. He pressed a quick, hard kiss on my lips as he walked us into the castle. I could do nothing but hold on and kiss him back with as much emotion as I could muster.

"What's going on?" A voice interrupted our bonding moment. It was Jase.

Elation tingled down my spine, and my cheeks flushed. When both of my feet touched the ground, I lifted my hand and opened my palm, showing him the vibrant Star of Poison. It pulsed with life.

Jase's eyes left my face, glanced at my hand, and then grew large. "You found it. How?"

I shrugged. "With this."

Using my other hand, I touched the pendant hanging around my neck. "It was the light that led me to the stone, just like she said it would." *She* being the woman in white. I had yet to figure out who the women were that kept appearing to me, but without their help, I never would have been able to locate either of the stars. These ghosts wanted to save my dragons as much as I did. I felt sure of it.

Jase's gaze zeroed in on Kieran's wrists. "They're gone. Just like mine."

Kieran grinned, holding up his arms and twisting his hands left and right. "No more magical shackles."

Running his fingers through his hair, Jase's dimples appeared, his face beaming. "I can't believe it. We might actually do this."

"Do what?" Issik asked as he exited the great room. His muscular form was followed by Zade's.

"Break the curse," Kieran supplied. He held out his hand, and I gladly turned the Star of Poison over to its rightful heir. He held it up between his thumb and index finger for the others to see. "Olivia found the star."

"No shit," Zade cursed in wonder.

Issik was studying me. It was hard to read his expression, but even though I thought he would have been happy, he didn't look pleased. "Are you okay?"

"I-I think so," I stammered, telling myself not to worry about the burning in my chest. Most likely it would go away, or so I hoped.

He didn't believe me and had to check me out for himself. Cool fingers pressed against my chin as he examined my face. "The last time you touched a stone, you absorbed its powers."

I nibbled on my lower lip. "Uh, well, there was this green mist, and I sort of inhaled it."

"You did what?" Kieran, Zade, and Jase thundered. Issik was the only one who didn't say anything, but he shook his head.

"It wasn't like I planned on gulping down some poison. It just happened, and that was minutes ago. I'm still alive, so... no harm done."

I mean, did I feel different? Yes, but that was to be expected after swallowing a mystical mist. And although I didn't want to believe I now had another dragon breath swimming around inside me, the logic of it was I probably did, which meant I also had the burden of figuring out how to control it.

Jase snorted. "At this rate, you're going to be quite the formidable little human if you keep absorbing the stars. Tianna is going to want to get her hands on you for sure."

"We need to be ready," Kieran instructed, catching the eyes of the others. The room sobered quickly at the mention of the witch. "There's no telling when she will strike next, but it will be soon. She will have felt the crack in her spell."

None of us knew that "soon" was just minutes away.

"We will be ready for her," Zade vowed, puffing out his chest. His shirt stretched taut over his flexed muscles, making them visible through the thin cotton. "Star by star, we'll chip away at this curse."

I didn't want to be the one to bring up the obvious, but it had to be said. "What about your waning powers? Should you guys really be fighting a witch?"

It was as if I'd slapped each of the descendants across the face.

They all wore shocked, how-dare-you expressions. The descendants considered themselves fierce warriors who could take on any foe, no matter what size or how strong—male, female, witch, wraith. Weakness was not an option.

I commended them for their bravery and believed in their abilities, but it didn't change the fact that I worried about something happening to them. Too many times we'd stared death in the face.

The four dragons looked grim as we walked into the main hall. "Olivia, we have little choice. It isn't just about our survival. The entire isles are depending on us to keep them safe," Jase reminded.

Kieran closed his fist over the Star of Poison. "We will fight until we take our last dragon's breath. This is our responsibility as the last royal blood of our kind. We must stand against her."

"Even at the cost of your own life?" I argued. "Wouldn't that defeat the purpose of trying to save the dragons from extinction?"

Issik's face softened, losing some of the harshness that had materialized at the first mention of Tianna. "You care for us. We care for you as well, and understand the graveness of our situation. If anything ever happened to you—"

"What Issik is trying to say is we'd die to protect you, no matter the cost," Kieran finished.

I swallowed back a swell of emotion. They would risk the existence of dragons—of the Veil Isles—to keep me alive. I didn't feel worthy of such devotion, and what I didn't say was I was willing to die to save them too. Ironic.

Who would die first?

Because death was imminent, wasn't it?

Was it possible, was there even a slim chance, that all five of us would live to see another year?

A shiver of foreboding scampered down my neck, causing the hairs to stand up. I suddenly felt as if Issik was hugging me in the center of a wintery blizzard. "You should probably put that somewhere safe."

I indicated the stone clutched in Kieran's large hand. A piece of me wanted to hold it again. Something about the crystal called to me. I wanted to keep it close, tuck it under my pillow, but it wasn't a good idea.

Distance, that's what I needed. Taking my advice, Kieran went to safeguard the star someplace secure, and hopefully magic proof—if such a place existed.

Needing a few minutes to get my wacky emotions under control, I started to walk out of the great hall, toward the stairs.

"Where are you going?" Issik demanded, blocking off my path like a giant boulder.

I had to think quickly. They wouldn't voluntarily let me out of their sight. "To change. These clothes reek of poison."

The ice prince lifted his brows. "Is that so?"

"Yeees?" I replied, looking guilty as hell. Why was it so hard to lie to them?

"Olivia." His voice had dropped below freezing.

"Issik," I rumbled back, rolling my eyes. "I'll be five minutes. I'm in the castle with four dragons. How dangerous can that be?"

"Be quick. I want us to stick together tonight." Issik stepped out of the way.

I strutted down the hallway, allowing myself a few minutes of solitude. The castle was deathly quiet, which I took as a bad omen. Nothing good ever followed a silence so complete.

Nudging the door to my room open with my foot, I peeked inside. It was just as I'd left it. Canopy bed, wicker dresser, clothes on the floor—nothing amiss.

It didn't take me long to change into something more appropriate for running and kicking ass. Both were probably in my future. At the last second, before I headed back downstairs to join the descendants, I grabbed the dagger Jase had given me, and tucked it into my boot. It couldn't hurt to be armed. Feeling more confident, I shut the door to my room and turned the corner.

Fear slapped me in the face, and the feeling was followed by the hissing of a snake—correction, multiple snakes. I knew that sound was bad news. It was my nightmares come to life.

I shuddered, sucking in a fortifying breath. *Don't turn around. Don't turn around. Pretend you didn't hear anything.* If only I could. Willing it away wasn't going to make what I was certain was coming my way any less real. My chest heaved as I took a breath and spun.

Holy dragon balls.

My head tilted to the side, transfixed by the figure headed toward me. "Is that… Medusa?" I mumbled to myself.

A woman stood in the center of the hallway leading into the great hall. I couldn't tell what color her hair was due to the numerous snakes twining around her neck and body. They slithered up her legs, wrapping around her waist and into her hair.

I wanted to puke.

Or faint.

Most definitely, I wanted to scream.

The red silky gown she wore clung to her like a second skin, moving fluidly as she swayed toward me. My feet backed up with each step she took forward, and yet, she somehow gained ground on me—the magic of a witch.

I was afraid. It helped to admit it and accept it. This wasn't the first, nor would it be the last time I'd be shaking in my boots because of our fight with Tianna. And regardless of how scared I felt, I was determined to not give up.

Not now.

Not until the last second before the summer solstice.

The warmth in the hallway was eaten away by Tianna's presence. She might have draped herself in snakes and slapped on a different dress, but the wickedness that lived inside her was the same. Clouds of mist crawled along the wooden floors, and up the veins of ivy clinging to the ceiling.

"If you came for the stone, I don't have it." I was shocked to shit that my voice hadn't quivered.

"But you did find it, didn't you, dear? I felt the power of the stone leave its vessel, and attach itself to something." Tianna poked me in the heart. "I'm guessing that something is you."

"Nope. Not this time," I lied, keeping my chin firm.

"You're not a very good liar, Olivia."

"And you're a bit—"

Tianna placed her index finger and thumb around my lips. Then she pinched them shut, cutting off my impulsive response. I couldn't help myself around her. She brought out the demon inside me. I wanted to wrestle her to the ground, and strangle her with one of her disgusting pet snakes. The witch clucked her tongue at me, while I shot daggers of pure hatred tinged with a healthy dose of fear in her direction.

"Someone needs to learn to hold her tongue when speaking to her elders." One of her snakes agreed. It lunged forward at my face, hissing in anger. Its forked tongue tasted the air around my cheek, making me cringe in revulsion.

With my mouth clamped shut by her slim fingers, the words I attempted to throw at her came out in a muffled shrill.

"Cat got your tongue?" She laughed like it was the funniest line in the world. "Maybe this will help." She released my pinched lips.

I was two seconds away from spitting in her face. "What is with you and the reptiles? Couldn't you enlist some Care Bears to do your dirty deeds?"

"I'm going to assume that is some kind of insult." She regarded me with distaste. "Enough of the cute banter. You and I have a show to put on." Her slim fingers reached for my hand.

I jerked my arm away from her. "I'm not going anywhere with you."

Tianna put her hand on my shoulders and twirled me around. "You don't have a choice. Now move it, sweet cheeks." She shoved me forward. "I need you to give a believable performance."

I didn't see how that would be a problem, considering the fear I felt was very real. Mentally bracing myself for the fight to come, I berated myself for not putting my hair up into a messy bun or ponytail. Strands of hair kept falling over my face, making it difficult to see where I was going, and for what I was about to do, I needed a clear view.

Tianna was at my back, and I was glad she couldn't see my

scheming face. It was a stupid plan, but it was the only one I could come up with under duress. Tianna had another thing coming if she thought I would be a pawn in her quest to get the dragon stars.

Not happening, witch.

On a whim of courage, I whipped out the blade inside my boot and pivoted. The knife thrust into Tianna's chest. I took a step back, leaving the weapon embedded inside her. Why wasn't she bleeding? Not even black blood oozed out of her.

Tianna threw her head back and laughed. She made quite the scene to behold, standing in the dim corridor in a ball gown with a dagger shoved into her heart. She pulled out the blade from between her breasts and smiled.

"Was that supposed to hurt? I'll give you points for effort, but really, Olivia, I'm disappointed in your originality. You couldn't have possibly thought a mortal blade could hurt me." Another haunting laugh filled with superiority released from her lips, as she chucked the blade across the hall.

But that wasn't the only thing she tossed.

Her hand swung toward my face, and the witch backhanded me silly.

I flew down the hall, landing near the stairwell hard enough to knock me unconscious. I barely held on as black dots swirled behind my eyes.

One good thing had come out of being slapped sideways. Mortal weapons might not be able to kill Tianna, but magical knives were fair game. Now I just had to get my hands on one.

No problem, I thought—heavy on the sarcasm.

"Olivia?" a deep voice called.

My eyes flew to Tianna. "No!" My scream took me by surprise.

Before I realized it, I was scrambling down the stairs and toward the sound of Issik's voice. Desperation tore through me. I had to warn them. My feet were flying over the steps, and by the grace of God, I didn't trip once or fall flat on my face. Issik was waiting at the bottom of the stairs, and I hurled myself over the last few and landed in his arms.

"She's coming," I panted, my eyes large with fright.

Issik took off with me in his arms, and I cursed the curtain of blonde hair that fell over my face. He burst into the great hall. "She's here," Issik hissed, handing me off to Kieran, who was still shirtless. The muscles in his arms and chest tightened as he set me on my feet.

They got into warrior mode. A wall of descendants stood in front of me. "I-I stabbed Tianna," I announced. My words came out in short bursts while I bent over to catch my breath.

"You what!?" four voices roared. Fire blazed in their eyes as the descendants judged me for a moment.

I pressed a hand gently to my cheek, and flinched at the sharp stab of pain. "Then the bitch hit me."

Based on the strength of their outraged shouts, I thought for sure the roof was going to collapse on us. Never had I heard such a low rumble. The floor vibrated under me. The chandelier above my head rattled. The walls trembled.

Zade cracked his knuckles. "She dies."

The others all seemed to be in agreement, making similar grunts of approval. Jase shook his head at me, running a finger over my jaw to take a look at the side of my face. "You're lucky to be alive. Kieran, get her the hell out of here. We'll take care of Tianna."

"No, you can't!" I pleaded, choking on the last word. Knowing she would come for the stone was nothing compared to actually having her in the castle, but not being able to see what she would do to the descendants scared me even more.

"Go!" Jase yelled.

Kieran's arms wrapped around my waist, and he lifted me off the ground. I twisted and kicked, flailing in Kieran's arms. "Put me down," I hissed. Being removed from the chaos that was descending upon me, threw me into a panic.

"Not on your life."

Kieran remained tense as he bolted out of the great hall, his longs strides swallowing up the floor. He took us to the rear exit of the castle that led straight into the woods.

Behind me, Tianna's voice echoed throughout the stone halls. I couldn't hear her words, but the high pitch of her voice, was followed by several profound male ones. This was the deadliest game of hide-and-seek I'd ever played. I wanted to quit, but that would mean the witch would win.

Never.

Kieran sprinted outside, and the sky was pregnant with dark clouds. Rain spat and sizzled on the ground, casting up a haze of smoke. As the storm gushed, the air carried the scent of upturned earth. Pine needles covered the ground like a spiky blanket, and a bolt of lightning painted the leaves in a cheerful glow of yellow.

Trees swayed heavily from the howling winds, like a thousand tortured voices. It was fitting the sun had decided to hide behind the clouds, while a lunatic witch was hunting me.

If there was ever a day for gloomy skies and traces of doom, that day was now.

As Kieran moved us deeper into the woods of Viperus, a roar thundered from above our heads.

Jase's dragon was circling the castle, his scales glistening from the mist of rain pouring from the menacing clouds. They weren't normal storm clouds, for they twisted and formed into a beast that lunged at Jase—another of Tianna's wicked spells.

"She's in the woods," I told Kieran.

His expression was gaunt. "I know."

He hung a sharp left, zipping over the ground with a speed that made me dizzy. His eyes were glowing and scales papered over his chest and arms. Kieran was tapping into his dragon, giving him extra strength and speed. This partial transformation fascinated me; I hadn't known he could.

"We can't outrun her forever," I stated. My arms were clinging to his neck.

Ducking under a large branch, he pressed on forward. "I don't plan on it. We're almost there."

"Where?" I asked, wondering what he was up to now.

"You'll see."

Jase came sweeping down from the sky in his dragon form, and barreled straight into a cluster of trees off to our left. I could guess what his target was. The witch. She was close, practically breathing down our necks.

Kieran felt it too.

Tianna was never alone in her fights. The prissy witch didn't like to get her blood red nails dirty. Instead, she had her cursed underlings do the honors. *Squawk. Squawk.* And here came the goonies.

"I fucking hate griffins," I mumbled, my eyes lifting upward. Through the trees, a pair of those evil assholes was locked on Kieran and me.

Kieran dropped me to my feet and pressed his forehead to mine. "Whatever happens, whatever you hear or see, you're not to leave this spot. Do you understand?"

What was so special about this specific spot? Did it have a protection circle? Or a secret trapdoor?

Turned out it was a tree. Not waiting for me to swear I wouldn't do something reckless, Kieran shoved me into the hollow of the tree before spinning around to shift. His large wing came up, blocking the entrance and keeping me locked inside.

Unable to help myself, I peeked through a small crack, needing to see what was going on, or sit in here going mad. Kieran roared, letting a mist of green poison exude from his mouth. It swirled around the griffins, who pawed at the ground, kicking up dirt. They were smart and held their breaths.

Huddled in the corner, I listened as the sounds of a battle echoed over Viperus. It was gut-wrenching—the claws, the roars, and the cries —but nothing was worse than not knowing what was happening. A reverberating silence ensued.

My heartbeat hammered in my ears as I cautiously crawled to the opening of the trunk. My fingers gripped onto the edge of the bark. Extending my neck and tilting my head to the side, I went to take a peek, but someone else had the same idea.

A griffin's head popped inside the hole. It shrieked in my face, blowing my hair back and spitting goo into my eyes.

Disgusting.

I scuttled backward on my ass, wiping a hand over my eyes. The substance was thick and sticky like snot. It also temporarily blinded me —at least I prayed it wasn't permanent. I told myself not to panic, but this was one of those times my body didn't listen to my brain, and I was moments away from losing my shit.

Blinking rapidly, I tried to wash away the film that blocked my vision, but it was to no avail. Fear clogged my throat. The griffin who had me trapped inside the tree trunk made a clucking noise, its beak brushing up against the side of my face. I froze, my heart jumping out of my chest.

Holy shit. It's going to peck me to death.

My hands flew out in front of me, warding off an attack I was sure would come.

Claws dug into my shoulders, ripping through my clothes. I cried out in pain as the nails pierced my flesh. The searing agony intensified when the griffin dragged me out of the hole. I dug my heels in, swinging my fists sightlessly. It was useless, but that didn't mean I would give in, never.

Opening my mouth, I tilted back my head and released a puff of tranquility. I could be aiming at anything, including one of my dragons, but one thing was certain, I hadn't hit the griffin holding me captive.

My feet were no longer on the ground. I couldn't believe what was happening. The griffin was hauling me off into the air. Where were the descendants? What had Tianna done to them?

Without me, the descendants would never find the last two stars.

They would perish.

The Veil would be destroyed by a witch, and all those who lived here would be enslaved, tortured, or worse.

No! No! Hell no!

Fucking great. I'd been kidnapped again. This time not by four incredibly sexy dragons, but by a witch with a vendetta.

To Be Continued...

ZADE

TAMING FIRE

FIRE

BOOK THREE

USA TODAY BESTSELLING AUTHOR

J. L. WEIL

CHAPTER 1

The griffin kept its sharp claws on my upper arms as it flew us over the Veil. Perhaps I drifted out of consciousness once or twice, because when I blinked, the landscape beneath us was no longer green, but barren, dry, and dusty as hell.

I wanted to thrash. I wanted to fight for my freedom. I didn't want to die. And I was most definitely going to hurl.

Jase. Kieran. Zade. Issik. I silently chanted their names over and over again to keep myself from dwelling on the horror of my situation. Were they searching for me? Dumb question. Obviously, they were. Without me, the key, they would never be free of their curse—Tianna, the witch, would win. I took comfort in knowing how important I was.

They wouldn't abandon me.

They wouldn't.

A little voice in the back of my head nudged free. *Are you sure? Everyone in your life has left you. What makes them any different?*

I rattled my head, banishing the dark thoughts from my mind. *No!* I refused to believe they wouldn't come for me. Some demons were harder to fight than others. It was the ones you couldn't see that often did the most damage.

The griffin tugged me along in the sky with gliding gait, sending harsh whooshing noises through the air, so different than the sound of dragon wings. Where the griffins had tattered feathers, my dragons had sleek wings like buttery leather.

We had been apart mere hours, and I already missed them something fiercely.

What would happen to me? Where were they taking me?

I longed more than anything to use my new powers on the foul beasts, but to do so would be a death sentence with no dragons to catch my fall. My time would come to strike. It just couldn't be twenty thousand feet up in the air.

We slowly began to descend, but not low enough. Although the clouds were no longer swirling around us, they remained about our heads, so out of place in the unforgiving environment below. Countless mountains of burnish red sand, and rock, carved the landscape in sharp plateaus. The wind rushed over my face, carrying traces of grainy particles and dust. The air lacked any moisture, making it tough to breathe in and out easily. It was a vile place, and I ached for the lush and vibrant lands of Viperus. I'd even take the damn snakes.

The griffin hurled me forward, releasing his sharp hold on me, and the world spun. I was falling.

My knees slammed into a giant nest of twigs, straw, and bones, causing me to groan and pain to shoot up my body as the branches scraped over my skin. I shoved myself up into a sitting position, ignoring the bark of my muscles. Bright red blood cascaded down one of my legs and I winced, my belly rolling at the sight of the cut marring my cream skin. I forced my gaze higher, telling myself not to think about the nest of bones, of who they'd been, of how they'd died, that I wouldn't end up like them.

The two cruel and vile faces of the griffins leered over me in the nest, and a chill slithered down my spine. *Were they going to peck me to death with their curved, razor beaks?*

My flight or fight response kicked in, and I peered over the side. Perhaps I could run or use one of my abilities now that we weren't flying.

Fuck.

The griffin's horrific nest was at the top of a pointed red sand plateau, so high I could nearly touch the clouds. So much for my plan to strike. Even if I managed to poison or tranquilize them, I had to find a way down. Without wings, I was screwed.

Now what, smarty-pants?

The countdown to doomsday had begun.

Four months—I had found the Star of Tranquility.

Three months—I managed to do it again with the Star of Poison, but also managed to get kidnapped.

Go me.

Talk about an overachiever.

"What do you want from me?" I yelled, surprised by the raspy rawness of my voice.

They only stared at me with vibrant amber eyes. I wanted to carve them out, and given the chance, I would.

"You can't keep me here forever," I hissed, not that I expected anything I said to set me free. Hell, they probably didn't even understand me.

The one who had carried me for god knew how long cocked his head toward me. Its wings flapped once, before blasting my face with a squawk. The foulness of its breath heated my cheeks, burning my nostrils. Feeling I might vomit, I threw my body toward the edge of the nest, and threw up what little I had in my belly.

Dragging the back of my hand across my mouth, I sat back and tilted my head to the sky. I screamed. I screamed in anger. I screamed in terror. I screamed in grief. My voice carried over the barren land, echoing and thundering through the nothingness, but no one was out there to hear my cries. My throat felt so raw and burned that I was afraid it was bleeding too. The cuts on my legs had clotted and were crusty with dried blood, but the aches and pains still pulsated throughout my body—every muscle and every limb.

Tears gathered in my eyes as I lay down in the nest of what felt like thorns. I couldn't stop the surge of emotions from bubbling up in my throat. Sobs dragged through my chest, racking my shoulders in violent tremors. I seemed to have lost track of time and drifted into sleep more than once, for when my senses finally returned to me, day had given birth to night.

Surrounded by darkness and starlight, the moon offered very little light, as if it too had hidden from Tianna's horrors. I tried to move, but my arms were tingling and weak, hardly able to hold my weight. With each tiny movement I made, the pain became worse than the last. I forced myself to try and get a bearing on my surroundings, or where the griffins had gone off to—were they still guarding me or had they left me here to rot? I didn't know which would be worse, being abandoned on top of a mountain I could never climb down from, or being the prisoner of Tianna's lackeys.

Shadows and wispy wind crept over the dry land, giving this place a petrified ambiance as my eyes adjusted to the blackness. I wet my lips, tasting the salt of my tears. *I would not panic. I wouldn't panic. I couldn't panic.* I told myself, reciting it like a chant.

No more tears. I had to keep my wits and figure out a way to escape. There was always a way. I might not see it at the moment, it might be days, but I would fight to live. I was a fighter, not a helpless ninny. If only I could use this one-sided bond in my favor, but no matter how long I thought of a way to convey my location, my mind was blank. Emotions weren't places.

Through the black night, my ears picked up the wispy beating of wings. I strained to identify what or who it could be. A dragon? A griffin? Or something else even wickeder?

My fingers clutched onto to branches of the nest, not caring about the rough bark digging into my sore flesh. The thundering of my own heartbeat drummed in my ears as a shadow appeared directly over my head. I scrambled to duck further into the nest, flattening myself as low as I could. Not that it did any good.

I knew without seeing their faces the griffins had returned from wherever they had roamed off to earlier. The stench of beast filled the air. One of them threw back its head, letting a shriek pierce the star-strewn sky above, as if it were answering a silent call my ears couldn't hear.

Landing on a corner of the nest, its front claws sunk into the straw and bones. It peered down at me as if it couldn't decide whether to eat me or smack me with its serpent tail. I'd rather choose option C—Let me go.

"No. No. No," I whimpered, shaking my head back and forth.

The creature bent down its massive eagle head as the other circled above us to keep watch. They appeared to work together, and the intelligence of the pair alarmed me. My hopes of outsmarting them dimmed, but shit, I had to believe I was wittier than two hybrid beasts. The griffin's coarse hair rubbed against my cheek and I ground my teeth, suppressing a shudder. The hot putridness of its breath was like acid on my face.

Click. Click. Click. Its beak clamped together.

Braced against my own terror, I tried not to think about what that beak could do to my nose, my eyes, and my ears. Too swift for me to follow, it once again snatched me in its claws, and took to the night. One minute I was in the nest, and the next I was soaring with darkness, the cool evening wind splashing over my pale cheeks.

I needed to be strong and didn't allow myself to think where they were taking me, or what Tianna had planned for me. She was undoubtedly behind my kidnapping. The griffins were merely pawns following orders.

My body went rigid under its claws, and I wondered if I would get my chance to fight back. Feathery wings spread out wide on either side of the griffin, slicing through the night as if it were liquid darkness. I concluded the creatures must have keen eyesight to see through such blackness. As we flew further, the air grew thicker with dust, clogging my nose and lungs. It was gritty.

The trip this time was shorter, still a distance away, but we hadn't left whatever barren land of the island we were in at the moment.

With a ripple of the griffin's wings, our altitude dropped, and its partner mimicked my captor's movements with eerie grace. It was awkward to be dangling from the claws of a beast, and I was grateful at the sight of ground closing in on us. In the night, the sandy floor looked nearly obsidian, but I knew it to be the same burnish red I'd see earlier today.

What was this section of the island? Was I even still in the Veil Isles, or had they flown me out of the barrier?

No. They couldn't have, not until the summer solstice. The curse didn't allow it, except for twice a year during the winter and summer solstices.

An outline of a mountain appeared directly in front of us and the griffin's sailed for it. Though, I didn't see the jagged opening on the side until we were flying through it, straight into a cave. The griffin's didn't stop, but continued to maneuver deeper into the mountain, a maze of tunnels and caverns in its depths. It only took a few twists and turns for the mental map I'd tried to memorize scrambled in my brain. Even if by some freaking miracle I managed to render them asleep or dead, I still had to find my way out of the labyrinth. Everything seemed bleak and hopeless.

My spirits were at an all-time low when a speck of light flickered up ahead. Someone was here. Someone was waiting, and I didn't have to think hard to guess who.

The griffins glided past two carved pillars and entered a vast chamber, glittered by more than a dozen floating candles around the room. Its flickering flames cast shadows against the rocky composite of coal and limestone.

Was this Tianna's secret lair? The villain always needed one, and my bet was she'd made herself quite cozy inside this secluded mountain, far, far from the four surviving kingdoms of the Veil.

Suddenly, I was propelled into the center of the room, onto the unyielding stone floor. My already bruised knees and palms screamed in agony as I slammed into the ground. How many more times were these damn assholes going to toss me about? I shoved upward and whirled, prepared to unleash a mist of poison, but the deadly breath got lodged in my throat. A few feet in front of me was the witch of darkness herself. Tianna was perched on a black throne.

That bitch.

I'd known she was behind this, but seeing her right in front of me stunned me for a moment, or perhaps it was the jarring of my body catching up to the trauma. My nails curled into my palms, a combination of fear and rage. I wondered if the descendants could sense my emotions right now. A part of me hoped not, I wanted to spare them the agony.

Tianna was as devastatingly beautiful as I remembered. Long, silky red locks of hair peeked out from either side of her black hood, spilling over her breasts. Her porcelain skin and delicate features were carved into my memory—a face I would likely never forget in both waking and sleeping hours. She would haunt my nightmares for years to come, and what I was about to face now would surely leave deep, wounded scars.

I braced myself, chin rising slightly. My nightmare was only truly beginning.

Those ruby lips curved into a false grin that didn't reach her calculative silvery eyes. Something about her was off, and the longer I studied her, the less I could decipher what it was. The answer had been on the tip of my tongue, only to be blown away like a soft eyelash on a baby's cheek.

This witch had managed to capture and isolate an entire island—imprisoning a rare dying species singlehandedly, and with little effort. She had lied to the five kings and abused their trust, all now dead, survived only by four of their sons.

The first moment of opportunity, I was going to cut her again. And again. I didn't care how many times I had to sink a blade into her heart. I would do so a million times until she was nothing but dust under my shoe. No matter how hard, I *would* get my grubby fingers on a weapon that would end her existence. I would make it my personal mission in life… other than becoming the dragon savior—or some divine name the descendants came up with for me.

"So nice of you to join me, Olivia dear," Tianna greeted, as if I'd kept her waiting. The witch looked me up and down, assessing and weighing, only to decide I was a pesky fly that was standing in her way.

"Like I had a choice," I huffed, brushing away the loose pebbles and dirt embedded in my hands. My eyes took in my surroundings, making note of any exits. I eased to my feet, regardless of the grumbling my body barked at me. It was important to meet Tianna on level ground, not coward on the floor in a ball, like I wanted to do.

Her lips curled into a scandalous smile. "Yes, my methods might have been abrupt, but those overbearing boys of yours were just hogging you all to themselves. I had to do something, for your sake, of course."

I scoffed. She had a warped way of twisting things, I'd give her that. "As much as I appreciate the gesture, I've got more pressing matters waiting for me." As she damn well knew.

Those silver eyes sparkled as if she enjoyed the game and banter. I was amusing her. "Why dear, after all the trouble I went to get you here, you wouldn't want to leave, would you? You must stay a night… or two." The way she lingered over the end of that sentence lead me to believe two might turn into days, weeks, or months. "We have much to discuss."

The blood in my veins pulsed, but I kept my face stoic, refusing to let her see the fear making my insides tremble. "Why are we wasting time? What is it you want from me? Why did you bring me here?" The questions rattled off my tongue one after the other.

Tianna tsked, shaking her head. "Humans are so impatient. All will be revealed in good time." Her long black nails tapped the armrests of her throne as she spoke. Turning her attention away from me, she focused on the griffins who had moved to flank either side of her. "Well done, my pets." Delicate fingers stroked the top of the griffins' feathery head. "I have no other need of you tonight. Go."

And like obedient dogs, the pair bowed their mighty heads to the ground, one leg extended, before exiting the chamber through the single entrance into the cave. Their nails clattered over the stone floor, echoing until they were no longer in earshot, leaving me alone with the witch.

Fuck.

I gritted my teeth together, blocking out the pain it took just to stay standing on my own two feet. Tianna's gaze snapped back to me, and my insides twisted at the way she smiled prettily. "Things had been quite dull around here until you came. I owe you thanks."

"I don't want your gratitude," I spat.

"No, I supposed you don't," she agreed. "Come now, dear, how about we make a bargain that will get us both what we want?"

Don't fall for her traps. A bargain with someone like her was surely a death sentence, no matter how she spun it. I needed to tread carefully. "How is that possible?" What I wanted was to shred her to ribbons.

She raised a thin brow, the same red as her hair. "I want this curse broken too. The game is no longer fun and has taken far too long."

"Maybe you should have thought about that before you cursed them," I blurted.

Her finger tapped on the bottom of her parted lips thoughtfully, flashing a row of white teeth. "Yes, well, where is the entertainment in that? Everyone needs a dose of spontaneity in their life, wouldn't you say?"

I nearly choked on air. "I've never been much of a thrill seeker," I admitted.

Her grin became twisted, to the point it was almost grotesque. I had known she was a perverse soul, but it became clear she was the type of person who enjoyed hurting others. "No time like the present."

"What is it you want from me?" I demanded, covering the quiver of my voice with sharpness. "I don't have the stones."

She rolled her eyes. "I'm not stupid, and neither are the descendants. I didn't expect them to let you carry them around in the bosom of your gowns, but you are right. I do want the other stones, and as for the two you've already found, that's where you come in."

"How so?" I dared to inquire.

"The Star of Tranquility and Poison are nearly useless to me now that they've gifted you with their abilities. That changes things a bit, and I'll admit, it was a twist of fate I didn't see coming."

And I bet that burned her ass.

"A minor setback, but nothing I can't undo."

Ice coated my veins. Was she implying she could rip the abilities from within me? They were a part of me now—a part of my soul. To remove them sounded painful. To hell with that, I wasn't letting her take what was mine, not without a fight.

"I've grown fond of the dragon's breath. Maybe you would like me to show you how they work." Faced with an opportunity to fight and flee or stay and become Tianna's pawn, I made a hasty decision and prayed I didn't end up dead. No time to strategize an epic plan—or any plan at all, I just acted.

Drawing a deep breath, I gathered one of the powers that resided within me. I was too distraught to distinguish between them. "Maybe you would like me to demonstrate how they work?" It was just the witch and me. My mouth opened, aimed in the direction where she still sat like a queen on her throne.

Before the mist ever left my lungs, her left hand rose, and she snapped her fingers into a fist. It was as if the witch had stuffed a sock in my mouth, blocking the poison from leaving my lungs. She laughed a haunting and throaty sound that filled the entire chamber. "That was a fool's attempt, little girl, but at least you had the guts to try, and that means something. You've got grit, which is good. You're going to need it."

Fueled by rage and desperation, I again tried to open my mouth, but this time to spew every vile name I could invent. Nothing came out. *Did the bitch just Little Mermaid me? Had she taken my voice?*

My fingers grappled frantically at my throat, but the loss of speech wasn't physical. She had spelled me and taken my ability to expel poison or tranquility. What. The. Actual. Hell.

Tianna cocked a brow. "Were you saying something?"

My eyes radiated at her with spears of hate.

"I think you'll see after some time that helping me will help you.

Now, if you promise to be a good girl, I'll remove the spell. Do we have a deal?"

Trick question? If I agree, was the deal just for my voice... or something more... something like helping her obtain the stones? I stayed silent.

"A nod will suffice," she pushed, staring at me with unyielding eyes, no room for negotiation. What choice did I have? That were the games Tianna played, ensuring she always won.

I nodded, my teeth clenched so tight my cheeks ached.

Her closed fingers opened and waved in the air. "There, that's better. Now, how about we have a civil conversation, girl to girl?"

"Nothing you do or say is going to make me help you," I seethed, my nostrils flaring.

"Your dragons are weakening."

That single statement had warning bells chiming in my ears. I went still.

"I can feel it," she continued, enjoying the pleasure each moment she taunted me brought her. "How long do you think they have left, before they won't even be able to save themselves? As they dwindle to just men with muscles—that will do very little against my magic—my power flourishes, strengthening with each passing day."

She was right, and the last thread of fool's hope I held slipped out of me. The only way I was making it out of alive, and still able to save the descendants, was by working with Tianna. If she wanted my damn abilities, she could have them, but I still didn't buy her excuse that the stones were useless. If that were true, then why had Jase and Kieran so hastily hid them from her? Why had she stormed the castle at the first sign of their return, demanding we hand them over?

I didn't trust her. She was up to something. She was keeping secrets.

But so could I.

"I offer you the chance freely to aid me one last time."

Immediately, I caught her drift. If I refused, she would find other creative and probably detrimental methods to get me to behave. I spit on her. "How's that for an answer?" For five whole seconds, I felt like a badass, and then reality hit me.

Her face contorted, shifting into the monster that lay beneath the pretty façade. I understood what a terrible mistake I'd made. She was going to make me pay for it and horror coiled in my gut. Similar to a viper, her slender fingers lashed out, twining around my throat. The sharp, fine tips of her long black nails dug into my tender flesh. My eyes hadn't even seen her rise from her throne, but here she was, towering over me like the devil's bride, supreme and evil.

"Why don't I give you the night to think on it, Olivia dear? I wouldn't want you to make any rash decisions you'll regret in the morning." Her fingers squeezed, cutting off my air supply and I gasped, my eyes burning from the lack of oxygen. "This is merely a taste of what will happen each time you disobey me."

My fingers scratched and clawed, tearing into her hands. All wasted effort that got me nowhere, got me no closer to breathing in the fresh air my lungs, my heart, my life desired. And it was only when the black dots of unconsciousness edged my vision, that she released her vicious grasp.

My knees buckled. The world drifted away as I fought off the blackness threatening to consume me.

Stay focused! Stay awake!

From within the swirling darkness, I searched for something to tether my mind to, something to keep me from falling into the depths of unconsciousness. I bit the inside of my cheek and the metallic tang of blood coated my tongue. Each breath I took was like swallowing glass, but it was the panting of my breath that saved me. It became my lifeline.

In. Out. In. Out. In. Out.

The quick, short, and uneven wheezes slowly morphed into long, steady breaths. The chamber of the mountain came back to me, along with the damp tang of mold and cool air. I didn't bother to get up again, but stayed huddled on the rough ground. Tianna's voice was muffled in the distance as if she was walking away. Did she plan to just leave me here?

I listened to the sound of locks clicking into place and my eyes snapped open. I could see no doors, no walls, but the throne room was gone. Poof like magic. Not like magic. Just magic. It was the only explanation. Tianna had sealed me into an enchanted cell.

Whore!

Even as I rushed to my feet to test the boundaries of my prison, I knew… there was no escaping. And yet, it didn't stop me from trying. I reached out with a hand. My fingers grazed a surface I couldn't quite identify. Smooth. Cold. Invisible. Flattening my palms, I ran both hands over the barrier, desperately searching for a gap, a break, an end to this nightmare. I traced the rectangular room with shaky, cut, bruised, and dirty hands a dozen times before I gave up finally.

My back pressed into one of the concealed walls, as I dropped my arms dejectedly to my sides, and took my first real look at my prison. Perhaps I'd blacked out after all, how else did I explain the invisible bars and change of scenery? Not that it was any better than the large chamber with its flickering candlelight.

The small box itself contained a tattered and grimy cot that street rats wouldn't sleep on, and an equally dirty, and what I guessed was supposed to be a toilet, but was more like peeing in a pot. I hated camping, and this was way worse than roughing it in the woods.

Shit. Shit. Shit.

Beyond the cage lay miles and miles of darkness—so much darkness—like an endless hallway. It was frightening, not knowing what awaited—what lurked in the shadows outside my clear cage—what creatures watched me—what prey stalked me. It could have all been in my head, a trick and part of Tianna's torture, but to me, it was all too real.

Couldn't she have bothered to leave me at least one candle?

Perhaps she had in a way. My cell wasn't flooded in utter darkness, but some unknown source provided a small bit of illumination—less than a nightlight, but it was enough to see. Everything behind the four walls was… nothingness.

I huddled into the corner, tucking my knees up to my chest and wrapping my arms around myself in a hug. I missed the griffin's nest—a thought I never imagined I would have. This place took icky to new levels and was worse than living in a twelve-year-old boy's gym locker.

My stomach rolled.

I was going to vomit.

Nothing but stomach acids would come out, considering I hadn't eaten anything all day, but the sick feeling would be the same. I reined in my breathing, doing what I could to keep the panic attack, and bile, at bay. What a freaking mess. Hell, I'd been a mess for the better part of a year, and it wasn't until I came to the Veil that I had started to see a light leading me out of the shadows, a light that gave me purpose, but now the darkness was back. It was all-consuming.

I needed my dragons.

And they needed me.

The last thing I wanted was to fall apart at the seams, to show Tianna weakness and allow her to win, but my lip quivered, and my eyes became blurry. Tianna might have left me alone, but not for a moment did I believe I was truly alone.

The silence was going to kill me. Nothing moved. Nothing stirred. I was encased in a tomb—my tomb.

Grave tears rolled down my cheeks and I let them. They weren't eloquent, but big, sloppy, ugly tears that shook my body and turned my face red. Not to mention the snot. Exhaustion slammed down on me, until I curled further into the corner of the room, dropping my cheek to the wall, and drifted off numbly.

Hours and minutes meant nothing to me while surrounded by blackness. Time was only measured by the arrival of my measly meals. The fact that Tianna was feeding me meant she needed me alive. My mind went back and forth between my importance and disposability. I clung to the thread of hope that without me, she couldn't find the stones. Though, I wasn't entirely sure how accurate the statement was, but it kept me sustained in the gloom.

I tried not to drink the glass of water all at once, but the few sips I allowed myself didn't easily quench my thirst. The bread I nibbled on was stale and tasteless, yet I forced myself to eat as much of the food as I could stomach, trusting the witch wasn't poisoning me. I chewed and swallowed, working my jaw to break down the cardboard bread.

A clanking of locks shot like a gun around the space, deafening in the silence. I blinked and scrambled to my feet, only to find myself back in Tianna's throne room. Legs crossed, the black material of her dress split down on either side of her thighs, cascading over the floor as the witch rested an arm against her throne. With nothing more than a twitch of her fingers, she had removed me from my cell, summoning me to her chamber. I hated the ease of her magic.

"I hope you slept well, Olivia dear," she purred, the fire of her hair spun in curls down her back. "As promised, I gave you the night to sleep on our agreement."

Did she honestly think tossing me into a cell of solitude and giving me a few stingy meals to eat was going to change my mind? That it would be enough to scare me into agreeing? Before the descendants, I might have very well given up already and spilled my guts, but after living with them, knowing them, and loving them, to betray the four dragon shifters would be like cutting out my own heart.

"Your hospitality has been most generous," I spat with sarcasm and venom.

"I take it you've come to your senses then?"

I smiled, despite my dire situation. "Not in this life." I braced myself for the temper I saw quickly flash across her eyes, but Tianna sighed, showing more control than yesterday.

"I'd hoped you would learn your lesson," she admitted, clucking her tongue. Her eyes shone as she stared at me, angling her head to the side.

Saying nothing, I held my chin tilted up and my lip stiff, keeping my face blank. No emotion to be found.

She flicked a finger in my direction. "Come. Let me show you something." Unfolding her legs, she eased to her feet gracefully, the silky material flowing onto the floor around her.

Did I really want to go anywhere with her? Hell no. Did I actually have a choice? Hell no.

Tianna moved with elegance, long legs carrying her slender frame as she moved to an opening at the right side of the chamber—opposite from where the griffins had dragged me inside the day before. The exit hadn't been there moments ago. I was beginning to think this mountain was filled with hidden passageways, secret rooms, and a network of underground tunnels controlled by her magic.

Clop. Clop. Clop. The clatter of my shoes on the uneven ground echoed through the cavern, but it was as if someone else guided my body. "Where are we going?" I asked, even though I told myself not to speak. My fear overruled my disguise at being unaffected by her tactics.

"I have my reasons for picking this specific mountain as my lair. I'm going to show you one of those reasons. This island isn't just known for its dragons, but because it has many natural elements of magic on its own. There was a time before the war when witches, warlocks, mages, elves, and magical beings of all kind sought to travel to the Veil Isles."

As we strolled down a path leading us deeper into the mountain, torches lit the way. They appeared a few feet in front of Tianna as she moved, igniting on their own—more magic. I tried my best to mark our path in my head, memorizing any small detail I could find.

"You seem to know a lot about the history of this place," I commented. I'd been under the impression that during the war the dragon kings had summoned her here, only to have her turn on them in the final hours of their warfare. How much time had she spent in the Veil prior to the war?

"I make it my business to know about the wonders of the world, but there was always something special about the Veil, and the pulse of magic energy here. It called to me."

Over Tianna's head, I could make out the arch of a doorway. As we grew closer, I noticed that the stone around the entrance was etched with runes that reminded me of seashells. I walked inside, a gush of cool, refreshing air bathed over my face, smelling of the sea. I swore in the distance my ears picked up the roaring sounds of waves colliding against the cliffs of the mountain.

"The magic calls to you as well, it seems," she considered, having stopped and turned slightly to watch me.

I said nothing in return. I couldn't really speak; my eyes too busy drinking in every inch of what lay before me. A pool like I'd never seen, not even in Wakeland. The water was vibrant in color, a swirling mixture of cobalt, turquoise, and midnight. A yearning to touch it rose up inside me so strongly, that I found my fingers outstretched of their own accord. Would it be sleek and silky? Warm? I was positive it would be.

Moonlight danced over the pool of water in the cavern, but how could that be? The chamber inside the mountain had no opening, no crack to allow in the night. Yet, tiny dots twinkled over the surface like a sky of starlight.

"Take a closer look," Tianna's silver-tongued voice enticed.

I cocked my head to the side, glaring at her. "Why, so you can push me in?"

She laughed, a haunting sound that had a wave spreading across the waters. "No, silly girl, so you can see." On light feet, she padded to the edge of the water, where it softly lapped over the stone floor. Crouching down, her hand waved over the water's surface, and the tang of magic tingled over my skin.

Curiosity got the better of me. I knelt beside the pool and peered in, realizing the pale moon was inside the waters not above. Another trick? Or was it magic, like she had let on during our walk? Was this one of the enchanted places of the Veil, like the Mirrored Shallows in Viperus Kieran had taken me to?

My line of thoughts was cut off, as soon as images began to form through the mist of the shimmery water. I leaned closer. The faces of Jase, Kieran, Zade, and Issik appeared. My heart jerked in my chest. God, how I missed their stupid, gorgeous faces—Jase's bright eyes, Zade's glorious skin, Issik's cool expression, and Kieran's lopsided grin.

But none of them were grinning now. In fact, their faces were somber and agitated.

My eyes were glued to the water and softly their deep, timbered voices floated up to my ears.

"Where is she?" Jase whirled on Kieran, his violent anger radiating off him, so deep, those violet eyes burned brightly. His face contoured with unbridled rage.

Kieran flinched. I'd never see him look so dejected before. His green hair hung over his eyes, shielding them from me. "She's gone," he whispered. "She took her."

Jase's fist lashed out, connecting with the right side of Kieran's cheek. I winced, my fingers digging into the rocky edge of the pool. Jase wasn't one to throw a punch and ask questions later. That was Zade. What was happening to them?

Don't fight. Please. Just find me.

Kieran did nothing to fight back as if he deserved the hit. It wasn't his fault I was captured. I wanted to tell him so, assure them I was alive, that I was okay, but I was hopeless to do anything but to watch them.

Zade paced the main hall in the castle of Viperus, while vines of greenery tangled along the high ceilings. "We have to get her back," the Golden God growled.

"We don't even know where she is," Issik pointed out, his words coated with sheets of frigid ice.

"Does it matter? Tianna took her," Jase snarled, hands fisted at his sides, looking like he was ready to go for round two with anyone who volunteered.

"No one knows the Isles like the four of us," Issik reminded, stuffing his hands into his front pockets. "The witch might have magic, but even with all the magic in the world, she won't be able to hide from us forever."

A lump formed in my throat. With this pool, Tianna got a front row seat at every move the descendants made, but even knowing it, I couldn't force myself to stop watching. We'd only been apart for two days, yet it felt like months.

Jase exhaled sharply. "Issik is right. We need to be smart. Tianna won't kill Olivia, not until she gets what she wants."

No one said it, but they were all thinking about the dragon stars.

"What do you suggest?" Issik inquired, his perfect face devoid of all emotion. The Ice Prince was ready for battle.

A shadow flashed across Jase's features. "We draw her out with a trade."

"No," I murmured. They couldn't hear me, but it didn't stop me from trying to will them to understand. If they gave in, gave Tianna the stones, we all lost.

The water rippled again, shifting the scene to a different day. The sun was beaming on the blue sky above, and the descendants were no longer in Viperus fighting or plotting. They were in their dragon forms, flying over a kingdom of gold with towers linked by bridges. An impressive sight—the dragons—the land was too, but seeing four powerful dragons with their wings spread wide, took my breath away. Each of them was so unique in coloring and physique, from the shape of their heads to the vibrant painting of their scales.

My heart became leaden by the weight in my chest. The two-way mental conversation didn't work through the magic of the pool. If they were speaking among themselves, I couldn't hear their words, which was for the best. The less Tianna knew of their plans, the better chance I stood at being rescued, but it didn't stop the ache inside me from spreading.

If Tianna knew of the silent communication she didn't lead on, but from the way they angled their heads, the flair of their nostrils, and the fire in their eyes, I knew something was brewing between the descendants.

The water stirred, taking the faces of Jase, Kieran, Zade, and Issik with it. Tianna's hand waved over the now stilled water once again, smiling sugary at me as if this made us friends. "This is a sign of good faith. You help me, and I'll let you see how your dragons fair, that they are still alive, as often as you like... assuming you cooperate that is."

"How do I know this isn't a dirty trick, just another one of your magic spells?" I so desperately wanted to spend the rest to the day beside the shimmering pool, but I couldn't let myself be swayed that easily.

"I think you know it is real. This isn't the first pool you've seen like this in the Veil. There are many. Some in plain sight, others concealed."

"What is this place?"

Tianna's eyes crinkled. "I call it the Pool of Mirrors. Although others before me might have given it a different name, for it has been here many, many centuries."

"How does it work? Could I make them appear?"

She waved her finger in the air and clucked her tongue. "You have not given me your word. But I will tell you that time has no bearing in the Pool of Mirrors. Past, present, and future circle like the moon orbits the Earth."

Meaning the visions were as unpredictable as Tianna herself. My eyes darted over the cavern. No windows could be found, and there was only one way in that was visible to me. This room was a dead end. "And if I refuse? What will you do to me? Keep me locked up in your box of darkness?"

The razor tip of her nail scratched along my cheek, a cool, deadly caress, and I felt the tender skin slice just at the surface. "Refuse me and I will make an eternity of hell for you, Olivia dear. The box of darkness, as you've named it, is a small fraction of what I can do. I *will* break you. You will beg me to kill you."

Color leeched from my face. "But you won't kill me."

She lifted her finger off my face, but the sting lingered, burning under the surface of my skin. "No. What I can do is far worse."

That was what I was afraid of.

"Your part is simple, dear. Lead me to the other two stars. We set out tomorrow, and every day after until I have them both in my possession."

If it were only that simple... I didn't dare tell her that despite the fact that I'd managed to find two stones, I had not done so on my own. Without the help of the women in white, I wouldn't have discovered a single star.

Perhaps there was a way I could deceive Tianna, at least until the descendants rescued me. If there was one thing I'd learned from the Pool of Mirrors, was that they were searching for me, and that gave me hope.

This was a dangerous game of lies and truths, yet I was willing to play it.

When I didn't refuse, she took my silence as agreement and I didn't correct her. Let her think I was yielding.

I was whisked back to my little prison just like before, with nothing more than a blink of an eye. Annoying and disoriented. I didn't weep this time, regardless of how much I wanted to do it. My lip trembled, but I bit down on it, hard, focusing on the pain instead of the emotional agony. No tears were shed as I lay on the cold, damp ground of the cavern. Dry-eyed, I categorized everything I'd seen today and learned. It might take me hours or days, but I would escape. I would free myself, and get the hell out of here. Alive.

Of course, I always had the option of sitting around and waiting for the descendants to rescue me, but after a few more days in the box, I realized, I wasn't the kind of girl who sat around.

I spent three days in the cell without a glimmer of Tianna. When she hadn't shown up to begin our search for a star, a growing sense of restlessness nagged inside me. Part of her torture, I was sure, as was allowing me a glimpse at what I longed to see, and then strip it away from me. Mind games. Her way of showing me she was in charge. I was allowed nothing unless she approved. Hell, she might as well dictate what time of the day I could pee.

I'd kill for a shower. Literally, kill.

Sadly, I was given no luxury.

I was becoming paranoid, overthinking everything. My mind needed to be sharp and attentive, but with no stimulation, but it was going slack. *Where was she? Had she changed her mind? Was I no longer important? Had she found another way?*

No! I couldn't think like that.

Right as I was on the verge of breaking down, the locks on my prison clicked open, and I was caught between relief and fear.

"You didn't think I'd forgotten about you, did you?" The sugary sweetness of Tianna's voice made my stomach pitch.

Two hideous looking creatures flanked her on either side—only coming up to her waist in height. Their leathery skin was a gangly green, making them appear almost sickly, and they had ears that were long and pointy, similar to those of elves.

Drawing my gaze away from the creatures, I glared at the witch. "How could I possibly think that? I'm your most precious possession," I replied, letting the sarcasm drip thick on my voice.

Tianna grinned, a corona of darkness appearing to swath around her. "I brought along a few friends, the reason for my delay. They'll do just about anything for a pretty bauble or a gold coin," she purred.

"What are they?" I asked, forgetting my manners, and failing to hide the disgust from my face.

"We'sss goblinsssss, girl," they hissed, speaking in perfect unison as if they were of one mind. Freaky.

Goblins? Really?

Wonderful. I was being chaperoned by two green goblins and a witch. This should be quite an adventure. I couldn't wait to get started. They also had a disturbing fascination with the necklace I wore at my neck, the one given to me in Viperus by the woman in white. It was this charm that had led me to uncovering the Star of Poison.

"Come," she instructed, waving her hand. "While we still have the cover of night."

I obeyed, although I nearly snorted at the idea of me finding a stone in the pitch black of midnight. Was it wise to mention I had a tendency of falling into holes, or tripping over basically everything? Nah. I'd let her figure it out on her own, she seemed to know so much about me already. Besides, I would probably be beaten for my clumsiness as it was. No use bringing it to her attention.

Stepping over the threshold of my invisible prison, the never-ending nothingness that surrounded my cage vanished.

"Take one of their hands," Tianna instructed.

"Why?" I inquired, glaring down at one of the goblin's fingers. He only had four. My insides cringed. Would it be slimy? Or rough with callous?

"Because they can willowphase."

"I don't know what that means."

She linked one of her elegant hands with the other goblin. "You'll see."

The goblin leered at me, holding out his hand. "It won't hurt," he assured, with a twist of his black lips that could be lying or speaking the truth. It was impossible for me to know.

On a sharp inhale, I placed my fingers inside the goblin's waiting, upturned palm. His four little appendages folded over mine. Tianna gave me a cold smile, her eyes biting into my skin like winter's frost. Before I had a chance to give another thought about what willow-phasing was, blackness gathered me up, the roaring of wind and speed echoing in my ears and rushing over my cheeks. The four of us were gone from that spot in the mountain, swiftly floating through space.

When my feet touched solid ground again, the darkness faded with it. The scent of ginger tickled my nose, and then I saw the evening horizon splashing the sky with hues of purple, pink, and orange as the sun sunk behind crags of black ash. At the base of a volcano, the ground was covered in lavish jade blades of grass.

This had to be Crimson—Zade's region. Was he near? I wanted to snuff the ember of hope that sparked inside me, but was afraid Tianna would see it.

We stood on the edge of the kingdom. Over my shoulder, dust of sand kicked up in the air. I didn't know the name of the territory Tianna used as her hideout, but it bordered Zade's lands.

A foreign weight settled onto my hands and feet. Curious, I glanced down and my stomach hollowed out. Chains of white silver were shackled to my wrists and ankles. I lifted my arms, testing their weight and was surprised to find them very light. This was going to make walking even more difficult than it already was for me.

A hysterical short laugh escaped me as I stared down at the shimmering metal. "Is this really necessary?"

"In case you get any ideas about running," Tianna explained, staring at me with a funny expression.

Oh, I had ideas all right, but they involved her eyeballs and a dull knife.

The two goblins prowled behind me, tendrils of their magic still glimmered over my skin. I shuddered, wanting to rid myself of the feeling. So, they could willowphase, jumping from different points in the world. A handy trick. Too bad one of the stars hadn't given me the ability to willowphase. It would come in quite handy right about now.

"Where are we?" I asked Tianna beside me. I wanted to hear her affirm my assumption.

Tianna's eyes sparkled. "Where isn't important, Olivia dear. Only what we need to find."

One of the goblins put his finger into my back and shoved. "Move."

Keeping my foot planted, I looked over my shoulder and glared down at the little pointy-eared man. "Push me again and I'll kick you."

Tianna chuckled, her lips pulling back into a wicked smile. "My kind of girl."

I blanched. The last thing I wanted was to be compared to her.

Crimson kingdom was sprawled across black sands, patches of green land, and a towering volcano—Titan Mountain—the only volcano on the Isles. I'd never seen anything like it, but that could be said for each of the regions in the Veil. They were all unique and impressive on their own. Through the puffy white billows of smoke from the volcano, Zade's ebony palace stood tall and powerful. It was made entirely out of obsidian, as I recalled, with sharp angles and piercing towers. He lived in a formidable kingdom that was sweltering hot twenty-fours a day. Even with the blanket of night, the air was stifling, making it almost difficult to breathe.

As we walked, sweat formed on my brow, the back of my neck, and beaded down my spine. I noticed one of the goblins had a slight limp to his gait, favoring his right leg. "What do you expect me to do?" I queried after a few minutes.

Did she think, like my dragons did, that I had some connection to the stars? That she could parade me around the kingdom, and I would lead her straight to the stone? They were wrong. I hadn't found them. It had been purely accidental. Or had it?

I guess I could say they had found me in a way and it hadn't been without help, but my lips were sealed tight about the women in white who had aided me. I wasn't sure how, but I knew it was important that Tianna didn't learn of them, and the roles they played in assisting me.

They were *my* secret weapon.

She blinked. "Whatever it is you do."

A snort/laugh rolled out of me—an action that didn't go unnoticed by Tianna.

"What is so humorous?" She sounded genuinely curious.

"Other than the goblins' faces," I insulted and shrugged. "Just that you think I'm going to be able to find the stars."

Her strides matched mine as we moved deeper into Crimson's smoldering heat. The expression on her face was one of pure boredom. "Why is it wrong for me to expect you to be able to do what you've already done?"

"You'll see."

She tugged on my chained hands and I stumbled forward. "Get to work." The little goblins at my back snickered.

Bitch. Bitch. Bitch. The word chanted in my head.

My feet dragged through the burning black sand, while the chains jingled into the night, joining a chorus of birds. I took a long shuddering breath, waiting to see if in fact, I would feel anything, a tingle of power, a pull of recognition, or a woman in white.

Nothing.

I felt nothing, but a balmy breeze rushing over my face, carrying the faint stench of burning fires—lava, I realized. Disappointment and relief swirled in my gut. A part of me wanted to find the stars quickly and be done with my imprisonment, the other part hoped I never found them. It would serve her right.

We continued to stroll about the land. "Do you sense anything?" Tianna asked for the fifth time in the span of an hour. She was driving me mad with her constant pestering.

"I can't concentrate with you badgering me," I barked, shaking my head. "Besides, I told you, it doesn't work like that."

"Bullshit. It's an enchanted object. Of course, it gives off a pulse of energy. All you have to do is find it—*want* to find it," she corrected.

"If that's the case, then why can't *you* find it?" I dared ask. "You have more magical powers in your pinkie, than I do in my entire body."

"True. Very true. The difference is in the signature of the magic. Not all mystical energy is the same. Like a thumbprint, it has a unique coding. If I were to come upon a spot charred from magic, a simple touch or taste would allow me to identify the user, assuming we'd ever crossed paths before."

A taste? I imagined Tianna licking the ground. "The stones… you've never touched them?"

"The crowns were destroyed, their stars lost, before I got the chance." The emotion that drove her was unmistakable then. Hunger. It was in her expression, in her voice.

And she was looking to make up for it now.

Over my dead body.

I ignored the tightness in my chest. This was going about as well as expected. Feelings I didn't want, clutched my insides, but I shoved them aside, focusing on the task and my impending doom.

For hours she dragged me around the kingdom, like a dog on a leash. Her eyes were always on me, watching me, looking for a flicker of recognition, hoping that I had felt something. The two goblins rarely gave me more than a few feet lengths in front of them. They occasionally mumbled to themselves, but were silent for the most part, waiting to take orders from the witch.

We kept far enough away from the castle, that I couldn't devise a plan to run and seek sanctuary behind the obsidian walls, not that I would make it with these chains *or* would even be protected from the witch there. On more than one occasion, Tianna had strolled into Jase and Kieran's homes as if she was a welcomed guest with an opened invitation. Nothing would stop her from grabbing me in Zade's home.

I took in the star-strewn sky. Were they out there, flying about the same stars? Searching for me*? I'm right here!* I wanted to scream. *Find me. Find me. Save me!*

Her eyes flickered with distaste. "They'll look for you, but they won't find you. Not as long as these two shadow us." She indicated with a tip of her dark red head to the goblins.

So something in their powers hid us from view? Damn. She was really taking the fun out of trying to escape. "You've thought of every-thing," I gritted between my clenched teeth.

"How else do you think I've survived for so long? It isn't because of my pretty looks."

"How ancient are you exactly?" I picked my words purposely, letting her know I thought of her as very old. She was vain enough to scowl a little deeper and I knew I hit my mark. A gleam of satisfaction glowed inside me.

"You never ask a witch her age."

I snorted. "If you're not immortal, how is it you don't age? Another spell?"

"Such a curious little thing you are."

If I kept her talking, it gave me time to ponder another escape plan, including how fast goblins could run with their little short, stocky legs. It was their mysterious magic I didn't understand and would get me into trouble.

I should have known better than to try and strategize while holding a conversation. My foot slipped on a patch of slick grass and I teetered to stay on my feet. A set of little hands grappled for my arms just as a thunderous roar burst over the volcano, nearly deafening me. The goblins fingers stiffened on my forearms.

That had definitely been the cry of a dragon.

My heart quickened, beating so fast I thought I might vomit. So close. My skin radiated with prickles. I inched away from the goblins whose attention had turned skyward along with Tianna's. *This is it. This is the opportunity you've been waiting for,* a voice bellowed inside my head.

Every instinct, every fiber of my being was screaming at me to run. *Go! Run! Now!* My eyes darted across the land toward the sound, toward the castle, judging the distance. Only a fool would try. Tianna would hunt me down and catch me, torture me with a spell, and god knew what else. This land was open, with little places to seek cover and hide. I would get but a mere few feet if I were lucky.

And then, I wouldn't be lucky at all.

I'd be punished in ways I didn't want to contemplate. I'd lose my privileges to the Pool of Mirrors, and I was anxiously looking forward to seeing the descendants again, even if only in a vision.

My eyes drew upward, searching for a large shadow in the dotted star sky, praying for the sight of those impressive wings. One of them was close, so very close, and I might never get this chance again. I had to get far enough away from my shadow goblins so I was no longer cloaked by their magic. If I could do that, I might stand a chance at being saved.

Again.

On the count of one… two…

Tianna's eyes pinned me as if she knew my body was primed to bolt. "It appears our search has come to a close for the night. Elon and Gor take us home." Her hand was on my shoulder before I could move a muscle, and just like that, it was over—my window closed shut with a snap.

I opened my mouth to scream, to hurl my voice across the night's sky, but darkness descended as my body was being transported.

Day one was a fail. On all accounts.

I wanted to cry, to rage, to kill. Not because I hadn't found the star, but because I was still confined. A fire like I'd never felt before rose up swift and deadly within me, scorching my blood to molten levels. Was this how Zade felt? Burning? Blistering? Pulse racing? The fire raged on. I could think of no way to extinguish the flames, except for a cold kiss from the Ice Prince. I nearly sighed out loud from the thought, only his cool breath could squelch the fever.

The moment we had willowphased from Crimson, back to inside the mountain, Tianna immediately locked me inside her box of darkness. I had begged her to take me to the Pool of Mirrors, but she slammed the door shut in front of me, clicking the locks one by one, and told me she was tired of looking at my dull face.

I took no offense to her slight, anger carpeting my senses.

It was impossible for me to eat that night. The sight of food aroused another bout of anger that made me want to toss the plate into Tianna's face. I didn't want her stinking stale, hard bread, her smoked meats, or nearly rotten fruit. I would rather starve than help her another day.

Sitting against the invisible wall across from the dingy cot, I let the coolness on my back soothe the burning of my skin. The plate remained untouched near the door. I should sleep. My eyelids were heavy, begging me to close them. They fluttered once… and again…

Something moved in the shadows outside my clear walls. The darkness seemed to ripple, and as I squinted, I told myself it was exhaustion playing tricks on me. Nothing was out there. No monsters waiting to shred me to ribbons. No dragons to rescue me. Only pure blackness.

The thoughts did nothing to rid the fear coiling in my stomach.

Are those eyes I see glowing?

Flecks of yellow danced in the shadows, far enough away that I couldn't make out what kind of face they belonged to. Friend or foe?

"Hello? I called.

The twin dots of yellow only stared.

I scampered across the floor to the other side of the wall, pressing my palms against the glass. "Help me," I pleaded.

The figure did not respond, nor acknowledge they heard me, but left me sitting in my cell. To be fair, I didn't even know if they would be able to free me. They would need magic to do so. Perhaps they knew they'd be unable to release me, so they had chosen not to reveal themselves. Tianna could have spies everywhere. They might be here to watch me, not help me at all, and yet, I couldn't shake the feeling as I stared into those yellow orbs, that they weren't here to harm me.

A crash of disappointment and severe loneliness, washed over me when the eyes disappeared deep into the shadows, no longer visible. I was once again alone.

My stomach tightened into a painful ball, growling at the discarded plate in the corner. I frowned at it and went to sit on the mattress. Dust of dirt and grim pooled out at my weight, but I didn't care.

Rain plummeted from the onyx and purple sky, thick and merciless drops soaking my face. My eyelashes stuck together and I blinked to see through the curtain of rain. In the corner of my left eye, I caught a shadow lurking, watching me. My skin crawled at the invasion. I didn't want to turn around, to face the prowler, but I had to know, had to see.

Wet tendrils of my hair flew out, whipping into my face as I spun. Brushing the heavy strands out of the way, I stared into the bleak grey. My fingers reached for the dagger strapped to my thigh, and shook as I gripped the handle, taking small comfort in the jeweled hilt. Where had I gotten the dagger?

In the distance, I made out the dragon form, but the rain was too dense for me to decipher which of my dragons was in danger.

I thought about shouting a warning to draw attention away from my dragon, yet the outline of his massive wings spread wide, soaring closer gave me pause. Seconds ticked by, but they drew out, feeling like hours. Blood splattered to a puddle under the dragon, turning the water scarlet, and my eyes darted up again. The dragon was no longer a beast, but a man, his gold chest painted with streaks of blood, whiskey eyes wide with shock.

"Zade?" My voice was smaller than I intended.

My head shook. No! No! No!

Rain sliced across my face, but I felt nothing. Not the cold. Not the wetness. I ran as fast as I could push myself. It wasn't enough. The last flicker of his fire left his eyes, extinguishing from his body and he fell.

I screamed.

I woke up crying, my voice hoarse and throat raw, sounding nothing like my own. My hand flew to my mouth as my crying finally ceased. Sweat beaded over my brow and in between my breasts. Sitting up, I braced my back against the wall and focused on my rapid breathing. The tang of blood had followed me from the dream, burning my nose. Zade's blood.

A nightmare. It was only a nightmare. Not the truth. Not a vision. Just a very, very bad dream. I repeated the words until they rang with truth, although it took longer than I wanted to admit.

How much time would it take of being locked up, being tortured before it changed me? Scarred me?

When I awoke the following morning, my plate had been removed and placed with a fresh hot meal. No longer able to resist the temptation of food, or the deep rumbling in my stomach, I gobbled it all. What good would I be to the descendants, or myself, if I withered away? The truth was without me they would die.

I refused to let that happen.

My despicable host arrived shortly after I finished eating, looking as enchanting as always. Her beautiful dress, the shine to her hair, the apricot scent of her skin all made me feel inferior, as if I was less than human.

I rubbed at my face. "Any chance there is a place to bathe in this mountain? Or do you like the stench of muck?"

Tianna snapped her fingers and the dirt vanished from my tattered dress, which was also mended, the grease disappeared from my hair, leaving it shiny and clean, smelling faintly of orange and honey. "Better?" she asked with a cocked slim brow.

Not precisely. She had spoiled my grand scheme to get to a body of water. It was in the depths of rivers, the lakes, and ponds that the women in white most often appeared. I needed their help once again. Stuck in my cell for hours, I had plenty of ways to plot and ponder my escape, but it hadn't work.

"Are we going out again?" I kept the hopefulness from my tone, refusing to let her see how much I wanted to get out of this box.

"No." She tapped a finger against her lips. "It became clear you don't know the first thing about magic, or how to use what you already have to find the other stars."

"And let me guess, you're going to teach me how to embrace it?"

"I plan to take it from you, Olivia dear."

I blundered a step backward. "I assume the abstracting of the star's power is a painful process."

Tianna sauntered closer, the ends of her black dress dragging on the ground. "The girl has a brain after all."

I bared my teeth. "Go. To. Hell."

Those light eyes had gone cold. She raised her hand as if she intended to hit me and I flinched, but the blow never came. "Hell couldn't keep me," she said it with pride.

Evil bitch. She was evil incarnate.

She perfected the expression of boredom as she fiddled with her ring. "If you want to keep me from plucking the wings off of your dragons, you will give me what I want." Her voice was flat.

"How can I give you the stones if I'm not allowed out of the mountain to search for them?"

"There may be another way," she dangled enticingly.

Did I dare ask? Was it a trap? "I don't understand."

Tianna caressed the ring on her finger. The stone was bright scarlet, matching the color of her bold lips. "A vial of your blood."

"My blood?" I echoed.

"Hmm…" She pursed her lips, mulling around the idea like fine wine, letting it marinate in her mouth. The prospect seemed to spark something of excitement inside her and those silver eyes brightened. "Yes, not much."

"That is all. Just one single vial?" I repeated to clarify there was no trickery to her offer. Once before I had offered up my blood. That day in the tomb of the kings had seemed a lifetime ago, but allowing the descendants to drink my blood had crafted an emotional connection between them and me.

She nodded, letting a slip of eagerness show in her expression, before she hid it once again behind her wickedness. It was enough to make me reconsider.

I bit my lip. "What will you use it for?" No way was I going to give the witch access to my emotions or something worse. I did not want a link between us, but if I were being honest with myself, I would have endured an eternity of being bonded to the witch if it saved my dragons.

She winked. "That's the real question, isn't it?"

Okay, so she had no intention of divulging her nefarious means with my blood. I gnawed on my lip harder, weighing my options. Everything in my body was screaming at me not to give her what she wanted. The descendants had believed blood was the key to the undoing of Tianna's curse. She had cast it with the blood of the kings, the descendant's fathers. I didn't grasp how my blood could be the key.

Was it wise to hand it over, no questions asked?

"Will you let me go if I agree to give you my blood?" Something inside me went cold and still at the thought of her having an essence of me at her disposal. Could she use it to curse me?

She shrugged a graceful gesture. "Perhaps. Perhaps not. It depends on your value. Not to mention, telling you would ruin my fun."

I didn't deign to make a response. My mind was whirling in a million directions, calculating all the risks.

"Last chance." She sounded so smug as if she knew she had her prey caught in her web.

How much was I willing to gamble for my freedom? I actually didn't delude myself into thinking she would let me go.

"I grow impatience of the waiting game. Time is up. I had hoped we could do this the easy way, but…" She stalked toward me, a smirk ghosting over her lips.

Pressing as far back into the corner as I could, my stomach tightened. For the descendants, I would sell my soul to the witch. I would give up my life for them to be free. "Wait." My voice was barely a horsed whisper.

Tianna lifted a brow, pausing a foot in front of me. "Yes?" she drawled out, tracing a sharp nail down the vein pulsing along with my neck. The slightest pressure and she'd get what she desired and I'd lose more blood than necessary.

I stared up into her silver eyes, realizing she was going to take my blood with or without my consent. If I were smart, I would bargain. If she was determined to have my blood, I wanted something in return, something worth my while. "Show me the descendants and I'll give you my blood." I kept my chin raised, defiant.

She smiled. "You have a deal, Olivia dear."

Exhaling, my shoulders slumped. Why did it feel as if I'd just made a deal with the devil?

T tried not to think about the consequences of what I'd done. Tianna was good on her word, bringing me immediately to the Pool of Mirrors. The enchanted cavern was silent when we arrived.

Seeming regal in her fine dress, adorned with gold jewels, Tianna strolled straight to the water's edge. "You're lucky I'm feeling generous tonight."

I gave her a flat stare, while her eyes glittered like stars.

"You've got five minutes, make the most of it," she snapped, her fingers gliding over the small pool.

My gaze turned to the waters. Anticipation, excitement, and fear danced in my blood—the blood she wanted. The turquoise water was tinged with gold, as if the sun was sliding into the horizon. No stars tonight, but streaks of summer, bringing with it warmth and the chatter of birds.

I was already on my knees as the water transformed into my mirror of the world outside this mountain. A heavy sigh escaped when I saw Kieran's face. His usually bouncing green eyes were slivers of poison, reptilian. Zade was perched on the edge of a long table, his legs, taut and muscular, stretched out before him.

Orange-red rays beamed through the window, to form a band of color against the polished ebony floors as Jase and Issik leaned against a wall of marble. Jase's jet-black hair was disheveled from the forking of his fingers through the strands, while Issik's jaw was locked. My heart bloomed with hope at seeing their faces.

They're alive.

"She was close," Zade growled, wrath twisting his features. "She was here. I sensed it deep in my bones."

"The witch probably cloaked her." Nastiness laced Jase's words.

Tianna chuckled huskily at my back, but I ignored her, focusing wholly on the picture in front of me.

"The important thing is we know she is alive. We've all felt her emotions," Issik said.

It gave them hope, I realized, that tether they had to my feelings was helping them.

Issik's glare suddenly hardened, like Icebergs, and his body bristled. The others noticed, becoming alarmed.

"What is it? What do you feel?" Jase prompted.

"S-she's sad," Issik murmured, eyes staring at nothing as he lost himself to the part of me that lived inside him. He rubbed his chest as if it ached.

Zade's lips were pale and tight. "We've searched every fucking inch of this isle, and not a speck of Tianna. We're no closer to finding Olivia than we were when she was taken."

Sadness flickered in Jase's stormy eyes and I swore I felt his agony deep inside me. I longed to wrap my arms around him, to comfort him, and absolve him of the guilt I knew he carried.

I leaned forward another inch.

Seeing Zade's sun-kissed face, the nightmare came rushing back. The rain. The fear. The blood, and panic beat against my chest.

"We promised we'd keep her safe," Kieran's voice broke, and my gut wrenched.

You did keep me safe! I yelled silently, willing them to hear me. I had only lived this long because of them.

Cold, glittering calm shifted over Issik's expression—his mask of frostiness. "We're not giving up."

"Issik's right," Jase mused. "Failing is not an option. This is bigger than Tianna ruling over the Veil forever, greater than her having more power than any single being should possess."

"We won't be so easily tricked again," Zade snarled.

"Time isn't on our side. There are only two stones left, and we know Tianna will use Olivia to hunt for the other stars," Jase admitted.

Their world rested on my shoulders.

A cold smile radiated from Issik's eyes. "We have a few tricks up our sleeves."

And so did I.

Before the descendants divulged their plans of action, revealing too much to the witch, I crept closer to the edge of the water again, my nose nearly touching the water, but this time I let gravity take me and tumbled into the pool. This place was magic, and I was counting on it being strong enough to keep the witch from plucking me out before I was able to summon the women in white—or one of them at least.

The low tide of the water rushed over me, and I was sucked into its depths. Biting down on my lip, I stopped myself from nearly yelping at the freezing shock of the temperature.

Help me! I called out into the water, not wasting a moment of this chance. *Come on. Come on.*

I had only seconds, a minute at the max until Tianna found a way to fish me out of here. I didn't know who or what heard my pleas, but the water suddenly rose up around me in a wrath of powerful waves that surged into a swirling typhoon. My body was swept up in the current, jerked from right to left in endless circles. Soon, I'd lost all focus, the world around me becoming nothing but a blur of turquoise sea.

Had this been a mistake, one that was going to cost me my life? I didn't know what to do. My lungs burned for air. My head pounded with pressure. I was dead. Surely, I would drown. There was no way out of the watery tomb encasing me. I had to take a breath. I needed air. I—

A jolt went through me and when I thought I could no longer stand it, when I was on the verge of passing out, the waves roaring around me stilled. The fire in my lungs eased, filling with fresh air, and the compression in my head released like a balloon. Following the sudden calm, the scent of autumn fires, wet leaves, and cinnamon wafted over me as I floated in the depths of the pool—with little effort on my part. I wasn't sure I was even still in the Pool of Mirrors. For all I knew, I could have been whisked to some other body of water, or some other land.

"Hello?" I called in my head, afraid to open my mouth.

The water in front of me swirled in circles until those rings formed images of a face I'd rather never see again. Tianna. Except, she was different. Younger, and she wasn't alone. A woman very similar in appearance stood beside her in a cream room that looked fit for a goddess. Decorative gold columns lined all corners of the space.

I watched with earnest curiosity as the young woman in her sheer pale blue dress crossed her arms, eyeing Tianna with worry. "Tianna, are you sure this is a good idea?" she asked. It was obvious in the way the woman fidgeted with the rings on her hand she was unsettled.

Tianna strode across the white marble floor, the golden train of her thin dress trailing behind her. The fabric swished over the room as she put an arm around the young woman's shoulder. "Corvina, it is the only way for magic to take its rightful place in the world. Why should we continue to hide who we are, what we're capable of? I'm tired of being shut off from other realms. There was a time when magic was worshiped. Humans bowed at our feet."

"But to double-cross the dragon kings, is that wise?" Corvina refuted.

Holy crap. I couldn't believe what I was seeing. This was a conversation from before Tianna cast the curse on the descendants, prior to her double-crossing the dragon kings, and before she went crazy.

Tianna gave Corvina a squeeze on the shoulder. "I can handle them. The curse will give us the stars and power to rule. We just need to be patient, sister."

So Corvina was her sister. What happened to her? Where was she now? So many questions, but all I could do was watch and see what unfolded.

"The only way to set things back to the way they once were, is to find the dragon stars," Tianna explained. "Then magic can once again be respected. We won't have to bow to anyone. They will bow to us." She grinned in that smug way of hers.

The vision was swept away with the tide, but brought someone else.

"Keeper of the stars, you seek my guidance."

I spun in a half circle at the omnipotent voice that sounded from behind me. Long silver hair haloed around a slim, and pretty face. Although her skin had an alabaster sheen, I could tell she had spent many hours in another life basking under the sun. I wasn't dumb enough to mistake the light in her grey eyes for anything other than wisdom beyond this world.

"You came."

"Our spirits have lingered for nearly a hundred years for the sole purpose to aid the one—the key."

Fabulous. *"I need to get a message to the descendants."*

"That is beyond the scope of our abilities. What we can offer is pieces of information regarding the stars."

"How am I going to get out of here?" The words had been

mumbled in my head as a question to myself, but the woman in white heard them.

"Help can come in different forms, and when you least expect it."

So not helpful. *"Who are you? Why are you helping me?"*

"We're the wives of the kings, the murdered queens of the Veil, and the mothers of dragons." Her voice joined with a collection of others as they spoke the words in unison.

In some part of my mind, I had known the women appearing to me had been the descendant's mothers. Something in each of them had been familiar. *"Which one is your son?"* I asked.

Her cool grey eyes filled with a mixture of pride, sadness, and love only a mother could have for a child. *"He is the dragon who breathes no more."*

Tobias, my mind hissed.

"Where do I find the Star of Fire?" I projected.

"The stones are like sisters. Like calls to the like."

"What does that mean?"

The water around us suddenly became agitated, rippling and swirling.

"She comes," Tobias's mother murmured, her gaze looking straight through me before her eyes returned to focus on my face. She lifted her hand, and using a wave she sent a phantom caress along my cheek. *"We'll meet again, daughter."* The sound of her voice began to fade. *"Be strong. Be brave. Don't lose hope. Our sons will find you…"*

Her body drifted toward the dark abyss below, the white material of her lacy dress engulfed by the shadows. She was leaving, her spirit pulled back into another part of the world where I couldn't follow.

"Wait!" I called out, my arm stretching toward her. *"Don't leave me. Not—"*

Fingers latched onto my honey-blonde hair and yanked, ripping me out of the water. I took a gasping breath of air, lips trembling as I let out a shriek of pain. My scalp was on fire, and strands of my hair twined around Tianna's alabaster fingers.

"You bitch," she hissed.

A string of curses was ready to roll off my tongue, but I coughed instead, spitting up water. My fingers flew to her hands, nails scoring over her flesh as I bucked and fought to be free of her clutches. Her deadly grasp only tightened, regardless of the skin and blood now under my nails. Caught in her own wrath, she was mindless of her soaked gown, or the blood dripping down her ivory hands.

"Was there a no swimming sign I missed?" Dumb. So dumb to taunt her in the midst of such animosity.

"A valiant effort, even if it was pointless. The pool doesn't allow you to communicate with those in the visions. That little stunt will cost you," she seethed with a low calm that unnerved me. What kind of creature was she that she could turn off her emotions with a flick of a switch? From boiling rage, to immoral eagerness as she regarded me now.

"I'm not the bitch. Try looking in the mirror," I snapped, unable to help myself. She deserved much more than a few scratches and nasty words. I recalled the vision with her sister and considered asking what happened to Corvina, but held my tongue.

Her eyes so full of hate and twisted excitement remained zeroed on me. "I'm going to enjoy this. You can kiss your freedom goodbye."

It would be a lie if I said her confirmation of my continued imprisonment didn't get to me. It stabbed me in the heart. But never for a mere flickering heartbeat had I believed she might let me go.

I was a tool.

And she wasn't done with me yet.

Tianna dragged me by my hair, hauling me out of the cavern and into the tunnels. Dress plastered to my skin and body shivering, I scrambled to keep my footing to no avail. It was an effort to try and keep my own panic and fear hidden, but for the sake of the descendants, I attempted to be brave, to be strong. My wild emotions would distract them from finding me, muddling their focus.

My struggles to break free were futile. When we entered into another chamber, she released me with a jerk, discarding me like trash. I wanted to curl into a ball and disappear into myself, but the witch had other plans. A flick of her hand and shackles appeared at my wrists, chaining me to the ground. I whipped my head upward to Tianna towering over me. My gaze was drawn away from her face to the shiny thin dagger fitted into her hand.

She smiled, cocking her head to the side. "A vial of blood was the agreement, but I never specified how I would take it."

The arms holding me up on the cold stone floor went weak. Deceived. I'd been a fool. "You tricked me."

"Tricked," Tianna mused, tapping the tip of the smooth blade against her nose. "How is it my fault you didn't ask?" Her words were like punches, hitting me with enough force to knock the air out of my lungs.

I shook my head and scooted as far away as the chains would allow. Not far enough. "No," I managed to get my mouth to say.

"A bargain is a bargain."

My face went pale. I wasn't getting out of this. No one was coming to rescue me.

The glint in her eyes was the most hideous thing I'd ever seen. A desire to cut them out shredded through me, but the only thing getting torn apart today was me.

The witch crouched down so we were at eye level and twirled the blade once in her fingers before pressing it against my cheek. Her brows rose as she met my wide, fear-stricken eyes. "Shall we begin?"

Counting on her malice, I braced myself against the pain I knew was coming, and prayed I was strong enough to withstand the torment she had planned. She didn't disappoint.

With slow movements, meant to prolong my torment, she pierced the flesh on my face, running the blade sideways from cheekbone to chin. A hiss escaped between my gritted teeth, fingers curling at the first sting. Every muscle, every bone down to the core of my soul begged me to run, but I couldn't. There was nowhere to go, no way to escape.

Again, she touched the end of the blade to my skin, a new spot this time—the top of my shoulder. I stared at the length of the weapon as it sunk through flesh. Something about the dagger held my gaze. Something about it was different. Not that I had much experience with being diced up like a piece of meat, but I knew—I felt the tang of magic transfer from metal to blood.

It was cursed.

A cry escaped my lips, and I slammed my eyes shut against the agony. When I opened them I gasped at the weapon causing me such torment. Part of the gleaming silver blade filled a quarter of the way with crimson fluid, and I instantly understood its magic. It was my blood the dagger collected, siphoning it from my veins.

Tianna's eyes glowed white, her pretty features contorting for a split second into someone much older. I blinked and the image was gone. Her lips curled—holding the same color that now filled her dagger. "Oh, don't look so miserable, Olivia. The fun is only beginning."

I blanched.

With each cut I felt my skin open up, felt the blazing pain, the flow of blood leave my veins. My arms slackened at my side. Dose after dose, biting pain after pain, she continued to make small cuts over my body. Arms. Legs. Back. Stomach. I was a human dummy for her to practice her voodoo.

Ear-splitting screams left me over and over again, my voice going hoarse and throbbing. The more I cried, the harder Tianna laughed, until I clamped down on my lip to keep from voicing my pain. Metallic warmth filled the inside of my mouth as another slash crossed my back. I had pierced my lip. It did very little to centralize the agony.

My entire body was now flaming, burning hotter than the center of the sun. I would have sworn she was peeling back my flesh. Silent tears streamed down my face and neck, intermixing with the channels of blood flowing over my body.

I went somewhere far, far away. A place she couldn't hurt me. A place free of pain. A place of love where I was surrounded by my dragons.

Time ceased.

I don't know how long she tortured me, or how much blood she'd stolen from my body. I had a faint recognition of her locking me back into my box of darkness, her voice a mocking whisper rippling in my ear.

Then there was nothing. No pain. No sorrow. No chains.

"*Olivia,*" a voice summoned me from within the darkness and despair. I groaned, not ready to wake and deal with the aftermath of what Tianna had done to me. At least unconscious, the pain, the horror, and the fear didn't breathe with life, but the moment I opened my eyes, it would hit me again.

Whether I wanted to come or not, the world came back into focus. Inky darkness still surrounded me, but differently, and I remembered… the box of darkness. I inhaled and immediately regretted the simple act of breathing.

I was lying on the cold floor of my cell—now stained a russet red by my blood. Remaining motionless, I took stock of my injuries, and gently tested the movement of my arms. I wasn't dead, which spoke volumes. Although I had many cuts on my body, none was life-threatening and all had clotted. Groaning, I braced my palms on the floor and used what strength I had left to push myself into sitting position.

The room spun…

"Good, you're awake."

I jumped at the deep male voice. There, under the cover of shadows in the corner stood a three-foot man. A goblin.

Alarm tornadoed inside me. Forgetting about the cuts and bruises covering me from head to toe, I clambered to the other end of the cage. "W-what do you want?" I stammered, hating the fear that overcame me.

"I'm not here to hurt you," he insisted, holding up both palms in a gesture of goodwill. His green skin wasn't as pasty as the other two who had escorted me to Crimson, and something about his speech was clearer, less otherworldly and more human.

Lies! He lies. Tianna sent him, my mind screamed. "I don't believe you."

"It is wise of you to mistrust after what you've been through, but I don't have time to explain. If you want to get out of here, you need to come with me. Now." A sense of urgency spiked his features.

"Did someone send you?" I asked, wariness tugging my lips into a thin line.

"Quick. We must be quick," he asserted again.

I shoved to my feet and winced, feeling like I'd aged a thousand years. "How can I trust you?"

Alight with understanding his yellow eyes watched me, and he carefully took a step toward me. "Not all creatures are loyal to *the witch*. Some of us know the world she promises is nothing but lies, smoke, and magic. Some of us remember the old."

He was offering me a chance to escape this place. And if it was a trap? I shuddered. My punishment would no doubt be far worse than what I had suffered last night. But could I pass up what might be my only chance at escaping… Time-pressed down on me, on us both. I could see the earnestness on his face, and the risk he took in coming here. If I didn't take his hand now, he would leave and take his offer of help with him.

Be brave. Be daring.

Fear wouldn't rule me.

So I placed my hand in his.

The familiar, cool darkness cocooned me. Weightlessness. Dizziness. Speed. The goblin willowphased, spiriting us out of the box of shadows to—

That was the question. Where was the goblin taking me? Was he friend or foe? It was too late to ask, unfortunately.

The next second, I was falling through the night until my feet landed on solid ground. I was free. I was a hot mess, but I was free. Chunks of disheveled hair were plastered to my face. My clothes and body covered in grime and dried blood, and to top it all off, I barely had the strength to stand up on my own two feet—my knees wobbled from the weight.

Eagerly, I gulped down steadying gaps of air, savoring the way they glided in and out of my lungs. Freedom, I could all but taste it.

"We're not out of the clear yet," the goblin announced, seeing the pure hopefulness slide over my features.

The sound of his gruff voice was a slap of cold water, reminding me I wasn't alone, and far from danger. Yet, I was out of the mountain. That had to count for something. "Why are you helping me?"

"Come," he ordered, not bothering to answer my inquiry. "We've no time to waste with questions. The wanderer waits to escort you across the Nameless Lands." His stubby legs moved quite quickly for his statue.

I was forced to jog to catch up. "Who is the wanderer?" I asked, figuring the Nameless Lands were this barren place of endless sand, formidable mountains, and dead brush that tumbled with the evening winds.

The goblin shrugged his shoulders, keeping a brisk pace and his eyes sharp. "Don't know, but he paid a hefty fee for your release."

Coin. It was true then, the myths of goblins and their treasure. My mouth turned down at the realization. How much had this *wanderer* paid? It had to have been a fortune for the goblin to risk so much to get me out of the witch's lair.

The night's sky was vast, sprinkled with starlight, and I let my eyes soak up the wonder. How long did we have before Tianna realized I was missing? Seconds? Minutes? I didn't think we would be lucky enough to have any more time than that. My eyes cut back to the goblin. "Thank you for helping me. I don't know how I can ever repay you."

"I've been compensated. You don't need to repay me," he mumbled, climbing over a dead fallen tree trunk.

I followed him with great effort, my body and limbs aching fiercely from the cuts. "What is your name?" I asked. It would be a name I'd never forget.

"My name isn't important."

Okay. Maybe it was better we didn't talk. I stumbled over my own feet countless times, but I never complained. I only hoped wherever we were going wasn't much farther. My energy was quickly waning.

"We're nearly there," he offered, noticing my apparent struggles.

The moon shone ahead, casting the sea of sand in silver shadows. In that moment, something emerged from behind a leafless tree. My heart knocked in my chest, seeing the figure hooded by a cloak, guarding their face against sight and the gritty winds.

Was this the wanderer? He had the look of someone with no name, no title, no home. I had known firsthand what it was to have none of those things. It felt as if my days of living on the streets had been a lifetime ago, not mere months.

The wanderer nodded at the goblin. "Orion." His eyes swiveled to me, taking in the cuts and bruises covering the parts of my body he could see. "She looks like walking death," he commented brusquely.

My chin rose as I met his scrutinizing gaze. Underneath the hood, his face was shrouded, but grey hair covered his chin and cheeks in a scruffy beard.

"She's stronger than she looks," Orion the goblin assured. "And stubborn," he added, folding his arms.

The wanderer thumped the staff I had just noticed in his hand to the ground and lifted his head. "Good. She'll need both to make the last leg of her journey."

I found the way they talked around me, instead of to me, to be perturbing. "I can hear you," I stated, finally speaking.

He sent a warning look in my direction, and I got my first glimpse of his face. A scar ran just under his eyes. It was too dark to see what color they were, but he had the kind of face that seemed weathered by long, harsh years. He reached inside his cloak and pulled out a pouch, dropping it into Orion's waiting hand. "Go now, my friend. Stay hidden. You know what *she* will do if she catches you."

Orion gave me one last look. "I bid you farewell and good luck, keeper of stars." He bowed his head slightly in my direction, before disappearing in front of my eyes.

A ripple of sadness trickled through me. One day I would find a way to repay him for his bravery and kindness. One day when the world wasn't going to shit. I was once again alone with a stranger, putting my freedom and trust in his hands. He had orchestrated my release, but I wasn't under any delusions he was a friend. Not yet.

"Why can't the goblin willowphase us?" I asked, staring at the spot the goblin had been only seconds ago.

His jaw tightened. "Because *she* can sense it. We don't want to attract any attention to us. It is a few more miles to the border. Can you walk?" Not waiting for me to respond, he started trekking it toward the moonlight, the darkness at his back.

Quickly, I fell in step beside him. "Why are you helping me?" I blurted.

"Does there need to be a reason to rescue a pretty girl from evil?" he countered, with a slight incline of his head in my direction.

"Most people wouldn't stick their neck out for a stranger," I mumbled, staring at the ground.

"In most places, the fate of the world isn't in jeopardy," he replied softly, regret and despair coloring his voice.

We walked in silence for a time, hours perhaps, and I took the opportunity to study the man who was a mystery. He was tall, even if his shoulders hunched with age, and though he carried a staff, he did not seem to rely heavily on it for support. Who was he? Why would he help me? How had he known I was in need of rescuing?

So many questions swirled in my mind, and I doubted he would give me the answers, but it didn't stop me from asking. I schooled my face into bland curiosity, keeping the pain I was feeling masked.

"Where are we going?" I asked, unable to handle the silence anymore. Talking helped keep my mind from what walking did to my body, and I hoped to gain insight on who this wanderer was. Two birds. One stone.

"To Crimson Kingdom," he replied in a flat tone. "That is as far as I can take you. After that, you're on your own."

"But—" I started to protest, but one cutting glance from the elderly man made me shut my trap. It wasn't that I was ungrateful for all he had done. I was afraid to be alone.

"Zade will be able to sense you the moment you step foot on his land, but so will the witch. She will be looking for you, searching for your scent." Which she had now, thanks to my vial of blood. "Zade must get to you before she does. It is your only chance."

The words were foreboding, but I'd take the gamble regardless.

This man knew of the descendants, knew them by name, and hearing that he was taking me to Zade had my heart skipping. "How do you know the descendants?"

The wanderer blew out a breath. "It isn't important."

So he wanted to remain a mystery. I cleared my throat. "What happened to this place?"

His eyes swept the horizon for a moment. "Without a ruler, the land dies. It is forgotten and all that lives perishes."

"This is the kingdom of the fifth dragon," I stated, voicing what I had already concluded. Tobias. He had tested the boundaries of his freedom from the Veil, paying for it with his life. Only the skeleton of his dragon bones had remained.

"It once was. Now it is known as the Nameless Lands," he declared. "A place the witch uses for her means."

"Do you know what it was called?" I paused to rest for a moment or two against the wide trunk of a desolate tree. My muscles were screaming, my stomach was famished, leaving me weaker than I should be, and I didn't know how much longer I could keep going.

Leaning on his staff, the wanderer gave me a wary glance. "We're nearly to the border. Can you feel it?"

That explained the flush in my cheeks, the exhaustion in my lungs. I nodded and pushed myself off the textured bark. "How did you know I was here? That I'd been taken?"

Our feet crunched over rocks and dried branches as we pressed onward. "I've dwelled in these mountains for many years. Nothing happens here that I don't notice. I spotted the griffins sneaking you off into the mountain," he confessed, looking over his shoulder, making sure I was still on my feet.

If he lived here then... "Have you ever encountered Tianna before?" I was prying, but the shadows in his eyes were like mine. Broken. Damaged.

His golden skin paled, and I immediately regretted the hurt my question caused to resurface. "We all bear scars from the witch's wickedness."

My gaze flickered to his face. Tianna had left her mark on him as well. I rubbed at my chest.

"There will be hell to pay for what she's done to you," he declared, with unbridled fierceness that smacked revenge.

My insides recoiled at the thought of more bloodshed to come, but another part of me rejoiced, wanting to join him on the crusade for vengeance. My own powers of poison and tranquility thrummed and pounded inside me, begging to be released, lashing through my lungs.

He watched me with caution as I tried to reign in the power that threatened to let loose. "You'll need to save that anger for when it counts. This night isn't over, although our time together is."

I dug my nails into my palms and took a few steadying breaths as I pictured the faces of Jase, Kieran, Zade, and Issik—my dragons. It was like a dose of cool smoke extinguishing the flame of fire inside me and the rush of power receded.

"Impressive."

I blinked. "My ability to get myself into shitty situations? You have no idea how impressive that really is."

If it weren't so dark, and the hood of his cloak didn't cast a shadow over most of his face, I would have sworn his lips twitched. My instincts were telling me he was trustworthy, that he really cared about what happened to the Veil and to the descendants, but until I was actually safe, I couldn't let down my guard.

We hiked a few more yards before the wanderer came to a halt where the rocky land gave way to black sands and mossy grass.

"This is as far as I go," he stated, the staff in his hand standing tall beside him. "Crimson is donned with rivers of lava, heat that can kill a man, and rocks as sharp as glass. Head straight for the castle. If you somehow make it into the walls, hide. Don't leave."

That wasn't likely to happen. One of them would find me before I made it that far. We both knew it. Well, that was if I didn't get myself killed before that by trying to avoid everything else.

I swallowed, staring out into the distance at the gleaming obsidian castle jutting into the night's sky. We had reached the border between the Nameless Lands and Crimson Kingdom. Fear hit me in waves, crashing into me again and again. Ally or enemy, there was something to be said for traveling with company, safety in numbers. The prospect of crossing over alone was both terrifying and joyous. I didn't know what waited for me in the foreign kingdom. Were the descendants there or miles away? The wanderer seemed confidant Zade would sense me, and I knew the dragons had those ties to their land, but going out there alone, knowing Tianna could come sweeping in to kidnap me again at any second, made my heart thunder in my veins.

Part exhaustion. Part fear. I might be sick.

Dragging my eyes from the intimidating land, I stared up at the wanderer. "How can I ever thank you?"

"Beat her, that's how. It's the only way any of us can be free."

"Any advice?"

The corner of his gray whiskers twitched. "Don't die."

Nodding, I crossed into Crimson.

The trees fell silent as I walked over the mossy earth, birds, and critters having darted for cover at my approach. Or maybe it was something else…they sensed something dark...

I felt it too.

Cursing under my breath, I glanced at the volatile land in front of me, so similar to the dragon. The air pulsed and throbbed with power, a hideous presence that loomed in the shadows. Tianna. She was searching for me and closing in fast.

"Run!" the wanderer hissed at me. "Run now. Swiftly. Run as if your life depends on it."

It did depend on it.

So I fled.

Eyes zeroed in on the tall obsidian castle, my feet flew over the mossy grass with patches of black sand. Even as the earth tilted under my feet, rumbled, I kept moving.

So close. I was so close to being free of the witch. If I had come this far just to get captured again… tortured… Tears fell in earnest at the thought, hampering my vision, but I couldn't stop running. Not to clear my eyes. Not to catch my breath. Not for any reason.

If I did, she would find me.

Perhaps she already had…

A howl echoed from the Nameless Lands, vicious and snarly. It was followed by another, and another, until fear pooled in my blood. *Shit. Shit. Shit.*

Faster. I had to go faster.

I couldn't stop myself from sneaking a glance over my shoulder. It was another form of torment, needing to see what hunted me. Sprung from a nightmare, the creatures were so dark they appeared made from a starless night. Three wolves of shadow and evil, eyes of midnight stalked toward the border between lands with frenzy.

Tianna's hounds.

My eyes slung forward and I forced my legs to move faster. My tattered dress snared on a branch and I hit the ground, grass and dirt scraping over my palms as I braced my fall. I didn't give myself time to wince over the pain, just shoved to my feet and raced for the castle, using the sliver of moonlight to be my guide. I didn't brave another glance behind me—I didn't dare.

Their panting breaths almost fanned my neck. The pounding of their paws dug into the dirt as they flew over the earth. I refused to let myself think of what would happen if they caught me as I careened over a small stream of flowing lava. The heat kissed my bare legs, but I barely felt the pain.

I should have known it wouldn't matter how far or fast I ran. Tianna had great power. She had years of knowledge of things I'd never understand. I didn't stand a chance pitted against someone like her.

So why try?

No! my mind screamed. *You can't give up. It is exactly what she wants. Don't let her win.* The words hissed and tingled in my mouth.

I had to survive. I really did, but her allies were too many.

Where did she hide them all?

It was a question I would regret asking myself because I was about to find out.

Hurry, hurry! Every muscle of my body beckoned.

My knees groaned as I pushed myself harder, focusing on the

towering castle. No matter how fast I ran, it seemed so out of reach. Sweat rained down my face and into my mouth. My strength was on its last thread, my speed diminishing. Stars danced in my vision yet I knew if I fell now, I wouldn't be able to get up again. I'd be surrounded… I'd be mauled…

Three dark shadows flew over my head, and a roar that shook the earth rang throughout the kingdom. The wolves snapped at my heels, sensing the urgency of the hunt. They'd found me. The descendants had come.

I stumbled at the sight of their figures in the dark sky, and the three sets of wings that took up the sky gave me hope. I forgot for a half a second about the hounds.

"Olivia!" My name bellowed from somewhere in front of me. A voice I'd dreamed about for days.

Jase, my entire body slumped with relief.

He was running toward me, feral rage smoldering in his glowing violet eyes. He was here. I could see him. Another few more feet and I'd be in…

One of the hounds rushed past my right with such blinding speed, I scarcely had time to react. The hounds surrounded me. A whoosh of air expelled from my chest as I hurled myself to a stop, and my feet dug harshly into the earth. I turned in a circle, shaking my head.

"No," I whispered, gritting my teeth. I had not come this far to get ripped away from the descendants again. I refused to believe it.

I wouldn't go down without a fight. Claws and teeth be damned. Nothing they could do to me would be worse than being caged again. I might not have daggers or arrows, but I wasn't weaponless.

The hound in front of me barred its razor canines, saliva dripping over its charcoal muzzle. He snapped at me and I jerked to the side.

"Olivia!"

Spurred by the sound of Jase's roar, wild instinct took a hold of me. I gathered what little energy I had inside me and summoned poison. I wanted the beast to suffer. Tranquility would have been too peaceful for what Tianna had done to me.

The poison buried inside me hurled through my lungs, flaring with elation. I unleashed my power, a burst of green mist erupting from my lips and traveling through the air as miniscule toxic particles. The hound snarled, backing away. He couldn't escape though. The poison swirled around his face, toiling its way into the beast's nostrils, down his lungs, until it weaved into its entire body. From there, it worked its magic, slowly killing the wolf.

I held my breath, but I didn't wait for the hound to die or the others to attack. I ran straight into Jase's waiting arms, a burst of energy boosting my legs. His scent hit me—sea and wild mountains—as he finally scooped me up into his arms, and in one smooth movement, he spun, taking us both to the ground. His strong body shielded me, while the power of Issik, Kieran, and Zade barreled into Tianna's mystical hounds. Flames, poison, and ice shot from the depths of my dragons, engulfing the evil beasts.

The wolves shrilled, groaned, and cried, their bodies writhing in agony as they were burned, poisoned, and frozen to death. Horrible sounds. Sounds that would live in my memory for years, along with the nightmares I endured in the mountain.

My breathing was chopping and raw, but I was safe—I was back where I belonged.

With my dragons.

I never wanted Jase to let me go. I was quite content to stay huddled on the earth for as long as he would hold me. It would take a crowbar and some serious muscle to pry my arms off him. I heard Jase let loose a breath he'd been holding, his face buried into my neck.

A rattling growl erupted from one of the descendants above us, and Jase lifted his head. As those violet eyes met mine, my body shook, and a small, broken sound burst from my throat. The primal wrath faded from his eyes.

He brought us up off the ground so we were knee to knee. "Welcome home, Cupcake," he whispered, his lips moving over my skin as he pressed a kiss to the curve of my cheek.

I'd missed them something terrible—missed the security they offered, the warm fuzzies, and even their bickering amongst each other. I drank in the sight of him, the familiar lips, the broad chest, and the messy midnight hair. He was exactly how I remembered, how I dreamed. "Are they—" my voice trembled.

"They're dead," Jase assured, helping me carefully to my feet. His eyes darkened as they roamed over my cheeks and arms. I probably looked atrocious and half dead, but I was too elated to feel any embarrassment. His thumb tenderly brushed over the cut along my cheek. "What did she do to you?"

My throat closed up and I shook my head, unable to speak of it yet. "She has my blood," I sobbed. That was all I could say.

Grim understanding glimmered in his eyes. "Come here," he murmured, and carefully swept me off my feet. I let him cradle me in his arms, carrying me off toward the castle.

My head rested on his shoulders, a hand over his beating heart. The kingdom behind me was no longer doused in shadows with the stain of Tianna's magic. Kieran, Zade, and Issik guarded us from the sky, soaring low enough I could make out the color of their scales, emerald, ruby, and white tinged with blue.

A humid breeze ruffled Jase's hair, brushing tendrils of silk off his forehead. The next time I lifted my head, the castle stood in front of us. Its sharp, spiked towers jutted up from the ground, like clusters of obsidian crystals, and the way the moonlight glinted off the angles took my breath away. The stronghold itself was as fierce and prominent as the dragon who ruled over the land.

Two pillars flanked an oversized front entrance, and the doors were wide open as if someone had left in a hurry—not bothering to lock up behind them. Inside the main hall, thick rugs scattered over the moonstone floor, a stark contrast to the palace's exterior darkness. Jase finally set me on my feet, and mere seconds later the elaborate curtains ruffled at the arrival of Kieran, Zade, and Issik.

The three stumbled in, haphazardly throwing on clothes. With unbuttoned pants and shirtless, we stared at each other, absorbing the first sight of one another. My eyes volleyed between them, heart stuttering, and suddenly Kieran was rushing across the floor, making his way to me.

Strong arms lifted me off my feet, his scent of pine and earth engulfing me. "I'm sorry," he whispered, his voice hoarse and quiet against my neck. "So very sorry."

Seeing him like this broke my heart into pieces. *She* had done that. Tianna was the only one to blame. I pulled back to meet his gaze, laying my hands on his shoulders.

"It's not your fault." I meant every word, and even managed to keep the wobble out of my voice, but Kieran wouldn't forgive himself as easily.

His usually sparkling emerald eyes were shadowed with guilt and remorse. "It is. I never should have left you. Not even for a second."

"She was determined to have me. If it wasn't then, it would have been another time." I had to help him see that, but I wasn't sure anything I said would make a difference.

Like Jase, Kieran noticed the mark on my cheek, and as he put me down on my feet, his gaze surveyed the rest of me. Issik and Zade came to stand shoulder-to-shoulder beside Kieran. They all shared identical expressions of murderous rage.

Kieran's jaw clenched tightly. "I wish I could undo it. I wish I could have spared your suffering, to have stood in your stead."

"I'm fine. I'm home. That's all that matters." My gaze shifted to the others. It was evident they were itching to get their hands on me.

"My turn." Zade butted in between us and swooped me into his arms, spinning us once in a circle. "Glad to have you back, Little Gem." He pressed his hot lips to mine in a quick kiss.

I smiled, my first real smile in days.

"Don't be an Olivia hog," Issik mumbled, plucking me from Zade's arms and securing me into his. Flutters of cold cascaded from his body, matching the radiance of ice swirling in his eyes.

Passed from descendant to descendant, they each took another turn squeezing me and I suppressed winces and groans my injuries caused.

All of us needing to believe this was real. I was home, where I belonged.

As the adrenaline of my escape finally left me, the dealings of the long night began to wear on me, exhaustion slamming into my body. A set of doorways stood behind me, leading into a pair of dim stairwells, and my eyes lingered on the passageway.

Somewhere up those flights of stairs was a bed, calling my name.

Zade barked orders to his staff and a flurry of women buzzed about the castle. Issik kept me tucked against his side, a hand at the small of my back, as if he needed the contact as much as I did. It wasn't long before most of my body weight was leaning into him. If he moved an inch, I'd tumble over like a log. Kieran was propped against the furthest wall from me, and I knew he had done so deliberately, giving me space I didn't want or need.

I thought I was doing a good job of hiding how serious my injuries were, but I was only deluding myself.

"She needs rest," Jase announced, eyeing me with concern. "And we need to attend to her wounds."

My ears had perked up at the mention of rest, and before I could protest, Issik scooped an arm under my legs, lifting me off my feet. A good thing, I wouldn't have been able to climb the infinite stairs. I had enough trouble maneuvering castles with a clear head. Imagining tackling that ascent with a pain muddled brain, and Jell-O legs that made me dizzy.

Zade slid his hands into his pockets. "I had one of the rooms made up for you in hopes..." his voice trailed off with sadness.

"It's okay. I'm fine," I lied, trying to reassure them, my fingers loosely secured around Issik's neck. He hadn't needed to finish his sentence. We had all hoped and prayed I would be back right where I was—home.

Kieran refused to look at me, his eyes focused intently on the floor. Zade's stare dipped to my right cheek. How long would they look at me and see the abuse I'd suffered? Would any lingering scars only ever remind them of my capture? I didn't want Tianna to come between us, not here, not now. I had escaped. Her evil wouldn't follow me home into the kingdoms of the Veil.

A flicker of fire ignited in his cinnamon eyes, making them more red than russet.

"Zade," Jase called his name in a low warning.

Zade blinked and nodded in the direction of the tranquility shifter. He took the stairs on the left, a hand shoving into his hair as he took the corner. Issik followed. I studied his face, while my head lay on his shoulder. It was too heavy for me to keep upright, and besides, he made a fabulous pillow—cool and not to firm, his body loosening. My head fit perfectly in the space beside his neck.

Each of the castles had a unique style and Crimson was no different. My half-lidded eyes took in the luxurious fabrics, the rich furnishings, and the gleaming floors. Zade's home was polished, refined, and loved. A clock chimed somewhere on the first floor, echoing down the corridors until its ringing became a soft whisper in the distance. My perception of floors was dulled by my fatigue. We could have gone up two flights or ten when Zade finally turned down a hall and pushed open a single door.

My room was a dream and fit for a queen

Smoky glass walls lined the space from floor to ceiling, inviting the night inside. Open and airy, exactly what I needed after living in a box. A private bathing chamber with an oval-shaped small pool, and a porcelain marble sink lay behind a rounded glass door.

Issik sat me on the bed with a gentleness that contradicted the Ice Prince's usual demeanor. "Let's get you out of these clothes." His hands gently tugged on the end of the dress, and he indicated for me to lift up my arms.

I obeyed, cringing at the sting of pain that reached me. The material easily went over my head, and staring at it in Issik's hands, I only had one thought. "Burn it," I stated with more venom than I intended.

Issik peered down at me with understanding. He flung the dress to Zade, who took care of the rest, lighting up the ratted material in flames. Immense satisfaction flared through my veins at the sight. Zade took the burning dress and tossed into a metal bin used for trash. I did not mind the smell as I watched my past turn into smoke and ash.

Now that I was nearly naked in nothing but my undergarments, all the cuts I had suffered were visible to them. Issik sucked in a breath, his eyes turning a dangerous color of blue as he took in the damage done to my body. "I'm going to kill her," he promised darkly.

I fought the urge to cover myself up. The sounds of water running filled the adjoining room and the thoughts of a bath chased any bashfulness.

"Let's get you washed up," Issik murmured, softening his voice. The muscles on his cheeks were tight and I could tell it took effort to keep his anger restrained. I trudged toward the bathing room, gritting my teeth against the torment in my legs, arms, and back. Basically everywhere.

I beheld the steamy water, breathed in the oils Zade had added to the bath and nearly whimpered. Zade helped me out of the rest of my clothes as Issik kept me balanced and from tumbling into the water. I didn't have the strength to lift myself in and without saying a word, Issik picked me up and set me inside the round tub.

I hissed through my teeth at the first touch of water to a cut on my calf and blinked back a swell of tears. A chain reaction of pain speared through me as I sunk deeper into the water, but I didn't stop until I was fully submerged. I clamped down on my lower lip to keep from sobbing and centered my attention on the heat seeping into my muscles.

Zade picked up a cloth and dunked it into the water. He used slow and careful movements, washing the dried blood, dirt, and filth from my skin. "The oil will help speed your healing."

"Thank you," I whispered, leaning my head back against the tub and closed my eyes.

I must have fallen asleep because I awoke to Issik gingerly saying my name and the water had lost all of its warmth. "It's time to get out," he said and lifted me from the tub. I was wrapped into a warm towel and dried off as if I was a fragile glass doll about to break. Issik led me into the bedroom where Zade was rummaging through a drawer.

He pulled out a white T-shirt and slipped the soft material over my head. It smelled clean and faintly of Zade—spicy and citrusy. It became so quiet I could nearly hear my heart beating. Together, they tucked me into bed, firelight from the hearth flickering over their faces. The two dragons lingered near the bed, and I realized they were going to leave at some point soon.

"Will she come for me here?" I blurted out, suddenly. The thought of being alone sent my anxiety skyrocketing. Was there any place where I would be truly safe from the witch?

Issik's eyes met Zade's and the two shared a look. "She might try," Issik replied after a long pause. I appreciated the candor. Lying to me would have been worse.

"But she is cunning. Tianna doesn't do anything that isn't carefully crafted. She got your blood. It might be all that she was after," Zade added, attempting to give me a semblance of peace.

"You should get some sleep, Little Warrior. Your body needs it," Issik encouraged.

The sheets were cool and dry as I slipped in, bone tired, but I was afraid to close my eyes. Zade and Issik were hovering in the doorway as if they too were fearful I would disappear if they took their eyes off me. At that moment, I knew what I wanted, what I needed to allow my mind to relax—if only for an hour or so. Deep, restorative sleep was out of the question for tonight. I was surprised Jase wasn't here to knock me out as he was so fond of doing.

Two single candles flickered in the darkness and I was thankful for the light it provided in the room, but the shadows that danced on the ceiling made fear dig its claws into my chest. "Wait!" I called out as Zade and Issik were turning to leave. They halted and glanced back at me, eyes willed with expectancy. I gnawed on my lip. "Can you stay? I don't want to be alone."

The ice blue and cinnamon of their eyes brightened. "Who do you want to stay?" Zade inquired.

Fools. I wasn't looking to play favorites. "How do you expect me to pick between you?" I countered.

Issik cleared his throat. "Are you suggesting…?"

I swallowed, unable to believe it was precisely what I was proposing. I wanted them both to stay. My fingers tugged at a loose strand of thread on the bed. "If that's okay?"

Both their chests heaved in response.

To be frank, I wanted all four of them in the same room, wanted to be reassured they were safe, but I'd settle for two.

They didn't say anything, didn't have to weigh the consequences of what I was asking, but instead padded back to the bed and got in with me. The mattress dipped on either side of me at the same time, adjusting to their weight while they got comfortable.

Now I can sleep, I told myself, snuggling deeper into the sheets and closed my eyes.

Wrong!

Five minutes went by. Then ten. I should have been able to drop off into a deep slumber the second my head hit the pillow, considering all that had happened. That was not the case. Sharing a bed with Issik and Zade was causing my brain to malfunction. Not to mention what it was doing to my body. I gave up any pretense of sleep and opened my eyes, looking left and right at the descendants. They both had their eyes closed, but I could tell from their breathing neither of them was asleep.

"Can't sleep?" Issik's deep voice sounded in the dark.

Careful not to incite my injuries I was surprised to find they were now reduced to a dull ache. I turned to face him. His eyes were bright, the most mesmerizing color I'd ever seen, like the moon reflecting off sheets of ice. I almost forgot he had asked me a question. "No," I admitted.

Zade placed his hands behind his head, the movement drawing my gaze. "It will take time, but the memory of what you went through will eventually dull. And years from now, it will seem like nothing but a distant nightmare."

"I don't want to forget," I admitted. "Not until we've beaten her."

The flecks of amber in Zade's irises simmered. "You let us worry about that."

I refrained from rolling my eyes. As much as they wanted to shelter me, to protect me, I was a part of this. Without me, the curse would destroy them. Digging myself deeper into the mattress, I tried to get my aching body to relax between the two dragons.

Issik's cool breath tickled my ear on my right and Zade's warm breath on my left. It was like being caught in a snowstorm during the dead height of summer. My mind was filled with nothing but Issik and Zade. No Tianna. No torture. No pain. No sadness. No loneliness. Yet, I knew if I closed my eyes, all that horror would come rushing back. I couldn't sleep. Not yet.

Being surrounded by dragons wasn't enough. I had dreamed of being home, being with them that I acted without thought. Rolling up onto my elbow, I glanced down into Issik's handsome face. Oh, how I'd missed the angle of his cheeks, the fullness of his lips so serious. They drew my gaze.

Something in my eyes must have alerted him to my intentions. "Olivia," Issik warned, but I pressed my finger to his lips and hushed him, a second before my mouth replaced it. He didn't protest again or resist when my tongue grazed his mouth, silently asking him to open for me. To give in to me. A gush of crisp mint filled my lungs as we shared air, our tongues entangling.

When I pulled away, I was breathless.

My back lay on the mattress once again, as I instinctively turned towards Zade, placing a palm flat on his chest. I held his intense gaze as he looked down at me, resting up on his elbow. He had been watching me kiss Issik, and the knowledge had my own blood heating. I had no idea what I was doing, only that it felt right. Sliding my hand over Zade's firm muscles, I cradled his neck and pulled him down to me, sealing my tingling icy lips to his searing ones.

A river of fire exploded within me.

This was what I needed, the two of them washing away the stains Tianna left and replacing them with ice and fire.

"Are you sure about this?" Issik asked, giving me a choice as he too leaned over me.

I stopped thinking about the consequences of what I was doing, letting what I needed right now be all that mattered. "Make me forget everything," I breathed. "I need you both. I need all of you."

A ravenous hunger passed over Issik's features. "I've thought about having you in my bed since I first saw you, of all the places I wanted to caress you." He shifted his body behind me, pressing so close that I could feel him everywhere. "Should I start here?" He lifted a finger, idly circling my breast through my shirt, and my breath caught, heart beating hard and fast.

Zade claimed my lips again, deepening the kiss and I hooked my leg over his.

"Or here?" Issik's fingers inched down my belly, over my hip to curve into the side of my thigh. I arched into his touch, sliding my fingers over Zade's bronzed chest. His shirt was unbuttoned from his hasty attempt at dressing earlier, but I wasn't complaining. Heat seeped into my hand, trailing up my arm.

If I had any reservations about being with two guys, they disappeared entirely at the first meeting of lips. Issik's cool fingers dipped under my shirt to circle my belly button, and I hissed at the combination of ice and warmth flooding through me, destroying my senses. Zade tore his lips from mine and turned his attention to my neck, his teeth scraped my skin and he dragged his tongue along the curve.

Hot. I was so hot. I was melting inside and needed to cool off. Flipping around, I switched positions, facing the Ice Prince.

Lifting my leg, I slid it around his hip in a silent invitation. Then I was on my back, Issik partially pressing me into the mattress with the length of his body. I savored the weight of him as his leg intertwined with mine, and the feel of his skin under my fingers—such power. My hand plunged into his blond hair as his lips crashed into mine, which gave Zade free range to roam other parts of my body.

God, help me.

Was it possible to die from pleasure alone?

Heaven? Hell? I didn't know which plane I was teetering towards.

Lifting himself up just enough, Issik peeled off my T-shirt, followed by his shirt so when he lay back down, we were skin to skin. My hips rocked up to meet his. A tingling sensation bloomed inside of me, and I craved more. He seemed to know what I needed without having to say a thing. Using his lips, he rained a path of kisses on each of my breasts at the same time that Zade's mouth found mine. I was feeling too much, so many glorious sensations. My hips writhed under Issik as he unleashed himself on my body.

Issik slid down between my thighs, his tongue stroking the sensitive points of my inner legs, so close to the center of me that ached with powerful need, and pulsed wildly. Expertly getting rid of the fabric that blocked his path, he slipped a finger inside me, and that part of me tightened around him. I bowed, moving against him anxiously. Zade captured the part moan, part sob of pleasure that escaped me with his mouth. The kiss was wild and branding, each of them marking me theirs. Somewhere in between the kisses, all barriers between the three of us had been shed. My nails found Zade's shoulders and dug in with need.

"You still okay?" Issik asked, his voice a growl of desire.

My moan was a plea on my lips and I pushed up with my hips, a tingling sensation building inside me. "Now. I need one of you now."

"We are powerless against you." Issik was breathing hard as he rolled me on my side, keeping my leg around his hip, and Zade nestled behind me.

"Only you. We'll take any part of you or of all you, but the choice is yours. Always yours," Zade whispered into my ear, nipping at the lobe.

Zade held my hips steady, his lips kissing my neck and shoulder, while Issik slid inside of me, his hardness filling me inch by inch. He took his time, allowing my body to adjust to his size. I couldn't take it anymore—the slow teasing—so my fingers clutched onto his shoulders and I thrust my hips, burying him deep inside me. A rumble tore from his lips and I trembled.

For a moment, I was just a frightened girl seeking solace, seeking to forget the world. Then we were fused together, two hearts beating as one. This was home.

I was encased in a battle of fire and ice, the two opposing forces raging through my veins. Issik withdrew slightly, his frosty eyes glowing as he studied my face. I was on the edge, so close to tumbling over as I moved my hips against him, urging him deeper. He obliged, thrusting back in. And out. Then in.

The three of us were a tangle of limbs and hands. Hungrily, my teeth scraped across the vein throbbing on Issik's neck and I was rewarded with a low rumble in the back of his throat. I flicked my tongue over his skin, tasting the frosty sensation of him.

Zade feasted on my neck with his lips, rubbing the hardness of him against my round behind, and the three of us moved in perfect sync. Together, Issik and I found release; shudder after shudder pulsed through our bodies in harmonious rhythm. I bit my lip to keep from screaming, but Issik growled my name as if it were both a thing of great pleasure and a curse.

In a flash, I was spun around, facing Zade who was eyes danced with animalistic need. He breathed my name when my fingers landed on the lower planes of his torso. The muscles there jumped at my touch, and I dragged my hands lower. He trembled, anticipating where my fingers were headed, and his mouth found mine.

I wasn't going to be deterred. They had done all the worshiping all the touching. It was my turn. Issik's hand glided to my breast, filling his hands with the weight. They weren't going to play fair. Neither would I.

My fingers wrapped around the length of Zade, my thumb rubbing over the sensitive tip. His teeth came down on my lip, growling into my mouth, and just like that, desire swept through me, so quickly, I hadn't been prepared to feel it so soon.

Even as I moved my hand, I felt the restraint beneath the skin. I didn't want controlled. I wanted him to be free, as they had freed me.

His fingers came to my shoulders, lifting me up and pressing me closer to him. My name tumbled from his lips in a half growl, half moan, when he sheathed himself inside me with a slow thrust, thawing the ice left behind from Issik. I nearly came undone around him instantly, the cold and hot combination heightening everything for me. He pulled out a few inches, the muscles in his back stretching and tightening under my nails and slid back in with one powerful thrust that sent my body singing.

"Don't move. Just hold on, I need to—"

I couldn't figure out if he was talking more to himself or to me, but my hips weren't listening to anything he said. They clenched around the fullness of him and pushed upward, sinking him fully and completely inside me. "I want it all."

"Sweet Jesus," Zade moaned, his control snapping.

Issik sunk his teeth into my shoulder, and for a second time that night, I lost myself. The orgasm ripped through me. Seconds later, Zade followed, his body shuddering with pleasure.

For long moments afterward, the three of us lay together in a jumble of limbs and sweat. My body never felt so sedated before in my life. My bones were liquid. The cuts on my body were dulled by the sweet bliss still coursing through me. I was content to stay in bed forever.

What had I just done? Not one descendant, but two.

To keep things fair and stop any bloodshed from happening, I was going to have to sleep with Jase. Not that it was a chore, or something I wouldn't look forward to doing. Nope. Just the opposite.

Jase Dior... I didn't doubt every glorious inch of him would be worth waiting for.

I wouldn't keep what happened between us a secret. I wouldn't hide my feelings or my desires, not anymore. Life was too short, and I would find happiness wherever I could.

Weary and satiated, I closed my eyes and fell asleep with the stars, Issik and Zade on either side of me.

S pecks of blood sprinkled the ground. My blood. Her husky laugh echoed in my ears, a sound I couldn't get rid of no matter how hard I tried.

"I'm coming for you, Olivia dear," she purred, a nail tracing down the side of my temple as if a talon was scratching my mind.

Fear like I never thought I'd feel again paralyzed me. Twisting my head from left to right, I searched through the utter blackness for a sign of the witch. She was nowhere… and everywhere. My skin crawled with prickles of her magic.

No. I didn't want to be here. Not again. Not ever again.

Wake up! I screamed at myself. Wake the hell up!

Drip. Drip. Drip.

More blood splattered on the floor, a ground I couldn't see, but knew was there under my feet, supporting me in a sea of darkness.

A dim light appeared near my face and I glanced down. There was a dagger in my hand, the one she had used to siphon my blood. I tried to drop it, but my fingers wouldn't budge. Wide-eyed, I stared as my arm moved, turning the blade toward myself. I couldn't stop it. I couldn't prevent the dagger from slashing across the inside of my other wrist, couldn't stop it from stealing my blood. My body wasn't chained or restrained by her magical binds as before, but I was still a prisoner.

My mind wasn't my own.

Was she controlling me? Was that what this was?

The idea was terrifying.

Her chortled resounded again. Another game. Another reminder she was in control, and I was only a pawn in her game. "You're mine," she whispered in my ear. "They can't save you."

"No," I rasped, my voice weak.

"When I need you, I will call."

"No." This time, my voice was stronger and forceful when I rejected her demands. My hand lashed over my arm again. "I won't," I refused, burying the stinging of the knife on my skin, but my muscles moved a third time, scoring the flesh so my forearm was covered in marks and blood. "No!" I screamed.

The scream still clawed at my throat as I threw myself awake. I forced myself to swallow back the fresh fear that had followed me from sleep. The darkness still surrounded me, and the panic spread over me, heart racing. Ten seconds past before I realized my eyes were closed. I peeled them open, and welcomed the bright stream of light that encompassed the entire room.

Frantically, I rolled out of bed, clutching my stomach as I dashed to the bathroom. Vomit expelled into the toilet, my stomach heaving, while my fingers clutched the side of the porcelain bowl.

You're okay. You're safe. Just a dream. You're okay. You're safe. Just a dream. Just a dream. Just a dream... I muttered to myself with each calming breath I took.

I repeated the words until my chest eased and my breathing steadied. Though, it took great effort. Leaning back, I hugged my knees to my chest. This was real. But so were the cuts on my body. No new lacerations, only the old ones that were healing, as I would... with time... and once Tianna was burning in hell.

I sighed through my nose and unloosed my fingers, letting my legs stretch out on the tile floor. Bile coated my throat, and I pushed to my feet, moving to the sink to rinse out my mouth. Downing a glass of water, then another, I couldn't remember the last time I'd given my body fluids. The water was refreshing and crisp on my tongue.

My head lifted and I caught a glimpse of my reflection in the mirror. An audible gasp escaped my lips, as I took in the gnarly scar that ran down my once flawless cheek. It brought a harshness to the creamy color of my skin. Tears clouded my vision as I gently traced a finger over the tender mark. What had she done to me? She had broken me. Scarred me.

Even now, I still felt like her prisoner, and I loathed her for it.

Teeth ground together, hatred imprinted in my eyes to the point where I didn't recognize the girl who stared back at me. She was a stranger. If Mom could see me now...

I blinked, banishing the spiral of dark thoughts from my mind. The now was all that mattered. Not the past, but the future I had yet to carve out for me, for the descendants, for the Veil.

Rubbing a gentle hand over my face, I turned to draw water into the round pool sculpted into the floor. Marble surfaced the tub, and the water funneled from a spigot in the wall, splashing over the smooth bottom. Of all the castles, this bathing room was the closest to what I'd had at home. I hadn't known how much I needed that familiarity until this moment.

My fingers went to the hem of my shirt, only to find there was no shirt. I glanced down at my nakedness.

Holy crap.

A small smile twitched my lips as I remembered why. My night with the fire and ice dragons had been spectacular. Never had I imagined my body could feel such bliss, especially after the horrific pain it had felt the day before.

Less than a day. That was how long it had been since escaping my capture.

I dipped my toe in, testing the temperature and sighed. No matter how many baths I took, I doubt it would ever erase the stain Tianna had left on me, but didn't stop me from trying. I settled in for a long soak, resting my head against the edge of the pool. It seemed a lifetime ago when I had my first bathing experience in the Veil. Harlow. I sneered at her name now. The jealous mean girl. How much simpler it was having her for an enemy versus Tianna.

The water lapped gently over my shoulders, smelling of eucalyptus and lavender and eased the aches along my body. The cuts stung a little at first, reacting to the warmth of the water, but it was a different kind of sting—a healing one. I stared at the miraculous little bottle of oil on the edge of the tub, grateful for its healing abilities. I'd still be in bed if it weren't for the relief the oil delivered.

Even though I tried, I couldn't shake the horror from my dream or the feeling of foreshadowing. Had that been a warning? Had Tianna wanted me to know she was far from done using me? Was I now some kind of unknown spy in the descendant's life, feeding information to the wrong side? Was it safe for me to be here? Listening to the descendant's plans? Was I putting them in danger?

I didn't know the answers, so I couldn't be certain of anything.

It could have very well been only a nightmare.

I desperately wanted to believe that was true, but until I was absolutely certain one way or the other, I intended to be cautious. I refused to be the cause of their downfall, but swore to be Tianna's destruction.

A while later the bath water had gone cold, and my sudden solitude was no longer a place of sanctuary. I wanted people, the comfort of being surrounded by the descendants, and food. Plates of fruits, meats, and breads.

And coffee. Pots of coffee.

Hastily, I went through the motions of washing my hair and body, before draining the tub to towel dry. Wrapping the cloth I found in the bathing room around myself, I padded into the bedroom in search of something to wear, but stopped in my tracks. The view from my room at the height of sunrise was spectacular. The windows for walls made it feel as if I was right at the center of the land. Plains of grass. Blotches of black sand. Dazzling streams of lava. And the volcano. Rays of yellow and orange crested from behind Titan Mountain, the heart of Crimson Kingdom.

I quickly changed into some clothes I'd found in the dresser, and headed out the door in search of two things. The descendants and food. In that order. My bare feet were silent as I padded down the stairs, not bothering with shoes, and crept down the hallway, admiring the pieces of painted art lining the walls. The black and white tiled floor was cool under my soundless steps. Husky voices grew closer as I neared the first floor and I listened, following the sound of my dragons.

The tenseness in the voices floating up into the grand staircase had me pausing at the bottom landing. It was wrong to eavesdrop from the shadows, but I heard my name. My fingers clenched onto the banister as I listened.

"I hope you know what you're doing," Issik snapped, in that familiar stony tone.

"We don't have much time," Kieran reminded with a dangerous quiet tension that had the hair on my neck standing on end.

"Don't you think I'm aware?" Jase barked back, tiredness and frustration lacing his words.

"We can't sit back and do nothing, while the curse seals our fates and ruins our world," Zade added.

"Who says we are?" Jase countered. "Olivia needs time to heal, and we all know what Tianna is capable of. We've all been victim to her games."

I chose that moment to make my appearance, not wanting to hear them theorize about the ways the witch had tortured me. I'd lived it once. I wasn't about to relive it every second of every day.

A breeze carrying heat and citrus fluttered over my cheeks when I turned the corner, finding the four shifters in the dining hall. No surprise. If there was food in the vicinity, the descendants weren't far away. They had opened the terrace doors, letting the morning sun and warmth into the room. It wouldn't be long before that balminess turned to blistering temps.

All four heads whipped in my direction then, but I kept my palm steadied on the doorframe. "Good morning," I greeted quietly. My cheeks heated when my gaze passed over Issik and Zade.

Dear God.

How am I going to get through the day without thinking about what we'd done between the sheets?

Zade cleared his throat. "Join us. You must be famished."

I was, and I deliberately took a seat beside Kieran. He continued to look busy, pushing around his plate of food, a plate I noticed he had barely touched. This had to end. His guilt. I had to find a way to ease the remorse and blame he felt.

"Did you sleep well?" Jase asked, eyeing me as if I was a fragile doll about to break. I could feel them tiptoeing around me, afraid to say the wrong thing, but in this case, my cheeks flamed with embarrassment.

"I managed a few hours," I answered, causing Zade to smirk and Issik's eyes to actually glimmer with amusement.

The conversation picked back up while I helped myself to something similar to oatmeal, toast, and fruit. Jase handed me a mug of coffee as he discussed the security of Crimson Keep with Zade. Gratefully, I accepted the hot beverage, and thanked him with a silent smile, his lips curved in turn. The strong and rich aroma reached my nose when I lifted the cup and sipped, then proceeded to dig into my breakfast, savoring each bite.

My bowl of porridge was near gone when I tuned into the discussion around the table. They had moved from security, to finding the next stone.

"I saw you…" I took a moment to clear my throat, realizing what I'd been about to say without thinking. I guess I was ready to talk about it. "When I was being held," I finished. The entire table fell silent as four sets of eyes swung in my direction.

Jase brows furrowed. "What do you mean 'you saw us', how?"

I broke off an end of crust from my toast, steeling myself to trudge through the difficult question, but it had to be done. I didn't have time to be coddled or the luxury of waiting. "One of the chambers in the mountain contained a pool. The Pool of Mirrors, she called it. I was able to see you in the reflection of the waters. I saw that you were looking for me."

"That must be how she knows what we're up to," Jase concluded, sitting back in his chair. The others went back to finishing their meal, or sipped their coffee in deep thought at my revelation.

"More likely than not," Issik agreed, ice forming in his eyes.

"You were held in a mountain?" Zade asked, picking up on that little detail.

I nodded. "In the Nameless Lands."

Zade stilled, but I could tell his mind was wheeling. "It makes sense she would use Tobias's forgotten kingdom as her home. What a better place to hide."

"And watch," Kieran added, his hands propped over his plate.

Jase's stare was thoughtful, assessing. "What can you remember of the mountain? Any detail big or small could be important."

"I'm going to need more coffee," I muttered, gazing down into my empty cup.

"I think we all will," Jase agreed, smirking.

One of the kitchen staff came out moments later with another carafe of coffee, and I took a deep breath, preparing to dive back into those haunting memories I so desperately longed to forget.

"She's anxious and upset," Issik announced, looking at me with concern and understanding. "Maybe this isn't a good idea."

"No," I blurted. "I can do this."

Kieran's fingers reached across the table and intertwined with mine. I smiled at him. He and I were going to have a talk, but for now, we could offer each other support.

"The griffins flew me to the mountain. It was dark. I couldn't see much among the barren land, no landmarks that I recall, just dead trees, miles of gritty sand, and tumbleweeds blowing in the wind."

"Sounds like the Nameless Lands," Zade muttered.

I wanted to ask what it had been like when Tobias had been alive, but now was not the time. "The mountain was huge. I know that is not a lot to go on, but she had a network of tunnels that webbed inside it. Caverns. A throne room. And the space where she kept me."

Kieran's fisted knuckles went white against mine.

Issik barred his teeth.

Jase's jaw tightened.

And Zade lips turned down.

Before one of them decided to flip the breakfast table, I continued, and by the glare tightening the corners of Zade's eyes, my money was on him losing his temper first. "She took me out once to look for the Star of Fire," I confessed.

"You were here?" Zade interrupted, his hands flattening on the table and shaking the plates.

I nodded.

"I knew it," Zade roared, jumping out of his chair, and nearly taking the table with him. He had finally let loose that temper I had sensed at the surface. Pacing the length of the room, he combed a hand through his tousled hair, as if this was one of many times he'd done so. "I felt you, but by the time we arrived you were gone."

"It was the only time. She was testing me, looking for a connection between the stars and I. I tried to tell her it didn't work like that, but like the stubborn ass she is, she didn't listen."

Jase's lips twitched. "I hope you gave her hell, Cupcake."

A ghost of sorrow crossed over my features, but I quickly masked it. They needed me to be strong, not weak. "How long was I gone for?"

A muscled feathered in Jase's cheek. "Ten days."

"What?" Had it been that long? I couldn't prevent the shock or disbelief from leaking into my expression. "Are you sure?" My mind whirled. I knew I'd lost track of time, but ten days! How could that be? Had I really spent that much time in the void of nothingness?

"They were the longest days of our lives," Zade confirmed as two girls shuffled in to clean up some of the breakfast dishes. "How did you escape?" he asked, once the five of us were alone again. His legs stretched out under the table as he sat back down, awaiting my answer.

My fingers traced with the rim of my coffee mug. "A goblin willowphased me," I simply stated.

"A goblin," Kieran echoed, shifting forward in the seat beside me. Something in his tone whispered astonishment.

"He appeared the night after…" The words got jumbled up in my throat, but I barreled on, propelling myself to continue. "… after she took my blood." I settled on leaving out the bits about how she had precisely taken my blood. "A cloaked man was waiting for us somewhere in the Nameless Lands. He called himself 'the wanderer'."

That sparked suspicion in the descendants. "We've never heard of someone called the wanderer," Issik replied wearily. They made it a point to know everything that went on in the Veil, including the people who lived here. The unknown of this possible ally wouldn't sit well with any of them.

"He orchestrated my escape. I don't know why, other than he knew about the stars, about what we are doing. He brought me to the edge of Crimson Kingdom, and told me to head straight for the castle. I ran, and you know the rest."

The gold flecks in Zade's eyes brightened, even from the end of the table. "We might need to seek out this wanderer, and find out what he knows about Tianna and her whereabouts. If he knew you were there and how to get you out, he knows what mountain she dwells in."

The descendants launched into battle plans. I was too mentally out of it to hear much of what they were discussing. Only a few words popped out. Death. Revenge. War.

Kieran's body stiffened beside me. "Now is the time to strike, when we have the element of surprise. If Olivia can lead us to the mountain, we can take it down around her."

"You can't," I protested, my eyes volleying to each of the descendants, silently pleading with them. "She grows stronger as you weaken, it's like she is stealing your powers."

"Aye," Kieran agreed. "You're right. Some time ago we came to the same conclusion, but it doesn't change what we must do."

"A suicide mission? I won't have it," I argued. I couldn't lose them. Refused to allow it.

"Two of us will search out this wanderer, and the other two will accompany Olivia to pursue the Star of Fire," Jase instructed, taking his usual role as leader.

I tried to keep from grimacing. This was my role, the key to breaking the curse, and all I had to do was find four stones. It didn't sound like a monumental task, except it was when I had no idea how to locate the stars. Even after recovering two of them, I was as dumb-founded as I had been when I arrived in the Veil. I needed help. I needed a visit from the women in white. Pronto.

Then I remembered what I'd learned about the women in white. They were their mothers. I opened my mouth to tell them, but clamped my jaw shut a moment later. Was it wise to convey? What if Tianna was listening? She would already know of our plans, know of the wanderer who helped me escape. This was a secret that might be best kept to myself, for all our sakes.

Issik frowned, his arms folded around his expansive chest. "It's imperative we find the Star of Fire before Tianna."

"We beat her at her own game," Zade added.

"Eventually, we will kill her," Jase concluded with a scary calm.

"And in the meantime, she has my blood," I reminded. "What can she do with it? Why would she want it?" I asked the question that haunted me. My mind had already conjured a variety of nefarious dealings she could do with vials of my blood.

Jase rubbed at the scruff under his chin, his elbow resting on the arm of his chair. "Only a number of disconcerting things, but we don't know. Blood was always the key to breaking the spell, so we can only assume it has an important part in her plan, whatever that may be."

"She has tormented us for nearly a hundred years," Kieran added, his shoulders tense. "We believe she was always after the power in the stars. When she struck our fathers down, she hadn't anticipated the stars vanishing as they did, which prompted her curse. By putting our lives and our abilities at risk, she has forced us to unsheathe the power she desires."

"If by chance Tianna got her hands on all four of the stars, she would not only be able to rule over the Veil, but other dimensions as well, including the human realm if she chose it," Issik informed.

A gust of balmy wind blew in through the open doors, and even the air seemed unsettled at the idea of Tianna overtaking the world.

Jase brushed aside a strand of hair off his forehead. "There was a time before the war, when humankind knew of dragons, witches, magic, and all those other worlds now sealed off from ours. The five stones were separated, one given to each of the first dragon shifters, bestowing them each with the power of the stars. They were never intended for one person to wield all five."

"Such power would be destructive," Issik informed firmly.

A shudder went down my spine at the thought of someone like Tianna being in possession of the dragon stars. I'd been privy to a fraction of her cruelty and quest for world domination. My thoughts turned to my old life, and the people I had left behind when I came here. There were only a few I cared about. Outside of the Veil, I knew nothing about the other worlds, yet here we were. So many lives were at stake, more than just the dragons I loved. It was so much bigger than I had believed.

The tasks in front of me seemed daunting.

Jase rose from the table to hook a finger under my chin, lifting my hung face to meet his gaze. "You are not alone in this. And whether we've said it or not, we want you to know that you're more important to us than the stars."

My breath hitched, and I looked at each one of them to find only truth shimmering in their eyes. Swallowing the knot of emotion in my throat, I folded my hands in my lap. "What about the fifth star?" I inquired, my voice not yet steady.

"Its power was extinguished when Tobias, the last of his line, died," Jase answered quietly.

"What is going to happen to me when I find the four stars?" It was a valid worry. Would the power of four stars be as potent as five, since the last had been destroyed? Would I be some kind of Omni-goddess? I didn't want that kind of power granted to me, didn't want to be responsible for the weight that came with it. Would I become a target? Would all sorts of power-seeking beings, like Tianna, hunt me for what I commanded?

The descendants shared a loaded look, one they often had when they were hiding something. "We don't know," Zade finally spoke.

His admission was like a gunshot to the chest. Great. I loved the unknown.

We disbanded after breakfast, Jase, Kieran, and Issik claiming they needed to check on their kingdoms, promising they would be back before dark. When I asked what I should do while they were gone, Jase only said one word. Rest.

I didn't want to *rest*.

I'd go crazy cooped up in the castle alone, while the others tended to their lands. Zade had offered to give me a tour, and have me *shadow* him throughout the day—code for Zade was assigned babysitter duties.

If I didn't know better, I might think this was a well-composed tactic to keep me inside and safe, considering they had all denied my offers to come with them.

Zade went to speak with the staff and I called Kieran's name, but the poison dragon's steps never faltered as he exited the room, feigning not to hear me.

He couldn't avoid me forever.

Zade came up beside me, draping an arm around my shoulder. I realized then I'd been staring at the empty doorway, where the others had left. "They'll be back," he murmured near my ear, sending a blazing stream of hot air along my neck.

"I know," I sighed, leaning into him, but it didn't make it any easier, knowing they were out there alone. I worried.

"Asena will get you some fresh clothes, and deliver me to you when you're ready."

I snorted. Deliver him, like he was a piece of mail? Sometimes their choice of words threw me off guard. They were from a different world, and it was times like this when I was reminded of how different we were.

Asena appeared to be in her thirties, a curvy woman with shiny auburn hair. Her hazel eyes regarded me with friendliness as she slipped her hand under my elbow. The white apron she wore had a small splotch of raspberry on it, as if she'd just wiped her hands before emerging from the kitchen.

I let her lead me from the dining hall and through the corridors of gold and deep red, until we came to a large room on the third floor of the castle. My eyes roamed over the space, the champagne velvet settee, the shelves lined with fabrics of every color and texture, the soft dusty rose walls, and the rows of silky dresses. Opened mouthed, I stood inside the room while Asena flipped through one of the clothing racks.

She came back with a bundle of material draped over her arm. "I'm sure there's something here that will fit you."

Overwhelmed by the glitter and sequence, I took a seat in the plush chair. "Got anything that doesn't sparkle?"

She returned a few minutes later, holding a simple sundress in a sunny pale yellow. The fabric was light and would keep me as cool as possible in the heat of Crimson. I ran my fingers over the clean, lovely material, grateful for anything that wasn't covered in blood and dirt. I learned long before coming to the Veil what it was like to go without such finery. To go days without showering and have everything I owned shoved into one bag. It was a lifestyle I never wanted to go back to, but had taught me to appreciate simple things—like shampooed hair, and jeans without holes.

In a pair of embroidered slippers, I turned toward the door to hunt down Zade.

"Where do you think you're going?" Asena's voice immediately halted my movements.

My brows lifted at her.

"Sit," she ordered, pointing to a cream-colored chair in front of a vanity.

She had the same tone my mom used to get, and out of habit, I automatically took a seat in the high back chair without question. Her fingers lifted the strands of my blonde hair off my shoulders, letting it tumble down my back. The first touch of her gentle fingers had me flinching, but I forced myself to stay still and relax, degree by slow degree. She picked a brush from the vanity painted with little rosebuds and made work at untangling the knots in my hair still messy from the bath. Not to mention my night with Issik and Zade.

Color came into my cheeks at the memory.

Asena clucked her tongue. "You're nothing but bones." She didn't say it in a way to hurt me, but out of motherly concern. "It won't be long before the cook has you filling out."

"Thanks, I think," I muttered. How much did the staff of Crimson know about me, about what I went through? I assumed that after having been brought here for the exact reason I had, they had more knowledge than I was comfortable sharing.

Twisting my hair into a pair of braids, she wound them into a crown on my head. "We're happy to have you here, Olivia. You've given us hope." She put her hand on my shoulder and squeezed.

I smiled, meeting her welcoming eyes in the mirror.

The fiery dragon was lounging on the corner of a massive oak desk when Asena returned me to the main floor. He was looking over what appeared to be a map as he sipped on a cup of coffee. His study was elegant but masculine.

I moseyed my way inside and plopped down on the deeply cushioned chair behind the desk, since he seemed content to sit on the piece of furniture. "Is this the Veil?" I asked.

He nodded. "It's been so long since any of us has stepped foot in the Nameless Lands."

Leaning forward in the chair, I glanced over the map, looking to the section where Zade had an index finger pressed. *Lavadare*. That had been the name of Tobias's kingdom before Tianna killed him with her curse. "What if the wanderer doesn't want to be found? He was old and didn't seem interested in getting involved."

"He involved himself the moment he helped you."

True. "And what about Tianna? Isn't it a risk to go to the Nameless Lands looking for him with her so close?"

"You won't be going anywhere near the border," he stated with a dark glower.

"That wasn't what I asked," I pointed out.

"I know, but this is the first time in almost a hundred years that we have a lead on her whereabouts. Before, she was impossible to track, blowing in and out of our lives with the wind. Her magic doesn't leave a trail, not one that any of us can follow."

"Do you think killing her would break the curse?" I pressed, swiveling left and right in the chair.

He shrugged. "I don't believe it would hurt anything, but it would feel damn good."

Fine, I couldn't fault his logic. Especially when my own hands itched to wrap around her slender neck, and squeeze the life right out of her.

. . .

I spent the day with Zade, shadowing him, as he took care of a few kingdom matters. The castle was mesmerizing with its lustrous floors, handwoven fabrics, and impressive art pieces from paintings to pottery. Such luxury. It was late afternoon when he suggested we get some air, my tour of the grounds continuing while also giving him the opportunity to check on his lands, and me to hunt for the stone.

The others still hadn't returned as we stepped out into the humid air, and I found myself overlooking a garden of bold colors and manicured hedges. Crimson was a slice of paradise hidden from the rest of the world.

But for how long?

Once I broke the curse, what kind of creatures would wander in?

"It's more beautiful during the day," I admitted, my eyes soaking up every detail for duel purposes. Not only was it a stunning view, but also somewhere out there laid the Star of Fire. The most obvious choice was the volcano. It was the heart of Crimson, figuratively and physically. So, if it was indeed inside the hotter than hell volcano, just how did I plan to retrieve it? Of one thing I was certain, lava would melt my skin off on contact.

The sun seemed to absorb into Zade's golden skin as his twinkling eyes watched me. "Would like to go for a ride?"

I cut him a glance of eagerness. "Do you mean—?"

He was already taken off his shirt and his intention became clear. Those reddish-brown eyes brightened under the sun's rays, and he let out a low laugh. "We can cover more ground in the air, and we could both use the release."

I didn't have to be asked twice. For a girl who'd always been deathly afraid of heights, who hated every roller coaster ever invented, the prospecting of flying on a dragon's back gave me a zealous thrill. It didn't make sense, but I imagined it had everything to do with the descendants that allowed me to conquer the phobia.

Fingers lengthened to black talons, reddish gold scales blanketed over every inch of skin, and lastly, his body stretched, shaping from man to dragon. I'd forgotten how huge they were in this form, forgotten the predator grace, and the leather-like wings. His nails clicked on the stone ground as he adjusted to his dragon body, working out any lingering kinks.

Soon, I was astride his dragon's back, flying with the summer-shrouded heat. He kept us low, forgoing the mist of clouds. Below us, the world glided by, a land of lethal beauty. In between the lava rock and blades of vibrant grass, hibiscus and jasmine poked out their petals from the earth. We grew closer to Titan Mountain and my ears picked up the sound of lava gurgling.

My arms tightened around his muscular neck. "When was the last time that volcano erupted?"

"Fifty years, I believe."

Tall, mighty, and alive, the volcano was magnificent, but I also respected its natural power. Nature had its own source of magic. "Do you think the star is inside?" Every bone in my body was pulling me into the center of Mother Nature's fiercest beast.

Zade circled around the top of the volcano, smoke billowing up through the center. *"I've considered it, yes."*

"My gut tells me it is in there," I admitted.

"Should we check it out?" he mused.

"Are you serious? Is that safe?"

"You're always safe with me."

We were both driven by the ticking clock and curiosity. "Okay," I agreed, tightening my legs around him, and steeling myself. Some risks outweighed the consequences.

"Hang on," he instructed, but I was already clinging to him as if my life depended on it.

Blistering air blew over my face as he dived down into the steam, pulling right over the mouth of the volcano. Peering down, I saw that black, craggy rock lined the walls inside, and directly below us, a pool of bubbling lava glowed so brightly that my eyes burned. I clamped down on my lower lip to keep from crying out as the heat blasted me.

"We can't hover long. It's not safe for you," he advised, his voice sounding in my head.

I didn't ask if it was dangerous for him. This land was a part of him and he of it, but another minute and I'd probably be barbeque. The hair on my arms was already singeing.

"Do you sense anything?" he asked hopefully. *"See anything?"*

"Yeah, buckets of hazardous lava," I replied dryly.

His dark chuckle sounded in my head as he started to pull up again. My arms hugged his neck, securing myself when I heard my name.

"Olivia. Savior of dragons…" a voice I didn't recognize spoke directly to me.

"Wait," I called, placing a hand on Zade's scaly neck. Something at my core nagged at me, beckoning me with a song that seemed to say, *find me. Find me. I am waiting.* The voice was much like how the descendants projected their thoughts, broadcasted in my head.

"What is it?" Zade's form tensed, eyes going alert at the sudden change in my body.

Smoke and magic hung in the air. "I-I felt something, I think." Or I'm hearing shit.

Wings flapped on either side of his body, holding us steady over the volcano. A chill went through me. Odd, considering not a single part of my body was remotely cold.

"Quick, Savior. Find me."

"We must go," Zade hissed, and with a powerful stroke of his wings, he lifted us up and away from the volcano, from the voice, from the star I was more than certain was inside.

Shit.

If I was right, how the hell was I going to retrieve a stone from inside a volcano without melting to death? It was an impossible task. Without magic—

I stopped breathing.

Magic.

The answer to my dilemma was a source of power I didn't have.

"Are you okay? Your heart rate changed." Zade interrupted my internal freak out session.

The fact they could pick up on sounds as quiet as a hiccup in my breathing pattern was disconcerting. "Just working out some stuff."

"What happened? What did you feel?" he pressed.

"It's there," I confirmed.

We cleared the smoke and I took a gulp of fresh air, but the oxygen turned sour in my lungs. The sky was no longer ours alone.

A wraith.

Yet, something was different about this particular phantom of death. Cold lurched toward me, wrapping us in a blanket of colorlessness, a world devoid of humor, happiness, and love. Zade's body stiffened beneath me as he fought to get us out of the wraith's path. My body was shaking from the abrupt change in temperature, almost going into shock.

Eventful strands of swear words echoed in my head just as Zade darted for the ground, and the wraith shrieked, the sound piercing my ears. I recoiled against the noise. We hit the mossy earth with a jarring impact, and my muscles strained to keep myself seated onto his back.

"Don't move," Zade's voice warned in my mind. He had tucked his massive wings against his body, and crouched low to the ground, using the shadow cast by the sun to blend into the side of a hill.

The wraith inched closer. I forced my eyes forward, not moving a muscle, and kept my face blank. Not even my eyelashes moved. The wraith went rigid, sniffing the air around me. Once. And again. The darkness clung to his faceless form, shadows gathering around him. Only a pair of gold eyes glowed underneath the hooded cloak of midnight.

"No matter what it says, no matter what it shows you, stay still," Zade urged. *"Don't listen to its words. And most importantly, keep your mouth shut. Do not scream."* Desperation coated his tone.

What did he mean? The answer came seconds later, but I wished it never had.

Unlike Zade's smooth and rich voice, this creature's screech pitched violently into some deep part of my mind, hijacking my thoughts, and shoving in violent images that made me want to curl into a ball and tremble in a corner.

What. The. Actual. Fuck?

'So pretty. So tasty. So strange. I can smell your fear. Let me taste you. Just a small nibble of your soul. So strange. So powerful. Open for me...'

I tried to swallow, but the air in my lungs felt as if it had frozen over, a hundred times worse than kissing the Ice Prince who was the embodiment of winter. I wanted to run, my legs screaming at me to get as far away as possible. No! I must not move, I reminded myself, closing my eyes tightly.

'I will devour you. Every drop of your soul. Give me what I seek, and I'll stop the pain. It will all go away. Open for me.'

My teeth were clamped so tightly together that my jaw ached from the pressure. I wasn't sure how much longer I could resist it. More than anything I wanted to open my mouth and draw in air that wasn't like ice in my veins. I wanted warmth. I wanted to end this misery, to save us all. Flashes of blood, bone, and bodies littering over the kingdoms of the Veil, and in the throes of horror were my dragons. Dead. Mutilated. Wings shredded or torn off completely.

I wanted to scream, the cry rising up inside me like a bubble threatening to burst.

'Yes. Yes. Yes,' the wraith seemed to purr.

"Do. Not. Let. It. In," Zade ground out the words, as if it was an effort for him to project them. Was it possible the wraith was keeping him out? Or doing the same to him? I blenched at the thought.

This was part of the Veil the descendants had first warned me about, the lethal creatures that roamed this world and others like it. With that single thought, I found an anchor that tethered my restraint, giving me the strength to resist.

The descendants.

Their warmth. The way I felt with them. And the love I had for them engulfed me.

That was all it took for the cold to vanish from inside me, the wraith disappearing, and leaving behind a trail of stillness in its wake.

Zade exhaled through his nostrils, shaking his head.

"What was that?" I breathed, my lungs working to take in mouthfuls of humid air, thawing my insides.

"A devourer. It's an ancient type of wraith," he answered hoarsely.

Had this devourer tormented him with its images of death, and enthralling words of persuasion as it had me? "This was different than the others. Why couldn't we fight it?"

"The ones we've encountered were messengers of death, bound to Tianna by magic. No one has seen a devourer in centuries, even before the war. They feed on souls and have the power to infiltrate your mind. They use it against you, to break their prey into giving them what they need. By tapping into your mind, they can see what you fear, what you desire, what you hate. It is how they get you to drop your guard."

"Sounds delightful."

His body rumbled in a short chuckle. *"Fire is useless against a devourer, as is poison. I'm not sure if Jase could put it to sleep, but even if he could, it wouldn't kill the creature. Tobias might have been able to, but it's not an option with him gone. I never thought I would ever encounter one. Let's hope it doesn't return."*

We had enough to deal with. This devourer only added another layer of shit to our stack of mounting problems.

I trembled despite my body being warm again. "I can still feel its touch crawling around in my head."

"The effects will eventually wear off, but in the meantime, we need to warn the others."

Z ade kicked off the ground with his talons, shooting toward his castle and ten minutes later we were in front of Crimson Keep. The tremors racking my body had slowly started to subside. I twisted over to my back and slid down the side of him, my feet plunking to the ground.

He waited until I gathered my bearings and took a few steps back, giving him room to shift. His membranous wings tucked in, as the dragon became man. He rolled his shoulders and picked up his discarded pants, jerking them on with hurried movements. I was a little disappointed he hadn't taken his time. A quick glimpse was all I was rewarded of his golden body, and I could have really used the distraction. The devourer's essence still lingered in my mind, like a dark stain.

"When will the others be back?" I asked.

His eyes scanned the orange and purple horizon. "Soon. They're on their way now. I sent word." He took off toward the castle, leaving me to follow.

I doubled my steps to catch up. "How did a devourer get here? If they haven't been around for centuries, how did a creature like that suddenly appear? And why?"

Glancing over his shoulder, he sighed and slowed his steps so I wasn't jogging to keep up with him. "It was summoned."

I didn't ask who, for there was only one person capable of such magic.

Tianna.

We didn't have to wait long for the others to arrive. One by one they flew in all wearing identical expressions of wariness as they joined Zade and me in the lounge. The staff had brought hot tea, little sandwiches, and shortbread cookies while we waited. I sipped the aromatic tea, tapping my foot. Zade was reclined beside me, with more patience in his pinky than I had in my entire body. It took effort for me not to jump and pace the gleaming onyx floors.

Issik and Kieran were occupying the other two chairs, opposite to us. Kieran had an ankle crossed over his knee, while Issik wore his perpetual frown.

Jase was the last to arrive. I saw his reflection in the tile and my eyes flew to his face. He leaned a shoulder on the doorway, and some of the tension lining his back eased a bit. "What's going on?" he asked roughly, glancing between Zade and me.

"A devourer appeared today, while I was showing Olivia the grounds," Zade informed.

To Jase's credit, he did a bang-up job controlling the tick along his jaw. "Are you certain it was a devourer?"

"There hasn't been mention of one since decades before the war," Kieran added.

Zade nodded. "I wish it weren't true. It took us by surprise when we were flying over the volcano, coming close to us."

Kieran's fist lashed out, putting a hole through the coffee table, and sent little sandwiches flying. The action had been so swift, I didn't know what happened until wood was splintering and glass was shattering.

Issik glowered at Kieran. "Where the hell is your control lately? This temper isn't like you."

No. It wasn't, and I had a good idea from where it stemmed.

"How is this possible?" Kieran seethed, ignoring Issik.

"The ward on the portal is weakening," It was Jase who answered. The tranquility dragon always had a theory and was usually right—annoyingly so. "It would explain how Tianna was able to summon one," he continued. All dots connected back to the witch.

Cold rage flickered over Issik's beautiful face. "We must find a way to kill it. Our people aren't safe."

And neither were they.

I saw the worry gleaming in Kieran's eyes, hidden under the outburst of anger. "How do we kill something we've only heard about it legends?"

Now they knew how I felt. It was a horrible feeling.

"There's something else," Zade added, his expression somber. He caught Kieran's eye for a quick second, as if to say *behave yourself.*

Kieran rubbed at the back of his neck, taking his seat again, the ruined table between us.

Yet, Zade's gaze remained on him, until he was certain Kieran was stable. "Olivia believes she might know the location of the next star," he informed them.

Outrage shifted to hope in all of their eyes. "Where?" Jase was the one to ask, but I knew the glimmer of hope was about to be extinguished before it really had a chance to shine.

"It's as we feared. Inside Titan Mountain," Zade revealed, and as I dreaded, their expressions fell flat.

"Jesus," Issik hissed.

Dinner was quiet, everyone lost in their own thoughts, the heightened emotions of the day bouncing between them. I picked at my food, but no one seemed to notice my lack of appetite. It seemed all of our minds were in elsewhere and the dishes around the table were barely touched, though I did manage to down two glasses of wine. Perhaps not the smartest decision, but it took the edge off the mind invasion I couldn't seem to rid myself of—the violation had left a mark.

Afterward, Jase and I took to the library. I volunteered to help with the research, hoping the task would calm the uneasiness that still lingered inside me with a book and another cup of wine. This one I promised myself I would nurse, or one of the descendants would be carrying me off to my room. Still, I doubted any of them would have minded. It had been months since I touched a drop of alcohol, since before the douchebag stepfather of the year kicked me out of my own house.

Prick.

Frowning, I wondered why he crossed my mind. I hadn't given Denny a thought in weeks, and I wasn't about to start now. All I had to do was gain control of these fuzzy thoughts and focus.

Books lay scattered on the table between Jase and I. The tranquility dragon was lounging on the couch, long legs stretched out, and violet eyes pouring over an ancient text of lore, searching for answers— answers we were desperate to unearth.

I stared at the page and blinked. The words blurred before clearing again, as my eyes glazed over the page but didn't actually read the text. *Too much wine.* I'd pay the price in the morning with one hell of a headache, but for tonight, it was worth it.

"What are you smirking at?"

Looking up from the glass I'd been staring at, I peered into Jase's eyes. "Was I? I hadn't noticed. The wine might be going to my head." My lips curled into a small reassuring smile, but Jase saw through the guise.

His gaze roamed over my face, and whatever he saw there had him concerned. "Why don't you call it a night? We'll be resuming your training tomorrow. You'll need the rest."

"We are, huh?"

"You didn't think I'd forgotten?"

Curling into the chair, I shrugged. The hearth was crackling in the corner, its warmth beckoning me. "You're not afraid I'll poison you?"

He flipped the page in the book, one side of his mouth twitching. "We'll get Kieran to help."

I huffed out a snort. "If you can get him in the same room with me for longer than ten minutes."

Jase lifted a brow. "He's avoiding you?"

The wine glass danced between my fingers, making the deep red liquid swirl as I looked at him. "It's obvious."

"He had a difficult time during your capture. We were all sick with worry, but Kieran… he blames himself for letting Tianna take you."

"It wasn't his fault. She would have found a way whether it had been that day or a month from now. You've said it before. Her moves are calculated. She needed something from me, and she got it."

"Only time will tell what she will do with your blood," he replied, staring into the burning embers.

Nothing good.

Jase returned to his book, and I tried to do the same, but my mind kept drifting. Who could blame me? Between never knowing when Tianna would strike, the complication in recovering the Star of Poison, and Kieran plagued with guilt, I was a frazzled-hot-nearly-drunk-mess. The alcohol only dulled the shadows and aches for so long, but it couldn't rid me of the scars I now wore—both physical and mental. Those I would have to find a way to live with.

I rereading the sentence for the third time and huffed, closing the book to give my eyes a rest. It was pointless. I wasn't helping. Setting the book in my lap, I picked up my wine, and let my thoughts wander. It was no surprise Kieran's face popped into my head. He was still evading me and it had to stop. What I needed to do was hash this thing out with him.

I gnawed on my lip for a moment, before pushing to my feet, but Jase didn't look up as I slipped out of the room and into the hall, a testament to his worry. It was consuming him—consuming them all.

They were so close to ending their torment, but at every turn, something else stood in their way.

The main floor was empty, even the staff seemed to have scampered off to their rooms, or to their homes, not far from the keep. My feet clapped on the floor, echoing down the corridors. A flickering of light deep in the dark caught my eye, as I neared the sweeping stairs that led down into the dungeon—a place I'd rather avoid. If I turned to my right, the steps would take me upward, to the sleeping chambers, but that light…

What was down there? Who was down there? I angled my head to the side, a portrayal of curiosity.

This is a bad idea, Olivia, like your worse idea ever. Do not go down there.

My foot landed on the first step and carved stone covered the walls on both sides, boxing me in.

It's not too late to turn back now. You're not going to find Kieran down there.

I took another step. And another. My hand trailed along the metal handrail, guiding me down into the darkness. I clutched onto it tighter, fear clamping my chest and squeezing the deeper I went. The shadows were suffocating me, and every bone in my body was yelling at me to turn around, to run back up to safety.

But the light flickered.

I narrowed my eyes, watching as the glimmer of gold fluttered to the left, like a little pixie, and I was enchanted. A chill seeped into my bones but I rubbed at my arms, encouraging warmth. A heavy weight settled into the air, pressing down on me like I was wading through a pool of mud.

"Hello?" I called into the shadows, my blood pressure skyrocketing. *Not in the mountain. I'm not trapped.* The words did little to calm me. "Who's there?" I called out again.

No one answered, but I hadn't expected anyone to do so. My shoe scuffed over the floor when I reached the bottom, and I cradled my palms together near my mouth, blowing a puff of hot air onto them. It was cold as if a frost storm had moved into the dungeon. Careful eyes trailed the ball of light as it summoned me further into the dungeon. I followed until the shimmering flecks of light brightened, growing and growing. From the core of white and gold, the figure of a woman formed and the light shining from her body bathed the dungeon, banishing the darkness.

Her aura was cast in gold, skin shimmering as if she'd been dipped in glitter and sunlight, while her feet floated a few inches off the ground. Long, rich brown hair was braided off to one side, flung over her shoulder. Soft lips curved as she offered me a friendly smile, and her head slightly bowed at me with the grace and dignity of a queen.

She *was* a queen.

The dead queen of Crimson Kingdom—Zade's mother if my calculations were accurate, one of the women in white. They each appeared to me in their respective kingdoms.

"You are home," she announced, the words sounding as though they were as important to her as they were to me.

"I am. Thanks to your sons… and you, I guess." The women in white had aided me since day one and continued to do so. "How am I able to see you sometimes in the world, and others only in water?" I inquired, realizing this was only the second time one of them appeared to me outside of a pool or lake.

Her eyes flared with an unholy ambiance. "Our abilities to manifest in this realm are strongest during a new moon, when the veil between worlds is the thinnest."

Tonight was a new moon.

"As the moon cycles, it becomes more difficult to communicate, which is why our time is so important and limited with you," she explained.

"Why me? Why not appear to your sons?"

The ends of her white dress swirled on a phantom breeze. "Our tie is to you, to the one who will save the Veil."

Wasting no time, I got directly to the point. "The next stone is inside Titan Mountain. How am I supposed to retrieve it, when my human body can't withstand the heat?"

She folded her fingers gently in front of her. "You are never given a task that isn't within your power to complete. Just believing you can, creates a spark. The strength within you is not a burning flame you can see."

Great pep talk, but how was any of it going to help me retrieve the Star of Fire?

"You seem lost, daughter," she confessed, perceiving my confused silence.

I glanced up from the spot in the dark I had been staring, lost in my own thoughts. "I'm afraid," I admitted. "I don't know how I'm going to secure the star." My voice broke.

A tender smile curved her lips. "All things have weaknesses, have contraries. It is what we do with them that matters. They do not need to be a hindrance, but can be the light in the darkness."

Shoving aside the feeling of despair, I lifted my chin.

"What are you doing down here?"

My head whipped around toward the sound of Kieran's voice. His form was shrouded in shadows, but I could see the scowl lines creasing the corner of his lips. "Did you see her?" I asked.

"Who?" His face grew somber, and I could tell he thought I was referring to Tianna.

"The woman," I clarified. "In the white dress."

He shook his head. "I saw no one but you. How much wine did you drink?"

My shoulders sunk. "Either too much or not enough," I replied, staring at the spot where Zade's mother had stood.

"You shouldn't be down here, not alone. Where's Jase?" His green eyes were full of disapproval toward Jase for leaving me unattended.

"In the library. He probably thinks I went to bed."

"And you should have." He pivoted to escort me upstairs to my room, but I turned one last time to look behind me. Big mistake.

With the woman in white gone, taking the light with her, I was left in utter darkness. For a heartbeat, I'd forgotten Kieran was beside me and I that wasn't back in the box of shadows. My breathing became uneven and labored, panic suddenly escalating. I couldn't move, my feet felt glued to the floor. The dark caved in all around me.

"Olivia," Kieran murmured my name, his hands coming to frame either side of my face, holding my gaze. "Look at me."

I swallowed hard, pushing aside the sick feeling rumbling in my belly and threatening to rise. *Damn wine.* Yet, it was more than the wine. It was a nightmare that haunted me day and night.

"I've got you." He enfolded me into his arms, and I breathed in the familiar scent of woods and rain. I let him hold me, let him chase away the demons that haunted me, and led me into the light. "Come on," his hand slipped to the small of my back as he applied light pressure, urging me back toward the stairs. "I'll show you the way."

"I'm okay," I told Kieran, forcing my chin up and my back to straighten. "It was just the wine."

Liar. Such a small fib, but a lie nonetheless.

"Hmm," was all he said, lips pursed.

I only half-remembered him leading up to my room, my conscious mind going in and out of that place of fear. It was a quick way to sober up, that and the way my body responded to being close to the shifter. His fingers brushed against the base of my spine as we came to the doorway of my room, and I could feel his touch through the thin material of my dress. A blush stole over my cheeks.

"I wouldn't mention your little venture into the dungeon tonight. Some parts of the castle are off limits." He stepped back, no longer touching me, and I immediately missed his warmth.

"Kieran, wait," I called, not allowing myself a chance for second-guessing.

My hand reached for his arm, to prevent him from whisking off down the hall. The corded muscles under my fingers shifted as his brows rose in question. I angled my body toward him, feeling the pull inside me to the poison dragon. We shared the same power. He could sense my desire, and had been the first guy with whom I'd ever slept with. Yet, I never felt further from him than I did now. In theory, all that we'd been through should have brought us closer, but Kieran with all his roguishness, had the most heart. He felt too much. Some might see it as a character fault—Tianna came to mind—but not me. It only made me love him that much more.

Now, I just needed him to realize he wasn't to blame for what happened. "Can we talk?"

His shoulder leaned against the doorframe in a lazy gesture. "What's on your mind, Blondie?"

My eyes closed for a second, savoring the sound of the nickname he'd given me. "You."

A playful smile danced on his lips but didn't quite reach his eyes. "I don't see how that is a problem."

It was an attempt at his old flirty self, and I appreciated the gesture, but he couldn't fake the guilt in his eyes. I was going to put an end to it. He was putting on a show for me, attempting to make things good between us and I valued it, but I didn't want it to be work for him. He shouldn't have to pretend to be okay, not with me. "Glad to see you haven't lost your sense of humor entirely."

"Some things not even a witch can destroy."

I was glad to hear that, because I wanted my dragon back, not the sully man who doused himself in guilt and regret. That was just the kind of attitude Tianna would prey on and use against us.

My hand lifted to placed my palm over his beating heart and peered up at him. He didn't back away as I shifted my body closer to his, needing to touch him. "I don't want things to be weird between us."

"Are they?" He glanced up at me from lifted brows.

"You can hardly look at me," I answered plainly.

He frowned. "I'm looking at you now."

Smartass. At least this was more like the Kieran I loved. Mischievous. "Good. Now listen to me when I tell you that what happened to me wasn't your fault."

"I know." He said the words but they were empty, meaningless. Something you said to appease a friend, a lover.

That shit wasn't going to fly with me. "Do you?" I shot back, holding his gaze. "How long are you going to punish yourself? How long are you going to keep avoiding me?"

Finally, his charade cracked. The pad of his thumb glided in a feather-light touch over my arm, tracing one of the still tender cuts, and his eyes darkened. "I couldn't find—You were just gone and I—" The snag in his voice cut through me.

I circled his wrist with my fingers and leaned into his hand, pressing my body against his so I boxed him into the wall. The heat from his body seeped into mine. "There's nothing you could have done, and it doesn't matter now. It's over. What matters is what we do from here. I need you in my life."

For a long moment, we just breathed each other's air, the glow of love surrounding us like starlight. "I miss you," I said quietly.

Something akin to regret flickered in his emerald eyes. "I'm sorry for it," he apologized, brushing a strand of hair behind my ear. My cheek turned into his touch.

"I love you," I declared, the words tumbling from me before I had a second to think about what I was admitting, but once they were said, there was no taking them back.

His powerful chest exhaled as he released a breath, his fingers coming to circle my wrists. Those emerald eyes brightened.

When he didn't say anything, my self-consciousness reared its ugly head and I contemplated bolting into the room and shutting the door behind me. What if he didn't feel the same way? Was that why he was staring at me with an expression I couldn't read? I shoved those nervous, vulnerable emotions aside and tried one more time.

"Do you hear what I'm telling you? I love you, Kieran." I loved them all, but for now, Kieran needed to hear how I felt about *him* specifically... or so I hoped.

If he rejected me... I didn't know what I would do.

"You love me?" The incredulity in his tone squeezed at my heart. When was the last time someone had told him they loved him? It made me wish I hadn't waited. I needed it as much as he did.

I loosed a long, controlled breath. "Yes, you fool. I'm in love with you."

"I don't deserve it. I—"

My lips pressed to his, shutting him up. "Stop it right there. That is not true," I murmured. The pain he attempted to bury from his eyes was visible to me.

He brushed his knuckles across my cheek. "I've never loved someone the way that I love you." Those emerald eyes flared with unholy affection.

"Stay with me," I asked softly.

His chuckle rumbled against my ear. "I thought you'd never ask."

After a night of fitful sleep plagued with memories of Tianna, I rubbed my eyes and glanced at Kieran. Rays of orange sunlight gleamed through the windows surrounding the room, casting his face in a golden halo. The sky was cloudless and cheery, unaware of the gloom it might face in the coming months—if Tianna won.

With those less than inspiring thoughts, I dragged myself out of bed. The cuts on my body were healed, leaving behind little scars that would forever remind me of my time in the mountain. I peeked at a still sleeping Kieran, debating about climbing back in bed or drawing myself a bath. My skin still tingled from being in his arms most of the night. We had both needed the comfort of being held—of love.

My heart glowed.

I padded across the room to slip into the bathroom. Today, my training with Jase resumed. My muscles ached thinking about it. When I emerged thirty minutes later, a rumbling Kieran was sitting up in bed, shirtless, running his fingers through that messy green hair.

He glanced up, what looked like a half-eaten croissant to his mouth. "Hungry?"

I gulped, my eyes devouring the sight of him in my bed, scattering my thoughts before I focused on the tray of food on the little table. "Breakfast in bed," I stated, my brows lifted.

"Mila came by while you were in the bath."

"And who is Mila?" I asked, crossing the room to help myself to his coffee. I noted there was only one cup, and a single plate of those flaky pastries that smelled like almond and sugar.

"She works in the kitchen."

My eyes narrowed and something hot flashed across my heart. "Does she often bring you breakfast in bed?"

He smirked. "Jealous? It looks good on you."

I gave him a particularly rude finger, ignoring the laugh rumbling from his chest.

Damn dragons.

I went to scrounge up some clothes worthy of training in, something that wouldn't be too restricting and would give me free rein of motion. Settling on a pair of form-fitting shorts and a tank top, I sauntered over to the little table and plucked off a croissant. I was aware of Kieran's eyes on me, watching me while I dressed, lingering on my hips as I walked.

Good. Let him suffer.

I had been jealous of another girl, seeing him sprawled out on my bed. There was an intimacy between two people first thing in the morning that should be kept between them. I had wanted to be the first person he saw upon waking.

Taking a bite out of my pastry, I left Kieran in my bed, staring after me with heat in his eyes to go find Jase.

"Fighting against a griffin or goblin is different than going up against a witch or a wraith. Combat skills are as important as magic. You need to learn to defend yourself, as well as attack."

We were outside in a training ring that was set up not far from the castle, as Jase schooled me on the importance of learning how to defend myself. The sun was beating down upon us, though not yet at full height. I gave myself ten minutes before I collapsed from a heat stroke.

"Is there nowhere *inside* where we could practice?" I asked, shielding my eyes from the bright glare overhead. At least I'd get one hell of a tan.

His brows narrowed. "Not unless you want to accidentally poison the staff."

"Right."

"As I was saying," Jase continued. "An hour of training can make all the difference in a life and death situation. I hope you got some sleep, because I'm going to test your limits."

"Don't think I can handle it?"

He laughed and I almost regretted the taunt. "You're going to need that spirit, that fire."

I rolled my eyes, surveying the training space. Dummies and racks of weapons that contained blades, daggers, maces, axes, bows, arrows, and spears were scattered over the area. Did he actually expect me to be able to do anything other than trip on my own two feet? The last time I wielded a dagger, I'd stabbed a witch, who then kidnapped me.

We were both in trouble.

Jase rotated his shoulders, loosening up the muscles, and I followed his movements. "Do you remember the basics?" he asked.

"I remember how to run, and I can summon tranquility and poison easy enough."

He did his best to keep the amusement off his lips as he pressed them together to compose himself. "Running is not a cowardly feat. If it saves your life, does that not make it a strength worth having?"

"I guess. I'd never looked at it like that." I chose not to point out that I wasn't a fantastic runner either, for fear of having to do laps around the training ring in this heat.

"You can practice the magic on your own."

"So, no Kieran?"

A knowing sparkle glinted in his eyes. "Didn't get enough of him last night?"

I shot him a vulgar gesture that only made him laugh; the deep sound did funny things to my belly.

"He seems in better spirits, so whatever you did, thank you. Now more than ever we need to be united, and I wasn't sure he'd ever forgive himself."

My cheeks burned, and this was one of those times I was grateful they could only read my emotions and not my mind. "We, um, talked."

"Is that what you're calling it?"

My hands perched on my hips as I let my bitch wings fly. "For your information, Kieran and I did not sleep together."

"But you did sleep with Zade and Issik the other night," he pressed. Oh shit.

I rubbed at the back of my neck, contemplating my answer. "It just happened."

He jerked his chin into the direction of the ring etched into the clearing. "Things tend to *just happen* around you."

Following his direction, I sauntered into the ring with heavy steps. "What does my sex life have to do with protecting myself?" I countered, spinning around to find him directly behind me. My palms instinctually went out to keep myself from falling and flattened against his chest.

He glanced downward and gave me a disarming grin. "Just know that you've saved the best for last." Then he kissed the tip of my nose.

My blood heated at the insinuation behind his words as the wind suddenly stirred, carrying his scent—a combination of sea and something else. "I can smell the sea on you. Were you flying this morning?"

Surprised showed in his expression. "Your senses have gotten stronger. That's good. And, yes. I went to do a perimeter sweep. Now, start your circuit of warm-ups."

I rolled my eyes, but obeyed, going through a series of lunges, kicks, and stretches designed to loosen up my muscles. And then the real fun began. Sparring. My hands jabbed into his upraised palms, in a succession of one-two punches, but his hands never faltered as I hit them. Thirty minutes later, I wished I had never stepped foot within that white-chalked ring of hell.

"Keep your feet planted and dagger up," Jase ordered. Again.

He had removed his shirt shortly after beginning and I cursed him for more than the sore muscles. The hard planes of his bare chest caused quite the distraction. It was hard to concentrate on keeping my balance with his abs gleaming in the sun, begging to be touched… or fondled… or licked.

Focus, Olivia.

The fact that we had moved from sparring with fists to blades made my stomach queasy, but I pushed through the rolling and the heat, resorting to taking out my frustrations on the person delivering this torment.

"If I cut you with this, I'll never forgive you," I barked, sweat dripping in places it shouldn't be. I waved the steel blade in the air. If I allowed myself, I could still remember what it had felt like to sink one very similar into Tianna's flesh. A fat wad of good it had done me. The witch still managed to abduct me.

"And where is the logic in that?" Jase countered, looking as if his skin was born to glisten.

"Who said anything about logic. It's your fault I have the dagger to begin with, so you'll pay," I seethed between my teeth and lunged forward.

Jase's arm connected with my wrists, blocking my attack. "Less complaining. More focus."

I lifted my chin, rotating my neck from left to right to work out the kinks. "When are we going after the star?"

His arms dropped, wiping the back of his hand over his brow. "You're positive it's inside Titan Mountain?"

"As much as I wish it weren't so…" I finished with a nod.

His lips formed a grim line. "The right moment will come."

"Is there a reason why we haven't already gone after it?" Something flickered in his eyes, and my unease churned. "What aren't you telling me?" I pushed.

"Tianna. The Pool of Mirrors." The words were heavy and weary—I wasn't the only one who was drained.

I understood what he was telling me. "She's watching us."

"From what you've seen, I believe so, and if we go straight for the star without a plan of extracting it from the volcano, she could interfere. We don't know where in Titan Mountain the stone is. So many unknown variables."

"There has to be a way," I insisted. We were so close.

"I'm working on it, just as you should be working on your ability to kick ass. Again," he directed, crooking his finger at me.

Craning my neck to the side, I started again. Swipe. Pivot. Lunge. It was like a lethal dance, except I had two left feet. *Swipe.* The blade sliced through the air, coming close to Jase's golden skin, but on my next pivot, my heel came down on a rock and the world slipped out from under me. My hold on the dagger slacked, and the blade clattered to the ground, me along with it.

"Shit," was all I could say, my body unable to take the sweltering air and physical activity any longer. I didn't move but lay on my back staring up at the blue sky.

Jase leaned over me, dragging a hand through his hair. "Are you hurt?" He crouched down to inspect for himself.

I took a moment to catch my breath, and sat up, letting my arms fall at my side. "How am I going to learn any of this in a few weeks?" That was all we had before the curse was permanent, trapping them here forever, and eventually, killing the dragon line. For when the curse reached the summer solstice, the spell that kept them suspended from age would no longer exist, and none of us knew how fast time would catch up to them, if at all. "It's useless."

Impatience rippled across his features, those violet eyes flaring. "I never want to hear you say you're useless. It is anything but the truth. You are everything."

Whoa. My belly fluttered at the words. What girl didn't dream of an insanely gorgeous guy telling her she was everything? "I bet you say that to all the girls."

He blinked. "What girls?"

I smiled, placing my hand into the fingers he extended toward me. "Don't give me that. We're surrounded by girls that you've brought here," I pointed out the obvious.

His eyes took on a look of roguishness right before he tugged me to my feet so our bodies were flushed. "But none of them are you."

"Is this what you call training?"

My head turned toward the clipped male voice. Zade was lounging against the base of a tree with his arms crossed, head angled to the side as he regarded Jase and me with traces of skepticism.

Jase's fingers at my waist tightened, keeping me against his body. "Shouldn't you be doing something other than bothering me?"

"Probably, but I heard something interesting today."

"This better be important," Jase grumbled.

"Regardless, it looks like our savior could use some rescuing," Zade countered roughly.

Jase growled, the depths of his violet eyes glowing.

I stepped out of Jase's grasp—much to his chagrin. "What the hell has gotten into the two of you today?"

"We're done for the day," he snapped, glaring at Zade.

Jealousy seemed to taint the air between us. Why had I ever thought juggling four dragons would be a piece of freaking cake?

God, I could really use a piece of cake. Chocolate with strawberries in the middle.

I positioned myself in between the two nostril flaring dragons. Not exactly smart for a human, but whatever this was, it had to do with me. "What the hell is going on? Why are the two of you puffing your chest and acting all territorial? I'm not a goddamn toy you can pass back and forth to play with."

Zade's glare skirted from Jase to me. "Everything was fine until you decided to play favorites."

"Explain," I demanded.

Fire rippled over his features. "You picked Kieran. Why, because he's been moping around with his guilt? Did you feel sorry for him, so you told him you loved him?"

Jase's face went taut. "Is that the *talk* you had?" He added air quotes with his fingers to be dramatic.

Well, fuck my life. This was not supposed to happen.

I stifled a groan, before tossing my hair into a messy bun to relieve the mounting stress. "First off, I did not choose anyone. Yes, I told Kieran that I loved him, but the truth is I have feelings for all of you. I've never pretended otherwise. I'm in love with every single one of you. There. Are you happy now?" The words came out in one big long string, leaving me winded afterward.

"Yes," Zade and Jase both sighed, seconds before I found myself sandwiched between two walls of dragon shifter muscle. One sticky and sweaty and the other hot as Hades, literally. I didn't mind.

Did I really admit to being in love with them?

My pink face buried into Jase's chest. "If I had known the way to diffuse your tempers was to confess my love, I would have done so sooner." The chest under my cheek rumbled as Jase chuckled, and I tipped my head back. "The last thing we should be doing is fighting. We can't let Tianna divide us, or this whole thing falls apart," I murmured.

Jase's fingers ran over my hair, a lopsided grin on his lips. "Agreed."

Zade slid his hand into mine from behind me. "I'm sorry. I shouldn't have snapped at you. We knew this thing between us wouldn't be easy. None of us expected to feel so strongly about you."

"Is that your way of saying you love me?" I wanted to hear them say the words, needed to hear it or I would feel like a fool.

Jase bent down, skimming my ear with his lips. "Some things are worth waiting for."

My toes curled at the sensual, dark tone of his promise, alongside a smidgeon of disappointment. Patience wasn't a strong suit of mine, and waiting would allow doubt to weasel its way into my soul.

Zade wrapped an arm around my waist, tugging me away from Jase. "You've had her all day. Go find something else to do."

I rolled my eyes. "We're not starting this again," I moaned. It was a waste of breath. So, before either of them could start at each other again, I stepped away from them both, and strolled off toward the castle, toward a bath. Alone.

I took a quick shower to rid myself of the stickiness, of my own sweat, and the smell that surely came with it. Apparently, bathing multiple times in Crimson was the only way to keep cool.

Trudging through the main hall with damp hair draped over my shoulders, I went in search of something to eat, but found Kieran sitting at the table sharpening his blades. A beam of sunlight streamed in behind him, haloing around his form as he worked. His head tipped up at my approach, and he smiled in a way that made me forget why I'd come to downstairs in the first place.

I shook the mushy thoughts from my head and marched up to him, poking a finger in his chest. "Hey, dragon douche. Did you tell Zade that I was in love with you?"

He crossed his arms over his chest to prevent me from poking him again. Ha. He had plenty of other body parts I could kick, pinch, or knee. One particularly sensitive part came to mind.

"And if I did?"

My ass plopped into the empty seat beside him, shoulders sagging. "Why would you do that?"

Metal against metal echoed along the hall, as he resumed expertly sliding the blade over and over on the block. "I wasn't aware it was a secret."

Facepalm. I hadn't been trying to hide my feelings but had wanted to spare the furniture from being destroyed. In seriousness, I had hoped to get the chance to tell each of the descendants individually how I felt about them. It wasn't entirely clear in my own heart how I could love them so differently, yet similarly.

"It wasn't a secret," I sighed. "But that doesn't mean you need to go rub it in the other's faces. I'll have you know that I also happen to be in love with Zade. And Issik."

Kieran turned his attention to me. "Let me guess, Jase too?"

I nodded, folding my arms across my chest. "Do you have a problem with it?"

He rewarded me with a wolfish grin. "Only if you show favoritism."

Startled, I paused to stare at him. Each and every one of them never failed to surprise. "You're really okay with sharing me between the four of you?" Saying it out loud was as strange as the concept was in my head.

His right shoulder lifted in a nonchalant shrug. "I don't know. We've shared many things over the years, but girls were never one of them. I do know that I'm not willing to live without you."

"God, this is such a mess." I dropped my head onto the table.

A hand trailed down my spine offering comfort. "It doesn't have to be."

I raised my head to prop my chin on my hands and glanced at the table. It was covered in weapons. "Why does a dragon need seven blades?" I asked.

Kieran shrugged. "It doesn't hurt to be prepared for anything, especially when there might come a time when I can't rely on my other skills." He was referring to his dragon and his poison.

"What will happen to me once the curse is lifted?"

"You'll marry me," he said matter-of-factly with a wink.

I sat up, unable to hide the smile from creeping over my lips. "Oh, will I? Don't make me hurt you."

"You could go home if it was what you wanted. The choice is for you to make, and yours alone."

Home. The word echoed in my brain. *This* was my home. I didn't want to leave, didn't have anything to go back to. "If I go home, will you find someone else to marry?" A frown pulled at my lips. I didn't like the idea of them marrying. Not. At. All.

"As the last dragons, it would be our duty to find a queen." He kept his voice casual.

My stomach dropped like a bag of gold bricks, and it nearly made a loud thud. Despair hit me in waves, so I swallowed against the constriction in my throat. "Well, that settles it. I'm staying."

Kieran laughed, tugging on a damp curl of my hair. "Good, because I would have come after you."

Was it fair for me to expect them to share me, but not share them? The mere thought of any of the descendants taking a wife made me ill, and mad enough to spit flames.

It was my problem.

And I would deal with it when the time came. For now, they were mine.

Something tugged inside me, waking me up from a deep sleep that I wasn't ready to leave, but the tug was persistent, annoyingly so, giving me no alternative but to bat my eyes open. I didn't do so without a grumble. It was the distant hissing and popping of lava, flowing over rock, and rumbling in my ears that pushed me over the edge.

I blinked.

A sleeping Jase lay beside me. Moonbeams streaked over one side of his face, casting him in silver and shadow. The tranquility dragon was breathtaking to behold. He had stayed with me last night and not a single kiss or touch. I wanted to curl up beside him and rest my head on the spot of his shoulder that seemed made for me, but that thing nudged me once more.

'Olivia. Keeper. Claim me.' That pull inside me whispered.

Shuddering, I flung off the covers and rose from the bed, the voice guiding me. A white haze filtered throughout my room, but I thought nothing of it.

Barefoot, I walked into the dark halls of the castle, the staff long since asleep. My steps were silent as I continued to tiptoe down the stairs, fingers running along the stone walls. I reached the main floor and listened. Nothing sounded, except for the voice.

'Hurry. Find me.'

A warm breeze blew my hair off my shoulders when I went through the terrace doors, and into the night. Stardust gleamed overhead, bathing the grounds in a shower of silver. I crept through the garden and winced as I stepped on a shard of rock, a sharp edge lancing the arch of my foot.

Fabulous. Not only was I running around nearly half naked in the dead of night, but I was alone, and now I was also bleeding.

In a deep recess of my mind, I comprehended what I was doing was dangerous, but I couldn't stop myself from moving further and further from the castle. The thread inside me gave a slight yank, urging me to the left, toward the volcano. I could be walking into a trap. Tianna could swoop in from the shadows and steal me away. Or I could fall into a river of lava. Take your pick. All sorts of threats were possible.

And yet, I was powerless to do anything but keep traipsing along. In the distance, dark smoke billowed from Titan Mountain. I tried to focus on the path laid out in front of me, but that white film made my vision unclear.

I needed to keep my wits about me. Whatever was summoning me, didn't know me very well. The prospect of me getting to the volcano unscathed was slim to none. As though to prove my point, I stumbled over my own feet, going splat on the ground. Luckily, I caught myself a split second before my nose hit the earth. My palms stung, but I'd take a few scrapes and cuts over a broken and bloodied nose.

Son of a b—

The cord jerked, cutting off a string of curse words I had lined up in my head.

I shoved to my feet, no time to panic, or perhaps it was because of what summoned me, for there was no doubt in my mind, I was being controlled. But by whom? Or what? The only way to find out was to see this through, following the silent commands leading my body.

It sort of reminded me of when I'd been possessed by a ghost. My limbs and muscles were moving, but the orders weren't coming from my mind.

'Hurry. Hurry.' The tug seemed to shout.

My heart was beating harshly in my chest, pulsing in my throat. I had the volcano in my sights. Sweat glistened over my skin, the night-shirt sticking to my boobs, my belly.

'So close—hurry—you must not—'

"Going on a midnight stroll?" A firm hand wrapped on my fore-arm, halting my progression. I tried to shake off whoever had a hold of me, but it was futile.

The culprit spun me around then, and I blinked. *Jase,* my entire body seemed to sigh, except for the thread. It pulled harder, over and over again, attempting to get me back under its enthrallment.

"Olivia," he breathed my name, not letting me go. His other hand lifted to caress the side of my face, the pad of his thumb running along my cheekbone in a gentle butterfly touch. "Wake up."

My eyes connected with his, and the thread snapped inside me. The film that had been blurring my vision cleared as those glowing violet eyes stared into mine. "Jase?" my voice quivered over his name.

"You gave me quite the startle when I woke up and you were gone."

My gaze took in my surroundings, the bubbling brook of lava, the volcano towering above us. It all seemed like a distant memory. "I-uh. Why am I outside? In nothing but a T-shirt?" I asked, glancing at my skimpy attire.

"Shit," he swore under his breath. "Did you have to mention your lack of clothes?"

I whacked the back of my hand against his exposed abs. He didn't so much as flinch. I wasn't the only one who was wandering around outside in next to nothing. "That's all you can think about?"

"You brought it up," he so eloquently reminded me.

I shook my head, pressing my forehead to his slick chest. "What's wrong with me?"

His arms came to wrap around me, pulling me into his embrace. "Absolutely. Nothing."

Sweet. But not the truth. Something was definitely wrong. I remembered getting out of bed, climbing down the stairs and strolling out of the castle, but every second of it had felt like a dream, foggy and surreal. Until I was staring into Jase's eyes, and bam, the world came back into motion. We both knew something evil was at play.

I was still a prisoner. The witch still had me in her clutches, much like how she had the descendants trapped.

Find me, the star had called out again. At least I thought it was the star. It could have been a spell just as easily. My head lifted and I threw a sidelong glance at the volcano. Even now, I sensed the stone whispering my name like a lost song. "It wants me to find it," I murmured, the words tumbling from my lips.

"The star?" he said, seeking clarity.

"Maybe. I'm not sure. It could have easily been Tianna. How would I know the difference?"

He regarded me, eyes brighter than usual. "I'm thinking we might need to start tying you to the bed."

"Are you getting kinky on me?" The words escaped me. I had no intention of flirting with him, but when faced with what might have happened tonight if he hadn't shown up, I needed a way to lighten the fear that gripped my heart. It was easier to tease him, instead of dealing with my emotions.

"What am I supposed to do with you?"

I slipped my hand into his, twining our fingers together. "Take me home. I've had enough of the outdoors for one night."

Bending down, Jase swept me up into his arms.

"I can walk," I protested, trying to keep some shred of dignity.

"It's faster if I carry you."

I rolled my eyes but didn't object further. He was right. It would be quicker and less hazardous for both of us if he carried me.

The fingers holding me flexed, and I peered up to see what was bothering him. He was glaring at my feet. "You're bleeding."

Lifting my toes in the air, I surveyed the dried blood on my foot. "Oh. It's no big deal. I cut myself on a rock."

A scowl marred his lips. "Of course, you did. I never knew how fragile humans could be until I met you."

It was hard to fathom, considering the numerous girls they had brought to the Veil over the last ninety-nine years, but none of them were me—like the descendants were fond of saying. How right they were.

He stalked toward the castle and I rested my head on his shoulder, yawning. "I've never sleepwalked before."

"How about we don't make a habit of it."

"What am I supposed to do? Not sleep?"

"Afraid that isn't an option. You need a different type of sleep, one devoid of dreams."

"Don't. You—"

Too late.

Jase's lips met mine, but not in just any kiss, a kiss punched with tranquility. I felt the cool, calm ribbon down my lungs.

"I hate you," I managed to mumble, my body collapsing against his.

He lifted me in his arms, pressing a kiss to my temple. "No, you don't," I heard him say before unconsciousness took me under.

My foot had been cleaned and bandaged when I woke late the following morning. I rolled my ankle, testing its mobility and winced, the cut itself stretched with the motion. Edging off the bed, I eased to my feet, keeping the bulk of my weight off the arch of my foot and hobbled to the bathroom.

Jase had a shoulder propped against the wall when I emerged a few minutes later. "Next time you feel the need to go for a midnight stroll, wake me up. Better yet, do it on someone else's watch."

"How did you know?" I inquired.

"I sensed your fear. It woke me up," he said simply.

This was one of those moments I was thankful for the emotional bond between us, even if it was only one-sided, and split between the four dragons. "Does that happen frequently?" I hated to think my emotions interfered with their lives. I would not be a happy camper if I were constantly awoken by someone else's feelings.

He shrugged. "It happens."

Not the answer I was looking for right now. "What did I miss while I was rendered unconscious?"

His lips twitched, knowing I was jabbing at him for using tranquility on me. He was lucky I didn't poison his ass. "Let's go find out. I'm sure the others are wondering where we are, or if I'm holding you captive."

I was surprised they hadn't rammed down the door. "It would serve you right for letting me sleep so long."

"You needed it, Cupcake."

I scowled, awkwardly following him to the library where Zade and Kieran were sprawled about, each with a book in their hands. Gold shelves of books lined all four of the walls all the way to the ceiling. A trace of something old and magical scented the air, something more than just dusty books.

"What are we researching? A way to kill a devourer? How to bind a witch's magic? Or how to get the stone out of a volcano?" I asked upon entering the opulent room.

Kieran's twinkling gaze peeked over a large dark green leather-bound book. "All of the above."

"Great," I mumbled, taking an empty recliner. "Toss me a book."

Someone put a plate of food in my hands instead, ordering me to eat. "Do you really think we'll find something here that will help us?" I asked, forking a piece of buttered bread with cinnamon and sugar that looked like French toast.

Zade crossed an ankle over his knee, a book propped on his leg. "You think we should be out there doing something, instead of cooped up in the library flipping through books older than all of us?"

I lifted my brows. "Is that so wrong?"

Jase shook his head. "No. You're not alone in this feeling. But," he added. "Not all battles are won in the field. Some are won by being educated, prepared. It is as important to be educated as it is to be able to wield a sword."

"Have there been any other sightings of the devourer? Perhaps it went back to whatever hell it came from."

"Only one. In the Nameless Lands." Jase's voice was a bit tight when he answered.

I sunk back against the cushion, the half-eaten plate of food now neglected alongside a stack of parchments. "How many other forgotten, or creatures of legend will she resurrect?"

Beside me, the light winked out of Kieran's eyes. "Until she gets what she wants. Us. The Veil. The stars."

Issik strolled into the room with purposeful strides at that moment, and stretched out on the other side of me. "Where have you been?" I asked, seeing the exhaustion lining his eyes. And I thought I'd had a rough night.

His head hit the back of the chair. "Searching the Nameless Lands."

"Did you find the wanderer? Or the devourer?"

He shook his head. "Not a trace. He is exceptional at hiding his tracks."

This was hopeless. My fingers rubbed over the sides of my temples.

Zade was watching me with intensity, no doubt sensing my frustration. "Why does it look like you're working on an early headache?"

"I had a restless night," was all I said, assuming Jase had already filled in the others about my late night escapade.

Jase coughed to cover up the grin on his lips, and the other three dragons pinned him with equal glares of ill humor.

My ears flared with heat. "That's not what I meant. Not everything is about sex." I was in a mood. And not that kind of mood.

"We got to do something to stay sane around here," Kieran drawled.

I ignored him and grabbed a book. "What the hell am I looking for?" I asked, staring down at the jumble of words on the page. Was this even English?

Jase came to peer over my shoulder. "Pretty sure you're reading it upside down."

I stared at the book frowning. Why did I bother?

He flipped the book around in my lap. "This is a journal about the lore of beasts. You might find some information on how to kill the devourer in there. The language is old, but the drawings will be useful. If you see anything that resembles the devourer, we'll have Issik translate."

"He can read this?" The words lining the page were symbols that reminded me of runes.

Jase nodded. "His family was one of the last to still speak the language of the gods."

I glanced over at the Ice Prince. He was sipping from a glass, thumbing through a large book with a dragon shield embossed on the cover. "Are all these books filled with magic?"

The dim light beside Jase picked up highlights of his dark hair. "Most of them. The important ones were divided between the royal families for safekeeping, away from humans. In the wrong hands, these books could be catastrophic."

Like Tianna's.

My attention shifted to my book, curious about what kind of magic it beheld.

. . .

A half hour later, I no longer was curious but enthralled and a bit frightened. Once or twice I gasped at the pictures that stared back at me. Beasts with horns or multiple heads. Creatures with scorpion tails or no spines. Animals that could take the shape of anything it touched. So many different types of horrors.

It didn't matter that I couldn't read the text. The drawings spoke a thousand words.

We had spent most of the day in the library, when I raised my head from the book of beasts to roll my neck. Wariness shone on my dragons' faces, but they dutifully continued searching for answers, anything to give us the edge in this battle against Tianna. The descendants had come and gone from the room, attempting to wear off their restlessness, or satiate their hunger, but it had all been uneventful. So, I was altogether startled when the door to the library blew open and in stormed Issik, a frosty chill sweeping through the room at his wake. I hadn't even noticed he had left the library until that moment.

Jase's gaze went stony as he faced the Ice Prince. "What is it?" he asked disconcerted.

Issik's icy expression remained intact, but his eyes were swirling with cold blistering rage. "We just received word that Tianna has attacked Wakeland. Your kingdom is under siege, Jase."

I ssik's announcement caused a roar to rip throughout the castle, and Kieran and Zade jumped to their feet.

"How long?" it was Jase who spoke, demanding an answer from the Ice Prince.

A shiver danced down my spine. I'd never seen such lethal calm in Jase's eyes.

"Not more than ten minutes ago. She has sealed the keep with a spell, moving her army in from the borders of the Nameless Lands, and into the villages," Issik supplied.

Amethyst scales instantly papered over Jase's arms, spreading along his body. Without another word, he tore through the room, the others on his heels, and I was quick to scamper after.

"Jase," Zade called, daring to lay a hand on his shoulder.

Jase whirled, a growl curling his lips, but Zade's fingers tightened their hold, in understanding. If it had been his home, Zade would have erupted into a blaze of fire. I marveled at Jase's control.

"We need to think this through. It could be a trap," Zade urged.

"I have to go."

Kieran shot Jase a calculating look. "No one is saying don't go, but let us help."

Jase's eyes glittered like burning starlight as he gave a short nod. "We don't have much time. She is making a point, letting us know she can take what is ours. We need to show her we're not so easy to conquer."

"We can't leave Olivia," Issik said. No one argued that point.

"Damn right you can't. I'm coming with you," I declared.

Issik's face was as cold as ever. "It's too dangerous. If she is there..."

Zade didn't so much as blink in my direction. "And if it is a trap? As much as none of us want to admit, we can't go up against Tianna alone. She would pluck Olivia right from under our nose."

Silence followed.

Cool anger simmered under the surface of Jase's expression. "We're safer in numbers. She comes with us," he ordered, and didn't wait for anyone to argue as he immediately shifted, becoming a deadly dragon, a warrior with murder gleaming in his eyes. He hadn't even bothered to shed his clothes, the material ribboned to pieces on the floor.

Kieran and Issik were quick to follow, joining Jase in the sky. The heavy beating of their wings sounded like the hovering of helicopter blades slicing through the air, taking them higher away from me.

Nausea unfurled in my stomach as Zade turned to me. The magnitude of what I was about to fly into hit the defensive wall I'd constructed. Tianna. I was going to see the witch for the first time since she abducted me—tortured me.

"You okay, Little Gem?"

My heart stumbled a bit, but I lifted my chin, pushing through it. "Let's go," I said tightly.

Understanding painted in his features. Zade barked orders to his staff and returned to my side, holding out his hand. "You forgot this." He offered me what he so zealously held, and I glanced down.

My dagger. The one Jase had given me over a month ago. The white of my knuckles showed as I took the blade.

"Just in case," he added, when I lifted my eyes to meet his in question.

Every inch of him was thrumming with the urge to shift and he didn't give in until I nodded, signaling that I was ready. Securing the blade to the outside of my thigh, I caught the tail end of Zade's transformation to a fire-breathing dragon. He shook out his head, the sun glinting off his red-gold scales, before sinking to the ground for me to climb on him.

I'd be lying if I said I wasn't scared shitless. The prospect of seeing Tianna again sent a spiral of terror rushing through my veins. I'd never been in a battle, let alone one with a witch. My expectations were horrifying, but my concern for the descendants and the people who called Wakeland their home, trumped all my fears and reservations. To save my dragons, to protect my home, I'd sacrifice myself—I'd fight Tianna to my death.

Zade shoved off the ground to join the others, and the wind tore at me. I clung onto his neck fiercely as we climbed into the sky. *"No matter what happens, don't let go of me,"* he instructed.

My legs and hands tightened against him in response.

"We'll be keeping higher in the sky, helping Kieran clear out the villages. Jase and Issik are at the castle," he informed with smooth precision.

Wakeland approached in the distance, and it was the blinding lights and thunderous roars echoing throughout the Veil that held me enraptured. When we grew closer, I gasped. The lake I had retrieved the first star from was stained red. I didn't want to think about what had caused the waters to turn the color of blood.

"Olivia?"

Forcing myself to breathe, I realized that no air was flowing into my lungs. "I'm okay." My mouth had gone dry at the sights around me. "Do it," I rasped. We couldn't afford to waste another second. Those people in the villages were counting on us.

Zade opened his jaw, letting a stream of fire rain upon Tianna's army during our first pass over the farming village. Suffocating heat filled the air, followed by the stench of charred flesh and cries of agony. Nothing about fighting, about killing, was glorified like the movies showed. It was heartbreaking. Defeating. Gut-wrenching. And bloody.

I had not anticipated the sheer force of Tianna's army—of her powers—of what she was capable of. To make such a violent move made me think she was threatened, perhaps by me. She wanted the stars and the power they wielded, but to do so, she would have to go through me.

My gaze found Kieran on the ground, standing across the bridge as he spewed a vile mist of poison on Tianna's soldiers. They were made up of goblins, griffins, spirits from the otherworld, and other creatures I couldn't identify—and probably didn't want to know.

By some small miracle, I spotted no wraiths. Yet.

Would the descendants be taking on both her army and the witch herself, assuming she showed her face? Her curse had weakened their powers, but even then, they were magnificent. I quivered thinking about what the four of them could do at full strength. This wouldn't have been much of a battle.

Below us, the screams of those who had made a home in Wakeland pierced the air, rising over the battle. So many. They didn't stand a chance against Tianna's ranks, not with mythical abilities the creatures possessed. I didn't know how the witch was able to band together such numbers. What did she promise them? Were they ensnared in her web of spells like the dragons?

I squared my shoulders. "Bitch," I hissed. How could she do such a thing?

In that moment, two griffins flocked at either side of Zade, blocking him in between them. Their beaks clamped with sharp snaps toward me, and I don't know what happened. Something inside me took over. Perhaps it was Jase's lessons, or newly awoken instincts, but I didn't hesitate. Opening my mouth, I let a stream of poison burst from my lungs, blowing the green mist into their feathery faces. The toxic vapor found its way into their nostrils, vengefully sizzling and burning through every inch of them. Shrieking in agony, they fell, hitting the ground with a thud that could be heard from the clouds.

Damn, that felt good.

"Remind me not to get on your bad side."

Zade circled back around over the village, drowning a cluster of troops in a ring of fire. She had turned Jase's kingdom into her own twisted hunting ground. Why? For no other reason than she could—for sick pleasure.

Below us woman and children ran, seeking coverage and protection. Kieran slammed his jaws over a pair of goblins before they had a chance to willowphase out of danger—like they had been doing, popping in and out of the village. Their bodies tumbled to the ground, followed by their severed heads, dropping out of Kieran's mouth. Blood dripped from his lips.

The sun, tinged in pink, rose higher as if it knew blood had been spilled this day. We glided through the village's streets, surveying the destruction and searching for any lingering soldiers. Then over the howling winds, my ears picked up a scream.

Crispness settled into my vision, the roiling of my power swirling in my chest. Left. Right. Left again. My eyes darted over the cobblestone street, but no sight of who was calling out for help. Zade's muscles were strained underneath me. "There." I pointed to the bridge.

A trio of awakened dead was taunting an elderly woman. Her frail fingers gripped the wooden banister as she backed away, and it was clear then that Tianna would use any willing body, dead or alive, to fight her battles.

"Hang on tight!" Zade dropped in a near vertical dive, heading straight for the dead. He soared with speed and accuracy, and my heart thundered against my ribs.

If he didn't—Oh, my god we were going to—

At the last second before impact, Zade pulled up, the talons on his feet sinking into two of the walking dead, and tearing them open. He used his tail to whip the third, sending it flying to the lake as its body split in two from the force. After he raised us to the flawless clouds again, his grip loosened, dropping the remaining pieces of the other two he'd had in his clutches.

"You good?" he asked into my mind, his deep voice filled with concern.

"As good as expected." I wasn't sure I would ever forget the sounds, the smell, or the terrifying feeling it gave me.

"Let's find Jase and Issik, see if they need any help with the witch."

Zade changed our direction, slicing through the blue skies with Kieran to our left. Together we headed for Wakeland Keep. The castle had an eerie shimmer that swathed it. Zade perched us on top of one of the towers, giving us a view with an advantage. Kieran sat on the twin tower, poised for the next attack.

The tower trembled beneath us as Jase landed on the ground, letting a roar of pure rage echo throughout his kingdom. Issik kept to the skies above the lake, picking off any remaining soldiers guarding the castle. Two died instantly, frozen and then splintered by the spikes of his tail. Their remains shattered like glass.

I glanced at my four dragons, relieved they were alive and unharmed, but that respite didn't last. At closer inspection, I saw the weariness in their eyes, in their bodies, in their powers. She had done that.

What more was she capable of?

I thought of my own scars and the ones now left on Wakeland. How many more innocents would suffer for her greed for power?

Jase released another rumble from deep within his chest, letting it shudder over the land. Tianna had encased his home in one of her wicked spells. Why? What did she hope to achieve? Was it me she wanted? Was it to shove her dominance over the descendants, make them grovel at her feet?

As the thought crossed my mind, the front doors to the keep parted, and she appeared. Tianna strolled from inside Jase's home like she was its queen, her black-laced gown flowing like fluid night behind her. Her scarlet lips curled.

I loathed the fear that sprang inside me at my first sight of her, the way my breath came out jagged.

"Easy," Zade crooned in warning.

Should we do something, strike her now? I didn't dare speak, didn't dare distract any of them. This was when they needed to rally their focus and powers.

Tianna strutted toward Jase, her bright, calculating eyes meeting his. "Took you long enough."

Jase cut her a glare. He didn't dare look away. *"What do you want?"* his dragon voice boomed into our heads.

Tianna's answering grin was a slash of white lightning across her attractive features. "I see you got your pet back. I hope I didn't break her too much."

Four growls erupted from different corners of the castle.

The witch hadn't spared me a single glance, but she knew I was here. My blood brimmed with a cocktail of panic and wrath.

She clucked her tongue at the fierce protectiveness rumbling from my dragons. "I heard the four of you liked to share. I didn't think you'd mind if I borrowed, Olivia."

Borrowed, my left asscheek! As if I were a cloak or a pair of shoes.

"Release the spell," Jase demanded, refusing to play her little games.

Tianna pouted, disappointment radiating in her silver eyes. "Not so quick, Tranquility Heir. You can have your precious little kingdom when I get my star. I want the Star of Fire," she stated, finally laying out her cards—her demands.

"And if I refuse?" Rage darkened Jase's violet eyes to near blackness.

"Let's just say that would be very unfortunate for all the little trophies you've collected over the years. How disappointed your father would be to see his legacy collapse."

Oh, how I longed for the power the Star of Fire would grant me. I'd light her ass up right now if I could.

"We don't have the Star of Fire."

"No?" she sung, tilting her head to the side. Her lips curved into a new smile, while she tapped a sharp nail against her lips. "But your pet knows where it is. Don't you dear?" And for the first time since the mountain, Tianna's gaze slid to mine. My skin felt as if a thousand spiders were crawling over it, shadows and darkness unfurling around my soul. "Such a remarkable thing she is," she mused.

I lifted my chin a fraction in defiance and schooled my features, refusing to let a flicker of emotion show. A cool mask of indifference slid over my face, but the dragon under me didn't show the same restraint. Zade let his roaring fury loose, unveiling a river of fire down toward the witch.

When the flames reached Tianna, they went right through her. The edges of her form rippled like water before stabilizing.

Another spell. She was fond of tricks and illusion.

Tianna threw her head back and laughed, a haunting sound. "You didn't think I'd actually show up, did you?"

Jase inclined his angular head. *"Too afraid to face the four of us. I'm not surprised."*

"It's you who fears me, sons of dragons, as you have for the last century. My reign has just started, while yours is ending before it even began."

"Our time isn't over yet," Jase seethed.

She tapped at her wrist. "Yes, tick tock."

"Release the spell on the castle. You've had your fun."

"Such impatience. You have until the end of this month to bring me the Star of Fire, or another kingdom will fall to their knees before me." Her eyes once again shifted toward the tower where Zade and I were perched. A smile of wickedness bestowed on her lips. "Olivia dear." She savored the sound of my name on her tongue. "You are so much more than I bargained for. I have plans for you. Big plans."

Heat itched along my cheeks and neck, and my body betrayed me, trembling at her dark promise. *Never again*, I told myself. Never again would I let her break me.

This war against Tianna had become mine. A mere human I might be, but I alone had been chosen by the stars. Who knew why they spoke to me, why they gifted me with their powers. I couldn't say I was happy about it, but I was grateful if it allowed me to save the descendants.

"Don't touch her!" Four different, yet equally grim voices resounded in my head.

"The choice is yours. Live under my command, or don't live at all. Either way, you will not win. It will take everything the four of you have to fight me—which as I understand isn't much—and even then, it won't be enough to beat me. So you see, the decision is simple. Give me the remaining two stars and I give you my word your pet will live. If you refuse..." she shrugged, her slim shoulders lifting in a careless, bored manner. "I'll make her *my* pet."

The kingdom trembled under the deafening roars that exploded from a deep and primal part of my dragons. She had threatened what they considered theirs. Me. And the instinct to protect, ingrained in every scale covering their fierce bodies, flared to life.

"You have quite the mess to clean up. Give me the star and I'll make sure the other kingdoms don't suffer the same fate." Then with a wave of her hand, she was gone.

J ase's unyielding gaze roamed over his castle entombed in Tianna's spell, grieving all those inside now frozen by her magic. Issik dropped down beside him, the sun glittering off their scales.

My eyes circled Wakeland, seeing the destruction Tianna had left in her wake. Never had I witnessed a battle. And nothing could have prepared me for the aftermath, for the lost lives, for the fallen stone buildings, for the blood.

A grueling moan of despair thundered from deep within Jase's chest, leaving him powerless to do anything to aid those trapped inside his home. I wanted to run into his arms, offer him what little solace I could, but I knew it would do hardly any good. He was suffering from grief, helplessness, and uncontainable wrath.

The worst part was that this war wasn't over. It had only just begun. Tianna hadn't been defeated, and the events of today would stay with me long after it ended, regardless of who won. I would never forget. Coming to the Veil had changed me forever, just as this first battle had left a different kind of scar on my soul.

A trembling hand lifted to touch the side of my cheek, where Tianna's mark marred my tender skin. More proof that I'd never be whole again, though I was more concerned about the internal damage left behind, than my vanity. If a visible scar was the worst affliction I received, then it was a small price to save those I loved, to save the land that had become my home.

"Will he be okay?" I asked Zade, staring down at the purple dragon who paced back and forth outside the castle, searching for the tiniest whole in Tianna's hex.

"Since the curse was cast, this has always been our worst fear. That she would attack our homes, the people we protect. We won't let her win. That is the only way any of us will be okay."

Heaviness settled into my heart.

We could do nothing to help those inside the castle, but the village beyond the lake was in need of aid. Kieran stayed behind with Jase, while Zade, Issik and I went to see what we could do for the others. The quiet lake still ran red as we flew over, and the little village was a flurry of panic and commotion. My heart stumbled in my chest. It would take months to rebuild what Tianna had destroyed in mere minutes.

When my feet touched the ground my knees nearly buckled, but Issik was there to lend me his sturdiness. He slid an arm around my lower back, catching my elbow with the other, and hauled me against him. "I got you, Little Warrior. You did well, for your first battle."

He had shifted before Zade and I had landed, tossing on a pair of pants that was always stashed in the villages. Blood crusted in speckles over his face and chest, but I didn't care how dirty he was. I used his shoulder as a pillow, resting my cheek on him. "All those people…" I murmured.

"We'll rebuild," Issik promised quietly.

I recognized a few of the faces among the throngs of people. Women limped along, seeking the healers. The air reeked of blood. I did what little I could to help, tending and cleaning wounds with fresh water, while Issik and Zade made arrangements for any of those who were displaced from their homes.

It wasn't until much later when Zade flew us back to Crimson Keep, and tears streamed down my cheeks only to be whisked away by the blustering wind. Every part of me ached. My legs. My arms. My back. My soul. My heart. Not a section was untouched by what had unfolded. I gave in to the exhaustion and lay onto of Zade's powerful dragon body, the scales brushing against my cheek.

I must have dozed for a bit, for when I woke, Kieran was lifting me off Zade and into his arms. "You're safe, Blondie," he whispered near my ear.

"Is he here?" My voice was raspy. I needed water, I needed sleep, but not until I knew they were here, together with me. Only then could I see to myself.

"No. It might be some time before he is able to get away. His kingdom is in ruin. He needs to see to his people's safety. They rely on us."

Just as I relied on them to keep me protected.

I stifled a yawn. "What time is it?"

He moved with grace and ease through the castle, not in the least burdened by my weight. "It is late. You need to rest."

"So do you," I added, watching a few green strands of his hair fall to frame the sharp angles of his face. Pieces were stuck together with a dark substance. Blood. My nose wrinkled. "But first you need a bath."

Those full lips curved. "Aye, I do. And I'm not the only one."

He carried me upstairs, to what I thought might be his room, fetching a glass of water and ordering me to drink. I obeyed, taking a long sip from the onyx goblet. My fingers were slightly unsteady, clenching the cup. "Thank you," I murmured. "What do we do now?" I asked, looking up at him expectantly.

"There is nothing more we can do tonight. Let's get you cleaned up and in bed. Tomorrow we'll regroup. Decide what needs to be done." Kieran held out his hand for me to take.

I nodded, not knowing what else I could say and put my hand in his.

He led me into the bathing chamber, and I followed him on wobbly legs, seeing him flip on the spray of hot water that cascaded from a spout in the stone, like rainfall. Kieran was quiet as he stripped the clothes from my body, not in a sensual way, but with loving purpose, and yet, my body tingled on the places his fingers grazed.

Steam had begun to fill the room when I stepped into the opened shower. The water hit my skin and my bones whimpered. Kieran sauntered in behind me. "It will be quicker if we bathe together," he replied at my drawn up brows, a bit of light coming back into his emerald eyes.

"You don't say?" I stepped back, allowing him more room in the space and dropped my head back into the cascade of water, soaking my hair and face.

Kieran watched me with male appreciation.

He was so tall and perfectly formed that I couldn't help but watch him as the water ran off his body, stained a pinkish-red. Not from his blood, but those of the enemy.

I took a piece of cloth hanging on a rack and lathered it with a bar of soap to wash the dirt and grime from his golden tattooed skin. I studied the ink, a painting of his life, of memories he held dear. Vibrant roses with sharp thorns, tangled with vines. A snake winding up his entire arm with glittering gems for eyes, much like the one carved into his castle.

Each tattoo told a story.

"Let me help," I offered, my voice hardly above a whisper. I took the soapy cloth, dragging it over his arm, and circled around to his back. My breath caught. A splotch of purple marred the skin on the top of his left shoulder. "You're hurt."

His eyes glanced over at me. "The bastard got a lucky shot. It will be gone by morning. Nothing to fret over."

I'd be the judge of that. With tentative fingers, I brushed over the bruise and unease pitted in my belly. They could have been seriously hurt today. The thought made me sick. How would I ever manage if something did happen to one of them?

Drawing up on my toes, I pressed a soft kiss to the bruise.

A long breath escaped him, his body letting go of the tension for the first time in hours. "Olivia." My name became a worship on his lips.

He turned to face me, so much gentleness radiating from his eyes. "You worry for nothing. I will be fine. So will Jase."

I gnawed at my lower lip, his eyes tracking the movement. "I don't like it when we're separated. It makes me feel vulnerable."

He took my face in between his damp hands and kissed me. When he pulled his lips from mine to brush his fingers down the column of my neck, his face was grave. "We're only stronger because of you. We can't win this war without you. The Veil needs you."

I only hoped I didn't disappoint or let them down.

The sun was once again shining when I awoke, rested and starving out of my mind. I rubbed at my eyes, and blinked at the bright light streaming in through the wall of windows. It was only for those first blissful moments of clearing my mind from sleep that I was at peace, and then the terror of what happened steamed rolled through me.

Jase!

Had he returned?

Was he alone?

I rushed from the bed, flying out of the room and into the corridor. It didn't matter that I scarcely knew my way around Crimson Keep. I had to see him, needed to confirm with my own two eyes that he was okay. My bare feet padded over the cool marble floor and down the steps, until I reached the main level outside the kitchen.

Deep voices came from inside the room, and without hesitation, I pushed open the double doors to find Zade and Issik at the long island —a mess covering the tabletop.

Is that flour on the Ice Prince's cheek?

My eyes darted around the room, searching for Jase. He wasn't anywhere to be found, but neither were any of the staff. "Where is everyone?" I asked, gradually walking further into the room.

Zade paused his task of slicing a loaf a bread to look at me. "I've given them the day off. Some have traveled to Wakeland to help, others are taking time to grieve."

Issik expertly cracked an egg into a bowl. "We're making breakfast? Are you hungry?"

"Uh, I'm starved. Is Jase back?"

Shadows flickered into both of their eyes, and I almost regretted asking, but I had to know. "He returned a few hours ago," Zade finally answered.

"And the castle? Was he able to find a way to break the spell?"

Zade only shook his head.

Dread spread inside of me. Poor Jase. I thought about all those who lived inside Wakeland Keep, including Harper. Were they terrified? Could they even feel in their frozen state?

"And Kieran?" I inquired, plopping into one of the chairs situated alongside the center island. Issik placed a cup of coffee in front of me, and I offered him a meek grin of thanks.

"He went to put his kingdom on high alert, and then we'll do a sweep of the Nameless Lands," Issik said.

Warming my fingers on the sides of the cup, I mulled over his words. "Is it wise for him to go alone?"

Zade's hand tightened on the knife. "We don't have much of a choice at this point."

"Did you warn your household?" I directed at Issik.

He nodded. "My lands have been on locked down from the beginning."

I gave him a funny look. "What does that mean?"

"I've enclosed my villages and castle in a tomb of ice," he explained.

"We all have our own defenses," Zade added, seeing the astonishment creep into my face. "Safeguards to protect the people during war. I only wish we would have done so sooner. If we would have known that Tianna…" His voice trailed off, but I didn't need him to finish.

I placed a hand over his on the counter and squeezed. "You can't blame yourselves. In nearly a hundred years, the witch has not made a volatile threat to your kingdoms. To you directly, yes, but not your homes."

Issik's jaw tightened, steeling himself for what was still to come.

I ate the food they put in front of me without tasting a bite. My eyes kept straying to the doors, waiting for Jase to come strolling in, midnight hair disheveled from sleep. As much as I wished it, he remained behind closed doors.

D ays wasted by and with them, my frustration grew. For once, I knew the location of the stone, but the dragons forbade me from retrieving it. The atmosphere in the castle was grim, and although the emotional bond between Jase and I was only one-sided, I swore my heart felt his pain, his suffering. I couldn't explain it, but I knew he needed me.

Jase didn't feel the same way.

An impenetrable armor had suddenly erected around him like a fortress of night. Anger and vengeance simmered close to the surface. It was difficult to see my born leader dragon become a man I didn't recognize. Gone was the starlight in his violet eyes. Gone were the once annoying dimples I longed to see.

I knew little of war, and even less about evil witches. But this, the waiting for the right time, the right place, or whatever it was the descendants were holding out for, felt like waiting for rain during a draught.

By the third day, I'd made up my mind. I knew what I must do and who I needed to ask for help.

The women in white. In this case, Zade's mother.

Summoning one of them was tricky. They didn't always come when I asked, and she might very well not appear, but I had to try. This was one secret I hadn't shared with the descendants… I had no doubt if they knew what I was up to, they would insist on coming along, and I couldn't let that happen. With them there, the late queens wouldn't be able to show themselves. Life on the other side wasn't something I even wanted to comprehend.

Rain plummeted from the heavy clouds sweeping over Crimson Kingdom and had for the better part of the day. It showed no signs of letting up, but that suited my needs. The difficult part of my plan would be getting outside without a dragon shadowing me, or noticing I was missing. They'd given me extra attention since the attack on Wakeland.

I waited until the castle had gone to bed and Zade was sleeping beside me, the last few days wearing on all of us. "I'm sorry," I whispered against his lips right before I pressed my mouth to his, blowing a stream of tranquility into his lungs. Insurance to make sure he didn't sneak up on me in the middle of my chat with his mom, assuming she answered my request.

Guilt followed me as I wiggled out of bed to dress, tiptoeing from the room. I was breathless by the time I made it passed the training area, to a field of tall wildflowers and mist. The moon wasn't full, only a crescent sliver missing. My hair was plastered to my face as the rain sliced through the air. This was a risk, but going off what little I knew of the late queens, it was the best shot I had.

The only way to end this torment was for me to go into Titan Mountain and find the star. Yet, the scorching temperature and pool of lava made it impossible for me to do so. I wasn't a witch. I had no spells to protect me from the heat. Perhaps I should have struck a bargain with Tianna, tricked her somehow in giving me the fortification I would need to go into the volcano.

That was where Zade's mom came in.

The mossy grass cushioned my feet as I walked, listening, flowers tickling my calves. I swallowed nervously. "Hello?" I called out, feeling like an idiot. Was there a proper way to summon a ghost? "I need your help. Please."

My only answer was a chorus of crickets, probably complaining about the evening rain. I didn't blame them. Beads of rain dribbled over my face. Coming out here alone was a risk. I just hoped it wasn't one I would regret.

"Hello," I called again. "Please, help me." I spun in the glade filled with flowers of sunlight and firelight, gleaming under the stars. Everything in Crimson seemed to burn; the trees and flower were no different.

Sticking around for a few more minutes, my arms hugged my torso as I stood in the rain, waiting. And waiting. My spirits sunk, and I turned to retrace my steps back to the castle.

"Have you found a way to obtain the Star of Fire, Olivia Campbell?" A haunting, soft, female voice cut through the patter of raindrops hitting the earth.

I turned, my drenched hair whipping with my moments.

Zade's mother, the former queen of Crimson, stood a few feet before me as she hovered an inch or two over the ground. Her cloak of white draped around her, the snowy hood framing her golden face. Hair the same dark shade of Zade's spilled out over her shoulders in loose curls. She looked every inch a ghostly queen.

How long had it been since I'd seen her last? Two weeks? It might have as well been a lifetime ago. "No. That's why I'm here. I need your help."

"Tianna's army is growing. You must claim the star. It is yours."

"Yes, but how can I claim it without killing myself in the process?"

She angled her head, considering it as if she had long forgotten how fragile humans were. "I only know what I can see, and even then, it is only a possibility."

So freaking helpful. "There must be a way."

"All the resources you need are at your fingertips. You must seek refuge in its rival," she said.

My brain whirled. Another mystery for me to solve. "Do you know what will happen if she is able to retrieve the star before I do?" I asked, since she seemed awfully chatty.

Her cloak flitted with the wind and something distant moved into her eyes. "Death and destruction will reign, in this world and others."

My stomach dropped.

"Even a single star could make her power mighty and wicked," she explained and I could have sworn she shivered beneath her cloak.

"I don't want anyone else to die."

"It isn't the stars that will win the battle rising on the horizon. You, Olivia, and you alone are the key to stopping the war before it truly begins," she confessed with that calm voice.

Lightning struck, slashing across the sky in a spear of white angry light. My eyes darted upward at the crack of thunder that followed. When I glanced back to the spot Zade's mother had hovered, she was gone.

I wrapped my soaked arms around myself, knowing the time had come for me to get out of the rain and back into the safety of the castle. Lingering would only bring trouble. The storm brewed an ominous omen as I dashed over the lawn with haste.

I snuck back through the castle, much like I had slipped out not long ago, and after changing into dry clothes I lay beside a sleeping Zade. It would be hours before he stirred, which gave me plenty of time to think… to strategize… to outmaneuver the witch.

I didn't sleep that night. I just lay in bed, my mind wheeling over all that had been revealed. And in the early hours of sunrise, while the sun chased the storm away, a plan formed. There was only one rival to something as hot as a volcano. Zade was that hot and Issik was the only one capable of combating such heat.

A dumb plan that would no doubt end badly, but it beat sitting on my ass and doing nothing. The others might be content to brood and pace, but this girl was breaking out her superhero cape.

With some help…

T'd been through every room on the first floor of the castle, gone up and down the stairs twice, searched both towers and still, Issik was nowhere to be found, but I'd been assured the Ice Prince hadn't left the grounds. Where could he be hiding? I ascended the staircase again. Every step had me convincing myself this was a stupid idea, but it was the only one I had. If I didn't act now…

It might be too late.

Time was pressing down on us, with another month coming to a close. My mind replayed the attack on Wakeland. Tianna had known I knew the location of the Star of Fire. What puzzled me was why she hadn't demanded I retrieve it right then and there, but that would have involved her actually being present, instead of a mirage—an illusion.

Tricky, tricky witch.

With her Pool of Mirrors, it was damn near impossible to be one step ahead of her, not when she constantly glimpsed at the past, present, and even the future. We might already be doomed, but it wasn't going to stop me from trying to save my home. I should have found a way to destroy the pool when I'd been her prisoner, but the idea of ruining an item of magic left a nasty tang in my mouth.

I passed a hall of open sleeping chambers, peeking my nosey ass into each one. *Where the hell is he?* My teeth ground together.

Sure, when I actually wanted to find him, he was nowhere to be seen. Every other day, one of them was stuck to my side, but nooo, not today. Today they suddenly decided to give me all the space in the world.

I lost count of the number of doors I searched before seeing the familiar whitish-gold hair. Today he had it tied back at the nape of his neck. The sun from the roof tower warmed my cheeks as I stepped outside. "You are very hard to track down," I admitted, sounding breathy.

Issik was sitting on an iron chair, sipping a clear liquid straight from the bottle. His attention was focused on something I couldn't see, a place in the distance. I could only guess it was Iculon.

At the sound of my voice, he turned his head in my direction, brows lifted. "I like to come up here to get away, to think."

Heat rippled off the obsidian tiles blanketing the roof as I padded over to him and slipped into his lap, wrapping my arms around his neck. "The view is breathtaking," I said, staring out into the vast, endless sky.

Issik's hand moved to cover my knee. "Is everything okay?" he asked.

My lips slightly curved into a smile, turning on the charm. "I need your help."

His eyes slid to mine, cool and questioning. "This is going to get me in trouble, isn't it?"

I squeezed his hand, appreciating the callouses against my tender skin. "Before you say no, hear me out."

"I'm listening," he conceded, inclining his head toward me.

"I want you to take me inside the volcano." There. I'd said it. Clear. Cut. And dry. No point in beating around the bush. None of us had the time.

"No," he stated flatly and without hesitation.

I had expected a decisive no. If he had agreed readily, I would have been disappointed, but I wasn't giving up yet. "You're being unreasonable."

"Me? I'm not the one who is suggestion a suicide mission."

My fingers toyed with the ends of his ponytail. "Are you saying that going into Titan Mountain would kill you?"

His features remained impassive and unyielding. "No. Zade and I are the only ones who can withstand the heat, but for two different reasons. The volcano would welcome him, the heir of the kingdom, because he was born from part of this land."

I prayed I hadn't underestimated my persuasive skills. "And you are his polar opposite. You're exactly what I need to get me inside the volcano. It makes sense," I pleaded.

He rubbed at the stubble on his chin, little white whiskers. "You don't think we've considered this, contemplated all possibilities?"

"I don't want you to just fly me into the volcano, I want you to freeze it, just long enough for me to find the star," I explained.

Issik cringed and opened his mouth to object, then clamped it shut. I watched as he brood over the idea. "There must be another way. It's too dangerous, Olivia. A warriors heart you have, but even the greatest warriors know when to walk away from a fight."

I refused to walk away. Not from this. "We need to nullify the threat, and the best way to do that is to cool off the volcano. After we get what we went there for, Zade can thaw the lava if it doesn't naturally do so." My guess was not even Issik's dragon breath of ice could contain the molten lava living inside the volcano for long, but I had to try.

His eyes flickered as he warred with the idea. "I should tell you no and walk away, but I have a feeling you'd be stubborn enough to go to Titan Mountain on your own, and I can't let you do that."

My lips started to curve in victory, maybe too soon.

"But..." His hand slid down to my thigh, sending a tendril of ice through my clothes at his touch. "I could lock you up in your room."

Color drained from my face. "You wouldn't dare," I hissed. He knew what I'd been through with Tianna, how she had locked me up and of the nightmares that still kept me up most nights.

Those crystal icy eyes softened. "No, I wouldn't, but I probably should."

Laying my palm over his chest, I savored the steady beat of his heart. "Issik, you know this is the only option we have, and we need to act before Tianna has a chance to see what our plan is."

"And just what is our plan?"

"It's easy. You ice the volcano, we fly in, I snatch the stone, we leave."

He shook his head, knowing damn well it wouldn't be that simple. Not with me. "Do you fully understand what you're undertaking? You will have the power of three stars residing inside you."

I hadn't thought about what it would mean for me. All that

mattered was saving them, but now that Issik had mentioned it... I chewed on my lower lip, contemplating the implications. "Is that something I should be worried about?"

Issik's chest exhaled against me. I was still in his lap, and neither of us stirred. "None of us know if your human body will be able to sustain harnessing the four abilities. The magic of the stones was meant for the most powerful dragons, the kings. When we set out to break the curse, we had no idea the stars still existed."

A part of me had blocked my mind from thinking about the consequences, only because the first two stones had given me unimaginable skills, but even with that power I still felt like me. My physical body hadn't changed. "This is something the four of you have discussed, and never thought to mention to me?"

He lifted a hand, brushing the pad of his thumb over my bottom lip. "We didn't want to worry you for nothing, especially since you handled two with fair ease. Jase wanted to test your abilities, your limits, see how your body responded over time."

So my lessons were more than learning to protect myself. Jase was lucky he was in a dark place. I would have marched up to his room, kicked in the door, and gave him a very loud and vulgar piece of my mind. "And what was the almighty Tranquility dragon's conclusion?"

The corner of Issik's lips twitched. "Inconclusive. But we're all concerned. This isn't just about freeing us from the curse or protecting the home we love. You're a part of this, and protecting you is as important as the rest."

I inclined my head to his so we were nearly cheek-to-cheek while I stared out into the clear blue skies. I'd been through too much, endure too much pain to turn back now or to be frightened of who I might become. "What's life without a little risk?"

Issik's arms wrapped around me. "We're about to find out," he murmured, breathing in the scent of me. "You know the others are going to kill me."

I turned my head slightly towards him and pressed a kiss to his cheek. "I'll protect you."

He sighed. "That's what worries me."

Just days ago, I'd seen such horror and sorrow, and now, I was gearing up to a battle of my own. The blade Jase had given me was strapped to the outside of my black leather pants, and another smaller one hidden in the inside of my boot—which I'd swiped from the training area earlier in the day, after I'd spoken with Issik.

The Ice Prince's face was a mask of patience as he stood in the foyer, ready to carry me into the fiery depths of Titan Mountain. I wasn't prepared for what I was about to do, not mentally or physically, but I had little choice in the matter. This was my destiny. Whether I ever dreamed it would be of such importance or not was inconsequential. For now, I'd face what was ahead, and the consequences that came with my choices.

My choices.

Not Tianna's.

Not Jase's, Zade's, Kieran's, or Issik's.

This wasn't only about them or the witch who cursed them. It was about me. About the people who lived here and their future.

"Have you changed your mind?" Issik asked, peering down at me.

I winked. "Not a chance."

We stepped out on the veranda as stars sparked into existence. His shift from man to dragon was as beautiful as that first snowfall that glistened on the trees with silver, like they'd been dipped in stardust. He was all frost, animal, and magic.

Every inch my Ice Prince.

He waited until I was seated on top of him, tilting his angular head so he could see me with one eye. *"Time to take that ride."*

He leaped off the edge as he had the first time, to save me when I fell from the balcony at Wakeland. Each dragon had its own flying technique. Issik's happened to be plummeting at a vertical drop before unfolding his wings.

It scared the ever-loving crap out of me each time.

With every foot, we flew faster and faster over the kingdom, staying close to the surface. "How pissed are the others going to be?" We had left in the dead of night, waiting until Zade, Jase, and Kieran slept.

"If we come back with the star, it won't matter what we did."

I wasn't so sure if that was true, but I liked the way Issik thought. "How old is the witch?" I asked. If she had cursed them a hundred years ago and still managed to look as if she was only twenty, I'd say that's one hell of an aging spell she was cooking. She was a witch, not immortal, at least I believed.

Issik dipped under a low hanging branch, making sure to clear it enough so not to whack me in the head. *"Older than any of us, possibly older than our fathers. She was not born here in the Veil."*

"How is she able to stay so young?"

"We've never figured that part out. A spell, no doubt, but she must draw her youth from somewhere, someone, or something."

And we knew it wasn't from the stars. "Do you think she knows what we are going after the stone?"

"She can't keep tabs on all four of us every second of every day. Even the witch needs sleep. Let's hope fate is on our side tonight."

I was going to need more than fate. A hell of a lot more. I sighed, taking a moment to appreciate the night, the balmy breeze on my face, and the dragon who trusted me. It could all end tonight.

"Are you having second thoughts?" he mused, feeling my tension, my melancholy.

He could sense my emotions, my rising doubt, but I answered him with the truth. "I'm nervous and scared, but it doesn't change what I have to do."

"In case I haven't told you how brave I think you are. You are, you know. Brave. Bold. Brilliant. And resilient as hell." I swore I heard a smile in his voice and it made me chuckle, relieving some of the tension tight in my shoulders. *"And I don't need a bond or stone to tell me how much I love you."*

My arms wrapped tight around his thick neck and I pressed my cheek against his scales. "I love you too. So much."

In the silence that fell between us, I scrambled to find any scrap of bravery hiding inside me. I wanted to make Issik proud, to show him I was indeed brave, regardless of the fear making my insides tremble. We swept up with the rolling hills, approaching our destination.

Titan Mountain.

There it was. I swallowed, my fingers clenching against Issik, and the dragon loosed a breath, causing a chill to ripple in my bones. My chest sank.

The obsidian mountain itself didn't glow, but the pulsing lava inside made it seem as if it were. We circled over the mouth of the volcano, and being this close, the mountain felt ancient. Wafts of heat drifted toward us, causing my skin to glisten with a fine coat of sweat.

"Have you ever been inside a volcano?" I asked, staring into the pit of rich molten fluid, ebbing and flowing below us, its sparks of embers floated in the air.

He circled over the top of the mountain, keeping a healthy distance above. *"Believe it or not, no. And I'm hoping this will be a one-time thing."*

"You and me both," I muttered. "We'll be in and out before anyone misses us," I assured over the howling wind.

"Are you trying to convince me or yourself?"

"Does it matter?" It didn't change how I felt about sneaking out, deceiving the others.

"Here we go, Little Warrior. Hold on tight."

My mouth went a bit dry.

Taking us higher in the air, Issik maneuvered himself into position directly about the mouth of the volcano. When he was satisfied, he plunged, unleashing a stream of ice as he dove in, to squelch the heat before it reached us. My knees squeezed against him, holding myself firm on his back.

Underneath me, his already cool body turned frigid, ice filling his veins. Steam rose from the pit in blinding waves from the collision of fire and ice. Due to the sheer amount of lava, he barely had time to inhale before he was blowing out another stream of frosty dragon's breath.

When the idea had formed, I'd pictured what would happen to ride an ice dragon into a volcano and all that it would entail. But this... this battle with nature, fighting the natural order of things...

It was beyond anything my mind could even think.

Was it too much, even for Issik?

It was hard to fathom there was anything the Ice Prince couldn't withstand, couldn't fight. He was a born warrior in my mind, tough and ruthless. But the freeze had taken a considerable amount of effort and most of his power, draining my already weakened dragon. It caused a not so graceful landing. Flaring out his wings, he tried to steady us, but we crashed down onto the frozen pool of lava too fast, too unevenly. I lost my grip and tumbled off Issik, over the ice, the freezing glass scraping my palms and knees as I skidded on its surface.

"Are you alright?" Issik groaned, working out his own kinks as he stood to his full dragon height.

I shoved to my feet, testing the durability of my own limbs. Nothing appeared broken. "I'm fine," I assured, brushing at my pants and took in our surroundings.

Holy mother of God.

I felt as if I'd fallen into a giant crystalized crater. The walls surrounding us were a glossy black that reflected light from the stars, and the frozen lava that glowed under inches of ice.

"Good, now let's find what we came for, and get the hell out of here."

I understood his need to be quick. Something about being inside the volcano made me feel claustrophobic, as if the walls were closing in on me, suffocating me. It could have also been the air quality, but my lungs were burning, screaming at me to escape.

Without wasting another precious moment, I set forth to find the stone. That tug inside me that drew me to this place gave a yank. It was as if the other stars were trying to connect with the missing ones, as though they recognized one another, like long lost sisters destined to be reunited.

My eyes scanned inch by inch of the volcano walls, seeking out that tiny stone of power. Issik took the higher points, stretching his long neck and lifting up to his full dragon height as I stayed close to the icy surface.

'Keeper of stars. Key of dragons. Have you come to save me?' an otherworldly voice broke through the silence.

My entire body went still, an action that didn't go unnoticed by my companion.

"What is it?" Issik demanded.

Feet planted and body still, I moved only my eyes, trying to pinpoint the origin of the voice. "I-the star… it's talking to me."

Issik watched me as if he was attempting to figure me out. *"Well, that's new."*

"You're telling me," I mumbled.

"What is it saying?"

I resumed my search, allowing my instincts to guide me. The star was here, so close. "It wants me to find it."

"This isn't the first time you've heard its call, is it?" he guessed, noticing my not so shocked expression at the stone whispering to me.

"It called on me once before," I admitted, shaking my head. "The others didn't speak, not with actual words or voices. It was more of a feeling, a nudge."

"Your bond to them is stronger. It would only make sense that the link flourished with it."

Fabulous. Can't wait to see what weird shit happens next.

"Where are you? Where are you?" I chanted at the stone, knowing I didn't have long to linger. My eyes scanned the cavern, the moon directly above providing enough light to see. Why the hell hadn't I thought to bring a lantern? *"Tell me where to find you?"* I beseeched, projecting the thought into whatever thread that allowed me to hear the Star of Fire.

"Are you asking me or the stone? This talking inside your head is very confusing," Issik admitted.

I hushed him, and the only sound that trailed was my breathing. My ears stretched, trying so hard to hear something, but nothing. I groaned, rolling my eyes and there it was… the pull. As if I was playing a game of hot and cold. My eyes raked over the ground we stood on, searching the frozen pool of lava.

And I saw it. A flash of firelight sparkled in the center of the pit. It seemed to pulse with an unearthly heartbeat.

The Star of Fire, shining like a ruby behind a film of glass.

My chest thundered.

'Free me,' the stone whispered in a song, an invitation. *'Free me.'*

I took a step toward it.

How? How was I going to get it out from under two inches of ice without destroying the very thing allowing me to stand? Without the ice, the temperature would rise, the lava would flow. "Do you see it?" I asked Issik.

He exhaled through his nostrils. *"The thing under your feet? It's difficult to see with you stepping on it."*

I rolled my eyes and shifted to the right, crouching. "Any suggestions on how to get it out?"

"None that will be easy," he rasped, but I could already see his eyes calculating. *"Step aside,"* he advised.

"What are you going to do?"

'Claim me,' the star lured like a siren's song.

"Loosen up the ice a bit," he informed. *"We can't stand here staring at it. Nothing a spike and my claws can't fix. Find something to hold onto."*

I backed away a few steps and pressed my spine into the rough wall of the cavern. My palms splayed out on either side of me, gripping the igneous dark gray rocks. Issik slid his tail alongside him, so it was directly above the throbbing crimson stone.

Something cold went through me. A different kind of chill. Not Issik, but…

He lifted his tail, bringing the spikes clustered at the end down on the ice. The walls shook underneath my hands and my feet rumbled. Pebbles and debris rained over us, but Issik unleashed a wing, sheltering me from injury.

I waited a heartbeat or two for the dust to settle, but from within the swirling smog, a figure arose, born of pure darkness. I knew from the slim, female form, the blazing flowing hair, and flawless beauty of the face that stared at me with wry humor… I knew I was in deep shit.

Tianna.

"So glad you saved me the trouble of having to do all the dirty work," the witch drawled with a wicked smile.

Issik and I both blinked with surprise. In retrospect, we shouldn't have been the slightest bit shocked by her arrival. It had really only been a matter of time. I just wished it had been after I had the Star of Fire in my possession. Now it was a fight to see who got it first.

Tianna fought dirty, so my odds of winning weren't good. Not in the slightest.

My fingers curled into fists at my side. That fucking witch had the worst timing. One more minute. I only needed a single minute more. Was sixty goddamn seconds too much to ask for?

"On it," Issik's voice flittered into my mind.

"That's not what I meant," I groaned.

But it was too late.

The distraction was already in motion, and there was nothing I could do to stop it, except thank him and take advantage of the opportunity. I just had to reach the stone, touch it…

I shoved off the wall at the same time Issik hurled that thorny tail toward Tianna. The witch only laughed as his tail went right through her, destroying the illusion. On a ripple the witch disappeared, leaving behind the echo of her nail-grating laugh.

More games. More tricks.

She reappeared with a pack of shadow hounds on both sides of her, growling and snapping. I was forced to skid to a halt, or risked colliding with the witch.

"Grab the stone and get ready to fly," Issik ordered, his voice booming with authority.

The hounds made of nothing but darkness, fangs, and razor claws attacked, flying over sheets of ice as if their pads were made of grippers. They dashed past me, going for the real threat. Issik. That left the stone between Tianna and me.

Issik's teeth sunk into a hound's neck, cleaving the beast's head off. Its body fell to the ground. The Ice Prince swirled right, but the other three hounds were at his feet, snarling and clawing. They jumped onto his back, one by one.

"Olivia!" he bellowed. *"Now! Get the stone!"*

His voice snapped me into motion. I had to get to the star before Tianna did. I *would* get the stone.

She must have seen the resolve on my face. The air swelled with magic as I gauged the distance between the stone and me against Tianna's position. Her eyes seemed to read my thoughts.

"So brave," she crooned. "I wouldn't do that if I were—"

Too late. I lunged.

It wasn't a graceful dive. No. I more or less threw myself forward and belly flopped on the slippery floor, landing five feet from where the stone was nestled in shards of broken ice. I didn't let myself think about Tianna, about where she was. I didn't allow myself to dwell on the pain shooting through my body or the air that had been knocked out of my lungs. I forced myself to scramble to my knees and dragged my battered body across the ice. My knees sagged behind me, but I persevered as the star coaxed me, offering me the strength and encouragement I needed.

Issik let out a yelp just as Tianna's foot came down on my hand, crushing the bones against the ice. I cried out in agony.

"Give me the stone or… I can make this feel like child's play." Her foot pressed down harder to emphasize her dark promise.

My teeth slammed onto my lower lip, biting against the pain that ripped through my hand. A deafening roar that made my head ring resonated throughout the cavern, but I couldn't think about Issik and the hounds. Couldn't think about the regret of not bringing the others. Couldn't think about how Issik and I were going to go up against the witch alone.

I had to move now. Every inch felt a mile, and even with one arm pinned to the ground, I didn't stop reaching for the star. It was so close. I could nearly feel its pulsating energy at my fingertips.

Toying with me, she allowed me a few inches, and just went my nails were digging through the ice, searching, she shifted all of her weight. The crunch of bone fracturing hit me before the pain brought tears to my eyes. Black dots blanketed my vision.

I screamed.

And screamed.

With that bellow of agony, I released a deadly concoction of poison and tranquility. The green and purple mist swirled together—separate, but one moving force, giving me the opening I needed, leaving Tianna to deal with the mist of magic.

The earth shuddered underneath me. I didn't dare look, but I heard it and knew I had to hurry. My fingers stretched and stretched until I thought the tendons would snap. Every bone and muscle in my other hand was screaming at me, but I managed to pull myself up to the hole Issik had created. Water was pooling onto the ice, melting.

Hurry. Hurry. Hurry.

Inside the crystallized lava, the Star of Fire sparkled, such stark contrast as my fingers shoved aside the broken pieces, reaching for it again.

"Give it to me," Tianna shrilled, like a wild woman on the verge of losing her shit.

I don't know what kind of sorcery she had unfurled to combat the effects of poison and tranquility, but it hardly mattered now. She had released her foot from atop my broken hand. "Go to hell," I hissed and closed my fingers over the stone.

My triumph was short-lived. Tianna let a shriek that threatened to take down the volcano on top of us. I didn't have time to register what was happening to me, because the floor underneath me groaned.

Fuck.

Crackle. Creak. Crackle.

Horror coiled in my gut. The ice wasn't going to hold. This was it. The floor was going to collapse, taking the stone and I with it.

I had succeeded in finding the Star of Fire, had been able to beat the witch by getting it first, only to die.

I rolled over on my back, cradling the star and my broken hand against my chest. A hundred bright glamorous dots glittered through the mouth of the volcano, splashing my face with moonlight. I thought I might pass out, was close to dropping off into the splendid abyss void of pain, fear, and panic.

Yes, there was loads of panic coursing through me… along with something else. My breath became a ravaging flame in my lungs, burning and roaring. I tried to sit up, knew I had to move, had to get out of the volcano, but the shooting pain kept me immobile. The ice continued to crack and crinkled underneath me.

"Shit," I hissed.

"Naughty girl," Tianna taunted with a slow smile, hovering over me.

If I had the strength and the means, I would have ripped out her throat. Someday, I promised myself. Someday. Right now, I could barely move, hardly breathe. The witch made a move toward my closed fist, but the ground underneath us trembled, knocking her off balance. She fell a few feet from me.

I needed to move, but my veins, my bones, my muscles all felt as if they were baking in an oven. The Star of Fire was intense as it granted me its power.

"Get to your feet. Now!" a voice in my head demanded.

Not Issik, and yet it was familiar, but my terror was making it difficult to decipher who the voice belonged to.

"Olivia. Get up. You must!"

The sense of urgency had me moving and lifting to my knees. A scream ripped from my throat as the ground fractured in three different directions, and my legs found themselves on opposite sides of the floating glaciers. My balance teetered just as strong talons grabbed me, wrenching me upward, and not a moment too soon. I glanced down to see the little pad of ice I'd been kneeling on be swallowed by a bubbly wave of liquefied lava.

I sucked in a gasp of air through my teeth.

Zade used the powerful flaps of his leathery wings to lift us up before the heat scorched the skin of my muscles and bones. Not a pretty picture.

"Cutting it close, don't you think?" he asked snarkily.

"I could say the same thing," I muttered, staring at the ice being swallowed by bubbling lava. Tianna was gone, vanished from the inside of the volcano, and Issik was above us, flying out of the mouth.

"What were you thinking, going inside the volcano?" Zade scolded. His claws wrapped around me securely, but gently.

"That I had to get the star before the witch."

"You could have been killed. Issik knows better than to put your life at risk."

"Don't blame him. This was my idea." The stone was clasped tightly in my hand, its power swimming in my veins in a fiery delight. "It might not have gone as smoothly as I hoped, but I got the star."

We broke free of Titan Mountain, the night unfolding around us. *"I felt it, the release of my chains, but it doesn't look like the night is over yet."*

It had been wishful to think the witch had vanished and admitted defeat. Not her style. Waiting with an army of supernaturals at the base of the volcano, however, that was more her thing.

"Shit," I rasped, seeing the sea of warriors that greeted us, stretching out to the border of the Nameless Lands.

Kieran joined us in the sky then, flying beside Zade. *"Well, isn't this a picturesque slice of hell?"*

"Where's Jase?" I asked, realizing everyone was here but him.

Zade motioned with his head to the ground. *"Down there."*

Wonderful. Jase was on ground control.

What was the point of this? Did she think she could show up with an army and we'd hand over the stone? It was too late. I'd already been granted the power from the Star of Fire. It was swimming in my veins, burning like liquid fire.

"Get me down there," I ordered. I wasn't about to let Jase face her alone.

"Are you smoking crack? I am not dropping you right in the middle of a fight. Not happening, Little Gem." Zade kept to the skies with my disapproval.

I wiggled in his hold, but it was a waste of energy. There was no way I was breaking free from a dragon's strength, even one not at full force.

"You're going back to the castle, where I can protect you and the stone."

"Sorry to disappoint, but Olivia and I have unfinished business." Tianna's voice exploded around us, everywhere and nowhere.

"Go to hell!" Kieran yelled. He swooped down, releasing a stream of poison over her army.

She laughed. "So predictable. The four of you never change."

In the distance, where the villages of Crimson dwelled not far from the castle, smoking cinders burned. Her army had gone in and trampled the town, windows shattered, walls crumbled, and people screaming. It was much like the attack on Wakeland. So much for those protective measures.

Tianna was showing her dominance, letting us know she would find other ways to hurt the descendants if they didn't give her what she desired.

"How should I punish you?" she purred, and I could sense her slithering over my skin, like a serpent.

"Cut the bullshit!" I yelled. "Enough of the games. Show yourself."

A piercing roar split through the waning night.

Jase!

Zade's chest rumbled with unbridled fury at the state of his lands, and he shot toward the ground, straight for Tianna's army of misfits.

"Zade," Kieran warned, but the fire dragon was past reasoning. We all were.

Zade landed in the center of her ranks with a ground-shaking thud, and released a torch of inferno from deep within him. Fire rained over my head and the troops closest to us incinerated into dust. The ash of their bodies blew away with the wind. I coughed, trying to shield my face as I slipped out from under Zade's talons, and rose to my feet, cradling my fractured hand against my chest.

Desperately, I searched the mass of chaos for Jase.

Issik landed on the other side of me with Kieran at my back. I was walled in by dragons, a hurricane of toxic masculinity, all equally as fearsome. *"You're not taking what's ours. Not again. Not ever,"* Kieran growled.

Where the hell was Jase?

Through the smoke and the stench of charred flesh, a dark shadow materialized. The army parted, making way for the slim figure as it walked toward us. Her dress was covered in raven feathers that fluttered with her graceful and regal movements. I glared at the witch. Behind her, she dragged a silver chain that clanged through the darkness like death bells ringing. It was a leash.

I'd seen one like it before. My stomach threatened to heave, a tumble of nasty memories assailing my mind. Tianna gave the shackle a yank.

Would this nightmare ever end?

A figure stumbled forward, the spelled chains secured around his wrists and ankles, making walking problematic. My world stopped moving and the three descendants beside me stiffened. I shook my head, unable to believe what I was seeing.

"Jase." His name was a sob that trembled on my lips. I leaned against Issik's massive leg for support.

No. No. No.

This was bad, so fucking bad.

How had Tianna captured Jase? My best guess, while we'd been fighting for the Star of Fire, she had been distracting us with her illusions. The real her had gone for Jase, knowing he was alone, that his hatred of her clouded his judgment, and that his strength was diminished.

I had a theory about the descendant's powers dwindling. It seemed that from the moment I released the invisible bonds holding them to the Veil, their abilities weakened in a more rapid pace. The closer we got to breaking the curse, the weaker they became, and since Jase was the first dragon I freed from his chains, his power had drained quicker than the others. Of the four, it was Issik who seemed to be the most resilient.

"Let's make this simple for everyone. Give me the star and I'll release your dragon." Although there were four of us, Tianna was speaking directly to me, as if I made the important decisions.

Funny. But in this case, I did hold the ability to strike a bargain, the Star of Fire lay glowing in my hand. "And if I refuse?" I nearly choked on the words, emotion clogging my throat. I couldn't take my eyes off Jase.

Tianna knew there was nothing… nothing I wouldn't give to save them, including the stone now warm in my hand. I fumbled with it in my fingers, turning it over. Could I really give her the star to save Jase? He might never forgive me… but he would be alive.

Wrath twisted Tianna's face. "Then not all of you will leave here alive. The time of playing nice is over."

"Don't do it. Don't give her the stone," Jase begged, and I hated, absolutely hated seeing him stripped down to a prisoner, pleading. From the powerful, born leader he was, reduced to a dog Tianna controlled.

How could I not? I couldn't let him die. I just couldn't. It would break my heart into a million fragmented pieces. I couldn't do what he asked. He might be willing to die to save his brothers, to save me, but I couldn't… I refused to let him sacrifice himself.

It would kill me.

I squared my shoulders, taking a step forward. "How do I know that you won't kill him even if I hand over the star?"

"Olivia," Jase snapped. "You can't." He turned his violet eyes to Issik, Kieran, and Zade. "Get her out of here," he ordered.

"I'm not going anywhere. Not without you," I declared, shoving aside the tears that had gathered in my eyes. I gritted my teeth.

A little, cold smile curled Tianna's lips, as if she could see my resolve dwindling. "Smart girl. These chains keep him from shifting, a clever little spell."

"You must," Jase argued. "Now go—"

His demand was cut off as Tianna flicked her hand. Pain fractured in Jase's eyes, and he fell to his knees. Frantically, his hands flew to his throat, gasping for air that wasn't there.

"Stop!" I screamed.

Her cynical grin only widened as she angled her head, in a condescending gesture that made me want to skin her alive. I wasn't the only one enraged by her actions.

Issik stomped the ground in icy fury. Kieran and Zade tightened their ranks around me, while the army at Tianna's back hissed and shifted on their feet, eager to attack. It was only a matter of moments before a fight erupted.

I could barely hear, could barely think about what Tianna was offering, what Jase was barking. Kieran spread his wings, the moonlight highlighting the veins that ran the length of them, and pure terror hit me. They were going to leave him here… with her.

Kieran moved to pick me up, but I ran forward, toward Tianna, ignoring the searing pain in my hand. "Fine. I'll give you the stone. But you release him first."

"*Olivia*," four voices hissed in objection.

I raised my brows. "Do we have a deal?"

"If you cross me…" Her white teeth flashed with every word. "Your suffering will be long, and I plan to be very thorough."

"Sounds delightful," I snapped, ignoring the silent pleas of the dragons behind me.

With another wave of her hand, she released the spell preventing Jase from breathing. His palms sunk to the ground as he gulped in air, releasing the burn in his lungs. "No," he rasped.

I kept my focus on Tianna. If I looked at Jase, I would break and I wanted nothing to get in the way for what I was about to do. Fear no longer gripped me, not for myself.

Placing one foot in front of the other, I moved further away from my dragons and toward Tianna, stopping just short of where Jase was slumped to his knees. "Go," Jase breathed. "Run."

"They really are magnificent," Tianna admitted, her silver eyes glittering. "It's a shame they wouldn't yield when I gave them the chance."

"Release him," I demanded just as Jase shoved off the ground and lunged at me.

Tianna snapped and his chains tightened, cranking him backward. His wrists were ringed with blood, but he didn't seem to notice.

"The stone for the dragon. That's the deal. No tricks."

I snorted. That was rich coming from her, but I held out my hand, opening my palm to reveal the glowing crimson stone. It pulsed with a burning light.

Like a woman possessed, her eyes brightened, fixed on the star. She lifted her slim fingers, nails painted black, and reached for it. In a simultaneous movement, she released the chains holding Jase prisoner, just as her fingers grazed the stone.

Jase exploded into his dragon, brutally towering over us. *"No!"* his voice thundered in my head.

But it was too late.

Something unexpected happened, something no one predicted, least of all me.

Together Tianna and I held the Star of Fire and the next second we found ourselves ensnared by the stone, trapped in our own little bubble. Untouched by the world around us. Unable to move. An unending flame of energy surged from the star, joining my power with the witch's.

Her life seemed to flow to me, her power mine for the taking.

Those silver eyes blanched.

Power shuddered through me, a void of ruthless magic flowed and flowed, a dam ready to burst. The star became a vessel and linking me to Tianna's magic. What the hell was happening? I tried to pull away, but it was useless, the energy of the stone was too powerful.

I had to let go or risk being incinerated to ashes.

"Olivia?" Kieran's voice whispered in my head.

Kill her. Kill her, the words chanted in my head. Not the stars, not the dragons, but my own voice. *Strike now. Kill her.*

I didn't know how.

Someone cried out my name again. Zade? Jase? I wasn't sure. I couldn't move, couldn't speak.

Nothing I did released the hold the star had. My fingers wouldn't budge. My muscles wouldn't listen to the commands of my brain. Tianna and I were trapped by the stone, held captive by its power.

Then something inside me splintered.

Fire exploded out of me. Not in a dragon's breath, but in a burst of energy. I had no other way to explain what happened. The molten flames had gathered inside me, and I was a glittering figure of flaming gold.

"What have you done?" Tianna hurled at me, pure rage contorting her features into something not quite human. Her eyes faltered as she stared at the stone in our hands.

"Olivia!" a voice roared. Not just any voice. Jase's.

Power burst from the stone in a white-hot light that shot through me, delivering an equal blinding blow to Tianna. Sparks showered over us and we were each thrown back, severing our link to the star.

I crashed to the floor, my head cracking against the ground.

The four dragons yelled my name again and again, but it was too late.

Seconds later I blacked out, only to find that I was staring at myself beside five ghostly women dressed in white. I recognized their faces. They were the mothers' of Tobias, Jase, Kieran, and Zade. The fifth, the one I'd never seen, I knew to be Issik's mother. She had the same white-blonde hair as her son, as well as those piercing eyes.

I gaped down at my body, a sick sense of dread overcoming me. One of my legs was oddly angled, definitely broken and blood pooled around my head, soaking into the ground. I tried to reach out, to touch myself, but it was as if I was far away. Another dimension possibly, no longer in the world of the living, yet somewhere in between life and death.

A flash of black caught the corner of my eye, followed by another and another. The four descendants rushed to my side, dropping to the ground beside me, while tears glistened in their eyes. They were in human form.

"What happened?" I sobbed to the women in white hovering close to me.

"You're on the brink of death," Jase's mother answered in a calm and leveled tone. Compassion settled on her pretty features.

"Tianna," I whispered. My eyes searched for the witch, just as Zade stood up, his face twisted into something animalistic and snarled. Tianna was sprawled on the ground a good twenty feet from where I was, but appeared in far better shape than me. She got to her feet, dusting off the folds of her dress.

"I'll kill you," Zade seethed. "You, traitorous piece of filth. You'll pay for what you've done to our families. What you've done to her."

A cruel smile tipped at Tianna's lips; white teeth gleaming. "Yes, well, now that I've got this…" She held up the Star of Fire in between her fingers. "You'll have to find another way."

Zade launched himself at the witch but her magic sent him sprawling backward, and then she hurled another blast at Kieran who had surged forward right after Zade. One by one the descendants launched themselves at Tianna, and wave after wave she countered their attacks with her spells.

My heart squeezed with pain, seeing them attack her and get knocked down again and again. They were relentless in their pursuit, but the witch was too strong. The army behind her was gone, misted by her magic. She stood alone against the descendants and still they lost.

It was my fault. I had failed them, failed to keep the star safe. If it hadn't been for me, Tianna never would have been able to get her hands on the Star of Fire. Jase had begged me not to save him, but I hadn't listened, couldn't bear the thought of him imprisoned by the witch.

And now…

Squeezing my eyes shut, I blocked myself from the fight. A deafening roar raged over the valley that shook the ground, but Tianna only laughed, tormenting them.

"You can come with us if you like." Tobias's mother extended an arm toward me. "You only need to take my hand. There will be no more pain, no more suffering."

I couldn't lie, the prospect of both had me considering it. I was so tired, so battered and beaten. This fight… I didn't know if I had the strength to continue, but as my eyes opened and I stared at the four dragons surrounding my body, all I could think was there would also be no more love.

I wasn't ready to let go of how they made me feel.

My head shook. "I can't. I must go back, for them."

"Good," Kieran's mother said with a nod. "They need you. This battle is far from over."

The former queen of Crimson smiled gently. "We'll send you back now, but this isn't goodbye, daughter."

"We will meet again," the five of them said as one.

Forming a circle around me, they each placed a hand on my shoulders, and everything around me went black. Silence fell and suddenly I was floating, soaring to a fleck of glittering silver light, like a tiny star beckoning me home. Then I was gasping for air. My eyes fluttered open and I was staring into Kieran's startled emerald eyes.

"Olivia?" His fingers brushed the blood-crusted hair away from my forehead. "You're alive," he whispered. "How?"

I was lying on a bed of gravel, the night sky sprawled out above me. No pain. No broken bones. No blood. The trip back to the living had somehow miraculously healed me. No. the fallen queens had healed me. I don't know how the women in white managed it, but I was eternally grateful.

"The other side kicked me out." My voice was scratchy and rough.

A chuckle of relief rumbled through his chest, and he leaned down, pressing a kiss to my lips. "I love you," he murmured.

"Get out of the way," a husky voice demanded. It was Zade. He stared down at me with glowing eyes of fire, and dropped down on the other side of me. "It's true."

I only smiled.

"Don't you ever die on us again," he demanded, cupping my chin in between his fingers. He turned my face left and right looking for injuries.

"See, that's the problem. The four of you are more important to me than my own life, so if dying was the only way to save you, I would gladly take my last breath."

I loved them. Deeply. Madly. Truly.

Issik and Jase were also there. They each took a hold of my hands, and I relished in their steady touch. We were together again, safe. That single thought brought it all rushing back to me.

I sat up slowly. "Where is she?" I asked.

"Gone," Kieran replied, caressing my cheek with a knuckle.

"For now," Jase added, and a warm breeze ruffled his hair.

I gulped. "And the star?"

Ice hardness radiated from Issik's eyes. Not at me, I realized, but the witch. "She took it."

"I'm sorry." My voice was quiet when I spoke, and dread sunk in my gut. "I never should—"

Jase's brows furrowed. "Don't say it. Don't apologize. You're alive. That's all the matters."

"We'll get the stone back," Zade promised, but it didn't change the feeling of failure swimming inside me. I had let them down. "Besides, the chains binding me are gone, and the star's power transferred to you. I'd say tonight was still a win."

A hole formed in my chest. I couldn't say anything else, so I let Issik and Jase helped me to my feet, and I released a wobbly breath. We didn't know what Tianna had planned with the Star of Fire, or if she could use it at all.

Still, nothing good could come from it being in her possession.

"Let's get you home," Zade urged, gripping my hand.

Night was slowly receding, and in a few hours the sun would break, giving birth to a new day.

We'd survived. Tianna might have taken the Star of Fire, but I had stolen something from her. Magic.

I didn't know what to make of the change. It was more than the power of the three stars. Something else swam in my veins now. I wasn't sure how I felt about having a piece of her inside me, or what it meant, but when Tianna found out there'd be hell to pay. She didn't seem like the kind of witch who took kindly to stealing. It hadn't been my intention to take even a shred of her magic, but what was done was done.

"Are you okay?" Jase inquired, watching me with careful eyes. "What you did back there with the stone… that was unbelievable. You were literally engulfed in flames, your entire body."

"How did you do that?" Issik asked, the awe resounding in his deep voice.

That seemed like a lifetime ago, like a dream. Had I really burst into flames? Looking at my skin, you'd never be able to tell. Not a mark on me, no residual effect. "I don't know." My own surprise was written over my features. "It just happened."

Kieran only shook his head at me. "You're a bundle of surprises."

They had no idea.

Keeping Titan Mountain at our backs, we walked the border

between Crimson Kingdom and the Nameless Lands, heading for the castle—toward home. In spite of the suffering my body endured, my legs were stronger than they'd been before. My hand was healed, no longer shattered and I had more energy it seemed.

We were about to cut inward, going around the river of lava that flowed through the heart of Crimson when a movement caught the attention of the descendants.

Jase held out his hand, stopping us. "Wait. There is someone out there."

The four dragons went into warrior stance, regardless of how weary they were feeling. All I could think was, now what. Hadn't we had enough trouble for one night?

A hooded figure stood in a whirlwind of dust. He grew closer, and as my heart sped up, recognition immediately hit me. I knew that man. It was the wanderer, the one who had broken me out of Tianna's prison. What was he doing here? Had something happened?

The wanderer stopped in front of us and leaned on his wood staff, the wind ruffling the hood covering part of his face. The four dragons surrounding me all stiffened.

"Tobias?" Jase whispered.

To Be Continued...

ISSIK

THAWING FROST

BOOK FOUR

USA TODAY BESTSELLING AUTHOR

J.L WEIL

CHAPTER 1

A ray of orange light cleaved through the darkness, as I stared at the wanderer in front of me, my mouth gaping.

Tobias?

The name rang in my head. This wanderer was the fifth dragon, the one Tianna's curse had supposedly killed years ago. How could that be? He was an old man, nothing like the four healthy and strong descendants flanking me.

"Tobias?" Jase called, his violet eyes a mixture of disbelief and suspicion. "Is that really you?"

I had no idea how they recognized their friend, under the white hair peppering his cheeks and chin. It covered most of his weathered face, leaving just the twinkle of his silver eyes visible under the hood.

Tobias nodded, and I swore his lips curved under the forest of hair. "It's been a long time," he confirmed in a deep, gruff timbre.

"How can this be? How are you here?" Zade asked, scrutinizing Tobias from head to toe as if he still couldn't believe it was true.

The descendants weren't about to take his word for it, regardless of what their intuition was telling them.

"We saw you, your dragon bones," Kieran clarified, while the sun glinted off his green-flecked hair—it laid flat for once, brushed back by his fingers.

Drops of sweat slid down Tobias brow as he wiped it. He had to be miserable in this heat, and under that cloak. "She killed the dragon, but not the man. The aging spell wore off, and the years caught up to me in a matter of weeks."

"Why didn't you come to us?" Jase questioned, a hurt scowl marring his lips.

Tobias' features pinched in a wince, when a gust of sandy wind hit his face. "As an old man? What could I possibly do to help you? I have no powers. No kingdom. Nothing to offer." Sadness flickered in his dove gray eyes. He'd lost everything. "I'd have only been in your way."

"Why would that matter?" Kieran challenged. "You're our friend, our brother."

A burdened sigh left Tobias' chest. "I couldn't leave my lands, even if the witch had destroyed them."

The Nameless Lands. They had once been alive, a place of beauty and life. Now they lay barren and void of life, except for Tianna and her army of warriors.

"You saved me," I reminded. "I wouldn't have escaped the witch's prison if it hadn't been for you."

Tobias's eyes scanned over the scar that ran along my cheek—a nasty gift from my time captured by the witch. "I'm glad to see you made it safely to the castle."

"I wouldn't be here if it wasn't for you. If there is anything I can do to repay you…" My words faded with the weight of truth.

I owed Tobias my life. My spine rocked with a shudder to even think of what else Tianna might have had in store for me. Would I still be in chains? Locked in the box of darkness? Would I have gone insane by now? I banished the thoughts from my head and shifted my body closer to Issik, who was nearest to me. His coolness gave me a reprieve from the sweltering heat of Crimson.

A curt nod was Tobias only answer.

Instinctively, Issik's fingers went to the small of my back, guiding me to lean into him, but he kept his gaze centered on Tobias. "Why have you come out of hiding now?" There was nothing friendly about Issik's tone.

I wondered the same thing. What made him risk the witch finding him? He had remained hidden for years. Perhaps she had discounted the old man, no longer considering him a threat. From what I knew of the wanderer, that was a very dumb move on her part.

Tobias's eyes narrowed a tad at Issik's protective gesture before they shifted, landing on me. "I have something… for you."

"For me?" I echoed, my brows pinching together. What could he want to give me?

Tobias nodded. "I know you're tired, and it has been a trying night. Meet me in two days, after you've rested, and before you travel to Iculon."

Jase stepped in front of me, and the maneuver wasn't lost on any of us. He would protect me, even from someone who had once been a friend. "Why should we trust you?"

To some degree, it was unnerving that Tobias knew of our movements and plans, but by process of elimination, it would only make sense we'd be heading to Iculon to recover the Star of Frost—the last dragon stone.

"You shouldn't trust anyone. The witch has eyes everywhere," Tobias warned, although we'd figured out that much on our own. "I don't expect you to blindly follow me, but can you afford not to come if it could mean destroying the witch? I have something in my possession that will aid you in your quest. It isn't wise to speak of it."

His gaze took to the skies, just as a gust of wind howled through the valley between the two lands. His fear of being overheard or watched was valid. Tianna did have spies all around us, and magic to see where her spies could not.

Meanwhile, Zade was monitoring Tobias's every move. I couldn't decipher if they were happy to see him, or wary of their friend. Maybe both. "What aren't you telling us?" he demanded.

Tobias lips curved into a tentative smile. "Come and I'll show you."

"Where?" Jase asked, his tone neither soft nor gentle. At that moment, he was every inch a dragon warrior with flaming violet eyes.

Tobias didn't so much as flinch, he himself having been a fearsome dragon. "At the border between these lands and Issik's kingdom. Dawn. She moves more freely during the night."

The four dragons shared a look, something passing between them that neither Tobias nor I were a part of. "We'll be there," Jase agreed.

"Until then," Tobias breathed, lifting his wooden staff to take a step back.

"Tobias, wait," Kieran called.

The wanderer paused and glanced up from under his hood, those silver eyes lit with question.

"Will you not come with us? Will you not join our fight? We are your brothers."

Not in blood, but in every other sense of the word they were. My heart cracked a little at the hope in Kieran's voice. I had no idea how they were feeling about seeing their old friend, knowing he was alive, but so frail, and without his power of persuasion.

Traces of remorse shone through Tobias's expression. "I can't. My place is here." His gaze indicated the barren land sprawling behind his back. "I will help with what I can, but I won't leave my kingdom. Not until this body has taken its last breath."

Jase bowed his head ever so slightly. "As you wish."

Issik's fingers fisted at the small of my back. "Let it be known that if you double-cross us, or if you harm Olivia in any way, I won't hesitate to give you that death you so desire."

I swallowed at the icy sharpness in Issik's words, glad I wasn't at the receiving end of the warning.

Yet, Tobias's eyes glimmered with amusement. "You haven't changed at all, old friend. I would be disappointed if you had." He gave Issik and the others a tip of his head, before he turned and hobbled off into the grainy air of the Nameless Lands. Within minutes, his outline was blurred by the winds of sand.

I wasn't looking forward to the journey back to Crimson castle. I wished we could willowphase. Perhaps the descendants should consider having a goblin, or two, in servitude in their kingdoms. It would make traveling a hell of a lot quicker and easier. I didn't mind flying, but this walking business… not for me, especially in my current state of sheer exhaustion. My legs strained to keep me upright, stumbling with nearly every step. I could no longer feel my feet.

"Come here, before you fall on your face," Jase murmured in annoyance.

He got no struggle from me as he lifted me into his arms. I swore I spent almost as much time being carried by them, as I did flying on their backs. I wrapped my arms around his neck, a frown taking over my lips. "What took you so long?" I muttered, stifling a yawn.

A low chuckle escaped his lips. "Pardon my thoughtlessness."

Soon, it became difficult to keep my head up, so I gave in, resting it between his shoulder and neck. "I'm not as helpless as you think," I declared, wincing at how weak my voice sounded.

Jase's face tilted slightly toward me, and the wisps of his breath touched my lips. "You were never helpless, Cupcake." His golden chest glistened in the sun as the first rays of morning crested the foothills.

"I missed you," I murmured, though I didn't need to tell him why I had.

Since the attack on Wakeland, Jase had more or less checked out, his anger becoming a living thing inside him. Not having him around had been lonely, which was odd since I was rarely ever alone, but I had missed him all the same. Tremendously so.

Smugness tugged at the corners of his mouth. "Is that so?"

"Yes. Believe it or not, I need you in my life."

With my confession, the drumming of his heart became a little faster under my palm. "Good, because you're stuck with us. You've become vital to my life."

His words made my breath catch. After a night like we had, I needed to hear I was still important, that they still cared for me as I did them. My eyes drifted to where Kieran, Zade, and Issik walked a few feet in front of us, talking amongst themselves. I couldn't hear what they were saying, but seeing them together had me thinking about what happened tonight—what we had gained… and lost.

"I'm so sorry," I whispered, tears of guilt and remorse dampening my eyes.

Sensing the sadness that hit me in mounting waves, Issik looked at me over his shoulder.

Jase stilled. "For what?"

"I lost the Star of Fire," I whispered, my shoulders sagging in defeat. My body might have healed from Tianna's torture, but I bore internal scars that still ached.

Failure.

I felt as if I had failed them. I hadn't been strong enough to protect the star. Tianna took it from me, and it almost cost me my life.

Jase's lips grazed over my cheek as he leaned closer. "You have nothing to apologize for. Nothing. You did not fail. What you did— standing up to her like that—took guts. You should be proud of yourself. I know that I'm proud of you."

Emotion clogged my throat, impeding my ability to say anything in response. How could he not hold me responsible for losing the star? But he didn't. I could see it in his star-flecked eyes. "I'm going to get it back," I managed to say. If it was the last thing I did, I would return the star to its rightful home. It belonged to Zade, and I wouldn't stop hunting for it, even long after the curse was broken.

Jase's powerful chest heaved an exhale. "I believe you. As much as the idea cripples me with fear—you against the witch—you might be the only person who can take the stone from her. I don't like it, but it is not my place to interfere with fate. If you were meant to recover the Star of Fire, I won't stand in your way. I will stand beside you. Always."

I rubbed my cheek against his, my arms tightening around his neck. "Thank you." I never wanted to let go. His trust in me melted my heart. Because of his confidence, I could find the courage to keep moving forward.

My Dragons gave me purpose. They gave me a home. And most of all, they loved me.

The faint scent of honeysuckle and burning leaves floated in the air, and my eyes closed.

I must have dozed off, because the next thing I knew, I was being tucked into bed—a soft blanket draped over me. Under hooded lashes, I stared up at Jase, now perched on the edge of the bed.

His tender fingers swept strands of hair away from my face. "Your eyes…" he murmured.

I blinked, opening my eyes a bit wider, the wonder in his voice pulling me further away from the haze of sleep. "What's wrong with them?"

Shadows crept over his features. "They are… glowing."

My nose wrinkled. Was that all? From the expression on his face, I thought that I'd perhaps gained a third eye on my forehead or something equally as dramatic. "I take it that's a bad thing?"

His thumb glided along the column of my neck, leaving behind tingles in its wake. "I wouldn't say bad, just different for a human."

News flash: I doubted I was only human anymore. I was becoming less and less the girl I'd once been. "I'm not so sure I am still human," I replied, voicing my thoughts.

"How does the prospect make you feel? To be something different, someone capable of magic?"

I chewed on my bottom lip. "Tired. And unsure of myself," I admitted, pausing for a moment to ponder if I should tell him about the other thing that had happened tonight. Picking at a thread on the blanket, I forced my eyes upward. "When Tianna touched the star, her power passed between us. I think I took a piece of her magic."

Worry coiled in his eyes, before he shielded them with a blank slate. "Interesting. As much as the idea frightens me, it could be something we can use against her. She won't be happy you stole her power, which puts an even bigger target on your back. You're sure that's what happened?"

Rubbing at my wrists, I thought back to those seconds when Tianna and I had been ensnared by the star. The strange tang in the back of my throat. The tingles that coursed through my veins, were so different than the fire that had raged alongside it. Tianna's power was dark and alluring.

"Anything is possible, but I…" My voice trailed as I gathered my thoughts. "I can feel it," I admitted, shifting on the bed so I could lay a hand in between my breasts. "Right here. It's like a little seed of magic has rooted inside me, sprouting into something more. Something dark." I risked glancing up, nervous of what I might see in his face.

Would he see me as tainted? Would he think I was wicked?

"Your power grows stronger. She felt it tonight, and that will make her think twice about going head to head with you next time."

Next time. The words echoed in my head. It was inevitable the witch and I would meet again, regardless that I wished otherwise.

The Star of Frost was out there, waiting for me. *Like calls to like—* that's what the women in white had told me. With the powers of tranquility, poison, and fire swimming inside me, I hoped locating frost wouldn't be difficult, but I also prayed it would be enough. After the loss of the fire stone, I was uncertain how that affected the descendants' curse. Would the portal be opened? Would the descendants be free? Or must I have the stones in my possession?

Tianna stealing the stone was a setback, but only time would tell how big or small that misfortune was. I had every intention of stealing it back and returning the star to Zade, the rightful heir.

Jase leaned down and kissed the tip of my nose. "Now, get some sleep." He moved to pull back, but I placed a hand on his forearm, and his brows lifted. "Do you want me to…"

I knew precisely what he was offering. "No tranquility."

Although, after everything that had happened, it was a tempting proposition. I didn't want the nightmares that would surely come. I didn't want to think about my eyes glowing, or what other changes I could expect from my body. I didn't want to think of anything at all.

"Stay with me," I whispered.

Jase didn't hesitate as he pulled back the quilt and settled in alongside me, the bed groaning as it adjusted to his weight. "Always," he murmured, opening an arm for me to curl into.

There were undoubtedly a million things he needed to discuss with the other descendants. He was probably dying for a shower. His skin still faintly smelled of smoke and sweat—which I found oddly comforting—but he put all those things aside to hold me as long as I slept, because I asked and it was what I needed.

He calmed me in a way no one else could.

I ssik paced in front of the onyx fireplace in Zade's study the following morning, his movements cold and sharp. His blond hair was unbound, dangling to the scruff on his chin. The gray tunic he wore stretched over his broad chest.

"Are we seriously considering meeting with Tobias in the Nameless Lands?" Zade growled from behind his massive ebony desk.

"We don't know anything about him, or why he's been hiding all these years. For all we know, this could be a trap. He could be working with Tianna. He *is* in her territory," Issik pointed out to us.

From my position on the chaise, my eyes trailed his movements from one side of the hearth to the other. "Actually, no. Tianna invaded *his* territory. Did you forget that he orchestrated my escape?" I reminded them, not sure why I felt the need to defend Tobias. It wasn't as if I knew the old man well.

Issik threw a glance in my direction that felt like chips of ice. "He could have helped you to gain our trust."

"There is no point in us snapping at each other," Jase snarled at Issik from the chair across from mine. A low wooden table sat between us, with books and parchment scattered on top of it.

I stifled a snort at his tone. That was rich. He was right there with the others, barking and puffing out his arrogant chest.

"Do any of us believe Tobias could have sold us out?" Shadows from the firelight danced over the side of Kieran's face. He leaned against the wall near the heart, arms crossed over his forest green shirt.

Sorrow doused the fire in Zade's eyes. "Not the Tobias we once knew, but Tianna is capable of turning even the most loyal of friends against one another. He has been out there in the Nameless Lands, alone, for years. We can't be sure the witch hasn't corrupted him, but we also can't disregard this meeting. If Tobias knows of something that could help destroy Tianna, I think it is worth the risk."

"I agree," Jase sighed. "I don't like it, but we can't continue to let her terrorize our kingdoms." It was evident in his expression that he was thinking about his own castle, and the spell now preventing him from entering his home.

My heart bled for him, for the people stuck inside.

Issik's jaw clenched. "She has half of the creatures in this world under her spell. It would be naive of us to think the same couldn't be done to one of us."

Zade's hand raked through his slicked back, coffee-colored hair. "If that's true, why hasn't she already pitted us against each other?"

"Because she needs you," I answered plainly. "It is the only way she can get the stars. Her goal has always been to gain the power of the dragon stones."

The air simmered with rage. Four dragons each expelling their hatred for one woman simultaneously. From across the room, Kieran's eyes blazed a bright green. "I'm going to peel the skin from her body, and poison her slowly."

"Knowing Tianna, she might thoroughly enjoy the experience," Jase coolly added.

I pressed my lips into a thin line, understanding Kieran's need for revenge and justice. "We need to go to the Nameless Lands. I don't know him as you guys do, but it feels important." I couldn't give them a solid reason. I only had intuition and this tug in my chest telling me to go.

I was asking them to trust me.

Four sets of eyes studied me with a mixture of intrigue, confusion, and doubt. "It's settled. We leave in the morning," Jase decided, giving the final word on the issue.

I stood on what seemed like the edge of the world. Wind and sand spun out before us, making the visibility dodgy. Red and gold danced on the horizon as morning broke over the land. We stood atop a dune, overlooking the barren desert that was the Nameless Lands. Even with the dawn's breeze, the air was thick, causing the thin material of my clothes to cling to my body. My lips were dry as I licked them.

We had stayed within Crimson until we reached the southern point of the kingdom, where it crossed over into the Nameless Lands. In the distance, snowcapped mountains to the northeast rose up to the sky.

Crossing borders into new territories never failed to awe me. It was so different from Earth, where the lands gradually merged into one another. In the Veil, the lines were more definite. I could feel, smell, and immediately see the difference. It was kind of similar to teleportation.

Although Crimson was visible over my shoulder, it looked as if I was peering through a mirror into another world. Gone was the sweltering heat of the previous land, replaced by a dry warmth. The air was grainy here, and the ground felt different, heavier.

Howling winds and our shuffling steps through the sand were the only sounds. I buried my face deeper into the scarf wrapped over my nose and mouth—my protection to keep the dust from invading my lungs.

The Nameless Lands was my least favorite place of the Veil Isles. Endless miles of lonely earth stretched out before us. Not to mention the memories of being imprisoned here. I hated the fear that coursed through my blood, the urge to run, the scream held back in my throat. As if I needed a reminder of the suffering I'd survived, the scar on my cheek tingled.

My hand rested on the hilt of the dagger strapped to my thigh. The weight of it gave me a small amount of security. Jase, Zade, and Issik were glaring in opposite directions, searching for any sign of Tobias, or danger of a magical kind. Kieran flew overhead, a lookout in case Tianna decided to cause trouble. Being this close to the mountain she used as her home was a risk. His shadow drew circles over the ground.

We were all in place, waiting for the former dragon to show.

A cut of muscle shifted under Issik's shirt. "If he doesn't appear in five minutes, we're out of here."

I rubbed at my chest. The blood inside my heart pumped harder the farther we traveled into the Nameless Lands.

Where is he? I silently asked, scouring the horizon for any sign of movement. I loathed being in the Nameless Lands. *Run. Run. Run,* my mind begged. I had to push aside the desire to flee, and steady my breath.

"He'll show," Jase stated with certainty.

"He better, if he knows what's good for him." Zade's nostrils flared. "I'll track his ass down and drag him here myself."

"I'm right behind you," Issik muttered, his eyes becoming sharp slits.

The three of them circled me, each taking up a similar stance—arms crossed, legs slightly apart. Their bodies made a shield, blocking a large part of the wind and sand from reaching me—a clever maneuver on their part, though restlessness licked the air, making me tense.

Seconds later, Tobias appeared out of thin air with a little green goblin at his side.

Willowphase. Of course, he would teleport, but I couldn't help but wonder if Tianna was able to track the use of magic. Was it a good idea for him to be teleporting around the Nameless Lands with her presence so near? Would she show up, magic blazing? An army surrounding us?

Panic clawed at my chest.

Issik nodded toward me, a gesture I realized was intended for Jase, who weaved his fingers through mine instantly. A steady stream of calm flowed into me, and I sighed.

"Took you long enough," Zade bit out, unfolding his thick arms.

"Some things can't be controlled," Tobias replied cryptically, but his features appeared tired. The goblin peered up at him, concern flaring in his beady black eyes. I'd put money on this goblin being the same one who broke me out of my imprisonment, but I couldn't really remember him.

"We came as you asked. What is it you have?" Jase prompted, wasting no time in getting to the point. "None of us want to linger here, and we don't have time to squander."

Tobias held Jase's stare, his expression unreadable. "This." He pulled out an object from the lining of his black cloak, opening his palm for us to see.

I gasped, my heartbeat thundering in my ears.

Jase whistled through his teeth.

Issik glowered—nothing unusual about that.

And Zade's dark eyes widened. "Father above," he muttered.

A stone, identical to the other three I'd found sat nestled in Tobias's hand. It was a beautiful amber color and it gleamed like the sunrise at our backs, but something was different from the other stars—it lacked its spark.

Was I actually seeing what I thought? Could this be…

The Star of Persuasion?

"Where did you find that?" I asked Tobias, stepping forward to get a closer look, but a hand landed on my shoulder, and the sudden chill that radiated down my arm clued me to Issik's presence.

Tobias's eyes darkened. "I've spent years searching my kingdom, hiding from the witch, and flying under her radar. There is no part of these lands I've not touched. The *where* isn't important."

"How do we know this isn't some kind of trap, a spell from the witch herself?" Issik challenged, his hand still firmly resting on my arm.

The stone looked very real, but I understood his hesitation and distrust.

"I'm an old man, with nothing else to lose," Tobias reminded. "Before I die, I would like to know that I did something to save the home I love. I want to see it returned to its former glory, and I will do everything these weak bones will allow to make it so."

I was unable to look away from the stone, my eyes drawn to it, and yet, I waited for a kernel of recognition to flicker in me. However, the power of the other stones inside me, didn't pulse or thrum with excitement at their reunion with their long-lost companion. No desire to touch it whispered in my ears. So strange. It was as if there was very little life left inside of it—if any at all—and that nearly made me call Tobias a fraud.

Yet, as I opened my mouth, I felt it—the tiny sputtering of magic.

A speck pulsed at the center of the stone, so small that I almost didn't see it with my human eyes. It could have easily been mistaken for a trick of the sun. "What did you do to it?" I asked softly, lifting my gaze to meet his.

Tobias's sharp eyes studied me with intent from under his hood. "You're able to sense the lack of power?"

Still waiting for him to answer my question, I nodded.

His tall frame shifted, as the glint in his eyes focused on me. "Its power is gone. It died with my dragon, but I thought it might serve you in your quest." He offered the Star of Persuasion to me. "Take it," he insisted.

I waited to see if the descendants were going to object. My head angled to the side, and I regarded the stone again before I moved to grasp it. Issik didn't stop me, instead, his hand slid from my shoulder, letting me go.

The stone was neither cool nor warm, but a neutral temperature as it touched my fingers. A low hum murmured in my blood, so faintly that I wondered if I was only imagining it, wishing for it. The power of persuasion—what a dynamic gift. The idea both thrilled and frightened me. I flipped it over in my palm, rubbing its smooth surface. Up close, what looked like winds of sand swirled through the crystal's veins. "I'm not sure its power is gone completely." My voice was low, muffled by the scarf and carried away with the wind. I shook my head. "It's so faint."

Jase, Zade, and Issik gathered around me. Did they feel anything when they looked at the stone? From the scowls marring their faces, I guessed not.

"If there is even a crumb of power left in the star, I wish you to have it," Tobias confessed. "You've been chosen by the dragon stones. It is you and you alone who shall wield the power and join the dragons. The curse is nearly broken, but your fight won't end there."

Kieran's shadow passed over our heads, blocking the dawn's rays for a brief moment. My fingers closed around the stone. "Thank you." Pulling the scarf down from my face, I offered him a smile.

"Don't thank me yet." A ghost of a smirk curled under his beard, but it didn't last long. "It was fate our paths crossed, Olivia, Keeper of the Stars, and Savior of Dragons. You are meant to save this world, to save *them*." With the words, I could have sworn regret and sadness flickered in his eyes.

I swallowed the lump of emotion that sat in my throat. "I'm sorry I wasn't here before… to save you." My apology was sincere.

He nodded, sinking further into his cloak. "Protect her. Protect the stones," he urged the descendants, and grabbing the goblin's hand, they vanished from our sight.

A thump sounded behind me, followed by a gust of wind and a looming shadow. *"Someone want to tell me what that was all about?"* Kieran asked in our heads.

"It's time to go," Jase ordered.

Despair wormed its way into my belly. What Tobias said about Tianna's torment not ending with the opening of the portal to this world struck a chord inside me. We had come so far, and yet we had so much left to battle.

Upon our return to Crimson Keep, the castle was a flurry of activity as the staff prepared for our departure tomorrow.

The stone made its way around the room, each descendant taking the time to inspect the glossy amber crystal. Jase held it up to the window, shifting it with the light streaming through the glass. "Nothing happened when you touched it?" he asked.

Candles flickered along the mantel, which had been lit by Zade, while I tucked my legs underneath me on the couch. "No. At least not like the others. It was obvious when the surge of magic flowed inside me from each stone." The descendants each had sensed the transfer of power identical to theirs.

Perched on the coffee table in front of the couch, Kieran leaned toward me. "But you still believe there is a trickle of power left inside?"

I nodded, taking notice of how his light gray tunic stretched across his broad chest. "I do. I can't explain it, but maybe if we had the other stones, then this one would come alive again," I suggested, unsure where my brain had plucked the idea from exactly.

My thought sparked something in Jase, who moved away from the window to sit on the couch beside me. His long legs stretched under the low table. "That's an idea worth exploring another day." He passed the stone to me.

"Until then, we need to keep it somewhere safe," Zade confirmed.

The stars had been stashed in their perspective kingdoms, hidden away from Tianna. Not even I knew where the descendants had chosen their hiding places to be, except for Zade's. I offered the Star of Persuasion to him. "Until we recover the Star of Fire," I said, "you'll keep it hidden." It felt right to give him Tobias's stone. To keep the stars on us could be devastating—a single attack from Tianna and we could lose everything.

For a few seconds, Zade just stared at the stone, considering it. "It should stay with you," he concluded, lifting his eyes to mine. His fingers closed around my hand to secure the star in my palm. "It's where it belongs."

No one objected.

So be it. "I will keep it safe," I vowed, pressing my hand to my heart, and I swore the stone pulsed once, like a sigh of relief. My eyes drifted to Issik in the corner of the room. He'd been quiet since we'd come home—unusually so, even for him. I'd nearly forgotten he was there. His distrust of Tobias lingered like a dark aura around him.

"What Tobias said about the fight not being over even after the curse is broken, do you think it will come to war?" I asked, looping my arms around my drawn-up knees. My golden hair fell, framing my face. The stone was still in my right hand, and I had no intention of letting it go.

Jase's eyes churned with burdened thoughts. "All this time we've searched for the one to break the curse. We had foolishly believed your blood would save us. As the years passed, our hope of ever being freed seemed like a dream. Then we learned the blood was only a small portion of the cure. Tianna is cunning, masking her true desire for the stars with some ridiculous curse."

"The origins of the dragon stones has always been a closely guarded secret, held only by the founding kings of the Veil. Some legends claim the gods once lived with us in the Veil, and other worlds like ours. They gifted those worthy with magic, and thereby mystical creatures were made—dragons, witches, faeries, trolls, nymphs, and so on."

Issik's deep, cool voice was hypnotic, like a bedtime story on a cold winter's night.

"But magic comes with a price. Some abused their abilities, wanting and demanding more from the gods. It's never a good thing to demand anything from an immortal. When the gods bestowed the stones to the five dragon kings, they enchanted the crystals to harness their abilities, and the kings crafted them into different weapons of their choosing."

Jase's face grew solemn. "I don't believe any of us want war, but if a fight is what Tianna is after, we'll give her one."

"When we get to Iculon, it might be wise to do some reading on the stars," Kieran suggested. "Most of what we know about them comes from stories passed down through the generations."

I was looking forward to seeing Issik's castle, but the cold temperatures I could do without.

"What will you do if your full dragon powers aren't restored once the curse is broken?" I was asking all the tough questions, but someone had to do it. "Will you be able to defeat her?"

Jase rested his head on the back of the couch, huffing. "My ego says we could without question. There was a time when a witch of Tianna's skills never would have stood a chance against a single dragon, let alone four of us. But the circumstances have changed, and we need to accept our current limitations. Though, even if our abilities are only a fraction of what they once were, it won't change my heart or my drive to kill the witch. We'll find a way. *That* you can be certain of."

I trusted them with my life, so did everyone who lived here. Snuggling deeper into the couch, I stared at the candles flickering over the fireplace. A feeling of dread swept through me. Tianna would stop at nothing to gain the power she desired. It was no longer just about breaking the curse. She would come for me—for the stars, and the power they entrusted to me.

I knew it.

Tianna knew it.

But did the descendants know?

The four of them continued to strategize, and plan for the upcoming travel to Iculon. I was lost in my own thoughts and theories, none of which I hoped were true, but there would come a point when I would have to face my future, whatever that may be.

It might have been five minutes or an hour after my mind wandered off, but the mention of my name refocused my attention on the conversation.

"We're going to need to get Olivia outfitted for the journey tomorrow." Kieran winked at me.

"I'll have Juniper see to it," Zade agreed.

My fingers twined together, tightening around the star. Tomorrow we left for Iculon—the coldest kingdom in the region. I was as ready as I'd ever been.

A snow-kissed breeze fluttered over the tip of my nose while we flew, and my cheeks grew red as I bristled at the cold of Iculon. I snuggled deeper into my hooded cloak, the navy blue velvet fabric felt soft on my face. It was decided I would be flying with Zade into the snowcapped mountain region. His warmth would keep me from freezing, and protect me against the blistering winds that whistled through the quiet land.

After crossing through a corner of Jase's kingdom, the unmarred blue sky transformed into a smoky gray, marking the edge of Iculon. The initial cold had stopped the air in my lungs, but the shock had soon given way, allowing me to breathe in the chilled mist. I'd never tasted air so crisp and pristine. Snow covered every inch of the ground, blurring the lines of where the mountains stopped, and the flat land began.

Zade crested a mountain, and on the other side, a lake of sheer ice spanned for miles. Crystals of light aqua sparkled like jewels under the frozen surface. He dipped down, sensing my amazement and wish for a closer look. His expansive, dark red, almost black wings sliced through the air with ease.

Holding on to his scaled neck, I peered over his shoulder to look down at the wondrous lake. Our reflection glanced back at me—a rider on a majestic red dragon. "It's beautiful," I whispered in awe.

"Don't let its beauty fool you. This place can be as cold and ruthless as its ruler."

Another dragon snorted in my head. Issik. *"You didn't see me bitching about the heat. Suck it up, lava boy."*

A deep snarl rumbled up Zade's throat, bringing a smile to my lips. I missed the banter between them. Things had been so serious lately, that there wasn't much joshing going on between my dragons.

I had to agree with Zade, but I kept the thought to myself. No point in stirring up trouble. Of all the kingdoms, Iculon was the most daunting, and the task in front of me seemed equally as formidable. Then I got a glimpse of Issik's home.

Unlike the sharp angles of Crimson Keep, Issik's castle was all curves. Five domed towers made of arched windows circled upward, each one slightly taller than the one to its left. Their round roofs were shiny and smooth, scalloped like dragon scales. Thinner towers of glass jutted up to the clouds like shards of crystal. Hell, the entire multistory castle could have been constructed of glass for all I knew, and it was encased in a shimmering shield of blue magic—Issik's shield.

What would the castle's interior look like? Would the floors be made of ice, and the furniture of packed snow? I shuddered at the thought. The castle seemed so remote from everything, lonely even, I had seen only one small village on the other side of the lake, the smoke drifting up in stacks from the numerous chimneys. My gaze sought out Issik in the sky. It took a certain kind of prince to live in a castle such as this.

Balconies and staircases wrapped around the castle, going up and up. My awe made me momentarily forget the cold. I was grateful no trouble had befallen us during the journey. The last few days had taken a toll on my body.

"You're awfully quiet. It makes me wonder what is going on in that pretty head of yours," Zade pointed out, breaking me from my thoughts.

"I'm just drinking it all in. I can't believe we're going to be living here."

"The quicker you find the stone, the sooner we can get back to someplace warm."

I chuckled under my breath, a curl of warm air escaping my lips. "What if I like it here?" I challenged.

He snorted. *"You would be one of the very few who prefer Iculon over the other kingdoms. He might be handsome, but his sunny disposition keeps many from getting close."*

My braid slipped free of my hood, falling over my shoulder as Zade descended. Poor Issik. My heart grew heavy for him, for the loneliness in his life. I glanced at the castle of ice. If he asked me to live here with him, would I be able to withstand the cold, to be happy here?

I'd like to think I could.

Issik's castle was nestled in a valley surrounded by craggy mountains. Not the easiest place for dragons to land, but Zade and Issik both made it seem effortless. Zade landed on the uneven ground with a thud that shook the earth, kicking up snow under his clawed feet as they dug into the rock underneath.

Dragon shadows danced around us, and I noticed Jase and Kieran were still in the sky. "What's going on?" I asked, watching their dragon forms circle the castle and then take off in different directions. They had to be weary from the journey. I hadn't even done anything physical, and I was bone-tired.

"Border patrol. They'll do a sweep of the kingdom," Zade replied.

My gaze followed them until they were nothing but dark specks in the gray sky, before I slid off Zade, and turned to the castle. Issik and Zade shifted, leaving them both naked in the dead of winter. My cheeks burned, but I kept my eyes focused on them. They might be completely comfortable with their nakedness, but it still made me blush, even though I appreciated their physique.

Ahead, stood two glass doors that were easily twice as tall as the ones back on Earth. The glass was etched with a symbol as intricate as a snowflake. Iron framed the glass.

"If you don't open those doors, I'm going to freeze my balls off," Zade barked, his teeth chattering.

Issik glowered before slipping a hand under my elbow to help me make the slippery climb to the castle. "Maybe then you wouldn't be such a hothead."

The massive doors groaned open under Issik's command, and I got my first glimpse of the majestic frost castle. Inside, the halls were silent. The soles of my shoes clattering against the flagstone floor were the only sound. I found its emptiness strange for such a large estate. Where was the staff? I remembered Issik mentioning that his home was protected by a magical barrier. Was that the reason for the solitude?

The main hall was a glass dome with creamy white furnishings. A chandelier hung in the sitting room off to the left, its teardrop crystals sparkling from the firelight. The hearth was roaring and crackling, filling the room with toasty warmth. An oval velvet settee sat under the chandelier near the fire. White, carved stone framed all the doorways, and fur rugs overlaid the gray floors. No curtains covered the windows, letting in the glistening of the snow, ice, and mountains.

I lingered in the threshold, trying to picture Issik living there. From the paintings on the walls, to the tile floors, his home was nothing like I had imagined. No igloo vibes here. A half smile curved my lips at my silly assumptions.

A young woman, near my age, came flying around the corner then, a bundle of clothes clutched in her arms. The shuffling of her footsteps had preceded her, and I spun toward the sound, to find her skidding to a halt in front of me.

"Oh!" she gasped, gathering the clothing more securely as she gave me a look of wide-eyed curiosity. Her obsidian hair fell in waves down her back, while sincere admiration shone in her striking azure eyes. "You must be Olivia." She gave a slight bow with her head. "The kingdom has been buzzing about you for weeks. We've wondered when we'd get the chance to meet you."

The honor and respect she showed me were a first, her high regard for me made me nervous. I didn't want to mess up this first impression.

"I'm Juniper."

"It's a pleasure to meet you," I replied, hoping I'd find a friend in Juniper. Her demeanor and smile instantly made me feel relaxed and welcomed. I needed both at the moment.

Issik cleared his throat. "Now that the introductions are out of the way… Juniper?"

Twisting toward Issik and Zade, Juniper walked toward them, giving both a graceful bow and then handing them each a pile of clothes. She didn't bat an eye at the two naked dragons. "Where are lords Jase and Kieran?"

Lords? This was the first time I'd heard anyone give the descendants titles. I knew they were royalty here in the Veil—kings, actually, since their fathers were gone—but the title still sounded strange.

The Iculon castle seemed so formal, but not in a cold, uncaring way. Pride and joy were evident in Juniper's face, leading me to believe she was very happy here.

"They'll be here within the hour," Issik informed her. "You can leave their clothes here. I know they will be as grateful as I am."

"Everything is ready for your arrival," Juniper assured him.

"Thank you. I don't know what I'd do without you," he assured, slipping the pants over his hips. The dragons had no shame. How long would it take for me to be as comfortable with their nakedness?

Zade, now fully clothed, strutted into the sitting area, and poured himself a drink. The dark cherry liquid swirled in his cup as he brought it to his lips, sucking it dry in one gulp. "Hopefully, that will warm me up."

"How can you still be cold?" I asked, walking into the room after him. Although the large fire added warmth, the overall temperature of the castle stayed at a pleasant coolness. Not the frigid, shivering kind.

Zade moved to stand in front of the roaring fire, a shudder rolling over the muscles of his back. "My blood isn't made for such a climate. Perhaps you should keep me warm, now that you share my power." A wicked gleam twinkled in his cinnamon eyes.

"How about I get you a fur coat instead?" Issik gruffly replied.

A giggle broke the silent glare between the Ice Prince and Hot Lips. I'd forgotten about Juniper. "Ignore them," I suggested, rolling my eyes. "I do."

She giggled again, and the sound echoed throughout the glass castle. I'd missed the sound of laughter in my life. Juniper gave me a bright smile. "We're going to be fast friends, Olivia. I just know it."

God knew I could use a friend.

After excusing herself, Juniper bound out of the room as lively as she had arrived, and Issik and I left Zade in front of the fire to tour the rest of his home.

"I thought the castle would be freezing. How is it so… tolerable?" I asked. In the Veil, there was no such thing as air conditioners or heaters. For all their finery and magic, they still lived without much of the technology we had on Earth.

"It's controlled with a spell."

Magic. I should have guessed.

"My father kept a healer on staff who also had other talents," he explained. His tone indicated there might have been more between his father and the healer. An affair possibly?

We walked up the stairs and down several drafty hallways. The craftsmanship in each kingdom never failed to impress me. Iculon was as opulent as the others, but in its own refined way.

"Juniper seems nice. Has she been here long?" I asked, longing to fill the quiet with chatter.

Issik thought about it for a moment. I could only imagine how the years blended together after so long. "Two years, I believe." His fingers forked through his silky blond hair. "Most of my staff has been with me for years. Juniper is the youngest in my care."

Was there anything between them? Something more than lord and subject? More than friends?

"Here are your rooms," Issik gestured, swinging open an ivory door. He leaned on the edge of the frame, waiting for me to pass through it.

"Rooms?" I echoed, lifting a brow.

My suite could have been an apartment in Chicago. When I first walked in, a sitting area with a small table for two greeted me. Through the next door was the sleeping chambers, having a joined bath and dressing room. The scent of lotus flowed from one room to the next, pure and sweet, and shimmering silver swirls adorned the soft blue walls.

"Does this room suit you?" Issik asked from his position by the doorway. He had been watching me as I explored.

Grinning, I spun to face him. "Are you kidding? I feel like a princess."

A smile played on his sensual lips—a rare treat from the Ice Prince. I wanted to make him smile every day of his life. "Good."

"It's so big. I don't know what to do with myself."

"It was my mother's."

I swallowed. "Are you sure it's okay that I stay here?"

He nodded. "She would be honored for you to take her rooms. You're royalty to me. I want you to be happy here."

My finger trailed over the ivory dresser, a hint of a smile on my lips as I looked at him. "How could anyone not be?"

Issik's icy blue eyes twinkled.

I only meant to lay down for a few minutes, the soft white bed was an invitation I couldn't resist. Yet, when I woke up, the sun was sinking low behind the mountains, immersing the room in hues of blues and pinks. The sunset was magnificent, and I was tempted to brave the snowy balcony.

My arms stretched upward as I sat up, while the low embers from the hearth in front of the bed toasted my toes. I padded over to the bathroom to wash my face, and unravel the braid from my hair—crimped locks cascaded over my shoulders in golden hues. I stared at my reflection, wrinkling my nose at the dusting of freckles that had darkened from my time in the Crimson sun, but the shadows that lurked under my eyes were fading. Turning my face to the right, the scar running along my cheek still shocked me. It was my face, but a roughness now marked more than just my skin.

I was different.

Swirling spots suddenly hurdled through my head, and I clutched the sides of the sink, hunched over with my eyes closed, and waiting for the black dots to cease. With slow, steady breaths, I inhaled and exhaled, riding out the dizzy spell until it passed.

What the hell was that?

Food. I needed to eat. It had been hours since breakfast.

Straightening, I stepped out of my quarters and set out to hunt down the descendants. I was a little surprised to find no one keeping guard at my door. They'd become relentless in their duty to protect me.

Speaking of protecting…

My fingers dug into my pocket, fumbling for the stone. I relaxed at the feel of the smooth surface against my fingertips. Perhaps it wasn't the smartest idea to carry it around with me. I needed to find a secure place for it in my rooms.

Either I was getting acquainted with castle life, or the circular layout of Issik's home made it easier for me to find my way around the palace. Effortlessly, I hung a left at the bottom of the staircase, and went toward the deep voices emanating from down the hall. My steps halted alongside an ivory pillar, needing to steady myself as another wave of lightheadedness shot through me.

Damn this dizziness.

However, it lasted no more than a few seconds. The scent of something savory wafting in the air made my stomach rumble, and I stepped away from the pillar to find Issik and the others lounged at the table in the dining room. Jase and Kieran had already returned from their patrol of the grounds, but the room went silent at my approach.

I paused at the empty seat, my hands resting on the high back of the chair. "What is it?"

Suddenly, their food became very interesting, and no one met my gaze. Something had happened.

Kieran shifted in his seat. "Jase and I ran into a small problem during our patrol."

My gaze bounced between the two, expectantly. "What kind of problem?" I finally prodded, seeing as they weren't voluntarily offering the information.

Jase lifted the crystal decanter of red wine, and poured himself a generous portion. "The portal. It's weakening, leaving the Veil exposed for other creatures to slip in." His voice remained calm while he spoke. "Kieran and I found a pair of dusanac roaming the western border."

A chill scurried down my spine. "Oh," I replied, sliding into the seat. "Do I want to know what those are?"

"No," was the uniform reply from everyone at the table.

I scrunched my nose while Issik poured me a glass of wine.

"It's nothing Jase and I couldn't handle," Kieran added, noticing my face had lost a shade of color.

This time. But what about the next time? Or the one after that? It made me nervous when they went out to fight. They might have been born warriors and bestowed magical gifts, but under the circumstances, I couldn't help but worry.

Until the curse was broken, and their strength was restored, they were vulnerable.

A bowl of thick, creamy soup and a basket of bread was placed in front of me. My lips curved into a smile of thanks to the older woman while I picked up my spoon. The first taste of soup was blissful, and it was an effort to keep from sighing. Ripping off a hunk of bread, I dunked it into the steaming bowl, letting it soak in the broth. The bowl was empty in minutes, and it wasn't until my spoon scraped the bottom that I became aware the descendants were watching me.

"You look... better," Zade offered, his chin propped against his closed hand.

"I'm going to take that as a compliment."

"I only meant that a bit of rest did you good," he mumbled, stuffing bread into his mouth.

If that was the case, then why did I still feel so tired? My body felt off-centered, like my equilibrium had quit on me.

"Have you had any inclinations on where to find the Star of Frost?" Issik asked, leaning forward.

Focusing on my plate, I shook my head. "Not yet." How did I tell him everything about me felt wrong? I would figure it out. My body probably just needed more sleep, a chance to decompress. In a few days, I'd be as good as new.

"We'll begin our search tomorrow, if you're feeling up to it," Jase informed, his food forgotten.

I swallowed, forcing my face to stay neutral and not hide the anxiety I felt. Mentally, I was more than ready to see this curse end. I just hoped my body and the stones cooperated. "I'm ready," I assured him with a soft smile. "What about the creatures Tianna is summoning through the portal?" I asked, nibbling on the last roll of bread.

Kieran swirled his wine before taking a sip. "You don't need to worry about that. We'll take care of them. It is our responsibility as the leaders of the Veil to keep our kingdoms safe, but when venturing out, we'll need to take precautions. Lucky for us, the conditions in Iculon don't make it a desirable place to seek shelter."

With that settled, silence fell over the room. We were all thinking about the future and what it held. My mind kept going back to the portal, and the untold dangers we might come up against. I wasn't fond of things trying to kill me.

Of all the other kingdoms, and the people who lived there, Iculon had the smallest population. Was leaving the other lands unattended wise? Of course, the descendants would monitor their lands, but it wasn't the same as them presiding over their kingdoms daily.

We lingered at the dinner table for a few hours, drinking and the dragons reminiscing about old times—times before the Great War and how different the Veil had been. Seeing the descendants relaxed from the wine, and the pleasant conversation was a nice change. They needed this, a few hours without responsibility, without the war looming over their heads, and without constantly thinking about being cursed.

I was careful this time to not overindulge in spirits. My head felt fogged enough without being drunk. The meal had done very little to still the spinning in my head. Although my body yelled at me to lie down, I couldn't make myself leave. Being with them like this—free of inhibitions—was something I wanted to treasure. I imagined this was how they were before being cursed by the witch.

Fun. Playful. Wild. Yet still, royalty—powerful and commanding.

Every so often Issik would glance at me, worry creasing his forehead. The emotional bond between us made him perceptive to what I was feeling. "Kieran, will you escort Olivia to her room? It's late. We could all use some sleep."

My eyes met Issik's, and I gave him a stern look, calling him out on his subtle command for me to go to bed.

He bowed his head slightly at me, as if saying, "You're welcome."

What was I to do with these meddling dragons, always thinking they knew what was best for me?

Sighing, I conceded that going to bed was wise. The chair scooted across the cool tiled floor as I stood, but then the room gave a horrendous lurch, and I stumbled. The smell of the woods after a rainfall surrounded me as I fell into strong arms.

"Hey, there," Kieran murmured near my ear, his hands steadying me. "How many glasses of wine did you have?"

"One," I mumbled, trying to make my eyes focus on his dark green tunic.

"Hmm." His lips pursed in an amused half smirk. "If you say so."

He lowered a shoulder, and I backed up a step, anticipating the maneuver they were so fond of using on me. "I can walk," I stated.

Kieran winked. "Where's the fun in that?" Still, he didn't try to lift me into his arms again, letting me lumber my way to the base of the stairs.

My hand gripped the banister for balance as I kicked off my satin slippers. A sigh left my lips. "I've been dying to take my shoes off," I explained at Kieran's lifted brows.

A wicked grin spread over his lips. "You're not required to wear them."

"Now you tell me," I muttered, bending down to pick up my discarded shoes. My bare feet were silent on the stairs, and I kept a hand running up the smooth banister. Such a sophisticated home for a brooding dragon. "Did you know Issik's family?" I asked, curious about who they had been, particularly the woman who had chosen to spend her life in a frozen tundra. She must have loved Issik's father very much.

Kieran strolled beside me, keeping close as if he sensed something was off with me. "Not well. Our fathers would summon the council of the five kingdoms twice a year, to discuss the state of the Veil. At around age five, I was instructed to attend the meetings with my father as the heir of Viperus. It was at these conferences that I met the other descendants. Although we were required to listen in on discussions, the five of us often found ourselves getting into trouble."

They had once told me that prior to the curse they hadn't been friends. "What were your parents like?" I inquired, hoping it wasn't too painful of a question.

"Normal, I guess."

"I find that hard to believe."

His full lips curved upward. "If you take out the dragon aspect, my life growing up was average. My mother made sure I had balance between being the prince to a kingdom and just being a boy. I spent most of my childhood playing and running around with the staff's children, terrorizing my tutors, and exploring the woods surrounding my home. They never treated me as a pampered prince. I had classes, the same as everyone else, but between those, I was given extra studies regarding the kingdoms and my position as the dragon heir for Viperus. My mother was loving and kind. She had an affinity for plants. They thrived under her attention."

What a perfect match for a king whose home was nestled deep in the woods. "Did you have any siblings?" Not once had any of the descendants mentioned brothers or sisters. I was an only child myself. Had they wished for a younger sibling to play with as I had?

"Like the other descendants, we all grew up as only children. It's part of the dragon gene. Only one heir is ever born to a dragon."

"Are they always male?" The folds of my dress swished in black waves as I climbed.

Kieran's hand quickly slipped under my arm, catching me as I tripped on the hem of my skirt. "It is rare for a dragon to have a girl, but not impossible. Jase's grandmother carried the dragon line in his family."

His grandmother had been a dragon. I was utterly fascinated by the family history of the descendants. "I wish I could have seen the Veil before the Great War."

The grin on his face was infectious. "You would have loved it."

"I already do." I wanted to tell him that I'd seen his mother, that she was beautiful and had helped me, but I stayed silent.

He leaned in, pressing a kiss to my lips, and the lightheadedness returned.

It's just the kiss, I told myself. *Kieran's kisses always leave me dizzy.*

True, but this? This was different.

"Olivia?" he murmured.

"Hmm," I replied, my voice sounding as if it was a million miles away from my body.

The pad of his thumb brushed over my cheek. "Are you feeling okay?"

"I-I'm not sure. My head…" The shoes fell from my grip as I lifted my hands to my temples—the whirling wouldn't quit. Suddenly, the stairs tilted and spun.

A cool hand pressed to my forehead. "You're burning up."

I was? Strange. I didn't feel hot.

The ground was swept out from under me, and I didn't protest his offer to carry me this time. "You need to be in bed," he informed in a disapproving tone, that was out of character for the rebellious poison dragon.

"I need to find the last star," I mumbled, even as my head fell onto his shoulder.

Kieran snorted. "Not tonight you don't."

"You smell good."

A low chuckle rumbled against my body, and the sound followed me into the darkness that swallowed me whole.

In the distance, the shuffling of feet and grumbling of deep voices crossed over the canyon in my mind. The grumblings intensified, disturbing my sleep. Why was I so tired? And why was it so hard to wake up?

It took considerable effort, but I peeled open my eyes and found all four descendants in my room. Two were sleeping in chairs, while another paced at the foot of the bed, and the fourth stared intently into the low-burning hearth.

What was going on?

Why were they all in my room?

Had I been hurt?

I wiggled in the bed, testing out my limbs. Everything seemed to be in working order, so I sat up and cleared my throat, finding it scratchy and dry. Water. I needed water.

"Olivia?" Issik breathed. He was the dragon pacing over the snow white rug on my bedroom floor. At the sight of me stirring, he halted dead in his tracks. His eyes flew to my face, and the next moment he was at my side, pressing a hand to my forehead. The others jumped up and surrounded my bed like a flock of mother hens.

"How are you feeling?" Kieran anxiously asked.

Ten seconds ago, I would have said fine, but the sudden movement of sitting up had thrown my stomach for a loop. "I'm going to throw up," I rasped.

The descendants backed up in unison.

Before I could further embarrass myself, I rolled out of bed and stumbled into the bathroom to hurl what little was in my stomach into the sink, but once I was finished, the nausea disappeared. I washed my face with cold water, rinsed out my mouth, and was pleased to see my skin had a tad of color to it.

What was going on with me? Had I eaten something bad last night? It couldn't have possibly been the wine. A single glass wouldn't have given me a hangover like this one.

Trembling steps took me back to the room, and climbed onto the middle of the bed. Folding my legs, I searched their gazes. "What happened?" My voice sounded odd in my head—stuffy, like my ears were filled with cotton balls.

"You collapsed and have had a fever for two days," Kieran replied first from his reclined spot in the chair. His black pants and tunic were wrinkled, as if he'd been in the same spot for hours.

Two days! What? How the hell had two days gone by? "I've been asleep the whole time?"

"In and out. We were beginning to worry," Jase confessed from the foot of the bed, where he stood frowning at me.

I'd lost two days that could have been spent looking for the star. "What caused me to get so sick?" It hadn't been like any illness I'd ever had before, definitely not the flu or a cold. But what was it?

Issik leaned a shoulder against one of the four posts at the corners of the bed. His eyes moved over my face, searching for something. "We don't know," he finally answered.

Jase's brow arched, the scowl lifting from his face. "We were hoping you could tell us."

"Me?" I forked a hand through my disheveled hair, wracking my brain for my last memories. "I remember being dizzy most of the day, but didn't think much of it. Kieran and I were walking up the stairs and…" I hit a black wall—slammed into it, to be more accurate. I pounded on the mental block in my memory, but it wouldn't budge; it wouldn't crack.

"You fainted," Kieran supplied, seeing the struggle and confusion on my face.

"On the stairs?" It was the last place I remembered. "And I didn't break my neck?"

Kieran put a hand to his heart, looking wounded. "I'm insulted. You were in my arms. Do you not remember me carrying you? Furthermore, do you honestly believe I would let you fall?"

"No, of course not. Given my history, it isn't unreasonable to expect that accidents will occur around me. I'm not used to having someone around to catch me. Thank you."

His emerald eyes sparkled. "Always. It was my pleasure."

Zade snorted from the other side of the bed, the deep red of his shirt bringing out the flecks of gold in his eyes. "You'd take any excuse to get her into your arms."

"And you wouldn't?" Kieran challenged.

Slowly, my fingertips massaged my temples, and I considered fainting again just to put an end to their banter before things got out of hand. A cup of tea appeared in front of me.

"Drink this," Issik commanded.

Eager to soothe my dry throat, I obeyed. The tea was sweetened with honey and something fruity like passionfruit. I sipped half of the cup in silence, and the sudden quiet had me studying them. They were acting weird.

Something was wrong, but what?

Lowering the cup of tea to my lap, I shot the four of them a look, daring them to avert their gazes. "What aren't you telling me?"

Zade shifted on his feet, and Kieran's eyes darted to the rumpled bed around me, avoiding my questioning glare. Jase rubbed at the back of his neck, the chest muscles under his white tunic tensing.

A rumble of irritation sounded at the back of my throat. "Someone better explain."

Jase huffed. "You are the most troublesome female."

My arms crossed over my chest. "And whose fault is that?"

Kieran's lips twitched.

"You were glowing while you slept," Issik murmured, waiting for my reaction.

I blinked. "What did you say?"

"We'd never seen anything like it," Jase admitted, but he didn't sound happy about it. In fact, his lips were turned down again. "Your skin was emitting a white glow, like you were bathed in starlight."

If I hadn't been in shock, I might have found the idea of glowing fascinating, but given the numerous unusual events in my life recently, this was probably not a good thing. "Am I dying?"

"Doubtful. If you were going to die because of this, you'd already be dead," Zade assured.

Issik's hand thumped the back of Zade's head. "Smooth."

"What the idiot is trying to say," Jase began, "is we believe the illness might have been caused by the exorbitant amount of changes your body has gone through over the last few months. These past few days in particular."

They had expressed their concerns before about this, and it appeared those concerns had finally caught up with me. "What am I supposed to do about it? We can't afford for me to spend days in bed."

Jase sat on the edge of the mattress. "Well, for starters, the next time you start to feel unwell, you tell us. Other than that, I'm not sure we can do more than hope your body has stabilized after resting these last few days."

My fingers tapped the side of my teacup. "I swear that even if my pinky tingles, I will let you know."

Snickers followed, and as hard as Jase tried to keep a straight face, his lush lips gave out into a smile. Leaning in, he brushed those lips over my cheek. "How many times are you going to stop my heart?" he whispered.

"Today?"

He shook his head at me.

I placed the teacup on the nightstand and stretched, realizing for the first time I was in my nightshirt. Someone had changed my clothes. My gut clenched. Which one had it been? *Get it together. It's not like they haven't seen you naked before, and it doesn't matter who.* They had cared enough to watch over me and keep me comfortable. All of them. Softening the tightening of my lips, I lifted my eyes.

"Did anything happen while I was… indisposed?" Like had they found any information on the Star of Frost? Had Tianna made any threats while I'd been dozing? Did any other creatures slip through the portal? So many gloomy possibilities.

Kieran crossed his long legs at his ankles, his features relaxed. "It was as quiet as a mouse around here, other than your snoring."

"I do not snore," I protested as I flung one of the pillows on the bed across the room at him. He laughed as he caught the pillow missile, using his dragon reflexes.

"So, I guess I shouldn't mention the drool?"

"Not if you don't want me to set fire to that pillow on your lap," I warned him. It was an empty threat.

He lifted a single brow. "You can do that?"

Suddenly, the feathered pillow resting on Kieran erupted into flames, and I squeaked at the sight of the blaze engulfing the silk like it had been doused in gasoline. He jumped out of his chair with ninja-like agility, tossing the fiery pillow to the tiled floor close to my bed.

As I scrambled backward—oblivious because of how close to the mattress it fell—Issik reacted, moving around the bed with inhuman speed. He put the flames out with a burst of ice. The lovely white fabric was now charred with black soot, and frayed. And just at that moment, I teetered toward the ground.

Zade caught me, depositing me back onto the safety of the mattress as four dragons scowled down at me. In less than a minute, the room had erupted into chaos, all caused by me. This had to be a record.

Shit. I hadn't meant for that to happen. It was only a fleeting thought, and yet...

The pungent scent of burnt fabric filled the room, while Kieran waved off the plume of smoke. Issik's ice blue, dragon eyes stared at me with a mixture of bewilderment and exasperation.

"Sorry," I mumbled with a sheepish look, tempted to pull the covers over my head. "I didn't mean for it to catch fire. I never would —" Emotion clogged my throat. What had I done? What was happening to me? I would never intentionally hurt Kieran, but I hadn't been able to stop the power from releasing. It had been a simple thought and whoosh, the pillow had gone up in flames.

"Hey, Blondie," Kieran murmured. His finger hooked under my chin, tipping my face to meet his. "You have nothing to apologize for."

I wasn't surprised he didn't hold me responsible, none of them would, but it still didn't change the fact that I was unpredictable, and potentially dangerous. A time would come when I had to deal with the changes happening to me, and that time was sooner rather than later. None of us could afford for me to become a loose cannon, especially when we were so close to ending this curse.

"Zade, any thoughts on how to control this?" Jase pressed.

I knew they didn't mean to make me feel like an experiment, but I couldn't help but feel as if I was on display, a puzzle they had to solve.

"None of us have that kind of magic," Zade replied, his hand scratching at his chin as he continued to stare at me.

Kieran's eyes looked me up and down. "I'm not sure any of us have the skills to teach her how to wield magic. She seems to be able to manipulate our powers in ways we can't."

My gaze fell, and I analyzed the quilt as though it were the most interesting thing.

"I'm curious now about what she can do with our other abilities," Jase added.

I rolled my eyes and dropped down onto the bed, groaning.

A soft knock sounded on the door, and Juniper poked in her head. I was sitting at the table in my sitting room, and I waved her forward, glad to see a friendly face. She carried a tray with broth and crackers that she laid on the far corner of the table.

"I'm glad to see you're awake. They've been going mad with worry and driving everyone crazy."

"I should probably apologize then," I mumbled, distracted by the food.

She chuckled. "Are you hungry?"

"Starving," I admitted, giving her a grateful smile. "Thank you, Juniper, for the food." My stomach growled at the aroma of the savory broth, and my mouth watered. "It smells delicious."

"Our cook is the best in the Veil. This is her special brew that is guaranteed to cure all ailments."

Juniper wore a simple teal dress that came to her calves. The sleeves were a short bell cut over her slender shoulders. She might choose to live in the coldest region of the Veil, but she looked like she had stepped straight out of summer. Which reminded me, it was spring-time, regardless of the snow and ice surrounding the castle, and summer was around the corner. Suppressing a sigh, I picked up the spoon on the tray next to the bowl of broth.

Juniper smoothed the folds of her dress. "The entire castle has been worrying about you. We're glad to see you're up and about." So the staff knew I'd been sick. What did they think of me? I was supposed to be some savior, and yet, I'd been knocked out cold for two days.

"Will you stay with me? I don't like to eat alone." The descendants were either busy taking care of kingdom duties, or snoring in my bed—like my current assigned babysitter, Zade. I didn't blame him for being exhausted and had left him undisturbed in my sleeping chambers.

She glanced over her shoulder at the door, then at the empty chair in front of me. For a brief moment, I thought she might refuse. "I have a few minutes before anyone notices I'm gone." The iron legs of the chair scraped lightly over the floor as she sat with a poise I'd never possess.

My shoulders straightened a fraction, as I tried to match her posture without looking like a fool. Juniper was bred to live in castles and stand beside dragon kings. Me? I didn't know how I fit into this world. The Veil was my home; I didn't question that anymore. This was where I wanted to be—with the descendants. But what happened after? After the curse was broken? After Tianna was dead? After we saved the world?

I sipped on the spoonful of hot broth, testing my stomach's ability to keep down food. It was divine, and my greedy appetite wanted to gulp it down all at once, but I forced myself to go slow, savoring the flavors of chicken stock and herbs with hints of onion. "Do you like living in Iculon?" I asked, blowing on the spoon.

She shrugged. "I like the quiet and the solitude. The other castles already had full staffs, and although we're always given a choice, I wanted a simple life without drama."

"It doesn't get lonely?" I was genuinely curious about her life here. It was so different than the other kingdoms, so remote and harsh, and yet this girl was sweet and lively in a refreshing way.

"Not usually. There is so much to do to keep up a castle, particularly since Issik keeps a smaller staff than the others." She played with the charm hanging around her neck, a pretty little medallion. And as she gnawed on her lip, I could tell she had more to say but wasn't sure if it was her place.

I offered her an encouraging smile. "I'm glad you're here."

She smiled in return. "You're not like I pictured. He's different with you, you know? We all noticed the changes in him, over the last few months since you arrived."

"How so?" I prodded, eating another spoonful of soup. She had piqued my interest.

"Warmer, if that's possible."

Dabbing at the corners of my mouth with a napkin, I leaned back in my chair. "Warm is not a word I'd normally use to describe the Ice Prince."

She lifted her brows at the nickname I'd given Issik. "You care about him."

I nodded. "I care about all of them."

The approval on her face reached her eyes. "We might have only just met, but I can't help but hope once the curse is broken, you choose Issik and come to live here. Call me a hopeless romantic, but you bring out the best in him. He needs someone like you to thaw that frozen heart. He's in love with you. And it would be great to have a friend close to my age," she added in earnest.

My belly fluttered. It hit me in the heart knowing that other people could see what I felt, but as full as my heart was with the descendants, a part of me was afraid. What would happen after the curse was lifted? Would I be forced to choose between them? Would they still care for me as they did now? And the big question that haunted my future: Would they marry? They were royalty, the last dragons, and were required to continue their lineage. I understood their responsibilities. I just didn't know how I would fit into their lives, and that hurt. Unexpected tears stung my eyes as I lowered my lashes, stirring the broth in aimless circles.

"I didn't mean to upset you," Juniper said quietly, having noticed the gleam in my eyes before I could avert my gaze. "I'm sorry. I should get back—"

My hand laid over Juniper's, stopping her from jumping up from the table and bolting, before I got the chance to explain my sudden shift in emotions. "You didn't," I assured her, lifting my glossy eyes to meet hers. "I'm being silly." I brushed the tears away before they could fall. "It's been an insane few months, and I never expected to fall in love. I don't know what to do about these feelings," I attempted to explain, unsure if she knew what I meant.

She observed me as I collected myself. "You're in love with all of them, aren't you?" Intrigue glistened in her expression.

"Is it that obvious?"

"If someone pays enough attention, but I don't think you need to worry about gossip. Most of the people in the Veil would be glad to see the four dragon heirs happy and smiling. Other than a few glimpses from time to time, they haven't been truly happy since the day the curse befell them. It would be a welcomed change. But that's not to say the others wouldn't be jealous. Many have tried to claim the heart of a dragon, but until now, none have succeeded."

"You don't find it strange?"

"It's not for me to judge. If there is one thing I've learned, is that nothing is impossible. Who knows? This might be exactly what fate planned."

I chewed on her words, unsure if I believed in fate. I wanted to believe we carved out our own destiny. "I never imagined I'd feel so strongly about four different men. I'm unsure how to handle our relationship, to find a balance between the five of us." My body also was attempting to find balance amidst the powers I now held. Perhaps they were linked? Or perhaps I was reading too much into the connection between the power of the stones and the dragons. Was that the reason I had such intense feelings for the four descendants? Because I'd been chosen?

Could it be destiny after all?

"I'd say your instincts have been leading you, and it's worked so far. Don't overthink it. Let what feels right guide you. They are as puzzled by you as you are by your feelings," she offered with more wisdom than her youth suggested.

I chuckled. "Keeping the descendants on their toes is my full-time job. I knew I'd like you."

Juniper had been right about many things, including the healing properties of the broth. I was feeling more stable and almost myself again.

Almost.

We set out on foot, the snow crunching under my boots as we walked. It was so densely packed in some places, that the descendants took turns lifting me over patches to keep from falling behind. Rogue flakes of snow sputtered from the overcast sky, and the winds howled like a lone wolf looking for its pack.

It had taken some convincing to get the dragons to venture out of the castle with me, but after two additional days of being fussed over, I needed fresh air and purpose. I must have said the words "I'm fine" at least a hundred times, but still, they wouldn't let me lift a finger. It wasn't until I threatened to go out on my own that they begrudgingly agreed.

However, as soon as we were about to leave, Kieran had dragged his feet, being a total diva, and stalling our departure in the hopes I would change my mind. Then, they each had come up with something they had to attend to before we left. After Issik announced he had some papers that had to be signed, I put my foot down, warning him that those damn papers that were suddenly so important were about to go up in flames.

And because they all knew how temperamental my abilities were, we had left the castle promptly.

Tugging the deep purple cloak closer around me, I tipped my head down into the hood to escape the bristling winds. Why the hell were we traipsing around on foot? I much preferred to travel by dragonback. Jase wanted to keep close to the castle for our first journey out, with the portals only partially shielded by the curse, he didn't want to take any chances of running into something nasty.

I didn't doubt Tianna had her eyes on us. In fact, I swore I could feel them staring at us from the shimmering surface of the Pool of Mirrors.

Bitch. The word seethed in my mind, fueled by every cut, every drop of blood spilled, and every person she'd hurt.

"Who do I need to kill?" Zade asked beside me. His proximity chased away some of the cold. It was handy to have him around in the frozen tundra.

Then I remembered. I had fire of my own. There was no reason for me to freeze to death, assuming I didn't accidentally set myself ablaze. It might not have been the best time to test out my magic, but the urge to let the tingle of fire spread in my veins was strong.

My teeth ground together. "The usual. A witch with the ugliest shade of red hair." That was a lie.

In truth, her hair was like autumn at midnight—a beautiful wine color that tumbled down her back in lush waves. She didn't deserve hair so stunning, and considering how old the hag was, it was obvious she was completely fake. Spelled, from her flawless skin to her perfect boobs. Knowing that she used magic to keep her looks and her youth, made her vain—a weakness worth exploiting if the opportunity ever presented itself. I had once seen her without the glamour. Once was enough. "Hag" wasn't a strong enough word to describe what I had seen in the mirror's reflection.

I shuddered.

"Her time will come," Zade promised.

"Whose time?" Kieran asked, bounding through the snow to catch up to Zade and me. The glimmer in his emerald eyes reminded me of a kid tromping through the first snowfall of the year.

"Never mind. Just keep your eyes open."

Kieran lifted a hand, shielding his squinting eyes from the glare of the sun. "It's hard to see with all this snow reflecting the light."

"You learn to adjust," Issik grumbled, having no problems at all as he moved. The man was born to maneuver through this land effortlessly, while the rest of us struggled.

"I'd rather not," Kieran mumbled.

This was going to be my day—a constant soundtrack of bickering dragons. It might have driven a normal person crazy, but I found some comfort in the banter—a familiarity and unity. They were like family in the way they interacted. I was part of something. I belonged.

"You figure out how to track these things yet, Blondie?"

I shot Kieran a sideways glance. "It helps if you stand on your head, and spin three times in a circle. It gets the energy flowing."

A snicker escaped Zade, while Jase rubbed his hands together to warm them. "So, you haven't felt anything since coming to the castle?"

Sighing, I refrained from pointing out that half of my time there had been spent unconscious. "No." My fingers stroked the star inside the lined pocket of my cloak. Now would be a great time for those stars to give me some kind of hint.

Nothing.

· · ·

We walked for over two hours, never wandering too far from the castle. Every part of me was stiff, aching, and frozen to the bone. Turned out even my powers had limitations. The fire in my veins had died out an hour ago, draining me to the point where I was tempted to just plop down in the snow and rest. Five minutes was all I needed. My body pleaded with me to stop as my feet dragged on over the harsh terrain.

Not a whisper or a tingle of the star had spoken to me.

Beyond the foothills gleamed the crystal castle, and I kept the sparkling glass walls in my sight as motivation for my feet to keep moving. One foot in front of the other. The tip of my nose was red, and my cheeks stung from the blistering cold.

We had avoided the bordering evergreens on the north and west sides of the castle. The woods were dense, and flecks of snow stuck to the needled branches. Issik's gaze kept shifting toward the snow-veiled woods. A deep glower came onto his face.

"We need to get back to the castle," he announced after yet another glance at the trees. "Something's coming."

A growl split the air and got carried by the wind, making it sound as if it went on for miles. We all came to a sudden halt. "Shit," Jase hissed, taking a stance in front of me. The muscles on his back rippled through his heavy black cloak.

"Is the devourer still out here?" I asked quietly. The devourer was a shadowy monster I'd rather not meet again.

"Yes," Jase said in a clipped tone.

Pulling the flaps of my cloak further around me, I moved to stand closer to Zade for both protection and warmth. "Do they growl?" I asked.

Zade slipped an arm around my waist, tugging me into his arms. His cinnamon eyes weren't looking at me, but in the direction the growl had been heard. To my great dismay, a series of cries called out, one after the other, as if the beasts were talking to each other. Whatever was coming, wasn't alone. "No. That was something else," Zade answered.

"Fun," I replied, heavy on the sarcasm.

Jase turned so he and I were back to back. Whether it was a conscious decision or not, the descendants moved to surround me from all angles. The earth went silent as the five of us listened, and scanned the surrounding evergreens piled in snow. Something was hunting us.

I didn't have the enhanced hearing they did, so I relied on the language of their bodies to warn me. Their muscles hardened; their eyes glowed; and scales papered their arms and neck as they called their dragons to the surface without fully completing the shift.

"We should go now," Issik suggested. His fingers had elongated into razor-sharp claws, and although his mouth was saying one thing, his body was poised for a fight.

The winter breeze stirred Kieran's spiky green hair. "It's too late. They're here."

Six shadowy figures emerged from the towering pines, with eyes so black they appeared to be made from the depths of the underworld. Covered in thick fur, the creatures stood on four legs. Sharp claws curled from their massive paws, digging deep into the snow for traction. They had the appearance of wolves, but on a much larger scale. Beside their erect ears, polished horns curled like talons.

They were creatures of nightmares told to little children to scare them into obedience. Their eyes haunted me the most, filled with a greedy bloodlust that chilled my soul. I had a hunch these creatures killed for sport. Tianna wouldn't need to spell them to do her bidding. These animals would tear apart anything that crossed their path.

Including us.

"What are they?" I whispered, not that putting a name to the creatures would make killing them any easier. There really should be a handbook of mythical creatures.

"Direhound," Issik hissed, his fingers flexing the claws that extended in place of his human nails.

"Are they… friendly?" I gulped, distributing my weight evenly on both feet in the snow. I knew it was a dumb question, but at some point, our bad luck had to run out. Right?

Not today it appeared.

The pack of predators paused at the edge of the clearing, eyeing us, their white teeth bared in greeting. Removing his hand from the small of my back, Zade cracked his neck. "Does that answer your question?"

Loud and clear. "Okay, guys. What's the plan?"

Several glares fell on me, but I ignored them. I'd proved I could fight alongside these warriors... sort of. "Don't die," Jase instructed me, removing a dagger from inside his boot. "And don't do anything stupid."

My fingers curled around the smooth ebony hilt of the weapon Jase offered to me. "I like it. Simple."

"Now might be a good time to try out those new skills, Blondie." Kieran grinned, flashing a pair of dragon canines that had lengthened in his mouth. These partial shifts weren't something I was used to—a blend of human and dragon. Did it take more or less of their strength?

I'd have to worry about that later.

As if a signal had been given, the six direhounds surged forward, paws flying over the snow and icy ground with an ease that made me groan. Issik drew back a clawed hand and sliced it across one of the direhound's throats as it lunged for him. Blood sprayed the pure white ground, but the beast clamped on to Issik's arm, taking him down with it.

A scream lodged in my throat, but I had my own problems.

Kieran and Zade were each engaged with a direhound of their own, leaving Jase and me still back to back while three direhounds circled us, their teeth gleaming with their snarls. I wanted to run—the muscles in my body imploring me to get as far away as possible—but I clamped my jaw tight.

I was done running.

Screw this.

Screw the witch.

I stared at the direhound in front of me. Its soulless eyes were like a portal into the pits of hell. The animal's breath came out of its nostrils in short pants. Up close, its size was intimidating—as large as a bear. One swipe with a paw and I'd be out cold. Terror gripped me.

If I was going to learn to fight, to truly defend myself, then I needed to stop thinking I was helpless and feeling like a frightened kitten. "You want me. Come get me," I taunted it, keeping my voice low.

"Olivia," Jase hissed. "Are you trying to get yourself killed?" His back flexed against mine, while he kept his eyes zeroed in on the direhounds in front of him.

"I'm doing what Kieran suggested. Testing my powers."

"I didn't realize that included taunting them," Jase snapped.

"I'm multitasking."

The direhounds were growing impatient, the thirst for the kill growing in their eyes. From either side of us, the sounds of flesh tearing, bones crunching, and teeth gnashing filled the air, but I couldn't look to see how the others were faring.

"Brace yourself," Jase hissed through his teeth. "They're about to—"

In a uniform attack, the three beasts rushed forward—one at me and the other two went for Jase. The hound was only a few feet from me when it leaped. Its giant paws unfurled in the air. Bewildered, all I could do was stare, waiting for contact.

Whoosh.

I landed on my back with a jarring impact, my head hitting the snow with a dizzying thud. Hot metallic blood pooled on my tongue, and I swallowed it as I scrambled to get up, but the beast was quick, a whiff of my fear filling its nostrils. Its front paw smashed down on my shoulder, pinning me in the compacted snow. Saliva dripped from its canines onto my face, and I grimaced, the slime falling down my cheek slow and thick, like a slug.

The direhound's head leaned forward so that its cold, wet nose touched mine, panting its foul breath over my face. Death stared down at me from those black pupils. Was this how I met my end? Killed by a furry beast on steroids?

I wanted to give up, to just let go. My body felt so cold and tired, and the creature was so strong. Hadn't I already been through enough? A dark void seemed to come over me, feeding and fueling a seed of doubt until it spread like wildfire.

"Olivia!" one of the descendants bellowed.

That dark, pitiful place I'd been sucked into vanished on a phantom wind, and I remembered who I was, what my purpose was, and what I could do. Venomous power coursed through my body, sharp and cool. My palms surged forward, clasping the direhound's chest as my nails dug in, past the thick fur and the undercoat to flesh. The beast snarled in warning at the piercing of my nails.

"Suck on this, asshole." I released the toxin that had been gathering inside me. Poison seeped from my fingers and into the animal whose eyes went wide at the first trickle of venom, but I held on, even when it jerked its head.

The beast let out a scream that was eerily human, and I knew the poison was doing its job. My ears rang as the creature took its last wheezing breath, collapsing on top of me. I didn't have time to recover. Using both my feet and hands, I pushed at the carcass of the direhound, rolling it off me.

Shoving to my feet, I took in the scene before me. The white ground was soaked with blood and grotesque body parts I didn't wish to identify—I didn't want to risk losing the contents of my stomach.

"Jase!" Issik's roaring warning made my head whip around as I sought out each descendant.

Two of the direhounds had the tranquility dragon pinned to the ground. They had been smart enough to avoid Jase's dragon breath by holding the side of Jase's face to the snow with a paw. Angry scratches ran down his neck and had torn through the side of his shirt, blood soaking the material. Those stormy violet eyes connected with mine, silently commanding me to run, to save myself.

I didn't think, only reacted. Something about seeing the beasts on top of Jase, snapping its fangs and growling in his face, severed the thread on my control. Molten fire burned through my veins, the switch between powers as simple as blinking. Poison gave way to fire. Rage or a wild instinct to protect what was mine burst out of me.

Sensing my approach, the direhound sunk its teeth into the fleshy part of Jase's shoulder. It dug in deep, blood oozing out of the side of the mutt's muzzle and dripping down Jase's arm. My gut twisted in a white-hot rage that cut through my senses.

Ropes of fire unleashed from both my hands, one end wrapping around my wrists, the other snapping free toward the direhounds. Fire hissed as it connected with one of the beasts' back, dissolving a patch of fur. I smacked the other in the muzzle, and a shriek of pain pierced the air.

Nostrils flaring, the beasts faced me, identifying me as their biggest threat. I didn't hesitate when I pulled the whips of flames back toward me. Sensing my intent, the duo charged, their paws pounding into the ground. Someone might have screamed my name, but I couldn't hear anything past the roaring in my own head.

My cloak splayed out around me, the wind picking up the ends of the velvet material. Flicking my wrists with a calculated precision I didn't know I possessed, the ropes of fire wrapped around the direhounds' throats, and with one quick yank, I snapped their necks. The crunching of bones was music to my ears. Satisfaction like I'd never felt before coursed alongside the power swimming in my veins. They were companions, one feeding off the other.

It scared the shit out of me.

I liked the power, the feeling of being feared. What did that say about me? About who I was becoming?

The fire inside me fizzled out, the flaming ropes and my energy dissipating with it, and I sunk to my knees in the snow.

"Holy shit," Zade breathed. "Did you see that?"

"Olivia's a badass." Kieran gave me a wicked grin.

I was something all right.

"Will he be okay?" I asked. It wasn't the first time I'd posed the question, and unless someone gave me an answer, it wouldn't be my last.

Jase was lying on a couch in the main sitting room, cradling his shoulder. Issik had ripped off his shirt moments ago to get a better look at his injuries. The groan of pain from Jase's lips cut through me. We had made it back to the castle, but Jase wasn't out of the woods yet.

"The direhounds' fangs carry a poison that paralyzes their prey. It allows them to bring their hunt back to their den, and that's when the true torture begins," Issik explained while his fingers made quick work of assessing Jase's injuries.

A shiver ran down my spine. The thought of Jase being hunted like that—dragged back to a cave to be torn apart piece by piece—made my stomach churn. "It won't kill him?"

Issik examined the crimson scratches that ran down Jase's side. They were smooth marks, as if they'd been made with a blade instead of claws. "Depends on the amount of poison in his bloodstream, and how deep the bite is. If he had been bitten multiple times, it could have stopped his heart. Direhounds are lethal creatures, and not from the Veil."

I sat at the end of the coffee table Issik had pulled up to the couch, and my fingers gently stroked Jase's midnight hair. "They came through the portal?" I kept my voice low.

Beside me, Issik frowned, staring at his friend. "I'm afraid so."

"What is the point of breaking the curse that seals the portal if it lets in every nasty creature out there?" Frustration mingled with my worry for Jase.

Unable to sit still, Issik began to pace the room. "The problem is that without our full abilities, we can't close the portal, so it remains partially open. Tianna's curse is a magical beacon, attracting them. Once the curse is lifted, the signal will be gone."

And until then, we were supposed to somehow fend them off and search for the last star. Talk about making an absurd task impossible. The odds continued to be stacked against us.

Zade tended the fire at the front of the room, the crackling of wood filling the quiet room. Jase's golden complexion had become ashen as he drifted in and out of consciousness. "How long until the poison wears off?" I whispered.

Issik halted his pacing long enough to drag a hand through his hair. "Hours, but hopefully the antidote Kieran is making, will shorten the paralysis."

Jase moaned again.

I hated this feeling in my chest. It felt like my heart was going to plunge out of my rib cavity, and shatter into a million pieces. Jase's brow was damp with sweat, after a fever had consumed his body, and there was nothing I could do to help him.

Crouching down beside me, Issik took my hand, threading our fingers together. My eyes lifted to his, realizing he was watching me. The expression on his face was one of admiration and gratitude. "What you did out there… it was impressive. He might not have been here if you hadn't reacted. The poison works quick and hampered his ability to shift."

To be honest, I was doing my best to forget about what I had done. It wasn't the killing that bothered me, but that I had enjoyed the rush of magic—the power it gave me. "It doesn't seem real."

Lately, Issik and I were emotionally in sync, more so than the others. Sadness was a reoccurring theme in my life. He blinked, and calmness came into his eyes. "The guilt is normal, as is the relief at saving his life. It can be confusing."

"Is this the part where you tell me it gets easier?"

Was that a tiny smirk on his lips?

"I could lie to you and tell you it gets easier, but it doesn't. You have to learn to deal with it, to compartmentalize all the feelings, and trust in yourself."

I shook my head. "If only the emotions I felt stopped at guilt and relief. It's so complicated."

"Try me."

"A part of me liked it," I admitted with a heavy sigh. "Using magic, having power. I wasn't useless or afraid."

"You were never useless. Not to us," he assured. "Power can be an addicting thing. You're smart to fear it, but also know it can be controlled. You don't have to let it control you."

My throat tightened, and I nodded, praying he was right.

Issik's lips pressed against my knuckles as he lifted my hand for a soft kiss. "Remind me not to piss you off," he murmured. "I would hate to go head to head with that flaming temper of yours."

His words coaxed a smile from me.

Kieran had given Jase the antidote, and he was sleeping soundly now—free of pain. The feverish sweat left his body, and I draped a throw over him. I lingered until he dozed off, while Zade slouched in a chair near the hearth, promising to watch over him through the night.

I retreated to my room with the sole purpose of bathing and sleeping. In that order. Discarding my clothes on the chair in the corner, I strolled into the bathroom in only my undergarments to turn on the water, waiting as it heated.

Why don't you heat it yourself? a voice purred in my head. *Why wait?* It was my voice talking, but it felt all kinds of wrong.

"Shut up," I hissed, rubbing at my temples.

Magic wasn't to be taken lightly or used on a whim, and right now, I wanted to forget I had any extraordinary abilities. I wanted to scrub away the tingle of power that radiated from my skin. I wanted a night of normalcy, and a bath with scented bubbles that foamed higher than the tub itself.

Slipping a hand in, I tested the water temperature and removed the last bits of my clothing. I let the water rush over my body as I stepped inside, and pure delight made a moan slip through my lips. Pink bubbles popped and snapped all around me, their rose scent tickling my nose.

I stared at my body, the rouge tint of my skin, and my hands. I didn't recognize them. Turning them over left to right, it was hard to believe what these hands were capable of. No signs of magic stained my fingertips, or revealed the flames that had morphed into a lethal weapon.

Gone was the girl I once knew, and I wasn't sure I liked who she was becoming.

My eyelids grew heavy as I allowed my body to relax. The heat of the water seeped into my muscles, but I refused to close my eyes. For in the darkness, the direhounds returned with their soulless eyes, and gleaming teeth. Yet, that wasn't all I saw. Even scarier was the woman who stood with her hair flying out like flames licking the air. Her bright eyes shone with ruthless anger, and whips of fire twined around her arms.

Her picture haunted me, refusing to leave me.

After soaking in the bath for nearly an hour, the chill that had resided in my veins finally dissolved, along with the bubbles. Stepping out, I found a cup of hot tea and cream on a tray in the sitting room, with an assortment of cookies. They were the best thing I'd ever tasted, and it piqued my hunger.

Bundled in a robe, I rubbed at my chest, at the emptiness that wouldn't go away, and strolled to the bed. I picked up the Star of Persuasion and sat on top of the fluffy mattress, turning the stone over in my hands. Dying embers in the hearth washed the room in a soft light, and as I held up the stone, flecks of yellow and orange seemed to set the crystal afire.

Ancient power resided in this little stone. At first glance, it appeared dull and lifeless, but if you looked closer—really looked— you could see the beauty long since forgotten. It called to me, to my blood, and I longed to answer and make it whole once more. I could fight this feeling all I wanted, but it wouldn't change my destiny.

I was the keeper of the stars, the savior of dragons. I would do whatever it took to save them, including losing myself. If the price was my soul, I'd gladly give it.

In that acceptance, I finally found the peace I'd been seeking for days—or perhaps longer.

Slipping the crystal under my pillow, I lay down. Being in the chambers of Issik's mother made me feel protected. It didn't really make sense, but in a way, I felt closer to her, as if she would look out for me, even while I slept.

Perhaps it was the wards around the castle I was sensing, or being tucked away so remotely from the rest of the kingdoms. Regardless, there was a quiet in the air I found comforting. Jase was going to recover, and the knowledge lightened my heart.

With the fire glowing in my room, I closed my eyes and slept. No nightmares. No dreams. Just the soundless sleep my body so desperately needed.

The following evening, I found myself alone in my bedroom. After sleeping until noon, I had spent most of the day keeping Jase company. He had gained much of his strength back, including the use of his tongue. By midday, he was barking orders to the staff, and grumbling about being treated like a baby instead of a king.

I was relieved to have the tranquility dragon alive and well, but this was another setback that cost us time—time we didn't have to lose. We all felt the hands of the clock ticking by, like a bomb about to explode in our faces.

Flipping the amber crystal in my hand, I stared at it, willing the thing to do something, give me a sign. It lay dormant between my fingers, dull and void of magic. I couldn't keep carrying it around with me; it was careless. The star might not have the power the others held, but it also wasn't just a stone. Therefore, it had to be protected. I couldn't explain it, but above all the rest, this star felt important, as if one day, it would shine again. Of course, the whole idea was absurd. I had too much fantasy in my real life, and I believed anything I dreamt up could happen.

Surveying my chambers, I became hell-bent on finding a spot in the suite to hide the stone. Under my pillow wasn't what I would call a safe or inventive location. If I were the witch, it would be the first place I'd look.

As I walked from room to room, I tapped my finger on my lip, eyeing the ornate knickknacks scattered over the dressers, shelves, and the fireplace mantel—a carved jewelry box, an ivory clock, and detailed sculptures. I rummaged through the hand-painted dressers and armoires, before looking at the vases filled with colored stones on top of the nightstands.

Hmm, I wonder…

Picking up one of the vases, I was surprised at its weight and was thankful I managed to hang on to the glass without dropping it. Raw-cut crystals of milky white, rose quartz, and one eerily similar to the Star of Persuasion were inside. The idea of hiding the star in the vase held promise, but as I chewed on my lip, I realized it would be easy to forget which one was indeed the Star of Persuasion.

My search continued. When had I become so bad at hiding things? Living on the streets, it had been an everyday occurrence—stashing my belongings where no one else would find or steal them. Now, I couldn't even stow a crystal out of sight.

Pathetic.

Refusing to give up, I turned my attention to the hearth. Was it possible there was a loose brick in the stone surrounding the fireplace? It worked in the movies. It seemed like a longshot, but what did I have to lose? Running my hands along the wall, I pushed and knocked at the bricks. This was stupid, and it proved to be a waste of my time. The hearth was solid.

I leaned a hand against the mantel and stared at the elaborate, silk-draped bed, wondering if I should slice a hole in the mattress. My nose scrunched at the idea of destroying something so beautiful, and that had belonged to a queen. I couldn't do it.

A ray of moonlight, softly streaming through a small crack between the ice blue curtains, called my attention. I traced the line to where it landed on an ivory statue sitting above the mantel, just a few inches from my hand. A female with full curves was swept up in a wave at her feet. Upon closer inspection, I realized she had pointed ears like an elf. Her face was young and beautiful. The long strands of her hair blew in an eternal breeze. The wave beneath her was supported by an oval base just big enough to hide the Star of Persuasion under it.

It was a fleeting thought, but my skin tingled, and I swore the crashing of the sea wave echoed in my ears. Compelled to pick up the statue, I wrapped my fingers around the cool stone, just as a draft blew down from the flue, causing the orange flames to sway.

What is going on?

Would anything normal ever happen to me again?

I tried to pick up the statue from her perch on the mantel, intent on inspecting the base, but to my surprise, she wouldn't budge. Repositioning my grip, I tried again and noticed something odd. I could twist her, so I did. She made a complete circle before clicking to a stop. The slab of brick in front of me groaned, and small pebbles crumbled to the ground.

What the—

The outline of a rectangle broke through the bricks, opening a sliver to reveal a secret door. Could this be real?

Releasing the statue, I let my fingers trace the rough outline, needing proof it wasn't a trick of the eye. The bricks were jagged and coarse under my touch. I should have alerted one of the descendants of my find, but my curiosity urged me to take a peek, I needed to see what was behind the door.

Leaning my shoulder into the bricks, I shoved against the door, and it swung open, revealing a dark passage on the other side. From the black depths, a stale breeze blew over my face, twirling the strands of my hair. My dragons should know better than to leave me alone, even if only for a night. This was going to lead to all kinds of trouble.

I glanced back into the room, at the ruffled bed, at the clothes strewn over the chair, at the door leading to the sitting area. If I took a step into the tunnel, what would I find?

"Olivia..." a soft voice called, disappearing like a shooting star through the night sky.

My head whipped back toward the opening in the wall, and at the same time, the Star of Persuasion pulsed in my hand. I opened my palm and stared down at the stone. Its center burned brightly, in rhythmic beats.

Interesting.

One thing was clear, it wanted me to go into the tunnel, to find whatever waited for me down there.

Going with my gut, I took a single step through the door, and unless my eyes were suddenly playing tricks on me, I saw the star beat faster. Excitement rippled through me alongside a dash of unease. Using the light emitting from the star, I held it out in front of me, and moved deeper down the passage. A staircase appeared not too far from the entrance, the steps under my feet seemed very old and went on forever. From the cobwebs tangling in my hair, and the things that scurried away at my approach, this tunnel hadn't been used in years—decades, more likely.

A chill hung in the air, but considering where I was in the Veil, that wasn't surprising. Did Issik's wards extend to this part of the castle?

My footsteps were light and cautious, the only sound in the eerie quiet. The deeper I traveled, the darker it became until I was surrounded by nothing but stark midnight, and with it, came those ugly nightmares I longed to forget. My breathing quickened.

You're not trapped in a box. You're not a prisoner, I reminded myself. *You're free. You're safe. You're powerful.*

Hold up. I halted. I was powerful. I did have abilities, so why wasn't I using them? The Star of Fire might be gone, but the magic of the stone lived inside me. I proved it yesterday when I had taken down those direhounds, but my confidence in wielding magic wasn't without concerns. My abilities had changed, and I couldn't say if it was because of Tianna or the combination of the stars. I had no choice but to learn to control it… or be controlled by it.

Letting the burn of fire roar through my blood, I snapped my fingers, and a ball of flames flickered over my hand like a torch. The warm glow heated my face, but didn't harm my flesh. Wicked cool. Perhaps having magic wasn't all bad. A smile tugged at the corner of my mouth, and I continued my descent.

Once I reached the bottom, I rotated the star left to right, watching it flicker at different intervals. Before me were four paths—each identically dark and dusty. It was hard not to think about the spiders and rats that might call this underground home. A shudder rolled through me.

I am not afraid. I am not afraid. I am not afraid, I chanted over and over again.

"*Olivia…*"

The echo of my name reached me from one of the tunnels, in a female voice that caressed me as a mother's touch would. I could be walking into one of Tianna's traps. It could be her voice luring me into the dark, but that didn't explain the sudden weird behavior of the stone in my hand.

My human ears couldn't detect which tunnel the voice had come from, unfortunately. So, using slow movements, I scanned the amber crystal over each opening and chose one of the paths on the right, based on the increased pulses of the stone. "I hope you know what you're doing," I mumbled to the star.

With each step, the passage grew colder and dampness chilled the air. A drop of water hitting the stone floor echoed from somewhere in front of me. The flames over my fingers sputtered, but I pressed on, letting the stone be my guide.

How much would it suck if I got lost down here? Would the star also lead me out?

I passed multiple round doorways and other passages, but the star continued to navigate me straight.

Soon, an arched door came into view with a silver dragon standing proud on its hind legs, emblazoned on the wood. A blue light shone from under the door and onto the stones. My teeth gnawed at the inside of my cheek, considering my options. If I opened this door, I couldn't take back what I found—good or bad. I would have to deal with what lay behind the unique passage alone.

The sputtering flame at my fingers extinguished as I closed my fist. Between the luminous amber stone and the light under the door, I didn't need my fire to see.

As I placed my hand on the metal handle, a gust caused the hairs on my arms to stand up and my skin to prickle. The cool breeze carried the whisper of my name once more, and my blood hummed as if what was behind the door called to me. Was it the Star of Frost? Had I found it so quickly?

Pressing down, the handle clicked, and I gave the door a shove. Dust sprinkled from the hinges, getting into my eyes and nostrils. Briefly, I turned my face into my inner elbow, and coughed before taking a step forward into the unknown.

The smell was the first thing I noticed. It reminded me of lotuses at midnight, an odd scent for an unused section of the castle. Glittering jewels greeted my stunned face. A treasure room? Was that what this was? Beautiful tapestries and paintings hung on the walls. Crowns, tiaras, necklaces, golden goblets, pearls, and so many other dazzling possessions covered the space.

In the center of the room was a desk with papers scattered on top, and I went over to get a closer look. It was a stack of maps, and places I'd never heard of in my life. Thumbing through the pile, I realized they must be other worlds. Ellemere. Hyren. Tulans. Larken, and so many more. A million questions spun in my head.

Would the portal—when opened—allow us to travel to these worlds? Did they all really exist? Who lived there?

A candelabra sat on the left corner of the desk, and I waved my hand over the top of the used wicks, lighting the three tapered candles. Firelight bathed the desk, casting shadows over the maps.

"You like history?" A light, female voice rang behind me.

I jumped, my heart hammering in my chest, and as I whirled around, my leg banged against one of the desk's wooden legs. Pain radiated from my knee, and I cursed, letting out a string of swear words.

A woman in white stood before me, clearer and more lifelike than any of her sisters had appeared to be. I was tempted to lift my hand and touch her, to know if she felt as real as she looked.

"Such a temper," she mused lightheartedly, with a twist to her lips. "It will serve you well for what is to come."

"It's you," I breathed, the air rushing out of my lungs in relief. Oh, thank God it wasn't the witch.

"I am Eira, the former queen of Iculon, and I have something for you, Olivia." She was as stunning as I remembered, her silver hair flowing down her back like a waterfall of starlight. Her crystal blue eyes twinkled.

"Is it the Star of Frost?" I tried to keep the hopefulness from my tone, failing miserably.

"Not quite," she replied, the humor vanishing from her eyes. "But it will be of importance one day, and it is imperative you keep it safe, keep it hidden. In the wrong hands, this item could be destructive not only to this world, but all worlds."

"What is it?" I asked. Could I really be trusted to keep another crucial item safe? Did I want that responsibility? Not that it mattered. I wouldn't refuse a request from the spirit of a dead queen, who had way more knowledge about this world than I did.

The queen reached into a wooden chest in the corner of the room, and pulled out a cloth-wrapped, rectangular package. "You must not share the contents of this with anyone—not until the time is right."

God, I hated secrets. "How will I know when that is?"

"You will know," she insisted, not answering my question in that annoying way the women in white did. A glimmer of pride shone in her eyes. "You've changed. There is a light about you, a glow of magic beyond the dragon stones."

I nodded, my stomach pitching. "The witch took the Star of Fire. I'm so sorry. I tried to stop her—"

She silenced me with a look. "It is not your fault, daughter. You do not owe me an apology. Everything that happens has a purpose, even if you don't understand it at the moment."

Was she telling me that Tianna was supposed to take the Star of Fire, because in doing so, I would be granted a seed of magic? I didn't pretend to understand the workings of fate, if I even believed in it. "I don't understand."

"Take this." She pushed the dusty package into my hands, her soft fingers covering mine, felt very real and very cold. "Now, go before something picks up your scent."

The package was heavier than it appeared, like I held a textbook in my hands. "Wait!" I called out before she disappeared on me. "Who would pick up my scent?" The sudden change in her eyes, to what looked like fear, had my heart racing.

"There are things in this world, creatures searching for you, and if they get a whiff of your power, these tunnels won't be safe for you."

I worked through what she was telling me. I already knew of the creatures slipping through the portals, but how would they get into the tunnels? Unless… "Are you saying there is a portal down here?"

"That is exactly what I'm telling you, daughter. Although my body is stronger here, I cannot stay long. Neither can you. It isn't safe to be outside the wards of the castle. Now, hurry." A ripple of something unearthly and cold traveled through the air.

Her eyes went wide, and she took ahold of my shoulders, pushing me toward the open door. "Run, quickly! Do not waver! Do not lose your way!"

A gust of wind surged down the hallway, kicking up dust and blowing my hair back from my face. The faint sound of something close to a growl had my feet moving before my mind could tell them. I didn't look back to check if Queen Eira lingered, regardless of how much I wanted to see her one last time. Flicking out my hand, I summoned fire, and ran back the way I had come.

I didn't stop running. Not even when I came to the endless stairs, or when I stumbled more than once going up the staircase. I didn't let up my pace until I hurled myself through the secret door, into my room, and slammed it shut behind me.

Remembering the statue, I twisted the ivory woman counterclockwise until the lock clicked into place once again. Only then did I allow myself a moment. Slouching against the sealed wall, my breaths came out in hard pants, the cloth-wrapped package still clutched to my chest.

Dropping it onto the bed, along with the star, I walked to the bathroom to splash cold water on my face. My heart was still racing, and the face staring back at me in the mirror was bone white. My hands shook as they gripped the side of the basin. *A portal. In the tunnels.* I didn't want to fathom what that meant.

After cleaning myself up and removing the spider webs that had clung to my hair, I sat on the bed, eyeing the wrapped bundle. I had more or less stopped panting, but my heart rate had yet to return to normal. Seeing what was swaddled in cloth, and an inch of grime, probably wouldn't help, but that didn't stop me from unwrapping the package.

Dust and dirt transferred onto the lush duvet, tarnishing its beauty as I peeled back the cloth, trying not to be disgusted. I made a face, crinkling my nose against the stale smell that lingered in the air from the dust. Crumpling the fabric, I tossed the ball into the hearth, and watched the flames burst to life once the material caught fire.

My gaze returned to my bed to behold a book, so I picked it up, laying it on my lap. Why would Queen Eira give me a book? Was there something inside to break the curse or stop Tianna? It seemed and felt ancient, like something that didn't belong in mortal hands.

I wiped off the cover, revealing the title embossed in silver lettering —The Book of Stars.

Holy shit.

Was this what I thought it was? A book about the dragon stones? Could it be? Did such a thing exist?

My fingers ran along the spine, tracing the thick leather cover. Silver lined the edges of the pages, and I swore the book was singing to me. A song with words I couldn't understand whispered into my ears— a deep and slow melody full of mystery and enchantment. The Star of Persuasion lay on the bed, pulsing with the song as if it were answering its summons.

I was afraid to touch the crystal. Would it be warm? Alive with restored power? Or was I being fanciful and foolish?

As I opened the book, a tingle slid down my spine, and I rubbed the goosebumps on my arms, scanning the first page. An embossed illustration of a silver tree with exposed roots wove down the page. The roots branched off into five different tendrils, each encircling a symbol —tranquility, poison, fire, frost, and persuasion.

Hours passed while I flipped through the pages. The book was written in a divine script I'd never seen before, which made it impossible to read. Notes had been scribbled along the margins, but even then, it made little sense to me. The plethora of drawings and pictures were what kept me mesmerized.

What was in this particular book that the women in white wanted me to find? I understood why they wouldn't want something of this magnitude in the hands of a witch like Tianna. The knowledge within this book would give her more power and ammunition than one human, witch, or anyone should ever have.

However, wasn't it all irrelevant if I didn't find the Star of Frost? Not to mention, I had to recover the Star of Fire from Tianna's greedy clutches. Did I really need to worry about what was inside the Book of Stars too? Had the women in white led me to the secret tunnels, and the treasure room, at this moment for a reason?

The unanswered questions were endless.

And the dangers...

A phantom breeze flowed through the room, carrying the distinct scent of lotuses. I shivered despite the warm fire beside me.

Now, I needed a hiding place big enough for the star *and* the book. I had thought it was problematic before... I clutched the book to my chest and the stone in my hand before kneeling to peer under the bed. Grasping at straws, I desperately searched for somewhere to stash the magical objects entrusted to my care. Why would anyone think I was capable of protecting something of this importance? I couldn't walk and chew gum at the same time!

"Where the hell have you been?" Boomed a voice from the doorway.

I jerked in surprise, bumping my damn head on the bed at the sudden intrusion. Swearing under my breath, I shoved the book and the stone in a dark alcove under the bed and turned to rise, rubbing the sore spot on the back of my head. On my feet, I faced a cross-armed, glowering Jase, and steeled myself for the bitch fest that was sure to come.

"Do you have to sneak up on me all the time? Make some blasted noise when you come into a room. Or, here's a thought, knock," I barked, not bothering to hide the annoyance in my tone.

His eyes narrowed. "What were you doing under there?"

"Glad to see you're feeling better." I was avoiding the question.

"I came to your room earlier. You can imagine my surprise when I found it empty."

Keeping my expression blank, I shrugged and smoothed invisible wrinkles from my dress. "I was restless and went for a walk." It was true. I just omitted the details about the walk being through a passage of secret tunnels.

"Hmm." Jase pursed his lips, clearly suspicious. "What trouble are you up to?"

I rolled my eyes. "Why am I always the one who is up to no good?"

He lifted an arrogant brow. "Does that question deserve a reply?"

My lips became a thin line. "You're so lucky you're recovering from a near-death experience."

"You know, I'm feeling much better." His hand shot out, snatching my wrist and tugging me against him.

My palms flattened against his chest while I peered up at him with a sparkle in my eye. "Is that so?" Flirting with Jase was safer than him interrogating me. Something about his eyes, and the way he gazed at me as if he could see my soul, made it difficult to keep myself from spilling my guts. He had a way about him that made me want to share everything, to lean on him, to open myself up completely.

"You know, I had it under control."

I snorted. "Not from where I stood. You scared me. I didn't like it."

"Now you understand how I feel, but I suppose I ought to show you my thanks." He pressed a kiss to the sensitive spot just under my ear, causing a shudder to roll through me. I tilted my head to the side, giving him unobstructed access to my neck, and he flicked his tongue over my skin. "I love the way you taste," he murmured, nipping at my ear.

Slipping my fingers into his hair, I let my eyes flutter closed. Jase's kisses held their own kind of magic, and each caress melted my bones, turning my core into molten lava. "Are you ever going to kiss me?"

He chuckled, sending goosebumps running down my throat. "Good things come to those who wait," he whispered, tracing my jaw with his lips.

"I'm not a patient person." And to drive the point home, I snuck my wandering fingers under his shirt, gliding my nails over his hard abs. I was rewarded as they rippled from my touch. I wanted my lips on him.

Jase's fingers threaded through my hair, tipping my face up to meet his gaze. A hunger lit those violet eyes as they fixated on my lips, our breaths mingling. "So I've noticed." He dipped his head, and I waited, poised on the edge for that mouth to meet mine, but he skirted to the side, kissing the corner of my lips.

"What kind of thanks is this?" I pouted.

"Let me show you."

Leaning down, he pressed his lips to mine in a kiss that shook the world. His mouth was sultry, soft, and warm. Jase Dior. The dragon who had whisked me off the streets of Chicago. The heir with dreamy violet eyes and a roguish smirk. I felt as if I'd waited since meeting him for this moment, and my restraint slipped away. I needed all of him. Now. And if the damn dragon attempted to leave me with just a few kisses and teasing touches, I was going to make him wish I hadn't saved his sorry ass.

I couldn't kiss him enough. He was the most potent drug in the world. Each kiss made me want more, and more, and more. A potent need rushed through me, and he growled softly into my mouth.

"Jase." His name came out as a whimper, a prayer, and a curse.

Skilled fingers ran down to the small of my arched back and somehow slipped the straps of my dress off my shoulders at the same time. The cool temperature of the room drifted over my exposed skin as the material fell to my hips. His fingers explored unabashedly over the planes of my belly, his lips slowing down with each touch.

The change in tempo made my head spin. From hot and fast to slow and gentle. I couldn't catch my breath, nor could I keep up with the sensations rocking my body. And then his hand rose up to stroke under the swell of my breasts, and I trembled, aching to feel his touch there. My body responded to him like a minstrel strumming the strings of a harp, creating something beautiful and enchanting.

I pushed him down onto the bed. Not only could I no longer stand on my legs, but I longed to feel him closer. Straddling him, I sunk my body onto his, the blond waves of my hair falling in a curtain around us.

My fingers fumbled with the button on his pants, while my lips teased the muscles of his bare chest. I wanted the barriers between us gone, to feel all the dips and curves of my body flush against his—that perfect fit between male and female.

In one swift predatory motion, Jase flipped our positions, and I savored the weight of him pressed into me. His body was warm and solid. His smoky purple eyes filled with a ravenous desire to travel the length of my torso. I watched as his gaze devoured my peaked breasts, before he dipped his head, and took one into his mouth.

My back bowed, coming off the bed. *God, he'd been worth the wait. So worth it.* The dragon of calm and peace was none of those traits as a lover. I became aware of every place those lips roamed, from the outer curve of my ear to the inside of my thigh.

Suddenly, he paused, and my eyes fluttered open. "Why did you stop?" I asked huskily, ready to bare my teeth at him.

"I just need a moment to look at you. I want to see you when I'm inside of you."

The core of my passion tightened in response to his words. I had to have him. All of him. Now.

I reached for him, and his fingers cradled my hips as he nudged himself at the opening of my center. My eyes were caught by the vibrant violet of his, and I stopped breathing, waiting, and waiting. My hips drew up, pushing the tip of him inside the warmth of me, but he held back. Biting my lip, I groaned. A wild, almost feral hunger swept over his features in response, and still, he took his sweet time torturing me.

The muscles bunched on his arms, as his eyes simmered. "I don't like sharing. Not what is mine. And make no mistake, Cupcake, you're mine." His teeth dragged over my lower lip. "Now, and for as long as I shall live."

What did that mean? I didn't get the opportunity to pry for more details. His lips were on mine again in a deep, drugging kiss that demanded all of my attention, and wiped every thought from my mind.

We were a tangle of limbs, kisses, and teeth. Heart to heart our bodies joined, and the world drifted away, leaving just Jase and I intertwined in my silky sheets.

I lay wrapped in Jase's arms, happily exhausted, sweaty, and smelling of him. A comfortable silence fell between us for a spell before he made love to me again. It was as sweet and smoldering as the first time.

My fingers drew lazy circles around his heart, and my thoughts turned to how only a day before he'd been poisoned by the direhounds. It was an image that would haunt me for years, seeing him unable to move or speak, seeing his body fight the venom of the beasts. "You could have died, you know."

Trailing up and down my arm, his fingers paused at the sound of my voice. Glancing downward, he gave me an arrogant grin. "I didn't though, thanks to you."

"Luck. That was dumb luck."

"When are you going to accept that you're amazing? I don't even think Tianna had any idea what she was unleashing when she cast that spell. If she had an inkling of the girl who would one day break our curse, she might have had second thoughts about wrecking her evil on the Veil and double-crossing the kings."

I laughed—a short sound that came out as part snort. "We haven't beaten her yet."

Jase kissed the tip of my nose. "No, but we will."

His sheer confidence in me, in our survival, was inspiring. He made me believe it. "I love you," I whispered, nestling my head into the crook of his arm.

"Not nearly as much as I love you." His fingers combed through my hair with each word.

A calmness I hadn't felt in a long time settled over me, allowing me to drift easily into sleep, but that was where the tranquility ended.

My dreamworld placed me in a long corridor lined with Grecian columns that shone gold under the sun's rays. Water trickled in the distance, and the air was perfumed with a bouquet of magnolias, freesias, and sweet peas from the vibrant gardens around me. The air was toasty and caressed my skin while I strolled through the hall, my heels clicking on the paved pathway.

I wore a flowing white toga that barely covered the important bits. The sheer fabric moved with the wind, exposing a large portion of my thighs, but I didn't care. In fact, I enjoyed the provocative attire and the attention I received. Gold bangles clanged together on my wrists, and my fingers were adorned with rings that refracted the light as I studied my hand.

Since when did I have a birthmark on my wrist? A crescent moon marked the inside of my arm.

It was then I realized this wasn't my body... or my thoughts.

My footsteps faltered, and I barely avoided colliding with a column in my confusion.

Behind me, a rich and sultry woman laughed. "When has my sister become so clumsy?"

My spine locked into place at the sound of that voice. It was one I would never forget, not for as long as I lived, and I had a feeling it would plague me long after I was gone. "Tianna," I whispered, but the voice that came out of my mouth wasn't mine. It was softer, and full of admiration for the woman approaching me.

I turned, and my heart felt like it had been ripped out of my chest in one quick jerk.

Tianna paused in front of me, a smile twisting her berry-stained lips. "Were you expecting someone else, dear sister? A lover perhaps?" Her mocking tone suggested Tianna's sister didn't have many lovers, and Tianna's spiteful grin implied she would have been jealous if that had been the case.

"What do you need, Tianna?" the sister I embodied asked in mild annoyance, as if she was upset her peace had been interrupted. I got the feeling the witch sisters didn't always get along.

"I need your help."

"I told you. I'm not going to get involved. I have no desire to rule the world."

"Corvina," Tianna dragged out her sister's name. "I can't do this without you." Her calculating look turned into pleading puppy eyes.

I could feel Corvina's resolve weakening piece by piece, and all I wanted to do was scream at her. "You underestimate your own abilities. We both know you don't need my help."

"Perhaps," Tianna conceded. "But are you willing to let me take the chance? The dragons have called for aid. This is the moment we've been waiting for—a chance to reinstate magic where it belongs, and the dragon stars will give us that opportunity. Don't you want to feel what our ancestors had before magic was contained?"

"I doubt the dragon kings are going to hand over the ancient stars, just because you said please." Corvina spun the rings on her fingers as she replied.

"They will if they want our help to end this war. And I don't need them all. Just one... or two," she added, tapping a long, onyx nail

against her lips. The grin on her face made me want to throat punch her. Lies. Lies. Lies.

Corvina knew her sister wouldn't quit, not when she got an idea in her head. She would harp, beg, and connive until she got what she desired. It was her way. And she still loved her sister. "If I go with you to the Veil Isles, this is the last thing you ask of me. I want no part of what you do after."

Tianna looped her arm through Corvina's, flashing her teeth in a wicked smile. "Deal."

Corvina didn't really believe her sister. She knew Tianna would never be satisfied. Not even after she obtained the power she coveted, but Corvina had plans of her own. She wanted to leave Mistaven—her home. She'd had enough of her sister's schemes, and longed for a life of her own making. Of love and children. Of happiness.

The dream shifted, and with it, the cries and screams of war raged around me. When the mist faded, I caught the glint of steel slicing through the air. The world was still hazy, blurring the face in control of the broad sword. I didn't have time to leap out of the way—or Corvina didn't—but at the last second, before the blade struck its mark, Corvina raised her staff. The edge of the sword sunk into the wood, and she hissed at the impact vibrating through her arms.

Grunting, she ripped the staff free from the sword, putting a step or two of space between her and the assailant. I squinted, trying to make out the shape of the face. A nudge of recognition poked at me, but it remained out of my grasp.

My heart thundered in my ears as the magic in Corvina's veins flickered. She knew she had to end this quickly. Her powers were wavering, leaving her to rely on training and determination alone. She fought like a skilled assassin, deflecting blow after blow with her staff.

To be inside her body, inside her mind, was staggering and empowering. This was how it felt to be a badass, to know how to truly wield magic.

An intoxicating feeling rushed through me so powerfully that my body sang. Corvina unleashed a burst of magic that slammed into her attacker, giving her a few breaths to regain her composure, but it wasn't long enough.

Darkness passed over the golden sun, and in that instant, Corvina and I both knew death was on the horizon. Sadness and regret mixed in Corvina's blood with her waning magic. She lifted her staff while sparks of power danced off her fingertips, preparing herself... but it was too late.

The sword swung again, a golden light erupting from the thin edge of the blade, and whooshing toward me.

It sunk into its mark, and I glanced down to see the glowing sword sticking out of my chest. The taste of something hot and acidic hit my tongue, while my blood oozed from the entry sight, soaking the fabric of my ivory war armor. My breath slowed, becoming irregular.

"What have you done?" Corvina wheezed, dropping to her knees. The pain finally registered, soaring through my heart. Agony had me screaming before I flew backward and hit the ground with a sickening thud.

This isn't real, I reminded myself. It is a dream... or a vision. I'm not dying. I am not Corvina.

The reminder did little to ease the pain. Tears stung my eyes as I looked up into the face of Corvina's killer. Her features came into focus —a beautiful face with creamy skin, flaming red hair, and silver eyes that glistened like stars.

"Tianna," Corvina gasped, blood trickling from the corner of her mouth, and I shivered at the sensation, it was so real.

Tianna had killed her own sister.

"Corvina," Tianna sobbed, dropping down beside her sister's bleeding body. "Forgive me."

"Why?" I gurgled, blood filling my lungs. It was the last thing Corvina ever said—a question that followed her into the afterlife.

I woke up gasping. My accelerated breathing was so harsh that my lungs strained. A sharp pang suddenly radiated from my chest, causing my hand to fly to my heart. I sighed out loud when I touched my cool skin. No blade. No blood. No death.

I was alive and unharmed. It was only a twisted dream of the past —Corvina's past.

Tianna's silence over the last week made me anxious, and this dream… it only solidified my fears. She was up to something, and I didn't dare let myself wonder what, or how bad it would be when she finally came out of her wicked cave.

How could she have killed her own sister? That took a special kind of monster.

The pain ebbed, but the memory of the dream lingered for hours, and not even the warmth of Jase's arms could banish the darkness from my mind.

I staggered into the kitchen with Jase behind me, and plopped into one of the high-backed chairs. A breakfast large enough to feed an army was laid out on the table. A cup of coffee was placed in front of me, and I grumbled a thank you before splashing creamer in, followed by heaps of sugar.

Kieran sent me a lopsided grin. "You're perky today."

Huffing, I gulped down half the contents of my mug. Some people sipped their coffee. I inhaled it. "Forgive me for not waking up with rainbows shooting from my eyes. Not all of us are morning people."

Kieran's grin only grew.

"The nightmares still keep you up?" Zade guessed from across the table, where he watched me with a perceptive eye.

Hating the insight they had into my subconscious, I sighed. Yes, the dream had kept me up, but it had also been my little venture into the tunnels, and Jase that had me all out of sorts this morning. The book I'd found was still shoved under my bed, and I was itching to do something with it. No clue what exactly, but the women in white had led me to it for a reason, and I owed it to them, to the descendants, and to myself to figure out what inside the book was so important.

"It's nothing I can't handle," I replied, staring into my cup and doing my best to pretend it was no big deal.

Yet, the secrets I was keeping were taking a toll. I hated the lies, even the ones by omission. It felt wrong, and I fooled no one, least of all the descendants. They had a pipeline to my emotions, so it was ridiculous to think I could hide how I truly felt.

"No one said you couldn't, but you don't have to. There are other ways," Zade offered.

"What sort of other—" I stopped myself from asking. The answer came to me before I finished. "You mean having Jase knock me out?" I slid the tranquility dragon a long side glance. He showed no reaction to the conversation, and went about his business filling his plate.

Zade shrugged, propping the side of his face on a fist. "Why do you make it sound like a bad thing? There is no shame in using our abilities for good. Not everything in our lives is about killing. Actually, before the war, our lands had been peaceful for decades."

"I didn't mean to sound ungrateful. I guess I'm still wary of magic." Particularly when the minuscule amount I had inside me was unpredictable. I didn't know what to do with it, or how it made me feel. In truth, magic frightened me. Not the actual use of magic, but the craving for more it instilled within me.

"No one will fault you for that. It is easy to forget you didn't always know magic existed," Jase offered beside me.

"Didn't you stay with her last night?" Kieran asked Jase nonchalantly, but there was no mistaking the insinuation in his emerald eyes.

Stabbing one of the sausages, I lifted it onto my plate. "Your point?" I hated the color that bloomed on my cheeks, giving away everything.

Giving me a lazy grin, he shrugged. "Explains the shitty mood. If I had to wake up to his brooding face, I'd be as surly as a starving wolf."

I rolled my eyes. "I assure you, Jase isn't the cause." My gaze met his violet next to me.

A round of snickers ensued, even Issik joined them, and the color on my face deepened. Nothing I said would help the situation, so I just kept my mouth shut.

Jase scowled. "As enlightening as this conversation has been, we have other matters to discuss. The direhounds we fought the other day, are just the beginning of the creatures that will be lured into our world."

The sweet taste of mango engulfed my tongue as I bit into it, as I thought about what I'd learned last night. There was a portal in the secret tunnels of Iculon Keep. That could be problematic *and* dangerous. However, if I told the descendants, they would definitely want to know how I'd come to learn of such information, which would lead to a slew of questions I wasn't sure I could answer—including the fact I'd been conversing with their dead mothers. So, I continued to shove food into my mouth, to keep from saying anything.

Leaning forward on the table, Kieran held a cup of something that definitely wasn't coffee in his hand. "If we could find a way to monitor the portal, we could stop them at the gate."

"It might make a difference in whatever battle lies ahead. We know Tianna isn't going to freely leave the Veil once the curse has been lifted," Issik tightly added. "And do we really want her to?"

Jase's fingers drummed on the wooden tabletop with the question. "The first thing we need to do is seal the portal. No one leaves. And then we deal with the witch."

Issik's face was a hardened mask when he glanced at us. "Our abilities won't be hampered by her curse any longer. She won't be able to take us all on."

"She managed to manipulate our fathers a century ago," Jase reminded us as a caution. The witch was cunning. No one believed she didn't have another agenda at play. Her thirst for the stars, for power, wouldn't end with the curse. That much we could guarantee.

Zade was quiet for a moment, his fingers clenching, unclenching, and clenching again. "Right now, our top priority is finding the last stone, and killing any creature that doesn't belong here. As long as the portal is ajar, our world is in danger. We need the last star."

All eyes fell on me, and I winced, the fork between my fingers freezing midway to my mouth.

"How are you feeling?" Kieran asked. The tattoo on his arm flashed from under the sleeve of his shirt as he crossed his arms.

His was a twofold question. "I'm fine," I insisted. Other than the nightmares, that was mostly true. "But I haven't had any inclination to where the last stone might be. Not yet," I said, predicting what they all were dying to know. The pressure was on. As long as the portal was open—even a sliver—the Veil was vulnerable.

Perhaps this was all part of the witch's master plan. The curse. The stars. The portal. The creatures. Destroy the Veil. Destroy the dragons. Gain a slice of the power of the gods.

The dancing snowflakes that fell from the late afternoon sky held my gaze, while I sat curled up on the center of my bed. A few days had passed by with little activity, which should have been good, but I couldn't figure out why it made me so rattled.

It could also be that Mother Nature had decided to curse me today with my monthly cycle. I stretched across the bed to grab the cup of hot tea that Juniper had brought me a few minutes ago, and winced at the pain slicing through my lower abdomen. Cramps were the devil. I breathed through the pain, my fingers digging into the duvet, and I swore under my breath.

I should be grateful. However cruddy and horrid I felt, it meant I wasn't pregnant. I couldn't imagine having a baby at my age, or in this world, with the cruelty of the witch who wished to rule over it. Not to mention, which descendant would be the father? Talk about a colossal fight in the works.

The tea was laced with a natural pain reliever. Juniper had informed me it would help ease the cramps. What I wouldn't do for a bottle of aspirin right about now. I glanced down at the cup. *Juniper, you better be right.* And drank half of it, eager to have the herbs kick in and fix me.

While lying in a fetal position, I noticed Jase show up to darken my doorway. My eyes flicked in his direction, shooting him an evil look only a woman could understand. He was dressed from head to toe in black—I called them his ninja clothes. The sleeves were cut off to showcase the strength of his arms, and he looked ready for battle.

"What are you doing still in bed, and why aren't you dressed? I waited ten minutes for you." We had resumed training yesterday—much to my dismay—but at the moment, the idea of moving at all made me groan. Jase, however, wasn't happy. Ten whole minutes was a lifetime for the punctual dragon.

"Training has been canceled for the day," I informed, shaking my head. "There is no way you are getting me out of this room. I'm taking a sick day."

Instant concern entered his eyes, and he crossed the room, sitting on the edge of the bed. His cool fingers pressed to my forehead. "You're ill?"

"Calm down." I swatted at his hand. "I'm not sick in that way. I'm… indisposed. That's all you need to know."

Lines creased over his brow as he continued to stare down at me. "Juniper mentioned you were unwell."

"I'm not sick," I emphasized, wondering how many times I had to say it before it got through his thick skull.

Jase's eyes narrowed as he looked me over. "You're not quitting on me, are you?"

Tugging on the blanket, I pulled it up to my chin. "Can't a girl just have a day to herself?" I huffed, nothing I said seemed to satisfy him or make the dragon leave me alone. Couldn't he see or sense my reluctance? Maybe it was Zade's connection that alerted them to my short temper and misery.

"What's wrong? You seem moodier than usual."

"You have no idea," I grumbled, picking at a loose string on the bed.

His fingers brushed a strand of hair off my forehead. "Well, if you're not truly sick, then there is no reason we can't do some drills. Perhaps we could take the day off from combat and work with your abilities, test your body to see how it is holding up with the three powers."

"You really are a hard ass, you know that? I'm tempted to tranquilize you."

His brows rose.

"I assumed with your expertise of women, that you'd be able to tell when it's *that* time of the month."

That stunned him. No more talk about training came from his full lips, and for the first time, Jase's cheeks grew red. He actually blushed in embarrassment. "Oh."

It was difficult to hide my smile at his sudden awkwardness. I took guilty pleasure in making the descendants squirm, which I hadn't expected to enjoy doing, like poking a bruise. I laughed lightly. "You should see your face." It was a memory I planned to tuck away for the next time I needed a good laugh.

"Um, if you need anything…" he stuttered, forking a hand through his obsidian hair.

God, could he look any more adorable? "I'm fine," I assured him. "I just need an entire plate of brownies, and some more of Juniper's tea."

Pleased to have an excuse to leave, he couldn't have jumped at the opportunity faster. "I'll have the cook whip you up a batch." And he would, I realized, because I had asked, and he wanted to make me happy.

"Thanks, Jase."

Bowing his head, he quickly exited my room with less stealth than he had arrived. I swore I heard him bump into a chair and curse under his breath before the room went silent, and I was once again alone. Geez, you'd think I had the plague, but at least the cramps had subsided for the time being. Juniper's brew of tea had done the trick.

The descendants took turns poking their heads in throughout the day, inquiring if there was anything I desired, but for the most part, they left me to nurse my cramps and let Juniper take care of me. Their concern was cute but unnecessary, as if they didn't quite know what to do around me. For all the females in their life, they really could have used some sisters. I still had the plate of brownies I'd requested earlier, but had already polished off two.

Snowflakes glistened on the window panes, sticking to the glass as the snow began to fall with gusto. I wiped the crumbs from the corners of my mouth and slid off the mattress to dig out the book hidden under the bed along with the Star of Persuasion. I'd been aching to take another peek inside, since I'd found the Book of Stars days ago, but the opportunity to do so alone hadn't presented itself until now.

Taking the book and the stone into the sitting room, I dropped them both onto the table as I took a seat. It was as I remembered, ancient, heavy, and alluring. My fingers ran over the leather jacket, tracing the symbol etched into the cover. The ink seemed to glimmer under my touch, and tingles pranced down my arm, warming my blood.

Magic calls to magic.

I didn't know where the words had come from. They were just there, echoing in my head, and ringing with truth. Did the powers granted to me by the stars call to other kinds of magic, like Tianna's, or what was in between the pages of this old book?

Only one way to find out.

Gingerly opening it, I leafed through the pages of the text, trying to make sense out of nonsense. I didn't know why I bothered with the book, I couldn't read the strange markings. Yet, the title was in English. It didn't make sense. Why title a book in one language, but have the script be in another? The book was so old, I found it hard to believe English was even a language when it was written.

Hours went by as I examined each page, staring at the intricate swirls, accents, and glyphs penned into the journal. I couldn't say why I'd spent the entire evening combing through the pages when I had no hope of deciphering the symbols, but something pushed me on, page after page. On the first floor, the clock struck ten, and I glanced up from the book, stretching my arms and neck.

The candle on top of the table flickered over the parchment, and the pot of tea Juniper had left for me hours ago had grown cold. I was about to call it a night, as I flipped one more page, when the Star of Persuasion pulsed with one vibrant glow of amber light. I stared at the stone that lay beside the book, wondering what had caused it to awake. The only time the star had ever shown any signs of life had been when I found the secret door, which in turn, led me into the tunnels and to the ancient manuscript.

Was it trying to tell me something?

My eyes swept the room, scanning for… I didn't know what. Trouble? A spirit? Tianna? I peered through the doorway that led into my sleeping chambers, but nothing stirred in the other room that I could see. So, what had caused the stone to react?

Another mystery to solve.

I returned my attention to the open page, and something about the markings there tickled the back of my mind. A tightness grew in my chest, my blood warming in a way that had the seed of magic within me awaking. What was happening? I stared harder at the scribbled marks. Were the letters wobbling? I blinked, and my heart thumped harder in my chest.

The marks weren't just blurry; they were shifting, reforming themselves.

My fingers clutched the sides of the table to keep them from trembling, while my mind tried to decide if this was good or bad. Probably bad, I concluded, but I couldn't make myself shut the book, or stop gaping at the glyphs that were now words—words I could read.

How was this possible?

My fingers ran over the text, unsure what I would feel when I touched the page, but the words were smooth on the paper. I did, however, detect a tingle of magic. The book read like a journal, with someone's notes jotted down for future reference.

"To restore what has been lost, place the object within a drawn conjuring circle. Do not break the circle until the words of restoration have been completed. Any interruption will negate its ability to restore the power. For the spell to work, there must be a kernel of magic left in the item. Without this, the amulet can't be revived.

Magic requires a sacrifice. A few drops of blood from the spell-caster must be deposited inside the circle. The three symbols born from the language of the gods should then be traced inside the space, using the blood as ink. If the ritual is done correctly, the object's magic shall be replenished to its full potential. This spell works best under the moon."

I swallowed.

Could it be?

Had I found a way to restore the power of Tobias' star?

Did I want to restore its power? Was it vital to breaking the curse or killing the witch? Was that why I'd been led to the book, to this spell? Question after question whirled in my head while I stared at the text, reading the lines again and again.

It really was a spell to restore power to an object of magical devices—an amulet, like the Star of Persuasion. Yet, whether the ritual actually worked remained to be seen. I stared at the stone still sitting on the table under the candlelight, and my heart quickened as I waited for a sign or a signal that never came.

Was I doing this? Was I really going to perform a spell, in my bedroom, with no idea what I was about to unleash? I pressed the heels of my palms into my eyes and rubbed.

"What should I do?" I whispered to the empty room. No one answered. No spirit. No voice.

The halls outside my room were still. Nothing stirred. Was it even possible for me to perform the ritual? I wasn't a witch, but the book had said nothing about needing magic. Was I looking for loopholes because I was afraid it would work, or that it wouldn't work?

What did I have to lose? And with that thought, my mind was made up, so I stood to my feet.

I stepped into the hall in search of something to mark the floor with —chalk or a stone. The castle itself seemed to be sleeping. Down and down the stairs I went, my feet soundless and frigid on the tile floor. It didn't take me long to find something that worked—a charcoal stick in Issik's office—and I managed to make it back to my room undetected as if fate wanted me to cast this spell.

Back in my quarters, I pushed the table to the far corner of the room, making space to work. I gathered my dagger from the dresser, the book and the star, and sat on the floor. Setting the supplies carefully beside me, I picked up the charcoal stick and reread the spell slowly. I didn't want to make a single mistake, not even the smallest of infractions. Satisfied that the first step seemed simple enough, I took the charcoal stick and drew the best freehanded circle I could muster on the white floor. Hopefully, the gods didn't dock me points for my lack of artistic skills.

The hair on my arms rose as I placed the persuasion stone in the center of the conjuring area, and a phantom wind whirled through the room—sending the flame of the candle on top of the table sideways. My eyes quickly swept the space to make sure I was still alone, and a ghost or something else hadn't wandered in uninvited. Anything was possible now, with the secret door to the tunnels in the other room. I didn't trust any little noise or movement as insignificant, but the air died down, leaving me alone with the book and the star.

Taking a deep breath, I returned my eyes to the page, reading the next step. Blood. This part made me squirm. Why did it have to be blood? Couldn't magic demand a different price, like a lock of hair, or a sprinkle of holy water? Not that I knew where to get that either, but it was a lot less painful than cutting myself.

My palms grew damp with sweat as I clutched the dagger, preparing to pierce my own flesh. *You can do this. Just a quick prick and a few drops of blood. No big deal.*

Then why had ice frozen my veins? Why was my hand shaking as I brought the tip of the blade up to my finger? If I didn't get my shit together, I was going to end up cutting off a limb. I had to do it quickly, and before I lost my will. Closing my eyes, I applied pressure and sunk the end of the dagger into the pad of my finger.

At the first sting of the blade, a flash of Tianna's face materialized behind my eyes, as if she had been summoned out of the darkness. I froze, my entire body locking up, paralyzed with fear. The air in my lungs stopped as I waited for the next cut of her dagger across my skin, but the pain never came.

My eyes flew open, banishing her demon, but the wild fear lingered. *She's not here. She can't hurt me.* I chanted in my head until I wasn't trembling anymore.

Focusing on the star once more, a calming wave flowed through me. With a deep breath, I held my hand over the circle while blood welled on the tip of my finger, running down my arm. I pinched my index finger and thumb together, watching the light liquid drip, drip, drip into the conjuring area. The bright ruby red dots shone under the golden glow of the candlelight.

I returned my attention to the page, studying the three symbols I was to draw. This was the final step. Dipping the charcoal in my blood, I set forth to copy the first mark, careful not to disrupt the outlined circle. When I finished the first one, I leaned back, inspecting my craftsmanship. Satisfied that it was the best I could do, I drew the other two glyphs in a line just under where the star sat. The marks left soot and blood all over the white floors, and I idly wondered how I was going to explain to Issik that I'd ruined his mother's chambers.

Yet, the thought instantly vanished because I had bigger things to worry about. What had I done?

A ring of pure white light lit up the circle, beaming upward as if it were reaching for the heavens. Its energy pulsed like a force field propelled off the light, warning me not to touch it or risk being electrocuted—or something equally as horrible. Every single hair on my body responded to the sudden change in the atmosphere, including the hair on my head that now floated around my face.

The bricks, columns, and icicles that made up the castle rumbled at the outburst of magic from my room. My fingers grasped for the table leg on instinct, reaching for something to hold on to in the quake. An amber light suddenly flooded the room, emitting from the star, followed by a humming that grew louder with each second, until it was a chorus of a thousand angels singing.

Heart pounding, I scooted back on my butt, putting some space between the circle and myself just in case things went boom. My hand lifted to shield my eyes against the torrent of light, but it was hard to take my gaze off the stone. A thread... no, not a single thread, but three strands inside me tugged me toward the circle.

I gave in, unable to fight the demanding urge, and moved closer, keeping my eyes on the star.

"Claim me. Only you have the favor of the gods. Only you, keeper of stars, can wield my power..."

Then that blinding light erupted, leaving the stone in the center of the floor. The marks vanished along with the circle. The Star of Persuasion glittered a deep gold with flecks of orange.

"Claim me..." the stars insisted, as if they were not four stones, but one star.

My fingers lifted, stretching toward the stone, but I hesitated a mere breath away. If I touched the star, I would be accepting the power that came with it—the ability of persuasion. It wasn't something to be taken lightly. Already, my body had shown signs of distress from absorbing the other stars, but that could have also been a reaction to the magic I'd stolen from Tianna. Either way, it was a gamble.

Fuck it.

I exhaled and plucked the stone off the ground, waiting for sparks to fly, for the magic to happen. The Star of Persuasion didn't disappoint. Power crashed into me like nothing I'd felt before, so different from the calm of tranquility, the viper of poison, or the scorching heat of fire. Persuasion was smooth and warm, like swimming in liquid gold. It was unforgiving and compassionate in the same heartbeat. My body rippled and contorted as I rode the wave of magic coursing through my veins.

From far off in the castle, a roar sounded, but I barely dwelled on what or who it could be. The other powers inside me all seemed to rejoice, swirling and mixing together like long-lost friends. With the side of my face illuminated by a small shaft of moonlight, and raw forces stirring in my essence, I never felt more alive than I did at that moment.

Or more frightened.

Thundering footsteps pounded outside my chambers moments before the door burst open. Four dragons loomed over me. My head lifted, with the Star of Persuasion still clutched in my fist.

"What the hell have you done now?" Jase demanded, his violet eyes piercing me with a glare that would have sent most girls running.

I released a long breath, hoping it would quiet the magic swimming in my blood. My hand lifted, and I opened my palm, revealing the glowing stone to the four dragons. Some things you had to see with your own eyes to believe.

As expected, utter silence fell over the room as their faces paled, and once the shock wore off, I had a lot to answer.

Jase pinched the bridge of his nose. "How?" was all he said, while the other descendants stared at me with their jaws still on the floor.

My arm fell back to my side. "I-I found a book." The response sounded lamer out loud than in my head, but I hadn't thought this far ahead. When I'd started this insane idea, I knew I would have to explain how I suddenly had the power of persuasion, but I naively thought I might have a day or two to digest the information myself. That was a fool's thinking when living with four magical dragons.

"A book?" Issik echoed as if I'd lost my mind. Perhaps I had with all this power inside of me.

"And you're just now telling us about it?" Jase rumbled. He towered over me in nothing but a pair of boxers, and it was then I noticed the others were all sparingly dressed. It was evident I had gotten them out of bed.

I sighed. My first night alone in weeks, and I'd still managed to get myself into a situation.

"Yes, but there's no need to get pissy with me. I fixed the damn stone. Isn't that what matters?" They were missing the point here. Sure, the castle had quaked for a minute, and I'd dabbled in a craft I didn't understand, but no one had died... yet. I guess the night wasn't over.

"I need to sit down." Zade pulled out one of the table's chairs that had been shoved in the corner and plopped onto it.

Jase bent down and picked up the Book of Stars. His brows lifted as he examined the title and thumbed through the pages, before his sharp eyes returned to mine. "Do you know what this is?"

"A book about the five dragon stars?" I phrased it as a question because, honestly, I wasn't sure what all the book contained.

Issik's intense eyes flipped from the book to me, a strange expression on his face. "It's written in the language of the gods. How did you read it?"

"Uh, I didn't." My fingers played with the stone in my hand, while I bumbled my way through an explanation. "What I mean is, I couldn't read it until tonight, when I stumbled upon a page with a spell. The letters rearranged themselves, and it became clear."

The four dragons shared a loaded look. "The letters moved?"

"Will you guys stop repeating everything I say? And why do you all look so shocked? Doesn't stuff like this happen all the time here?" I'd had to deal with all kinds of strange and difficult to believe crap since I stepped foot in the Veil, while they were more than used to it. "I don't understand why you aren't acting like I just found the holy grail of dragon books."

Zade cleared his throat from his seat, his elbows propped on his knees. "So, let me get this straight. You found the book, and then decided to do an ancient ritual to revive the Star of Persuasion."

I blinked. "Yep. Pretty much."

Jase passed the book to Kieran, who scanned a few pages before handing it over to Issik.

"This," Issik said, holding the book in the air, "hasn't been seen in centuries. How did you even find it?" He handed the relic to Zade.

That was another story entirely. "So, it *is* like the holy grail of dragon books?"

Kieran's lips twitched, his green eyes bright in the dim room.

"Something like that," Zade mumbled as he flipped through the pages, occasionally gliding his fingers over the illustrations.

"How do you feel?" Jase asked, crouching down beside me.

My gut tightened at the question. "Like I just swallowed a pill of sunshine. My whole body is tingling."

Kieran gave me a mischievous look. "Persuasion, huh? This should be interesting."

"You think we should find Tobias?" Issik asked.

Jase shook his head. "Without his dragon, he has no connection to the star. I don't think he'd be much help. Besides, he gave it to Olivia for a reason. Perhaps this was it."

Was he implying that Tobias might have known I'd find the book, and be able to restore the stone that had been entrusted to his family for centuries?

Kieran smoothed back his rumpled hair. "Who would have thought the book was hidden here this whole time? Issik, you never had an inkling?"

Issik stiffened. His cold eyes darted to where the book now laid on the table before they flicked back to me with an intensity that had icicles forming in the room. "Never. I'm very interested in how darling Olivia managed to find it. I've combed every inch of this castle multiple times in the last hundred years, and never once have I come across this book."

It was in that moment that I knew I could no longer keep the tunnels a secret. I told them about the door by the fireplace, the tunnels, and the treasure room where I'd found the book. I left out the part about the woman in white, but I mentioned the portal, confessing I had felt it rather than actually seen the opening into this realm, which was true. I'd only been told about the portal but had never seen it with my own eyes.

When I was done, Issik stepped closer. "Show me."

"Now?" I squeaked.

The stoic expression on his face made me squirm. "I get that you've had a long night, and are probably tired, but it would be a great help in securing our safety if you showed me the door. Growing up, I heard stories about the Westgard who built this castle—my great, great grandfather. He was said to have designed an escape route from the royal chambers. I spent my youth looking for the hidden doors."

Kieran snorted. "Leave it to our Olivia to find them in record time. It's what she is good at—finding the danger."

Wonderful. I rolled my eyes. "I'm not some world-renowned detective."

Zade's lips quirked to the side. "Don't underestimate yourself. From where we stand, you're that and so much more. You have no idea how special you really are."

Sighing, I placed a palm on the floor to boost myself up, when Kieran shot forward, taking my left wrist in his grasp. "You're hurt," he hissed, noticing the blood on my hand. He inspected the injury.

I'd completely forgotten about the prick to my finger. "It's just a small cut. The spell required my blood."

Four dragons scowled at me, a low rumble reverberating in the back of their throats like a pack of wolves. "The next time you get it in your head to do a spell, tell one of us so we can make sure you don't bleed out or something," Issik admonished.

I gave him a droll look. You'd think I'd cut off my hand. As usual, they were being over the top, but some small part of me was comforted by the fact that they cared so much. "I'll do my best." My reply earned me a few more growls of disapproval. No one was more surprised than I, when an answering growl came from the other room. "Tell me that was one of you," I blurted, jumping to my feet.

The descendants threw themselves in front of me, forming a first line of defense.

Cold sweat trickled down my spine. What were we dealing with? Was it Tianna? Had she sensed the spell? Did she know I had the Star of Persuasion and had come to take it from me?

Over my dead body. I wasn't about to let her get her pointy nails on another stone. This one belonged to me and me alone.

Another vicious roar tore through the room, causing a dull throb in my temples—the beginnings of a headache. The night had started to wear on me, and the prospect of going up against Tianna right now filled me with an exorbitant amount of dread. My fingers slipped through Kieran's, with him being the closest, and his hand tightened around mine.

"How did it get past the wards?" I whispered, the words burning in my throat. Was this my doing? Had I unleashed something else with the spell? Or attracted it with the magic I'd used? Whatever it was, the thing sounded like a rabid beast with a nasty bite.

Issik bent down to pick up my discarded dagger on the floor. Bursting into a dragon wasn't practical in the small space, and they had all rushed to my room without a single weapon, an action I could see they were now regretting.

"These tunnels might not be protected by the wards, and if there really is a portal in them…"

Just as I'd feared. I'd been warned by Issik's mother not to linger in the tunnels.

"I think it's time you showed us where this hidden door is," Jase advised, moving slightly to let me lead the way into the bedroom.

Zade grabbed the candle from the table, lighting the path to the other room. The logs in the hearth were still warm, their orange and red embers glowing softly in the gray ash. I went up to the fireplace mantel, sensing the descendants watch my every movement, and spun the statue. The brick wall to the right of the hearth groaned as a slender gap broke from the bricks, revealing the outline of a door.

"She wasn't lying," Kieran murmured.

Swiftly, I stepped back from the door. "I'm not imaginative enough to make this shit up."

"I can't believe it's been here this whole time." With the dagger in his hand, Issik moved to press his shoulder against the door.

"What are you doing?" I hissed. My hand grasped Issik's arm while claws scraped down the bricks from the other side. The moment he opened the door, that thing was going to pounce.

His glittering eyes met mine over his shoulder. "It knows you're here, Little Warrior. We must dispatch it. If it got into the tunnels, then it can get out. We can't allow this thing to run around the Veil or bring others."

Disbelief swept through me. They were going to go up against a beast while half naked.

I knew he was right, but that didn't make releasing his arm any easier. As dragons or warriors, I still feared for their welfare. If anything happened to any one of them…

Issik shoved his shoulder into the bricks, and the door gave, swinging open to the darkness. I didn't dare breathe while something stirred in the shadows. Two crimson orbs gleamed out of the blackness. Zade waved the candle in front of the doorway, lighting up the stairwell I knew led downward and deep into the tunnels. The flame grew brighter, flaring with my distress.

The creature was something sprung from the devil's nightmare. Horns wrapped around the sides of its three faces, falling in line with its bared canines. Rows of fangs poked out of its mouths as the beast let out another deafening roar. Its talons dragged over the floor with an awful shriek, and the ground trembled under its massive paw, slamming down in challenge. Animal to animal.

I blinked and blinked again, assuming my eyes couldn't focus in the dim light. Did it really have three heads?

Issik rolled his shoulders once before he plunged into the stark midnight of the passage, meeting the beast on the stairs. His name tore from my lips, but Jase and Kieran were there to stop me from mind-lessly running through the doorway after him. I struggled against their arms, unable to suppress the instinct to help Issik, to protect him as they always guarded and shielded me.

Still, the width of the passageway wasn't big enough for both of us to fight the creature. I would only be in the way, so I stopped straining, and watched with my heart in my throat as Issik took on the three-headed monster.

The creature gave one snotty snort and barreled toward Issik. With his feet firmly planted, Issik held his stance. The blade became sheathed in ice under his frosty grasp. At the sound of jaws snapping in rapid succession, my blood froze in my veins. Issik lunged back, swinging the dagger through the air at one of the beast's throats. Blood the color of sticky tar spurted from the wound, covering Issik's arm, but whereas one head now hung limply to the side, the other two released a shriek of rage and sorrow that vibrated from one end of the castle to the other.

It rose up on its hind legs and thrust his claws at Issik's chest, scoring his bare flesh with a bellow. Issik staggered backward into the room, but not before he pushed the dagger into the underbelly of the beast. Yet, the creature didn't fall. It stood on its back legs once more, advancing toward Issik like it was part man. Toward all of us.

What is this thing?

It tipped back its remaining two heads. Its craggy teeth dripped drool as it fixated on me with the anticipation of a kill, but to get to me, it would have to tear through four dragons. The bloodlust in its eyes was feral and not of this world. If given the opportunity, it would shred the descendants to pieces, bit by bit, enjoying each death, but the beast would save me for last. The intent of the animal was clear as it sized up our group.

I had to do something to stop it. The descendants needed an opening to cut off both heads, because I had a sinking suspicion that was the only way this creature from another world, a hellish world, would die. Issik gave no sign that his injury bothered him. His face tilted slightly to the side, the impenetrable mask of a warrior born to slay evil in any form.

My hands thrust out at my sides, power hurtling through me and singing in my blood. The stone in my grasp pulsed with fervor.

Kieran swore under his breath when he noticed my movement. "What are you doing?"

Shrugging him off, I squared my shoulders, and met the beast's eyes without flinching. "No," I seethed with a conviction that had the room buzzing with magic. "You won't hurt them."

"Have you lost your mind?" Kieran hissed between clenched teeth.

I couldn't break my concentration to answer him, or the beast would break free from the hold I now had on its mind. Apparently, I didn't need a manual to learn how to control someone or something, but I was going to give most of the credit to the stars. The combined abilities seemed to guide me, whispering what needed to be done, perhaps even informing me of the creature's weaknesses. Was that how I knew how to kill it? The stars had whispered it to me?

Something to ponder another time, when our lives weren't being threatened.

"She's using the power of persuasion," Jase whispered in astonishment, quickly followed by a command. "Zade, Issik, now! While the beast is still enthralled."

Zade stepped beside Issik, and together, the fire and ice dragons formed a wall of the hottest fire and the coldest ice—a combination that to any mortal would have been lethal—and some supernaturals as well. But this creature wasn't so easy to kill.

"We have to cut off its other heads," I informed them, while the wall of flaming ice kept the creature at bay for the time being.

"When did you become such an expert on killing beasts?" Jase shook his head. "Never mind, I don't want to know."

Issik held up my dagger. "Well, this will have to do." And with that, Issik lunged through the flames, the blade an extension of his brute strength. He brought his arm down with a force no mortal man would ever possess and cut through to the back of the beast's middle neck. It wasn't a clean beheading, but nearly. It took a second swipe to finish the job.

Thick, black blood coated the end of the dagger as Issik tossed the blade to Zade who caught it at the hilt, wrapping his fingers firmly around the leather binding. He turned to the last head, which snarled and snapped at him, waiting for any opening. Then he plunged the dagger into the top of the beast's head, through flesh and brain. The sound of the creature's cry was like a banshee's. Zade ripped out the knife, and used his next two blows to fully sever the head. It thudded to the floor, rolling toward Jase's feet, black blood streaking across the white tiles.

"I'm going to be sick," I muttered, my stomach rolling. That was something I desperately wished I could unsee. Kieran pulled me into his arms.

"I don't think it's safe for you to sleep here anymore," Issik wheezed, his breath labored from the exertion.

Hell, I wasn't sure I'd ever be able to sleep again.

I stood on a rooftop in the center of a city I never thought I'd lay eyes on again. Chicago. Skyscrapers jutted up all around me, tall and proud, crammed so close together it was as if they were stacked on top of each other.

Frowning into the evening wind gusting between the buildings, the air smelled of twilight and trash—a combination that wasn't pleasant, and one I didn't miss. A hint of rain hung in the air while nothing of interest happened below in the streets. No late-night partyers stumbling home. No nefarious deals happening in the back alleys. No taxis roaming the roads. The city and its twinkling lights were still.

And yet, I knew I wasn't alone.

My hand grasped onto the cool metal railing as I stared out over the city I had once loved, but now every memory was coated with pain. Why was I back in Chicago? More importantly, how did I get here? On top of a roof no less?

The building wasn't one I recognized, just another flat area with a makeshift garden, a few plastic lawn chairs, and a dodgy iron fence around the perimeter. The rooftop itself was in dire need of repairs, uneven and lifting at the corners. Water pooled in the pitted sections.

Once I had lived in a brick complex very similar to this one, and often hung out on the roof. It was where I'd snuck my first cigarette, and where I'd run to when I wanted to be alone or cry. The vast skyline always made my problems seem so small. Now, as I soaked up the view, I lamented that my problems couldn't be solved by a good cryfest or a long drag on a cigarette.

My life had changed, and there was no going back.

A blackbird squawked as it landed on the edge of the roof, drawing my eyes. The little critter shook out its ruffled feathers before tucking its wings to its sides. It watched me with an intensity that had a shiver running all the way to the base of my spine. Its claws clanked against the metal as the bird readjusted its grip, angling its head to the side.

Its silver eyes bore into mine, and I recognized the mocking look in them. The bird was laughing at me, and I could almost hear the haunting cackle that often invaded my dreams. It didn't matter what form or what world we were in, the thirst in those silver eyes was the same. What a bitch.

"Why am I here, Tianna?" I spat her name out like an old piece of gum, but kept my expression bored.

At that moment, a chill wind blew in from Lake Michigan, and with it, the blackbird lifted its wings, throwing back its head. Those wings became slender alabaster arms, the black feathers transforming into a flattering dress that hugged the curves of a woman. Strands of long red hair fell in waves over her bare shoulders, and in nothing but a few blinks, Tianna stood before me, her skin shining like moonlight.

"Olivia, my dear, such a beautiful night out in the city." She smiled

in that unmerciful way of hers—wicked and villainous. "I thought you would like a trip down memory lane, considering what day it is."

What the hell was she talking about? What was so important about today of all days? I didn't want to fall for another of her foul tricks, but my brain was still trying to work through what she was getting at with this parody. What day was it? In the Veil, dates hardly mattered, except for one. Summer solstice. It was less than a month away, which meant it was June.

My heart dropped into my stomach, and stayed there, twisting and churning as though a dagger had pierced it. Had it really been a year? June, my mind echoed. It was the month my mother had died.

Today was the one-year anniversary of her death.

I didn't want to know how Tianna acquired the knowledge. Having her be the one to remind me of the most tragic thing that had ever happened in my life, made me want to rip out her tongue with my bare hands. That was one way of silencing the witch.

"You didn't forget, did you?" She lifted a hand to her chest in mock surprise, the golden bracelets on her wrists clanging together. "I hate to impose on such a sentimental day, but I'm sure your mother would want you to honor her."

"You don't know anything about my mother," I yelled, the words punctuated with actual venom—a green mist of poison spewed from my mouth.

"Temper. Temper." She tsked her tongue, like I was a child to be scolded as she waved off the cloud of poison.

My fingers curled into fists, anger trembling through my body so violently, that it felt as if the ground was shaking with me. Did she want me to lose control? Was that why she taunted me, to judge how powerful I was?

"Your magic will do you no good here, seeing as this isn't real. This is all created from you. I just plucked out a few memories, and viola, we have the city to ourselves. You have quite the eclectic memory bank."

"Get the hell out of my head," I growled, baring my teeth.

Her scarlet lips curved into something ancient and sinister, reminding me just how old and dangerous she was. "I guess we've gotten the pleasantries out of the way."

The tapping of her spiked heels against the roof echoed through the city, and my eyes followed her every movement. I wasn't buying the whole "I can't hurt you here" act. She was a witch. Nowhere was safe, not even my dreams, and this had to be that—a never-ending nightmare.

"You stole something that belonged to me, you little thief."

I moved away from the banister, positioning myself in a less vulnerable spot—not wanting to be shoved over the edge of the building. My eyes never left hers. "I guess that makes us even," I retorted.

She laughed, and my chest tightened. "Not quite. You owe me something in return." Her voice was low and threatening.

"And let me guess, you want the Star of Frost," I asked with more bravado than I felt.

Her silver eyes took on a whitish glow that would have been pretty, if not for what lurked behind the look. "The dragons' pet has a brain, which is more than I can say for all the other girls before you."

"I won't give it to you," I assured, certain of that fact. The wind whipping over my face was cool, but fire scorched my veins.

Tianna took a step closer to me, the black feathers on her skirt fluttering. "There is only one minor detail... I have your blood."

"What does that even mean?"

"You'll see, my dear. You'll see."

I didn't like surprises, especially from a witch. "You're positive I can't hurt you? Because I'd really like to test out my new abilities on someone, particularly a worthy adversary."

Darkness seemed to gather around her, swathing Tianna in an armor of shadows. A flicker of intrigue sparkled in her eyes. "I'm flattered, but our time has come to an end." How quickly that twinkle had turned into something wolfish. "You have five days to get me the Star of Frost. Five days before I storm the castle. Issik's ice wards won't be able to keep me out. And remember, dear, I'm always watching."

Her warning slithered through the air until it was crawling up my neck, whispering its threats in my ear.

My heart beat so violently that breathing nearly became impossible. Yet, through the panic, an idea emerged, and I thought this might be an opportune time to test the limitations of hurting her in my dream world. I knew I only had a few seconds and had to make them count. The magic answered my call, unfurling inside and waiting for my command, but I didn't give Tianna a chance to see what I was planning. Without warning, I lunged at the witch as the tips of my fingers lengthened into claws made of flames.

"Not if you can't see," I roared, scoring my nails over her eyes.

Blood slid down her beautiful face, trickling into her mouth as she screamed like a banshee. Fast as a viper, the witch struck out with her hand, cracking her palm against my cheek. I went flying across the rooftop, tumbling onto the ground. Pain erupted from my hip, and my cheek stung, but I shoved myself into a sitting position. The sharp metallic taste of blood pooled on my tongue, and I spat at the witch's feet.

I smiled, my teeth stained red. "Go to hell." I could feel the witch's blood and flesh under my nails, and I hoped the wounds scarred, marring her beauty and taking her sight.

Ruby red scratches ripped her skin open on both sides of her face, scorched by the fire. "You will pay. You will suffer. And those you love will die!" She transformed back into the crow and took to the black skies.

I awoke in a dark room. Whiffs of rain, garbage, and burnt flesh still lingered in my nose, mixing with the scent of Issik—cool, crisp, winter pine. The dying embers in the hearth provided little warmth in the room, and I pulled the covers up to my chin.

Fuck.

What had I done?

It was hard to tell myself it had only been a dream, when every single moment of the nightmare had felt so real, from the wind on my face to the city lights, and the blood...

The feeling of her bloodied skin under my fingernails was still present… *My lip.* I touched the corner of my mouth—where the witch had cut it with one of her many rings—and in the glow of moonlight, sticky blood smeared my fingers. Both hers and mine.

"Bitch," I muttered, wiping my hands clean. That lying whore. Couldn't be hurt my ass. Good. I hoped her scratches and burns stung, and she got to feel some of the agony she was so fond of delivering. With any luck, the damage would be permanent.

I struggled to believe that I had turned my fingers into sharp, flaming weapons, or that I'd had the nerve to attack her, knowing damn well she would retaliate. Was I a glutton for punishment? Or did I just not care anymore? Perhaps I was just beginning to understand and embrace who and what I was, and the power that was mine to control.

Issik stirred beside me, his light blue eyes glowing like the moon high in the cloud-shrouded sky. The white sheet clung around his waist —blanket hog—exposing four dark gouges on his chest that had my face paling… again.

The creature was dead, but it didn't lift the worry from my heart. More would be coming, and would continue to hunt me down until I found the Star of Frost. Five days Tianna had said, but I had my own agenda. I would find the damn stone, not because she had ordered me to, but because it was the only way to end this curse and the torment.

With gentle hands, I traced the lines on his skin, measuring the width with my own fingers. The marks were at least three times the size of my fingers, and the cuts went deeper than he had let on. They weren't clean scratches, but serrated and messy that would leave long-lasting scars… like mine.

The Ice Prince and I had both endured wounds of war, and it made me sick with rage.

"Are you planning on setting the sheets on fire?" Issik's voice sounded in the silence, heavy with sleep.

It took me a few steady breaths, to calm the sudden inferno that had risen up and blazed inside me. I hadn't even realized I'd summoned fire magic until Issik spoke, but now I could feel it roaring within me like a living thing, ready to come alive.

Silently, he watched me gain control of my abilities, and rein in the fire burning off my skin in waves. His fingers gently caught mine and he slowly brought my hand to his lips, in a kiss of frost that cooled my flesh. Yet, my eyes were still on his chest.

"I'm fine. They'll heal," he whispered roughly.

My gaze lifted to his as I rolled onto my side to face him, but the sudden darkness that flashed in Issik's eyes had me instantly on alert. Was it Tianna? Had the witch already come to seek her retaliation for what I'd done? Had I truly harmed her? My body stiffened alongside his on the bed. "What is it? What's wrong?"

Issik continued to glare at me, a muscle at his jaw ticking. "You're bleeding." The pad of his thumb lifted to my split lip, and with a gentleness that defied the Ice Prince's demeanor, he rubbed at my bottom lip, inspecting the cut.

A rush of air expelled from my lungs. That was all? He had me ready to leap from the bed, magic once again tingling in my blood. "A gift, courtesy of Tianna," I informed him.

"How?" he demanded, wide awake and prepared to murder.

"How does she do anything? Dirty and with magic."

Clearly, Issik wasn't satisfied with my attempt to brush it off. He wouldn't let it go until he got answers.

A defeated sigh left me. "She invaded my dreams, but I'm not the only one waking up with a reminder of our encounter tonight."

He caught my drift, and by the scowl on his full lips, he wasn't pleased. A long silence followed. "What did you do?" he finally asked.

"I gave her a taste of her own medicine."

"Olivia." My name rumbled from deep within his chest.

With the memory still fresh, my face fell, and I lifted my hands to peer under my nails. "I don't even know how I did it."

"Did what?" he pressed, his patience balancing on a thin line.

"I tried to gouge her eyes out."

"You what?" His voice rose as he shot upright in the bed. "She could have killed you. Of all the reckless things you could have done…" He raked a hand through his blond hair.

I sat up after him. "It was a gamble, but I called her bluff. I want her to know that I won't quake in front of her. Not anymore."

Something akin to pride shone in his eyes, a grin tugging at the corners of his mouth. "You're something else, taking on a witch. I should wring your neck."

"I'd settle for a kiss instead." I batted my eyelashes at him in the nearly dark room.

He glanced down at me with a shameful look in his eyes that had a thrill dancing through me. "She's using your blood to keep tabs on you, to break into your mind, and God knows what else."

A comforting thought. "Probably," I agreed reluctantly. In hopes of steering the conversation away from the dream, I ran a hand over the lower half of his belly, feeling the muscles quiver at my touch.

"What did she want?" he asked, his eyes darkening.

"She…" I started to say, but then I remembered. Today was the anniversary of Mom's death, and it struck me like an arrow to the heart, leaving me paralyzed with gut-wrenching sadness. The wound in my chest opened, blooming until I couldn't control my breathing, or the panic from digging its claws into me.

Issik felt the sudden onslaught of sadness that barreled into me, as I gasped for air. "Olivia," he whispered my name, but I couldn't hear it over my ragged breathing. I only saw the word form on his lips.

Torn, I lost control of everything, of the room, my surroundings, my grip on reality, my powers, and most of all, of myself. It all spiraled swiftly away from me, as if I was back in that stagnant hospital room that smelled of sickness and hopelessness, and the doctor in his white lab coat was telling me Mom had passed on to a better place, one void of pain.

I had called bullshit then, yelling at the doctor, at the nurses who had rushed in to help. The screams and the thrashing had continued until there was a sting in my arm, followed by a welcomed blackness. For in the dark, there were no feelings, no hurt, no loneliness, just… nothing.

"Olivia," Issik called, more forcefully this time. His gentle fingers were under my chin, urging me to look at his face. "Just breathe," he encouraged, becoming a focal point for me. I conceded, working on slowing my breathing. "That's it, just breathe."

Regardless of my slowed breathing, the frenzy inside me wouldn't subside. I couldn't restrain the mounting power ready to wreak havoc. My wild gaze flew to Issik's, warning him of the storm about to hit. He needed to take cover, protect himself. I was on the edge. I had to get out of here, had to get air. Magic crackled in my veins, a combination of tranquility, poison, fire, and even persuasion.

Instantly, Issik seemed to understand. "Just hang on," he pleaded, but that was the thing, I couldn't. He jumped out of bed, flashing to the window at the far end of his bedroom, which was nearly as large as his mother's room—although hers was on the opposite side of the castle in a tower that went up multiple stories. The glass groaned as he lifted it to let in fresh air.

Before the crisp breeze could reach my scorched cheeks, unbridled magic ripped from me, on a sob that broke from my lips and exploded over the room. Fire licked the ceiling; poison curled over the floor in a pine green mist; tranquility swirled around me like a violet cloak of vapors, and persuasion's invisible force field blasted out of me, along with an echo of agony that rang over the castle, waking even the dead.

Swiftly lifting his arms, Issik threw out a shield of ice around himself, and if it weren't for his dragon speed, he would have been thwarted by one of those elements.

Kneeling on the center of the bed, I gawked in horror at the whirlwind of chaos I'd created. The release of both magic and emotion had purged my soul, leaving me raw and full of regret.

What have I done?

Using the last bit of strength inside me, I banished the powers of the stars, my hands falling slack at my sides. Tears stung my eyes with a mixture of guilt and sadness, but although the heaviness still pressed down on my chest, my breathing finally leveled.

Issik shattered the wall of ice, shards raining to the floor. "That was unexpected."

He was telling *me*. It wasn't every night I woke up and became a tornado of power.

The low fire in the hearth had extinguished, surrendering the room to complete darkness. Exhaustion weighed down on me as I curled myself into a ball. "I'm sorry. I'm so sorry," I repeated.

The mattress dipped with Issik's weight. His cool fingers brushed aside the damp hair plastered to my face. "You don't have anything to apologize for. Trust me, we've all lost control before," he assured me.

I couldn't look at him, so I kept my eyes averted, staring at the rumpled sheets. My gut was a tangle of twisted knots. "Still, I could have hurt you. If I had—"

One minute, I was wallowing in despair, and the next, Issik was kissing me. It was more a kiss of comfort than passion, but it made me feel alive, and I didn't know if I should be grateful or feel guiltier.

His fingers entwined into the mess of my blond locks, pulling me into his embrace. No other words were needed, not with Issik. He just understood what I needed and demanded nothing in return.

My little breakdown instilled in me a renewed sense of determination, to wipe Tianna from existence, and propelled me into action.

"Five days before I storm the castle…"

That had been her warning, and I wasn't about to test her limits.

Five days.

A lot could happen in one-hundred-and-twenty hours. This was the Veil, and nothing ever went according to plan.

So, I didn't have one concrete plan, but a loose one. Everything else was up to fate.

I plucked an apple from a bowl in the kitchen, and peeked into Issik's office. He and the other descendants were deeply engaged in a discussion about what had happened last night. Specifically, the elusive portal, Tianna invading my dreams, and the fact I could get hurt in them. Before roaming to the kitchen for a snack, I reminded them that I had also been able to injure the witch in return. We could use that to our advantage if the opportunity presented itself again.

That got shut down real quick by four overbearing, pain-in-my-ass dragons.

Didn't they see that they couldn't always protect me, not if we ever wanted a chance of breaking the curse? The stakes were much higher now, especially because I had omitted my looming deadline from my encounter with the witch.

The chime of a clock from the great hall rang through the castle, and I turned away from the den, taking a bite of the apple. Let them discuss portals and witches. I had one task—to find the Star of Frost.

That was exactly what I was going to do.

Today.

Before any of them noticed I'd been gone too long, I took the stairs to the fourth floor of the castle and hooked a right at the landing, toward the room that had been mine until last night.

God, had it really been less than twenty-four hours since I restored the Star of Persuasion? Time seemed to be in a weird loop of countless minutes sometimes, and then other times, hours flew by as if they were mere seconds. I couldn't get a grip on my days and nights.

The pressure was on, breathing down my neck like a shadowy beast about to devour me whole.

I fished the stone out of my pocket, holding it in my hand. "You better do your thing. I'm counting on you to find the last piece, your lost sister. Think you can handle that?" The star appeared to be in a helpful mood, the smooth angles glittering like gold in the sunlight. But that wasn't so unusual, the stones were known to pulse with life on their own. Except, what happened next was definitely not normal.

"Key of dragons..." An ethereal voice that was neither male nor female but something else entirely whispered in my ear.

The apple I held in my other hand dropped to the floor. It thudded on the ground with a crisp and juicy whack.

"Hello?" I called out, scanning the shadows for the source of the voice, but I already knew I'd find no one. It had come from within me, versus a person or spirit lurking around the corner.

"Your fate awaits you, and in it your future."

"Who are you? What do you know about my future?" I demanded, feeling like a fool.

"You are bound to this world, to us, in life, death, and beyond. We belong to you as much as you belong to us."

The fact that I hadn't started running and screaming yet, was a testament to how accustomed I'd become to bizarre things happening to me—including unexplained voices in my head. A shrink would have a heyday with me.

I bent down and picked up my bruised apple. "Are you the Stars of Dragons?"

"We are far more than stars. We are the spirits of gods long since forgotten. We are power, life, and death. We are you."

Oh man. That was a little too deep for me, a spiritual plane I wasn't ready to dissect, but I'd roll with it. "Great, then let's find the missing piece."

"She's close," the voice assured me, and I hoped it was one I could trust.

"Like in the castle?" I asked for clarity.

"Not precisely."

"Wonderful. You're about as much help as the women in white," I mumbled and continued to walk down the corridor.

S tanding in front of the door leading into my old chambers, I stare at the handle as if it would bite me the moment I touched it. Perhaps it would. Nevertheless, every bone in my body was telling me the answers I needed lay beyond this door.

I should leave, or at the very least, grab one of the descendants to accompany me on this suicide quest I was hell-bent on pursuing. Yet, my fingers reached for the ornate iron handle as if an invisible force was guiding me.

"Yes. Yes. Yes," the stars purred.

My hands met an unforeseen resistance when I turned the handle. "Shit." I exhaled. Issik had locked the door—no doubt to deter me from doing something stupid… as I was now.

"Unlock it," the voice inside me commanded.

How? I wasn't a thief or a master locksmith. I had no skills at breaking and entering. However, I did have magic. Surely, no little lock could keep me out.

I went through a series of ideas based on my powers, looking for the best possible option. Finding the key was out of the question, even if I could *persuade* Issik to tell me where it was. The idea had merit and I could practice my new skill, but I shut it down as swiftly as it had entered my mind. Some lines weren't meant to be crossed, and taking away my dragons' free will wasn't something I would ever do.

Unless it was to save their life, but even then, it didn't feel right.

Only one solution seemed likely to work. I just hoped I didn't set the castle on fire. Controlled and contained. I could do this. Although it would be a shame to melt something so pretty.

My hand covered the lock, sending a stream of molten heat into the crevices of the iron. I gave it a minute before I tried the door again.

A satisfied smile curled my lips as the handle clicked and the door swung open. Thank the stars.

The air in the bedroom of the former queen of Iculon was twenty degrees colder than the rest of the castle. The room was still stunning with its billowing white curtains, gold accents, and the lovely canopy bed frame. My skin prickled from the cold as I walked farther into the bedroom, and toward the hearth. A draft blew in from under the secret door. I had been driven to this room, to the tunnels.

I placed my ear to the icy bricks, listening for any movement or sound, like a snarling beast with teeth sharp enough to rip the arms from my body. Only the howling of the winds beating against the castle could be heard. No wet panting. No razor-sharp claws scraping against stone. No witch cackling.

It was now or never. If I didn't open the door, I was going to lose my nerve, and run back down those stairs into the safety of the dragons. My fingers trembled as they reached for the statue, spinning her in a full circle. *You have nothing to fear. You're not helpless.*

"And you're not alone," the stars reminded me.

Right.

With my chin raised, I put my shoulder against the brick door that had revealed itself. This was the worst idea, especially since last night there had been a three-headed beast at the entrance, who had wanted to gut me, and probably eat me as its main course.

I glanced over at the bed, where I'd left the Book of Stars. *Go,* it seemed to say. *Go. And be quick.*

Pushy book of magic.

I put a foot over the threshold, peering down the stairwell of utter darkness—correction: utter doom, because that's what it felt like to me. The descendants were going to have my head, and if I didn't want them to stop me, I had to go. Now.

My other foot lifted.

"What are you doing?" a menacing voice thundered, making me squeal.

Shit. I spun, glaring at a golden dragon with mahogany hair as he leaned a shoulder on the doorframe. "Goddammit, Zade. I nearly tumbled down these stairs and broke my neck."

His expression didn't change. The faint amusement sparkling in his eyes never dulled. "I would have caught you."

I released a breath that became visible in the cold air. "*So* not the point," I mumbled, willing my heart to come out of my stomach, where it had dropped.

"You didn't answer my question, Little Gem."

"What does it look like I'm doing?" I retorted with a mega eye roll.

His gaze moved from my face to the pathway behind me. "It looks like you need a chaperone. There's no way you're going in there alone."

My mouth dropped open wide enough for a swarm of flies to choke me. "So, you won't try to stop me?"

He shrugged. "If whatever you think we'll find in the tunnels is important enough to risk your life for, then I can't stop you. Believe it or not, I trust you."

I wanted to assure him it was important, but truth be told, I wasn't sure myself that it was. Still, I had to go back down there. "Thank you, Zade, for not being a prick."

"I let Jase hold that title," he quipped with a chuckle.

A snort flared out my nostrils. No matter what sort of situation we were faced with, the descendants never missed a chance to jab at each other, but it was always in a brotherly way.

"You ready?" His head tipped toward the opening.

Summoning my fire, I sent a glowing ball of flames into the darkness to light our path. Its warmth chased away the eerie chill that had enveloped us.

"You're getting good at that."

My lips curved into a half smile while I shrugged. "I guess. It comes naturally now." Which was scary to admit.

Together, Zade and I hiked down the endless staircase and, at last, we reached the arched tunnel entrances. I opened my palm and extended my hand, counting on the Star of Persuasion to lead us in the right direction.

"You've done this before," Zade commented, watching me carefully as I guided the stone to each opening until it pulsed with a vibrant, glittering beat. His eyes were transfixed. "Unbelievable."

"You have no idea."

We traveled through the long-forgotten, winding tunnels, taking a different path than when I'd found the treasure room. Our footsteps echoed against the stone walls like we were walking in a tomb. Not a pleasant thought.

Ice infiltrated my body, spreading all the way to my bones. I swore even my nose hairs had frost on them. Why was it so cold? I let heat surge into my fingers and rubbed my hands up and down my arms.

"I assume we're tracking the star?" Zade guessed, moving closer to lend me his natural warmth.

I nodded. "It's somewhere in these tunnels."

His cinnamon-colored eyes were staring far ahead, scoping out what lay beyond the darkness. "Beats the bottom of a volcano."

I smiled at first, but then I remembered what had happened after I found the Star of Fire. I'd lost the damn thing to Tianna. The guilt still weighed me down, like the witch was pressing on my chest with the spike of her heel.

"I'm going to get it back," I assured. It was a vow I planned to uphold, and as I spoke the words, something inside me stirred, wrapping around my promise, as if the stars were magically binding me to the oath.

Under the flickering light of my hovering flame, the muscle along Zade's jaw thrummed. "Not if it means losing you. I'd rather have you than a family heirloom."

Though I appreciated the sentiment, it was more than a trinket passed down through the generations. So much more. And we both knew it.

I said nothing more about the Star of Fire, our feet shuffling along the dusty tunnel floor. Moisture thickened in the air, growing inch by inch the deeper we went. Icicles trickled down the stone walls, reflecting the orange ball of light. If it weren't for the consistent pulsing of the stone in my hand, I would have turned back, but I continued forward. Until Zade halted.

"Do you hear that?" he asked, his body stiffening beside me. The fiery dragon had been on high-alert mode since we stepped foot in the maze of damp and musty corridors.

Stilling, I listened, catching only the drip, drip, drip of water and... "It's the wind," I whispered, turning to face him.

He nodded, eyes bright. "But it's coming into the tunnels, not beating against them."

"So, there's an exit?" I theorized, trying to follow his line of thinking about why the direction of the wind mattered.

Zade moved in front of me. Nothing but a straight path lay before us. "It appears we're going to find out."

In no less than five minutes of walking, we came to an archway covered from floor to ceiling in cobwebs. It was thick and intricately weaved, like no spiderweb I'd ever seen before, and living in the city, I'd seen my fair share of hairy eight-legged critters. But this, this was something else entirely. This made my skin crawl.

"Something has been busy," Zade muttered, running a finger over the silken strands, and testing their durability.

The ball of fire hovered overhead, casting a soft glow on the threads of white. "Have I mentioned how much I hate creepy-crawly things?"

"So, I shouldn't ask how you feel about spiders big enough to eat humans?"

I shot him a dry look. He was joking. Right? "Only if you want me to start screaming like a little girl." The star in my palm suddenly gave a thrum of energy that vibrated through my hand. "Uh, Zade…" I held up the Star of Persuasion for him to see.

Flecks of fire sparkled in the center of his irises. "It seems we need to get through this mess."

Of course, we had to take the giant-spider route. "How certain are you that whatever made this trap is long gone or very dead?"

His features remained stoic. "Do you want me to lie to you?"

I waited a beat before replying. "Definitely."

"Stand back," he ordered, pulling out a sword strapped to his side —bigger and deadlier than my dagger. I hadn't even noticed him carrying it. A blast of fire shot through the air, glancing off his blade and straight into the network of webs. Zade's head whipped around, surprise in his expression as if he needed to make sure the source had been me.

I grinned, my fingers still tingling from the heat I'd hurled at the webs.

"That's one way of dealing with it." He nodded his head in a moment of teacher-to-student appreciation. "Well done, Little Gem. Perhaps I'd be safer behind you." He swept a hand through the air toward the now open passage, bowing his head slightly.

My eyes rolled, and I grabbed the front of his shirt, pulling him into the tunnel with me. "Come on, let's get this over with." I had a feeling we were on borrowed time as it was.

The pungent smell of ancient things and dust faded while we walked, turning crisp and fresh. We were close. My teeth chattered, the air had turned several degrees below freezing. Without the power of fire in my veins, my fingers would have fallen off already. The passage became lighter and lighter until the ball of flames was a source of heat instead of light. I quickened my pace, slipping twice on patches of ice coating the floor, but Zade was always right there to keep me on my feet.

Soon, we came upon a scalloped archway, with marks carved into the stone of the opening similar to the ones in the book.

I marveled at the sight that opened up on the other side of the arch. Zade and I stood on the edge of a cliff, and across a ravine of startling turquoise waters, was a frozen waterfall of glistening ice. It plunged into the still waters below, disappearing in its dark depths. Splashes of gold glimmered on the surface, reflecting the sun's glow. Icy trees clustered around the water's shore, dipping their heavy branches into the pond.

The arctic winds battered my hair, and I gawked, awestruck by the sheer beauty of the frozen waterfall. "What is this place?" I asked, wonder and delight lacing my words.

"That's a better question for Issik, but I have a feeling even he isn't aware of this place." Zade stood close beside me, in case a gust of wind took me over the edge. The landing was small, just big enough for the two of us to stand.

It didn't look as if anyone had been there in decades. In truth, it didn't look like it even belonged to this world but to somewhere the gods themselves dwelled. The soft lapping of water below drew my attention. "How is the water unfrozen?"

Zade's shoulders were tight under his dark tunic. His body hadn't relaxed an inch since we'd stepped foot inside the secret tunnels, and now was no different. "It shouldn't be. Not here, not this close to the castle. It doesn't make sense."

Little did in the Veil.

The chilly wind pinkened the tip of my nose and cheeks, as I lifted my face to the sky. The star was warm in my hand, bursting with excited energy that beckoned me closer to the water. It called to the sparkling of power inside me.

I stepped forward, with only one thought running through my mind —find the star. A firm hand clutched my forearm, stopping me from tumbling right over the edge, and like I'd been splashed with cold water, I snapped out of it. Startled, my gaze met Zade's.

His gold-flecked eyes were bright with worry and tinged with anger he didn't try to hide. "Hey, what are you doing? I'm about to haul your ass back inside, star or no star."

My mind was reeling, and I was so confused. That sinking feeling of being on the brink of passing out crept up from some dark corner of my mind. "I—"

Then, I was falling down into the waiting world below.

Freezing air, swirling mists, and ice surrounded me as the drop shot my stomach up into my throat. My scream was smothered by the brisk wind hollering in my face. The rocky cliff, the frozen waterfall, and the dark trees were all a blur as I sped past, the kiss of winter embracing me.

I was going to die.

Where was Zade? Why hadn't he busted out as a dragon and saved me with those majestic wings? Why couldn't I see him?

The fall was endless. I tumbled and tumbled through the eternal sky, until I thought that perhaps I'd stumbled into a portal, but then the plunge stopped, and I was suspended in nothingness.

"We have been waiting for you," a collection of voices announced.

Five of them. The mothers of dragons. The women in white.

They materialized from the gray mists, the ends of their white, tattered gowns dancing on a breeze I couldn't feel, only see.

"You brought me here?" I asked, attempting to work through what was happening.

"You are not safe here. Things not of this world linger. They are drawn to you and the power you possess."

"Because of the stars?" I asked, my feet oddly dangling underneath me.

"It is more than the stars." The eyes of the five women seemed to glow an omniscient white as they continued to speak as one. *"It is the kernel of magic and how it has transformed the power inside you. Nothing of this magnitude has been born, or felt, since the gods walked this earth."*

Oh shit.

"But the stone. It is here. I feel it. I can't leave without it," I tried to rationalize.

"She comes on wind and darkness. Her sight has been impaired, but it's not completely gone. She has other ways to find you."

Tianna.

"She will stop at nothing to find the final star. It is her last hope. Desperation makes her deadly. But also weak. This is your advantage. You must protect the grimoire. It cannot fall into the wrong hands."

"You mean the Book of Stars?" I asked.

"It will be your key. Only you have the power to destroy the darkness that has consumed her soul. She is past redemption."

That was code for I had to kill the bitch. "How can I defeat her?" Even with my new abilities, I wasn't strong enough. She always had the upper hand.

"Your courage lies here, daughter." Together, they merged into one spirit, their five faces flickering over the one head. Their shared palm pressed to my heart. *"It is a rare gift. Trust in yourself. Let your heart guide you, and with it, you will find the answers you seek."*

I hated cryptic messages, even though this one gave me those feel-good vibes.

The one being spread out its arms. *"Now, open your eyes and truly see. Only then will you be able to find the final star."*

The five queens' forms shimmered, slowly fading away like the evening mist giving way to dawn.

What the hell had she meant by open my eyes? They were bloody open.

It was the last thought I had before the cursed falling resumed—

that sense of dropping off the highest cliff in the Veil, with no dragon to save me.

But I worried for nothing because Zade was there, and he did catch me, in a way.

I blinked, coming to with Zade calling my name. His hands were firmly on my shoulders, holding me steady. His golden skin was as pale as I felt. A shaft of sunlight beaming through the trees illuminated the side of his face.

"Olivia." He exhaled my name on a loose breath, and hauled me into his arms for a quick hug we both needed. Then he pulled back. "What the hell was that? Where did you go?"

Funny he should put it that way. My eyes glanced over the edge of the ravine, a brisk wind ruffling my hair. "I was here… but I wasn't."

His dark brown brows furrowed. "You're not making a lot of sense."

Still feeling unsteady on my feet, I moved closer to Zade on the uneven rock, seeking his strength. "It's complicated." Behind Zade, in the distance, a black dot stood out in the clear sky. It was miles away, but my blood chilled as I remembered the vision. "Zade," I rasped in a low warning. "We need to leave now. I don't have time to explain. You must trust me."

"Tianna?" he guessed.

"Yes, and something else. Something not of this world. We are not safe."

"What about the stone?"

The black dot seemed to grow wider, like a feral beast set on devouring the kingdom. "We have to leave this place before the witch finds us."

Glancing over the edge of the ravine, he slipped a hand to the small of my back. His fingers tensed at some unknown evil I couldn't see, but it caused caution to prickle my skin. "It might be too late," he murmured.

I caught the glow in the center of his eyes, and the claws that lengthened in place of his nails. Trouble had already found us.

"Whatever you do, don't make any sudden movements… or loud noises," he added, sizing up the threat still yet to make itself visible.

"Why?" I whispered.

Zade's eyes narrowed. "You don't want to know."

A distorted growl and gnashing teeth made my head whip toward the sound, turning my back on the tunnels. The good news: it wasn't a giant spider. The bad news: it was still huge, hairy, and ugly as sin. Not to mention the smell. I nearly gagged when the wind carried its stench to us.

The creature stalked out from the shadows, emerging from behind the frozen waterfall. Its white, milky eyes roamed over the waters, searching. Zade continued sizing it up, while the monster did the same to us as its claws clicked on the stone, moving closer. Its slitted nostrils flared, sniffing the air in our direction, and it was then I understood.

"The creature is blind," I whispered to Zade.

He nodded, having already come to that conclusion himself. "But that doesn't make it any less deadly. When the opening presents itself, I need you to run. Do you understand? You need to head straight to the stairs and into the castle. Issik's wards will protect you."

My hand squeezed his arm. "What are you going to do?"

"I'll be right behind you."

"Liar." If it was blind and had to rely on its other senses, surely we could use that to our advantage. "I can fight. Let me—"

"Olivia!" a voice bellowed from somewhere deep within the tunnels, a voice that eerily sounded like Issik's. The stone walls behind me shook with unrestrained fury, followed by a blast of ice that rippled out of the passage.

"So much for keeping quiet," I muttered, keeping my eyes pinned on the creature.

Right on cue, it threw back its hairy head, and answered with its own war cry—a challenge. The monster turned those milky eyes on me, as though it could see me, now filled with a ravenous desire to kill.

Zade flashed me his teeth. "Remind me to wring your neck when we get out of this mess." Rage transformed his features. "Run!" he snarled at me, right before jumping over the side of the cliff.

"Zade!" I screamed. Did he—? Had he—? The asshole had left me alone up here, away from harm, and had plunged off the cliff to battle the beast by himself. Always the valiant dragon, acting on instinct alone.

He had told me to run, but I found myself rooted in place, peering at the spot where he had jumped. Zade exploded into his dragon form before he reached the water. In the chaos of Zade's heroics, I'd lost track of the creature. *Where is it? Where the hell is it?* Then Zade disappeared into the coverage of the trees.

I sunk to my knees, crawling to the edge. My hands scraped over the rough rock, hard enough to make me wince, but it didn't matter. I had to see, had to know what was happening.

A roar that could only be dragon erupted. Zade shot upward, out of the trees, and the creature lunged from its hiding spot, slamming into Zade ten feet in the air. It sent the dragon whirling into the side of the cliff, rocks and pebbles showering into the water. Its ability to track Zade in the sky without seeing him was impressive.

Using its claws, the beast latched on to Zade's back. Zade rolled, flipping himself upside down to dislodge the beast, but its nails had dug deep into his dragon scales. The bastard had used himself as bait, giving me the chance to run to safety. Damn these selfless dragons. When were they going to let me stand and fight beside them? The time had come, whether they liked it or not.

Considering my options, I gnawed my lower lip. If I sent a ball of fire, tranquility, or poison, I could accidentally hit Zade, which would be epically bad for both of us. What should I do? Did I listen for once and run, even though every bone in my body begged me to stay and fight?

A black shadow in the sky distracted me, and the decision became clear. I'd forgotten about the black dot, which was now definitely a crow like the one I'd dreamt of last night. My eyes made out the wings as the bird glided through the sky, leaving me no choice but to run. I couldn't let Tianna find me and reveal how important this place was.

I jumped to my feet, frowning and glancing one last time at Zade and the creature. He would be fine. He was a freaking dragon, a fierce one at that. I had no reason to worry.

So, I turned and ran like hell.

And I kept running, letting the star in my hand guide me. It was as if it too understood the sheer importance of my safety, and putting as much distance as possible between the Star of Frost and myself. I didn't ease up my pace, not even when a high-pitched shriek pierced the air.

I slipped once, but was quick to regain my composure and forged ahead. More than once, I swore someone was following me, and the hair-raising feeling stayed with me as I twisted and zigzagged through the tunnels, the pounding of my feet slapping the stone. The Star of Persuasion was diligent in its guidance, warming and pulsing in my hand at each turn I needed to make. *Hurry. Hurry. Hurry,* it seemed to whisper in my ears.

"Olivia?"

At first, the sound of my name felt like a dream, distant and watery, but it rang out again and again, growing closer with each step. "Issik!" I called back and pushed my legs onward despite how badly they ached. My lungs were burning, and the maze of tunnels was endless.

Have I taken a wrong turn? Where is the staircase? Where is Issik?

Around the next bend, I finally saw him. He was there, rushing to me while loose pieces of his blond hair flew about his face as he ran. The Ice Prince was fast, reaching me in a few strides. He didn't give me a chance to say anything, but plucked me off my feet and hauled me back the way he'd come.

"Zade," I gasped, my breathing choppy and rough.

That made him pause as I'd hoped, and he set me upright, staring down at me with cold steel in his eyes. My legs felt as if they would collapse, but Issik's hands went under my elbows, preventing me from crumbling to the ground. "Take a deep breath," he ordered softly, and I obeyed. "Good," he said with a nod of approval. "What about Zade?"

"We were attacked," I managed to get out before stopping for another breath.

His irises crystallized. "Is he hurt?" he asked.

"I-I don't know."

"Shit." Issik gritted his teeth.

"Tell me you have more confidence in me than that, Little Gem."

That voice. That sweet, husky voice had the fire in my blood roaring.

I spun around, and there was Zade—naked, and looking worse for wear—but he was here... alive. He leaned a shoulder against the wall. Dirt and blood smeared across his chest and one side of his face.

My heart knocked against my chest, blooming with relief. "Zade, thank God." I slumped into Issik.

A lopsided grin curled his lips. "I told you I'd be right behind you."

He had. A sound part sob, part laugh bubbled out of me, and I took a moment to let my eyes examine him fully for any serious injuries behind the grime. He looked tired, but no real wounds that I could see in the dim corridor, other than a few minor cuts and scratches.

Zade stared back at me with mischief dancing in his weary eyes. "Stop. You're making me blush." His golden body appeared to glow in the dreary tunnels.

"He's fine," Issik snarled. "We need to get out of the tunnels."

"Agreed on all accounts," Zade replied, shoving off the stone wall and taking a step or two, but that was as far as he made it before he swayed.

Issik grumbled what sounded like a curse, before stalking toward Zade with me in tow. "Do you need me to carry you too?"

Zade slightly grinned, clearly exhausted. "If Olivia doesn't mind."

I rolled my eyes. How they could joke at a time like this was beside me.

Issik untangled his arm from around me and wiggled out of his sweatpants, leaving him in just his boxer briefs as he tossed them to Zade. "Put these on. I don't know how much longer my eyes can handle your nakedness."

Catching the pants, Zade tugged them over his hips with care. "You just want Olivia to stare at you instead of my… finer points."

A gruff noise of disgust escaped the back of Issik's throat as he gave Zade a shoulder to lean on. I slid away from Issik, allowing Zade space, and started to strut down the hall on my own. "Where are you going?" Issik barked.

"You can't possibly—" Yep. He could. Issik, one-handed, lifted me up against his other side, without breaking a sweat. I looped my hands behind his head and held on, too tired to fight him, or demand he put me down. Besides, I wasn't sure my legs would make the end of the journey. "You're impossible," I whispered in his ear. "But I love you." Then I rested my cheek against his.

"You and I are going to have a little talk later," Issik replied, his breath fluttering over my face, and sending a shiver of ice through my body.

The three of us hobbled up the never-ending staircase and into the sleeping chambers, plopping down on the lush, silk-covered bed. No one cared about the dirt or blood coating our bodies. I'd kill for a glass of water but couldn't move anytime soon.

Jase and Kieran found the three of us sprawled on the bed, and staring at the ceiling a few minutes later. They had each taken a different path to hunt me down, after figuring out I'd gone into the tunnels.

"Is anyone going to tell us what the hell is going on?" Jase demanded, looking less than pleased at our comatose state.

"And what happened to Issik's pants?" Kieran added, wickedness sparkling in his vibrant green eyes.

I took one look at Zade and Issik and lost it. Laughter rolled out of me, flooding the room. I laughed and laughed until I was curled in a ball on the bed clutching my sides as the uncontrollable hysterics worked through me. I couldn't help myself. The humor of it all.

Jase and Kieran looked at each other, then to the three of us. "What did we say?" Kieran asked, his nose scrunching in the most adorable manner.

Jase folded his arms, his lips stretched in a thin line. "Perhaps they drugged her."

Kieran eyed me. "Is she drunk again? That would explain why she went off into the tunnels."

"She's not drunk," Issik growled.

Zade sat up, wincing. "Someone get Issik some damn pants."

Oh, my God. I couldn't breathe. It had been so long since I'd let loose like that, and heard the sound of my own laughter. The release felt uplifting and freeing. It cleansed me of the tension, fear, and anger binding my body and soul.

Issik waited until I gained control of myself before peppering Zade and me with questions. "What were you thinking going off on your own?" he directed at us both.

Kieran had fetched Issik another pair of sweats, and tossed them to him on the bed. Issik slipped one leg in and then the other, standing long enough to pull them over his hips.

"You know damn well you would have done the same—*did*, if I recall correctly. Or did you forget the night you went into the volcano?" Zade pointed out to Issik's irritation.

Neither Issik nor Jase were having it. Kieran, on the other hand, stood in the corner smirking. That man thrived on the discord of others.

"That's beside the point," Jase retorted, in his best no-nonsense tone.

"She was already on her way into the tunnels when I found her. I couldn't let her go alone, not after we'd seen that creature. Plus, if there is a portal somewhere in that maze, she definitely needed protection." Zade wasn't the least bit remorseful.

"Tell me the blood soaking your shirt was worth it. What did you find?" Jase inquired of Issik, looming over the foot of the bed. His fingers gripped the iron post of the canopy's frame.

Crossing my legs on the mattress as I sat up, I turned the stone over in my hand. "The Star of Frost is definitely down there, but..."

Silence fell, a disturbing and horrifying quiet after the sounds of my laughter.

"There are other things that know it's there," I added.

"Tianna?" Kieran guessed, the gleam in his eyes quenched.

I shook my head, my eyes meeting Zade's. "I think it was guarding the star," I mumbled. That creature hadn't been there by coincidence.

Everyone's attention snapped in my direction, and Zade's brows came together as he mulled over the idea. "Guarding it? Could it be?"

"Makes sense," I replied, holding his stare. Bone-deep weariness had settled in, and my eyes were heavy. "Is it dead?"

Zade shook his head. "No, the bastard disappeared on me. It probably ran off to whatever hole it lives in, to lick its wounds."

My brows knotted and I blinked. "What do you mean *disappeared?*"

"Since when does a threat ever get away from the fire dragon?" Issik asked, picking up on the gist of what went down in the ravine.

A gust of warmth blazed from Zade as he sighed. "It wasn't one of my finer moments, but one minute it was clawing at me, and then it was gone."

Making a noise in the back of his throat, Jase strutted to the fireplace to stare at the ivory statue. "A creature that can cloak, or willow-phase like a goblin? Interesting… interesting indeed."

I didn't find anything intriguing about the tidbit of knowledge. I found it frightening. "I need to get to the star it's protecting."

"We'll find a way," Issik promised, with ice-cold determination.

We didn't have a choice. *"Five days until I storm the castle…"* Tianna's warning breathed down my neck.

The moon shone high in the sky. A dark shadow moved through the night, creeping over a slice of the glowing orb. A lunar eclipse.

Perfect. Just perfect.

I took it as a sign. What better night than tonight to decipher a spellbook? There had to be something else inside the Book of Stars that could be useful.

Two days had gone by since my last venture into the tunnels, and in that time, we'd spent most of our hours in Issik's library, poring over the text inside the ancient grimoire. It was a slow process. Issik was not fluent in the language of the gods, making translation challenging, but it seemed important to learn about what was between the pages.

Now more than ever.

With each passing day, the window for breaking the curse became smaller and smaller. Then there was Tianna's threat. I had only forty-eight hours until I found out if she would make good on her promise.

We were so close, so close. I could almost taste the sweetness of victory and freedom, could almost smell the air devoid of Tianna's dark magic.

And yet, the hurdles we faced seemed so much higher and steeper than any we had encountered.

I gazed one last time at the mist-shrouded mountains, and the shadowed moon before moving away from the window to join Issik on the couch. He had the book open on the table, which was littered with old parchments, dusty books, and empty cups of coffee and tea. We'd been at it for hours already, finding nothing of importance.

His hand rubbed over the back of his neck as I sat down beside him. He didn't tear his eyes away from the page he was trying to translate. From the furrowing of his brows, it wasn't going well.

Jase had a stack of books piled up on either side of his chair—one side to read from, and the other to discard those that proved useless. So many journals existed from the former kings, along with books of healing, agriculture, histories of the five kingdoms. Many of them had been brought here over the last two days from the other kingdoms—Jase's and Tobias's being the exception. Those were lost to us now.

In the front of the room, Zade stoked the fire—much to Issik's vexation—flanked by large frosted windows. I caught him a time or two scowling at Zade's back, while the flames leaped back to life under the fire dragon's gentle prodding. The dancing flames seemed to reach out toward Zade like a lover's hand.

While Issik and I worked on the Book of Stars, the others searched for whatever they could find on the creature guarding the last star. It was decided that this particular beast, was an obstacle we were going to have to deal with in order to retrieve the final stone. Zade's answer to the problem had been simple, just storm the beast. He claimed there was no way the creature could best the four of them.

Five, I reminded myself. I was not going to sit idly by, not when I had the power to fight.

Zade's idea had merit if their abilities weren't dwindling, and their strength with it. Although none of them would admit it, I could see the change, and if I could tell, there was a good chance the enemy could as well.

I knew how much it grated on their instincts to sit around and read books, when every bone in their body demanded they take action, but sometimes smarts outwitted brute strength. We needed to know what we were getting in to before going gung ho.

While I had enjoyed the slower pace and lack of excitement over the last few days, I wondered if there was something more I should be doing than researching. People in the villages were scared and uncertain, their lives on the line. Jase's home was still encased in a spell, the people inside trapped, or worse, dead. And there were things that didn't belong in this world sneaking through the unguarded portal. Without their full powers, the descendants could do nothing to protect the Veil from the darkness that lived in other worlds. As long as the last ribbon of the curse was still tied around Issik, we were exposed to all sorts of dangers.

"Anything?" I asked, snuggling up closer to Issik on the couch to peer down at the book.

"Not unless you want to control demons, or summon a God," he replied, frustration punctuating his words.

Sucking on my bottom lip, I contemplated the options. "It might come in handy."

Issik and Jase snorted in unison.

"There has to be an easier way than this. My eyeballs are bleeding," Zade groaned.

I was inclined to agree. Days of poring over books was wearing on all of us, but on Issik the most. It was *his* star we needed to find, *his* freedom waiting to be claimed.

"Let me have a look. You need a break," I offered, nudging him to move over with my hip. It was like moving a glacier.

Issik dragged his gaze from the book to look at me. Shadows darkened the tender skin under his eyes. "I'm fine. Besides, how will you translate?"

We'd been through this every time I'd offered to help with the book, which he'd declined every time. "I have this, remember?" I said, holding up the Star of Persuasion. "It led me to a spell before, perhaps it can do it again."

The stone hadn't given a flicker of light or a beat of warmth since we'd left the tunnels. It was as if it too was drained, and needed time to recuperate its energy.

Issik's head dropped to the back of the couch, waves of coldness radiating from his skin. "It could all be for nothing, just wasted time. We don't even know what we're looking for."

"Maybe, but the stars do." I placed the stone on the table beside the book.

"A lot of good that thing has been," Issik grumbled, waving a hand at the amber star.

With my lips turned down, I stared at the star. "I think it's out of juice."

The flames licking over the charred logs warmed Zade's pinched features. "Don't tell me we need to find a spell to rejuvenate it."

I shrugged.

"Not happening." Two words Issik was so fond of saying. Everything with Issik was *no*.

Instead, Jase was already plotting. He paced from one bookshelf to the other. "Olivia might be on to something."

Was I? Now, I was all ears and feeling smug as I leaned back on the couch, putting my feet up on the table. "Thank you."

Zade smiled as he stood up near the hearth, the firelight glowing on his back.

"Don't leave us in suspense," Issik muttered, disrupting Jase's thought process.

Jase's finger tapped the spine of a book tucked into a shelf, his sable hair sliding forward. He was still working through whatever it was he was considering. Jase was the type of guy you didn't rush when he had something on his mind. "Perhaps having the stones together is the missing key."

I thought I was the missing key.

How many keys were there?

Issik's frown deepened, his head lifting off where it rested on the back of the couch. "Is that a good idea? We've always been warned about the power of the stars, and the need to keep them apart."

Zade shrugged after he had considered it. "What is the worst that could happen?"

Issik's chin rose a fraction, his ice blue eyes narrowing. "The world blows up."

"Your input is appreciated, as always." Jase scoffed.

Kieran strolled into the room with a giant bowl in his arms and one of the housemaids trailing behind him with a tray of drinks. "I figured since we're pulling an all-nighter, we needed provisions." He placed the bowl of popcorn on the table, giving my braid a tug as he passed by to take a seat across from Issik and me in one of the deep, plush chairs. "So, what did I miss?"

Taking a handful of popcorn, I wrinkled my nose at him. My stomach rumbled at the smell of butter and salt. "They were arguing about the stars," I relayed to him, thumbing through the Book of Stars and shoving the popcorn into my mouth.

"Wait!" Issik blurted out, scaring me half to death. I nearly choked on a kernel of popcorn. He shoved the sleeves of his cream-colored shirt to his elbows. "Go back a page," he directed me with a wave of his hand.

Flipping the sheet of parchment over, I paused. "Here?"

He nodded, pulling the book closer to him, as his finger ran over the line of ancient runes. Everything about his demeanor changed while he read—from the concentration lining his forehead, to the twitching muscle along his jawline. His mouth set in a grim line, and the information suddenly made his face turn ashen. The brightness in his eyes faded and he cursed at the book.

"What's wrong?" I stared at the page of symbols, hoping it would translate itself in front of my eyes like the spell had done.

Issik's hand clutched the side of the table, ice spreading under his fingers and over the glossy surface on contact. The others stopped what they were doing to focus on him, sensing the sudden change in the room. All the heat was sucked out of the room, replaced with a frigid chill that had my breath clouding in front of me.

Finally, he swallowed and glanced up, his eyes fixating on me, but soon his attention went to the other descendants. "According to the book, if Olivia absorbs all five stars, the power will kill her," he addressed them as he spoke. Avoiding my gaze.

A grim silence descended upon us. Even the flickering flames in the hearth seemed to freeze, as if they too felt the magic of the book, the power of the words.

"It says a mortal's body isn't created to withstand the power of five gods, even if it is only a grain of their full ability," Issik whispered.

The air in my lungs vanished.

Jase angled his head to the side and studied the grimoire. "Are you sure?" He was questioning Issik's translation, needing to make sure he was confident. It was an error none of us could afford—me especially.

"Yes." Issik exhaled, a violent storm churning in his eyes.

Fuck.

Five stars. Not four.

I had doomed us all. The moment I'd restored the persuasion stone, I'd made finding the last star a death sentence for everyone, for the world. If I had never found the book, never performed that stupid spell, the Star of Frost would have only been the fourth. That was all I'd needed to break the curse.

What had I done?

Dust puffed up into the air when Issik slammed the book closed with a snap. His knuckles were white, and his eyes glittered like sapphires. "I forbid you from touching the Star of Frost. Do you understand me?"

My mind was whirling, and arguing with Issik was more than I could handle right now. "You're being unreasonable."

I understood it was a shock to us all, but did that mean we gave up? I wasn't ready to admit defeat. Not yet. No way. We'd come too far to say, "Screw it." Besides, Tianna wasn't going to just let this go. She had invested a hundred years into getting the power of the five stars, and sacrificed her sister to see the deed done. That was a kind of determination that shouldn't be ignored.

Jase gave me a sharp look. "This changes everything."

"Does it, though?" I countered, scooting to the edge of the couch.

"How can you say that? Do you want to die?" Zade growled, the words raw and angry. His eyes mirrored the flames clawing at the logs.

"What kind of question is that? Of course, I don't *want* to die, but not everything in life works out the way we want." My eyes flicked to each one of them. "I don't have a choice, or have you forgotten about the curse? More people will die if we sit around and do nothing. You will die!" I shouted, getting worked up.

A collective sigh went through the room. Issik stood up and stalked to the window, leaning his forehead against the cool glass. "If this book has a shred of truth to it, then the power of the five stars will kill you. I won't let that happen."

"We can't be sure," I argued.

Jase shook his head, and I knew they would gang up on me with the sole purpose of keeping me safe. "We're not willing to risk your life on a gamble."

I glanced at each of the descendants, seeing a similar expression on each of their faces, but I wouldn't be intimidated by a pack of dragons. Future kings or not. If I didn't find the Star of Frost, they wouldn't be kings at all.

"The choice is mine," I declared. "And I choose to save the stars. Save this world. Save you." I didn't need a moment to think about it. My mind had been made up months ago. This was my fate. This was what I was brought here to do. If I was being honest with myself, the choice really had never been mine, but that didn't mean I was going to let anyone dictate what I did or didn't do.

Issik whirled around, pinning me with a look that would turn most people to ice. He was ready to argue. I could see it blazing like blue fire in the center of his eyes. "I can't live without you," he finally said, his voice just above a mere whisper, and the emotion behind his words was gut-wrenching.

"Issik," I murmured his name. They were going to make this difficult for me.

"We can't let you do this. We'll find another way," Kieran urged.

"Our time isn't up yet. Give us the opportunity to see if we can find more information," Jase reasoned, looking to pacify the situation with his levelheadedness.

I wanted to point out that, in nearly a hundred years, this was the closest they'd ever been to breaking the curse. There was no other way out. This was it.

Slowly, I blinked, understanding that nothing I said or did would help them understand. It was wasted energy I didn't have, not after the long nights we'd endured. I nodded, saying nothing.

This setback was devastating. We all felt it. Hope had been sucked from the air, leaving us suffocating in despair. I hated the emotion. Hated the way it crawled on my skin, making me feel stained with uselessness and failure. They might as well tattoo "loser" across my forehead. They meant well, but their love for me was clouding their judgment. In a way, part of me was overjoyed, thrilled even, by the depth of their feelings—to know they ran as deep as my own.

They didn't want to live without me.

But...

My eyes shifted to the window to see if the eclipse was complete. The red moon burned in the sky. An omen. A blood moon. If I believed in prophecies and fates, then this would be a sure sign of bloodshed to come.

S omeone stood at the foot of my bed.

I could sense their presence. The feeling of being watched had the hairs on the back of my neck rising, yet when I opened my eyes, no one was there.

My heart beat wildly in my chest as I slowly sat up, surveying the room. Jase slept beside me, sprawled out on his belly across the bed, while his back rose with even breaths. Earlier that night a gloom had settled over the castle, and even the staff seemed to make themselves scarce, taking the chatter and livelihood with them. It had become a frozen tomb.

I wanted to defy the descendants, argue that they were killing themselves for me, but their stubbornness made it impossible for them to see reason. Finding another way wasn't an option, not when we were so close, and out of time.

Sleep was a joke. I just tossed and turned, the sheets a tangled mess in the bed. Jase woke me a few times, whispering in my ear or pulling me into his arms. My body was so tired. I felt the exhaustion every-where—in my bones, in my magic, and deep within my soul. But the dreams continued to plague me all through the night, the whispering of Tianna's voice.

And here I was again, awake in the middle of the night, that bead of magic inside me pulsing at the presence I was certain was in the room with me. The stars didn't seem to care about the consequences the book warned about. They, more than ever, encouraged me to complete what I'd started. The pull to the ravine in the tunnels nagged at me day and night. I didn't mention the internal struggle I was in with the power of the stones, knowing the descendants would only blame themselves. So, in silence, I suffered the demand they imposed on me, suffered the sleepless nights, suffered through the dark promises of pain and death Tianna vowed in my dreams.

But something was going to have to give.

And I was afraid that something would be me.

Would that really be such a bad thing?

It was what I wanted too. At least, I believed it was. At this point, it was difficult to decipher between my desires and what the stars wanted. The two had blurred together, muddying the lines of me and them. The separation between the two was almost nonexistent.

Perhaps I should give in.

I found it hard to resist, like a scratch I couldn't reach, and I just wanted the irritation to stop. I didn't want to fight anymore. I wanted to win, and to do that, I needed the five stars. We'd become one. My willpower was at its weakest when the dragons slept, like now, as if the stars or Tianna—perhaps both—knew the right time to wear me down, and when I was the least protected.

"Olivia…"

My eyes swung to the open door, toward the sound of my name. The women in white. Was it them calling me? They might have answers I desperately needed, a way to work around the death omen predicted by the Book of Stars. I refused to believe this was it. There had to be another way. There just had to be.

And who better to ask than the queens of the Veil?

Focusing on Jase, I checked to see if he had heard or felt anything. He was the lightest sleeper of the four dragons. Go figure. The tranquility dragon. The irony wasn't lost on me.

He was going to hate me in the morning, but I had little choice. This was something I had to do for all of us, and they *had* wanted to look for another way; this could give us that, even though I wasn't holding my breath for a miracle. I would accept the answers the women in white gave me, whether I liked them or not.

In sleep, Jase's ruggedly handsome face was peaceful. It was easy to see why I'd fallen so hard and fast for him. Any girl would. He possessed such a striking combination—obsidian hair, violet eyes, pronounced cheekbones, and his lush mouth parted slightly. I could gaze at him under the moonlight for hours. I burned the memory of his face in my mind, alongside Zade's, Kieran's, and Issik's.

Pressing my lips together, I blew Jase a kiss dosed with his own power. "Forgive me," I whispered as I swung my legs over the side of the bed. My toes touched the cold floor, and I slipped on a robe before sneaking out of Jase's room and into the dark hall.

The thought of igniting a fire in my palm crossed my mind, but I found the darkness wasn't a hindrance. In fact, I could navigate fairly well, my feet knowing where to go without being told. The silky cream material of the robe dragged behind me, making swishing sounds as I moved toward the staircase.

Lotuses didn't scent the halls like I'd grown accustomed to, roses did instead. I followed that scent to the main floor, and from there, into Issik's library. Without a sound, I pushed open the door and walked into the empty room, surprised to see the fire in the hearth still glowing. It had been hours since the five of us had been in this room. The aroma of roses was so strong that it almost choked me, turning the sweet scent into something potent and foul, like rotting flowers.

"The book," a woman's voice whispered. *"Open the book..."*

I didn't have to be told which one she was referring to, only one book mattered—the Book of Stars.

A slice of moonlight came through the window, falling upon the grimoire where it laid on Issik's desk, out in the open for anyone to see. Such a thing of magic and ancient secrets should be kept under lock and key, I thought, stroking the cover. The contrast was strange as I felt the buttery texture of the book under my fingers, and the condemnation of the words inside tumbled through my mind. Everything about it felt wrong, as if they weren't my fingers, and the thought hadn't been my own.

A purr of approval escaped me as magic zapped from the book to me, and a smile curved my lips. *"Hello, beautiful,* a voice that wasn't mine said. *What hole did you crawl out of? Let's see what sorts of sordid information you've been keeping hidden between these pages, shall we?*

My fingers turned the thin sheets of paper, my eyes scanning over text I'd nearly memorized at this point, but I was seeing it through a new set of eyes. This was wrong. How I was feeling, the smell of the room, the chaotic whirling of magic that rose up in my veins, it made my blood run cold, like there was nothing I could do to stop it.

The words on the parchment were no longer foreign as I mumbled the translations through my teeth, skimming over the pages. What was I looking for?

Answers.

Right. A way to retrieve the Star of Frost without killing myself and my soul.

Unfortunately, that wasn't what I found.

My finger paused on a page near the back of the book. A drawing of a five-pointed star was sketched under a paragraph, capturing my attention. *"Well, well, well. There you are,"* the voice in my head crooned in absolute delight.

Lifting my hand, I traced the lines, a smile tugging at my mouth. Excitement and victory bubbled in my stomach. My eyes devoured the spell written on the pages, reading it over and over again, until I could recite it word for word.

This feeling of being not quite in control of myself was familiar, and I was afraid of what it meant, afraid to realize the truth of what was happening to me. The women in white weren't guiding me, or waiting for me in the library. They were nowhere to be seen.

"Thank you, Olivia, dear. I'll see you soon."

As if someone had snapped their fingers in front of my face, waking me from a trance, I blinked. The memories of the last hour were hazy as I tried to recall why I was in the library and not in bed with Jase. I glanced down at the book, and it hit me like the crack of a whip across my back. My knees buckled.

Tianna.

The bitch had used me, used my blood. But that wasn't all. She could read the language of the gods.

I steadied myself on the desk, staring at the aged parchment. She had been after a spell, this spell. Again, I traced the lines of the five-pointed star, and my heart thundered in my chest so hard I thought it would burst through my ribs. A chill slithered down my spine. The runes that moments ago had been easy to read meant nothing to me now.

A strangled sob broke through my trembling lips. "Dear God, what have I done?"

Issik found me in his library moments later, curled into a ball on the floor and crying. "Olivia?" his soft voice called. The confusion and gentleness in his tone only made the tears come swifter and harder.

My shoulders shook with emotion. Had I condemned us all because I was weak? Because I struck a stupid bargain with the witch? A deal that had seemed like everything at the time, but now... now I wondered if I should have been stronger. Then, she wouldn't have been able to use me.

Tianna wouldn't have the spell.

His body dropped down beside me, his arms brushing up against mine as I hugged my knees to my chest. I felt his presence rather than seeing him, because my face was buried in the tops of my knees. Cool fingers brushed aside the curtain of hair around my face. "What's wrong? Tell me what happened. Why are you down here alone?"

In between those words, I heard the unspoken questions. *Why are you crying? What did you do now? Where the hell is Jase?*

Dejected, I couldn't bring myself to look at him, feeling as if I'd already lost everything, including the descendants I loved with all my heart, and there was nothing I could do about it. The tears kept flowing, and when it became clear I wasn't ready to talk, Issik scooped me off the floor, gathering me into his arms.

I didn't go willingly at first, not feeling like I deserved the consoling he so freely gave, but it only lasted a few seconds. I couldn't deny myself the comfort and solace of being in his arms. Even in this, I was weak.

I was broken.

Lost.

A failure.

I couldn't stop shaking, but Issik never let go. He continued to hold me, saying nothing. Sometimes the patience he exuded impressed me. Jase was often the calm one, but Issik had a quiet restraint that seemed endless.

My face buried into his neck, breathing in the crisp and wintery scent of his skin. Being close to him, and relying on his strength helped settle the raging storm of sadness inside me. I didn't understand how this bond between us worked, and I usually considered it to be one-sided, but perhaps they also could counter the emotions I was feeling.

Finally lifting my head, I dried my eyes with the back of my hand. "I didn't mean to wake you," I sniffled, knowing it had been my sorrow that had disturbed his slumber, prompting him to find me.

"My bond to you isn't a hindrance, or something you should apologize for. Your sadness was so deep it cut through me like a steel blade. I've never been so afraid. I-I thought…" He shoved a hand through his disheveled hair. "It doesn't matter now. You're okay?"

I wasn't. Not really. Yet, I nodded, biting my lip. I had to tell him what had happened, what I had done. "Tianna came to me."

Blue shards crackled in his eyes, like water freezing, and his body went hard and tight underneath me as if he was ready to leap to his feet. "Where is she?" he growled, murder in his eyes.

"She's gone. She got what she came for." His brow lifted, but I shook my head, reading the question there. "Not the star."

"How did she get past the wards?"

"Me," I stated flatly. It was the truth.

"I don't understand."

"She used my blood to control me."

He let loose a colorful string of words I didn't understand. They sounded ancient, foul, and beautiful in the way he let them roll off his tongue. "What was it she wanted if not the stone?"

My eyes shifted to the desk where the Book of Stars still sat open. "A spell," I answered, my voice cracking at the admission of what I'd been powerless to stop. It was embarrassing how easily she'd manipulated me. I had magic and more power than I knew how to wield, and yet, I hadn't been able to stand up to the witch, hadn't even realized I was being used until it was too late.

Issik's sharp gaze followed mine to the book. "She was able to read it?"

"Yes." If I closed my eyes, I could see the page as she read it, word for word, and the picture of the five-pointed star was inked into my memory like a tattoo.

He pushed to his feet, taking me with him and depositing me on the nearby couch before strutting back to his desk. "Is it this one?" he asked, holding up the open book for me to confirm.

I didn't want to look, to see the drawing on the page, but my eyes lifted. "I'm sorry. I'm so sorry," I said, feeling the pressure in my chest bearing down on me again.

Cool fingers framed my face, and I helplessly lifted my gaze to his, finding concern in his eyes. "There's nothing you could have done. Do you understand? This is not your fault. Besides, she can't perform this spell without all the stones."

That didn't stop the dread from tangling in my stomach. She had a plan.

And I had no idea what it was or how to stop it.

Every point in my body was numb—a hollow, cold silence that threatened to drown me. And when I did feel something, it bounced between guilt, grief, and anger until it ate me alive. Then the numbness returned, freezing my insides. It was like that for most of the following day. The descendants gave me the space I desired, but I couldn't decide which was better—the utter nothingness or the flood of emotions.

I was in some sort of free fall that never ended, and I didn't know how to stop it, how to pull myself out of the darkness.

How the hell could I find the last star and fight off a powerful witch when I couldn't leave the room?

Outside Kieran's windows, nothing but clear sky and snowcapped mountains could be seen. The castle was so removed from everything and everyone. I sat in the corner by the window, gazing at the frozen kingdom.

A knock sounded at the door, and I forced myself to look toward it, tearing my focus from the glass. Kieran's expression was uncharacteristically solemn as he walked inside, spying me in the corner near the window.

He strode to the bed and sat down. "Did you eat today?"

"I'm not hungry."

"Do you want to talk about what happened?"

Thinking about it made my throat close up. "What's there to say?" My voice was flat, and my heart crumpled. How could I save them now? To do so would condemn us all.

Kieran's face was a grim mask, and it was a reminder of just one more thing I'd ruined—the twinkling in his emerald eyes. "Don't let her win. If you fall apart now, the bitch gets what she wants."

A faint ringing started in my ears. "Didn't she already?"

He rubbed his hands over his thighs. "We still have the stones, don't we?"

I shrugged. "She has me. I have the power she desires, and she means to take it from me, to use me as a sacrifice."

Kieran was on his feet and at my side in a flash, taking my hand as he sat down at the window seat with me. "We won't let that happen," he vowed.

Regardless of how dire and gray our situation currently was, Kieran still believed with that big heart of his that there was hope. I wished I could steal a sliver of that optimism for myself. I sighed. "Just promise me you will find a way to end her."

"We're not letting her take you from us."

Did any of us really have a choice? I pasted on as much of a smile as I could muster for his sake. He seemed to need it.

Kieran could see that I wanted to be alone and wasn't in the mood for conversation, but he was reluctant to leave. In the end, he slipped out of the room without me even knowing.

Once I was alone, I paced the floor for a good while, gnawing at my lip until it was swollen, red, and irritated. My slippers scuffed against the gleaming white tile, the silky material of my dress swishing with each turn I made.

Kieran's words echoed in my head. Had I just given up completely? Was I going to let her win? Was there anything I could do to stop it? Without the last stone, what could I do?

Something pecked at the back of my mind, something I was missing—a clue or a piece of the puzzle I needed to solve. It was there, within my reach, all I had to do was grab it, but the damn thing evaded me like a slippery devil.

There was a reason the women in white had led me to the book, and the book had pointed me to the revival spell. They wouldn't have doomed their own sons. The Star of Persuasion was my key to retrieving the final stone, but how?

It didn't matter. I had made up my mind.

Changing out of the flowy dress and into something more practical, I slipped into the hallway. I tiptoed down the hall, making the climb up the two flights of stairs, and from there, I let myself into my old room. This place was part of it. The tunnels, the ravine, the beast, it was all connected.

My mouth went dry as I paused in front of the hearth and stared at the statue.

Voices from behind the fireplace wall, deep within the secret tunnels, taunted me as an ancient wind blew in from the chimney, sending the dying embers dancing. I glowered at the door in front of me, a filthy string of curses reeling through my head.

I knew what I had to do.

I might very well be walking into a trap, but it mattered little to me anymore. This had to end, and sitting around doing nothing, sulking while waiting for Tianna to show her wicked face would drive me mad. If I was going to die, I wanted it to be on my terms.

With my dagger tucked into my boot, the stone in my hand, and the Book of Stars secured inside my red cloak, I returned to the tunnels, to where the Star of Frost had called to me the moment I stepped foot inside the secret door. I hurried through the dark passageways, going straight for the ravine. I had a plan—a loose, ill-thought-out plan, yet it was something.

An icy chill pricked my skin, and magic trembled at my fingertips the deeper I went, alerting me to the presence of others. "If you're watching me, see this," I muttered, flipping off the witch and her prying eyes.

I wanted her to find me, to see me. *Come get me.*

Approaching the ravine, a brisk breeze kissed my cheeks, and I nearly stumbled on a rock. A curse slipped through my gritted teeth, my breath clouding in front of my face as I drew my cloak closer around my neck. I could smell the snow and the water trapped in the ice waterfall.

By the time I made it to the arched opening that led to the cliffs, I was out of breath. The star in my hand was throbbing with energy, sensing the nearness of its sister, the Star of Frost. I could relate, for I too felt it—that gleaming thrill in my blood. My powers seemed to rise up in unison.

One foot at a time, I stepped onto the jutting cliff, watching the frozen, cascading water, the ends of my cloak billowing behind me. *Where is your furry guardian?* I had to deal with the creature before I could even get close to the stone.

How the hell was I going to get down there? I peered over the edge, surveying the drop. I kicked a rock over the side and listened to hear how long it took to hit the bottom. This was one of those times it would have been damn convenient to have one of the descendants with me. They would arrive soon enough, but I needed to be down in the ravine when they did. It was imperative I retrieved the star before they came storming after me, or else everything we'd been through these last few months would be for nothing.

It shouldn't have been this easy, but perhaps it was because this was the path I was meant to take. The answer to my problem appeared in front of me.

Standing where just air had been a moment before, the creature bared its teeth, sending a low warning rumble out from its beefy chest. I could have sworn the ground under my feet trembled. Temperamental beast. I lifted my hands in the air and backed up a step or two, letting the creature know I meant no harm—not unless it tried to bite my head off, of course. Then shit would get ugly.

"Hey, there," I murmured. "Good, uh, boy." Assuming this thing had a gender.

With sharp and wary eyes the beast snorted, shooting some sticky substance through its nostrils onto the ground.

Gross.

"I'm not going to hurt you, but I do need your help." My hands might have been a tad shaky, but I managed to keep my voice even and calm.

The black fur on its neck raised as it tilted its head to the side, regarding me. It took a step closer, sniffing the air around me to take in my scent. A short barking sound came from the back of its throat, similar to a cough or a sneeze but much deeper and scarier.

"I hope that was a yes."

Taking a moment to collect myself, I gathered the power of persuasion. It swirled with the seed of Tianna's magic and settled in my throat. What I said next would be laced with an irresistible potency that not even the beast could deny… or so I hoped.

I cleared my throat, lowering my hands. "You're going to let me climb onto your back, and then you're going to take me to the stone you protect." I stared him dead in the eyes, letting my voice croon over him and watching as his eyes turned glassy. "Oh, and under no circumstances can you attack me," I added.

The beast didn't move a muscle, but continued to stare with that blank look. I took that as a sign and shuffled closer, sliding one foot and then the other as quietly as I could. A massive paw thudded on the ground in front of me, and the beast dipped its head to bow forward.

My arms shook as I reached for it. "I can't believe I'm doing this," I mumbled under my breath, moving with care toward the creature's back.

It remained surprisingly still while I hoisted myself onto its wiry hide, and used a fistful of long fur to grip onto tightly. The beast pranced under my weight, its feet fumbling on the cliff.

In a soothing gesture, I ran my hand along the side of its neck. "Easy," I purred. "Easy."

To my shock, it relaxed under the command of my voice, and I realized traces of power were still flowing through me.

With a shake of its head, followed by a snort, we were fully engulfed in a cool ripple of darkness, suddenly riding on the midnight breeze. It whisked us off the cliff, our surroundings disappearing. It took only seconds for the feeling of weightlessness to set in, and a different sort of freedom that couldn't be found in this world spread through me. It went beyond the boundaries and laws of mortals, witches, and even dragons. This creature was born from darkness itself.

From the blackness, the world materialized again. I was in a narrow ice cavern that seemed more like a bridge. On either side of the path, were two moonstone pillars that glowed like stars in twilight. One side of the bridge had a wall of ice so shiny, that I could see my reflection. The other had icicles of various shapes and sizes.

Fascinated by the sight, I swung my feet off the beast, and hopped down to the slippery floor of frozen water. Everything in this place was made of sheer ice. Telling the creature to stay, I inched my way along the bridge, trailing a finger along the frozen wall. We were behind the waterfall, in a small alcove.

My head lifted upward, taking in the canopy of ice that twinkled over my head. The air was cold, cutting right through the warm material of my cloak. My gaze roamed the length of the ceiling and down the waterfall, causing my heart to leap in my chest.

Encrusted in the sheet of ice falling over the cliff was the Star of Frost. It emitted a pearly blue light, creating fractured rainbows that glinted off the frozen water all around it. I raised my hand, pressing my fingers to the glacial surface. The heat from my touch melted it slightly, leaving an imprint of my palm.

The beast whined at my side, as if it could sense what I was about to do.

"There is no other choice," I told it, my brows set.

Fire flooded inside me, but I hesitated. All I had to do was press down on the ice, and the flames would do the rest.

If it were only that easy.

This could very well be the end of me. So many regrets, so many wishes, so many things I longed to do with my life. And still, I had fallen in love not one, but four times. Who could say that? Some people chased love but never found their soulmate, and I had been blessed four times over.

This was for them. A gift for how cherished they made me feel, treasured, beautiful, and loved beyond belief. For the future of the most magical men in the world.

My vision blurred, and even then, I didn't realize I was crying until the warm tears slid down my cheeks. I dug my flaming fingers into the dense ice, melting it like a torch.

It took less than a minute to reach the stone.

Holy crap. I'd done it.

The last star was only inches away from my fingers. I just had to reach out and—

Abruptly, the beast bound to its feet, its low warning growl echoing around us, and I twisted my head to see what had raised its hackles. My dragons had arrived, looking none too pleased with me. The Star of Persuasion pulsed in my hand, as if urging me to return my attention to the Star of Frost, to seize it now, before the descendants could stop me.

I gave the stone a twirl in my palm, a reassurance that I wasn't going to let anything derail me from my plan.

"Olivia." Issik stepped forward, my name sounding like a curse on his lips. "What are you doing?"

"I think it's obvious," I answered softly.

Jase and Kieran eyed the beast that continued to stand between me and the descendants, issuing a ferocious rumble in warning.

"We talked about this, and agreed it was a bad idea," Issik sternly reminded.

"You did," I shot back. "Not me. I agreed to nothing."

"Olivia." This time it was Jase who called to me, his calmness radiating out of him like sonar waves, but I didn't hesitate.

My hand shot up, sending out a shield of fire to vaporize the mist of tranquility. "Nice try."

"Have you lost your mind?" Kieran whispered.

Slowly, I shook my head. "I wish I could claim insanity." Didn't they see this was the only way? Why was I the only one who understood? Well, and the stars.

"You weren't even going to say goodbye," Zade choked. Raw pain emanated from his cinnamon eyes.

I blinked back a fresh bout of tears. "I hate goodbyes," I sobbed.

"Then don't do it," Jase begged with a passion that speared my heart.

I glanced at him, picking up the panic in his violet eyes, but it didn't change what I must do. "How did you—?"

"I felt a spike of fear in our bond," Jase admitted, taking a step forward.

Of course. Their connection to my feelings was a thorn in my side, but it had saved my life on more than one occasion. I supposed I should have been grateful because it allowed me to get to this point. "You brought me here for this reason. Why won't you let me save you?"

"Unforeseen circumstances have unfurled. We never imagined this would be the sacrifice we'd have to make for freedom. I can't live like this... without you." His violet eyes pleaded with me.

"If I don't do this, the witch wins. Isn't that what you said?" I directed at Kieran.

The other descendants glared at him. "I did. But I didn't mean for you to kill yourself. I just couldn't stand to see you so... broken."

"Which is entirely our fault," Issik admitted.

"You promised to stand beside me. Always," I reminded, hurling Jase's words back in his face.

The hue of purple in his eyes fractured with pain as he too recalled that promise.

"Don't leave us. *Don't* do this," Issik whispered, and as my eyes found his fallen face, I didn't think he had ever begged anyone for anything... and probably wouldn't again.

It broke my heart, splintering it into a million jagged edges. "I love you. Can't you see how much I love you all?" I dared to meet their eyes, and wasn't surprised by the mixture of hurt, anguish, and betrayal that flared in them. I had lied to them, gone behind their backs. The anger was justified, but it wouldn't change what I had to do... not if it saved their lives. "There was never a choice. Not for me. I'm sorry."

"Olivia!" the four dragons bellowed.

I grabbed on to the Star of Frost.

I ssik's face was set with feral rage as he whirled toward me, to stop me from touching the Star of Frost. "No!" he yelled.

Yet, nothing could stop what had already begun.

The energy burst through me, and my stomach churned as ice coated my tongue and teeth. My body shuddered from the assault of power transferring into me from the crystal in my grasp. I backed away from the waterfall, my eyes fixated on the stone. The air in my lungs felt like a blizzard. It took my breath away, making each inhale and exhale excruciating—like a thousand needles pricking my organs.

It hurt like hell.

I might have cried out and stumbled, for I heard someone call my name, but it was overrun by the surge of magic. Unforgiving and ancient, it encompassed every crevice of me. A flash of blinding light came from behind my eyes, and I knew the power of frost was mine.

A cloud of darkness misted my eyes. Black dots swirled like savage snowflakes, and I feared this was it, the end, just as the Book of Stars had predicted. Death was on the horizon, sucking me into its cold arms, pulling me into its never-ending depths. Oblivion was whispering in my ear, and I longed more than life itself to see, to touch, to tell the descendants I loved them one last time, but fate had other plans for me.

My time was up, and my only consolation was I had done it. I'd broken the curse.

Something inside cleaved through me, breaking my soul into five sections. Tranquility. Poison. Fire. Persuasion. And Frost. I threw my head back as a scream ripped from me, because what I was feeling, what was going on inside me, was too much for any one person to handle, and I crumbled to the ground.

I screamed again, my voice raw and shrill until I no longer recognized the sound coming out of me. It wasn't normal. It wasn't human.

Shadows wrapped around me like claws in its final sweet and grim embrace. Cold, numbing, and unforgiving, death pulled me into its depths until everything disappeared, even the sound of my heartbeats, and there was nothing left…

…

Then my screams began anew.

I became anew.

Something otherworldly. Something bewitching. Something divine.

The book had been right. I had died. But I'd also been reborn as something… different.

Not human. Not a witch. Not a dragon. Perhaps, somewhere in between.

The ice underneath my fallen body wasn't biting cold as it should be. I told myself to breathe, to open my eyes—simple human actions we do without thinking—but suddenly, I found everything so profound.

From the purity of the air, to the gentle caress of wind on my skin. My senses were heightened, making the world around me brand new.

I lifted my unblinking, sharpened eyes to the descendants, seeing them in a different light—clearer, defined, and vibrant. They were even more magnificent with these eyes. Given the luxury, I would have marveled at the sight of them for hours, but the expressions on their faces mirrored one another's as they stared at me. Terror and awe.

Beyond the shock, I could sense they felt a shift in their own abilities.

The curse was broken once and for all, and the release of it was written on Issik's face as he stared down at his hands, turning them over, and over again. Those invisible manacles were gone, which meant I had only seconds until the witch descended and the real fun began. She would know the moment the descendants were no longer held captive under her spell.

"Olivia?" Jase's voice was hesitant when he stepped toward me.

I held up a hand, warning him not to touch me—still unable to speak. What would I even say?

"We need to get her out of here. Now!" Zade thundered, shaking the ice walls with the boom of his voice alone.

Kieran's gaze went over his shoulder to the ravine outside the icy alcove. "I think it's too late."

The good news: I hadn't died yet.

The bad news: Tianna had come to collect what she considered hers.

Me.

A crow squawked, and the cavern went pitch black. From the darkness, Tianna rose as if she danced with shadows. Her laugh echoed over the ravine, followed by clapping. "Bravo. Bravo. What a performance. I don't think I've ever seen anything so heartfelt and tragic since Romeo and Juliet."

Instantly, I leaped to my feet, stumbling a bit. My equilibrium was off, thanks to this new body I hadn't had time to grow accustomed to yet. My fingers tightened on the two crystals, and I slipped them into my cloak for safekeeping. That was when I saw the glittering labyrinth of colors under my skin.

However, I didn't have time to examine or theorize what the fuck was happening to me. Tianna's sudden appearance sent a series of growls rippling through the dragons, but she dismissed their warning with a wave of her slim, alabaster hand, like they were nothing more than a pack of disobedient dogs. Scars raked over her eyes, a brand of my gift.

My eyes volleyed between Tianna and the descendants, finding I was the one who stood between the witch and the dragons.

"How does it feel to be free, boys? A long time coming, I'd say, but I didn't come to chat." She turned those heartless milky eyes toward me. "You've changed." She held up something in her hand, twisting it around. It was a black crystal, and at the center, something moved.

Holy hell.

It was an eye.

The witch had concocted a seeing stone to compensate for the loss of sight I had taken from her. The eye roamed over me from head to toe, taking in the network of swirls and whorls that covered my body, glowing like an iridescent rainbow. "Aren't you just intriguing? You get more fascinating each time we meet." A grin spread over her dark cherry lips. "I'm going to enjoy killing you."

A roar shook the stones, and the surrounding ice cracked as Issik burst into his dragon. The cavern groaned from the sheer mass of him, sending shards of lethal crystals raining down upon us. Shit was about to get real.

"Touch a hair on her head, and I'll paint the Veil with your blood," Jase threatened with a terrifying calmness that I'd never seen in his expression.

"You'll have to take each of us down to get to her," Kieran added, his claws lengthening over his fingers as he let a part of his dragon emerge.

"Olivia, give me your hand," Jase demanded, stretching out his fingers across the cavern.

It would have been so easy to lift my arm and intertwine my fingers with his, and yet, I hesitated.

Why?

Why the hell would I do that?

A sane person wouldn't have even given it a second thought, and here I was, caught between the witch, who had made my life hell, and the dragons, who had been my salvation.

I knew this war hadn't been won, not yet.

Tianna clicked her tongue at Jase. "You never could learn how to share." She spun on her heels, and that eerie eye in the stone gave me a mocking look.

Icy, glittering rage tingled through my blood. "You and I have unfinished business."

"You read my mind. Shall we?" She held out her black-tipped fingers.

I couldn't bring myself to look at the descendants, keeping my gaze centered on the witch. "I'm sorry," I told them, my voice hardly a whisper, right before I placed my hand in hers, leaving behind the silver-tipped mountains, the comfort of the castle, and above all else, my dragons.

"Olivia!" Four voices screamed.

Another roar ripped through the cavern, and Issik sent a blistering stream of ice in Tianna's direction, but her power had already engulfed us. A whirlwind of magic and darkness swathed me like a cloak. Large feathered wings of her crow form enveloped my body.

What had I done?

Shadows surrounded me as dark as a starless night, swallowing me whole. I might not have been able to see anything, but I could feel the witch's presence, her triumphant laugh echoing in my ears. My body was weightless as we soared through space, using the wind and night as an ally. There was no way out, no way to stop the journey I'd begun. I had no choice but to see it through to the end.

Tianna swept us from the hidden cavern in Iculon, to the barren and unforgiving kingdom of the Nameless Lands. Although the shadows and wings had released their hold on me, my body remained unmoving, staring at the expansive, rough, and rugged land before me.

Storm clouds shrouded the sky above, and a mist hung low over the sandy ground, making it appear like grains of coal. Lightning speared the sky, and it was during the brief flash that I saw her. She was waiting under the shade of a gnarly, half-dead tree. The branches that were covered in leaves sagged toward the ground, as if they couldn't bear the weight.

My legs seemed to know what to do without me commanding them, or perhaps it was the witch leading me like a marionette doll. I stepped toward her, nausea and panic rising up inside me, but I forced my chin to lift while I moved forward.

"Welcome home, dearie," Tianna purred when I halted in front of her, a wicked grin on her crimson lips. "Let's catch up."

I pressed my nails into my palms, letting the pain center me, reminding me of what was real, for the witch was known for her tricks and illusions. "I'd love to, but we have a score to settle first."

"Oh." Her lips formed a pouty circle as if she was sincerely disappointed. She held a scepter in her hands, the creepy eye crystal was embedded into it, and the sight of her with the magical weapon produced a memory of the night she had betrayed the dragon kings. She had wielded a similar scepter then, except this one was made of bones—dragon bones.

Oh, my God.

They were Tobias's bones.

That bitch.

I was going to kill her. Or die trying.

Noticing that it caught my attention, she twirled the scepter, and its silver tip glinted in the moonlight. "Imagine what it would look like with five beautiful jewels. Dragon stones perhaps…"

The words were meant to taunt and enrage me. Well, she succeeded. A sudden upsurge of violence roared within me, and I would have struck the witch had it not been for her dark hold on my mind. Cool-tipped nails squeezed my free will into submission.

Tianna ran her fingers down the smooth length of the scepter, a predatory hunger in her sightless eyes. "Before you decide to be a hero, we have some unsettled business to attend to, and then, my dear, you and I can have that duel you crave."

"I'm not giving you anything," I spat. "It's too late. The curse is broken. The stars you so desire have been found. You lost." To prove my point and to let her know I wasn't afraid, I summoned a serpent from the mist. Long and sleek, its green scales gleamed, poison coursing through its fangs. The snake's forked tongue licked the air at her feet, coiling around her legs.

She chuckled, and the sound made me want to punch her in the throat. She extended her fingers toward the hissing snake as if she was going to stroke its triangular head. I narrowed my eyes, willing the beast to strike now, but the creature stared into Tianna's hypnotic eye. A moment later, the traitorous reptile wound itself up her slender arm, settling its head across her neck.

I silently cursed all the gods.

She had taken my magic and bent it to her will. If she could do that with a simple smile or glare of her evil eye, I was doomed.

"Silly girl, that bit of magic you stole from me is just a speck of what runs through my veins. Besides, I don't care about the stones. It's the power I want—the power that is now inside you." Moving closer, she grabbed the end of my chin, holding my face steady and firm. "The stones are useless without their energy."

"Why didn't you just hunt down the stars yourself then? Why curse the descendants at all?"

"The gods are fickle beings. When they crafted the stars, and granted the five dragon kings a fraction of their own powers, they did so with caution and stipulations. You see, I am unable to touch them in their true form due to some ridiculous notion about my heart and soul. The stars only grant those who have pure intentions with their gifts."

My mind was reeling. When she had touched the Star of Fire, I'd received a piece of her magic. The star had extracted her power, giving it to me. But if she couldn't harness the stones' powers directly, then how did she plan to gain the power for herself? I was terrified to ask.

"You're a vessel," she answered, reading the question in my eyes. "I needed someone whom the gods deemed worthy to bestow their powers upon. It was the only way to release the magic from the stones themselves."

That still didn't explain why the hell the stars had chosen me. I was no one special, and I couldn't say that my heart and soul were pure. I'd done things in my life I wasn't proud of—stolen, cheated, lied. I was no freaking saint.

"How will you get the power from me?" I had an inkling it was going to involve pain. And blood.

She raised her arm with the snake still twined around it, and brought its head to her nose. Puckering her lips together, she breathed a puff of black smoke into its face, and the creature born from my power died at the hands of hers. "With magic, of course," she replied, dropping the limp creature to the ground.

"The spell. You mean to use the spell from the book to extract the power from inside me."

She tapped the end of my nose with the tip of her long, ebony nail. "I bet you were a straight-A student, weren't you?"

I snorted. Her question didn't deserve a response.

Her finger trailed up the seam of my cloak. "Since I can't physically touch the stars, I had to get creative. I needed a human that was pure of heart. That's where you came in, dearie."

Unblinking eyes stared at her with despise. Tianna had manipulated the descendants the whole time, in this elaborate scheme to grant herself the power of the gods.

My hand darted to the inside lining of my cloak, whipping out the dagger I had stashed there, and I held it to my own throat. "I'll die before I let you take it."

Tianna's scepter flung out towards me, magic tingeing the air. The dagger flew out of my hand and straight into my hers with nothing more than a twitch of her pinky. I could smell her anger. Her milky eyes darkened to the color of tar.

"I can't have that." She angled her head to the side. "Any other secret weapons stashed inside the cloak, or do I need to search you?"

She would enjoy humiliating me like that. "Go to hell," I seethed. "I'll never help you."

"That's why I have this." She produced a vial out of thin air, filled with a thick, crimson fluid. Blood. My blood. "A little insurance to make sure things go as planned."

Shit. Shit. Shit.

My face remained calm, even though a series of swear words went off in my head once again. The little vial gave me a nasty, sinking feeling in my gut. I had known from the moment I'd struck the bargain with Tianna for a vial of my blood that it was going to come back and bite me royally in the ass. Well, that moment had arrived, and it was devastating.

Reaching inside me, I let the power of ice coat my veins, preparing to hurl it at that stupid vial of blood. If I froze it and shattered the tube, she would have nothing to hold over my head, nothing to force me to succumb to her will.

It was imperative I destroy it.

My hand lifted, and I cast it out toward the witch, but sensing the power gathering within me, Tianna tipped back her head and took a swig from the glass tube. With a Cheshire grin, she licked her lips, sampling my blood like an exemplary wine. Before the arrow of ice could reach its mark, something inside me flipped. My magic sputtered and then was completely snuffed out, causing the arrow to halt mid-flight. It dropped to the ground, shattering into a hundred pieces.

A lump formed in my throat, and I attempted to swallow it. What the hell had I been thinking? Yes, I had broken the curse, but I had stupidly believed I could take her on alone—without my dragons—in some foolish dream of protecting them like they had done with me for months. I'd been prepared to die to save them, but this… this was a colossal fuck up. I had walked right into her sticky web, and was now trapped in a cocoon of her magic.

I tried to scream. To thrash. To fight. To summon every ounce of power within me.

Yet, it was useless. There was nothing I could do to stop the darkness of her magic from taking me prisoner. Again.

"Don't fight it, dearie. It only makes the connection between us more difficult, and by difficult, I mean painful… for you," she added with pleasure. "Your blood is now a part of me, which gives me a direct line to you. Clever, isn't it? Magic can be cunning if the wielder knows how to use it."

And she'd had decades to master her craft. I, on the other hand, had had just a few pathetic weeks, and my lack of skills showed in how easily she outmaneuvered me every step of the way.

"I'll give you points for trying. You never give up. There is something to be said for your tenacity. Now," she spun her pointer finger in a circle and sauntered closer to where I stood, rooted in place, "how about we get this ceremony started? We wouldn't want any… unexpected interruptions."

She pointed the scepter in her hands toward me, and my legs trembled as I fought against her command of my body. I gritted my teeth, sweat dripping down my forehead, but no matter how much I strained, my legs moved, carrying me across the barren plain a few paces.

"I promise this won't hurt… much." She laughed, and the sound made me want to shove her scepter up her ass. One of her pointed nails raked across my bicep, tearing through my flesh.

Hissing between my teeth, I dropped to my knees, the drawing from the book glowing in my head. The cut on my bicep was throbbing, blood trickling down my arm, but I ignored the pain.

"Your blood is the key…"

They were right. It had been the key. It had been what linked us together. What had led me to the stars. What Tianna used to keep tabs on me. And now it would be what destroyed us all. I had to find a way to turn the tide in my favor.

Tianna placed my dagger in my hand. "You'll need this."

My fingers closed around the familiar hilt and weight of the blade. I wanted to plunge the dagger into her black heart. I wanted it more than life itself, but that wasn't what Tianna willed. Biting down hard on my lip, I dipped the end of my blade into my cut. The deep red, lustrous blood became my ink to copy the five-pointed star from the book onto the sandy earth. Nevertheless, the symbol itself wasn't enough to complete the spell. I needed the five stars.

Two of the stars were on me. Tianna had one. But the other two were hidden in Viperus and Wakeland. Just how did Tianna mean to complete the spell without them?

My mind was whirling with possibilities even as I opened my palm and eyed the Star of Persuasion glowing a radiant, rich amber. Mine. This dragon stone belonged to me. The truth of that rang through my body, and the stone shimmered in response as if to say I belonged to it.

Was I really going to let the witch take it from me?

There had to be a way to stop this spell. I needed to find a loophole. And quickly.

I pressed the stone onto the top left point of the bloody star. On contact, the two lines extending to the next points lit up with a pure white that glittered like starlight.

Holy. Fucking. Shit.

Tianna's eyes lit up with wild hunger. "Yes," she murmured softly, her fingers gripping on to her scepter. "Now the next," she instructed me with a hint of impatience in her tone.

Unearthing the Star of Frost from my cloak, I nestled it into the bottom left point, the center of the stone lambent under the moonlight. Another white line emerged.

A tear slipped from my eye, falling down my face. I was relying on blind instinct, trusting the magic of the stars to reveal a Hail Mary that would put an end to this torment.

"The stones will only answer to you, as long as their power floods your veins. You must call them," she whispered in my ear. "Magic to magic."

I shook my head. "No," I uttered in a voice so weak, so quiet, that it sounded pitiful.

"You will," she demanded.

I had no choice. She had stripped that away from me.

Stretching out my right hand so that my palm faced toward Wakeland, I called forth the power of tranquility, summoning the crystal to come to me, to return and claim the magic that was rightfully its own. As she had stated, I was simply a vessel to keep the power safe until this moment.

I blinked. That was all it took for me to feel the thud of something in my open palm. My fingers closed around the cool, violet stone that reminded me so much of Jase's eyes, and I let loose a low breath. Placing it at the top point of the symbol, I watched as another line illuminated.

It was at that moment that I fully understood my role to the stars, and what I was fated to do.

My hand lifted to summon the Star of Poison when a deafening roar vibrated from the skies. The magnitude of its anger shook the ground under my knees.

Then another sounded. And another. My heart stopped.

Tianna's head whipped toward the dark clouds, the eye in her scepter searching for the first sign of the descendants. "Hurry," she hissed, waving the end of the scepter toward me.

Elation spiraled up through me. They had found me. Their presence gave me the courage of defiance, and only one thought echoed in my head. *I will break the spell that binds me. I will break the spell that binds me. I will break the spell that binds me.*

My hands fisted into the cool grains of black sand as I repeated the words over and over again, until there was nothing but truth in them. The three stones thrust into the earth, and the ones still in my blood intensified each time I recited the phrase.

I will break the spell that binds me.

Scorching heat blazed from the clouds, and a wind stirred with a cold that froze bones. Tianna cast out her scepter with her back to me, her feet planted on the ground, preparing to take on four full-fledged dragons. She was a powerful witch, and I didn't want to underestimate her evil nature. Her thirst for godly power made her a snake in the darkness.

Four dragons descended from the black skies. Daggers of lightning shot across the darkness that had wiped out all the stars and moonlight.

Magic simmered and brewed, becoming a song in my blood. I had to keep pushing against the binds of her energy that commanded me. I shoved, kicked, and pounded against that dark power holding me prisoner with my own abilities. Harder and harder I pushed.

My breath became a flame in my throat.

Ice wrapped around my heart.

My voice transformed into a chant of persuasion in my head.

Venom hissed through my veins.

And a steady calm of tranquility grounded me to the earth.

My attention returned to the spell, to the stars, and they purred in my presence. Like a rubber band snapping, the blood-hold Tianna had on me severed. It seemed the witch had limits after all.

It was my turn to take control.

Now was the time to strike while the witch was otherwise engaged with the descendants. I wasted no time in summoning the other stones. Lifting both hands in the air, one to the east and the other to the west, I invoked poison and fire, allowing their mystic energy to fuel my blood. Behind me, the flashes of magic, the snarling of teeth, and the vicious glory of battle raged, but I didn't dare look, didn't dare distract myself.

My right hand burned with fire and my left with fatal poison as the stones flew to me. An inhuman scream of madness reverberated around me, only to be overpowered by a blast of fire that sizzled and cracked in anger over my head. Yet, the ice in my blood kept the flames from burning the hair off my body.

I had to end this.

Positioning the Stars of Poison and Fire into their points according to the drawing, the last two lines lit up, completing the five-pointed star and leaving one last thing to do.

I swallowed, said a silent prayer to any gods that might be listening, and dragged my palm along the bleeding wound on my bicep. My bloody hand slammed onto the earth, fingers spreading wide into the center of the star.

"No!" Tianna bellowed, but it was too late.

The glowing white lines flowed like a river of starlight to the center where my fingers dug into the sand. The dragon stones hummed, and I listened, the voices of the gods whispering in my ears. Like a sleeping enchantress had woken up inside me, my head fell back to the sky. Pure, undiluted power pumped through my veins, a thousand times stronger than the stones had separately. Together, their power was endless.

I had done the one thing the descendants warned me about—combined the five stones into one.

At the center of the star, where my hand had been, laid a single luminous stone. Clear in color, like a diamond, it reflected a prism of tiny rainbows even in the weak moonlight. Picking it up, I prepared to unleash the storm raging within me.

"What have you done?" Tianna's angry voice hissed. "You little bitch."

Truth be told, I hadn't expected to make it this far, but that didn't mean I hadn't planned for what I must do next.

I stood, my movements fluid and graceful as I turned to face the witch, my magic building like ice lightning hitting a tsunami, that was burning with blue flames of poison. The magic inside me was a weapon. I was a weapon, like bullets firing in the night, arrows taut against a bow, a blade hissing with the winds. I was all of those things if I willed it.

Behind Tianna, my dragons formed a formidable wall of muscle and vengeance.

My chin lifted, knowing I must look like some alien, something not human, but I embraced it, welcoming the power granted to me by the stars—by the gods. "Your reign of terror ends today."

Although violence and anger rippled off her body, Tianna gave me a wry grin. "I hope you have the force to back up that threat, dear." She summoned the darkness to her in waves, pulling from the night surrounding us. She was greed and corruption, and from the pits of hell, her army was born. Creatures from other worlds and beasts made from smoke and evil magic lined up beside her. With a nod of her head, chaos erupted.

The descendants roared like dragon warriors, and set forth to destroy her soldiers while I took care of the queen witch. For good.

Tianna gave a silent command and then attacked. She flung out her scepter, hurling a dozen silver-tipped arrows at me, which undoubtedly were dipped in some sort of toxin.

Suddenly, time slowed in my eyes, and I became aware of each arrow slicing through the air toward all the vital parts of my body. My power rebuked her onslaught of filth. Lifting up my hand, I halted the fleet of arrows dead in the air, and swatted them away like nothing more than pesky flies.

Meeting her gaze head on, my lips curled into a wicked grin of my own. "Your magic is useless against me now."

Her face twisted with anguish. Those once beautiful eyes that were always full of hate, bitterness, and trickery showed an emotion I'd never seen on Tianna's face before—fear.

Around us, the descendants fought through ranks of Tianna's demon infantry. The sounds of searing flames, hissing poison, crackling ice, and the thuds of bodies hitting the ground in numb submission, surrounded me from all angles. Yet, I drowned out the noises of war and focused all that I had on the witch.

Sheer power trickled into my fingers, and I unleashed it. The white, fierce magic of the stars burst out of me. Through the blackness, my power shined, seeking out the infernal evil that lived inside the witch. The next second, chains of starlight wrapped around her tightly, binding her spells.

Tianna thrashed with a crazed rage against the shackles, but she couldn't break free from my dominant hold.

Confidently, I strutted forward across the dry land, my feet gliding over the earth until I was nose to nose with the witch. "How does it feel to have your abilities reduced to nothing?" I asked, kicking the scepter that had fallen to the ground.

With her arms pinned to her sides, her scarred eyes glared with malice, stinking of desperation. "You think you won? You think you bested me?"

I was going to incinerate the bitch.

"Yes." I bared my teeth. I was not a tool. Not a weapon to be wielded for warfare and glory. I rallied the last of my magic. "This is for my dragons. This is for Tobias…" I hissed into her ear. "This is for Corvina." And then, I detonated.

Tianna screamed.

I struck her again, my blood humming in approval. Her cries grew, cursing me to seven different hells, but I didn't waver in my retribution.

"And this," I whispered, letting the well of power surge up inside me until it was overflowing, "is for me." I couldn't tell where my body began, and the stars' energy ended. We were one. I blasted her one last time with everything I had left, destroying every drop of magic she had in her black blood.

The spell finished, and a ragged breath flew out of me as I swayed on my feet—my abilities and power depleted. Strong arms caught me before I fell, holding me against his solid, bare chest. Kieran. It was his scent of dewy woods that gave his identity away. "Is she—"

I shook my head. "She's mortal. Her magic is gone."

Tianna was on her knees. Her head hung so low that she could very well be dead. A curtain of glossy red hair covered her features, hiding them from my view. I watched as the strands of her vibrant hair withered, turning a dull gray.

She lifted her head, raising glittering eyes of horror to me. All her false beauty and youthfulness was gone, leaving behind a frail old woman. "How-how could you?" she croaked.

Feeling nothing but pity for the corrupt witch, I stared back at her. "For love," I replied softly. "Something you'll never understand."

The army of darkness had been vanquished the moment her magic was stripped from her. Now, the four descendants stood at my side in their human forms, and I leaned closer against Kieran, drawing on the strength of his arms.

We had done it.

The curse was broken.

The Veil was safe.

My work was done. And I could go home.

The thought stopped me. Where was home? What happened next? Would they ask me to choose between them? Would I bounce between kingdoms?

"Claim it," a cluster of voices coaxed inside my head, almighty and familiar. The stars. They were a part of me, and I a part of them. *"You know what to do. It's your destiny. It has been since your birth, Olivia, Savior of Dragons."*

I shook my head, unable to believe what the gods were suggesting.

"This land, is yours for the taking. Claim it..."

"Olivia?" Jase called, sensing something was going on inside me.

Were they suggesting what I thought? That I could claim the Nameless Lands? I could bring them to life? My eyes swept over the harsh and sorrowful kingdom, and my heart wept for what Tianna had done to it. "How?" I asked, ignoring the dragon for the moment.

"Give it a name."

"That's it?"

The descendants looked at me with concern and confusion. They were talking amongst themselves, but I pushed aside their voices, focusing on the stars.

"Your power, our power, will reshape this land. It will be yours to rule, to govern, to protect, to nurture, to cherish as long as your blood flows."

It couldn't be so simple, so normal, could it? Did I want a kingdom? I didn't know how to rule, how to be a queen. What they were proposing was insane. And yet, I couldn't deny I was tempted. A home. This place would be mine. No one could take it from me, or kick me out. It would be *mine*. My children's… and their children's.

What the hell. Wiggling out of Kieran's arms, I dropped to my knees.

"What is it? What is wrong?" Kieran asked.

"There's one more thing I must do," I replied, feeling the tether of their powers flicker inside me. I was so tired, but somehow, I found the strength to let magic dance in me once again. I threw my head back, letting loose the power of the gods within me. "Aylin!" I bellowed, thrusting the stone into the earth.

An electric pulse surged from my fingers to every crevice, every particle of sand, down to the deepest roots of the trees, to the very core of the Nameless Lands. Life flowed from the stone into the soil and beyond, the land taking what it needed to repair itself and start to heal.

The Nameless Lands weren't nameless anymore. Now, they had an identity. The kingdom of Aylin. We were united. Joined.

Beside me, the first bud of life rose from the dirt—a single blade of grass—and I grinned.

Four different voices echoed in my head, and as I shifted to face the descendants, I could sense the bond between us from ruler to ruler. Dear God, I was the ruler of a kingdom—my kingdom.

Zade's lips curled. "The queen of Aylin," he stated, testing the name on his lips. "I like it."

If any of them had an objection to what I'd done, I couldn't see it in their faces as I stared up at them, but there was someone who did— someone whom I had momentarily forgotten.

A war cry of rage and desolation shouted from behind me, and I spun to see Tianna charging toward me with my dagger gripped in her wrinkly hand.

Suddenly, Issik was in her path, his look was savage, unyielding, and vengeful. He struck out, grasping Tianna by the throat with one single hand. Without her powers, she was nothing. She was mortal.

His ice-tipped claws dug into her chest, freezing her black heart, and then he ripped it out of her. Tianna's inky blood sprayed over his forearm and bare chest, splattering over his glorious face.

Her shriek splintered throughout the Veil.

And then, a blissful silence ensued.

Issik crumbled her frozen heart in his fist. Shards of ice rained over the ground, and as the pieces of her heart thawed, they shriveled. A gust of wind blew through, scattering the dead particles of her soul.

Her mouth was agape in a frozen, eternal scream of death. The last traces of her magic winked out, and with it, the dominion of bitterness and wickedness was annihilated.

The witch was dead. Truly. Forever. Dead.

I ronically, I found myself unsure of the future without a purpose or a task in front of me. What was I to do with my life now that Tianna was no longer a threat? The Veil was protected. The portal safeguarded. The descendants' powers were restored to their full glory.

And how magnificent they were.

Never had I thought they could be more impressive and majestic than they already were. I'd been wrong, and their kingdoms thrived under their rule. The four kings of the Veil.

Then there was me.

The keeper of stars.

The savior of the dragons.

The queen of Aylin.

Who would have ever thought a homeless girl from Chicago would become the queen of her own kingdom, and have power beyond her imagination? Certainly not me.

What would Mom think of my life? I'd like to think she'd be proud of me, of the woman I'd become, but perhaps not of the mess I'd created with my love life.

Four dragons. I had four gloriously gorgeous dragons who wanted me… at least I thought they did.

Gnawing on my lip, I stared out the window of my newly crafted castle of gold. It shimmered under the sun. The kingdom of Aylin had blossomed into a land of beauty over the last week. With its rolling green hills, fields of wildflowers, sparkling ponds, and flowering trees, it was truly a paradise. Every day I found something new to marvel.

Yet, there had been a hole in my heart these past few days. A part of my life was missing, and creating a home, building a castle, restoring the land had all been a distraction to what was really bothering me inside. The days and weeks after defeating Tianna had been a bustle of activity. The descendants had kingdoms to attend to, and people who depended on them, leaving me to tend to my home.

What was I supposed to do with a kingdom? Was I to be granted a crown of diamonds? Was I to just sit around all day, lounging in the gardens and eating fruit from the trees? Tobias had visited me once to thank me for bringing life back into the land that had once been his. He refused my offer to stay, informing me his days in this world were coming to an end and not to cry for him, regardless of the tears that had fallen down my cheeks.

With a heavy sigh, I turned away from the window and wandered to the fountain that sat in the middle of the foyer. Compared to the descendants' homes, mine was modest, but I didn't need or want a large home to get lost in. The castle was built, after all, by my own magic and imagination, a weird concept to wrap my head around, but I loved being surrounded by things that were mine.

And still, I was lonely.

Other than the occasional visits from the dead queens of the Veil, my castle was quiet. The women in white seemed to know when I needed company or guidance, as I did now. I had a feeling they would be with me always, queen to queen. We shared a bond.

As though I had summoned them, the five of them rose from the sparkling basin of the fountain. Their forms were not entirely solid, but more real now that Tianna was gone. *"Why do you look so sad, daughter?"* Eira asked, Issik's mother.

Roseria looked at me with concern in her warm brown eyes, much like her son Zade's. *"Is your new home not to your liking?"*

Were they kidding? It was everything and more than I could ever need. It had literally been born from my dreams, my wishes, and my desires. Magic was a marvelous thing, though I still had so much to learn about my newfound abilities. They weren't to be taken lightly. I never wanted to let the power I had corrupt me, so I needed to make sure I stayed grounded.

The material of my white dress swooshed against my legs as I moved to sit on the edge of the stone basin, the trickling water filling the room with a soothing sound. "I love my home. I love my kingdom. There is nothing more I could hope for."

"Nothing?" Wisteria, Jase's mother, asked with a single raised brow that reminded me eerily of her son.

Her tone had my eyes narrowing. "What are you implying?" It wasn't lost on me how unique and possibly odd some might find my situation—the fact that I frequently held conversations with the ghosts of dead queens.

"Perhaps you should seek them out, if they are too stubborn to come to you," Kelaya suggested, the queen of Viperus. Since these almost daily chats had started, I had learned a great deal about the mothers of my dragons, including their names. They appeared to be less bound by the laws of the world since the curse had been lifted.

My nose wrinkled. "Why would I do that?"

Adara sighed. She was Tobias's mother. *"I'll never understand young love. If you want something, you need to take it."*

"So, you're suggesting I just stroll into their kingdoms and kidnap your sons?"

A series of laughs echoed throughout the foyer, so light and girly for five ghosts who were so wise and dignified. *"You know that was not what I was suggesting,"* Adara replied, a smile still upon her lips.

"What if they don't want me?" *What if they make me choose?* I silently added. I couldn't possibly pick just one. I couldn't. The thought made me sick. And they deserved a queen who would stand beside them, give them children, and love them wholly. I couldn't do that, not if it meant I had to pick between the four of them.

Wisteria clucked her tongue, and I felt a phantom touch against my cheek as she brushed aside a strand of loose hair. *"You have nothing to fear. In your heart, you know what you must do. It is the only way you will ever find genuine happiness."*

My fingers played with the star of the gods in my hand.

The great thing about being a ruler in the Veil was I had a direct connection to the descendants, which came in handy when phones weren't a thing. After spending all night dwelling on what the women in white had said, I finally came to the decision that we needed to have a talk, and I was desperate to see them.

It had been too long.

I summoned the dragons to Aylin. Since I didn't have wings, and hadn't quite figured out how to willowphase, I was more or less stuck at home. It was driving me bananas.

Pacing the garden from one hedge to the other, I soaked up the sun as I continued to stare into the cloudless sky, searching for any sign of my dragons. They were still my dragons… I hoped.

Beating wings in the distance alerted me that they had arrived, and the sound had my blood racing. Seconds later, four dark specks appeared at various points in the sky. Zade and Issik's kingdoms bordered mine to the north and east.

Nerves and excitement spiraled through me, and I thought I might be sick. That would make one hell of a reunion. My fingers turned the stone in my hand as I fought for patience, and to keep from throwing up. The star of the gods had become a source of comfort, and I often found myself reaching for it in the long nights alone.

Issik was the first to touch down, his massive dragon feet landing with an icy thud in the courtyard, which was designed large enough for dragon landings. My feet flew over the cobblestone pathway, racing to the patch of grass in time to see him wiggle the pants over his hips, although he didn't bother with a shirt. I had a stack of clothes waiting on the edge of the gardens for such occasions, when the descendants showed up in dragon form.

A smile came to his lips as his eyes found mine just as I reached him. His cool breeze kissed my cheeks, smelling of winter's first snow-fall. "Hey, Little Warrior," Issik greeted in that deep voice and pulled me into his arms. His lips were on mine a moment later, drinking from my mouth like a man dying of thirst.

I barely had time to catch my breath before I was spun around to face Zade, who had arrived moments after Issik. Molten heat engulfed me. "Little Gem," he murmured against my lips, chasing the cold from Issik's kiss away.

Next was Kieran. He didn't bother with clothes, coming straight to where I was being mauled by Issik and Zade. He flicked the tip of my nose before planting a quick kiss of greeting on my lips, causing my pulse to hammer. "It's been too long, Blondie."

I couldn't agree more. "I missed you too," I agreed with the biggest grin on my face.

Picking me up off my feet, Kieran spun me. While the world was blurring around me, I sensed Jase, his unmistakable tranquility. When my feet touched the ground, I didn't wait for the dizziness to pass before launching myself into his arms, welcoming the blissful calm that radiated from his skin. I drew in his scent like clean air.

Jase rained kisses over my face. "Olivia," he sighed. My arms went around his waist, and I held on tight. He was content to keep me there for as long as I wanted, neither of us pulling away, not until three males cleared their throats.

They were here. All of them. And my heart had never felt so full, so complete. The gleaming, golden castle was at my back, but their eyes were all on me. A thrill made its way through my veins, making me realize how much I wanted them in my daily life.

"Love what you've done with the place," Kieran offered with a lopsided grin.

I beamed. "It's home."

"I can't tell you how happy we are that you've chosen to stay," Jase confessed, looping a free hand around my waist, and walking with me toward the palace.

The others fell in step alongside us. "Why Aylin?" Issik asked, surveying the grounds.

"It was my mother's name. It means paradise, and that is exactly what I want this place to be. A reminder of her and of all that is good in my life."

"It's beautiful," Kieran agreed with a wink.

An awkward moment followed with the pleasantries out of the way. Zade offered me a wicked grin that was all dragon. "We've tracked down and hunted most of the creatures that managed to slip in through the portal these last few months."

"You've been busy," I admitted. While I'd been lounging around in paradise, rearranging all the furniture they had sent my way, and sulking, they'd been out making sure the Veil was once again a safe place. Why hadn't they asked me to help? I was more than capable of taking down the bad guys now that I was… hell, I didn't know what I was, but I had enough power to protect this world.

Violet glittering eyes swept over my face. "Have you settled in okay?" Jase asked.

I nodded, wondering how weird it would be if I just stared at them for hours.

"But…" Issik prompted, the faint smile in his eyes fading as he sensed my hesitation and the loneliness I tried to hide.

Having the four of them here with me again, being in their presence, I wasn't sure I could let them go this time. I shrugged in an attempt to keep things lighthearted and protect my heart. The fear of rejection, of no longer being wanted was making me feel vulnerable. I took a deep breath and told myself that whatever happened, I would survive it.

"I wanted to talk to you." My feet got caught up with each other, and I stumbled, but Jase was there to keep me from eating grass.

Color stained my cheeks. I had all this power, and I still tripped over my own damn feet. I sure as hell didn't expect my body to start tingling. My tattoos shifted and moved on my skin, that now glimmered like a rainbow on the surface of the sea.

The four of them stopped walking, most likely for my own safety. "What took you so long?" Zade replied, slipping a hand under my elbow, his eyes bright with delightful humor.

Kieran was at my other side, a hand at the small of my back. "We've been going crazy waiting for you to figure out what you wanted."

What? All this time they were waiting for me?

I couldn't decide who to look at because they were all equally important, so I kept my gaze centered on my twining fingers. "That's the thing… I don't know what I want, except the four of you. I don't know how to be a queen, or what is expected of me."

Issik slipped a finger under my chin, tipping my face upward to meet his gaze. "We won't abandon you. Not ever." The expression I saw there had my heart squeezing.

Zade's hand slid down my arm to entwine our fingers. "We're forever in your debt."

"Veil Isles will only have one queen," Jase offered softly. "That is, if she will have us—all of us."

"I don't understand." My brows scrunched.

Kieran looked into my eyes, into my very soul. "None of us are willing to live without you, or to let the other make you his queen, so we've decided it's time for a new era, and it is only fitting that the one who saved us becomes the Isles' one queen—the queen of the Veil."

My legs wobbled. I hadn't gotten used to having my own kingdom yet, and now they wanted me to rule over the continent. I was young and inexperienced. What kind of queen would I make?

"What about having an heir?" It was the only way they could ensure the dragon line didn't die. With the curse broken, they could once again mate and have children.

"Our relationship might be unconventional, but we have a proposal for you," Jase explained. The four of them looked at each other before turning those vibrant eyes to me. "You share the power of five dragon stones, making you the ideal mate. Our sons and daughters will be stronger."

Zade brushed a thumb across my cheek, leaving a trail of warmth behind. "We only ask that you spend equal time between our kingdoms and their people, including yours. You will help us rule the courts of the Veil."

It was too good to be true. I wanted to throw myself into each one of their arms. My joy and relief overwhelmed me.

"This is ultimately your choice, and it isn't all or nothing, but we're all in agreement on what we want," Issik confirmed.

Tears of pure happiness glistened in my eyes, of belonging, of love —a well of emotions. "I've never wanted anything more."

"We'll make you happy," Jase promised.

"I know."

A disarming grin hooked the corners of Kieran's lips. "So, whose kingdom is first?"

Here we go again.

I laughed as the arguing of the four descendants broke out in my gardens. Some things never changed, and I wouldn't have it any other way. My chest bloomed with unconditional love for these four dragons.

The End.

Thank you so much for joining me on this journey into the lives of the dragon descendants. I fell so much in love with these characters and will miss them dearly. Hopefully, I gave them a happily-ever-after that fantasies are made of. I ventured into new territory when I decided to write a reverse harem, and I hope I did it justice.

A NOTE FROM THE AUTHOR

Thank you so much for reading Thawing Frost, Dragon Descendants, book 4. I truly hope you have enjoyed reading it, if you have, please show your support by leaving a review. It only takes few moments, visit the series page:

Dragon Descendants
https://amzn.to/3zEzrIJ

For the latest news about new releases, sales, upcoming books, giveaways, and more join my news letter today!
http://www.jlweil.com/vip-readers

NEXT FROM J.L WEIL

Turmoil

A Dark High School Romance,

Elite of Elmwood Academy Book 1

They call themselves the Elite—four boys from the wealthiest and most prominent families in Elmwood, which somehow gives them the right to be righteous A-holes.

Gorgeous.

Arrogant.

No regard for rules.

And Brock Taylor is the worst of them all. I wish I had known that before I slept with him. A night I just want to forget. But Brock won't let me. They aren't just high school boys. They're four guys with an agenda, and I'm out of my element.

***Turmoil is a full length 80k dark high school romance novel, the first in the Elite of Elmwood Academy series. This series is not RH and ends on a cliffhanger. It is recommended for 17+ due to language, sexual assault, drugs, and drinking.*

Exclusively on Amazon! FREE on KU!

https://amzn.to/3oLKSZ3

THE COLLECTION

ABOUT J.L. WEIL

USA TODAY Bestselling author J.L. Weil lives in Illinois where she writes Teen & New Adult Paranormal Romances about spunky, smart mouth girls who always wind up in dire situations. For every sassy girl, there is an equally mouthwatering, overprotective guy. Of course, there is lots of kissing. And stuff.

An admitted addict to Love Pink clothes, raspberry mochas from Starbucks, and Jensen Ackles. She loves gushing about books and Supernatural with her readers.

She is the author of the International Bestselling Raven & Divisa series.

ABOUT THE AUTHOR

Don't forget to follow her!

www.jlweil.com
www.facebook.com/jenniferlweil
www.twitter.com/JLWeil
www.instagram.com/jlweil